THE MYSTERIOUS FREEBOOTER

Also Available from Valancourt Books

GASTON DE BLONDEVILLE
Ann Radcliffe
Edited by Frances A. Chiu

CLERMONT
Regina Maria Roche
Edited by Natalie Schroeder

THE CASTLE OF WOLFENBACH
Eliza Parsons
Edited by Diane Long Hoeveler

THE VEILED PICTURE
Ann Radcliffe
Edited by Jack G. Voller

Forthcoming Titles

THE MONK
Matthew G. Lewis
Edited by Allen W. Grove

ZELUCO
John Moore
Edited by Pamela Perkins

THE FARMER OF INGLEWOOD FOREST
Elizabeth Helme
Edited by Sandro Jung

THE NEW MONK
R. S. Esquire
Edited by Elizabeth Andrews

Gothic Classics

THE MYSTERIOUS FREEBOOTER

or,

THE DAYS OF QUEEN BESS

A Romance.

FOUR VOLUMES IN ONE

Francis Lathom

Edited by James D. Jenkins

CHICAGO:
VALANCOURT BOOKS
2007

The Mysterious Freebooter by Francis Lathom
First published by Lane & Newman, 1806
First Valancourt Books edition, April 2007

Library of Congress Cataloging-in-Publication Data

Lathom, Francis, 1777-1832.
The mysterious freebooter, or, The days of Queen Bess : a romance : four volumes in one / by Francis Lathom ; edited by James D. Jenkins. - 1st Valancourt Books ed.
p. cm. -- (Gothic Classics)
Includes bibliographical references (p. ix).
ISBN 0-9777841-9-3
1. Scotland--Fiction. I. Jenkins, James D., 1980- II. Title. III. Title: Mysterious freebooter. IV. Title: Days of Queen Bess.
PR4878.L175M97 2006
823' .7--dc22

2006200778

Published by Valancourt Books
P. O. Box 220511
Chicago, Illinois 60622

Typography by James D. Jenkins
Set in Dante MT

10 9 8 7 6 5 4 3 2 1

CONTENTS

EDITOR'S NOTE

The Mysterious Freebooter; or, The Days of Queen Bess was first published at the Minerva Press by Lane & Newman in four volumes in 1806. It was Francis Lathom's eighth published novel (he would go on to publish eight more, as well as four collections of short stories) and the greatest success of his career.

The book met with immediate popular success and a fair degree of critical acclaim, with the *Critical Review* for July, 1806 declaring that, "Mr. Lathom has most disdainfully rejected all assistance from grammar, style, and harmonious construction. And yet, when we had finished the work, we forgot our displeasure at the errors of the composition, in our regret that the story was concluded."

Unlike most of Lathom's novels, for which a single edition generally sufficed to meet public demand, *The Mysterious Freebooter* went through at least four editions in Lathom's lifetime, being reprinted by Newman in 1818 (again in four volumes), and in sumptuous one volume octavo editions published by Jaques & Wright, London, in 1828 and again in 1829. And yet its popularity seems to have endured even beyond the latter date, with another author borrowing the title for the anonymous *The Mysterious Freebooter; or, The Bride of Mystery* (1844), and allusions to it being found as late as 1851, in the novel *The Fair Carew, or, Husbands and Wives,* in which one of the characters peruses "the last volume of the *Mysterious Freebooter*...with a vacant smile."

The present edition follows as faithfully as possible the text of the 1806 first edition. Minor variants in spelling (e.g., god-daughter/goddaughter, recognise/recognize, etc.) have been retained to maintain the flavour of the original work, as has Lathom's sometimes idiosyncratic use of punctuation, which involves a superabundance of commas, dashes, colons, and semicolons. Only in the case of obvious typographical errors or punctuation likely needlessly to confuse modern readers have I chosen to make slight alterations. Particularly significant additions are noted in brackets and alterations in footnotes.

The 1828 and 1829 reprints do not feature any substantive change from the first edition, but eliminate a large number of punctuation marks and alter others, substituting colons for semicolons, dashes for colons, etc., as well as occasionally "improving" run-on sentences. However, I have chosen to follow the first edition because the run-on sentences and frequent dashes contribute to the sensation of a plot that moves along at breakneck pace. The action is so continuous that the author/narrator scarcely has time to finish one sentence and begin another.

Rather than repeat here the biographical details of Francis Lathom's life, thus swelling an already large book to even larger proportions, I refer the reader to my introduction to the Valancourt Books edition of Lathom's *The Castle of Ollada* (1795), where he will find a variety of information, biographical and bibliographical, about the author and his works.

Finally, I would like to acknowledge gratefully the proofreading assistance of Jessica Calabrese, and Professor Allen Grove of Alfred University, who provided the copy of the first edition from which this edition has been set.

James D. Jenkins
Chicago

December 31, 2006

FURTHER READING

Other works by Francis Lathom available from Valancourt Books

The Castle of Ollada (1795). Edited by James D. Jenkins.
The Midnight Bell (1798). Edited by David Punter (*forthcoming*).
The Impenetrable Secret, Find it Out! (1805). Edited by James Cruise.
Italian Mysteries (1820). Edited by James D. Jenkins.
The One-Pound Note and Other Tales (1820) (*forthcoming*).

Books discussing Francis Lathom and the Gothic novel in general:

Frank, Frederick S. *The First Gothics.* New York: Garland, 1987.
Macconochie, Arthur A. *Francis Lathom: Forgotten Goth.* (MA thesis, University of Virginia) Charlottesville, Va., 1949.
Nause, John D. *The Eclipsed Orb: A Study of Francis Lathom, His Life and Gothic Romances, Plays and Experiments in Forms of Fiction.* (PhD dissertation, Dalhousie University). Ottawa: National Library of Canada, 1989.
Potter, Franz J. *The History of Gothic Publishing.* London: Palgrave, 2005.
Summers, Montague. *The Gothic Quest.* London: Fortune Press, 1938.
Varma, Devendra P. *The Gothic Flame.* New York: Russell & Russell, 1966.

PREFACE.

No apology can be required for writing a Romance, after the many eminent persons, of both sexes, who have, for centuries past, deemed it no degradation to employ their talents in this species of composition.

Story-telling is of ancient and reverend* origin; and provided the tendency of the story told, be moral, there can be no fair objection raised to its being made the entertainment of hours devoted to relaxation.

But I have heard it objected, that the characters of Romance are usually of too high a sphere, to be capable of that effect upon society in general, as examples for imitation, which they might prove, were they drawn in the more humble stations of life; and to this I reply, that, as it is from the example of the great, that the bulk of mankind is accustomed to regulate their actions, there is at least no mischief to be apprehended from endeavouring to make the great perfect, if the lesson, conveyed through the medium of a fictitious tale, can be supposed to carry with it any weight of the kind.

Romance, from its earliest periods, has, in the persons of its heroines, taught the female world, that it is virtue which can alone give lustre to their rank and beauty; and, in those of its male characters, it has instructed the stronger sex, that they are to regard themselves as the natural protectors of the weaker, to treat the objects of their passion with the most profound delicacy and respect, and to expect the hand of her whom they love, as the reward of their virtues: and if this conduct be shewn to produce happiness to those who move in a high station, it will naturally produce the same desirable consequence, if pursued by those in an inferior rank of life.

Another objection which has been raised to Romance is, that it frequently assumes the right of placing deceased characters in situations through which they never passed, and of giving to historical facts false dates, and erroneous terminations: As this charge is, in some instances, applicable to the subject of the following volumes, I feel it incumbent on me to prepare an answer for those who may bring it against me, and this it is—"A Romance," says Dr. Johnson,

* In reference to the Theagenes and Chariclea of Heliodorus. [Lathom's note.].

"means a fiction, a tale of wild adventures of love and war;" which explanation must, I think, be sufficient to prevent any one from reading them under the idea of gaining from them correct historical information; and prepare them to encounter those anachronisms and misstatements which the author has been guilty of, for the purpose of augmenting or enriching his tale. Those who have perused the history of their own country, with that laudable attention which the subject demands, will not, I am inclined to think, be displeased at meeting some of its features in the guise of Romance; and those who have never examined into the events which have preceded their entrance upon the stage of life, cannot, at least, complain of *their* ideas upon the subject being confused by such scraps of the history of their mother country, as a Romance furnishes them with.

After the daily instances which we have of this species of composition meeting with the greatest success, I should have deemed it quite superfluous to have written a line of defence for one more added to the number, were I not aware that *some* of the reviewers are like hornets, looking out for a hole in a man's jerkin, through which they may drive their stings; and that, probably, if I had not confessed myself conscious of some deviations from historical truth, in the matter contained in the following pages, they might have placed them to the score of my ignorance, and have taken the pains of writing me a lecture upon the subject: which trouble I now spare them.

The reviewers are, in my opinion, a very ancient community, and deserving of some respect for their antiquity. My ideas of the remote period from which they have had existence, are founded upon this expression of Solomon—"Oh that mine enemy would write a book!" and I am always tempted to understand from this sentence, that there were reviewers in his days, and that some publication of his had fallen under the lash of their censure, and provoked this wish from his lips. I have for some time entertained this opinion of myself, and I think I am bound in charity to publish it, for the comfort of my brother-labourers in the toils of book-making, in order that it may console them for any mortifications they may meet with, at the hands of those gentlemen, since if so wise a man, and so powerful a sovereign, as the great Solomon, could not, even in those days of good order and decency, escape their censure, how can insignificant individuals expect to be shielded from it, in this age of freedom and irregularity?

To be sure, it is difficult to reconcile ourselves to the kind of rifle-fire, with which these literary gunners shoot at us, from behind trees and hedges, as it were, leaving us uncertain who it is that pops at us; but then, we should consider that their trade must live, as well as ours, and that it appears an essential part of their history, to give weight to their oracles by their obscurity: if they were to put their names to their performances, as we do to ours, the names would very frequently destroy the effects of the criticisms.

But this assertion is by no means made of *all*. There are amongst them *many* men of excellent dispositions, unprejudiced opinions, and good natured hearts, who, to speak from my own knowledge of them, and from what evidence can a man speak better? have treated my repeated trifles which have come before their inquisitorial bar, with lenity and indulgence—by whose advice I have profited, and by whose remarks I have been instructed.

But my readers are doubtless impatient for the conclusion of my Preface, that they may proceed to investigate the merits of my Tale; I shall, therefore, detain them with only one more observation.—"Is there no certain way," enquired of me the other day, a young friend of mine, who was just turning author, "to gain a favourable sentence from the critics?" My reply to him was this—"There is one habit, from which I never intend to deviate myself, and which, if it be not, *ought* at least to be an author's infallible passport to their approbation—that of making his pen a constant servant in the cause of morality; in which case, if his execution be condemned, his motive must be approved, a decision which cannot fail to impart satisfaction to his mind, upon this reflection, that, if he cannot gain *entire* applause, it is infinitely more desirable to be pronounced the possessor of a good HEART, than of a good *head*."

For the Poetry interspersed through these Volumes, the Author is indebted to several Friends.

THE *MYSTERIOUS* FREEBOOTER

CHAPTER I.

By how much unexpected, by so much
We must awake endeavour for defence;
For courage mounteth with occasion.

KING JOHN.

It was during that hostile period when the continued inroads of the borderers, whose course was marked with death and devastation, called for the utmost vigilance of the government, and rendered the fortifying and garrisoning of the northern castles an object of the greatest importance, that Lord William, Baron de Mowbray, received from his sovereign, Queen Elizabeth, the commission of Warden of the Borders, appointed to controul and chastise the Moss-troopers, whose ravages had risen to so alarming a height, as to attract the particular notice of those in power.

Placed in this dangerous but honourable situation, he conceived it his indispensable duty to execute the arduous employment entrusted to him with the greatest promptitude. Accordingly, with all alacrity, he strengthened his residence by every means in his power; he erected a double wall, cut trenches, and surrounded the whole by a deep moat, over which a drawbridge led to a massy iron-cased gate, and huge portcullis; around the roof were erected battlements planted with cannon; and over these a garrison of three hundred men, selected from his vassals, and trained by himself to arms, were appointed to do duty.

The office upon which Lord William had now entered, accorded but ill with those dreams of family comfort in which he had hoped to pass the evening of his days:—but light was his repugnance to the bloody business of the field of battle, when compared with the heart of his motherless daughter, the beauteous and gentle Rosalind, which sickened in her breast as she dwelt in imagination on the scenes of blood and rapine to which she must now unavoidably become a witness.

Lord William had scarcely completed his fortifications, ere he was called upon, by the voice of danger, to an exertion of the greatest fortitude.

The clouds of evening were just closing in the parting day, when the sentinel at the drawbridge dispatched one of his comrades to the Baron, with information that a Moss-trooper, sinking under fatigue and famine, was lying at the foot of the bridge, and imploring, in terms of the most vehement entreaty, to be permitted to see Lord William, whose life, he said, was in imminent danger.

Every Moss-trooper was of course the decided enemy of a man placed in a situation like that in which Lord William now stood—the prime foe, as it were, of their ravaging bands; and so strange did the information appear to him, that he hesitated for some moments how to reply to it.

Irwin, his first leader, thus addressed him: "The instance of an enemy passing over to the side of his foe is by no means a singular one; it may be caused by his having deserted, for a length of time, from his own party, to whom he now fears to return, dreading the chastisement due to his crime: It is also possible that it may be occasioned by a prepossession for ours; and it is still more probable, that the hope of future reward and preferment have been his inducements to this step. Whatever the motive, a single individual is incapable of committing injury within our walls. Let him, so please your Lordship, be searched, to prove whether he conceal about him any instrument of death, which it may be his desperate purpose to level at your person; and this done, let him be brought before you."

"But should he come merely as a spy upon our strength," suggested the wary Baron: "this is a supposition which has escaped you."

"That will be easily discovered," replied the leader who had before spoken, "and if such he appears, we have chains and dungeons, to prevent his carrying back the information that may be required of him."

"Let him be brought into the castle hall," said Lord William, "and I will meet him there."

Irwin called upon some of his men to follow him, and they proceeded to the drawbridge, at the foot of which they found the Moss-trooper of whom they had just received intelligence. His garb was of the common Scotch plaid; a breastplate of rude workmanship covered his chest, and an iron cap bound his brow; sword he had none; nor was there any weapon of death concealed in the scanty folds of his garment.

Irwin bade him rise and follow him; he complied with Irwin's order, but his strength was so greatly exhausted, that he would have fallen again to the earth, had not two of the soldiers given him their support.

Lord William was in the hall, prepared to receive his stranger. "If you are Lord William de Mowbray," exclaimed the young man, the moment his eye fell on the person of the Baron, "oh save me, in mercy save me! say but that you will not deliver me into the hands of Allanrod, and I am your slave for ever."

"Who are you?" asked Lord William, "and who is this Allanrod, of whom you speak?"

"I am the veriest wretch that breathes upon this earth," returned the man, "and he, the vilest monster Nature ever issued from her womb."

"By your garb," replied the Baron, "you are a Moss-trooper."

"I have been," answered the man, "but by your good-will, I am henceforth an English soldier."

"And who is Allanrod?" asked Lord William.

"The chief of the band into which I was deluded, and have now abjured," returned the stranger. "My father was—oh that he was so still! an humble peasant in the Tiviotdale; myself and one dear sister, all his household—and happy was our little family—no wish beyond ourselves, till Allanrod, a second fiend, broke upon the paradise of our tranquillity—lured me with tales of glory, and my sister with his vows of love!—Tempted by a small command which he gave me in his band of ravagers, and still more by the promises of favour that he would heap on me, I left my native vale; scarcely was I gone, ere he returned, and with brutal violence attacked my sister's honour; my wretched, grey-haired father, who stood forth in her defence, he murdered—struck to the earth—and while he lay a bleeding corpse, my sister, still more wretched, fell a victim to his lust!"

The youth's voice was no longer audible; it was drowned in the contending feelings of his heart; he hid his face in his hands, and continued silent.

Lord William urged him to proceed to the conclusion of his tale, and after some minutes pause, he went on thus:—

"Intelligence was brought me of the horrid deed:—I flew to Tiviot, and arrived there just in time to catch my sister's dying breath; and for her, to hear me pledge an oath to Heaven of vengeance on her's, and my lost father's murderer.—Admit me to your ranks, and for my own revenge I will be a lion in your cause, when opposed to the savage Allanrod—You know not whom you have to fear in Allanrod; more of the demon than the man, there dwells within him; wild, ungoverned, cruel, and ferocious are his passions; dire is his enmity to England and its Sovereign; but still more against your person, than the nation, or its Queen, does his hatred appear to be directed; for from the moment that he learnt the commission to which you were appointed, he has been collecting forces to subdue your power. His strength is now all raised; I have watched him for the completion of my just revenge, and the present hour alone is yours, to save yourself from falling into his power, and mine, to execute my vengeance on him. He is now on march towards your castle; his forces now move in divisions; within three miles of your abode, these divisions are to unite; and so great are their numbers, that fatal to you must be the event of the day, if you once suffer them to gain this union. The first division Allanrod heads himself. Do you march out boldly then, and attack it on its way. Entire victory must be yours, for small is the division he leads; and their chief being once cut off, his other forces will lose all spirit to attack your castle.—Say 'aye,' good Baron, and the blow that levels Allanrod shall be my own. I am no hypocrite, and I confess that it is not *for England*, but *against Allanrod*, I fight."

Lord William inquired of the young man, at what distance from his castle he supposed the first division of this Allanrod's troops might now be?

He replied, that he had for some days past been an unobserved spy of their progress, and that he conjectured them to be now at the distance of about thirty miles: "thus," continued he, "according to the speed they usually proceed at, they will reach this castle by noon on the day following the morrow."

Lord William next demanded of him to point out the exact route in which they were advancing; this he readily answered, and particularized the spots where he supposed the first division, headed by Allanrod, would halt on that and on the following night.

To the Baron's questions of what had been the rank, title, or name of Allanrod, before he had taken upon him those he now bore? the youth declared himself unable to reply; and Lord William then commanded him into safe custody, telling him that he should deliberate on what use to make of the information he had brought him.

Why the freebooter Allanrod should bear a greater and acknowledged hatred to him, than even to the government to which he was a rebel, was an ænigma which Lord William found himself unable to solve. He dismissed his attendants, and being left alone with his leaders, submitted to their judgment the propriety of following the advice given him by the deserter from Allanrod's camp.

All the leaders, and in particular Irwin, declared it their opinion, that the tale of his misfortunes had worn the appearance of having proceeded from a heart unacquainted with deceit; they could see also, they said, no motive but his hatred to Allanrod for the step he had taken, since in the very moment he had declared himself on their side, solely because they were the foes of Allanrod, he had not endeavoured to impose himself upon them for a friend to the English cause, which one well schooled in the lessons of hypocrisy would doubtless have made his first point of information, as the one most likely to ingratiate himself into their favour.

The Baron coincided in their opinion; but there were still two nights and a day before them for action, ere (as the deserter had said) the enemy could gain the castle; accordingly he determined to give the present night to cool reflection upon his pillow, and not to form his resolution till it was past. Before he retired to his chamber, he again called the youth into his presence; again he heard his tale, and was still more convinced that it appeared the tale of nature and of truth; so forcibly did the countenance and emotions of Donald (for such was the young man's name) present themselves as vouchers for the veracity of his words.

Lord William arose with the dawn, resolved to march and surprise the division of the enemy headed by Allanrod, which the youth

Donald had described as the most advanced body, in their quarters that night.

Donald was again questioned on the strength of this advanced body; and having positively asserted that it consisted of not more than eighty men, Lord William resolved to take with him only one hundred and twenty of his own soldiers, in order to leave his castle in the better security during his absence.

According to the custom in those days, his one hundred and twenty companions, with their leaders or captains, destined for this enterprise, and whom he had selected from amongst his best men, were divided into fifty mounted as cavalry with matchlocks, forty foot with pikes and broadswords, and a body of about thirty archers and slingers, who brought up the rear; these were intended to be placed in ambush, and to commence the charge with a shower of arrows on the first onset.

Every thing being prepared for their departure, it was agreed, as the distance they had to journey could not exceed fifteen, or at most eighteen miles, to begin their march under cover of the night, that they might have a greater chance of keeping themselves concealed, and bursting upon the enemy unexpectedly.

During the whole of the day, Lord William had been employed in superintending the preparations for his march; towards the approach of evening he entered the apartment of his daughter, to bid her farewell previously to his departure. The child of woe, he found the beauteous Rosalind, hanging over that lute, of which the tones had no longer power to soothe her aching breast, where eternal sorrow had settled its abode; of the hue of grief were her garments, like the colour of the fortune which had marked her fate; a sable robe flowing to her feet, alone composed her dress, save the single band of pearls which confined its folds round her waist; her light brown hair hung in unrestrained tresses upon her shoulders; her blue and heavenly eyes were dimmed with weeping; a faint tinge of the rose's hue still painted her cheek, just sufficiently to recall to remembrance how beautiful it had once been; and her neck of milky whiteness, even when not contrasted with her sable robe, gained from it the pureness and lustre of unfallen snow.

The Baron took the hand of his daughter, and leading her back to the seat from which she had arisen at his entrance, he placed himself by her side. A silence of some minutes ensued, but the eyes of each were eloquent. "How happy had been my life, had a daughter been obedient to my will!" passed in the eyes of Lord William; and—"How wretched has the exercise of parental authority made his child!" in those of Rosalind.

"You have doubtless heard, my Rosalind," Lord William at last began, "that the temper of the times calls me from my castle; the enterprise upon which I am now setting out, I am taught to believe, is one of little hazard to the safety of my troops or myself; but the fate of the field is uncertain; and however secure of victory in my opinion, it may be the will of Providence that I shall never return;—will my daughter vouchsafe a parting embrace to a father whom she may never again behold?"

"Heaven avert the evil that you mention," returned Rosalind: "you have been cruel, very, very cruel to your only child; but I cannot forget that you are my father, though you have so severely used the authority of a parent over a child towards me."

"Should I return in triumph, the conqueror of my sovereign's foes, wilt thou quit this garb of woe, cast off these frowns of sorrow, and consent once more to visit with me that court, of which thy youth and beauty would be the grace, and to which my gracious mistress has so oft invited me to bring thee?" asked Lord William.

"Do I ever, my father," returned Rosalind, "reproach you with the miseries that load my aching heart?—do I ever breathe a sigh of malice aimed at your feelings?—never, witness Heaven, have I done this!—be then the reward of my patient sufferings, that my future days be those of obscurity!—force me not into busy life, where my wretchedness would be exposed to the gaze of every unfeeling eye. O, in this one point, 'tis all that I have left to ask, do not constrain my feelings."

Lord William returned a cool reply to the request of his daughter, and then proceeded to inform her that she need not be under any dread from the incursions of the borderers during his absence, for that he should leave the greater part of his strength in the castle for her protection.

To life and death Rosalind was equally indifferent—thus with apathy she heard his declaration.

The first bugle was now sounded, for the body of men who

were that night to march out, to begin accoutring; on its sound, Lord William rose to quit his daughter's chamber; Rosalind rose also, and throwing her arms round the neck of her father, she imprinted on his cheek the first kiss which her lips had for the last four years bestowed on him.

Even into the eyes of Lord William de Mowbray, the tear of parental affection started; he returned her embrace, and would probably have pronounced a blessing on her head, had he dared to have blessed, where his conduct had fixed a curse;—in unbroken silence he left the apartment.

He repaired to the castle hall, whither Donald was again summoned to meet him. The youth came forth; his appearance more composed, and his strength renovated by the care which had been bestowed on him.—After a short and friendly conference, the Baron submitted it to his option, whether he would join the party then preparing to march, or whether he would prefer to await the event of that night's rencounter with Allanrod and his men, at the castle.—"Your late hard faring," said Lord William, "has apparently rendered you unfit for the march; and were not this the case, consider what you have to dread should you be taken by Allanrod's party, and submitted to the tyranny of his chastisement;—all this you are risking, only to add to my strength one additional arm, of which I am not in need, for I could increase my numbers to three hundred, with ease to myself."

Donald thanked the Baron for his consideration, but was resolute in becoming the avenger of his own wrongs: "By this hand," he exclaimed, "must perish the murderer of my sister and my father."

Lord William finding him earnest in his entreaties, yielded to his prayer; and an English soldier's garb was given to him, instead of the one which he now threw off; a sword was girt by his side, a pike put into his hand, and he was appointed to march by the side of Irwin.

"You are very young," said Lord William, who was present at his equipment, and during that time more particularly observed his features than he had before done.

"I have not yet seen quite twenty summers," Donald replied.

As his bonnet was exchanging for a cap corresponding with his English dress, Lord William again addressed him—"I have somewhere met with a countenance very much like your's, and did I not know it to be almost an impossibility, I should think that I had really seen you before."

"It is not improbable, my Lord," replied Donald, "if you have travelled in Scotland; the scenery round Tiviotdale is much resorted to by strangers, and my poor father and I have often been their guides to its beauties."

"I have been in Tiviotdale," returned the Baron, "but it is some years ago, and I do not recollect the particulars of my visit."

The second bugle was now sounded, and every one dispersed, in order to be ready at the signal for marching, which would very shortly be given. Meanwhile the evening bell tolled, and the usual guard of the castle was mounted on the ramparts. The third bugle then sounded, and the two parties having taken leave of each other, the massy gates were unlocked, the drawbridge was let down, and the cavalcade, headed by their chief, sallied forth.

The country lay before them wrapt in the stillness of night; no warlike instruments gave notice of their march; all was secrecy and silence.

CHAPTER II.

What may this mean,
That thou, dead corse, again in complete steel
Revisit'st thus the glimpses of the moon,
Making night hideous; and us fools of nature,
So horribly to shake our disposition
With thoughts beyond the reaches of our souls?

HAMLET.

For a length of time past, the fair Rosalind had allowed herself no air or exercise, but what she took in an evening on the eastern rampart of the castle, which led by an easy communication to the apartments appropriated to her use; from this spot she beheld the departure of her father, and his chosen men; she continued to watch the red glare of their glowing torches, which, reflected on the steel armour, threw its broad masses of light over the whole body of men, till a narrow path, winding between two mountains, concealed them from her view; and all traces of them, save a faint lustre, which rose from their torches into the air, were lost in the gloom of night.—Then, reclining her head on her hand, she leant over the battlements, listening to their footsteps, which, owing to the stillness of the night, were heard when they themselves were no longer visible. At length they died away also, and a solemn stillness prevailed, broken only at intervals by the sentinels relieving each other from their posts, and the iron tongue of the castle clock, which sounded awfully, by the contrast of the stillness in which it was heard.

Night was stealing upon evening, but still Rosalind continued to wander in the air. The moon was now rising in cloudless majesty, attended by a sparkling train of glittering stars, and throwing her silvery honours on the regal brow of Skiddaw, monarch of the mountains; while an unruffled lake at its foot, a rival of its glory, appeared like an immense sheet of silver studded with burnished gems.

Entranced by the scene she was beholding, Rosalind stood wrapt in reflection. "Why," she cried, "is man the only piece of mechanism which this globe contains, of whose nature discord forms a part?—all above is harmony and peace; 'tis but on earth, where man has a sway, that discord has existence:—The silver moon sails calmly through the fleecy clouds, which separate obediently to clear her azure path;—the stars, irregularly scattered through the firmament, know no hostile jarrings to disturb their movements, or obscure their lustre.—'Tis now the hour when nature asks repose; hushed are the songsters of the grove, and every animal seeks repose but man—Insatiate man alone awakes—man, that should be the brother and the friend of man, awakes to plan the destruction of his fellow beings; subject as he is to innumerable infirmities of mind and body, short as is his own natural existence, he awakes to curtail a few moments of his allotted portion of life from his fellow-creature!—Happy those who die, if this it be to live!—O ye bright orbs, that now reflect your beams on me, say, do ye contain the dead within your blessed abodes?—are ye the resting places whence the departed good look down on suffering mortals, and waft to them those sighs of pity, which communicate fortitude to their bosoms under the trials of existence?—If such ye are, a sainted mother, and a murdered husband, have their dwelling with you.—O spirits of bliss, if it be permitted you to administer consolation to the living, twine your wreaths of peace around my aching head; shed the balm of comfort upon my bursting heart; endue me with resignation to the will of Omnipotence, till the hand of Death shall release me from anguish, and call me to the blessed reward of meeting you again."

Rosalind continued standing with her eyes fixed on the planets to which her address had been directed, her every thought lost in scenes far distant from the spot on which she stood, till a faint sound, which resembled her own name, made her start from the trance into which she had fallen, and look hastily around her. She was at that time standing on a projecting part of the rampart, which had an opposite side, that encircled an angle of the castle; and upon this she either saw, or fancied she saw, a dusky figure moving upwards, as if in the act of rising from the glacis below. A momentary fear seized her, but she had not been accustomed to suffer childish apprehensions to subdue her reason, and she exclaimed—"Who is that?—what seek you here?"

"It is only I, my lady, only Gertrude, coming to look for you," returned a voice behind her, which she instantly recognized to be that of her faithful attendant—"It is only I, my Lady; whom did you think it was?"

"I was rather startled by a shadow, I believe," replied Rosalind, and casting her eye towards the spot where the appearance of a figure had before struck her imagination, nothing but the unbroken line of the massive wall now met her sight.

"If you were startled at only seeing a shadow, my lady, what must they be that see a real substantial ghost?" cried Gertrude. "I would not have been in poor Philip's place to-night for all the wealth in the castle.—Pray come in, my lady; don't keep abroad; you don't know how dangerous it is to stay here;—come in, and I'll tell you all about it; I came on purpose to warn you."

"To warn me! of what, Gertrude?" asked Rosalind; "and who is this Philip, of whom you speak in terms of so great pity?"

"Why to be sure, my lady, though you do go very little amongst the inhabitants of the castle, you must have heard me speak of Philip Watkins; he was born in the same village where I was; it is he that you have heard me say got such a terrible thorn in his foot when he was getting me a blackbird's nest;—if you don't remember the story, I'll tell it you again any other time; only it has nothing to do with the ghost Philip saw to-night."

"Ghost!" echoed Rosalind, casting her eye involuntarily to the spot where she conceived that she had seen the appearance of a figure.

"Aye, my lady, a dreadful black ghost: did you never in your life happen to see a ghost yourself?"

"No," replied Rosalind, "nor any one else, I believe, who had the courage to convince their senses of the delusion which they mistook for one."

"Oh, my lady," cried Gertrude, "don't say so; pray don't be so wicked; they don't belong to this world, and should be respected.—Old Ambrose the porter has seen it before; and Simon Williams saw it from the watch-tower last night; only I never heard of it till Philip was brought into the hall to-night in a fit at the sight of it.—Pray, don't stay here, my lady, pray don't; I dare not keep with you, indeed, if you do, for it was on this side of the castle that they both saw it walking;" and away she ran towards the door in the turret which led to Rosalind's apartment, still calling upon her to follow.

Rosalind complied, for the night was far advanced, although its serenity would perhaps have tempted her to have walked longer, had she not been interrupted in the manner she had been. The moment Rosalind was within the turret, Gertrude, who stood waiting her approach with a lamp in her hand, shut the door, and having fastened every bolt upon it, she exclaimed, "thank Heaven we are safe in the castle, and pray its goodness we may be safe, now we are in it."

With the utmost good humour, Rosalind chid her for her weak apprehensions, and endeavoured by every argument to reason her out of her alarm; but the occurrences of the evening were at present too strongly imprinted on the mind of Gertrude, for it to be divested of them by the power of words only; and she proceeded to relate her tale.

"You must know, my lady" she said, "that it is now three evenings ago, as old Ambrose was returning from the village, where he had been on a visit to his sister, the poor old woman, my lady, at the foot of the hill, that you may remember broke her leg the day she was eighty, and that every body thought must have died of it, and now she is quite finely again; is not it a wonderful recovery?"

"Yes, it is," answered Rosalind; "but proceed in your story without interruption."

"I am only explaining a little as I go on, my lady," resumed Gertrude. "Well, old Ambrose came hobbling along, he can't walk very fast, since he has had the rheumatism—looking down on the ground and picking his way for fear he should stumble; when just as he was turning the eastern angle of the castle moat, he happened to lift up his eyes, and there he saw, O mercy on us! a tall ghost, all in black from head to foot; and the moment he saw it, it vanished away from him in a noise like the hissing of serpents!"

"Probably," said Rosalind, "the old man's alarm was occasioned by the shadow of a tree; and the motion of its leaves, agitated by the wind, created the rustling noise he heard."

"No, no, no, no, my lady," exclaimed Gertrude, "he might have been deceived once, but last night he saw the very same appearance again, on the very spot where he had seen it before, and it vanished away from him again, just in the same manner; this was about eight o'clock in the evening:—and now it is come out that Simon Williams saw the very same spectre at midnight, stalking backwards and forwards before the eastern rampart, where you were walking this very night.—Heaven be praised I came and called you away before the dreadful hour strikes."

Rosalind was silent—no faith in spirits was growing in her mind; but the information conveyed by Gertrude of the appearance of a figure in black near the rampart, seemed so strongly to vouch for her senses not having deceived her in regard to the dusky form which she had believed herself to have seen that night, that she could not immediately collect her thoughts to reply to Gertrude's account.

Gertrude mistook her silence for alarm, and exclaimed, "I wish I had kept it all a secret from you, my lady, since I see how much it has frightened you; for I know it will be impossible to withhold the rest of the story from you, now you have heard part of it; and what I have already told you is nothing to what is to come about poor Philip."

"I own I am rather surprised by what you tell me," replied Rosalind; "frightened I assure you I am not.—Amidst the calamities which you know I have suffered, you have always seen that I had still consolation left me within my own breast; it arises from the consciousness that I have never committed a voluntary fault; this knowledge is my talisman against all fear. If there be spirits, either good or evil, permitted to revisit the earth, I still rely that the virtuous power is the superior; and that the innocent will not be allowed to suffer for their appearance."

"What a comfort it is to hear religious words, when one is terrified almost out of one's senses!" exclaimed Gertrude. "Heaven bless you, you talk as well as poor Father Anthony did, rest his soul!—Well then you won't be frightened to hear with what art this black ghost managed to-night to get into the castle-court, will you, my dear lady?"

"If it had really been a spirit," replied Rosalind, "according to the nature of such aerial beings, it need not have used the art you describe it to have practised, for introducing itself wherever it wished to be;——but proceed."

"Why you see, my lady," said Gertrude, "this evening, when Lord William and his troops left the castle, many of our men who were not destined to go upon this expedition, went over the drawbridge with their comrades, intending to march a little way with them; but your father would not allow it, so they were forced to return back to the castle;—all directly repassed the bridge but old Ambrose and Philip; they stood chattering, Heaven forgive them for it! on the other side; when all on a sudden, they don't know whence it came, nor whether it walked, nor whether it flew—but all on a sudden, as I said before, there stood before them this tall black spirit, all in armour;—it had one foot upon the drawbridge, when they first saw it;—poor old Ambrose fell upon his knees, and began to pray;—Philip rushed up to it; for he was terrified enough, as you may well think, at the idea of what might become of him, if he suffered a ghost to go over the bridge while he was the sentinel on it; and was just presenting his pike at it to prevent its proceeding, when it lifted up its beaver, and they saw its face;—and oh, my dear lady, what do you think it was?—the face of a corpse, pale and emaciated, with a streak of blood down the left cheek.—Philip dropped down in a fit, old Ambrose was stupified with fright and astonishment, and the ghost walked over the bridge!"

Gertrude now paused for Rosalind's reply, who said, "Is that all you have to tell me?"

"All, my dear lady!" exclaimed Gertrude, "and is not that enough?—the ghost, you see, has got within our walls, and who knows what may be the end of his visit.—Poor Philip was brought into the hall in fits, and is scarcely recovered from them still, nor can I believe he ever will perfectly, for had I seen such a dreadful——Oh Jesus, what's that?" cried she, interrupting herself in her story.

"Only the clock striking midnight," replied Rosalind. "You see, by your present apprehensions, how sounds we are the most accustomed to, have the power of startling us, when our minds are weakened by tales of folly or superstition.—Thus simply, I make no doubt, might the ghost of this night be accounted for, if reason had been suffered to exert her influence upon the minds of those who thought they saw a phantom."

Gertrude remained incredulous, and would probably have talked the whole night of what she knew nothing, but from hearsay, that deceitful intelligencer, had not her mistress, by undressing herself, and getting into bed, given her a signal of silence for the night; and Gertrude was obliged, though with great reluctance, to retire to the adjoining apartment, where her bed stood, and where she was compelled either to hold her tongue, or talk to herself;—the latter she preferred, probably for the same reason that boys whistle in a dark night upon the road, that they may hear no noise but their own; and thus Gertrude fairly talked herself to sleep.

Rosalind, although free from every apprehension that agitated the mind of her loquacious attendant, did not so soon lose reflection in sleep; for although she had no faith in the supernatural existence of the black figure that had appeared to Ambrose, and his companions, still she could not forbear making it a subject of thought, and attaching to it some degree of credit, from the similarity of their account of the phantom, to the sable form which had that night appeared to her on the eastern rampart.

CHAPTER III.

All comfort, joy, in this most precious lady,
Heaven ever laid up to make parents happy,
May hourly fall upon ye!

KING HENRY VIII.

And now, whilst Lord William and his party are on their march, and his daughter Rosalind locked in the arms of sleep, we will step back a few years, for some particulars which are necessary to be learnt, before we proceed in our story.

The first of the De Mowbray family on whom the honour of knighthood was bestowed, was John; he received it in the field, at the hand of Edward the Third, under which prince he signalized himself by his bravery at the famed battle of Cressy, in which battle the Earl of Flanders fell by his hand; and on his return to England, he was farther rewarded, by being created a Baron, and receiving from the Crown the gift of an extensive domain in Cumberland.

From this time the family of De Mowbray was constantly about the court; its character was that of wariness, rather than depth of understanding; and it was a quality which it so used, as to protect itself from all the storms of court intrigue, and to hold itself in favour with each succeeding monarch.

At the period of the death of Edward the Sixth, the situation of the De Mowbrays, for the first time, seemed in a state of doubt: fate appeared undecided whether to place the crown on the head of the ambitious Mary, or that of the placid Jane Grey; and during this indecision trembled the house of De Mowbray, who being universally known and acknowledged, as adherents, and firm ones too, to the Protestant religion, dreaded the accession of Mary to the throne; but the wariness of Lord William's father, Thomas, exerted itself with success to re-establish their safety.

Convinced that a hasty change from the Protestant to the Catholic religion would not impose on the keen-sightedness of a princess like Mary; that though she might appear to tolerate them for such a change, still the natural fire of her temper might only be smothered, till an opportunity should present itself for her to revenge on them the religious persuasion which she would believe them in their hearts still to follow; he wisely conceived that some effort must be made, some step taken, by which he should purchase her favour, without any obligation to ideas of religion.

Accordingly, perceiving that Jane was too coldly received as Queen, to be likely long to hold her seat upon the throne, he kept himself retired from all public observation of his opinions, till he should see her established upon it, or Mary in her stead fixed upon the seat of power; and no sooner had the unambitious Jane resigned all pretensions to the sceptre of royalty, than Lord Thomas de Mowbray, with every display of zeal in the cause of the new monarch, joined the party who arrested the Duke of Northumberland, and several of his adherents at Cambridge; and having assisted in conducting these objects of Mary's inplacable hatred to the Tower, and taken steps that it should be understood by her, that he had been thus active in her cause, he contented himself with retiring for the remainder of her reign into his native county, where he had the good fortune never to be disturbed by the bigotry of the Queen, as he believed, and as probably was the case, in return for the shew of service he had made to her on her accession to the throne of England.

In the same year that was marked by the death of Queen Mary, died also Lord Thomas de Mowbray, and his successor was his son William, to whom our readers are already introduced, and who was then in his twenty-third year.—Lord William's person was rather commanding than handsome; his complexion dark, and his eye keen, though it conveyed neither the intelligence of a depth of understanding, nor a conciliating disposition; his mind was formed in the true mould of his predecessors, the nursery of wariness and craft; and with the re-establishment of the Protestant religion, stepped forth De Mowbray, vaunting himself not a little on being the head of a family which had not swerved from its religious tenets, during the whole period of the last reign of persecution.

Elizabeth, although possessed of a solid and refined judgment, had a foible, which opened a way to her heart for Lord William de Mowbray: with her it was a sin, in those whom she permitted about her person, and these with her were intimates, for confidants she had none, to arrogate to themselves the slightest degree of that authority which she considered, and was resolved to maintain, her's alone and indivisibly; and Lord William possessed both the art of flattery, and the meanness of licking the dust she trod on, with an ingenious policy, that concealed his views, and displayed only his humble sentiments of adoration and loyalty.

Thus placed amongst the favourites of his Queen, Lord William dreamt not of love, his thoughts being solely placed upon the aggrandizement of his power and wealth, till Elizabeth recommended to him to wife, Ann Cecil, a woman of exquisite beauty and accomplishments, the orphan niece of her favourite minister, Cecil, afterwards Lord Burleigh. To this proposition no man could return a negative whose heart was disengaged; here was the double inducement of person and fortune for it to fix upon: and the Queen herself became the negociator of the marriage; it was solemnized at her court with the utmost splendor; and after the ceremony, she hung upon the bride's neck a chain of diamonds, adding, that she pledged herself to become the sponsor for their first child, if a female.

Lord William now hugged himself indeed, in the reflection of the use he had made of that policy so truly the talent of his family; and Elizabeth, if ever she perceived the colours of self-interest shining through the veil of loyalty which he hung over them, had too good a knowledge of administerial œconomy, to confess a discovery, which, for the credit she owed to herself as Queen, if confessed, must rob her of so valuable an assistant at the helm of state.

Lady Ann de Mowbray was all gentleness and virtue; more attached to the solitude of her castle, its gardens, and adjoining woods, than to the gaieties and festivity of the court.

Lord William's time was divided between his sovereign and his wife; and Elizabeth was satisfied that he had her's and his country's interest too much at heart, ever to be absent, when either called upon him for his services.

About a year after her marriage, Lady de Mowbray became pregnant, and at the accustomary time, she gave birth to a daughter. Again fortune smiled upon Lord William, and he flew to bear the information in person to the Queen.

Elizabeth reminded him, in the most flattering terms, of her promise, in regard to the child; and bidding him not delay the christening longer than was necessary to the health of the mother, as she was eager to visit Cumberland, which was a new country to her, sent him back without delay to attend the recovery of his wife.

The Baron returned home, where he was busied not less in assuring himself that every care was taken of the babe on whose head honours, undreamt of by its infant brain, were going to be poured, than in those preparations which he conceived it necessary to have made against the royal visit.

In the chapel of the castle was erected a canopy of purple velvet, fringed with gold, under which the Queen alone was to have her place during the ceremony of the baptism; and into the most superb chamber of the castle, was introduced a bed of crimson velvet, richly embroidered with the royal arms in gold and jewels; the hangings of the chamber were of tapestry, purposely worked for the occasion, and in the centre compartment, opposite to the foot of the bed, was this device—*"Rejoice, ye walls which have entertained her people's blessing, and her people's pride*—ELIZABETH!" The rest of the apartment was divided into four sections—In the first was depicted, Commerce; in the second, Agriculture; in the third, Peace; and in the fourth, Plenty—the whole superscribed—*"England in* 1565."

The infant daughter of De Mowbray having attained the age of six weeks, and her mother being sufficiently recovered in strength to attend at the ceremony of her baptism, Lord William set out for London, whence he intended himself to become a part of his royal mistress's escort into Cumberland. He found the Queen prepared to attend his invitation, and a few days after his arrival, she set out.

Queen Elizabeth was in person extremely pleasing, if not critically beautiful; and there was besides a certain majesty in her manner, which made her look the Queen she was; added to this was an engaging affability in her conduct, that endeared her to her subjects, and won her the esteem of her people: no wonder then, that thus extolled through her kingdom, the homage, the reverence, and the marks of affection, which she received in every town and village through which her journey lay, kept her in excellent good humour and spirits, and brought her to De Mowbray Castle, prepared to be pleased with her reception, had it not been equally splendid and flattering as she found it.

Her congratulations to Lady de Mowbray, were of the most affectionate and complacent nature; her inquiries after her infant god-daughter, the most flattering to Lord William; and her affable conduct throughout the household such as gained her its universal adoration.

The day for the baptism being arrived, Lord William, in the most adulating terms, ventured to inquire of her Majesty, whether the infant, in whose early fate she was condescending to take so strong an interest, might be honoured by receiving the name of her sovereign? Elizabeth replied to the question as if she had foreseen that it would be submitted to her decision; and her reply won the heart of Lady de Mowbray, as strongly as she was already possessed of Lord William's. "No," she said, "your daughter's name must not be Elizabeth; I do not withhold it from you from any motive of pride, but out of consideration to your wife:—Lady de Mowbray never knew but one parent—that one was her mother; of her she was extremely fond, and being deprived of her, I know she will derive much satisfaction from giving the name of her parent to her daughter; therefore let her be named Rosalind."

Lord William bowed, and affected gratitude for her command; Lady de Mowbray felt it with all the warmth of an affectionate daughter, who really venerates a lost parent, and wishes to perpetuate her memory.

Lord William had certainly been better pleased, if the Queen had waved the compliment which she had paid to his wife's feelings. The name of Elizabeth he would infinitely have preferred; it would have appeared, though indeed it were only appearance, to have allied his child to her whose name she would then have borne: the Queen, however, was still her godmother; and to this reflection he reconciled his mind.

The name of Rosalind was accordingly given to the child—Elizabeth imprinted the first kiss on her Christian god-daughter, and put into the hands of her father a purse of five thousand marks of gold, as the dower of her nominal child.

The day was passed in the utmost festivity at the castle; no brow could wear the frown of care or displeasure, where a benign sovereign set the example of smiles; and real happiness gave lustre to the wine which sparkled in the golden goblets, and infused soul into the revelry that resounded in the hall of De Mowbray Castle, on the day of fair Rosalind's christening.

CHAPTER IV.

But hark!—that crash!—with tenfold rage
The warring elements engage:
Loud and more loud the impetuous thunders roll,
And "earth unbalanc'd" shakes from pole to pole.

HERBERT.

From this day nothing of moment occurred to the family of De Mowbray, till the little Rosalind had attained her sixth year; it was at this period that Queen Elizabeth concluded her advantageous treaty of commerce with John Basilowitz, Great Duke of Muscovy, and Lord William's presence was demanded at court during the negociation.

Lady de Mowbray had not quitted the county in which her castle stood, since the birth of her daughter, and the Baron had been nearly six months absent from them, when a day of hard travelling brought him, at the close of a sultry evening in the month of September, to a wood within three miles of the borders of his own estate. He was on horseback, attended only by two servants; the blackness of the clouds foretold a thunder storm, and he spurred on his steed, in the hope of reaching his castle, before the tempest should rise to the violence which the appearance of the sky threatened—large heat-drops were already falling, though it could scarcely be said to rain, and short gusts of wind, rustling between the trees, announced the elemental war at hand.

He urged his horse into a swifter pace, but the tempest was more rapid in its movements; the vivid lightning began to stream in forky spires along the burning sky, and the thunder to roar amongst the surrounding mountains. Still partial drops of rain only were falling, and Lord William still spurred on his horse;—but suddenly, with a tremendous crash, a thunderbolt burst nearly over his head, and a ball of fire, which dropped from it, fell upon a knot of trees, at the distance of but a few yards from him; an instant conflagration ensued, and the wind, which was rapidly increasing in strength, bore along the flakes of fire in every direction. Lord William was himself startled at the sight, but his steed was terrified beyond the Baron's power to govern him.—Darting into the thickest of the forest, the animal flew with the swiftness of an antelope, carrying his alarmed rider through almost impenetrable passes, and wounding his head against the hanging branches of those trees between the boles of which he flew with him. Still Lord William continued to keep a firm seat, till a violent flash of lightning again caused the horse to start out of his path, and with this motion his rider fell from him

Lord William lay for some time almost insensible; his head was much bruised, and the pain he felt in it was violent. On his endeavouring to move, a still worse discovery took place; he found that he had broken his leg. His attendants had been separated from him; they must be uncertain where to seek him; his voice could not be heard at the distance of a stone's-throw from him, in the raging contention of the elements; and his case appeared, for the present at least, hopeless.

Night had almost assumed her sablest hue, and none of Heaven's luminaries shone forth to alleviate his distress, save the lightning, which continued to dart through the atmosphere with unabated fury; and by its flashes he discovered that he was lying very near to the brink of a piece of water, which by its situation he knew to be a small lake to the southward of his castle; and he felt an immediate sensation of gratitude arise in his mind, at having been providentially saved from being plunged into it.

His pains increased, but still the roar of nature's discord gave him no opportunity to call for assistance; and he was also unacquainted whether his cries were likely to bring him help; for as this lake was situated at a distance from the high road, it was a long time since he had visited it, and he was quite ignorant whether there were any cottages in its neighbourhood.—One only assurance gave him comfort; this was, that his attendants would beyond all doubt call numbers to their aid, and not relax in their search till they had found him.

Thus passed full an hour, and patience, urged by pain, began to lose its virtue. He called aloud for help, and the thunder, which was now receding in hollow murmurs to the distant mountains, left spaces of silence for his cries. The lightning also was now but a faint shadow of its former fierceness, and the stars were beginning to start from the cleared sky, whose fullness had before impeded their appearance; by the faint light which they gave, he discovered something like a habitation at some distance from him, and imagined that he could perceive the faint gleam of a lamp within it; the apparent dimness of which seemed to be accounted for, by its being placed at a great distance from the casement.

Again and again he called; the light glided nearer to the window, and then vanished. He called again, with all the strength he could exert. The door of the cottage was opened, and a figure appeared at it with a lamp in its hand. The figure paused, as if uncertain whether it had been deceived, or had really heard a voice. Lord William repeated his entreaties for assistance, and the figure, which he quickly saw to be that of a man, advanced towards him.

In few words, the Baron explained to him his name, and the accident that had befallen him, entreating his care and humanity till he could be conveyed to his own mansion.

The stranger was a man of about fifty-five years of age, of an open and interesting countenance; his dress was that of a shepherd, but his manners were those of higher birth; he looked with the utmost compassion on Lord William, and still forbore to reply to his request, or to give him help.

"Will you not serve me?—have you no pity for my sufferings?" asked the Baron.

"Shall I go instantly to your castle, and bring some of your vassals hither?" asked the stranger.

"The distance is four miles," replied Lord William, "and should you leave me here, to go upon that errand, wounded as I am, I may perish in the damps of the night."

"I hope not," returned the stranger. "Heaven avert it!"

"Cannot you take me into your cottage?" asked the Baron; "you look compassionate, but you act———"

"I am not strong enough," interrupted the man, "to bear you to my cottage alone; and you cannot lend yourself the least assistance, with your limb thus disabled."

"Is there no one but yourself in the cottage?" inquired Lord William.

"I'll bring you something to comfort you," said the stranger hastily, after a short pause, which appeared to convey a doubt how to answer, and was moving away.

"Oh, for Heaven's sake do not leave me thus," exclaimed De

Mowbray. "I will reward you liberally, if you will procure assistance to carry me from the wet ground to shelter."

"I never was paid in my life for an act of humanity," returned the man; "but I can do no more than I can."

"Can no assistance be procured?—Is yours the only cottage?" asked Lord William.

"The only one within two miles," was the answer.

"And you are quite alone in it?"

"If I were to bring a boy of eight years old to help me, I don't believe we together could lift you."

"If you have only such a boy in your cottage, pray make the attempt," returned Lord William; "you know not what I am suffering."

"Nor do you know now much I suffer," returned the man; "it is very contrary to my nature, to hesitate about serving my fellow creatures."—He paused again, then added, "however unwillingly, I must leave you here a few minutes; but, by my soul, I will return to you as speedily as I can;" and so saying, he moved hastily towards the cottage.

Lord William followed him with his eyes; he saw him enter the cottage, and having for a moment lost sight of the lamp, it again appeared in an upper apartment; here it remained visible for at least ten minutes, and then again it vanished, and was quickly seen below advancing towards the door; the stranger came out first, the lamp still in his hand, and close upon his heels trod another man, wrapped in a long cloak; the latter continued standing in the door-way, and the man who had before been with Lord William came again to him.

"Lord William," he said, "if I consent to introduce you at this moment into my cottage, will you swear to me, that whatever you may see within it, or whomsoever you may see in it, you will never disclose having seen to the world?—these are the only terms upon which you can enter it."

The demand was strange; but the torture of the Baron's head and leg was such as urged him to any promise for the barter of friendly assistance; and he swore to comply with the stranger's request.

"I have one more condition," said the man—"that you will suffer me to tie this bandage before your eyes, which shall be taken off the moment you are placed on a bed in my cottage: if you consent to this, a word from me will bring the person whom you see yonder to my assistance in carrying you to the cottage, and you shall be treated there with every tenderness due to your sufferings; but if you attempt to remove it, that moment, heedless of your wounded state, we drop you upon the ground; and further calls upon our assistance are in vain."

De Mowbray would probably have complied again, had not distant lights, and voices calling loudly on his name, turned his attention from the terms to which he had been on the point of agreeing; and he replied to them with all his strength, while the stranger by his side, exclaimed in accents that seemed to proceed from the bottom of his heart, "Are these your Lordship's attendants?—Heaven be praised that they are at hand!"

Immediately on the sound of voices, the man who stood in the door-way of the cottage disappeared, and the door was closed. In a few moments Lord William's attendants were by his side; and the stranger explained to them the mangled state in which their master lay.

The two men who had been separated from De Mowbray in the tempest, having in vain sought him in the wood, till nightfall had put a period to their search, dreading that some fatal accident had befallen him, had proceeded to the village, which was little more than a mile from the spot where the ball of fire had fallen; and having here collected together a number of the peasantry, to whom they related their fears for their lord's safety, had returned into the wood with firebrands, with which they had separated into different paths in search of him.

A litter was immediately composed of the boughs of trees, and upon this Lord William being extended, with a bed of moss to rest his broken limb on, his vassals proceeded with him towards his castle.

Melancholy was the meeting for Lady de Mowbray; but she allowed not the idle indulgence of her own sorrow to unfit her for the attention she owed to a suffering husband. The surgeon of the household was instantly by the side of Lord William's bed, and the fracture having been set and bound up, and the bruises on his head dressed, Lady de Mowbray became his nurse, refused to quit his chamber during the whole of the night.

Thus did she pass the second, third, and fourth nights; but with the fifth, the privation of rest to herself became wholly unnecessary, as Lord William's recovery promised to be as speedy as the nature of his wounds would permit, the surgeon declaring him entirely free from danger.

CHAPTER V.

No wealth had he, no garland of renown;
Slow pass'd the minutes thro' the live-long day,
Till from the upland mead, or thistled down,
He watch'd the sun's last lustre fade away;
And if, perchance his little heart was gay,
It beat to hear some merry minstrel's note,
Or goat-herd caroling his roundelay
On craggy cliffs.

MRS. ROBINSON.

In the course of three months, Lord William de Mowbray had recovered the use of his limb, although he could not yet exercise it with the firmness he had once been accustomed to do.

Often during his confinement, had he reflected on the strange occurrences which had attended the evening of his receiving the fracture, which now confined him to his castle. The apparent feeling of the stranger for his situation, with his reluctance to introduce him into his cottage, furnished a frequent subject for his thoughts. Lord William had bound himself by an oath, never to have disclosed any particulars which he might have seen in the cottage, had he been conveyed into it; and by the same sacred promise, he regarded himself to be bound not to send any one to the cottage, upon the business of scrutiny. For although Lord William did not always pay strict observance to the commands of honour, where the overstepping of their bounds promised advancement to his own views, or desires, still it was not his nature to trespass wantonly upon the comforts or secrets of an humble cottager. What appeared the strangest part of the mystery, was, that the man at first should have given him to understand that he had only a boy of eight years old within the cottage, and that immediately after, a figure of full stature should have appeared at the door, for whose sake, it seemed probable, that the terms of secrecy to which he had been enjoined were made; as the man who had come to his relief had used no endeavour to conceal his own countenance, but had mentioned the bandage to be placed before the Baron's eyes, as the condition of the other's coming to his assistance.

One of the men who had been Lord William's attendants on the night of the tempest, was that Ambrose who was now grown into years, and the present porter of the castle; he was a native of the neighbouring village, had lived in the service of the late Lord Thomas, and had often been honoured by being made the companion of Lord William's sports when a boy; hence the distance between master and servant had not been so rigidly preserved between the Baron and him, as with his other attendants; and contriving one day to have him alone with him in his apartment, he began his enquiries thus—

"That cottager, whom you found by my side, on the night that I fell from my horse, was a kind, civil man; who is he, Ambrose? do you know him?"

"Merely by report," replied Ambrose: "the nearest cottage to his, and that is at the distance of about two miles, belongs to an aunt of mine; I have heard her mention that she had such a neighbour, and she called him Matthews."

"What did she say of him?" asked Lord William.

"Very little, so please your Lordship," answered Ambrose; "they live too far from each other to have much intercourse."

"Has he any family?—is he married?" went on De Mowbray.

"He has been," replied Ambrose, "for I recollect that I have heard my aunt speak of his grandson Edward."

This was all Ambrose knew—thus Lord William was obliged to suspend his inquiries. After a pause, he said, "Take this purse—carry it to Matthews—tell him that it is sent to him by Lord William de Mowbray, in gratitude for his assistance, on the night which he cannot fail to remember, and that my services are at his command."

Ambrose received the purse, and was leaving the chamber to obey his master's directions.

"Ambrose," said Lord William, "if you should pass near the cottage of your aunt, step in, and inquire if she knows whether the situation of Matthews is such, that my farther assistance might be acceptable to him;—there was something in his countenance that prepossessed me that night in his favour, and this prepossession is not a little enhanced by the recollection that he tendered me his help in the hour of my necessity."

Ambrose now departed, and the Baron impatiently awaited his return: so natural is it to the mind of man to wish to undraw, if it be but a single thread of the veil which obscures any occurrence, that has met its knowledge in the guise of mystery.

Ambrose performed his lord's commands, but he reversed their order in the execution of them, by going first to the cottage of his aunt. Here the conversation, as it is natural to conclude, began with an account of where he was going next, and upon what errand.—"Ah!" cried dame Tabitha, "old Matthews is a charming man; so worthy, it does one's heart good to hear him talk; and so sensible, he is as entertaining as a history."

"Where could a shepherd gain so much learning?" inquired Ambrose.

"He is no shepherd," cried Dame Tabitha, "he lives upright, on his means."

"Indeed!" said Ambrose; "and how many has he to maintain on what he possesses?"

"Only himself and his grandson," was the reply; "a boy of about eight years old, or a little more;—poor man! he has outlived all his relations, as he told me, but this boy; pray the saints he live to be a blessing to him, and that the good man may not have to go to his grave without one of kin or kind to follow him!"

"But as he is neither shepherd, nor husbandman, why does he live in this lonely spot?" asked Ambrose.

"May not it be his pleasure to live in solitude?" returned the dame; "he never told me, and what right had I to question him on his actions?—He has lived in the world, as I have found from the discourse I have had with him; and most likely he has seen enough of its ways to be weary of them, as I am, and as you will be, before you come to my years, though you are so fond of gadding to court with your lord now."

Here Ambrose would have chatted away on the delights of the metropolis, had not Tabitha interrupted him with, "aye, aye, all very well while you are young; there's a time for all things; when you are my age, you'll think as I do;—come, go your way to Matthews, or you'll not get home again before midnight."

Ambrose drank another cup of his aunt's mead, and departed.

He trudged on without any adventure for the first mile: he had still full half another to go, and had just jumped over a ditch, which led him by a nearer way through a copse to the cottage of Matthews, than the high road did; when he heard the sound of voices close by him; he stopped to listen whence they proceeded, and perceived, at a short distance from where he stood, Matthews sitting upon the stump of a tree, with his back towards him, and his grandson, Edward, on the ground by his side, and cutting something out of the branch of a tree, which he soon found the youth intended for an imitation of a pike.

A cluster of bushes formed a tolerable screen between them and Ambrose; and creeping to where their foliage was the thickest, he paused a few moments, with the desire of overhearing what subject their conversation was upon.

"Why should I not be brought up to be a soldier?" asked the boy. "I shall never be happy till I learn the use of arms.—I know I am too young to go to battle and fight yet, but I might be learning how it is done."

"Time enough to learn that," replied Matthews, "when thy strength is equal to its toils and hardships.—What canst thou wish for beyond the enjoyments of peace and plenty, that thou hast in life? is there aught left thee to desire?"

"Oh yes," returned the boy, "and I am sure you can't be angry with me for telling you so, since you have always charged me never to conceal my thoughts from you.—I should like—oh, how I should like, if the great Baron that lives at the castle yonder, would but take me to be one of his pages!"

"Do you then wish to leave me, Edward?" asked the old man.

"Oh no, that I don't," returned the boy; "but I have heard you say that you understand the use of arms; perhaps Lord William would give you employment too."

"No, no, my child," returned Matthews, "my days of strength

are past; thine are not yet come; we are both unfit for what thy inexperience longs us to be practising."

"What! ain't I fit to be a page? I am almost nine years old."

"No, Edward," said Matthews, "you must not be the page of the proudest Baron in the realm."

"How oddly you talk! you are always telling me how bad it is to be idle, and when I want employment you oppose my seeking it."

The old man did not reply.

"Was my father a soldier?" asked Edward.

"Yes, he was," replied Matthews.

"And he was your son, and you let him be a soldier; I think if he was alive, he would have let me be one too. Did he die in battle?"

Matthews rose from his seat, and Ambrose directly sprang from his concealment and moved up to him:—"I was on my way to your cottage, sir," said he, addressing the old man; "I come from the Baron de Mowbray, who sends you this purse, in requital for the assistance you rendered him on the night when his leg was broken by a fall from his horse."

"I would," returned Matthews with emphasis, "that it had been in my power to have afforded him relief adequate to the feelings of my heart."—He paused, and then proceeded thus—"I have taken means to inform myself of Lord William's health, and it gives me extreme satisfaction to learn his amendment—return him my most grateful acknowledgments for his intention in sending me the purse, but I must decline the acceptance of it.—Say also, that I shall seek a time to thank him more fully."

"Let us go to the castle and thank him," exclaimed Edward, "and then perhaps we shall see the soldiers performing their exercise."

"Good night, Sir," said Matthews; "I pray you execute my message punctually:" and having said this, he took the hand of Edward, and walked away from Ambrose.

The Baron awaited impatiently the return of his messenger, and when he arrived at the castle, he was instantly admitted into his Lord's apartment.

Ambrose related with exactness, all that had passed between him and his aunt, as also the conversation which he had overheard, from his covert behind the bushes, and his subsequent one with Matthews; and then retired.

When reclined on his pillow, the Baron felt a stronger inclination than ever to gain an explanation of what had appeared mysterious to him on the night of his accident. From Matthews's words, "that he should seek a time to thank him more fully," he conceived it possible that he might only be wanting an apt opportunity to explain to him what he had witnessed; and he accordingly resolved, as soon as he was able to go the distance, to call in person at Matthews's cottage, under pretence of making his verbal acknowledgments to him.

In about three weeks, Lord William was able to put his design into execution, and taking with him only Ambrose, he set out on his visit to the cottage by the side of the lake.

It was now the middle of January, the weather cold and frosty; the Baron was on horseback, and Ambrose walked by his side. At the distance of about a quarter of a mile from Matthews's cottage, Lord William looking forward, said, "who is this that comes running towards us?"

"It is Matthews's grandson," replied Ambrose; "and see, my Lord, he observes us, and quickens his pace."

In a few moments they met—"O Sir," exclaimed Edward, addressing Ambrose, "how very glad I am to meet you! I was coming to the castle; my poor grandfather is taken so ill, that he thinks he is going to die; and I am running to the castle with a message from him, to implore the good Baron to come and visit him;—do you think he will condescend to comply with my grandsire's request?"

"Set your heart at ease, my boy," returned the Baron, "Lord William will be at his cottage in a few minutes; I myself am he." So saying, the Baron dismounted from his horse, and telling Ambrose he should walk the rest of the way to the cottage, directed him to mount and make all possible speed back to the castle, and return without delay to Matthews's cottage with the surgeon of his household.

Ambrose obeyed his directions, and the Baron walked on with Edward.

"Has your grandfather been ill long?" asked Lord William.

"Only since yesterday evening; but he says he is sure he is going to die," replied the boy, the tears rolling down his cheeks.

"You love your grandfather, I see," said the Baron.

"I have never known any body else to love," returned Edward; "I have never known either friend or relation but him, and should he die, I have nobody to care for me or to protect me."

"Come, come," said the Baron, "do not fear the worst, he may yet recover, and live many years."

"O no, I fear not," returned the boy, "when I left him just now, he trembled and shivered so much, I scarcely expect to find him alive when I get back, though I left him sitting over the hearth; and I had piled all the wood upon it that it would hold too; but nothing could warm him."

A very short time brought them to the cottage; Edward ran in first; "Oh, he is dead, he is dead!" exclaimed the youth, and threw himself in anguish upon the floor, on which the old man had fallen from his seat during his absence, and on which he now lay senseless.

"You alarm yourself too much," said the Baron, who had followed Edward close upon his heels; "he is not dead, he breathes still."

"But he will die, I am sure he will," cried Edward.

"Let us replace him in his seat," said Lord William, "and endeavour by simple means to keep life in him, till one shall arrive who better understands the operations of nature."

They succeeded in placing him on his chair, and Edward, by the Baron's directions, bathed his temples and the palms of his hands; after some time he opened his eyes, and threw them wildly around without any expression:—at length they settled on Lord William: on seeing him, the blood mantled in his cheeks; his lips moved as if he would have spoken, but no sound proceeded from them; with much difficulty he raised his hand, and pointed towards Edward; the tear of supplication stood in his eye, and he kept it fixed on Lord William.

"Is it my protection for that boy, you wish to ask?" said De Mowbray.

Again Matthews struggled with greater violence than before to speak; the exertion overpowered him quite, and he sunk back in his chair.

"Now he is dead, and I have no friend left me!" exclaimed Edward, falling at his feet, and burying his face between the old man's knees.

Lord William thought as the youth did, but he forbore to confirm his fears, by letting fall his own suspicions; earnestly did he pray for assistance from his castle; and as the time passed on, and no signs of animation were visible in Matthews, he began to conclude that it would indeed come too late.

From what was just past, it was evident to the Baron that Matthews's motive in sending for him, had been to implore his protection for his grandson; but might it not have been possible, he thought, that if the power of speech had been permitted to him, he might have had some secret of moment to disclose to him—some discovery to make, some explanation to convey relative to the mystery of that night, on which he had before seen him. It was still possible that the art of physic might recall the dying embers of his life into a momentary blaze, before they should be extinguished for ever; and his anxiety for the arrival of the surgeon swelled the minutes into hours.—At length he came, escorted by Ambrose. Matthews was not yet dead, he pronounced, but the hand of Death was upon him.

Ambrose and the surgeon conveyed him to his bed, and proper means were used for recalling his senses. All endeavours for a time proved ineffectual—life was drawing to its close, and his disorder was merely the last flickerings of the lamp before it expired for ever.

The Baron placed himself by the side of the old man's bed. The medicines which the surgeon had administered, had induced a composure resembling sleep; his breathings were audible, and his shiverings had ceased.

"He will never use them again," said Edward, the tears streaming down his cheeks, and removing from a table in the apartment some scattered papers which lay upon it, and the implements for writing.

"What are those?" asked the Baron, pointing to the papers.

"They are," replied Edward, "verses which he writes in the night, when I am gone to bed; he is very fond of passing his time in writing, only he never does so when I am up, lest I should be melancholy for want of conversation.—He wrote that last night," added the boy, putting a paper into Lord William's hands, which he found to contain:

AN ODE TO WINTER.

Winter bound in icy chains,
Slowly creeps along the plains;
Naked branches shivering stand,
Withering under his command;
If a single leaf appears
Still bedew'd with Autumn's tears,
The tyrant views, with envious glance,
The glittering diamonds it sustains;
He breathes around, and nought remains
Of Autumn's richly-tinted stains,
Unless a hidden spray escapes awhile perchance.

Imperious now he sits on high,
Scattering whirlwinds from the sky;
Spreading devastation round,
He skims the earth, and seas profound;
Waves that gently kiss'd the shore,
As they lav'd their golden bed,
Now with thundering fury roar,
Dashing every mainmast head:

While wash'd from off the shattered deck,
Yet clinging to the buoyant wreck,
The sailor sees, in wild despair,
A foaming billow high in air;
Desponding, yet still firm and brave,
He stems the awful mighty wave;
Till mountains over mountains roll,
From east to west, from pole to pole,
And plunge him deep within a watery grave.

Various troubles now assail
The humble tenant of the vale—
Labour, that gives with every meal,
What pampered luxury ne'er can feel;
Labour, that smooths his rugged bed,
And seasons high his oaten bread,
Stern Winter, with terrific frown,
Denies; and rules the world alone.
The polished plough-share strives in vain,

To sever Winter's icy chain;
The adamantine soil repels
With sullen firmness every stroke,
With vegetative life it swells,
Yet cannot break the galling yoke.

'Tis night; the sun his light withholds;
While cottag'd industry unfolds
Her simple work—her evening care—
No precious moment can she spare.
Contentedly the weary sire,
Sits o'er his dying, scanty fire
Till cold and chill, on either hand,
A group of cherubs shivering stand,
Begging a brighter blaze may rise,
With lisping tongues, and pleading eyes:
Thus nature pleads; nor ever pleads in vain;
The father eyes his little store;
One log, he thinks, can't make him poor;
And soon each face reflects a smile again.

The ling'ring sand now wasting shows,
The hour approaching for repose.
The pallet's spread; the mother sees
Her infant offspring laid at ease,
Then strait retires, but not to rest,
For cares unnumber'd fill her breast:
The spectre, poverty, an inmate here,
Within her breast excites no fear;
But wasted famine's haggard eye,
Bespeaks too hard a destiny;
Her fortitude within her dies,
And even hope, reluctant flies:
But soon upborne on silken wings,
A beauteous seraph comfort brings,
Religion, never-ceasing, bounteous power
Of those who seek her in affliction's hour—
Religion brings her peace when hope is fled,
And dries those tears her eyes in anguish shed.

No sportive matin song of birds,
Ushering in the crimson dawn,

No distant sound of lowing herds,
Awake to life a Winter's morn;
No cowslips gild the dewy lawn,
No ruddy blossoms deck the thorn;
The modest daisy hides its head,
Beneath its cold and watery bed;
The flaunting poppy, pert and gay,
Attendant on a summer's day,
Resigns its soft Lethean power,
And sinks the victim of an hour.
Stagnation reigns in every withering leaf,
And mourning Nature looks absorbed in grief,
Till Phœbus sheds his many-coloured rays,
And on the glittering surface softly plays;
Dissolving quickly then the snow,
Falls trembling from the mountain's brow;
And soon no vestiges remain,
Of all that whitened o'er the plain.

Thus ends the reign of Nature's icy foe;
Whilst, first of gifts that from her bosom flow,
Spring returns with aspect mild,
Violet crown'd, her loveliest child:
Now again the ruddy thorn,
Glitters with the dew of morn;
Buzzing round sweet cowslip bells,
Bees suck nectar from their cells;
The vivid flash from beauty's eye,
When tell-tale love is lurking nigh;
The pleading look, the starting tear,
That parting lovers often wear;
The balmy kiss, the gentle sigh
Escaping, yet it knows not why;
All hail the lovely bloom of opening Spring,
While Cupid's arrows flutter from its wing.
Give me a heart to enjoy her various charms,
For by her power, misfortune she disarms;
And hours of tears, and days of grief and pain,
Are lulled when Nature smiles, and Spring resumes her reign.

The lines which Lord William had just read bore evident marks that they proceeded from a mind which had enjoyed the benefits of education, and not from that of a rude shepherd; and this conviction made him still more earnest to derive, if possible, from Matthews, some account of himself, before his death.

As evening drew in, the surgeon recommended to the Baron to return for the night to his castle, saying that it was extremely uncertain how long the existence of Matthews might still be protracted; and promising to send for him immediately, if any material change should take place; but the desire of fathoming the mystery which appeared connected with the boy, to whom he was so extraordinarily called, by his helpless state, to give protection, prompted him not to quit the spot; and he sent home Ambrose to account for his absence.

During the night no alteration took place in old Matthews; about seven in the morning his respiration became more difficult, and opening his eyes, he endeavoured to lift himself up in his bed, which Lord William perceiving, lent his assistance to raise him on his pillow. Matthews turned his eyes upon him, a faint smile of pleasure sparkled in them at the sight of the Baron, and he pressed his fevered hand upon that of De Mowbray, as if to thank him for his presence.

Edward came to his side;—Matthews recognized him;—the boy understood that he did so, and throwing his arms round his neck, hung weeping upon him.—Matthews held him there some minutes, while he appeared to be in silent prayer; then disengaging himself from his embrace, he turned his head towards the Baron; he endeavoured to address him, although unintelligible words alone proceeded from his lips, of this he did not himself seem sensible, but continued to speak: at length, "protect, protect him!" were distinguishable; on this Matthews paused;—"I will protect him," replied Lord William, "while he continues worthy of my favour." Again Matthews spoke, his agitation appeared violent; he seemed to be wishing to convey to the Baron an idea how very worthy the boy was of such favour, but one word only was articulate in all he spoke, and that was "*noble.*"—But whether the epithet had been applied by Matthews to his mind, or to his blood, the Baron was undecided, although he conceived that the old man had endeavoured to indicate the latter.

Anxious still for some clue to the mystery of that night which had introduced him to Matthews's acquaintance, he requested the surgeon and Edward to leave him for a few moments alone with the dying man. They complied, and Lord William lost not a moment in advancing the inquiry, for the purpose of making which he had required their absence;—whilst he spoke, he saw the eyes of Matthews fixed on him; and when he had made his demand, they still continued the same;—he repeated his question, and took the old man's hand in his, by pressing which he hoped the more earnestly to engage his attention to what he was saying. His eyes still continued unmoved; he breathed a faint sigh, sunk back on his pillow, and expired.

The Baron stamped with his foot upon the floor, and Edward with the surgeon immediately came up. On hearing the event of the last moments, expected as the issue of his grandfather's illness had been by him, still the acuteness of Edward's sorrow was as violent as if the shock had been sudden; so true is it, that hope hangs on the last thread of a valued existence, and does not fly us till that thread is divided past repair.

At this moment arrived Ambrose, and two other servants from the castle, with refreshments for their lord, who directed them to proceed to the village, and procure proper persons to perform the due offices to the dead body; and commanded Ambrose not to leave the cottage till the interment had taken place, concerning which, he said, he should in the course of the day issue his orders.

This done, he directed Edward to collect for him all the papers which had belonged to his late grandfather; they composed only a small roll, which the boy took from a drawer in the chamber; and the Baron receiving it at his hand, invited Edward to accompany him to his castle.

Edward entreated to be permitted to remain with the corpse of his grandsire, till it should become a tenant of the earth; but to this request, the Baron replied, "No, Edward, that must not be; I have promised you my protection, which promise includes in it my friendship; and consistently with these titles, I cannot permit you to pay an attendance inimical to the return of peace to your own mind."

Edward again kissed the cold lips of his grandfather, and bursting into a flood of tears, gave his hand to Lord William, and suffered himself to be led away by it, from that humble cot, which had hitherto been the scene of all his boyish griefs and joys.—Happy age! why are thy hours so fleeting? why are thy minutes the painful prologues to the bitter tale of life?

On their arrival at the castle, the Lady de Mowbray was just risen, and the breakfast-table spread: Lord William introduced to her his young charge; and the little Rosalind, who had just completed her sixth year, smiled her welcome to the first being so near her own age, whom she had yet seen admitted an inmate of the castle walls.

The Lady de Mowbray, whose gentle soul expanded in tenderness to every child of sorrow, exerted herself, with the most happy art, to repel the flowing tide of grief that streamed down the cheeks of the youthful Edward; but although she soothed the anguish of his heart by her motherly attentions, still she could not prevail on him to join in their meal; his heart was overcharged with grief, and at the present moment he loved it as his best friend, for it filled up every vacancy that his lost friend had filled before.

With the first opportunity, Lord William examined the papers he had brought with him from the cottage, but to his disappointment, there was no information to be gathered from them. Some contained only lines of poetry, and others essays on various subjects, which he thought appeared to have been written for the instruction of Edward. Not a single word was to be found in them, concerning the family, fortunes, or name, of him by whom they had been written.

At the due time, the interment of Matthews took place; and the sorrow of Edward was again awakened to its keenest pitch, by attending the body to the grave. But friendless as he had conceived his case to be, the poor Edward had many consolers and many comforters; the peculiarity of his unfortunate situation, added to his engaging disposition, won him the hearts of the whole castle, as well as those of its Lord and Lady.

A few days after the funeral, Lord William took occasion to talk apart with Edward; there might still, he thought, be a clue to the unravelling of the mystery concerning Matthews, within the breast of the youth himself, although he might be unconscious that the intelligence he might have it in his power to give, was the solution of any dark occurrence; for this purpose, leading him one day into the garden, he thus began—"How old do you say you are, Edward?"

"I shall be nine years old on the first of next May," the boy replied.

"And how many years have you lived in the cottage by the side of the lake?"

"Ever since I can remember; I never lived any where else till I came to this castle."

"And how long had your grandfather lived there, do you know that?" inquired the Baron.

"No, that I don't indeed," replied the boy.

"He had not always lived there, then, I suppose?" Lord William said.

"I dare say not," returned Edward, "for I have heard him talk of London and Scotland, and many places that he had been in, he said."

"He must have found his cottage a very solitary place, after having been accustomed to the busy scenes of life; but I suppose you had visitors?"

"No, never," replied Edward; "nobody came to see us, except by chance any of the peasants round about the neighbourhood had business with my grandfather."

"Indeed!" returned De Mowbray; "are you sure nobody ever came to your cottage as a visitor, either by day or by night?"

"I never saw any body in the daytime, I am sure," answered the youth; "and what should any body come for in the night?"

That was what the Baron wished to discover; but the means seemed as far distant as ever. They walked on some minutes in silence, Lord William watching the countenance of the youth, but unable to discover in it the reflection of any sentiment in his heart which betrayed him acquainted with the subject at which the Baron was hinting.

"Do you remember the night on which I fell from my horse near your grandfather's cottage, and broke my leg?" asked De Mowbray.

"Oh yes, very well," replied Edward; "he told me of your accident when I awoke in the morning; and he often made inquiries about you of the peasants, and was quite pleased to find you were getting well."

"Then you were asleep when it happened, and knew nothing of his coming out to give me assistance till the next morning?"

"No, nothing; he told me of it then; he said, I had been in bed an hour or two when he heard your cries."

"Was he alone when you went to bed?" asked the Baron.

"Yes," replied the boy; "you forget, my Lord, that I told you before there never was any body with us; why did you think there was?"

"I thought I saw another man besides your grandfather," replied the Baron, "and guessed it might have been some unfortunate straggler, from the bands of the Scottish ravagers, to whom his humanity had tempted him to give shelter."

"Indeed you were mistaken," returned Edward, "for I am sure there was nobody in the cottage but us two."

The ingenuousness of the youth convinced the Baron that he was really unacquainted with a third person having been the inmate of the cottage that night; indeed it was natural to suppose, that whatever deed had been passing in it at the time, that required secrecy from the world, would have been concealed from a boy of eight years of age. He was not sure that it would be right in him ever to inform the boy of what he knew; the present, he was certain, was not a time for such communication; he therefore discontinued the subject, and they returned together to the castle.

CHAPTER VI.

We are as twinn'd lambs that did frisk i' th' sun,
And bleat the one to t'other; what was chang'd
Was innocence for innocence; we knew not
The doctrine of ill-doing; no, nor dream'd
That any did.

THE WINTER'S TALE.

SEVERAL years passed on, during which Edward was the universal favourite of the inhabitants of De Mowbray Castle, and very frequently the playfellow of the little Rosalind.

Wary as was the general conduct of Lord William, he had not the judgment to understand that those intimacies which are contracted in innocence of heart, are more difficult to be broken off than such as are formed upon passion; thus, while he considered them as too young to love, he foresaw no growing mischief in a partiality which he conceived to proceed merely from an equality of years, and a liking for the same sports and toys.

But young as Edward was, his soul was naturally of that manly disposition, that the ball and kite would have been looked upon with contempt by him, with any other companion in their exercise than Rosalind; but with her, although he did not yet understand the nature of his feelings, every trivial amusement became of the highest consequence; and an accidental feather, which she had in sport blown along the air, was a treasure worthy to be hoarded in his breast.

Still Edward found time for the grand passion of his heart, which was the rival of his sports with Rosalind, and this was that of endeavouring to make some proficiency in the use of arms. The Baron perceived his martial disposition, and took pleasure in having him instructed in the science he loved: he was observant of the lessons he received, and did credit to those who were, by turns, his tutors.

Lord William often reflected on the mysterious manner in which Edward had been thrown upon his protection; sometimes he felt inclined to trust to him the mystery which had attended the first night of his introduction to his grandfather; but this idea was always overruled by the consideration that such knowledge might fill with anxiety and melancholy the heart of one whose conduct, during the time he had been an inmate of De Mowbray Castle, had been the most deserving.

About the time that Edward had attained his fourteenth year, was the period at which the incursions of the borderers called so strongly for the counter-exertions of the English government, that the Queen commanded the fortifying of all the castles on the borders of the kingdom, amongst which that of De Mowbray was one of the principal.

Young as Edward was, he was extremely alert in attending Lord William during the time that the castle was receiving additional strength from the architect; and the zeal with which he lent such assistance as his youth enabled him to give to the preparations for repelling the foe, added to the Baron's knowledge of his love for arms, induced him to promise the youth, that in the new troops which he was about to levy, he should be an active member.

Edward already thought himself a hero of renown; already he saw a gigantic Scotchman dead at his feet, and his pike smoking with his blood; his heart leaped with joy at the idea, not because he was to become a murderer, but because he was to become a brave soldier: cruelty was no inmate of his heart; he would at any time rather have gone a mile out of his way, than have trodden on a helpless worm.

When he first saw Rosalind, after the promise made to him by Lord William—"Oh, Rosalind!" he cried, "I never can be sufficiently thankful to Lord William. I am to be a member of his new troops, when they are all raised."

"And shall you like that?" said Rosalind, the words faltering on her tongue.

"To be sure I shall," replied he. "Oh, what havoc I shall make amongst the foe! It will be glorious!"

"How can you talk so about killing people?" asked Rosalind. "What have they done to you, that you should thus seem to enjoy the idea of their death?"

"Why," rejoined he, "are they not the enemies of our country?—the enemies of our good Queen, who is the favourer of my protector?—and who is, what I like her still better for, the godmother of Rosalind?"

Rosalind smiled, then said—"But should you be killed yourself?"

Edward looked at Rosalind, then at the ground, then again at Rosalind; and for the first time ventured to thank her anxiety for him with a gentle kiss, which she scarce felt touch her cheek. Lady de Mowbray entered at the moment; the action did not escape her, but she did not notice that she had seen it. Lord William almost immediately followed her into the apartment, and Rosalind enquired, with an agitation which he did not observe—"when the new troops were to be raised?"

Lord William replied—"Oh, some time hence, when our castle is fortified."

The words "some time hence," Rosalind flattered her own wishes by giving the utmost latitude imaginable to; and composure quickly returned to her spirits.

Whilst the preparations for repelling the incursions of the Moss-troopers were forwarding with all possible alacrity, amidst the daily labourers at the castle, was an elderly man, a mason by trade, who having represented himself to Lord William as a widower, the father of a large family of children, whom he was unable to support by his labour with any degree of comfort, petitioned employment for his eldest boy, who he said was about fourteen years old, and able to assist in carrying stones and mortar. The Baron assented to his petition; and on the following day appeared amongst the workmen, the boy, whose name was Hubert.

Edward, constant in watching the progress which was making in fortifying the castle, saw, in turn, every workman employed in it, and amongst the rest, Hubert caught his attention. The lad had a fine countenance, though a cloud of discontent hung over it; his limbs were well formed, but the scantiness of his cloaths had exposed them to many hardships, of which they bore the marks; shoes he had none; the soles of his feet seemed of equal hardness with the flints on which he trod, by the unconcern with which he moved over them, when heaviest laden; uncovered, like his feet, was his head; and his dark brown hair hung in matted folds about his face and neck.

Edward eyed him with attention; and whilst he looked at him, he drew a comparison between his own happy situation and the comfortless one of poor Hubert, exposed to the biting winds of March, and shivering under burdens too great for his strength and age. The lad climbed the castle wall with a stone on his shoulder, and moved out of Edward's sight.

Towards evening, Edward was again on the ramparts; as he was approaching towards an angle of the castle, he heard a voice say—"Why, you are cold, boy!"—"Aye, and hungry too!" was the reply. He turned the angle, and saw Hubert beating himself with his arms, to produce circulation in his almost frozen blood. It was already dusk, the workmen were departing, and amongst them, Hubert almost immediately left the ramparts. On the following morning, Edward took with him a slice of meat upon a cake of bread, and with these he went in search of Hubert. Before he had delivered his present, he met the Baron.

"What have you got there, Edward?" he asked. "What, hungry so soon after breakfast!"

"I hope you are not angry, my Lord?" replied Edward. "I hope I have not done wrong; but it is to give away." And he then related his intention.

Lord William was a character which is very common in the world at the present day, and most probably was not singular in those he lived in; he was a good man in every respect where it did not interfere with his own views to be so; thus he only chid Edward for apprehending his displeasure for such a trifling liberty, and was passing on, when the object of Edward's charity appeared in view, and Lord William stopped to observe him.

"Here, Hubert," said the youth, advancing towards him, "here is a piece of bread and meat for you."

"You can't eat it yourself, I suppose," returned Hubert, without stopping to take it.

"You draw a very unkind inference from my action," replied Edward, not a little hurt; "and what I did not expect from you."

Hubert's father appeared in sight at the moment Edward spoke.

"Come hither," said Lord William, calling to him; "your's is an insolent boy, and deserves punishment: this youth just now offered him some food, out of compassion to his comfortless appearance; and instead of thanking him, he told him that he supposed he could not eat it himself."

"Pray, my Lord, forgive him," said the father. "I have tried every means in my power to alter his disposition; but I cannot by any method break him of speaking exactly what he thinks upon every occasion. I am sure he did not mean to offend—he has one of the best hearts in the world; and I am certain he is hungry enough too."

Lord William was going to reply, when he was interrupted by the yelping of a dog behind him. The mastiff belonging to the castle had, out of tyranny, hunger it could not be, snatched a bone from a cur belonging to one of the workmen, whose apparent ribs eloquently told the hungry state of his stomach, and who was now bewailing his loss.

Hubert came running up to Edward, "I beg your pardon, Sir,

for what I said," he cried; "pray will you give me the meat and bread now?"

The hand in which Edward had at first held it out to the lad, was still extended with it; and as he did not withdraw it on Hubert's request, the lad took it into his. "Thank you gratefully, Sir," he cried, and running up to the howling cur, laid it down before him.

"What is that for?" asked Lord William.

"To reward him, my Lord," said the lad, "because he was run down for being poor."

"He *has* one of the best hearts in the world!" exclaimed Edward, "and I wish Lord William would let me ask him to dine at the castle."

Lord William smiled at the earnestness with which Edward advanced his petition; and with a caution to the lad not to speak his thoughts again with the freedom he had just been guilty of, he gave him his permission to dine with the servants at the castle that day.

From this time, there was a something, inexplicable almost to himself, unless it could be accounted for by that reverence which a mind of discernment naturally feels for a noble and honest heart, which led Edward to throw himself perpetually in the way of Hubert; and to him, and him alone, the lad relaxed in that roughness of temper which he maintained towards every one else, and which proceeded from his sense of Edward's benevolent feelings towards him, and from gratitude for the many favours which he received at his hands.

In the course of about three years, the castle was in a state of such forwardness, that Lord William began to raise the men, who were to render that strength a terror to the enemy.

Edward was now on the point of completing his seventeenth year, and the Baron realized the promise which he had made to him, by giving him the command of a small body of men, into which number the *surly* Hubert, for by this appellation he was generally known, voluntarily enlisted.

At the close of another twelvemonth, Lord William seeing his plans of defence drawing towards a state of perfectness, and all the levies of men which he had demanded raised, judged the present an expedient time for going to London, and basking for a while in that sunshine of favour, which the Queen would doubtless warm him with, in return for his alert execution of her commands, and which would render him the envy of the court. Another motive also impelled him to this journey; his Rosalind, the god-daughter of her Queen, had never yet been introduced to the metropolis: Elizabeth had never seen her, since she had held her an infant in her arms; her charms were now beginning to expand into the most lovely bloom of perfection; and he hesitated not to conclude, that she would be no sooner seen, than some exalted alliance would offer itself to her acceptance, as the possession of her hand would be deemed a never-failing passport to the favour of the Queen.

To Lady de Mowbray he accordingly imparted his intention of setting out, as soon as the necessary preparations could be made for their journey: she had never visited the court since she had become a wife, and from causes confined to her own breast, she felt a reluctance ever to return to it; but the will of her husband was absolute; and she also considered it becoming that Rosalind should not be withheld from a visit to the Queen, who had so frequently asked to see her: she therefore acquiesced in his plan.

To Rosalind, the sensation of leaving home was a new one, and she knew not whether it inspired pleasure or pain. There was something too gratifying to the heart of youth, in the idea of being received at court as the child of her sovereign, not to inspire her with some degree of pleasure; but it was counterbalanced by the wish that she had a brother to share her joy; and she wished that Edward were that brother; but he was to stay at home, exposed to attacks from the enemy; he might fall before she should return, and she might even have no nominal brother to relate her adventures to. These were feelings which she could not subdue, and with a blush, she whispered them in her mother's ear. Lady de Mowbray endeavoured to rally her out of her ideas, but as she spoke, the tear stole down her own cheek.—"Why do you weep, my dearest mother?" said Rosalind.

"Not at any present unhappiness, believe me, my child," she replied; "thoughts are intrusive visitors, that will come unbidden: —before I die, you shall know whence they proceed."

The Baroness here broke off the conversation, and the necessary preparations for their journey prevented Rosalind from dwelling so much on her mother's words, as she otherwise might have done.

To Irwin, his first leader, Lord William deputed the chief command in his absence; and under him, Edward was appointed to a post of the next importance.

On the morning of their departure, Edward attended them to their horses; the bustle of preparation had allowed them scarcely a moment to bid farewell.—Rosalind caught one unobserved, as she passed through the castle-hall, to say—"Take care of yourself, Edward; do not run heedlessly into danger, should you have to encounter the foe. If you should be killed before I return, I shall wish I had never known you as"——she hesitated.

"As what, dear Rosalind?" asked the youth.

"As my brother," she replied.

"And should I be safe and well at your return, shall you be as glad to see me as if I were really your brother?" he rejoined.

"Oh yes," she answered; "but should you have exposed your life to danger, I shall not love your memory, though I am sure I shall weep for your death."

The Baron was already on his horse, and calling to her to follow thus not another word passed—Edward pressed her hand in his, and they parted.

CHAPTER VII.

Thou cam'st on earth, to make the earth my hell,
Tetchy and wayward was thy infancy;
Thy school-days, frightful, desperate, wild, and furious,
Thy prime of manhood, daring, bold, and venturous;
Thy age confirm'd, proud, subtle, sly, and bloody.

KING RICHARD III.

THEIR reception at court was as flattering as Lord William had predicted it would be; and the charms of his daughter created all that admiration which communicates the glow of pleasure to the hearts of fond parents.

Lord Burleigh, it has already been said, was the uncle of Lady de Mowbray; thrice had he visited Cumberland since the birth of Rosalind, and at every visit his conduct had been the most attentive, and apparently kind, to his niece; still it had been evident that her acknowledgments of it had not proceeded from the heart, but were the result of politeness, and that she looked upon him with something like awe and distrust.

At the period of Lord William and his family visiting the court, the Queen was lending her assistance to the Protestants in France, to whom she had sent many of her troops; and a decisive battle shortly expected to take place, which would restore them to their rights, and put an end to the religious broils which then agitated the sister kingdom.

Lord Burleigh paid the same attention to his niece, which he had ever been remarkable for doing since her marriage; and appearing one day in the utmost good humour, which disposition he seldom shewed, even if he felt it—gravity being the natural tone of his temper—Rosalind perceived her mother collecting, as it were, her strength to speak, and with a half-choaked utterance she said, "Where, my Lord, is now my cousin, Harry Cecil?"

"He is honoured by bearing the arms of England in France," returned Lord Burleigh.

Lady de Mowbray sighed, and nothing farther on the subject passed.

When the family of De Mowbray had been about two months at the court of Queen Elizabeth, and she had finally asserted the justice of the Protestant claim, the English troops were recalled from the Continent; and a day, at a short distance from their return, was appointed for them to receive the thanks of their royal mistress. This day was destined by the Queen for festivity; in the morning she gave notice that she should receive her warriors in her drawing-room, and promised to her court a splendid ball in the evening.

Lord William de Mowbray understanding, that although the Queen had not expressed it, she still expected it, as a compliment due to the anticipated pleasures of the evening, that such of the nobility as were invited to share in them, should attend her in the morning, and be present at her reception of the officers on their return from foreign service, the Lady de Mowbray and her daughter composed part of the levee, which was very numerously attended. As god-daughter to the Queen, Rosalind always found the place of pre-eminence yielded to herself, and on that morning she and her mother happened to stand at the right hand of Elizabeth—a situation which gave them an opportunity of particularly observing each officer as he approached the throne.

To Rosalind, every face which came up to receive that mark of the royal favour, which was conferred in the liberty of kissing her Majesty's hand, was a new one; to her mother, the countenances of some of the veterans in service were familiar; and next to the Queen, she became the object of their notice.

Whilst Lady de Mowbray was engaged with these in conversation, Rosalind's eyes were observing the succession of claimants for the Queen's smile, and amongst the number, one particularly arrested her attention; and the impression he made on her senses was almost that of fear.

His figure was so tall, as even to be gigantic; his limbs appeared cast in the same mould with those of Hercules, and his broad shoulders seemed like those of another Atlas, capable of bearing another globe; the lines of his face were hard, and his penetrating, dark eye, beamed with ferocity rather than courage; still his countenance was indisputably handsome; and from the necessity of confessing it to be so, the keenness of his features appeared the more dreadful. He seemed at least forty years of age, and Rosalind thought that he might probably be more; but his person was such as did not betray the full sum of his years. He was cased in a complete armour of polished steel, studded at the points with gold; at his back hung a cloak of tyger skin, intertwined with a crimson scarf, richly embroidered with gold, to correspond with the ornaments of his armour; and in his hand he held a helmet, on the top of which nodded a forest of black plumes, and which, when placed upon his head, must have raised him a couple of feet in height above his companions.

He was announced as Lord Rufus de Madginecourt.

On retiring from the foot of the throne, he cast his eyes around, as if in search of some face which he might recognise; they fell on Lady de Mowbray, and he moved up to her. They entered into a conversation which denoted them well acquainted; and the firmness of De Madginecourt's voice corresponded with the strength of his form.

Lord William came up to the spot where they were standing, and after a few introductory sentences had passed between him and Lord Rufus, he said, "my Lord, I have a daughter, who must congratulate you on your return, as her father's friend;" and having said this, he led Rosalind forward by the hand.

Lord Rufus received her with the smile of a courtier; but as his eyes encountered her's, they sparkled with the fire of admiration, and he exclaimed, "By Heaven, De Mowbray, all the lilies which the Court of France can boast, must droop before this English rose.—Your father and I, lady," he continued, addressing Rosalind, "are old friends, and we must become better acquainted;—let this kiss," and he imprinted one on her glove as he spoke, "be the bond of my claiming your hand for the dance this evening."

Rosalind had no plea for refusing his request, but the insufficient one that she should have liked any other partner better; and timid of a refusal, she bowed acquiescence.

In the evening, Lord Rufus appeared divested of his armour, and splendidly attired; his attentions during the evening to Rosalind were marked, but she could not help considering them, and she hoped her idea was a just one, as the effect of vanity—inspired by seeing himself the partner of a woman, whose hand was that night the most in request, from the partiality with which the Queen treated her, rather than of any preference he felt for her person.

Rosalind's opinion was by no means a fallacious one: Lord Rufus de Madginecourt was descended from a family, which had for many reigns been of the first importance in the kingdom; he was now himself its head; and as such, in addition to his being known to be a firm adherent to the interests of the Protestant cause, and an implacable enemy of the Jesuits, who were the open foes of Elizabeth, he had been received at court with a great degree of partiality by the virgin Queen.

Lord Rufus, eminently proud of his family, vain of his person, and covetous of wealth and honour, had misconstrued, or rather turned to his own wishes, the favour of Elizabeth, by suffering himself to believe that her partiality for him extended beyond friendship; and that while the sons of monarchs, nay, even sovereigns themselves, were denied the participation of her throne, good fortune pointed to himself as the destined partner of her exalted situation.

A man less proud than himself, might have perceived that vanity was the only motive from which the Queen invited all the young noblemen of England to be continually about her person; he might have seen that her favours were equal, to the end that she might not lose the homage of one youth, whom it flattered the predominant passion of her breast to believe she held in the chains of adoration, not as a Queen, but as a female of superior personal charms.—To believe herself such, and to believe that others viewed her in the same light, was the only foible of a Queen, otherwise of an unimpeachable judgment and conduct; but even while acted upon by the only weakness that had place in her breast, she had still sufficient wisdom to determine within herself, that this indulgence should never lead her into repentance, by inducing her to give up that supremacy, which must have died away from her, into a husband's power, had she ever admitted a partner to her throne.

Blinded thus by a vanity, which had not that command over itself which the same passion possessed in the heart of the wary Elizabeth, Lord Rufus saw only the favours which he himself received at the hands of his sovereign; and believing himself the only man to whom they were extended, he already considered himself as the chosen participator of the English throne.

His false hopes were just risen to their climax, at the time at which the English troops were sent into France; and a command of importance, to which the Queen had appointed him, seemed, in his imagination, to decide the crown of glory, his. Ever haughty and imperious, his conduct was now more so than it had been before;—he saw that it offended, but he relaxed not of his dignity, self convinced that its enforcement would soon be allowed as his right.—Anxiously did he pant for his return, to prove it such; and exultingly did he triumph on this day, when ranged amongst the nobles of the court, he looked upon himself as the all-powerful Jove, in whose hand the resistless thunderbolt of power would soon be grasped.

He knew his person to be good; he had on this evening given it every advantage of splendid dress—to him a real advantage, for his height admitted the richness of his robes as such, when on any other person they would have looked the very pageantry of folly. Resistless he beheld his appearance, and desiring every part of his conduct to be alike deserving of approbation from the Queen, he asked the hand of Rosalind for the dance, not because her beauty and innocence claimed her every tribute of admiration—not because she was the daughter of his friend, De Mowbray, but because she was the god-daughter and favourite of the Queen.

Lord William was an attentive observer of the conduct of Lord Rufus towards his daughter; he judged it the opening of a growing passion, inspired by her blaze of beauty; and he felt no small delight in the conquest he conceived her to have made.

Rosalind herself feared what her father hoped and believed; and never had solitude appeared to her so irksome, as the festivities of that night; she longed to be walking on the ramparts of the castle, or indeed to be any where, rather than where she was; nay, she almost thought it cruel in herself to be revelling in an amusement from which her friend Edward was excluded.

The Lady de Mowbray was even more depressed in spirits than her daughter; her cousin Harry Cecil, had fallen in France; and she could not forbear paying the tribute of silent sorrow to his memory.

CHAPTER VIII.

For what is wedlock forced but a hell,
An age of discord and continual strife?
Whereas the contrary bringeth forth bliss,
And is a pattern of celestial peace.

FIRST PART OF HENRY THE SIXTH.

Three weeks were now only remaining of the time which had been set apart for the visit of the De Mowbray family to the court, and Lord William had resolved not to prolong it, as he judged that a farther absence from his castle, at the very period when it was first become capable of being rendered of material service, would wear an appearance of neglect on his part, which might, in all probability, offend his Queen.

It was now the month of May, and short as had been Rosalind's stay in the metropolis, she felt anxious to return to the country. Her taste was purely simple, and she preferred the beauties of nature to those of art: the rising of the summer was her favourite season of the year, and she knew that in London she should see little of its charms. Towards the close of February, when she had left the country covered with the desolation that winter spreads from its withering hands, which open only to disperse bleak winds, frozen air, and driving snows, she had found so many artificial causes conspiring to soften its rigour in London, and to change the face of the season, that she dreaded lest the months of summer should be as much transformed as she had seen those of its opposite season; and this idea lent its aid to other causes to make her desirous of returning into Cumberland.

Almost all the youths of the day who frequented the court, had fluttered round Rosalind's charms during her residence at it; but none had been sufficiently wounded by their lustre to seek the balm of possession for their cure: probably more than one had been withheld from a declaration of their passion by the watchfulness of Lord William, from whose frown they recoiled, none wishing to lie under the stigma of a refusal; and on almost all he *had* frowned when they had read his countenance, in order to learn from it his sentiments of their pretensions to his daughter's hand, since he had entertained a hope that she had fixed her image indelibly on the heart of Lord Rufus.

On the morning appointed for their departure, the Queen insisted on meeting them at breakfast early, as that meal was prepared to favour a long day's journey; the cold sirloin, with its wonted attendants, in those days, of ale and mead, graced the board. Lord Rufus was of the select invited to be present at their setting out; and the repast being concluded, a most gracious farewell from the Queen led them to the hall of the palace, from whence Lord Rufus attended them to their horses.

As soon as they were left to the privacy of their own party, the Baron demanded of Rosalind whether she regretted quitting the metropolis? Her answer was in the negative: and he then proceeded to questions which, although enveloped in ambiguous terms, she understood as inquiries whether her heart was returning from it as free from chains as he believed she had taken it thither; her answers were such as left him doubtful, and the conversation after some time took a turn. Lady de Mowbray had not joined in it; she had merely said, on quitting the city—"I shall never see London again;" and neither her husband, nor her daughter, made any reply to her observation.

Their journey was pleasant and safe. Towards the afternoon of one of those days when spring lavishes her smiles in the richest luxuriance on the earth, after refreshing showers have given new vigour to the vegetative world, and called forth that perfume which the healthy bed of nature exhales, when the sun casts a golden lustre on the glittering drops which hang sparkling on the flowers, and the birds hail its triumph over the cheerless rain with their songs, Rosalind's eye caught the lofty towers of De Mowbray Castle, as her horse bore her slowly up a hill, from which its battlements seemed warring with the clouds.

To most females of her rank and age, the sight would perhaps have occasioned a sensation not entirely pleasant. "Here," they would have sighed out, "I shall be immured at least for months, perhaps for years to come, in solitude! and oh, how bitterly shall I experience the reverse of this scene from those of gaiety I have just quitted!" But exactly the contrary were the feelings of Rosalind; a quick pulsation throbbed in her heart at the sight, and she exclaimed aloud—"We shall soon see Edward now; and oh, how much I have to tell him!"

They presently descended into a vale, where the castle disappeared from the sight of Rosalind, and nothing met her eye but the easy hills which formed its sloping sides, and which glittered like a bed of emeralds under the feet of the cattle which were browsing on their produce. As they again emerged from the vale, the castle once more became the prominent feature in the landscape; and the next to it in attraction was a body of Lord de Mowbray's men, who were seen drawn out on a velvet turf without the castle walls, in the act of practising the pike exercise, and on whose arms the declining sun shed its rays of crimson light.

On approaching this body, Lord William perceived at their head his chief leader, Irwin, and eager to inquire of him whether any matter of importance had occurred during his absence, he turned aside his horse from the road, saying that he would follow his wife and daughter to the castle.

No sooner had they passed the drawbridge, and entered the first court, than Edward was by their side, and Rosalind's cheek, for the first time, suffused with blood at beholding him; perhaps the blush was produced by the lesson of love which the different sensations with which she had beheld every other man, since her absence from home, could not have failed to have taught her.

The Lady de Mowbray was a silent spectator of their pleasure at meeting; she was fatigued with her journey, and retired almost immediately to her chamber.

"Thank Heaven, you are safe and well!" said Rosalind, the moment they were alone.

"Ah, Rosalind!" replied he, "can you think so kindly of me still, after the many men of rank and fortune who have, no doubt, sought from you that esteem you honour me with?"

"For shame, Edward," she returned; "don't you know me better than to think I could desert an old friend for any new acquaintance?"

"And have you not seen any one during your absence," replied Edward, his eyes sparkling with pleasure and triumph, "whom you have considered worthy the name of friend, which you honour me with?"

"No, indeed, I have not," she answered; "friendship must be founded on esteem, and how can I esteem those of whose interest in my happiness I have had no proof but their own words, equal to one like yourself, from whom I have received so many of a different nature? I know only their actions; I know your heart."

"Do you indeed?" said Edward with a sigh, half-pleased by the confession, half-fearing that she did not know it.

"Yes, I have known many instances of your goodness of heart," she said.

"I have never had an opportunity of doing you any service in my life; would I had been so fortunate," he replied; "or rather let me be thankful that you have never stood in need of the acceptance of any at my hands."

"But if you have never done me any, have not I been a witness of those you have conferred on others? and do you think me so selfish that I can only commend such benefits as I receive myself? Did not you give all your money to the poor woman that had her cottage burnt down, when you had been hoarding it for almost two months, to buy yourself a new sword with, and the first too you ever were to have?"

"That was selfish in me," replied Edward, "if you knew the truth."

"How can you speak so ill of yourself?" returned Rosalind, "when you know such was not the motive? Was it selfish in you to risk your own life by jumping into the lake after the poor woman's child, which had fallen into it, on the evening we went to visit the cottage where you lived with your grandfather?"

"Yes, it was indeed," replied the youth; "I was too proud of both those actions for them to deserve any name but that of selfishness; for I was so sure they would give you pleasure, that the satisfaction I received from their performance took away all the merit of my self-denial in the first instance, and my danger of being drowned in the second."

The Baron now came into the apartment, and Edward's conversation was immediately directed to him. The castle had been free from all assaults during Lord William's absence, and the neighbourhood very little infested with ravagers; to this account Edward added, that the fortifications were entirely completed, and that every workman had received his discharge.

Edward supped with the Baron and his daughter; and at an early hour the two latter retired to rest, to seek refreshment in sleep from the fatigues of their journey. Every favourite piece of furniture appeared to Rosalind an old friend after a long absence from home; and on entering her chamber, she cast her eyes around, to assure herself they were all in their proper places. Her lute lay on a table in her closet, and she could scarcely forbear even then calling forth some of the tones which she loved to hear it express; but she contented herself with a promise in her own mind, that it should be the first thing she did on rising in the morning; and she then entered her bed, where she slept with a serene composure which had been unknown to her, while revelling in the splendour of the court.

On the following morning, Lady de Mowbray was so unwell as not to be able to descend into the breakfast-room. For some days previously to her departure from the metropolis, she had complained of unpleasant feelings and faintness, which had been solely ascribed to her being at that time obliged to use greater exertions of strength than she was accustomed to do at De Mowbray Castle, where she was in the habit of visiting but little. During her journey, the sensations of which she had sometimes, though very seldom, complained, were placed to the same cause; and the physician still believed that her present inability to leave her chamber, proceeded from her strength and spirits having been too much called into action during her absence from home. But the illness of Lady de Mowbray continued to increase with each succeeding day, and the art of medicine gave no relief to a frame which was sinking under nature's debility. In the course of two months her approaching dissolution was so evident, that the physician ventured to announce to her family that his skill could not save her.

The Baron de Mowbray loved his wife, if not with the rapture of an impassioned lover, at least with that affection with which it became him to behold the mother of his child; and on the receipt of this intelligence, he expressed a sorrow which he really felt.

The lovely Rosalind, whose gentle nature, and whose sex, had allied her more strongly in affection to her mother, although she had never been defective in filial duty to her father, could scarcely support life, under the idea of the loss she was doomed to sustain; incessant tears flowed from her aching eyes, when she sought the solitude of her chamber to indulge her grief unobserved; and when she returned to the apartment of her mother, her heart was almost broken with the full tide of grief which she struggled to confine within her own breast.

In a gradual decay of nature, such as was the case with Lady de Mowbray, the animal strength faints and revives at intervals, like the last efforts of a dying lamp, and flatters with ungrounded hope, till a delusive blaze flames forth, the signal of its power being gone for ever.

A hectic colour had for two successive days tinged the cheeks of Lady de Mowbray; her voice had been stronger, and she had taken the refreshments which had been offered to her with a better appetite than she had done for some weeks before. Rosalind observed the change, and almost ventured to believe that it was the omen of amendment.

On the evening of the second day, the Baroness was sitting up in her bed, supported by pillows, and by her side sat her ever-watchful daughter. "My Rosalind," said her mother, "do you not recollect that on the day previously to our departure from this castle on our journey to the court, you spoke to me of your friendship for Edward, and hinted to me your apprehensions of never seeing him again? I endeavoured to rally you out of your fears; but as I spoke, the tear stole down my own cheek. You enquired the cause. I promised you that I would one day make it known to you—that moment is now at hand, for I feel that I shall not be long with you."

The tears now burst from the eyes of Rosalind, in spite of her efforts to subdue them.

"Do not weep, my sweet child," said the Lady de Mowbray; "death is but a short sleep, into which you will soon fall too, and then we shall be reunited." She kissed her daughter, and added—"Let your father be called to me—I have something yet to say to him before we part; if I defer it, my strength may not be equal to my inclination."

Lord William was summoned to the chamber; he approached the bed. Lady de Mowbray extended to him her feeble hand; he took it in his, and she spoke thus—"I feel, my husband, that my time on earth is short; it is still in your power to render the few moments I have to pass on it, happy ones—perhaps the happiest of my life."

The Baron entreated her to speak, declaring himself devoted to the will of rendering her happy by any means in his power.

"Have I," she asked, "proved myself to you a dutiful and affectionate wife?—Have I added comfort to the years I have lived with you?—Have I done any action that has made you repent your union with me?"

"Witness Heaven!" exclaimed the Baron, "that I consider you to have conformed, in every respect, to the character of a good wife, and an affectionate mother."

"Grant me then," she said, "for the fortitude I have shewn through life, the petition I urge to you on my bed of death.—De Mowbray, when I gave my hand to you, my heart was rent from his, with whom Heaven had united it:—life is in me past recall;—his spirit has already flown to happier realms; and it is now no sin to make confession of the truth.—From the hour of infancy, until that day when ripened sense pointed out to us too keenly the agony of separation, my cousin, Harry Cecil, was the only heart on which mine had ever reposed, in friendship or esteem.—I was an orphan—so was he—dependant both on my cruel uncle Burleigh.—He knew our love, but he forbade our union, with threats, which, desperate as they were, I knew him capable of putting into effect.—I was not allowed to speak in my own cause; and he gave you my hand:—Once become a wife, I resolved to perform, for duty's sake, what I could not do for love: you had been deceived, though I had been wronged; and I resolved that my conduct should never open your eyes to repentance.—You had not been the aggressor towards me; and I felt that I owed you good only for the situation to which you had raised me. I wrote to Harry Cecil, and charged him never to see me again; I obtained his promise.—The exercise of my duty towards you, you returned with an affectionate kindness, that gained you my love.—This child was given us to make the bond indissoluble."

The tears of the Baroness choked her utterance, and she fell upon the neck of Rosalind. Lord William stood as one entranced at what he had heard, and unable to reply. In a few moments she proceeded thus—"Heaven is my witness of the gratitude I have ever felt, that with me a forced marriage has been a happy one.—Witness also is the same Heaven of the blessings I have implored upon the head of him who has made it so.—But oh, I have known the dread attendant on the idea of being forced into a tyrant's arms; and the only pang I now feel, the only care that haunts me, as I tremble on the verge of the grave—the only tie that makes me wish to linger here—lest my poor child be ever exposed to such a misery. Soon will she be, as I was, without a mother to protect her, or to plead in her defence.—Pardon me, De Mowbray, that I should seem to hint a doubt of your protection equalling what mine and yours united have hitherto been; but I well know how men are urged by pride, how worked on by ambition, and how little feeling for a woman's love these passions leave within their hearts.—O, let not our child be such a victim!—oh, let me die happy—say that you will give my Rosalind to the man of her heart."

The Baron pressed the hand of his wife in silence; he felt his pressure returned with a grasp beyond her present strength, and he foresaw that it was the grasp of Death.—Her eyes were already dim, and her lips white; the exertion of the last half hour had hastened her scene of life towards its close, perhaps more speedily than it would else have drawn to it.—Her other arm was wound round the neck of Rosalind.—In accents scarcely audible, she repeated—"Give, oh give my Rosalind to the man of her heart!" and with a faint sigh, she expired.

The Baron immediately called in her attendants, and resting the fainting Rosalind upon his breast, he led her away from the scene of death.

Rosalind's tears would now no longer flow; the existence which she had so earnestly prayed to have protracted was fled past recall; and an entire stagnation of faculty, which denied her even the relief of tears, now bound up her feelings. Her attendant, the simple Gertrude, who was the niece of Ambrose, and had lately been admitted into her service, tried in vain to gain her attention to the words of comfort which she bestowed on her; but Rosalind heard her not; all sense lay buried in her; and she was almost as devoid of life as the corpse whose inanimation she bewailed.

The Baron, like his daughter, sought the solitude of his chamber; but he bewailed their common loss with a grief less poignant than her's; he was a worldly man, and the life of her whom he had just lost was not of sufficient weight in his scale of power or advancement, to create him any serious sorrow at her death;—he bewailed her as a wife whom he had loved, not as a privation, of which time would never efface the impression from his mind. He dwelt on the confession she had made of her heart's engagement ere she had known him; he felt that she deserved every remuneration for her conduct towards himself; and he believed it an impossibility that it should not be his wish, as well as her own, to give their "Rosalind to the man of her heart."

De Mowbray Castle had in former times been a religious foundation; hence its chapel was still extant, and in the use of the family;—in this chapel, accordingly, were the remains of Lady de Mowbray to be deposited; here was to be laid the stone that would close up all her earthly honours.

The eighth evening after her decease was appointed for her interment; the ceremony was performed by torch-light, and the gloom which pervaded the scene tended to string the wretched feelings Rosalind already experienced, to a higher pitch of misery.—Leaning, half-dead herself, upon the arm of her father, she followed that clay which was still dear to her, even though the life which had rendered it amiable had forsaken it:—the vaulted passages which led to the chapel, in the repetition of the slow steps which paced them, seemed to send forth murmurs in unison with the moment; and from the insufficiency of the torches to produce an even light as they were carried through them, their lofty roofs appeared to spread a sable canopy over the melancholy procession.

As they descended the steps which led from the last of these winding passages into the chapel, the organ poured forth its plaintive tones upon their ears:—Rosalind could no longer subdue her emotions, and the tears burst from her eyes, while groans of agony fell from her lips.—Still she retained sufficient strength to support herself, with the assistance of her father and Edward, from falling to the ground; but when the earth was thrown upon the coffin, and even that was hid for ever from her sight, all her little remaining fortitude died within her, and she sunk senseless into her father's arms.

For a length of time, the spirits of Rosalind gained little amendment from the state of depression into which her mother's death had thrown her. Seldom could she be induced to quit her own apartment; and then it was only to stroll through the gardens, or along the ramparts, attended by Edward, or the Baron.

Heavy was the heart of Rosalind, even after reason had chased from her breast the violence of grief, and reflection began again to exert its powers in her mind; she felt—inexplicable to herself was the feeling, but she could not divest herself of it, that all her happiness had died with her mother.

CHAPTER IX.

For 'tis the mind that makes the body rich:
And as the sun breaks through the darkest clouds,
So honour peereth in the meanest habit.
What, is the jay more precious than the lark
Because his feathers are more beautiful?
Or, is the adder better than the eel,
Because his painted skin contents the eye?

SHAKESPEARE.

NEARLY six months had elapsed since the death of the Lady de Mowbray, when on a winter's evening, which called for the most cheering blaze a wood fire could emit, the Baron, who, from respect to the feelings of his daughter, had spoken but little of his wife since her decease, produced a casket, in which, he said, she had told him, a few days previously to her death, that she had deposited some small legacies, which she wished him to distribute, when she was no more.

On opening it, he found her jewels inscribed to her daughter; several trinkets of small value, directed to her favourite servants; and a parcel superscribed for Edward, which contained a ruby cross, that Lord William recollected to have heard her say, had been given to her by her cousin Harry Cecil; and on the paper that enclosed it was written, *"Accept a mother's gift."*

"Next my heart will I wear it!" exclaimed Edward, "for she who gives it has indeed been a mother to me."

The tears of Rosalind flowed afresh as she looked upon the ornaments, which brought to her memory the form of her who had been accustomed to wear them.

The Baron himself did not see them without emotion; he called in such of the domestics as had bequests assigned them; and he had just distributed the valued legacies, when a shrill horn was heard on the outside of the castle walls, which was immediately replied to with a louder blast by the sentinel in the watch-tower.

Lord de Mowbray sent out to inquire the cause;—the servant returned with information, that a courier, then waiting at the foot of the drawbridge, had brought the letter which he delivered into his Lord's hands: the Baron broke the seal, and as his eye passed rapidly over the characters which the paper contained, pleasure sparkled in it;—turning to the servant, he commanded the courier to be admitted, and every attention to be shewn him in the castle;—then addressing his daughter, he said, "My Rosalind cannot fail to recollect Lord Rufus de Madginecourt, to whom she gave her hand at the dance; he is travelling, this paper informs me, into the north, and will make my castle his abode for a few days on his journey towards his own; he will arrive to-morrow by the hour of dinner."

Rosalind certainly did recollect him, and the same unpleasant feelings which had attended her first sight of him, accompanied his image to her memory now.

The Baron proceeded without delay to give orders for the reception of Lord Rufus;—a splendid entertainment he directed to be provided in the castle;—he commanded his forces also to draw themselves out on the walls, and salute the entrance of his friend within them: he then retired to rest, his brain filled with floating ideas of his daughter's conquest, his hopes of which have already been hinted at;—and Rosalind laid her head upon her pillow, with the anticipation of something disagreeable, she could not decide what, arising from the intended visit.

Lord Rufus passed a more uneasy night than either, at an inn about twenty miles from De Mowbray Castle, where he rested on his journey.

At the time when Lord William and his family returned from the court, it must be remembered that we left Lord Rufus soaring on the wings of pride, towards the point which he vainly imagined would ensure him the summit of his earthly wishes, by making him the joint sovereign of his country with his Queen. Blind, we have already said, he had hitherto been to all the attentions which Elizabeth had bestowed on the other nobles who resorted to her court, and clear-sighted only to the favour with which she had honoured him, which his own vanity prevented him from seeing as it really was, of an equal nature with that conferred on other courtiers. But his eyes had lately been opened, and he had fallen from the pinnacle of his imagined glory, into the very abyss of madness and despair. Although he had not been able to distinguish when others enjoyed equal favour with himself, yet he had become immediately clear-sighted, on one being selected by the Queen to be blessed with honours and countenance superior to himself; and this had occurred within a short space of time, to Robert Dudley, the younger son of the late Duke of Northumberland, whom Elizabeth had created Earl of Leicester, and to whom her partiality was such as could not escape the dullest perception.

In him Lord Rufus saw the downfall of his hopes—the execrated period of his self-raised expectations! All he now desired was that the Earl might in like manner fall the victim of his wishes; and had he not dreaded the utter ruin of himself being the consequence of such a step, he would have put a period to his rival's hopes in death. Rage, for a length of time, alone filled his breast, and choked up the powers of his mind; gradually the natural policy and cunning of his disposition began again to assume their sway, and he considered that next to sharing the throne himself, the succeeding step was to be second in honour. To this attainment the road appeared to him easy and open. The Queen's first favourite was her god-daughter, Rosalind de Mowbray; the father of that god-daughter was his intimate friend; thus he conceived that to ask, and to obtain, would be the short prelude to the preferment which he sought.

On this errand was his present journey into Cumberland taken. Still the disappointment of the past rankled more in his breast than the expectation of the future animated his heart; and there was even a possibility, though he considered such a possibility to be the very shadow of a shade, that the prize he now aimed at obtaining might, by some unforeseen obstacle, be withheld from his possession; a second failure of his schemes he felt his already irritated system very ill-suited to bear up under, and he truly dreaded the event of a negative.

About an hour before noon on the following day, the shrill clarion announced the approach of De Madginecourt's train; it was instantly replied to from the castle, and the drawbridge let down.

Lord Rufus was numerously attended, and with the most condescending smiles to those in arms who saluted his arrival, he entered the first court of the castle. Here he dismounted; the bridle of his horse, while he alighted, was held by his page, a boy of about fourteen years of age, of a most interesting person, and intelligent countenance, to whom, on entering the castle hall, he gave his helmet to bear at his heels.

Here the Baron de Mowbray stepped forth to give his friend welcome, leading in his hand Rosalind, whose native charms gained additional lustre from the simplicity of her dress, which consisted only of a long robe of black silk, which flowed to her feet, and was confined round her neck and waist with a single string of pearls. Lord Rufus met her with a smile of ecstacy, while studied adulation flowed from his tongue, with all that ease which is natural to a man whose intercourse with refined society has taught him how to make design appear the involuntary act of nature.

Edward and Irwin were next introduced to his Lordship, on their entrance from the command of their troops, which had been drawn out upon the ramparts against his arrival; and the sumptuous repast was then served up. That every sense might be alike regaled, the pillared hall rang with the sound of various instruments, and the minstrels sang the tales of Valour and of Love, the defeat of France on the Plains of Agincourt, and on the hills of Cressy; the contest of the Roses; and the praises of their present Queen; and these were followed by love-ballads and romances.

The repast being ended, the health of Rosalind, proposed by the lips of Lord Rufus, went round in an overflowing goblet; and she then left the hall, that her presence might not prevent the free circulation of the wine, or be a restraint upon the revelry of the hour.

She retired to her own apartment, to which her attendant Gertrude soon followed her. Without any other female except this simple attendant to exchange a sentence with, Rosalind had allowed her, since the death of her mother, a much greater degree of familiarity in her presence, than she would else have done to a girl in her situation; and Gertrude had returned the confidence reposed in her with the truest affection and esteem for her mistress. Entering hastily into the apartment, she said—"Joy to you, my dear Lady. I hope I don't offend you. I beg your pardon with all my heart if I do; but I must be the first to wish you joy, if all that is said be true."

"What is said, Gertrude?" asked Rosalind.

"That the noble Lord Rufus, about whom there is all this bustle now in the castle, is come on purpose to make your Ladyship an offer of his hand," returned Gertrude.

"If such is his intention," replied Rosalind, "I am sure it is unknown to me; and if such were the case, do you really think it would be the occasion of joy to me?"

"Why, my Lady," rejoined the girl, "they say he is the first and richest nobleman in the land; but then, to be sure, if one's heart don't go with one's hand, or is gone any where else before, as I may say, why then, indeed, that alters the case; at least, I am sure if I speak of myself, gold would have no weight with me, if the other scale were filled with love."

Rosalind smiled.

"Aye, my Lady," went on Gertrude, "I've always had my guessings; whether right or wrong, I've always kept them to myself. I say nothing to any of them below. There are his Lordship's attendants all dying to have a peep at their new lady, as they call you; they say they have heard your Ladyship is so beautiful; just the wife for a man of his Lordship's rank and wealth. I'll believe it when I see it, thought I; but I kept my thoughts to myself."

Rosalind continued silent; Gertrude went prattling on, and at last hinted, pretty plainly, at the nice couple which, in her opinion, her lady and the charming master Edward would make.

"I have no thoughts of marriage," said Rosalind; "it is certain that I shall never give my hand where my esteem has not proceeded it; and I confess that Edward is the only man, except my father, whom I have ever yet thought worthy of possessing it. But then you are to recollect, Gertrude, that my esteem may be bestowed without my hand, though my hand shall never be given without my esteem."

The goblet had been so freely circulated in the castle hall, that the Baron did not require the presence of his daughter at the evening repast; and having understood that she was not desired to preside, she retired at an early hour to bed.

Rosalind's sleep was disturbed, her dreams various and distressing; one in particular—during the influence of which she imagined herself in a lonely wood, where she met a coffin, borne on the shoulders of skeletons, and the lid of which being opened, displayed to her sight the mangled body of Edward.

She awoke, chilled with horror at the recollection of her dream, and unwilling again to commit herself to the tormenting power of sleep. Her lamp was burnt out, a faint light shone through her window-curtain, and imagining that day was beginning to dawn, she arose, drew on some of her cloaths, and went to the window; just as she reached it, the castle clock struck five. She was now convinced that it could not yet be daylight; she drew aside the curtain, and perceived the moon floating in silver splendour through a peaceful sky opposite to her window.

She felt a reluctance again to return to bed; thus [she] stood gazing on that planet which had often before been the subject of her admiration and reflection. The season was that of the depth of winter, and the ground was covered with snow, the surface of which the biting air had hardened into a sparkling substance, which being reflected upon by the light of the moon, appeared as if the earth was sprinkled with myriads of stars. As her eyes wandered over the scene before her, they fell on a distant object, of which the dusky colour attracted her notice by its contrast to the whiteness of the snow, and which appeared to be in motion; a few moments discovered to her that it was a human figure, and as it approached nearer, she saw that it was tall, and wrapped in a dark-coloured cloak. It continued to advance towards the castle, and, in a short time, she lost sight of it, as it turned an angle of the walls which led to the drawbridge.

She would probably have thought no more of what she had seen, supposing it to have been some person belonging to her father's household, that had been to the village, and was returning by the advantage of the moonlight to the castle; but in a few minutes more she heard footsteps on the rampart which ran under her window, and, on looking down, she saw the same figure moving hastily along.

The sight rather startled her, but she felt convinced that it must be somebody belonging to the castle; it could be no enemy, or he would not have gained admittance across the drawbridge, from the sentinel. Still she felt desirous of knowing who this midnight wanderer could be, and what his business abroad: there could be only one reason, she concluded, for his passing along the eastern rampart, and that must be to gain admittance into the castle by the postern-gate, to which it led. The window of her closet commanded a view of the court, into which was the entrance from the postern-gate, and she resolved to go to it, and ascertain whether her suspicions were just.

Arrived there, she saw no one in the court below, and observed that the gate was shut; but almost immediately she saw it glide back on its hinges, and the muffled figure pass through the portal. It looked round, and then cautiously locked the door on the inside. This done, it proceeded across the court; and even now Rosalind would probably have thought no more of the circumstance, had not the figure stumbled in its progress, and the cloak fallen from its shoulders in its effort to recover its balance. It stopped, and turning round its head, as it again drew the cloak upon it, the light of the moon fell on its countenance, and Rosalind discovered the features of Lord Rufus de Madginecourt.

The discovery surprised her, although she could not account why she should be surprised at any action in a man's conduct, with whose character she was so little acquainted, as she was with that of Lord Rufus.

He passed out of sight, and she continued at the window in thought. Sometimes she argued with herself the possibility of her having been mistaken in the countenance which she had believed herself to have seen; but truth would not be refuted; her view of him had been too good for a mistake of this nature. Whether she should mention what she had seen, was her next point of debate with her own mind; and on this she concluded, that as his actions could by no means concern her, it was her wisest plan to be silent upon them, lest her being known to have observed them should draw forth from any lips a reflection upon her having left her bed at that hour in the morning.

With true pleasure she hailed the light of day; and no sooner did the crimson-fringed curtains of the east announce the rising of the sun, than she called up Gertrude, and began to attire herself for appearing in the breakfast-room.

Lord Rufus and she entered it together; he beheld her with all the studied admiration he had done on the preceding day, and she looked upon him with even more dislike than she had at first seen him with; her unpleasant feelings with regard to him being now heightened by the concealment which had attended his entrance into the castle that morning.

When breakfast was ended, Lord William proposed that they should ride out for an hour or two, and fly their hawks, to which his guest readily assented, and their horses were led forth. A milk-white steed, with gilded trappings, bore the imperious De Madginecourt; proudly he neighed on receiving his rider, and proudly Lord Rufus bestrode his favourite horse. Of a commanding figure and person, Lord Rufus never looked to greater advantage than when mounted on horseback; it was therefore his favourite amusement; for, like all men whose passions are relax, vanity held a place in his heart; and he now triumphantly gave the reins to his steed, which sprang wildly forward with his rider, and gave him an opportunity of displaying to Rosalind, who had attended her father to the drawbridge of the castle, his skill in the art of horsemanship.

On their departure, Rosalind returned to the breakfast apartment, where she had not been many minutes before a gentle tap upon the door asked for admittance; she rose, and opened it. The solicitor for entrance she found to be the page of Lord Rufus, who advancing into the room with a small silver box in his hand, said—

"Lord Rufus de Madginecourt, my Lady, commands me to request your acceptance of this trinket, as a mark of his esteem for you."

Rosalind knew not how to reply; she felt repugnant to accepting any present from a man to whom her soul was as averse as it was to Lord Rufus, and who she feared might construe her acceptance of his gift into pleasure at receiving it, instead of seeing it in the only light in which she could induce herself to take it, that of not hazarding an affront to a guest of her father's by a refusal.

After some moments hesitation with her own mind, she coolly said—"Your Lord does me unmerited honour; pray return him my thanks, and accept that piece of gold for yourself."

The page put the silver box upon a table, received his reward from the hand of Rosalind, and, with a low obeisance, he quitted the room, saying—"Alwin is your Ladyship's slave."

Vexed by the necessity she had been under of accepting a gift thus forced upon her, by a man to whom it was unpleasant to her feelings to be placed under the slightest obligation, the box lay some time untouched; at last she took it into her hand, and, opening the lid, she found it to be only the case for a rich diamond necklace, in the centre of which, encircled by stones of great value, was a picture; she examined it, and found it to be the resemblance of Lord Rufus himself.

The discovery which she had dreaded was now too clearly made, that Lord Rufus intended to ask her in marriage; no other motive could have authorized the gift she now held in her hand. She looked upon it some time with a disgust heightened by contrasting with his image the one which her mind drew to rival it; hence followed a train of ideas which wound her senses to the keenest pitch of feeling; and unconscious that she spoke, she exclaimed aloud—"Never shalt thou be the rival of my Edward!"

A sigh behind her recalled her senses from herself to outward objects; she turned hastily round, and observed Edward on tiptoe, leaving the apartment. His eye met her's; he hesitated in his pace; confusion glowed on both their countenances.

"I entreat your forgiveness, Rosalind," stammered out Edward; "I did not intend to listen to what you were saying; I did not come into the room on tiptoe, but you were so occupied, that my steps were unnoticed by you, and I could not help hearing what you said."

Rosalind blushed still deeper than before, but she did not speak; and Edward was again moving slowly out of the apartment.

"You are not going," she said. "I have much to say to you."

He was by her side in an instant.

"Edward," she went on, "I have always considered you as my brother; the dying gift of my mother warrants the name by which I call you;—to whom then ought a sister to disclose her griefs, but to the brother of her affections?"

"Speak out, dearest Rosalind," he returned: "if you have wrongs, I will redress them, if I am able; if that is not in my power, I will not prove myself unworthy of your confidence."

Rosalind shewed him the contents of the box she had just received, and explained to him her dread of what declaration might not follow such a present. The manly lip of Edward quivered as he repelled the rising tear; for the first time in his life he felt the dread of losing Rosalind, at a moment too when her innocent confession had filled his heart with joy and gratitude; speak he durst not; had he allowed his tongue the privilege of speech, he could not have restrained the drops of sorrow that would have started with it from his eyes.

"And yet," said Rosalind, "surely I fear too soon, too vainly.—I am my father's only child—her, he calls his darling hope; surely he will not, by unkindness, wither in its bud the blossom which should cheer his age, which I would live to be, would he henceforward cherish me with the same affection he has hitherto done."

"Oh, Rosalind," exclaimed Edward, "that I were any thing but what I am—that I did but know myself——"

"Are you not good, virtuous, and brave?" asked Rosalind. "What more is requisite to make life happy? If you were a Prince, you could not more excel in those qualities than you now do; thus you are a Prince already in that which is most excellent, and best worth loving."

"It is not in fathers, my dear Rosalind," returned Edward, "to content themselves with such inheritance in sons, as philosophers might prize—with them, especially with men who rank in society as highly as Lord de Mowbray does, wealth and title are the only pre-eminences which they seek in marriage.—Lord Rufus has both."

"And you——" said Rosalind mournfully.

"Shall ever be much blest in being still your brother," said Edward, interrupting her.

Rosalind burst into tears, and fell on his neck; for the first time their arms entwined each other. Edward raised her gently from his shoulder; and as he led her to a seat, his eye fell on the window, and he saw Alwin, the page, standing in the garden opposite to it, and looking inquisitively into the apartment.

Rosalind's eye turned to the spot where she saw Edward's fixed, and she observed the page.

"Call the boy in," she said, "and I will send back his Lord's present by him who brought it. You shall be present at my returning it."

"I entreat you not," said Edward; "if it be for your happiness to return it, let it be conveyed back to him through the medium of Lord William; do not put it into the power of that boy, whose pertness and vanity bespeak him a favourite with his Lord, to convey to him a message of his own moulding, upon a subject of this nature."

"Do you think he had been long at the window?" asked Rosalind.

Edward understood the modest fear that was concealed in the question; he endeavoured to evade an answer, but she understood that the page had seen her face reclined on Edward's neck. "Well, be it so," she said; "I am sure my father loves me, and I will see him in private ere I sleep."

CHAPTER X.

He says, he loves my daughter:
I think so too; for never gaz'd the moon
Upon the water, as he'll stand and read,
As 'twere, my daughter's eyes; and, to be plain,
I think there's not half a kiss to choose
Which loves the other best.

THE WINTER'S TALE.

HAD Rosalind been the only female who was that day to have sat at her father's table, she would have made it her excuse for remaining in her own apartment, as she had already given her presence once to Lord Rufus in the banquet-hall; but on this day the family of a nobleman in the neighbourhood having been invited to the castle, in which were a mother and her two daughters, she prepared herself without hesitation, to take her place at the dinner-table.

She did not enter the hall until Lord Rufus and some of his companions were already there with her father; thus she had no opportunity of speaking to him alone: after some time, he moved up to her, and whispered in her ear—"From a hint which has been given to me this morning, I expected to have seen a new ornament gracing your neck to-day, Rosalind; or has your modesty, at a first gift, kept you from wearing it? Methought you would have been proud of the display."

This remark confirmed her fears, and she said—"Pray let me see you in my chamber to-night, before you retire to your own."

The Baron returned an affirmative nod, and mixed amongst his guests.

At dinner Lord Rufus was, as he had been on the preceding day, the occupier of the seat adjoining to that of Rosalind; his eyes were the legible prologues to what his lips were intending shortly to convey; but the presence of the company restrained him from more particular attention. After the feast, Rosalind saw him no more, as she retired to her own chamber on the departure of the guests.

Wrapped in busy thought, she sat waiting the coming of her father till the clock struck twelve; she had already enquired for him once, but had found that he was engaged in conversation with Lord Rufus and the gentlemen who composed his party. She now sent again to ask concerning him, and Gertrude brought her information that he and Lord Rufus had retired together into the Baron's study.

The heart of Rosalind beat more anxiously than before; she could not fail to conclude of what was their conversation; she dreaded lest her father, lured by the splendour of De Madginecourt's offer, might be led into some rash promise, in which her future happiness might be involved, and she could hardly forbear sending to request his immediate presence.

An hour and a half more passed, and still she heard they were together; at the expiration of that time, one of the Baron's servants called Gertrude from her mistress's chamber, desiring her to inform

Rosalind, that on account of the lateness of the hour, his Lord must defer seeing her till the morning.

Rosalind, on hearing this message, suffered herself to be undressed, and Gertrude to draw the curtains round her; but although reclined upon a bed of down, sleep refused its balm to her agitated mind.

Alwin had faithfully communicated to his master Rosalind's manner of receiving his present, and he had equally taken care to represent to him the full extent of what he had afterwards witnessed in the breakfast apartment between her and Edward.

Alwin was the acknowledged favourite of Lord Rufus; and the reason of his being so was, as Edward had supposed, his artful exercise of qualities which were useful to a man who possessed De Madginecourt's spirit of intrigue. The boy had, from almost an infant, been in his service, and proved himself an apt scholar in those lessons which his Lord had given him, for mixing the meanness of cunning with the playful childishness natural to his years, and exercising them to the best advantage, in gaining such intelligence as suited the favourite scheme of his master, whatever at the time it happened to be.

During their morning ride, Lord Rufus had communicated to De Mowbray his intentions concerning his daughter, and the present he had that day sent to her. Lord William received his proposal with evident marks of that joy with which it really inspired him; and in answer to De Madginecourt's question of whether the Baron believed her heart to be disengaged? he had replied, that he was certain it was so. Upon this intelligence, Lord Rufus returned triumphant in his own idea to the castle; and De Mowbray experienced an exultation at the completion of his desired plan, which he knew not how to confine within his own breast.

But this vain suitor, and inconsiderate father, who should have recollected that the heart most intimately concerned in an affair of this important nature, should have been the first consulted, met with a severe check in their progress towards their air-built castle, when Lord Rufus, requesting to speak in private with the Baron at night, informed him that Alwin had seen his portrait thrown down in disdain from the hand of Rosalind, and her cheek, bedewed with tears, rested on the neck of Edward.

It was some time ere Lord William could be induced to believe that the boy had not been deceived, or was not deceitful in the information which he had conveyed to his Lord; and when convinced that his report was actually founded in truth, his reply was, that his daughter had ever lived on terms of the greatest friendship with the youth Edward, and that he doubted not but that she was imparting to his confidential ear the first emotions of her joy.

Lord Rufus was too well acquainted with the history of the heart, not to know what is the nature of a friendship between two persons of opposite sexes, at the age of Edward and Rosalind; and he represented his opinion to the Baron.

The Baron, in his heart, was not less suspicious of the truth than was Lord Rufus; but not hesitating to decide that his arguments in favour of De Madginecourt, backed by his wealth, his rank, and his passion, would easily turn the girlish affections of his daughter away from the youth who lived only by his bounty, he still maintained his first idea of sisterly friendship to Lord Rufus; and they parted for the night, the Baron promising to commune with his daughter before he saw him in the morning.

The Baron, as it has been already said, retired from his conversation with Lord Rufus to his own chamber. The observations of the page Alwin perplexed him in the regulation of his conduct; not less did his daughter's request of seeing him that night render him at a loss what to expect from her lips; at all events, he judged it best to prepare himself for meeting her with a night of cool reflection; and for that purpose he urged the lateness of the hour as an excuse for his not seeing her before he went to bed.

Lord William slept little that night; he feared that Edward was regarded in a nearer light by his daughter than that of a nominal brother; now the idea had once started into his brain, he recollected many circumstances which confirmed him in believing it to be a just one, and which, at the time, had escaped his notice, or at least his reflection. After much debate with his own mind, he determined to meet his daughter, in such a manner as if it were impossible for him to doubt that what she had to communicate was her joy and pride at the conquest which Lord De Madginecourt's present of his portrait shewed her to have made of his heart. Should he find her communication to be of a different nature, he resolved, first to endeavour to wean her mind from Edward, by holding him up to her view as an object derogatory to the honour of her affections. Should not these means succeed in bringing her over to his fondest hope, there were others left behind, of which he meant as yet to say nothing.

The sleep of Lord Rufus was very little disturbed by the occurrences of the day; he had no real love for Rosalind, to keep him waking with the reflection that a rival might be possessing the heart he coveted; he doubted not but Lord William would be sufficiently clear-sighted to his own interest, to exert his authority over his daughter in the bestowing of her hand, if he could not command her affections along with it; and his motive for marrying her was not of that nature which could suffer any anxiety about the terms in which he received it.

At an early hour in the morning, the Baron entered Rosalind's apartment; early as it was, he found her risen, and prepared to receive him. After the usual salutations of the morning, she took from her table the present sent her by Lord Rufus; and extending her hand with it towards Lord William, she said—"I have to request of my dear father that he will return this into the hands of Lord Rufus de Madginecourt, with any apology for my not accepting it, which he may deem best suited to the occasion."

Lord William did not open his hand to receive it, but spoke thus—"I commend, my dear Rosalind, the delicate principle upon which you refuse a gift of this nature; but you are still to be informed of the motive from which it springs—Lord Rufus asks your hand in marriage."

"My motive for returning it," replied Rosalind, "is still as strong as ever; for Lord Rufus, in the offer of his hand, confers on me an honour I am incapable of accepting."

"Incapable! why incapable?" exclaimed the Baron, who now expected to hear the name of Edward advanced as the cause.

"Because," answered Rosalind, "Lord de Madginecourt, my dear father, is a man whom, as your friend, I shall always make it my study to treat with politeness, and, if I can, with friendship; but were he not your friend, so far from loving him as a husband, I could not even feel happy in his presence."

"Childish prejudices, my Rosalind!" cried the Baron, "too weak to inhabit a mind of education like yours! You can give him friendship, you say, as being my friend; will not this induce you to give him love as my son?"

"Never," returned Rosalind; "if he persists in asking that, I fear I shall forget he is my father's friend, and repeal the indulgence I was, on that consideration, willing to allow him."

"You are firm in your replies," returned the Baron rather warmly.

"I have been taught by a fond parent, now no more," replied Rosalind, "that women, like myself, have only one period of existence at which our resolution is not sinful, and may be instrumental to the happiness of our future lives—it is when we are called upon to bestow our hearts where we are incapable of bestowing the passion that alone renders them valuable."

Rosalind's firmness was solely in her words; the tears were trickling down her cheeks, and her lips were pale. The Baron maintained silence; the recollection of Lady de Mowbray, which Rosalind had called forth, softened for a while that pride which was steeling every feeling of his heart, and interrupted him in the volley of praise which he was going to pour forth on the wealth and worth of Lord Rufus.

A few minutes recovered for him his utterance; and he set before her all the arguments which he had devised during the night, to tempt her into an acceptance of De Madginecourt's hand.

Rosalind continued to oppose them with the placid reasonings of the heart; and the progress of an hour left the Baron entangled in the web of his own sophistry, and unable to support his pleas—so infallibly does Nature in her pleadings ever triumph over her foes.

But still, though perplexed in his arguments, De Mowbray felt himself possessed of a father's authority, when his eloquence failed him; but he judged it the wisest plan not to exert it too suddenly, lest, if a determined air accompanied his words, if his daughter once decided it cruelty in him thus to urge her inclination, that decision might render her desperate, and stamp the utter ruin of his hopes; he accordingly concluded with requesting her to promise him that she would for the course of one month, endeavour, by every means in her power, to alter her opinion of Lord Rufus, to reflect on the honour that awaited her as his wife, and to exert herself for the happiness of a father who sought only her welfare.

Although convinced within herself what would be the issue

of such a compliance, that were the month a century, her opinion would still be the same, she consented to this proposal, annexing to it only one condition of her own—that at the present time, she undoubtedly did not regard Lord Rufus as the man whom she could ever consent to receive as her husband, the present which he had sent to her must remain in his possession till she had changed her sentiments concerning him.

With reluctance the Baron received it at her hands, and repaired to the breakfast-table; from attending him to which Rosalind excused herself.

On the entrance of Lord Rufus the Baron met him with an assumed smile; and with some comments on the delicacy of feeling natural to a girl of her years, he told him that it was her wish to be allowed a month for her decision, which he left Lord Rufus no reason to doubt would be in his favour, as he informed him that she had not spoken a single sentence to him, in their conversation that morning, relative to Edward, whom, he was now convinced, she regarded only in the light of a friend, or she would not have passed by so favourable an opportunity of declaring a warmer esteem for him. This was one artifice which he used to blind Lord Rufus to his daughter's real sentiments; another was, that of not returning to him his portrait, but retaining it in his own hands, and by his silence relative to it, leading him to believe it still in Rosalind's possession.

In compliance with her father's commands, Rosalind was constrained to appear as usual at table, and to receive those attentions from Lord Rufus, which tended only to render him more odious in her sight.

No opportunity had occurred for her to see Edward alone for a single moment, since that morning when she had so innocently breathed forth the confession of her heart; but Edward had not required this avowal to tell him that their sentiments were the same, though various causes had withheld him from making a display of his own affection; nor did Rosalind now want to see him, in order that a repetition of the same professions might convince her of his truth and constancy, more than she was already convinced of them.

Edward was about this time very little seen at the castle; a tower of strength had for some time past been erecting at the foot of a bridge which crossed the river running through the neighbouring village, and which pass, by being ably guarded, it was believed would materially impede the Moss-troopers in their incursions into the kingdom; and the command of this tower had been given by the Baron de Mowbray to Edward.

To him and Rosalind the cause of his removal from the castle appeared obvious; but it gave them no anxiety; they loved too truly, and too disinterestedly, for either to fear that absence should weaken the affection of the other.

Rosalind was in doubt whether Edward knew the terms to which she had been compelled to agree regarding Lord Rufus; she wished him to know them; but no safe method of conveying the intelligence to him presented itself to her relief.

Edward was at this time arrived at his full growth and strength; in form he was tall, well proportioned, and active; his person more than ordinarily handsome, yet manly and commanding; his hair black, and falling in short curls on his forehead and neck; his eyes extremely dark, and unusually expressive; in these beamed the intelligence of his mind, and on his lips played the good humour and benevolence of his heart.

Rosalind united in her person all the fascinating beauties of a Venus, and the modest graces of a Diana; exquisitely fair, her light brown hair hung in shining ringlets on her neck, as on a bed of polished ivory; her soft blue eyes sparkled with sensibility, her lips emulated the smooth ruby, and she spoke only to complete the witchery her face had begun.

Ill-fated pair! how little did ye dream, when ye first felt the glow of affection for each other warm your youthful hearts, that the innocent passion would lead you to misery! How little did ye then understand, that the noblest sensation of the breast is snapped from its stem by the withering hand of pride, and the purest sources of Nature's happiness turned from their course by the greedy finger of avarice!

Oh Love! passion omnipotent and pre-eminent! how nobly dost thou display thine own superiority!—how gloriously assert thine independence! when, amidst a host of contending foes, thou risest still above their menaces and frowns, unshaken in stability; and when enclosed within the thorny circle of the world's prejudice, still findest a heart's-ease garland for thy breast in constancy!

CHAPTER XI.

Ah me! for aught that ever I could read,
Could ever hear by tale or history,
The course of true love never did run smooth.

SHAKESPEARE.

Day crept on after day, and as the expiration of the fatal month drew nigh, Lord Rufus wore on his countenance a smile of joy and triumph, whilst on that of De Mowbray was painted a sullenness which had heretofore been unusual to it.

Lord William fed his friend with a belief that a ready affirmative to his proposal would flow from the lips of his daughter, whilst convinced himself that her opinion was unaltered. He grieved that it was so; and he grieved still more that his pride urged him to compel her to enter into an alliance which she abhorred; but he could not bring himself to sacrifice the honour of an union with the first nobleman in the kingdom, to the whim, as he regarded it, of a girl, whose opinions he considered as originating in caprice, and whose inclinations he doubted not would easily adapt themselves to any man, once become her husband.

Accordingly the determination of Lord William was, that Rosalind should become the wife of Lord Rufus; and being thus resolved with himself, he directed all his subtilty to make Lord Rufus believe it her voluntary act, though virgin coyness rendered her cool in the display of her sentiments.

On the day previous to that which concluded the month of trial, Lord William addressed his daughter with these words: "To-morrow, my Rosalind, expires the time which my indulgence has permitted to your girlish reserve. I hope that it has been long enough to teach you to act with discretion in an affair of which you must see the importance to your happiness and my own—not doubting to find your opinion in concurrence with mine, I shall take an opportunity of seeing you alone to-morrow evening."

He did not wait for a reply, but immediately turned from her.

Rosalind burst into tears, and left the room. Her departure was not unobserved by him; and the cloud with which she alone seemed to darken his future hopes for the first time irritated him against her; and the word "obstinate" fell unintentionally aloud from his lips. And alas! how often does it fall from the tongue of parents, when daughters cannot accommodate their feelings to the convenience for which fathers wish them to marry!

On the following afternoon, when Rosalind left the castle hall after dinner, Gertrude met her, as usual, to attend her to her chamber; but on arriving in the gallery which led to it, Rosalind turned to the opposite side of the mansion, and with a slow step proceeded along.

"My Lady," said Gertrude, "you are wrong. Whither are you going?"

"Into the cedar-chamber, Gertrude," replied Rosalind.

"What, the cedar-chamber where my dear lady died?" exclaimed Gertrude; "sure you won't go into it this afternoon: consider nobody has been into it since the day her sad remains were taken out of it; it is all hung with black yet, you know; and indeed I think you had better not go till to-morrow morning, if you wish to visit it.

"To-morrow morning, Gertrude," answered Rosalind, "would not suit my purpose in going into it; it must be tonight."

"To-night!" echoed Gertrude. "What then, you have heard the nonsense that the servants and people talk; but sure you can't believe that it is so, my Lady?

"That what is so?" asked Rosalind in surprise.

"Oh, nothing at all, nothing, if you don't know," returned Gertrude.

"You have said too much," replied Rosalind, "to escape a confession now. What is it that is said?"

"Why, if you insist on knowing, my Lady—nothing more than that an odd kind of a shadow has sometimes been seen near the door of the cedar-chamber of late—that's all," said Gertrude.

"If you mean to hint to me," returned Rosalind, "that my dear mother's spirit haunts the room in which she breathed her last, oh, may it be permitted to visit her unhappy daughter!"

"Why, my Lady, to be sure you would not wish to see such a sight?" cried Gertrude.

"What, not desire to see my mother—and such a mother too as mine was! Oh, that it were possible for me to see her now, and to gain comfort from her lips!—But fear not, Gertrude, that my wish should be accomplished; there is no intercourse between the living and the dead."

"Sure, my Lady, begging pardon for saying so, we hear of ghosts in the bible, you know."

"Not since the revelation of God's will to man in the person of his Son," replied Rosalind; "before that period, such appearances, we are told, were accidentally permitted on earth, for some especial purpose of the Creator, but now are no longer necessary."

"If it be so, my Lady, and I dare say you know best, because you have had so much good learning, what a pity it is that amongst the many other comforts the new testament has for us poor sinners, it don't mention that there are to be no more ghosts; I am sure it would have been a great happiness for many of us if it had."

They were now arrived at the cedar-chamber; the door was not locked, though the apartment was in disuse. Rosalind entered first, and Gertrude followed her with a slow and cautious step, which did not shew her thoroughly convinced of her lady's doctrine. The room was still cased with black, and the large knots of sable plumes, which had been placed upon the bed to grace the funeral pomp, were still hanging over it. The hour was that of twilight, and the portion of day which was admitted by the high and narrow casements, such as rendered the appearance of the whole scene so dark and melancholily awful, as might have shaken a stronger mind than Gertrude's with superstitious fears.

Rosalind fell on her knees before the bed, and continued for some time in silent prayer. Gertrude stood close by her, anxiously desiring to look on every side at once, as if expecting to behold some object of alarm at every point of view, and yet so timid as not to be able to raise her eyes from the ground.

The moment Rosalind rose, "Come, my Lady, let's go," cried Gertrude, hastening towards the door.

"I am not going to depart from hence," said Rosalind.

"Not going to depart!" exclaimed Gertrude; "mercy bless us! Why, in five minutes time it will be quite dark; we shan't see our way out of the gallery into your apartment."

"Then go you down whilst there is light to shew you your way," said Rosalind, "and bring me up a lamp."

Gertrude had rather have argued upon this command than have obeyed it; but, however reluctantly, she was obliged to do the latter. In a short time, Gertrude returned with a lamp in each hand, which provision she had made for lighting herself down again, lest the want of such a convenience should have obliged her to have continued a partaker of the gloom in which her lady, so unaccountably to her thinking, seemed resolved to remain. Rosalind saw her intention, and telling her to inform her father, when he should inquire for her, where she was, sent her away.

With her eyes fixed on a portrait of her deceased mother, which hung suspended over the wide and cheerless chimney-piece, Rosalind sat awaiting that interview with her father, on which she believed the fate of her future days to depend. With reflection for her only companion, her memory strayed back to the days of her happy childhood, and so crept on through every circumstance of note in her life to the present;—with a mind abstracted from the world, she dwelt on many days of bliss that would return no more; the sigh escaped her lips, and the tear stole down her cheek;—thus, absorbed in thought, she sat, till a rustling noise roused her from her reverie.

She started, and looked round her; the noise was repeated more gently than before, and seemed to proceed from behind the black drapery which covered that end of the room against which stood the head of the bed; she took up her lamp, and went to the spot; the arras was unmoved, and was hanging equal with the wall in every part. It must have been the wind, she believed, that had shaken the hangings; and thus convinced, she felt almost angry with herself that Gertrude's prattle should for a moment have caused her to suppose the noise she had just heard to have been produced by any other cause.

As she was returning towards her seat, she heard a footstep approaching along the gallery, which she imagined she recognized to be her father's; and she was not deceived, for in a few moments he appeared at the door. Entering but a few steps into the apartment, he said—"Why does my Rosalind choose this chamber for our conference?"

"Because," replied Rosalind, "it is the spot peculiarly sacred to the memory of my mother; and at a subject like the one that we are about to discuss, I would, if possible, have both my parents present."

Lord William cast his eyes around the chamber, with a countenance on which was depicted a mixture of regret and dissatisfaction; he then returned slowly to the door, and having closed it, he seated himself on the same couch on which Rosalind was sitting.

"Although you have lost one parent," he said, "can you doubt, my child, that the loss has diminished to you any of the parental affection I owe you?"

"I hope it has not, my Lord," replied Rosalind; "I hope ere we quit this chamber, to experience a proof of it—to find in your heart that double portion of affection which would have been divided between you for an only child, had my mother lived."

"You know, Rosalind," rejoined Lord William, "that my wishes are for your happiness and grandeur."

"Alas, my father," answered Rosalind, "how sickly a companion do you give happiness to thrive under, when you join it with grandeur! It is the deadly nightshade twining round a healthy vine to rob it of its sweets! If you would give me happiness, give it to me in its most enchanting garb of affectionate tranquility."

"Lord Rufus," returned the Baron, "loves you too well not to grant you every indulgence which can contribute to your enjoyment of happiness according to your own ideas."

"Oh no, my Lord," replied Rosalind, "if it ever becomes his right to be the dealer out of happiness to me, my felicity ends the moment such a right commences."

"You speak too firmly on conjecture and prejudice," answered De Mowbray.

"What can you oppose to my ideas, that shall confute them with any degree of certainty?" asked Rosalind. "Surely it is more reasonable to seek happiness in humility, than to encounter misery for the sake of wealth."

"You allow love, then," said the Baron, "no place in the heart of Lord Rufus?"

"If it has," replied Rosalind, "and that love be for me, I should be unjust to him, as well as to myself, in giving him my hand, for I have no love to return him for his."

"But you are not incapable of the passion," answered the Baron, with a satirical smile.

"I am incapable of deceit," answered Rosalind; "and if to esteem one above the rest of his sex—to feel for him as a brother, when other men pass unheeded by, is love, I hesitate not to confess it."

The Baron breathed a groan of contempt.

"But hear this also, my father," continued Rosalind: "force me not into the arms of Lord Rufus, and I bind myself, by the same indulgence, never to ask of you to receive the man I love as any other than my friend, if you shall refuse to call him your son."

"I call him *now* my dependant," exclaimed the Baron; "for I know your minion, though I have concealed from you my knowledge—Edward; he whom I raised from beggary and want, to my protection, and whom one instant is enough for me to crush again! My dependant!"

"But as your dependant," cried Rosalind, "in the confirmed superiority you hold over him, does it not become you to be *more* kind to him, than if he were your equal, only because he *is* your dependant?"

"And is my kindness to extend to making him my heir?" roared out the Baron.

"It is not required of you," replied Rosalind. "You have drawn me into speaking of him, when I meant only to have spoken of myself. You have said that you would supply to me the place of my lost parent, by added affection on your part. You said my happiness was your desire. Send Lord Rufus hence, and I will bind myself, by a solemn vow, never to become the wife of Edward."

The Baron was going to reply, when a deep sigh was echoed from the other end of the chamber. He started up, and seizing the hand of Rosalind, he exclaimed—"Who is here concealed to overhear our conversation? Confess, I charge you, who your hidden witness is."

"On my sacred word," replied the trembling Rosalind, "there is no one concealed that I am acquainted with: indeed there is not."

After a pause, the Baron let go her hand, and moved towards the spot from whence the sound had proceeded. The place was nearly the same where Rosalind had heard the noise before, but somewhat further removed from the bed. The Baron passed his hand over the arras: no impediment obstructed its progress. He looked around, and under the bed: nothing was to be seen or heard.

"Did you not hear a voice?" he asked, returning some steps into the middle of the apartment.

"I thought I heard a sigh," replied Rosalind; "but it was probably the wind that caused it. That corner of the arras was shaken by it before you came in."

"Was it?" said the Baron, his countenance becoming a little more composed. "I dare say it must have been so. There can be no one concealed, for I have felt the wall uninterrupted along the whole side of the chamber."

He again threw his eyes round the room, returned to his seat, and spoke thus:—"Rosalind, I should not be the affectionate father I profess myself, did I not suffer my parental authority to over-rule your scruples, where I am convinced the enforcement of it is for your eventual good. I am sorry my child should be so unlike me in her ideas of propriety and real happiness: I trusted that the month of deliberation which I gave you would have been much more than sufficient for opening your eyes to the good that presents itself to your acceptance; and as I see you still blind to it, it becomes my duty to treat you as I should be compelled to do, were you a timid infant shrinking from the taste of a medicine, on which your life and welfare were depending."

"If Lord Rufus be the loathsome draught you mean," replied Rosalind, "I have sufficient firmness to declare, that I will not swallow poison at a father's hand, although he be so prejudiced as to believe it a wholesome drink."

"You are now," said Lord William, with a forced smile, "becoming the very infant which I spoke of. You conceive the draught to be nauseous, and push it from your lips, without courage to make the experiment of its flavour."

"Can you wonder at that, my Lord?" asked Rosalind, "when, if the draught prove bitter gall itself, 'tis drank for life?"

"But if those who have studied its powers tell us that it is desirable," asked the Baron, "how then?"

"Ask them if they have tried its effect upon themselves?" returned Rosalind.—"But drop, my Lord, this allegory: plain reasonings best suit a discussion of interest like this. You are rich yourself;

you stand high in honour: my alliance with this man cannot make you more prosperous, then why desire the sacrifice to be made?"

"Should I die," returned the Baron, "would you not want a protector?"

"The daughter of Lord William de Mowbray is a sufficient protection," answered Rosalind: "besides, I possess the additional one of my sovereign's favour."

"That sovereign may die: the times may alter," said De Mowbray.

"May not Lord Rufus die too?" asked Rosalind. "He has counted full your years, though you judge him an equal alliance for your daughter."

"The more matured by experience his years, the higher the honour of his condescension," returned Lord William—"and the more ignoble it would be in us to turn such an alliance from our door: me it becomes to guard against the falling of such a stigma on our house. I have pledged my word to Lord Rufus that you shall become his wife; and I will not sully mine honour by a broken promise."

"Though the heart of your only child be broken in its fulfilling!" exclaimed Rosalind.—"Oh, my mother, why art thou not now alive, my mother!"

"Shame—shame!" cried the Baron. "Thy wish is blasphemy against a father's affection."

"I have no father!" sobbed out Rosalind, in a voice almost choked by contending feelings. "If I had a father, I would not lament a mother's repose from the cares of life; but the nature of him who was my father, is changed: he makes his child the tool of his ambition, and throws off love for pride."

"Rosalind," exclaimed the Baron, in a voice almost as much stifled as her own, but with different sensations, "degenerate girl, kneel, and thank thy mother that the semblance of thy voice to her's spares thee my bitterest——"

"Oh, do not curse me!" shrieked out Rosalind, falling at his feet. "How have I erred? I cannot change my nature, any more than Lord Rufus can alter his; I do not condemn him, because his is such as I cannot love; let not him, on that account, condemn me; and let not a father, whom Providence has gifted with reason, err in such wilful blindness."

The Baron's eyes were fixed on her, but he spoke not.

She rose, and took his hand.

"You recollect my mother," she said, "or you could not have compared my voice to her's. I thank Heaven that you have so strong a recollection of her! and I will now venture to tell you why I asked you hither."

She led him towards the bed; standing by its side, she continued thus—"It was on that bed my mother breathed the sigh of death; upon your bosom rested her head; her arm was wound round my neck, and, in the struggle of departing life, she clasped me to her face, to imprint upon my lips her dying kiss: Scarcely she breathed: the tale of her crossed love had worn her strength to its feeblest extremity. Once more she spoke—'Give my Rosalind to the man of her heart!'"

Every feature in the Baron's countenance became fixed, and it was difficult to read in them what was the predominant emotion in his soul.

Rosalind sunk upon her knees before him, and went on speaking—"Just now you compared my voice to that of my mother's—Oh, think it her's once more—think that they are her arms, which now twine themselves around your knees—think that they are her lips, the sanctuary of inviolate truth, that now repeat—'Give my Rosalind to the man of her heart!'"

Pride, rage, and affection, were impetuously tossing in the heart of Lord William. In the tumult of the two former passions, the softer feeling was overwhelmed, and he burst from the innocent supplicant, in an ungovernable ecstacy of rage.

Rosalind fell to the ground, with a faint shriek, and, at the same instant, a voice exclaimed—"Oh, spare her—spare her!"

De Mowbray's features fell: the stupor of astonishment seemed for a moment to lock up his every sense; then snatching the lamp from the table, he hastened with it towards the arras; but in his haste he hit it against the flowing curtains of the bed, and it went out.

His passion and disappointment were now beyond all bounds. He called aloud for assistance; and having, with some difficulty, found the chamber door, he repeated his calls in the gallery. They were quickly attended to, and several domestics appeared with lights.

He repeated the search he had made on hearing the sigh, and with the same ill success: nothing was to be discovered behind the sable covering which yet dressed the apartment. Puzzled, and almost alarmed by the occurrence, he rushed out of the room, and commanded that Rosalind should be conveyed to her chamber.

CHAPTER XII.

Hail! thou house of death!
And thou, the lovely mistress of these shades,
Whose beauty gilds the more than midnight darkness,
And makes it grateful as the dawn of day!
Oh, take me in a fellow-mourner with thee!
I'll number groan for groan, and tear for tear;
And when the fountains of thy eyes are dry,
Mine shall supply the stream, and weep for both!

ROWE.

In a state of wretchedness of mind, which it was almost beyond her strength to bear, Rosalind continued for some time to traverse her chamber in silence and solitude, save the presence of Gertrude, who stood, statue-like, observing her mistress from one corner of the apartment, and who did not at all hesitate to conclude that she had seen the dreadful shadow in the cedar-chamber, of which the report was gone abroad in the castle.

In about a couple of hours, a knock at the chamber door called Gertrude to it: it was one of the Baron's servants, who put into her hand a letter for Rosalind, and departed. The paper contained these words.

"Rosalind, you have this evening so far despised my authority, that it becomes a justice in me to myself to exert its power over you; prepare yourself, therefore, to become the wife of Lord Rufus de Madginecourt, on the fifth day from the present one.—Your father affectionately, if you merit his love,

"De Mowbray."

The paper fell from the hands of Rosalind, and she sunk down upon the bed. Tears would no longer come to her relief: the iniquity, the cruelty of her father's conduct, froze them in their source. To her his nature appeared entirely altered since the arrival of Lord Rufus; but such was not the case: his nature was the same as it ever had been—kind, where it did not interfere with his views to be so; relentless, where his firmness was to produce him the completion of any desired plan. An instance of this nature had never yet occurred, in which Rosalind had been concerned; thus she believed that part of his character, which accident had not yet made her acquainted with, newly assumed.

In a short time, she recovered herself sufficiently to send Gertrude to her father, to request his presence in her chamber. Gertrude returned, and brought her intelligence that he was engaged with his guests, and could not leave them. Rosalind could not thus calmly bear a refusal to her petition, and taking up her pen, she wrote to him, requesting that as he would not indulge her by visiting her himself, to inform Lord Rufus that it was her wish to see him.

She dispatched her note, and after some time Gertrude returned again, with information that Lord Rufus was, like himself, engaged, and could not be interrupted.

Rosalind believed that her father had not communicated her request to Lord Rufus, and in this supposition Gertrude confirmed her.

"My die is then irrevocably cast!" she cried. "A father dooms his only child to be the victim of his pride, drags her to the altar, a living sacrifice to his ambition, and blasphemes the blessing which he there bestows on her, by fixing an everlasting thorn in her heart! Oh, heavenly powers, will you suffer such cruelty to pass without redress?"

"Ah, my Lady," said Gertrude, "I never saw the happiness of poverty before; but it strikes me now, that my humble situation in life is a much happier one than your's: for as my father is only a poor delver, and I have nothing more to expect from him than the life he has given me, if he were to be as cruel to me as the Baron is to you, and would not let me marry the man my heart was set upon, it would be no loss to me to run away from him, and please myself; but if you were to do so, what a great fortune of riches you might lose by such a step! and I suppose indeed that keeps you from it."

"Oh, that there were time allowed me to ask the intercession of my godmother, my queen!" exclaimed Rosalind.

"But there is not half time enough for that," returned Gertrude: "five days are not enough for a man to get to London in, let alone the coming back besides."

"I will not become the wife of Lord Rufus," said Rosalind, "except force compels me to it!"

"And Mr. Edward has not been to the castle for a week and more: he is always at the new tower in the village now. What a thing it is of him to be absent at this time! surely, my Lady, it would but be right to let him know what is going forward?"

"Not for me, Gertrude: it would not indeed," replied Rosalind. "Is that a step," she added, with a smile, "that you would take, were you in my situation?"

"That I am sure I would, my Lady," returned Gertrude; "and I can't see the indelicacy, begging pardon, of a lady's doing it, any more than a poor girl like me. If you did not love him, you would not marry him; and if you do love him well enough to marry him, why not accept the same service from him, as if he were your husband already?"

"But I have promised my father not to think of Edward in the light of a husband, if he will not urge me to accept Lord Rufus as one."

"But he does urge you, you see, my dear Lady; and I am sure his brow looked as stern as a lion's, when I carried your note to him," answered Gertrude.

A pause ensued.

Gertrude broke it.—"What a pity it is Mr. Edward is not here to give you advice, my Lady!"

"On no account send to him," replied Rosalind; "for while you imagine that such a step might give me relief, it would in reality only add to my unhappiness. It is enough for me to meet Lord William's scorn myself: let him continue where he is, and avoid it."

The clock now struck eleven, and Rosalind dismissed her attendant. Conscious that sleep would not visit her pillow that night, she continued wandering about her chamber, till another hour had passed away. She had not been long alone before she conceived an inclination (it was one of those which hearts overburdened with grief cannot explain, yet find imaginary comfort in) to visit her mother's grave that night, and spend some time by it. When the midnight hour had sounded, she opened the door of her chamber, and stepped into the gallery, to listen whether all the family were retired to rest. Not the sound of a single footstep pacing the marble hall, or lofty passages, met her ear—not the faint flickering of a dying lamp caught her eye.

With a light in her hand, she moved cautiously forward, treading gently, lest she should herself be overheard. Arrived at the top of the great staircase, she paused: the sounds which she had that night heard in the cedar-chamber, recurred to her memory, and, in spite of her fortitude, a cold chill ran through her veins. She resolved to rally her strength of mind, and the most potent medicine which presented itself for its revival, was the conviction, that whether it were the voice of a human being, or of supernatural agency, which had that night been heard by her, it was a voice friendly to herself.

She descended the stairs, and crossed the marble hall, in the immense space of which, the single lamp which she bore in her hand appeared a speck of light quivering in an universe of gloom, impenetrable to her sight. Hasty were her steps, till she had reached the vaulted passages on its opposite side; and here the shutting of a distant door struck upon her heart, and suspended her respiration.

She was approaching towards the apartments which Lord Rufus inhabited in the castle, and the recollection of her having seen him abroad, at the early hour in the morning which she had once done, led her to imagine that circumstances might again bring him from his chamber on this night, and that it might be the sound of his door she had now heard.

She shaded her lamp in the folds of her dress, and looked around to discover if a light was any where visible: darkness and silence prevailed on all sides, and she ventured to proceed. With the swiftness of an antelope, she flew through the corridor into which opened the door of Lord Rufus's dressing-room. She had now nothing to fear from any part of the family; the succeeding passages which led to the chapel, were unconnected with the inhabited part of the castle, and seldom resorted to, except on the Sunday. She reached the chapel without interruption. She looked around her; for the most courageous wish to be certain that no danger lurks near them; and having assured herself that she was alone, she placed her lamp in a niche of the wall, at a short distance from the tomb of her parent, and then sunk upon the cold marble that enclosed her form. Her tears now came to her relief, and, in fervent prayer, she began to regain her composure of mind.

A shrill but distant whistle awakened her from her meditations and devotion. She started up, and took her lamp in her hand. The whistle was repeated. It sounded from a narrow passage, leading into one of the aisles of the chapel, which wound into vaults and cells now in disuse, since the main building had been converted from a religious purpose into its present state, and which, she believed, opened upon the northern rampart.

Fear seized her: the sound predicted the approach of some human being, and she knew not whom or what to suppose it: if she fled, her lamp might discover her retreat; if she put it out, she despaired of retracing her way to the marble hall. In this dilemma, her heart beating high within her breast, she was standing, lost in irresolution, when she heard the fall of approaching footsteps. Excessive terror urged her: the idea of self-preservation for the moment alone filled her mind, and, blowing out her lamp, she stationed herself behind a massy pillar, where she hoped to escape observation. Scarcely was her lamp extinguished, before some animate being ran against her, with a violence that almost threw her down, and at the same instant a cold and clammy substance was pressed against the back of her hand: all her courage forsook her; she shrieked and fainted!

The sounds of—"Rosalind—dearest Rosalind! 'tis I—'tis Edward!" recalled her into life; and she found that it was indeed Edward who supported her in his arms!

"Rosalind," he said, "how is this? Why do I see you here at this hour of the night?"

"I have been at prayer by my mother's grave," replied Rosalind. "Oh, Edward, how little did I imagine that it was you, by the sound of whose steps I was so much alarmed!—But you were not alone; it could not have been you who ran against me, when I stood behind the pillar?"

"I have a friend with me," replied Edward; "but he was by my side when I heard your shrieks, and flying to your assistance, found you lifeless on the ground."

Rosalind turned to observe the friend of whom he spoke, and recognized in him the countenance of the so-called *surly* Hubert.

"I beg your pardon, Lady," said Hubert, "not for myself, but for my dog, who I am sure would ask it for himself of you, if he were able; for he it was, no doubt, that created you the alarm of which you have just been speaking."

Hubert was standing at some distance from Edward, and, by his side, was a large mastiff, which fixed its eyes on Rosalind, and seemed to be wagging its tail in approbation of its master's apology.

This dog was the same which had attracted Hubert's compassion when a cur, on the ramparts, the first day of Edward's introduction to him; and which, pitying for its poverty, he had since bought of its master and attached to himself:—the dog's name was Lion.

Convinced, at the sight of the dog, that it had been his cold nose which had touched the back of her hand, Rosalind could scarcely forbear a smile at her late alarm; and being now relieved from the terror that had before filled her mind, her thoughts wandered into another channel, and she returned to Edward the question which he had before advanced to her—"How is it that I meet you here?"

Hubert's eye caught that of Edward, and he retired to a greater distance.

When he was out of hearing, Edward spoke thus—"I have all this evening been watching for an opportunity of seeing you. I knew this to be the day on which your answer to the proposals of Lord Rufus was expected, and——"

"You were then acquainted with the month which was given me for consideration?" interrupted Rosalind.

"Oh yes—yes," returned Edward. "Nothing has passed during that time in the castle, with which I have not taken means to gain acquaintance, though I have been seen but little in it: but knowing the decision you were to give this day, I could not forbear making an attempt to see you."

"But why enter the castle by those dismal vaults?" asked Rosalind.

"Because I must not be seen in it," he returned. "The Baron has commanded me not to leave the tower in the village for an instant, on pain of his most violent displeasure. I see the motive of his command, and although I endeavour to preserve the appearance of obeying it, my heart will revolt from such discipline, and lead me hither by stealth."

The tears burst from the eyes of Rosalind; and Edward held her to his breast for some moments in silence.

Edward spoke first.—"Hubert is my sincere friend; gratitude for kindness I have shewn him, has bound him to me; he admitted me by the entrance from these vaults, which opens upon the ramparts, some hours ago, and I remained here, whilst he sought an opportunity of informing you that I was waiting to see you; but, alas! he sought you in vain; you were not in your chamber, but in conference elsewhere with your father."

"Oh, that was a dreadful hour!" said Rosalind.

"At eight o'clock I was obliged to depart, to place the guard for the night at the tower, in order that my having been absent might not be suspected by the soldiery, amongst whom are, no doubt, spies upon me from Lord William. That done, I pretended to retire to rest; but with the midnight hour I again stole forth, and found my trusty friend awaiting my arrival on the rampart. Here it was my intention to have remained, whilst he proceeded to the chamber of Gertrude, and entreated her to give you information of my being here, and of my wish to see you. Guess my surprise, when I found you in the very place where I most longed to behold you, and least expected to find you."

"And this is now, perhaps," exclaimed Rosalind, "our last meeting; I have but four days yet to call my own; the fifth gives me to wretchedness, and to De Madginecourt."

"Is it thus decreed?" cried Edward. "Oh God! Oh Rosalind! that I were any thing but what I am!—an unknown!—and I would swear the sun should never rise upon that deed!"

"Vain were the oath, my Edward," returned Rosalind; "vain all that you or I can do to save me! What can avail our words, our prayers, with hearts steeled against pity, like my father's?"

"I would not use either," returned Edward; "prayers with the cruel are but edges to their resolution, and sharpen their vengeance to cut the deeper. If I loved thee less than I do, Rosalind, I could save thee, sweet!"

"What mean you by this riddle?" asked Rosalind. "How am I to understand that you love me too well to strive for my happiness?"

"Did I not value you too dearly, to lower you a feather's weight in fortune's scale, I might say, give your hand to a dependant, and be the name of wife your security against an unjust father's persecution."

"Oh, Edward," cried Rosalind, "you speak of impracticable chimeras; were I willing to throw myself into your arms, you know, the priest could not be found who would join the hand of De Mowbray's daughter in marriage, without his sanction and especial command."

Edward struck his hand with violence against his forehead, and turning his face aside from Rosalind, stood wrapt in thought. He saw the force of her remark. Wedded they could not be. Attempting her to fly with him, without the name which could alone disunite indelicacy from the act, he recoiled. Convinced also was he, that in this point all argument would have been lost upon her, had his heart even leant to the means;—thus, to become the wife of Lord Rufus appeared her inevitable fate!

"In spite of my father," said Rosalind, "I will see Lord Rufus to-morrow; I will set before him my aversion to an alliance with him—I will implore his mercy. If he has a heart, he will not surely join with a father in an act of cruelty against his child."

To this resolution Edward returned only a sigh of despair.

How swiftly fly the hours which lovers steal to interchange their pleasing griefs! Scarcely had it appeared to either a minute since they had met; and the envious clock now striking three, warned Edward that ere the expiration of another hour, he must be in the village at the post of glory.

Hubert advanced, and told him that it was necessary for him to depart.

"Promise me," said Edward, "that you will be here to-morrow at midnight, and inform me of the success of your interview with Lord Rufus."

"I will indeed be here, Edward," she replied; and with a silent embrace, whose eloquence was most expressive, they parted.

CHAPTER XIII.

> There's one did laugh in his sleep, and one cry'd murder!
> That they did wake each other. I stood and heard them.
>
> MACBETH.

Cautiously Rosalind retraced her steps through the vaulted passages, scarcely allowing herself to breathe, lest any sound which threatened a discovery of her nightly visit might escape her hearing. A footstep alarmed her, but it was only that of a sentinel on the ramparts, which sounded through a grated window in the lofty passage. A few minutes after, she heard the guard relieved, and now she trembled, lest they should by any means discover Edward in his retreat from the castle. She paused a few moments; all became hushed again, and she went on.

Arrived at a flight of steps, which led into the corridor upon which opened the first of the suite of apartments occupied by Lord Rufus, a chill of fear again pervaded her frame; she could not forget her having seen him abroad at the early hour she had once done; and she could not conquer her alarm lest he should be again returning to his chamber, or leaving it, just as she might happen to pass the door.

At the distance of a few paces from it, she stopped to assure herself that all was quiet; she listened—all was still; and she was on the point of proceeding, when a wild laugh burst on her ear, accompanied by a blow, which seemed to strike the floor of the room, and resembled the noise of some one falling with great violence. Her every nerve trembled, and she could scarcely hold the lamp in her hand; a momentary silence ensued, and she then heard a voice, which it was impossible not to recognise for that of Lord Rufus, exclaiming—"Die she must—if she will not kill herself, I must do it for her!—it is but one stab, and all is over!" The terror of Rosalind was wound to a pitch of such excess, that it was with difficulty she could forbear calling out; her knees seemed bending under her, she fell against the wall, and with difficulty kept herself from sinking to the ground.

A soft voice within the chamber spoke next—"My Lord, my dear Lord, pray come to bed again!" it said.

"There, there!" exclaimed Lord Rufus, "'tis done! 'tis done!—nobody knows it, and I am myself again!"

"My Lord! awake, my Lord! pray awake!" rejoined the other voice.

A momentary pause was followed by a deep groan. De Madginecourt then said, in a softened tone—"Oh, Alwin my boy, these nights are dreadful—dreadful! I must have air."

Rosalind now imagined that their steps were moving towards the door, and exerting all her remaining strength, she fled towards the great hall. Here the beating of her heart was so violent, that she was again apprehensive of sinking, and clung to one of the marble pillars for support; she, however, heard no pursuing step, and from this circumstance, she derived such comfort as, in a short time, regained her sufficient strength to bear her to her chamber.

She threw herself into a chair, her brain bewildered with such a chaos of ideas, that it was for some time incapable of reflection. Of whom, she enquired of herself, could it be that Lord Rufus had spoken in his sleep? *Was* he a murderer, or did he intend to *become* one? Of the crime she decided him equally guilty, whether it were already perpetrated or only planned; and this knowledge put the seal to her determination of never becoming his wife—avoid the dreaded ceremony how she might.

She had told Edward, that it was her intention to request an interview with Lord Rufus, for the purpose of setting before him the injustice of which he was guilty towards her, by suffering a father to treat his daughter with the cruelty to which she was now subject on his account; but, aware that the heart which is capable of executing or commanding the death of a fellow-being, must be callous to the voice of suffering, she now resolved not to see him, if even he should himself request admittance to her presence, in consequence of the note which she had on the preceding evening sent to her father.

To him she felt no hesitation in determining not to impart what she had that night overheard in De Madginecourt's apartment; blinded as he was by prejudice, he would, beyond all doubt, accuse her of having fabricated a tale to the injury of him with whom she wished to avoid an alliance; and her want of a sufficient reason for having passed his door at that hour in the morning, would give colour to the very imputation he would wish to put upon it. Once she believed it possible that effective means might be taken for frightening the truth out of the page Alwin; but she considered that as he was the only domestic allowed to sleep near his Lord, and this she knew to be the case, he was doubtless well instructed in replies to any questions which might be put to him; and even if that were not the case, without her father's assistance, which she was certain of not having, she was not possessed of the power of obtaining the desired explanation from his lips.

She resolved not to quit her chamber that day, but to see Edward again at the hour she had promised to meet him in the chapel, and be guided by his advice.

At dinner the Baron sent to request her presence in the hall. She replied to the invitation, that she was unwell, and begged for the indulgence of remaining in her own apartment.

Rosalind had not tasted repose on the preceding night, and in the evening she laid herself upon her couch, hoping to sleep awhile, and gain strength for the ensuing night, which would be passed in waking. She had not been long reclined when a rap at the door called Gertrude to open it; and on the outside she found Alwin. He was come, in the name of Lord Rufus, to enquire after her health, and to request permission to visit her.

She returned in reply, that she was too much indisposed to admit a visitor, and Alwin departed with his message.

"What a proud, saucy urchin that Alwin is!" said Gertrude, as she shut the door upon him; "he gives himself more airs than any of his Lord's attendants besides, or all of them put together I may say; and I wonder what for, for my part."

Rosalind did *not* wonder, but listened attentively to hear whether Gertrude knew more.

"The little fool is as proud as a horse, to-day," Gertrude went on, "of a fine diamond button his Lord gave him this morning to loop up his hat with. I am sure he has luck on his side, and indeed the proverb seems made out with him, that it is better to be born with good luck than good fortune, for they say it is not to be believed how fond Lord Rufus is of that boy, and what a number of handsome presents he is always making him."

The reason was plain to Rosalind, but she made no comments

on Gertrude's observations, and, in a short time, fell into a slumber, which was attended with distressing dreams, and from which she awoke about two hours before midnight, unrefreshed.

At her accustomed time of retiring to rest, she dismissed her attendant; and when her hour of appointment with Edward was come, and she believed all the inhabitants of the castle to be locked in sleep, she left her chamber, sighing that the cruelty of a father should drive his only child to steal through his mansion like a midnight plunderer, for a moment's repose on a heart of friendship.

With all the fears that had attended her on the preceding evening, she again moved cautiously along, shuddering as she passed the door of Lord Rufus's apartment; but safety guided her footsteps into the chapel. She had not left her chamber till the hour had sounded twelve; thus she found Edward ready to receive her.

"Heaven bless you, my dearest Rosalind," he exclaimed, pressing her to his heart.

"It has protected me through dreadful terrors since I beheld you last," she returned; and then related to him the occurrences of the preceding morning, in her return to her chamber.

Edward's opinion was, like her own, that any appeal to the humanity of the Baron, upon the plea of what she had heard Lord Rufus utter within his chamber, would be without effect. How then was she to escape the hated fate that awaited her?

"Oh Heaven!" exclaimed she, "thou alone hast power to interpose, and save me from the dreadful sacrifice of my eternal peace!"

"Heaven has presented us the means," returned Edward: "it rests alone with my Rosalind to accept or refuse them."

"What are they?" asked Rosalind.

"Not for your rank—not for your inheritance, which, by the step I shall propose, becomes uncertain to you, but for yourself alone, to rescue you from misery, I will now ask whether Rosalind will become the wife of the humble Edward?"

"You know," replied Rosalind, "that were my mind prepared for this step, our union is impossible."

"No—no, it is not impossible!" exclaimed Edward. "I have, at this moment, a friend within call, who is willing to unite us by the most sacred bonds of religion."

"Who can he be," asked Rosalind, "that dares thus to hazard Lord de Mowbray's displeasure?"

"One," replied Edward, "whom ill fortune has sunk into necessity: he is a priest, of the catholic persuasion, who, driven by the laws of our present sovereign from the exercise of his office, lives in obscurity, in the neighbouring village. Want presses upon the poor old man, and he has consented, for the reward I have promised him, to unite us by the ceremony of our own church."

A silence ensued. Edward broke it.—"Will not my Rosalind," he said, "consent to save herself from the horrors of a forced marriage?"

"I shudder," returned Rosalind, "to assent to a deed, on which I know a father's curse will fall!"

"Is it not his cruelty, in attempting to fix a curse for life on you, that drives you to it?" returned Edward; "and have you not, my Rosalind, the consent of the parent whom you most value, to my becoming her son? Look at this cross," continued he, producing it as he spoke, "the legacy of her deathbed to me: is it not inscribed to Edward, *as a mother's gift*? She had herself been torn from the heart of her affections, and did she not confess her apprehension of the same fate awaiting her daughter, when she implored your father to give you to the man of your heart?"

"Oh that she had lived, to have received his promise to that effect!" exclaimed Rosalind. "How much agony might have been spared to her child! Oh that she were now alive, to give her sanction to our union!"

"It is already given: she *has* called me *her son*," said Edward.

The tears flowed swiftly from the eyes of the trembling Rosalind, and as Edward supported her agitated frame in his arms, he continued to whisper his entreaties for her happiness into her ear. But three days were yet her own, before the hated De Madginecourt was destined to become the master of her person. Edward urged, that he might be prevented from meeting her again, before the dreaded time arrived—that the priest might refuse again to accompany him. Hubert appeared in view, at a distant part of the chapel. Edward called to him, and directed him to bid the priest advance to the altar.

"Oh, Edward—Edward!" faintly articulated Rosalind, and hid her face on his neck.

"May Heaven desert me," exclaimed the youth, "when your happiness ceases to be my first, and only care!"

Slowly he led her towards the altar. The priest, a venerable aged man, stood forth. Her tears ceased to flow: she *almost* ceased to breathe. The ceremony was read; and Rosalind was a—WIFE!

Edward extended his arms to bestow the first embrace of a husband; and Rosalind sunk senseless into them.

Some time elapsed, ere she again awoke to sense, and it was then only to give vent to her tears. Scarcely able to move, she leaned upon Edward, and he conducted her to her chamber.

With the early morning it again became Edward's duty to return to the tower in the village, and he was constrained to leave Rosalind overwhelmed with tears, with his vows of tenderness, and promise of meeting her on the succeeding midnight, for her only solace.

Dreadful became the reflections of Rosalind, when left to the solitude of her own chamber.—Edward—her beloved Edward, she now feared would be made the victim of the Baron's revenge, for having been the means of rescuing her from becoming the sacrifice of his pride: the idea almost maddened her, and she now wished that her hand were her own to bestow on Lord Rufus, that the act might save him she loved from her father's anger.

The day crept slowly on with Rosalind: Gertrude was her only companion. In the afternoon, she felt an unconquerable desire to visit the cedar-chamber; she wished to see her mother's portrait, and almost to ask it whether it approved the step she had taken. Accordingly whilst Gertrude was at dinner, she repaired to the apartment where her parent had died. Arrived at the door, she endeavoured to enter; but the lock resisted her efforts, and she was obliged to return disappointed towards her own chamber.

Lord de Mowbray, she concluded, had caused it to be shut up, in consequence of the alarm he had received there, on the night she had been in conference with him in that apartment. As she returned slowly through the gallery, her thoughts resting on the mystery of the voice which she had on that evening heard in the cedar-chamber, looking towards her own apartment, she could just distinguish (for the evening was coming on, and the light, admitted through the long and narrow casements of the gallery, feeble) the figure of a man gliding into it.

Supposing it either her father or Lord Rufus, she stopped, as she felt a reluctance to encounter either of them; and she continued wandering near the head of the great staircase, in anxious expectation of Gertrude's return from dinner.

Presently she heard the wards of a lock creak, in the opposite gallery to that in which was her chamber. She turned her head to the sound, and saw the face and arm of a man thrust out of the door of the cedar-chamber. She thought he beckoned to her; but at the same instant a step was heard in the distant part of the gallery, and he drew in his head again hastily, and shut the door:—the step was Gertrude's, who appeared with a light in her hand.

Rosalind directly retired with her attendant to her chamber: no one was in it. She framed an excuse for going into her closet, and thence into the chamber where Gertrude slept. No one was to be seen, nor were there any marks of any one having been there. The circumstance rested on the mind of Rosalind: as she had not seen the figure return, she feared there might be some secret outlet from her chamber, with which she was unacquainted, but which might be known to Lord Rufus, and of which he might take advantage for visiting her, in opposition to her wish of not seeing him. No one but her father, she could suppose it, who had opened the door of the cedar-chamber; and if it had been he whom she had seen there, she was as much puzzled to guess why he should have visited it, as she would have been to have decided how any one else could have gained admittance into it; at all events, she concluded that she must have been deceived in supposing the figure, whoever it was, to have beckoned to her.

The most soothing balm which a mind bending under the burden of anxiety can taste, is to repose its sorrows in a kind and sympathizing heart, though it be a heart gifted with neither profound sense, nor eloquent arguments, for our consolation: the tear with which it meets our's, renders it of inestimable value to our feelings.

This sensation did Rosalind experience, when she reposed the history of her sorrows and the confession of her marriage, in the breast of the artless Gertrude, from whose tender sensibility and unaffected sympathy, she derived a most consolatory relief.

With the sounding of the midnight hour, Rosalind opened her chamber door, and anxiously awaited the coming of Edward. Time passed on, and no approaching step cheered her listening ear. She left her chamber, and wandered towards the grand staircase leading into the hall. All was silent. She knew not what to imagine, nor what to fear: she dreaded lest he had been discovered in leaving his post, or in entering the castle; still she hoped he was safe, and only delayed by some unforeseen circumstance. The clock struck one. Anxiety became too powerful to be borne. She supposed that she might have mistaken his words, when she had understood that he would come to her apartment, and that he might now be expecting her arrival in the chapel, as on the two preceding nights. Impressed with this idea, she delayed not a moment to proceed towards it: too wretched to be shaken from her purpose, by any of those alarms which had before agitated her mind, she was now experiencing terror for the safety of a husband.

Arrived in the chapel, no friendly voice welcomed her approach—no cheering lamp blazed in the niche, where his before had held its station: all was silence and darkness. She moved towards the passage which led to the vaults opening upon the ramparts: extending into it the arm which bore her lamp, she looked anxiously forward, but void alone met her eye. Still she hoped he would come, although it was now evident something had occurred to detain him beyond his promised time.

She seated herself on the steps of the altar—of that altar at which the sentence of her future life had so lately been pronounced, past all recall. The clock struck two, and still he came not. Another hour was lingered out by her in anxious expectation. Again the clock sounded, and no Edward was arrived. The twilight of the morning would now soon be breaking through the dark clouds of night: she durst no longer be absent from her chamber; and, in a paroxysm of heart-broken sadness, she returned to it, and threw herself upon her disconsolate bed.

In the morning the Baron de Mowbray entered her apartment: a smile of triumph was painted on his countenance, beneath which she foresaw some evil to herself to be lurking.

"I know," he said, "that it will give my Rosalind pleasure to be informed of the promotion and honour of her friend and favourite;

I am, therefore, myself the first to inform her that Edward is appointed to the command of a regiment, which forms a part of the troops our queen is about to send into Flanders."

Rosalind would have spoken, but her efforts to articulate were ineffectual.

"The nature of the times presses for hasty steps," the Baron went on: "he had but a few hours to prepare for his departure. He commenced his journey to the coast, whence he is to embark, yesterday."

"Gone!" exclaimed Rosalind—"Gone without seeing me!"

"You informed me yesterday, by your servant," returned the Baron, "that you were too unwell to admit visitors, when Lord Rufus and myself made the enquiry. This I told him, and promised to bear you his apology."

"Apology, my Lord!" cried Rosalind.—"Pardon me, but I cannot be deceived into a belief that Edward was content to send me an apology, instead of a farewell from his own lips; nor can I credit that it was his voluntary act to leave me at this important moment. You have driven him hence, that his presence might be no impediment to my accepting the hand of Lord Rufus. But know, my Lord, that if I never see him more, he has left an impression on my heart which will prove a breast-plate of steel to guard me from that monster's arms."

"It is well that you are thus provided with a champion in his absence," returned Lord William, with a satirical sneer: "and what may be this mighty talisman that forms the armour which you vaunt of—is it love?"

"Pure as the source from whence our affection flows," replied Rosalind, "it is a safeguard to the breast that nourishes it; for it teaches that breast to preserve its own honour, for the sake of that heart's honour with which it is united."

"Love, with all its enchantment," answered the Baron, "is not always strong enough to draw a magic circle of security round the heart it inhabits."

"Because the violator of such enchantment," rejoined Rosalind, "employs such wicked arts to break the spell, as love is too innocent to have devised for its formation; still, when too grossly aggravated, and too cruelly beset, it has a tower of safety to retire to, where it assumes a name on which even few ravishers, monstrous as Lord Rufus, dare intrude."

"You seem well schooled in arguments to back your weak prejudices," answered Lord William; "think you you should be as great an adept in their practice?"

"The most harmless reptile, my Lord," replied Rosalind, "may be stung by an envenoming serpent, till, by a sudden effort of desperate strength, it shall rise, and free itself from the tyranny of its oppressor. Such do I consider myself;—trodden upon by the joint persecution of yourself and Lord Rufus, I have turned, and asserted my freedom."

"Aye, your freedom!" echoed Lord William—"Are you sure of that?"

"My release from an alliance with Lord Rufus, is for me liberty enough," answered Rosalind.

"And what charm has ensured you this release?" asked the Baron, half laughing.

"By assuming that name which had made *him* my tyrant," answered Rosalind, "the name of *wife*."

A silence of some minutes ensued. The eyes of Lord William flashed fire: those of Rosalind were sunk, and fixed upon the ground. The blood which had, on the first sound of *wife*, fled from the cheeks of the Baron, began again gradually to return to them, and he exclaimed, in a tone of mingled doubt and passion—"This is a trial of falsehood to deceive me; but it will not pass."

"It is no trial," returned Rosalind, the words faltering on her tongue, "but the last effort of a motherless child, to ensure herself a protector, when cast off from the affection of her father."

"Is Edward thy husband?" roared out the Baron.

"He is—he is!" replied Rosalind.

"Is he?" exclaimed the Baron; "then may those curses which await the——"

"Oh, hold, hold—in mercy hold!" interrupted Rosalind; "he is now *your son!*"

A groan of passion burst from Lord William's lips, and, darting a look of venom at his daughter, he rushed out of the chamber.

CHAPTER XIV.

There's mercy in each ray of light, that mortal eyes e'er saw;
There's mercy in each breath of air, that mortal lips e'er draw;
There's mercy both for bird and beast, in God's indulgent plan;
There's mercy for each creeping thing—*but man has none for man!*

M. G. LEWIS.

The miseries of the unfortunate Rosalind appeared now to be wound to their most poignant acme; and she even thought that she should have experienced less wretchedness as the wife of Lord Rufus, than she now felt in the belief that Edward had been driven from England on her account; and as she considered the indignation which her father would bear against him, now he had learnt that the union which he had dreaded had been effected.

Edward was torn from her—perhaps for ever. She endeavoured to pray, but her mind was too much agitated for the office, and she flung herself into a chair, scarcely able to encounter the light of day.

In the evening, Lord William again appeared in her apartment. In the most solemn manner, he commanded her to confess to him, by the hopes she entertained of her soul's felicity, whether or not she was the wife of Edward. His tone struck terror to her heart, and sinking at his feet, she implored his pity and forgiveness; but the tempest of his impassioned mind was too wild to allow him either to feel for her distress, or attend to her justification of herself; and uttering dreadful menaces against her disobedience and Edward's temerity, he left her.

On the following morning, Rosalind was proceeding to the door which led from her closet upon the rampart; Gertrude hastily followed her, and with a tear starting in her eye, she said—"Alas, my Lady, grieved am I that I am compelled to tell you such unpleasant tidings—but you cannot pass that door; the key is taken from us; you are the prisoner of these apartments; it was your father's command that you should be confined to them quite alone; but I implored not to be taken from you; and as I promised solemnly not to let you out of them, the Baron gave me leave to stay with you. I hope you are not angry that I accorded to such conditions, rather than leave you alone; indeed, it was my love for you, my dear Lady, that impelled me to do it."

"Am I then a prisoner in my own father's mansion?" said Rosalind—"denied the common air, which Nature allows to the guilty as profusely as to the good? and am I deprived its blessing, because I am unfortunate? Oh, Gertrude! kind girl! thou art now the only solace of my afflicted heart!"

"I will be as far as I can, my Lady," returned Gertrude; "and when I am deficient in consoling you, you must attribute it to my want of power, and not my lack of will, for indeed I love you dearly; you are the kindest and best, as well as the most injured lady; and let all the world turn their backs upon you, Gertrude will do all in her power to serve you."

Thus spoke the honest-hearted Gertrude, whose sentiments would have shamed the noble inhabitants of De Mowbray Castle, had they seen through any sense but that of prejudice; and truly did she act up to her declaration, in her endeavours to rob the hours of her mistress's imprisonment of their heaviness, by her prattle and attentions; but still they crept on with painful slowness. No tidings could she gain of Edward; not a breath could Gertrude ever gather of his fate, in her conversation with the other domestics of the castle. Sometimes Rosalind was inclined to believe that her father had forbidden them to mention, in Gertrude's hearing, any intelligence which might have been received of him, wishing to deprive her even of the solace of having his name repeated to her by her attendant; but in this point Gertrude's uncle, Ambrose, who was, in fact, the friend of Rosalind in his heart, declared her mistaken, as he was certain that whatever his Lord might know of Edward's fate himself, it had never transpired from his lips to any one in the castle.

Lord Rufus departed on the second day after the discovery of Rosalind's marriage had been made to her father; but whither he was gone, Gertrude heard not.

From this time five months had passed away, during which Rosalind continued a prisoner in her chamber, and saw no human being but her faithful attendant. Her father, so far from visiting her, never enquired after her at all; he concluded that she was alive, or that her death would have been reported to him; for her happiness or health, it was evident, from his commands respecting her imprisonment, that he cared not—nay, it was often a doubt even to himself, whether he did not wish her dead, rather than the wife of Edward. It was true, he conceived—for even disappointed men, like Lord William, endeavour, in their own breasts, privately to extract some good from the most hated circumstances—that it was possible Edward was her equal in rank; the word "noble" had escaped the lips of him who had called himself his grandfather on his death-bed, and been spoken in reference to the youth; but whether of his birth, or his mind, it had at the time been a point of doubt with him, and was so still. If noble by birth, of whom was he the heir? and why had he been thus obscured in the early years of his life? On this he had often reflected, and found himself now as little able as ever to solve the enigma; the chances, he feared, were greatly in favour of his being only the simple Edward, the grandson of the plain old Matthews; and, upon this fear, he could not bring himself to bend to the necessity of the occasion, by acknowledging him as the husband of his daughter, but was resolved to keep their union a secret for ever, unless such a proof as he wished for, of his equality to his daughter's rank, should ever appear in his favour: it is also true, that he might have procured him to be declared the heir to his own title and estates; but this was poison to his pride, in his idea, hugging a serpent to his bosom, which had been nursed into presumption by the weakness of a headstrong girl, who had defeated all his plans of aggrandizement; and he made a vow within his own heart, never to perform that lenient act towards those by whom he conceived his dignity and authority to have been so grossly and contemptuously insulted.

His days were passed in superintending the military concerns which were transacting at his castle, and repelling the incursions of the borderers, by sending out detached parties to route them from their holds, in which skirmishes his men, from the advantage which they possessed in having been more regularly trained to arms than the freebooters had an opportunity of being, were usually successful. His leisure hours were passed in disturbed reflections with his own mind, during which he generally wandered about the ramparts, or paced the marble hall of the castle. Irwin was always the companion of his meals; and sometimes he added to the society of the table his other leaders.

Wretched and more wretched as the days crept on, and no intelligence could be gained by her of the fate of her husband, Rosalind conceived the idea of addressing a petition to her Sovereign, requesting her intercession with her father, and explaining to her the full history of her unfortunate situation; but she found, by the means of Gertrude, whom she directed to make enquiry to that purpose, that the Baron's strict injunctions had been issued to every individual in the castle, not to receive any letter from his daughter for delivery out of it, without first bringing it to him for inspection: she still for a while believed that some inferior domestic might be won by a bribe to convey it for her into a proper channel for reaching the Queen; but overawed by the dread of what cruelties her father might inflict on her, should her emissary be tempted to treachery by the hope of meeting a second reward at the hand of Lord William, she desisted from her design.

Great as Rosalind had already, and justly too, believed her portion of woe, the period was now come, which brought with it a discovery that gave its keenest edge to the sharp tooth of misery which preyed upon her heart. This discovery was that of her being destined to become a mother!

Incessantly did the tears of Rosalind now flow. "Unfortunate babe!" she would exclaim, "who hast not yet beheld the light, to how bitter a portion of sorrow mayest thou not be born!—no father to welcome thy entrance into life—a grandsire, cruel to thy parents, who will perhaps revenge on thy innocent head the crimes of which he thinks them guilty, a mother worn down by affliction, who will cradle thee on a breast of anguish; and when thou lookest up to her for a smile of joy, will check thy fondness with the tears that fall for thy unhappy birth! Oh God! thou hast still mercy to bestow, and art, perhaps, most merciful, when thou withholdest it from the mother, to bless her doubly in bestowing it upon her child!"

Scarcely two months were now wanting to the time at which her babe would see the light: not once had Lord William visited her, since the day on which the confession of her marriage had been made to him. Frequently since her discovery of her present situation, had she entreated to see him, but in vain; he had returned contemptuous, sometimes brutal, replies to her messages borne to him by Gertrude: still she was resolute in her desire of seeing him; with the gloom natural to her present situation and misfortunes, she had most strongly imbibed the idea that the birth of her child would be the period of her own existence; and her anxiety to see her father proceeded from her wish to recommend to his protection her yet unborn babe, whom she dreaded he might doom to share the neglected fate of its unfortunate parents, although it could not be otherwise than innocent of their faults.

The Baron still continued deaf to the entreaties of his daughter to visit her; and Rosalind became wretched beyond bearing, at the idea which haunted her, of dying without having recommended her infant to his protection, and having received his promise to that effect.

At length she wrote the sentiments of her harassed brain, and putting them in the hand of Gertrude, besought her not to leave her father till she had prevailed on him to peruse them. Interested in the fate of her mistress, Gertrude implored the grant of her request, in terms which led the Baron to suppose that some extraordinary cause must exist to render her thus resolute in her entreaties; and his curiosity being thus excited, was probably the cause of his receiving the letter at her hand, and breaking the seal.

Gertrude waited to see no more, but ran back with the joyful, as she believed it, intelligence to Rosalind.

The paper fell from De Mowbray's hands when he had perused its contents. He had believed that Fate had exerted all its ingenuity in tormenting him, when it had given the hand of his daughter to the unknown Edward; but he now found it subtle in its plagues beyond his belief, when he learnt that an offspring of the hated marriage was about to enter the world, and his protection implored by his daughter, as her *last* request, for the child of the man, against whom every indignant and rancorous passion of his heart was raised.

Edward, he considered, subject as he was to the fate of war, might be cut off from a return to England; his daughter might have been weaned from his memory, and induced to form an alliance in a sphere suited to her birth, perhaps even with Lord Rufus de Madginecourt himself; but now a perpetuation of the act which he wished to have for ever buried in oblivion, and which he was satisfied to be little known in the world, was about to start up, and hand down to future ages what he deemed the disgrace of his family.

Rage was too cool a term for the emotion of his soul; every

nerve quivered with hatred, disappointment and dread.—The passion of pride cannot be supported without the aid of vices more heinous than itself; it is a fact which has often been asserted, and as often proved, before the days of Lord William, as since his time; his conduct serves only as another example to illucidate its truth. He resolved the babe should die!

This resolution was the event of a sleepless night, and when he arose in the morning, assuming a composure in reality foreign to his mind, he wrote to his daughter, informing her that she might rely on his protection for her child.

Rosalind kissed the paper which contained the promise, and thought her father still was kind.

On the first opportunity, Lord William took occasion of conversing apart with Mr. Wilmot, the surgeon of his household, and this conference called for the exertion of all his wariness and subtilty. The Baron knew Mr. Wilmot to be a man strongly educated in those prejudices which support the dignity of high birth, and scarcely consider even as minor sins, those alliances which infringe on family rank and honours. Thus far he knew him suited to the purpose of his present conference with him; but then, he likewise knew him to be a man of so strict principles and religion, that he would fly off from him the moment he saw him deviating but a single hair's breadth from the path of rectitude, though he was certain of his utmost assistance in the support of those prejudices which corresponded with his own sentiments, while they demanded no sacrifice of honesty or honour.

Artfully then did he disclose to him the pregnancy of his daughter; and having, with equal art, brought him to confess that he thought it necessary, to the honour of his family, rather to bring up the child at a distance from the castle, than to permit it to live within its walls as the acknowledged offspring of Edward and his daughter, he told him that he had a service to require of him, towards the forwarding of his plan, which was to pronounce the child still-born; as he feared that if the mother knew it to be alive, it would be impossible to remove it from the castle; and thus the disgrace, which he so much dreaded, would, without his consent to this proposition, be indelibly fixed on the honour of his house.

With this demand Mr. Wilmot was for some time unwilling to

comply. He first demanded whither the child was to be sent? and in reply to this question, Lord William showed him a letter forged by himself for the purpose, which contained an agreement, and promise of secrecy, as from a farmer's wife in Westmoreland, to bring up the child as her own, on condition of receiving a yearly sum from the Baron.—"She believes it," said Lord William, "a natural child of my own."

This letter hushed Mr. Wilmot's scruples in part: his other objection was—the pain it would create to the mother when she should be told, that all the pangs she had endured were without a recompence:—but this objection, after some time, the Baron also over-ruled, by representing to Mr. Wilmot how much more in favour of her happiness it would be for her to believe her child had never existed, than to know it alive, and constantly to be desiring to see it, without the possibility of so doing, which the Baron said would undoubtedly be the case, as he was resolute in never suffering it to know its parents. Upon this argument Mr. Wilmot yielded, and it was then agreed between them, that, at the time of the child's birth, Mr. Wilmot should declare it still-born; and, upon this plea, take it away from the chamber, that its sight might not affect its mother, and instantly bring it to the Baron's apartment, who would, against that time, have a confidential person in readiness to convey it without delay into Westmoreland.

Thus far all had gone well with the Baron in his plan; but that confidential person had more to perform than Mr. Wilmot guessed, and he was yet to be sought for.

Cunning is a mean quality, the surface of sense, which floats upon it, like a froth, and partakes not at all of its solids. This was the Baron's master tool; and, in the exercise of it, he believed himself keen and sharp-sighted: it was true that he could exercise the talent, if it may be admitted to the name, with sufficient skill to make it serve his purposes; but he wanted that depth of perception which looks into character, and does not chuse improper objects for its villanous confidence—that judgment which gives security to foul deeds, as far at least as they are capable of concealment; for every crime is but for a time delayed in bringing to the light; and when the wicked seem most to prosper, they are but sinking deeper into that gulph from which they are one day to find the impossibility of emerging.

The Baron looked around his household for a countenance which should seem the index of a heart impressive to the touch of gold, and suited to his purpose. No face appeared to him sufficiently gloomy; no lips pouted enough with discontent to tempt him into a trial of their souls. Time was creeping on, and yet no minister for his dark plot was found. One evening he had strayed to the village, and was returning thence in the dusky hour of twilight; in passing the newly-erected tower, he hailed the sentinel, and the voice that replied to him was that of Hubert.

CHAPTER XV.

If the midnight bell
Did, with his iron tongue and brazen mouth,
Sound one, unto the drowsy race of night;
If this same were a churchyard where we stand,
And thou possessed with a thousand wrongs;
Or, if that surly spirit, melancholy,
Had bak'd thy blood, and made it heavy, thick;
Or, if that thou couldst see me without eyes,
Hear me without thine ears, and make reply
Without a tongue, using conceit alone—
I would into thy bosom pour my thoughts.

KING JOHN.

THE Baron moved on slowly towards his own castle—Hubert, the subject of his thoughts.

Those who have not the skill of searching deeply into characters, are always much biassed by the name a man bears in the world. Hubert had acquired the name of *"surly."* On this the Baron reflected; and from the sternness of his countenance, doubted not but the epithet was a just one. He remembered the day when he had refused Edward's bounty, on the walls of the castle, while yet a boy, with a moroseness which had indicated a sourness of temper, and a spirit of dissatisfaction, at his indigent lot. Many trivial circumstances Lord William called to mind, to prove to him that his temper was not softened into greater complacency since his situation had become ameliorated by his entering into the troops of De Mowbray Castle. For this sternness of temper, he could himself see no reason, but that of a bad heart: he thought it impossible for a man to be dissatisfied with the inferiority of his situation, and not at the same time to be capable of any crime which would amend it. Thus knowing Hubert's bluntness of temper great as ever, he conceived him to be the very man whom gold could tempt, and whom remorse would never goad.

Thus agreed with his own mind, he resolved to enter into conversation with him on the next night of his being stationed as sentinel on the same post where he had that evening seen him, and which would happen on the eighth day from the present time.

The expected evening being arrived, the Baron sallied forth at the proper hour for seeing Hubert. The evening was bleak, the rain fell from the skies, and the north-east wind poured its sharpness over the heath, which skirted the village. The gloominess of the evening rendered the approach of night apparently more sudden than usual, and when the Baron reached the watch-tower, substances, but not features, were any longer discernible. The quick step of the sentry, hastily pacing his allotted portion of ground to preserve his limbs from numbness, led the Baron immediately towards Hubert. It was a night when the Baron believed that no one, whose business did not call him into the air, would expose himself to the roughness of the weather. Thus he spoke to Hubert, without hesitation, having no fear of being overheard—"A cold night this to be upon guard, sentinel," he said.

"My Lord de Mowbray, by the voice," returned Hubert.—"It is a colder for you to be abroad from choice; for such *you* must be."

"When I am on an errand which gives me satisfaction in the performance," replied the Baron, "a glow of pleasure warms my breast, which counterbalances the cold without. I come hither, Hubert, on purpose to seek you."

"For what?" asked Hubert, the gruffness of his voice not at all relaxing into complacency, though the words of Lord William were poured forth in tones of the utmost kindness. Hubert had more insight into men's hearts, than the Baron gave him credit for possessing: he knew how seldom the great seek the little, except for their own convenience, and he did not want to be told that such must be the motive of the Lord de Mowbray's exposing himself to the inclemency of the night to seek a poor sentinel.—"For what?" asked Hubert, still continuing to perambulate his spot of ground.

"I have perceived in you," the Baron went on, "a soul superior to the rank of life in which fate has destined you to move. Justly is fortune depicted blind: the partial hand with which she distributes her gifts daily proves her so; but the sense of perception of which she is deprived, nature has placed in the judgments of men, and they become willingly faulty in the point where her blindness is her excuse, when they do not rectify the faults into which her infirmity leads her."

Hubert was silent.

Lord William walked by his side, and continued speaking thus—"Perhaps you do not understand what I mean to say, Hubert: I wish to tell you that I think it the duty of men in my situation of life, when they see a mind like your's, superior to the rank it has been born in, to transplant it into a more prosperous bed of life."

"Has your Lordship just come to a sense of this duty," asked Hubert, "that you have chosen this hour of the night to inform me of it?"

"Oh, no, no," replied Lord William, "it has been long in my thoughts; and the reason which has kept me from avowing to you my feelings, is this:—I reflected that a mind like your's would indignantly refuse an offer of service, which it would, from the nobleness of its nature, conceive to lay it under an obligation to the man at whose hands it was received; I have therefore anxiously awaited a moment, when I might ask of you a benefit in return for such service as it is my desire to confer on you, that thus a mutual obligation might relieve us both from the unpleasant idea of either being the debtor of the other."

"There is some reason in what you say," returned Hubert: "the friendship which only lays a poor man under an obligation to a rich one, is but increasing his misery, by rendering him dependant in competence, while he was free from that clog in his indigence."

The sentiment was natural to the disposition of Hubert, the Baron considered, and not at all contrary to the feelings he wished to inspire him with; he therefore rejoined—"Your ideas correspond with my own:—to serve you, on a system of equality, is my wish.

But as your advancement here in Cumberland would but create for you the envy of your fellows in situation, and for me their hatred, originating in their jealousy at seeing you singled out for my favour, I must first point to you the necessity of your enjoying your good fortune at some distance from hence."

There was a secret chord in the heart of Hubert which vibrated with joy at the idea of possessing the means of leaving Cumberland, and he replied—"I am not so attached to my native county, as to regret departing from it."

"Nor perhaps," said the Baron, "to your native country?"

"Perhaps not," replied Hubert: "to a man who has money, every country is the same."

"It is indeed," answered the Baron; "and sometimes a foreign one more friendly than his own; for, in fact, old friends are the worst acquaintance for a man who rises suddenly into prosperity; they think themselves authorized, upon the privilege of long acquaintance, to dive into his secrets, and if they cannot fathom them, they consider themselves at liberty to use very unwarrantable remarks upon his change of situation. I myself believe it impossible for a man who experiences either a sudden change from affluence to poverty, or from indigence to wealth; to be comfortable on the same spot, in the two opposite situations."

"What is the service you require of me to equalize our obligations?" asked Hubert.

"The benefit I propose to confer on you, is five hundred pieces of gold," returned the Baron.

"The sum is large," grumbled out Hubert.

"It is," returned the Baron.

"And therefore seems to bespeak," added Hubert, "that the requital demanded for it, is of an extraordinary nature."

"One suited to the performance of a friend," returned Lord de Mowbray. "*You* are my friend: I have selected you as such, and will never swerve from my friendship, though you refuse to return me your's."

Hubert was again sullenly silent.

The Baron conceived him only reluctant in giving his promise, in the hope of an increase of reward, thus fearlessly proceeded—

"You know, Hubert, that I have a daughter. Hubert, that daughter has brought shame on me, and on herself."

Hubert stopped for the first time, and rested on his pike.

The Baron went on—"The service that I ask of you, is to hide a stain that is about to fall upon my house."

"Proceed, my Lord," said Hubert, his accents somewhat softened.

"Edward, the wretch whom I fostered," replied the Baron, "has returned my kindness with treachery—has stolen my daughter's heart! Would that had been all, and that he had spared her honour!—But, oh, madness to a father's brain, she is about to give birth to his child!"

"The Lady Rosalind become a mother!" stammered out Hubert.

"Aye, a mother!" exclaimed the Baron. "Thy voice falters, and I perceive that thou feelest for my unhappy situation. I could not doubt thou wouldst; thy heart is one capable of feeling for the dignity of man; and thou canst not want a keener spur to prompt thee into sympathy with me. But great as is my misfortune, Heaven has sent a balm for the wound which an undutiful child has made in my heart. Edward will see England no more: *he is, by my design, detained in Flanders*. Rosalind, since the moment of her fatal frailty, has been a prisoner in her chamber: no one has visited her but Gertrude, whose affection for her mistress will prevent her from disclosing her shame; and thus, with thy aid, good Hubert, the honour of my family may be re-established."

Hubert did not speak.

The Baron demanded—"Will you say it *shall*, and by your promise restore me to my dignity and peace?"

"But the means?" asked Hubert, hastily.

"That you be prepared to leave Cumberland, at the moment of the child's birth, and take it with you," replied the Baron.

"Never to return to its mother?" asked Hubert, emphatically.

"Never—never," replied the Baron, significantly. "She shall be taught to believe it born without life.—Oh, no—no; it must *never* return, or be known to have lived! It must be removed far—very far from hence: it must be rendered *impossible* for it to return."

"My journey hence must be precipitate when once begun, for

fear of a discovery," returned Hubert; "and 'tis not unlikely that this haste may prove fatal to the life of so young an infant."

"It is not unlikely—not at all unlikely, my friend," said Lord William, pressing the hand of Hubert in both of his as he spoke; "and should it so chance, the *six* hundred pieces of gold will be all your own, which else the maintenance of that young imp must lessen."

"Do you wish it rather dead, than alive in obscurity?" said Hubert, in a whispering voice.

"Dear, valuable Hubert," exclaimed De Mowbray, "judge of me as thou wouldst of thyself, if any blot were thrown upon thine honour, and thou couldst wipe it out, unseen, unknown by all the world. I trust me to thy fervor in my cause; but, Hubert, both for thee, and for myself, the grave is a security which no art can equal in the hiding up of those who live."

The steps of the soldiers who were coming to relieve the sentinel, were now audible.—"Hush!" said Hubert.

"Only say I may rely on thee," replied De Mowbray.

"Say no more," returned Hubert; "but let me have the child the instant it is born."

The Baron again pressed the hand of his new friend, and then fled into the shade, to avoid the sight of the guard which was advancing; and winding round a path which obscured him from the view of the newly placed sentinel, he returned back to his castle, his spirits elate with the success which had attended his enterprise, and extolling his own penetration into the character of Hubert.

CHAPTER XVI.

Blossom, speed thee well!
THE WINTER'S TALE.

But a short time elapsed before Lord William found a second opportunity of conversing in private with Hubert, and he was then more than ever pleased with his own discernment, and the fervour of his minister in his cause, as Hubert expressed something like alarm, lest Lord William should find any other person with whom he might prefer to entrust the business, before the time of the child's birth should arrive, and the sum of which he anticipated the possession, be thus lost to him; but this apprehension the Baron silenced, by his solemn promise of not swerving from their agreement, to which Hubert voluntarily added his own.

As the time of Rosalind's confinement drew near, the Baron took care so to arrange matters, that an exchange should be made between some of the armed men at his own castle, and those at the tower in the village, in order that Hubert might be on the spot, to attend him at a moment's notice.

An uncommon depression of spirits hung over Rosalind, as the hour approached which was to usher into being the unfortunate offspring of her love for Edward. Her health was as much impaired by her seclusion from the air, as were her spirits; and it appeared a doubtful case to Mr. Wilmot, who had been lately several times allowed to visit her, whether or not she would have strength to carry her through her agony.

At length the minute of her fate approached. Gertrude was alone permitted to attend upon her; and to her and Mr. Wilmot was entrusted her safety. Contrary to the expectations of the latter, she did survive the hour of birth; but so far had her strength been reduced by her pains, that her child was brought into the world during the insensibility of its mother. All Gertrude's care was fixed upon her lady, and this circumstance gave to Mr. Wilmot a most favourable opportunity for removing the child, as Gertrude, employed in her endeavours to recall her fainting mistress into existence, scarcely considered whether there was a child born or not.

The Baron was alone in his private apartment, when Mr. Wilmot entered with the child in his arms.—"Is it alive?" said he, on seeing the surgeon.

"Yes, it is," replied Mr. Wilmot; "and appears likely to continue so. It is a boy, and a fine one too."

"Thanks—many thanks, and acts of gratitude untold are thine!" returned Lord William, putting into his hand a diamond ring of great value, for which the surgeon having made a due compliment, retired to attend to the health of Rosalind.

The hour of this transaction was the dead of night; and in expectation of the child being brought to him, Lord William had stationed Hubert in a closet adjoining to the apartment which was dedicated to his own private use, and where Mr. Wilmot had now found him. No sooner was Mr. Wilmot gone, than the Baron called in the minister of his dark deed, and having wrapped the child in his presence, in a mantle, to prevent its cries from being heard, as Hubert passed with it through the castle, he gave it into his arms, and then putting into his hand a purse containing the six hundred promised pieces of gold, not a word was spoken, as had been agreed upon between them; and the Baron then preceded Hubert out of the apartment, in order to point out to him a private way of leaving the castle, which he had before told him he should do, when the occasion for secrecy arrived: and this outlet proved to be that which opened from the vaults of the chapel upon the northern rampart, and with which it is scarcely necessary here to remark that Hubert was already well acquainted. Arrived at the extremity of the dark and vaporous passage, the Baron said—"Farewell, my friend! May thy days be happy, and thy newly-acquired wealth lead thee to greater prosperity!"

Hubert bowed his head, but spoke not.

"I *may* rely then upon thy *care* of this child?" added the Lord de Mowbray, with a significant look, and emphasis.

"By my soul, *I will* take *care* of the child!" answered Hubert, and moved hastily on.

The Baron watched him till he was out of sight; and when he vanished from his view, he returned to his own chamber with a heart which felt lightened from a load of anxiety.

Mr. Wilmot was still with Rosalind. She had recovered from the fainting fit, into which loss of strength had thrown her, and her first enquiry had been for her child.

In the most feeling manner, Mr. Wilmot informed her that it did not exist. She did not appear to doubt the truth of his assertion, but she asked to see it in its state of death: he represented to her that it was unusual to submit an infant thus born to the sight of its parent, and that he had, on this account, out of tenderness to her, caused it to be removed from her chamber. Still she entreated to see it; but after awhile, finding him resolute in denying her request, she ceased to importune him, bending more to necessity, than a conviction of the impropriety which would have attended a mother's gazing on her child, although life had been denied it.

After the first week of her confinement was past, Rosalind began to recover much more quickly than Mr. Wilmot had augured she would; and when he thought her capable of tasting the air, with benefit to her health, he procured for her, from her father, the grant of the key which opened the door leading from her closet upon the eastern rampart, and its use was not again repealed by the Baron.

Slow and cheerless crept on the days of Rosalind, with occasional visits from Mr. Wilmot: Gertrude continued to be her only companion; and her only change of scene, from the sameness of her apartment, her wanderings on the terrace of the eastern rampart; here, in the solitude of her chamber, in her dreams, and in her prayers, Edward—her lost Edward, was the never-ceasing subject of her thoughts, and desponding melancholy the temper of her mind. Sometimes with this idea she would blend that of her lost babe, and picture to herself how it might, at this period, if life had been permitted to it, have been growing up into the resemblance of its father. When her spirits were acted upon by this imagination, she would burst into tears, and wish it alive, till returning reason pointed to the tyranny it might have experienced from its relentless grandsire; and she would then think it a blessing that it had never seen the light.

As time moved on, Lord William began in some degree to regain the composure of his mind: Edward he knew secured from a return to claim his wife—of Hubert he heard not, and as a considerable period had elapsed since his departure, he began sometimes to entertain a hope that he was no more; for however secure he felt of his fidelity, he felt also, with regard to the minister of his foul commands, as he had done of their object, that no security can equal that of the grave.

In the castle Hubert was looked upon as a deserter from the troops, and as such was universally despised, which idea the Baron himself assisted in propagating and supporting, in order to cover suspicion, and was himself most vehement in his execrations of his perfidy. Thus it is that a villain has not even the consolation of his fellow villain's good word; and if he knows that he has the secret applause of his companion in vice, or even can contrive so to support appearances, that he has the universal applause of the world, it is far more than outweighed by the reproofs of his conscience. Oh what a paradise is to its possessor that heart which can look in upon itself, from the taunts and calumnies of a universe in enmity against it, and still be happy!

CHAPTER XVII

Oh world, thy slippery turns! Friends now fast sworn,
Whose double bosoms seem to wear one heart;
——————————Shall within this hour
————————————break out
To bitterest enmity.

CORIOLANUS.

Nearly three years had elapsed since Lord Rufus de Madginecourt had quitted the castle of Lord William de Mowbray, on the discovery of that hand, which he had himself sought, being already given to another. He had departed in a gust of disappointed pride and rage, which he had no one to vent upon, and proceeded sullenly to a castle of his own, in the county of Durham.

Rosalind was already a wife; no existing law could therefore give her to him; hence there was no appeal from the destiny upon which she had rushed to avoid him; and complaints were vain, where no redress could be obtainable: to return to court, where another, and more material disappointment, stared him in the face, he felt as unwilling as he had been to quit the castle of De Mowbray, the scorned suitor of its Lord's fair daughter. Accordingly he resolved for a while to bury himself in the retirement of his domain, and to confine within his own breast the secret which, through necessity, the Baron de Mowbray had confessed to him of his daughter's marriage; and upon this he determined for two reasons—the first, because he was unwilling that it should be noised abroad, that the great and noble Lord Rufus had met with a refusal where a peasant had been accepted; the second, because he judged that if he did not himself reveal the circumstance of Rosalind's private marriage, it might, in all probability, never meet the ear of the world at all; and that Rosalind, by the death of her husband, whom he knew to be engaged in warfare abroad, might still be his, without a suspicion being entertained of his having sued for her hand before.

The third year since his departure from De Mowbray Castle was drawing towards its close, when Lord Rufus first began to discover that from having originally addressed Rosalind as a suitor, with regard only to her rank and favour with the Queen, he now entertained for her a more tender, or at least, a passion of a different nature; and it is by no means an uncommon instance, that the man who first thinks little of the woman with whom, from secondary motives, he seeks an alliance, shall, upon any mark of scorn from her, become the impassioned lover, in which character he ought first to have attempted a progress towards her heart; perhaps, and most probably indeed, the change arises from mortified pride, which sensation teaches him to adopt in future the same means for gaining his desired ends, by which he had seen others reach the attainment of theirs; however, let the effect proceed from whatever cause it may, such was the case with Lord Rufus.

With disappointment did he hear of the existence of Edward, on the arrival of every fresh news from Flanders; and at length despairing of his death, he wrote to De Mowbray, requesting him to appoint some place where he would meet him, on a subject which required their deliberate conference.

Lord William had his reasons for not inviting Lord Rufus to his own castle again, while Edward still lived, thus appointed a place for meeting, to which, at the time fixed, came Lord Rufus, and found the Baron there, ready to receive him.

The wish of De Mowbray to court an alliance with Lord Rufus for his daughter, when they had first met at the court of Queen Elizabeth, on his return from France, had not escaped him; and convinced that in seeking the alliance, his only consideration had been that of his superior rank and wealth to the nobles of the age, he doubted not, but that if he were now to shew himself ready to accept Rosalind, of whose marriage there was no existing proof, as his wife, Lord William would joyfully accede to any proposal which accorded with his favorite plan of aggrandizing his family.

Relying, therefore, on this expectation, and feeling that it was necessary to his happiness to possess Rosalind, even though already a wife, he, without hesitation, proposed to the Baron to lead her publicly to the altar, and to stifle her opposition to the plan, by promising, on these terms only, to spare the life of her beloved Edward.

The Baron de Mowbray had not shrunk from commanding the

murder of a helpless infant; and it may therefore be imagined that the unnatural sacrifice of a daughter would have appeared a lesser sin in his eyes; but this was not De Mowbray's temper. By crushing in its bud a blossom which had scarcely opened its sweets to the light, he deemed himself performing so essential an act towards the support of his house's dignity and honour, that the crime was lost in the service which it was to confer on the idol passion of his heart.

The proposition of Lord Rufus appeared to him the demand of his adjunction in an enormity, which might for ever blast that purity which he wished to bind the eternal partner of his name; the discovery, should such a discovery ever transpire, and nothing appeared to him more likely than that the rash step proposed by De Madginecourt might spirit on the parties, whom it so nearly concerned, into adducing proofs of their marriage, must instantly publish what the death of the child was for ever intended to hide. Thus, deciding from his feelings, as men are too apt to do, on the heinousness or innocence of the most important virtues, and most enormous vices, he considered the proposal of Lord Rufus an insult, and openly declared to him his opinion.

Infatuated as Lord Rufus now really was with the person of Rosalind, yet, like all men of strong passions, love was forgotten, at the moment when revenge stepped into view as the champion of frustrated gratification. "Remember," he exclaimed, "I have the secret of her base marriage; and if you give her not to me, I blazon it to the world!"

The voice of threatening was new in the ear of the haughty Lord William, and painful was it to him to subdue his fury; but his subtilty never forsook him at the moment of his need, and in a tone of composure, which it cost him many a struggle to command, he said—"The fate of a father who is unhappy in the connection of an only child, will at least gain as much sympathy in the world, as that of the monster who would induce that father to lead his daughter to a second marriage-bed while yet her husband lived. I have, you perceive, Lord Rufus, my tale for yours," he added, with a smile of triumph; "and it cannot be difficult to you to determine on whose side the opinion of a virgin queen would rank, when the object to whom this brutality is proposed to be offered is her god-daughter."

The truth of Lord William's remark struck forcibly to the heart of Lord Rufus; rage and disappointment choked his utterance, and his emotions became the more violent, as no ready means of vengeance upon De Mowbray presented themselves to him; in sullen passion he broke up the conference, and breathing curses on the mean spirit of the Baron as he quitted his presence, retired again to his own castle, more strongly than ever bent upon the accomplishment of his purpose, in proportion as fate seemed to have removed it farther from his grasp.

With far different sensations did Lord William return into Cumberland; the meanness of De Madginecourt's disposition, and the ambition of his views, had now been so clearly unfolded to him, that he almost began to repent of having ever required his daughter to bestow her hand on him. He could not forgive her union with Edward; but he thought it possible that if he had offered to her acceptance some man less repugnant to her feelings than Lord Rufus, she might not have rushed into an union with Edward, as a safeguard to her against becoming the wife of De Madginecourt. He believed that she had seen more clearly into his evil disposition than he had himself done; and he almost began to pity, though he could not pardon her. So true is it, that the slightest proof which our senses give us of any fact, wins us over in an instant to an opinion, into which the repeated arguments of others have not been able to induce us.

The Baron's first action on arriving at his castle, was to enter the apartment of his daughter. It was now three years since she had beheld him; his presence startled her, and she could scarcely support her frame from sinking to the earth, so many painful ideas, which the lenient hand of time had in some measure deadened within her heart, did his sight recall into life again. The Baron was little less agitated than his daughter; his step faltered, for he was unconscious what reception he had to expect from one whom he had so cruelly treated. But Rosalind, the amiable Rosalind, who, although seeing the persecutor in the father, could not still forget the father in the persecutor, advanced, and extended to him her hand.

The recapitulation of past events the Baron dreaded more than did his daughter; thus he proceeded hastily to repeat to her his late conference with De Madginecourt, and their enmity which had succeeded it. But alas! what availed to Rosalind their dispute? She was already protected by the rights of religion from becoming the wife of Lord Rufus; and she found, that although her father's eyes were opened to the atrocious character of the man whom he would have given to her for a husband, his heart was not in the smallest degree softened towards him whom she had made his son; for still with firmness he refused to reply to her enquiries after Edward, and still maintained, that to forget him must be the price of her entire return to his favour.

Still she fed on hope, the only medicine for an aching heart; but all its promises were deceitful, and the fourth year passed sorrowfully on, as the three former ones had done, since the birth of her child.—With the fifth, fate brought to her what appeared to be the climax of her misery—intelligence of the death of her beloved Edward. And here the scene becomes too painful for recital; let it suffice to say, that she felt as every breast wounded by the hand of cruel destiny must feel, when the master-stroke of misery bends its feebleness to the earth, and the perspective of its day presents no friendly hope to raise it up again—no ray of comfort to reanimate its exhausted nature.

When the Baron de Mowbray first employed means for sending Edward out of England, in order to prevent that union, which the youth was no sooner gone than he discovered to be already accomplished, he appointed trusty spies near his person, and from one of these he now received the intelligence of his death.

This information, as it may be imagined, was most delightful to the feelings of the Baron; and the object of his dislike being now for ever removed from the power of occasioning him any fresh anxiety, he used every tenderness in his disclosure of the event to his daughter, not doubting, or at least, most ardently hoping, that now he, from whom her separation had been to her a constant source of misery, was no more, she would in time be prevailed upon again to appear in the world as the heiress of De Mowbray, and the goddaughter of her Queen.

But long before a sufficient time of trial had been given to her spirits for such a change, a written application from Lord Rufus arrived to the Baron, for his permission again to become the suitor of his daughter.

Since Lord William believed himself to have discovered the real character and views of Lord Rufus, a proposal of this nature could not be received by him in any other light than as an insult; and, thus impressed, he returned a negative to his letter, written in terms of the warmest indignation against his presumption.

No farther tidings were from that time heard of Lord Rufus at De Mowbray Castle, and nearly three months more passed away, unmarked by any event but the incursions of the borderers, whose temerity, in advancing towards the English posts, was now becoming every day greater.

Rosalind, during the lifetime of her Edward, the prisoner of her father's will, was now the prisoner of her own inclination, and all his entreaties to her, to leave the solitude of her apartments, were ineffectual. Her hours were spent in weeping for him whom she was never again to behold, and in drawing forth such plaintive airs from the strings of her lute, which he had been accustomed to praise.

The Baron's hours were divided between his attentions to his daughter, whom he still hoped again to court into the world, and his superintendance of the military regulations necessary to be observed in his castle.

At this period then it was, and as it happened, on the very day which completed the fourth year of Rosalind's becoming a mother, that the Scotch youth, who called himself Donald, arrived at De Mowbray Castle, with information to the Baron of the danger that awaited him from the attack upon his strength, which was threatened by a freebooter named Allanrod.

And having now recapitulated all the events of moment which had occurred to the characters in our history, before the period at which we opened our scene, we will return to that night in which we left the Baron de Mowbray marching towards the enemy, and Rosalind locked in the arms of sleep, in her father's castle.

CHAPTER XVIII.

Foul deeds will rise,
(Though all the earth o'erwhelm them) to men's eyes.

HAMLET.

ROSALIND arose at early morn, and proceeded to the chapel: ever since she had learnt the death of her Edward, it had been her daily custom so to do; and the hour which she passed at prayer by the side of her mother's grave, was the only one which brought her consolation through the long and weary day. Here would she cling to the cold marble that encircled the mouldered frame of her parent, with a heart as frozen to every object, but the images of those whom it was now alone given her to behold through fancy's eye, as the icy stone she knelt upon.

It was always Rosalind's choice to proceed to her devotions alone; thus Gertrude's services not being at this hour in request, she sought her uncle, Ambrose, eager to hear from him some farther particulars of the spirit, which had for a few evenings past haunted the ramparts of the castle; and on the very last had occasioned so much alarm to him and Philip Watkins, the sentinel, at the drawbridge.

To her wish, Ambrose, with his bunch of keys slung on his arm, was the first person whom she met in the castle hall, and without delay she proposed to him her enquiry.

Ambrose shook his head sadly and significantly, looked around wistfully to see if they were observed, and then said—"Oh Gertrude, the times, I do verily believe me, grow wickeder and wickeder every day!"—He paused, then added—"Have you mentioned to your lady what Philip and I saw last night?"

"Oh yes," replied Gertrude, "I told her directly, and begged of her not to walk on the ramparts so late in the evening."

"And what said she to it?" asked Ambrose.

"Smiled, and treated it as an idle tale," returned Gertrude.

"Oh Jesu!" cried Ambrose, "had she heard the noise that I did, by the side of the moat, three evenings ago, and seen the face that I saw last night, beneath the vizor of the spectre——"

"Pale as ashes, and a streak of blood down the left cheek, had it not?" asked Gertrude, trembling as she spake.

"Aye—aye, even as you say," returned Ambrose. "Heaven be praised, the Lady Rosalind treats its appearance so lightly! I am glad in my soul she does. It was my intention, Gertrude, if you had not spoken to her of it, to have warned you not to have done so; and now I charge you, girl, as you love your uncle, never begin the subject to her again, nor enlarge upon it: if she should start it to you, drop it—do you understand me? as quickly as possible, and talk of something else."

"Why, I tell you, uncle," answered Gertrude, "it does not frighten her."

"But it *would* frighten her, if she knew all," exclaimed Ambrose.—"Oh Gertrude, I know, though thou art simple, thou art to be trusted; so I will tell thee why it would alarm her. Heaven forbid it be evil that I am going to say; but Heaven is my witness how true my words are! Philip Watkins said it, before I said it, though I believe I observed it first.—The spectre which appeared to us, is the spirit of my Lady Rosalind's husband! The pale face, with the streak of blood down the left cheek, which we saw last night, was the very picture of Mr. Edward."

"Mr. Edward's ghost!" cried Gertrude—"what can it mean?"

"Hush—hush," replied Ambrose, looking again cautiously around him, "I would not, for the world, that we were overheard."

"Nor I," answered Gertrude.—"But what can it mean, uncle?"

"I fear me," returned Ambrose, "it indicates that foul deeds have been abroad. I accuse no one—I condemn no one, girl; but I cannot stifle my thoughts. The Baron disliked his daughter's marriage: Edward was sent abroad, into Flanders—a villainous country, Gertrude, that Flanders, where the Jesuits still have much power; and I well know where there are Jesuits, men do not stick at the commission of crimes, because they get them wiped off their consciences by confession.—Idle, foolish ideas! The truth will prevail; sin will come to light, and all the absolution in the world has not power to make a murdered body rest in peace."

"Murdered!" echoed Gertrude—"Do you mean——"

"I mean nothing," interrupted Ambrose, "for I know nothing. I only am certain that spirits do not walk, without they have some evil to reveal, or when their consciences are overburdened. I got my knowledge in spirits from thy grandfather, Gertrude, who was esteemed to understand their nature well. Now I am certain Mr. Edward (bless his good heart!) cannot be raised from his grave by an unquiet conscience; thus it must remain, that he has some matter of importance to unfold—and what can I think it is, when I see the streak of blood on his poor, pale cheek?"

"Heaven grant he tell it not to me," replied Gertrude: "I should never live to make it known."

"No, no, no," cried Ambrose, "no fear of that: he will choose some one gifted with good sense for the purpose; perhaps myself, as likely as not. Gracious—gracious me! Heaven send I be not made the accuser of my master! But were I invited to that purpose by the spirit, I must perform its commands, Gertrude: disobedience would rank me on the side of Satan's legion; for my soul's sake, I must perform, if it commands."

Rosalind was now seen returning from her devotions.—"Here comes my Lady," said Ambrose. "Sweet sufferer! pray the powers of mercy, there is no more ill in store for thee!" Then turning towards Gertrude, he added, in a whisper—"Promise me not to reveal a word of what I have imparted to thee."

"Upon my faith, uncle, I will not," returned Gertrude; and Ambrose then moved out of sight.

Rosalind returned to her chamber, and throwing open the casement, admitted into her apartment the enlivening rays of an eastern sun, which was emerging, in golden splendor, from a bed of purple clouds. As she stood contemplating the beauties of the surrounding landscape, she could not forbear exclaiming—"How blest is every animal of this creation, but myself! How cheerfully are the bleating flocks browsing on the dew-bespangled grass; how jocundly are the birds singing on every spray; and how carelessly is the whistling husbandman proceeding to his labour, whilst I alone know only heaviness and care!"

Her attention was now directed to some flowers, which grew in her window; and as she pleased herself with examining their beautiful colours, and inhaling the sweetness of their scents, a rose bud, snapped from its stem, just as it was opening into bloom, caught her observation: the melancholy tone of her mind led her to draw a parallel between her own fate and that of the flower; and it afforded her a slender consolation to divert her thoughts from bitter reflection, by versifying her ideas in the following lines:—

Addressed to a Rose Bud, broken from its Stem.

Poor, luckless flower! and art thou too,
Ere yet thy leaves have nurs'd the dew,
A victim, at misfortune's shrine,
That still is wet with tears of mine?
Companion in the ills of life,
Because thou wert too sweet and fair?
May ill betide the cruel hand,

That pluck'd thee, ere thou could'st expand!
May it neglected droop like thee,
And seek in vain for sympathy!
Poor flower! my fate resembles thine:
Thy hopes are blighted;—so are mine!
I caught the transient glow of spring;
When days flew by on halcyon wing;
Thou too beheld'st the rosy morn,
When blushes mark'd thy early dawn;
But now alike, on clouds of care,
We travel on to meet despair.
Would in my bosom thou could'st lie,
Conceal'd from misery's searching eye!
But, serpent-tooth'd, she riots there,
And feeds the poisonous canker, care.
Shun then this talisman of woe,
That pines with sorrows none must know!
Thy griefs are transient; soon thou'lt be
Beyond the power of destiny.
Already do thy charms decay,
And all thy fragrance dies away;
But I must linger in my pain,
And never taste of peace again:
Year after year may roll away,
And sorrow mark each coming day;
Till quite exhausted by my woes,
I die, like thee, to find repose.

END OF VOLUME ONE.

THE MYSTERIOUS FREEBOOTER

CHAPTER I.

In God's name, cheerly on, courageous friends,
To reap the harvest of perpetual peace,
By this one bloody trial of sharp war.

SHAKESPEARE.

Lord William de Mowbray and his troops meanwhile pursued their march, under the stillness of the night, without any interruption, save what arose from the nature of their route; the difficulties of this kind which they had to encounter were indeed not a few. As it was of consequence to them to use whatever speed was in their power, they quitted the high road, which would have extended their journey several miles; and though attended by skilful guides, they found it by no means an easy task to wind up the unfrequented passes of the mountains which they were obliged to cross, or to ford the numerous rivulets which obstructed their progress.

However, these were difficulties thought lightly of by men who had been accustomed and inured to fatigue and danger, as most of Lord William's men had been, both before and since they had been taken into his service; and they made such good use of their strength and spirits, that ere the morning began to break, they found themselves within a short distance of the spot where Donald's information had given them reason to believe that Allanrod and his advanced body had halted during the night.

The cheeks of the youth Donald glowed with anticipated vengeance on the murderer of his father, and the ravisher of his sister's honour; and he could not forbear expressing his joy as they marched on.

The Baron presently commanded a halt, in order that he might have an opportunity for consulting with his chief leader, Irwin, on the measures best to be pursued at this crisis. The situation occupied by him and his soldiers, at the moment he issued this command, was one most favourable to the purpose of a short repose; it was a romantic glen, enclosed on all sides by rough and stupendous mountains, the frowning, craggy tops of most of which appeared to bespeak them impervious. Placing, therefore, guards at the avenues, which were alone believed accessible by De Mowbray and his commanders, the Baron seated himself, with his friend Irwin and the youth Donald, at foot of one of them; while his men reclined themselves on various spots suited to their inclinations; and their horses were permitted to browze upon the grass which the valley afforded.

A little refreshment was necessary to all after their march, and while they were taking it, Lord William submitted to his companions the propriety of remaining awhile on the spot where they now were, and dispatching from thence a spy or two, to gain, if possible, information of the enemy's situation. This proposal appeared to Irwin and Donald so perfectly judicious, that they strongly recommended its being put into execution without delay; and three of their party were accordingly chosen for the purpose.

One of these three was one of their guides, and to him Donald made it understood in what direction to proceed for gaining the desired information. It was not till this scrutinizing party was dispatched, that the Baron himself began to taste the refreshments which were necessary to the support of his strength; and as he pressed Donald to join with him in his meal, he perceived that the youth's fatigue was so great as to have entirely deprived him of a wish for food: he drank willingly of a flask of ale which Irwin offered him, but he refused all substantial nourishment; his agitation appeared every moment to be increasing, and the Baron besought him to endeavour to compose his mind, and not to suffer the recollection of the past, or the anticipation of the future, thus to harass his feelings, as it would entirely unfit him for the enterprise they were shortly to rush upon.

The youth replied—"Fear me not, my Lord; agitated as I am, and violently, too, believe me, that joy affects me more than pain, and that I will do my duty when we meet Allanrod—would to God that the moment was come!"

A shrill whistle, blown through the fingers at this moment, called the attention of the Baron, and he saw two of his spies returning with the utmost speed down the steep side of a mountain. The Baron sprang up to meet them, and as soon as they could be heard—"The enemy! the enemy!" burst from their lips.

"Do they come?" exclaimed Donald, "Thank Heaven! thank Heaven!"

Instantly the drum beat to arms, and Lord William and his men snatched up their rested weapons; every one was, in as short a time as possible, in a posture of defence; and, quick as were their movements, they had not an instant to spare; for already a body of freebooters appeared at the mouth of the only avenue which the Baron believed practicable for leaving the glen. To escape from the circle of danger which was environing them, Lord William thought the only means, to rush through the enemy by the strength of arms; and their only chance of conquering, to attack them on a level ground; as the fortune of the war must be indisputably against them, were the event hazarded in a spot where the enemy had the advantage of height over them, as they had in the present instance.

He had little time for reflection, but he could not help repenting that he had not marched earlier on the preceding evening from his own castle, which would have prevented his present surprise.

The enemy, aware of the Baron's intention of forcing a passage through them for his troops, stationed their strength at the point for which he was making, and opposed his approach towards it with the most obstinate vigour. Equally resolute did Lord William's men shew themselves in their attempt at gaining the pass; and a most severe contest ensued, in which the freebooters were repeatedly driven back, by the skilful use made by the English soldiers of their fire-arms; but although frequently repulsed, they returned, with the violence of wolves, to the attack; and the party of De Mowbray had still gained but little progress towards the mouth of the valley.

For a time, the effects of steady discipline and regular tactics prevailed eminently over savage ferocity and irregular vehemence; but Lord William now made a discovery, uncomfortable in the extreme to his feelings, which was, that the troops of the Scottish banditti, as repeatedly as they were driven back, returned to the combat with increased numbers; which discovery brought with it the sad conviction that Allanrod had already collected his forces into one body, contrary to the opinion of Donald, or the still more to be dreaded apprehension that Donald himself was an impostor.

He looked around for him, and perceiving him mixing in the English ranks, the momentary doubt which had arisen in his mind of his truth was dispelled, and he now thought that he had only been faulty in his calculations, and not so in his intentions.

All men are apt to judge from events, and Lord William was, in this respect, a man in the full sense of the expression. Burning with almost maddening disappointment and chagrin, that the issue of the present contest was likely to prove contrary to the opinion he had formed of it at its commencement, he began to believe that he had been guilty of an imprudence in following an enemy into their own haunts, uncertain of their strength and number; and to think that he would have done better in awaiting their arrival before his own castle, although the evils of such a delay had been fully represented to him, and upon that representation he acted: Lord William, in short, felt as all disappointed men do, who have not sufficient fortitude to restrain the effervescences of their passion within the bounds of sense and reason; and seeing the situation of himself and his men to be a desperate one, he rendered it still more so, by passing over the cool measures of management, and issuing a command for the exertion of a last and desperate effort for disentangling themselves from the lines of the enemy.

In order to atone for what he now thought his own oversight, in the first instance, of marching from his castle, he resolved to sell his life or liberty, which however he was destined to lose, as dearly as possible: fighting himself like a wounded lion, which turns in desperation on his hunters, he spurred on his men, both by the example of his own courage, and promises of immense rewards, to an emulation of his conduct.

Suspicious of Donald (for thus men are always, in circumstances which run adverse to their wishes, of those by whose advice they have acted), he again looked round for him: he saw him not; but he hoped, at least he trusted, that if he was not amidst the ranks, obscured from his sight by the clouds of smoke which were rolling through the air, that he was in search of the Moss-troopers' leader, Allanrod, against whom his vengeance had been so warmly denounced; and his hatred to whom he had declared to be his only reason for joining the English cause.

This Allanrod Lord William had not yet seen: his eye had met the forms of several, whom he conjectured, from their dress, and the posts of command they held, to be leaders in the savage band; but he had seen no one who appeared of eminence enough to bespeak him their chief, or who at all corresponded with the account which Donald had given of Allanrod; he had described him of gigantic height, and of a fierce and commanding aspect. At the present moment, it was impossible to make inquiry whether he was present or not; and thus the Baron was obliged, if he was not satisfied with doubt, at least to put up with it.

At length the archers of De Mowbray had expended all their arrows, and his horsemen had fired their last charge; although not without considerable execution, for great numbers of the slain and wounded of the foe strewed the ground. The fight must now, the Baron saw, be given up, or the event of close combat be hazarded; the latter he determined on, not abating a single spark of his lion's fire; and he accordingly urged on his men to attack the enemy shield to shield.

The command being given on the side of the Baron, the enemy accommodated themselves to the fresh charge which was preparing for them; and throwing aside their bows and matchlocks, drew their swords, and rushed like their foes, to closer combat.

The surrounding hills, still reverberating with the thunder of the musketry, now caught the direful sound of clashing swords; shield was opposed to shield, and pike to pike; every stroke was aimed with a ferocity on both sides, which seemed almost decidedly to render its direction fatal; and the earth was bathed with reeking blood. But short was the duration of this mad carnage; for suddenly a fresh band of the Moss-troopers appeared on the tops of those mountains which the party of De Mowbray had supposed impassable, and thence rushing down into the vale, decided the fate of the battle. Lord William and the few remaining men of his troops who were still alive, were completely overpowered, and enclosed by the enemy. Even did the Baron scorn to sue for quarter; his pride was about to receive a stab in becoming a prisoner, for which he would willingly have bartered his life; but fate had decreed it otherwise, and Lord William and his followers were surrounded and made prisoners of war.

At the mercy of this ferocious band, the few existing men of De Mowbray's party entertained but small hopes of preserving that life, which their Lord despised on the terms upon which he now held it: they had held down their conquered heads in despair and sadness, while their savage opponents triumphed over them, mixing with their insults threats of torture and death.

Lord William was offering up a silent prayer to Heaven, in the first despair of a vain mind foiled in its plan of glory, to be released from an existence intolerable, under the circumstances which at the present hour attended his, when one of the leaders of the borderers advanced, and having motioned with his hand to enjoin silence, he spoke thus:—"Our loved and venerated chief commands me to inform the conquered De Mowbray, that as the fortune of the day has placed him in his power, he must not expect him to yield his person to liberty, without the remuneration of a valuable ransom. In the meantime, he condescends to assure him that he shall experience no other ill-treatment than that of imprisonment."

"Who is your chief?" asked De Mowbray.

"Allanrod, the great and powerful Allanrod," replied the leader; "behold him on yon mountain's brow!"

Lord William turned his eyes the way the leader's hand was extended, and perceived, on the top of a craggy mountain, less elevated than the rest which fenced in the valley, a man of extraordinary hulk and height, clad in the Highland fashion, and leaning on a matchlock of enormous length, one end of which was rested upon the ground, and his arm laid across the other: every part of his dress and arms corresponded with those worn by the Scottish freebooters, except that of his head, and upon this he wore a helmet, the vizor of which was pulled down. But the eye of the Baron rested scarcely an instant on the form of the conqueror; it turned to a small figure, in the attire of his own soldiery, which was hanging on the arm of Allanrod, and which, though its countenance was turned from him, he could not hesitate to decide the treacherous Donald.

The Baron's feelings defied controul; and he exclaimed to the leader—"Tell me, I entreat you, is not he who leans upon his arm a youth named Donald?"

"I have no time for parley, sir," replied the leader; "my commission to you from our chief is delivered, and we must now on without delay, or we shall not reach our quarters by nightfall."

"It is he, by Heaven!" cried the Baron. "Curses on his villainous hypocrisy!"

His exclamations were unnoticed by the enemy, or, at least, not replied to; all their attention was directed to the commands issuing by their own leaders; and these were for them to leave a sufficient number of their party to take care of the wounded; and for the rest to guard the prisoners from the valley to their own fortress.

Maddening were the reflections of the Baron; he now perceived, or fancied he perceived, that he had been made the dupe of a tool from the enemy, commissioned to his castle for the purpose of drawing him into the entanglement which had just led to his ruin; and although he could not but think, that were the same circumstances to occur again, the plausibility of a tale like that delivered by the youth two evenings before, in the hall of his castle, would again lead him to pursue the same steps he had taken, still he felt enraged at himself that he had taken them, now he believed it probable that by observing a contrary conduct he had been safe.

CHAPTER II.

When I feel
These bonds, I look with loathing on myself.

CONGREVE.

It was now high noon-day, and the sun unobscured by a single cloud to soften its heat. Their way lay over steep mountains, and through rugged paths; and, owing to the weakness which they felt from their exertion in the battle, and the wounds they had received, the progress of both the conquerors and the conquered was considerably retarded.

As they moved on, the Baron looked sorrowfully around on his beaten troops, and found that the number of the surviving was scarcely forty; of these, his chief leader, Irwin, was one, but the wounds he had received were so great, as to oblige him to be borne on a litter, formed of the branches of trees.

About the time that the sun began to withdraw his light from the earth, and usher in the twilight of the evening, they entered upon a wide and dreary heath: for nearly three miles they proceeded along without any signs of cultivation or inhabitants meeting their eyes; from the slowness of their march in these three miles, the twilight had retired beyond the expanded curtain of night, and the pale silvery light of a rising moon alone gave a faint illumination to the scene.

The country continued wild and desolate in the extreme; no vegetation could yet be perceived, except a short brown grass, on which one solitary flock of sheep were picking their scanty meal; and here and there piles of enormous stones, the growth of ages, broke the melancholy sameness of the barren heath.

At last their road wound into a rugged path, on one side of which arose immensely steep mountains, clothed with a black furze, which gave to the scene a gloomy and funereal appearance, heightened by the shades of night, from which the eye of the traveller turned to seek relief on the opposite side of the road; and here it no sooner rested, than it shuddered at the sight of a deep gulf, from which there was neither natural or artificial protection, and which appeared expressly designed either to perpetrate or conceal a murder in; and there was not wanting evidence that of such a scene the spot beneath had been a witness, for a creaking noise drew towards it the eye of the Baron, and he found that it proceeded from the rusty chains of a gibbet, on which hung a half-decayed figure, which the wind agitated, and caused the links to grate each other in their motion.

The Baron shuddered as his eyes rested on the horrid object; the freebooters passed it with jocular observations on the fate of the unfortunate wretch, who had been placed there as a warning mark to those who were now treading in his path of iniquity.

As they drew towards the end of this path, the Baron perceived a speck in the horizon, which he conjectured to be a distant building: a short time convinced him that it was so; and as they advanced towards it, the conversation of the freebooters informed him it was their haunt.

For the first time since the commencement of their march, the Baron spoke.—"Is this the abode of your chief?" he asked.

The reply was in the affirmative.

"Is it a castle—a building of strength?" he rejoined.

"Oh no, no, it's no castle," replied one of the freebooters; "nor is there much strength in it, except that of some good muscles and hearts: it was once a monastery, but it is turned to a much better use now; what they used to pray for and never get, we fight for and always enjoy."

One of his companions was going to reply, when a horn, sounded from an advanced body of the moss-troopers, obliged him to silence, or at least prevented his being heard.

The horn Lord William found to be a signal to those at home of the approach of their comrades; for in a very few minutes many torches were visible about the building, and their light exposed to him the ruinous state it was in; for not one of the torches was as yet in the air, but gleaming along the vaulted aisles, and winding passages, which had once formed the beauty of the edifice, and which were now decayed, either by the hand of Time or violence, and appeared to leave almost the heart of the mansion naked to the light.

Those who now issued from the various outlets of the edifice with their torches, appeared, if possible, more ferocious than their companions; the triumph of the latter was instantly made known, and congratulations offered them by the former. Before this edifice they halted: the leader who had addressed Lord William on the field of battle, again approached him, and having commanded the prisoners of inferior rank to be led into the subterraneous vaults of the building, which had formerly been the cellars of the monastery, he preceded the Baron into a large gloomy hall, which appeared once to have been the nave of a church: it was faintly illuminated by an iron lamp, suspended by a chain from the roof, which served to discover the many obscure passages that branched off from it to the several parts of the building, and led to wide and lofty stone staircases.

Irwin was immediately taken up one of these: the Baron could not forbear expressing some anxiety for his fate, although he did not believe such expression calculated to procure him any additional advantages amongst the savage set they were now with; but the leader, who would have been considered a man of a most dark and forbidding countenance, to have been seen alone, but who, by comparison with the more ferocious faces he was now amongst, almost deserved the name of gentle, assured the Baron that every care his situation required should he shewn to him; and then desired the Baron to follow him to the apartment destined for himself.

The Baron's pride wanted relief as much as his body; and considering it a condescension, if not a mark of respect to his situation, in the leader to denominate that his apartment which justice would have allowed him to have called his prison, he followed with more complacency of temper than he believed he could, in his present trying situation, have commanded.

It may be urged—"What could he do but obey? he knew resistance or complaints to be in vain." To this it is replied, that it is a mind of more than common energy that can restrain its feelings in a situation so galling to its peace; and that it is the custom of the multitude most to murmur where murmuring least avails; because their complaints are always great in proportion to the greatness of their sufferings; and a sense of suffering takes away from them the power of reasoning upon the good or evil effect of bewailing their misfortunes.

Following the leader, he ascended a flight of stone stairs, although not the same up which Irwin had been carried, and passed into a long gallery, faintly lighted in like manner as the hall; hence they proceeded to some smaller stairs, which appeared to wind up a tower: there was here no lamp, and a torch was necessary to shew them their way. The stairs were extremely decayed, and even dangerous to pass; they were, however, few in number: thus, notwithstanding their ruinous situation, they soon arrived at the top of them. The leader drew from his pocket a key, and giving it to one of his attendants, ordered him to unlock a small iron door which presented itself to their view.

With difficulty the man turned the key in the rusty wards, and then forced open the door, from which issued a cloud of dust that almost blinded them, and proved the length of time the apartment had been unoccupied.

The man who bore the torch entered first; him the leader followed, and called to the Baron to come in after him. The Baron obeyed, but not without casting on his conductors a look of suspicion to which they replied by a malicious and satisfactory smile.

The room they had now entered bore every mark of having

been built for a prison: it was large and high; the walls of stone appeared once to have been plastered, but were now in many places, bare, and in others covered with a green and mossy dew; the roof was formed of beams of oak, worm-eaten, and black with age; and the only place for the admission of light was a small grated window fixed nearly at the top of the wall.

In the middle of the apartment stood an iron pan, in which wood seemed once to have been burnt, for ashes might be discovered in it, as also scattered about the floor. The only furniture was a small table and a chair; and in one corner stood a large oaken chest, over which hung a rude wooden crucifix.

Lord William looked around him with marks of dejection at the appearance of the place, which the leader observing, told him that it should be made more comfortable, and immediately gave directions for a fire to be lighted, and a lamp to be brought him; which being done, some provisions were set on the table, and a mattress and blanket spread for him on the floor; and the Moss-troopers then all departed, the chief observing that it would be very soon in his own power to shorten his imprisonment. The door was shut upon him, and he heard it locked and barred without.

The Baron, left to his own reflections, cast his eyes once more hopelessly round his prison, and, heaving a deep sigh, he threw himself into the chair, and felt his heart sinking within him.

The pride, the vanity of his life, which it had been his soul's passion to feed and to support, had met a blow, from which it might never rise again to its former dignity and honours: the Queen might believe that he had been faulty and rash, in marching towards the quarters of the enemy, and might withdraw her countenance from him, as a man without sufficient skill to guard the frontiers of her kingdom. From himself, his thoughts wandered to his daughter; what pain would she not experience at his not returning to his castle; for he believed she still loved him, notwithstanding the rigour with which he had enforced over her his parental authority. His own unfortunate circumstances softened his heart; and, now he supposed her to be regretting his absence, he thought he loved her more tenderly than he had ever done, and wished more ardently than he had ever done before, to clasp her to his breast.

The loud voices of the freebooters, who appeared in dispute, probably, he thought, about the division of the spoil, or else under the influence of intoxication, or perhaps both, sounded, at intervals from the lower parts of the building, and broke the silence of the night. At length, about an hour after midnight, universal silence prevailed, and the victorious crew beneath him appeared to have retired to rest.

He longed to know how his soldiers, and his leader, Irwin, were treated; but the wish was vain; and relying but little on the promise made to him by the leader who had conducted him to his prison, he felt for them a degree of anxiety which heightened his own unpleasant sensations; for, as we have before said, Lord William's heart always inclined to the side of feeling, where it did not interfere with his darling passion, to exercise his benevolence and humanity.

His march had been a long and weary one, and the cravings of nature impelled him to examine the contents of the basket which had been placed upon his table; he found in it a loaf of brown bread and some broiled fish; and by their side stood a stone jug of malt liquor, and a flask of spirits.

It was at this moment some small relief to him to find a supply for his appetite, and having eaten what necessity required, and drunk a draught of the spirits, in the hope of inducing sleep, he threw himself upon his mattress, having first trimmed his lamp, and laid an additional log of wood on his fire.

Painful reflection for a long time combated fatigue and drove off the approach of sleep; at last it stole upon him, but his slumbers were short and disturbed: he fancied that he heard various noises, sometimes of persons running up the stairs of his prison; then, as if the door of his apartment was unlocking. Several times he sprang from his mattress, and paced the room, to examine if any danger was lurking near him, and severely lamenting that he was unarmed: nothing, however, was to be seen or heard when he rose up; and believing that his fears might have been the suggestions of his hurried imagination, he again stretched himself on his hard bed. The dawn was now beginning to peep through the narrow casement that alone gave light to his prison, and feeling more secure as the darkness of night died away, he soon fell into a profound sleep.

When he again awoke, the strength of the light which entered his apartment proved to him that the morning was far advanced, as did his lamp and fire which were both exhausted.

He instantly began to use the light of day, for, more closely investigating his prison than he had yet been able to do, he examined the door; the bolts were all too firm to admit of the hope of an escape that way: he placed his table under the window, and upon it he put his chair, upon which he mounted; but the casement was still beyond his reach, nor could he, by all his endeavours, catch through it a glimpse of any object but the passing clouds. He descended, and his next step was to endeavour to lift up the lid of the chest, but it bid defiance to all his efforts: he kicked against it, and the hollow sounds which followed his knock seemed to bespeak it empty.

He continued to walk round and round his prison hoping to find some chink, some outlet which might flatter him with the hope of an escape; but all in vain; the walls appeared strong in every part, and fully capable of resisting the efforts of an unarmed individual to force a passage through them. He observed that they were not in every part bare, but that here and there fragments of tattered tapestry were still adhering to them; many of these which were within his reach he pulled away, hoping still same chasm might present itself to his sight behind them; but dust only followed their fall, and the wall beneath appeared perfectly firm in every part.

The leader had, on the preceding night, said that it would be his own fault if his imprisonment was of long duration; thus all he had now to do was to await in patience the proposed terms for his ransom.

He had not been risen more than an hour when one of the men appeared, and brought him his breakfast; with the evening his provisions were again renewed, and his oil and fuel replenished; but still no one but an inferior of the freebooter's party had been into his apartment, and he had heard nothing of the expected terms of ransom.

His night was not at all more easy than the former one had been; indeed rather less so, as he began to entertain suspicions that he was meant to be detained a prisoner for life, or perhaps to be delivered up to a death of torture.

Late in the evening of the following day, the leader appeared.

"I am glad to see you," said De Mowbray; "I feared that you had forgotten me: I have been expecting, ere this, to have heard from you. What are the terms of ransom which you mentioned to me?"

"I have purposely delayed visiting you," replied the leader, "lest, in the first heat of your disappointment at not being yourself the conqueror, which you know Allanrod to be, you should have spurned at terms which, on cool reflection, will no doubt appear to you as reasonable."

"I am fully prepared to hear them," returned the Baron.

"And foolish will you be," answered the leader, "if you do not as readily comply with them, and think yourself blessed in the easy terms offered to your acceptance. Remember, proud Lord," he continued, "that it is in the power of Allanrod to confine you here for life; to keep the spot of your confinement a secret, by detaining your captured soldiers here like yourself; and if the spot be suspected, and a force marched out to attack it in your behalf, it will be in his power to cut off your liberty by death. Reflect well on the superiority he has over you, and then hear his conditions."

Lord William's blood boiled within him. Conditions from the leader of a savage band of freebooters to the Lord of De Mowbray Castle, was a sound worse than poison to his ears; but policy commanded him to subdue his feelings, and with an effort which cost him many pangs he said, in a voice of composure—"Speak!"

"Promise to give your daughter in marriage to Lord Rufus de Madginecourt, and you are this instant free, and shall be conducted with honour to your own castle," replied the leader.

If the mind of the Baron had before been agitated, what were his feelings at this demand! Astonishment closed his lips, and he stood fixed in silence and surprise: his eyes encountering those of the leader—"Give my child to Lord Rufus!" he exclaimed, after a pause.

"As I say," returned the leader.

"Never, by heaven!" answered the Baron.

"Deliberate upon it for the night," returned the leader: "I will see you again to-morrow;"—and was departing.

"No deliberation, no idea of my own liberty shall ever induce me to sacrifice my daughter to the monster I know him to be," returned the Baron: "but stay—I conjure you, stay, and tell me how am I to understand this demand—as proceeding from whence, and from whom?

Is it urged by Lord Rufus himself, or by Allanrod, your leader, for him? Is Lord Rufus here? How is Allanrod interested in his happiness?"

"None of these points can be replied to till you have answered in the affirmative," said the leader. He then repeated—"I will see you again to-morrow," and departed.

CHAPTER III.

Now o'er the one half world
Nature seems dead, and wicked dreams abuse
The curtain'd sleep.

MACBETH.

THE Baron sunk into his chair, in a state of greater wretchedness of mind than he had ever yet experienced: to solve the mystery which had just been presented to him he found himself inadequate; but he plainly perceived that he had been the dupe of a plot deeply planned to win his consent to an union which his own soul now abhorred, not less than did his unhappy Rosalind.

Who could this Allanrod be, whose prisoner he was?—and how were Lord Rufus and he connected, as this demand seemed to bespeak them? were questions which he proposed to his own mind many different times during the night, and which he was obliged as often to dismiss from it again unanswered.

The transactions of the few last days appeared to him a dream: he could scarcely believe himself now awake. He felt suspicious of the truth of every occurrence of recent date which his memory registered as facts; and knew himself certain only of one thing, and this was, that be his own fate what it might, his consent should never be extorted to that man becoming the husband of his daughter, who would have been a sufficient monster to have led her to a second marriage bed, while yet her lawful husband lived.

In the morning the leader returned as he had foretold he should do.—"Well," he said, "are you determined?"

"Yes, I am," replied Lord William, "never to agree to your terms of liberty."

The leader placed on the table some paper, some ink and a pen. "When you change your mind," he said, "as there is no doubt but you soon will, write your consent on that paper, sign it, and order it to be given to the leader Monrose, who is myself; till then you will see no more of me, rest assured."

The Baron was beginning again to propose to him one of the questions relative to the connexion of Allanrod and Lord Rufus, which he had urged in vain the evening before; but Monrose interrupted him by saying—"Not a syllable from me till you have given your consent;" and with a malignant smile he left the place.

Two days passed unmarked by any event but increasing misery to the Baron; on the next he determined to tamper with the men who attended him, and to endeavour to open their feelings to his situation by the master-key of gold, which fits the wards of almost every heart. The first on whom he resolved to make the attempt, was the fellow whose observations on the gibbet they had passed, in their march had so much shocked him; and his reason for selecting him was, that he thought he did not appear to possess sufficient sense of feeling to bind him honest, even to his comrades in dishonesty. He it was who usually brought him his morning repast, and on this day he came to his wish.

"How long have you been a freebooter?" said the Baron to him, as an opening to the conversation.

"Long enough," replied the man, "to be much richer than I am."

"Perhaps your honesty has kept you poor," rejoined the Baron; "and though you are not above a robbery, you may, perhaps, scorn a bribe?"

"I was never tried," answered the fellow, with an arch smile.

"I have three pieces of gold at your service," returned the Baron, "in return for some information I want to gain of you."

"Respecting what?" asked the man.

"Respecting your leader, Allanrod," replied the Baron. "I want to learn how he stands connected with Lord Rufus de Madginecourt. Do you know any thing of their concerns?"

"A little, I believe," returned the fellow, with another intelligent smile.

"Then what say you to the three pieces?" rejoined the Baron.

"I say that if they were nine," returned the Moss-trooper, "and in my hand, my communication should be at your service."

Nine pieces were all the Baron had about him, but he considered them worth bartering for information upon so obscure, so mysterious a point, and one so greatly important to him; and he put them into the hands of the man.—"Now then, speak," said Lord William.

"Not a word," answered the man. "Now you see I have honesty to my chief, and know how to use a bribe, though it is the first I ever received;" and with these words he left the place.

To curse was in vain: the Baron clasped his hands, and paced his prison in an agitation which he would not at any other time have believed the insolence and treachery of so mean a wretch could have excited in his mind. He had never before been in a situation to lament the loss of such a sum, but it was now his all, and in more friendly hands might have rendered him the most essential service: he had now nothing of value left him with which to win the robbers to his cause, and he despaired of making an impression by any other means than those of gold on the heart of a freebooter.

At night a stranger appeared, with his fire and provisions; he doubted not but that the other had formed an excuse for not coming again into his presence.

For three successive days he saw only this stranger and another man, whose features were equally new to him. The first of the two seemed to be cast in a less rugged mould than were the general part of his comrades, and him the Baron resolved first to address: he had only promises to hold out to him; but he hoped to be able, in some measure, to prevail by these, as he recollected that none of the Moss-troopers could be unacquainted with his rank and wealth.

On the fourth morning he accosted him when he brought in his breakfast. The man did not reply, or raise his eyes from his employment, when the Baron spoke. He addressed him again; still he replied not. He spoke to him a third time, and with as ill success, the man not even looking towards him.

As he was about to leave the apartment, the Baron crossed upon him, and spoke once more: the man fixed his eyes on him, and having for some moments watched the motion of his lips, he shook his head, and pointing to his ears, indicated that he was deaf. The Baron made a sign to him not to depart, and the man waited patiently to see what he required. Lord William tore a slip from the paper which had been brought him by the leader Monrose, and on it he proposed a question, in writing, and shewed it to the man.

"I can't read," said the man, "but I'll send somebody to you that can hear you, directly."

He went away, locking the door after him, and leaving the Baron to lament a second disappointment. He had not many moments for reflection, before the door opened again, and another man appeared.—"Do you want any thing, sir?" asked he. "Murdoch thinks you do; and we are ordered to grant you every accommodation you may require."

"Indeed!" exclaimed the Baron, surprised at the question—"then tell me, who is Allanrod?"

"That is an accommodation he ordered us not to grant you," said the man.

"And do you refuse to grant any on your own account?" asked De Mowbray.

"You were unlucky the other day," returned the man—"you met with one of our chief's first favourites."

"Whom do you mean?" asked the Baron.

"His name is Frasier," was the reply; "he that got the nine pieces of gold of you: he has bragged enough below of his deceit to you."

The Baron was now animated with a spark of hope which announced a friend at hand; and bitterly did he lament that an enemy had snatched from him the only reward he had been possessed of, and which might now have been valuable indeed to him.

"Would to Heaven," cried Lord William, "that I were possessed of thrice that sum to bestow on thee! but I have not a single coin about me. I do not scruple to tell you this, because I think I read in your eye that *you* will not doubt the sincerity of any promise I make to you: and to shew you that my promises are not in vain, answer me faithfully to a few questions which I shall ask of you, and I will give you my written promise on this paper."

"Will you give me a promise for twenty pieces of gold?" asked the man.

"On my life I will," returned the Baron, with the energy he felt.

"Enough," replied the man; "then propose your questions; but do not betray me—it would expose me to torture, and render you no additional benefit."

The Baron promised most solemnly not to reveal what should be imparted to him, and then proposed his first question—

"What connexion is it that exists between your chief, Allanrod, and Lord Rufus de Madginecourt?"

"Connexion!" replied the man, "why they are———"

"Rascal!—villain!" exclaimed a voice, and at the same moment Frasier darted into the prison. "This I expected," he cried, "from your remarks when I shewed you my nine pieces: but I am in time to prevent your damned tattling.—Out imp! your life is not worth an hour's wear."

Violently he drove him towards the door, and was following him out.

"For Heaven's sake!" cried the Baron, "report him not: on my soul, he has disclosed nothing to me!"

"That was not his wisdom, but his want of time," replied Frasier; "and we, who exist only by honour to each other, are philosophers enough to consider the will and the deed the same."

The door was instantly shut, the Baron left without hope, and the unpleasantness of his feelings materially increased by the punishment which he dreaded awaited him who had shewed a readiness to become his friend.

The paper, upon which he had been about to give his written promise of a reward to the man who had been just hurried from his presence, was still in his hand. He had found one heart, which from interest, or perhaps partly from humanity and partly from interest, at least he wished to believe it so, had been about to become a friend to his cause; and he doubted not but there were others amongst the freebooters possessed of the same feelings, if he had but an opportunity of seeing them, and selecting one for his purpose: as he had not this opportunity, being aware that, now Allanrod's favourite, Frasier, had unfortunately been the first object of his temptation, none who were likely to incline to his suit, would be permitted to approach him; chance must inevitably be his guide in his future attempts at freedom: accordingly, having torn off a part of the paper he wrote upon it—"Lord William de Mowbray promises to reward with a thousand pieces of gold, him who shall give information at De Mowbray Castle that he is a prisoner in this building."

This done, he tied the paper to a piece of rusty iron, which he found on the floor of his prison, and again placing his chair upon the table under the window, he climbed upon it, and threw out what he had written: he had secured it from being carried away by the wind, and all he feared was that it might fall upon the roof of some lower part of the building, and thus be lost for ever. The chances were also much in favour of its falling into unfriendly hands. However, he must either submit to these hazards, or forego all attempts at liberty; and he resolved to repeat what he had that day done on every successive one, whilst any of his paper was yet remaining.

In the evening his oil and provisions were brought to him by the deaf man: he heard the voice of Frasier on the stairs, but he did not come into the prison.

Late in the night the Baron laid himself down to rest; the fatigue of mind which he had endured during the day inclined him to sleep, and he soon sunk into the lap of repose: but his imagination was too much disturbed for him to derive much refreshment from his slumbers; and dreams of a horrid nature floated in his brain. He imagined his daughter sinking under the ferocious embraces of Lord Rufus, and calling to him for assistance, while he stood by at a short distance, anxiously desiring to rescue her from her ravisher, but unable to move towards her: the agitation of his mind awoke him, and as he awoke, he heard the clock strike twelve.

In a short time he again composed himself to sleep; still dreams, of a like dreadful nature, haunted his fancy: he thought himself entangled in the labyrinth of a wood; a rough-looking figure approached him, and he besought it to point out to him his way. The figure beckoned to him to follow it, and he did so; but it appeared only to lead him still further into the entanglements of the forest: presently it knelt down, and scratching up a tuft of grass, discovered to his view, beneath it, the skeleton of a child; the figure, at the same moment, assumed the likeness of HUBERT, and darted at him a blow with a dagger. In an agony of mind he awoke, and started from his bed; his lamp was not entirely extinguished, and a faint light still proceeded from the dying embers of his fire: he cast his eyes fearfully around his prison, almost dreading to behold the form he had seen in his dream; as they turned towards the great oak chest, he perceived the lid open, and a haggard countenance appearing beneath it.

He started at the sight, and uttered an exclamation of surprise: the face immediately disappeared, and the lid fell down with a loud clap.

Terror seized him: he could not disunite the ideas of his dream and his waking observation; he believed the haggard countenance which he had just seen to have been that of Hubert. Could it be possible that he was one of the freebooters, and really determined on his life, as his dream had predicted?

"Oh that the child of Rosalind were living!" he exclaimed in mental agony; "oh that the black hour of my misfortunes were not deeper dyed by the recollection of my crimes!"

Trembling he staggered towards the chest (for security of the worst is better to endure than suspense), and endeavoured to raise the lid; but, as on all his former trials, it resisted his efforts; he again kicked against it, to ascertain whether it would now return the same sound of hollowness that it had before done; and the sound was still the same.

He retired to a corner of his apartment, anxiously listening, and expecting momentarily to hear some fresh sound of terror, or behold some object of alarm; but the silence of the night was unbroken, except by the echoes of his own quick breathings. After a length of time had elapsed, and neither sounds nor objects returned to re-excite his terror, he became almost ready to impute the impression of the past to his perturbed imagination, as being merely a part of his dream, or the consequence of it; but he could not pass the soothing impression on his senses; he felt too certain of having been really awake, and too strongly convinced that what he had seen was no vision of sleep, no waking dream, but a reality.

He traversed his chamber in an agitation of despair; a few minutes put a period to the life of his lamp, and he was constrained to pass more than two hours in dreadful darkness, ere the grey morning began to break through the clouds of night; and when the rays of day once more entered his prison, he felt a reluctance again to return to his mattress, and placed himself in his chair, where he hoped for awhile to forget his miseries in sleep; but thought drove off its approach, and though his mind was busily occupied by reflection, ideas crouded so fast upon each other, that he felt himself entirely incapable of so arranging them as to produce any thing like reasoning.

CHAPTER IV.

Look where it comes!
It harrows me with fear and wonder.

HAMLET.

About an hour after sun-rise, Lord William heard a drum beat; an immediate bustle seemed to ensue throughout the building; he heard the voices of the borderers calling to each other, and sometimes their hasty steps approached close to his prison. For a moment he entertained the faint hope of a rescue being near at hand; but as the noises seemed all confined to the inside of the building, the idea of its being attacked by any friends of his soon vanished.

In about an hour more, the single drum beat a call, and in a few minutes after it was joined by several instruments which played a lively march: for some time they appeared to be stationary, either on the outside of the edifice, or in some court within its walls. They then began to recede from it, and their sounds were heard by him gradually decreasing, till they died away amongst the whisperings of the floating breeze.

It was the first time since his confinement that he had heard the sounds of instruments, and he doubted not but that they were now used to lead the freebooters to some act of plunder and devastation.

During the day no one but the deaf man and the malignant Frasier attended upon him. About noon he again threw a paper out of his window, similar to the one he had let fall from it the day before: as the evening advanced, he determined to be sparing of his fuel and oil, that he might not again be left in darkness during any part of the night.

The whole day he had traversed his prison in the greatest inquietude of mind, and as the dusk of light began to add the gloom of nature to that which already obscured his feelings, Hubert was the only subject of his thoughts; nay, he even fancied that the passing breeze seemed to whisper in his ear—"Murderer of thy grandchild!" In agony insupportable, he wrung his hands, and from an aching heart his lips groaned forth—"How blessed are the innocent in misfortune, when compared with what the guilty suffer!" Still he attempted to flatter himself with the idea that his present conduct, in so resolutely refusing to sacrifice his daughter to Lord Rufus, must be of some weight in his favour in the scale of good, to balance his former cruelty to her and her child; his heart acknowledged it a feeble consolation; but he grasped at the only straw of comfort which there appeared in view for him to catch at in his present sea of calamities.

About midnight he sunk to sleep in his chair: how long he slept he knew not, but when he awoke his lamp was out, and his fire was also nearly exhausted; two or three expiring sticks were all that remained of it, and these threw a feeble light upon the wall on one side, leaving the rest of the room in dark shade. He directly rose to replenish the fire, and as he approached it, he heard a noise, resembling the rubbing of two pieces of iron against each other: he stopped, and listened; the sound of an opening door followed immediately after, and all was then still again.

Several minutes elapsed, and the sounds did not return: he heaped more fuel on his fire, which for the present rather choked than added to the little light which proceeded from it: suddenly a loud noise, like the falling of chains, burst on his ear, and seemed to proceed from the chest. He recollected the haggard countenance which he had once seen under its lid, and trembled: he doubted not but that the performance of some treachery was at hand, and he was unarmed, thus unable to defend himself.

He now heard something creak within the chest, and thought he could distinguish the drawing of breath. A loud snap in its inside made him start, and he stole into the shade, to observe what he could not fly from. The gloom he now looked through upon the chest was thick, and almost impenetrable by the slender light his fire afforded; but he thought he could perceive the lid lifted up: a faint gleam of light, which immediately appeared beneath it, convinced him it was open. All anxiety and dread, he durst scarcely breathe. The light increased gradually, but not to any great strength, and an armed head appeared rising up above the edge of the chest; its features, as well as he could discern, for the shade of its helmet was strong upon them, appeared black, and distorted; and he felt, for the first time, what excessive fear is. The figure continued to rise slowly up, its eyes rolling wildly about, as if endeavouring to look through the misty gloom that pervaded the prison; its right arm was now stretched out, and in this it held a lamp and a dagger.

Lord William continued involuntarily shrinking back from the appearance before him; and as he receded towards the wall, a violent blow on his head brought him to the ground: a loud crash ensued—a dreadful giddiness seized him, and in a moment all was darkness and silence.

When Lord William's recollection returned to him he found himself lying upon the ground, and totally insensible how long he might have lain there. He awoke from his stupor sore and bruised, and entirely ignorant where he was; the place to which he was transported appeared to his senses full of misty vapours, and a strong earthy smell assailed his nostrils.

The ground was clammy and uneven; and, in endeavouring to raise himself, he several times slipped down again.

He extended his hands on every side—all was vacancy: he moved on a few steps, and a stone wall, dripping with humid exhalations like that of a sepulchre, met his touch.

Guiding himself by this wall, he determined, if possible, to measure the extent of the place he was in, and endeavour to learn if there was no opening for him to escape by. As he proceeded, unwholesome vapours met his breath, and the dewy damps, which settled on his hair and clothes, ran down in drops upon his face and hands.

He trod on cautiously for a considerable time, his hands constantly held out to warn him of any obstacle that might intercept his progress. Suddenly a short but rapid declivity in the ground again threw him on his side, and at the same moment a deep groan struck his ear. With suspended respiration, he awaited its repetition; but no similar sound was heard; all was again profoundly silent.

He sighed aloud, thinking that it had perhaps been the echo of his own breath which had alarmed him, and willing to ascertain if it was so. No echo now replied to it, but at the moment when he expected to have heard it, the air close by him was cut by the rapid movement of some substance passing through it—and all was then again still.

He had heard no footsteps accompanying the sound, but dreading that danger was lurking near him, he made an effort to rise: he could not find the wall which had before been some protection to him in moving along; still he thought that a few steps might bring him to it. The ground became more slippery than ever: he again stumbled, and in his attempt to catch at something which might save him from falling, he encountered in his grasp a—skeleton!

He threw himself from it, as if a serpent had met his touch, and darting on one side, he again found himself by the wall: cold drops of perspiration burst from every pore, and a deadly sickness seized him; he groaned aloud in agony, and the spot where he now stood returned him the echo of his own voice in hollow sounds, which fear might have believed to have proceeded from the mouths of an hundred spirits.

Lord William stood chained to the spot, at a total loss how to proceed amidst the horrors he was existing amongst: at length, recovering, in some measure, his fortitude, as no fresh cause of terror assailed him, he thought he perceived the gleam of a front light at a distance: he fixed his eyes on it; it appeared of the same nature with that which had issued from the chest, on the opening of its lid that night; he fancied that it moved, but if it did, its progress was remarkably slow. He presently ascertained that it did recede from him, and considering that his only chance of escaping from this spot of horrors was to follow it, he moved boldly forward.

The ground became drier, and thus favoured his advances towards the light; he kept it still in view, and believed that he could discern by it a deep and lofty vault, into which he was entering: gradually the vault became narrower and narrower, and at length he moved along with one hand upon either wall. For a considerable time he continued to proceed, the light appearing to him to move at nearly the same pace he did, and becoming neither stronger nor paler, till on a sudden it totally disappeared. In this dilemma, Lord de Mowbray felt himself as much at a loss as he had ever been how to act; he dreaded equally to advance or to recede from the spot where he stood, and to remain there could not forward his hope of escape; he therefore determined, at all hazards, to proceed.

After a progress of a few moments, he found himself at the top of a flight of steps, down which his extreme caution just saved him from falling. He descended about a dozen steps of stone, and on arriving at the bottom of these, he again caught a glimpse of the light, and, as he believed, of the figure which he had seen rise from the chest. He again stopped to deliberate; was he really under supernatural influence?—was the spirit of Hubert haunting him? or was the living Hubert the agent of a plot for his destruction?

The clock at this instant struck three; it sounded loudly, and appeared much nearer to him than it had done in his prison: he started at the sound, for its reverberations beat from vault to vault.

The light was now again swiftly disappearing, and still fearing to be left in total darkness, he again quickened his pace; but his progress was almost immediately stopped by a grated door. He placed his shoulders to it, and it flew open with a noise which resounded through the place like distant thunder; and at the same instant he felt himself precipitated down several steps, upon a hard and flinty ground. He immediately raised himself up again, painful as was the effort, and looked around hastily for the light, but it had entirely vanished.

The dungeon into which he had fallen was so small, that its extent measured scarcely a dozen paces; but he could perceive in it no outlet, no means of quitting it, but by the stairs down which he had fallen, and which were so decayed and broken away, as to defy all his attempts to re-ascend them.

For a considerable time, he continued in this wretched situation, till chancing to raise his eyes to the opposite side of the dungeon to that on which he was standing, he saw a faint illumination playing upon the wall, which appeared to be the reflection of some light above his head: he turned his eyes to the spot, and discovered a cleft of considerable size, through which the moonbeams were gaining admittance. His heart leaped with joy; the cavity was not above his reach, and hanging upon it by his hands, he easily raised himself up to it. He perceived that it was indeed the welcome light of the moon which was cheering him, and a fine star-light night presented its beautiful serenity to his view.

He now blessed his unknown conductor, whatever his intentions might have been, and began to place all his strength upon his endeavours to force himself through the aperture.

Those alone who have been exposed to the situation in which Lord de Mowbray had been condemned to exist, can be adequate judges of the force with which the expectation of freedom arms the nerves; at another time, the Baron himself would have asserted his incapacity to rend the rock which pointed out liberty to him, and still denied him its enjoyment; now, with strength almost supernatural, he, by small particles, crumbled away the envious earth, till he was enabled to thrust his body into the aperture: from the descent to the ground was but a few feet, and, without hesitation, he leaped down.

On looking round, he found himself at the foot of a rocky piece of ground, on which stood the building where he had so lately been a prisoner. He raised his eyes, and beheld the very turret which had been the scene of his miseries, frowning upon him from the gloomy grandeur of the shade in which it was enveloped. He had however enjoyed but very few moments of exultation, when he heard the silence of the night broken in upon by the sound of footsteps. His heart sunk within him: if he was pursued, how dreadful might be the punishment decreed against his escape, although he himself had not been the original agent of it. He crept into a cleft in the rock, and here he endeavoured to hide himself; the sounds advanced nearer, and then again receded from him: thus they several times returned, and then again died away; and the Baron at last discovered that they were the footsteps of a sentinel who was pacing his allotted portion of ground on a prominence of the rock nearly above the cavity in which he was standing concealed.

Once more Lord William feared to move; one glance of the sentinel might destroy all his hopes of escape: he perceived, however, that the moon was rapidly withdrawing her light from the atmosphere, and knowing that there would be an interval of at least an hour between her disappearance and the rising of day, he determined to await that time for flying from the precincts of the castle; accordingly, when the orb of night had sunk below the horizon, he again ventured forth: the stars were also withdrawing their influence, and the country was now wrapped in the dark shades of night. The road towards his own castle he knew to be intricate, and he was unacquainted with the track which it became him to pursue.

After he had moved a short distance from his hiding-place, he discerned a path down the rock on which the castle stood; it was steep, and covered with knots of furze and loose stones, which rendered his going down it not only dangerous but difficult. Arrived at the bottom, he resolved not to proceed by the regular path, lest he should encounter any of his enemies returning to their haunt; but to deviate from the road, still keeping it as much as possible in view, and making it the rule of his progress.

He wandered on, through an immense valley, bounded on each side by lofty hills, and soon discovered that he was passing through that very gulf which, on the evening that he was conducted prisoner to the monastery, had struck him with terror as a spot suited to the dreadful purpose of murder. The gibbet was scarcely discernible at the present time, but the creaking of the chains met his ear, and he shuddered at the sound.

Over the range of hills which encircled the valley, he perceived he must climb, before he should quit the purlieus of his enemy's encampment, and with extreme difficulty and caution he arrived on their other side, without any obstruction but such as the ruggedness of the hills themselves presented to his progress.

Although the exertion was overpowering, he abated nothing of his speed, and as the dawn of day began to break, he believed himself at least six miles from the spot where he had so lately been a prisoner. Thirst was the most painful sensation he suffered under, and perceiving no cottage near, he slacked his drought at a rivulet; sweetened by liberty, the draught was delicious, and seemed to inspire him with fresh spirits and strength.

Morning was now beginning to break; the grey dawn had for some time mixed its lighter tints with the sable and retiring shadows of night; and the dappled clouds separating in large masses, unlocked the rosy gates of day.

CHAPTER V.

Rous'd by the cock, the soon-clad shepherd leaves
His mossy cottage, where with peace he dwells,
And from the crowded fold in order drives
His flock, to taste the verdure of the morn.

THOMSON.

About an hour after sun-rise, the Baron felt a faintness, the consequence of fatigue, seize upon him, which required some short respite of his progress; he accordingly threw himself down at the foot of an oak, where his bed was perfumed by the violets, which shrunk from view amidst the herbage; and here he lay for awhile, almost entranced, enjoying, in luxury, the beauties of the scene, and contrasting them with the horrors of the preceding days and nights; and but for the recollection of his imprisoned men, and the uncertain state of his affairs at home, he would for some moments have revelled in perfect happiness:—so exquisite is the air we breathe in that liberty which has for any time been denied us.

Short, however, were the moments of his blissful trance—a distant sound, resembling the tones of music, mixed itself with the rustling breeze that played upon his ear; it grew gradually louder, and he plainly distinguished the voices of warlike instruments: he was now as miserable as he had just before been happy; he doubted not but that the sounds portended the return of some of the Moss-troopers from a sally for plunder, and the dread of discovery again seized him; he crept towards some bushes, through the foliage of which he could catch a glance of that part of the country from whence the sounds proceeded, without exposing himself to view.

He perceived a long train of men, whom he instantly recognized to be Scottish freebooters, winding up the side of a hill, at the distance of scarcely a furlong from the spot where he stood: he could also perceive that they were laden with plunder, and he conjectured, heavily too, by the slow pace at which they moved. The road along which they must pass ran close by the present concealment of the Baron; to quit it, however, he judged more hazardous than to keep close within the cover it afforded him; and he therefore skulked down beneath the underwood, in a state of dread and anxiety, which equalled every unpleasant sensation he had before experienced.

The music continued to sound, and the rough voices of the freebooters were now audible, even amidst the din of their instruments. The Baron crept still closer to the earth, not daring to raise an eye from his hiding-place. They at length passed within a stone's throw of him. By the few words he overheard of their conversation, he discovered that they were conducting some prisoners to their fortress. He pitied those condemned to the cruel fate from which he had so recently, so unaccountably escaped himself, and from returning to which he yet scarcely thought himself secure.

At length they had all passed the spot, and he ventured to raise his head; but those he looked for were no longer visible, although the sounds of their voices and instruments were still reverberating on his ear: they had marched into a valley, into which his eyes were prevented from following them by a cluster of trees which grew at the entrance of it.

That this body of freebooters had been rencountered by him in his way, the Baron was glad, now he had escaped their observation; because the chances appeared in his favour, that he should not meet any of the party to annoy him during the remainder of his journey to his own castle. Inspired by this hope, he again set forward; the sounds of the instruments were now scarcely audible, and he saw his enemy at a considerable distance, proceeding along the upper part of a road, where their appearance was that of one moving body, separate objects being no longer discernible.

Lord William felt the want of sustenance growing upon him at every step; but still he wished to proceed a little, and still a little further, before he asked refreshment of any of the shepherds whose huts were scattered about, lest he should be recognized by any of them, as he dreaded what connexion they might have with the freebooters. Whilst he was thus debating with his own mind, he perceived three men coming towards him: he was at first startled at the sight, and felt undetermined whether he should avoid them; but perceiving that they were shepherds, and that they saw him, he collected himself as much as he was able; and assuming the manners of a weary traveller, besought their hospitality. They returned his salutation with great friendliness; and the eldest, who was the father of the other two, a venerable grey-headed old man, immediately invited him to his cottage, which he told him was situated on the other side of the hill, which the Baron was ascending when he met them.

One of the sons being left with the flock, the other returned back with his father and Lord William, and, after a few minutes walk, they arrived at the humble dwelling of the shepherds. The hut was as rude as it could well be conceived to be; the walls were of boughs, plastered with mud, and the roof of thatch, was in many parts quite broken away, and in others nearly overgrown with moss and weeds; the door was too low to allow a person who did not stoop, to enter it; through a few narrow chinks in the walls, was admitted all the light the cottage received; the fire was contained in a hole dug in the centre of the floor, and the smoke having no chimney to conduct it out, had dyed the inside of the roof with its dusky influence, and cast innumerable blacks on the beams and rafters, in finding a way out for itself.

Two or three wooden benches, and a rough-hewn table, composed all the furniture of the place, except some straw, which was scattered in one corner, and covered with sheep-skins for a bed. Every thing around denoted the poverty of its inmates; yet they appeared cheerful and contented; and with a most cordial welcome they joined many apologies for the humble roof beneath which they received him.

A female, of a hale and florid complexion, whose attire corresponded with the meanness of her habitation, rose, at their entrance, from her employment, to welcome the stranger; and at the command of the old man, she set before the Baron some new milk and some oaten cakes: the old man introduced her to his guest as the wife of his son.

Readily did Lord William partake of the humble but palatable repast which was placed before him; and he then threw himself upon the shepherd's bed, which, in a state of less fatigue, he would not have been emulous of pressing, but which now wore the most inviting form. After a few hours repose, he awoke, and found himself alone in the cottage, with a boy of about five years old, who appeared to have been placed there to watch his waking, and give notice of it to the woman; for the moment he opened his eyes, the child ran to the door, and calling out—"The stranger is awake," the female entered, and graciously enquired what she could do to serve her guest?

"Nothing further, I thank you," returned Lord William; "I am now sufficiently recovered from my fatigue to proceed on my journey."

The boy was standing by the side of the woman, as were two other children, apparently younger than he was: the Baron's eyes fell on the child, and he observed him to be remarkably beautiful, and of a most interesting countenance; his face was round, and lighted by a pair of arch and nearly black eyes; a vivid colour painted his cheeks; his hair was a few shades deeper than the flaxen, and his scanty raiment displayed the fairness of his skin.

"That is a very handsome boy," said the Baron. "He is your child, I suppose?"

"No," returned the woman, "they are all mine but him."

"And whose is he?" rejoined De Mowbray.

"My brother's," was the reply.

"He whom we left with the flock, when I first met your husband and father, I guess," said the Baron.

"No, another brother," the woman replied.

The old man at this moment entered the hut, with some firing, which he had been cutting: he had overheard their conversation as he approached, and patting the boy on his head, as he spoke, said—"Aye, Heaven bless him, I call him mine, for he has nobody else to look up to at present; all have not humanity enough to take care of their own."

Earnestly did the Baron, at the present moment, wish that he was possessed of the means of rewarding his hospitable entertainers; but being destitute of them, he promised that they should not be long without meeting a return for their kindness.

The old man replied, that a reward was what he did not wish for, nor think of;—he had but little, it was true, he added, but he had never found that little less, for relieving with it the hungry and weary traveller.

"With such ideas," returned the Baron, "thou art more blessed than affluence could make thee; thy comforts, however, may be increased, without endangering the purity of thy happiness—and depend on it they shall."

The Baron, by enquiring the nearest road to his own castle, had found that the cottage where he had met with so hospitable a reception was but a stone's throw from the valley where he and his men had been surprised by Allanrod and his freebooters. At this spot he quickly arrived; and although it had led him nearly a furlong from his road to visit it, he could not resist the impulse he felt to pass that way, and learn whether the banditti had possessed sufficient humanity to bury his soldiers who had fallen in that day's contest.

Having gained a sight of the tumulies which enclosed their bodies, he set forward again, with all the speed he was capable of making. But sixteen miles lay between him and his castle: it was now little more than noon-day; thus, at a moderate pace, he might reach its walls by sun-set. This idea inspired him with strength, and lent wings to his speed.

At length the turrets of De Mowbray Castle, rearing their heads above the groves which surrounded it, met the eye of their Lord; the sun was at this moment on the horizontal line, and its golden light painted the scene with a glowing influence, which communicated itself to the heart of the Baron, and almost drew the tears of joy into his eyes.

Nimbly he ascended the velvet turf which led to the moat of his castle, and eagerly he turned the last angle which lay between him and the drawbridge: on coming within sight of it, he found it down; this did not surprise him, as he supposed that some one had lately passed over it, or was about so to do; but on arriving at its foot, he perceived no sentinel near, nor any human being whatever in view. This startled him; he cast his eyes to the watch-tower; it was without its accustomary guard, and those places on the battlements which had for years past been the stations of sentinels were all vacant.

He crossed the drawbridge, and arriving at the gate of the first court, he found no obstruction to his entering it; the heavy portcullis hung suspended in its chains, and gave free access to the interior of the building. In the utmost astonishment he stepped forward. What were his sensations on entering the second court, when fragments of the broken walls met his sight, scattered on the earth, and mingled with the balls of the musketry, the snapped blades of swords, the barrels of match-locks, the unbent bow, and the useless sling.

Plainly did these bespeak that his castle had been besieged in his absence, and too clearly did the state of the drawbridge and portcullis declare that the enemy had conquered, and despoiled his mansion. "Where was his daughter?—was the building deserted, or were there still some remaining within its vanquished walls, to tell him the sad tale?"—were the instant questions which he proposed to himself, and rushed towards the castle, to gain a reply to. The doors stood open; wildly he entered the castle hall, and called aloud upon his household, in various names, to which no answer was returned. He rushed into the first apartment which presented itself to him—it was the saloon, where oft the assembled group of joy had made the vaulted ceiling ring with the echoes of the dance and song; now how altered its state! every feature denoted rapine; the heavy chairs alone remained of all its sumptuous furniture; the golden tripods, which had supported the fragrant exotic, and the blooming shrub, were no longer there; the silver lamps were torn, with their chains, from the walls, and the ewers and basons of massy gold, which had been the containers of the scented water devoted to the refreshment of the partakers in the dance, were alike no more to be seen.

"Allanrod, accursed, damnable Allanrod! these are thy ravages, these are the marks of thy savage fury," exclaimed Lord William, as he gazed on the scene before him. "Doubtless, from my castle was thy ruffian band returning with their wealthy spoils, when I this morning beheld them from my covert;—perhaps at that moment my faithful servants passed me, the prisoners of thy inhumanity—nay, perhaps at that instant my unfortunate child was led thy captive, unconscious how near to her was her unhappy father, ignorant of her fate—unable to succour her if it had been known to him!"

It was still possible, he thought, though hardly probable, after the demand which Allanrod had made of her for his friend Lord Rufus de Madginecourt, that she might be in her chamber. Thither flew the Baron. The stairs which led towards it bore indubitable marks of the avarice and ferocity of the spoilers of the building; spots of blood, strips of garments, and broken weapons, lay every where scattered amongst such articles of furniture as the ravagers had rejected.

The door of Rosalind's apartment stood open—no one appeared to meet him at his entrance—he called on his daughter, but his invocations were in vain—he clasped his hands in agony, and stood almost maddened by the idea of what atrocious sufferings she might have been condemned to, or still might be reserved for.

In a state of mind that bade defiance to cool reflection, the Baron continued to run from one apartment to another, in the vain hope of at last finding some individual who might reply to his interrogatories: at length despair seized him, and overpowered equally by his recollection of the past, his ideas of the present, and his anxieties for the future, he sunk, overpowered in body and mind, upon a couch.

The shades of night were beginning to close in the day, and the gathering darkness added to the misery of De Mowbray's mind. Still he did not attempt to quit the castle; he knew not whither to go at so late an hour, and he felt equally unwilling to remain where he was: his mind was too much harrassed to admit of any resolution or plan, and he continued to lie where he had thrown himself down.

The apartment to which chance had led him was the cedar chamber, in which the Baroness, his wife, had died: this alone appeared to have escaped the fury of the spoilers, and at the present moment he could scarcely avoid believing that fate had preserved the solemnity of this scene entire, to add one more pang to the tortures of his soul. There is a state of frenzied grief to which the mind is driven by accumulated sorrow, in which it almost wishes, rather than dreads, an increase of misery and terror; imagining it almost impossible that it can feel more than it already does; and almost desiring that it may experience enough of horror and affliction, to end all feeling at a blow.

In this situation was De Mowbray; he felt, as it were, prepared to see the spirit of his wife approach him, and demand the cause why he had not given Rosalind to the man of her heart? He recollected the awful, the unknown voice, which had called upon him to spare Rosalind, on the night when in that chamber she had fallen in supplication at his feet, and he had declared to her his resolution of yielding her to the detested Lord Rufus; he expected to hear the voice again address him, and his feelings were worked to that pitch of horror, that something like disappointment attended the failure of his expectations.

Then came to his mind the remembrance of his parting with Hubert, and the innocent countenance of the babe whom he had committed to his mercy. To this idea succeeded the recollection of the terrible visage which had gazed on him from the chest in his prison, in the fortress of Allanrod; and which he believed himself to have followed through those vaults into which he had so unaccountably been introduced. Had this been Hubert, or the spirit of Hubert?

His tongue was parched within his mouth, a burning fever drank his blood.—"O God!" he cried aloud, "thy punishments are just, but they are severe. O Power Omnipotent! accept my repentance; let the infant spirit of him whose blood I have spilt plead to thy mercy for my offence! my weight of woe already crushes me to the earth—forbear, forbear to torture me further—I am humbled before thee."

CHAPTER VI.

To what new wonders am I now reserv'd?
Providence and Heaven!
Oh, failing eyes, deceive ye not my hope?—
Can this be possible?
This little cross:—I know it by sure marks—
——————rising thoughts,
And hopes and fears o'erwhelm me.

AARON HILL.

We now return to Rosalind, whom we parted from on the day succeeding that which was marked by the setting out of Lord William and his men from the castle, to meet the advanced body of Allanrod's troops.

Rosalind slept peacefully, although the rumour of the black ghost, which had been seen on the drawbridge, and on many parts of the ramparts, interfered with the repose of some of the inhabitants of the castle, and caused them curiously to watch the burning of the lamp at midnight, dreading the appearance of its flame turning blue.

But although Rosalind experienced no anxieties on account of the spirit which her household so universally dreaded, still her mind was rendered ill at ease by those which she derived from other sources; for her father she could not help feeling a degree of interest, notwithstanding his conduct towards her had been so unlike that of a tender parent; and for the life of Gertrude, her only female companion, and whom habit and affection combined, had taught her to consider in the light of a kind friend, her alarm was not less than for the safety of her father.

Gertrude had suddenly been taken ill, and from the first moment of her indisposition, her disorder had worn so alarming an appearance, as gave Rosalind the most serious uneasiness on her account. Bereft of her, she should be deprived of every one whom she now looked upon with any degree of affection, and whom she considered as feeling any real love for her. Mr. Wilmot, the family physician, had been nearly two years dead: his loss had only been replaced by a youth in the castle, to whom he had, at leisure hours, given some little instruction in the art of medicine; and Rosalind trembled for the safety of her servant, committed to the care of his slender skill.

Day and night, Rosalind herself attended upon her with unremitting care and attention; she did not for an instant suffer herself to quit her apartment; even her devotions, which she had for a length of time been accustomed to perform in the chapel, were now offered up in the chamber of Gertrude.

As she one night watched by her bed, observing her to be fallen into a slumber, she amused her thoughts, and kept herself from sleep, by composing the following—

ODE TO HEALTH.

Thou, who mak'st the cheek to glow,
Health!—prime blessing here below,
What can all the world bestow
    If thou'rt not nigh?
What to soothe the voice of woe,
    Of pain and misery?
Need Experience tell his tale?
Ah! too surely riches fail!—
But thro' the ragged path of fate,
Altho' a thousand ills await,
    Tho' thorns around,
    And stings abound,
And numerous brambles scattered lie,
To wound the naked feet of Poverty,
Yet with the wretch, if thou wilt stay,
Thou strew'st with roses still his way.

    See on his crimson couch of state
        The wealthy Croesus laid!
    Around physicians wait,
And livery'd slaves, who with officious aid,
    Attend his anguish'd eye,
    All ready at a glance to fly—
Vain, vain their help! The fever-heated brain

Rages; nor can the icy poles allay the pain.
—"Oh for yon beggar's ease, yon beggar's health,
"A moment grant it, and take all my wealth!
    "He, by some greenwood side
"Contented ope's his wallet's humble store,
    "And quaffs the clear, cool tide
"Of the fresh rivulet; happy, tho' poor!
"Presses the grassy turf in thoughtless sleep,
"While I, worn out, eternal vigils keep."
The tantalising thought adds keener fires;
He storms, he madly rages, and—expires.

    Riches oft tempt excess;
The costly wine, and viand season'd high,
    Contain the slow disease; nor less
The enervating bed of Luxury.
    With palsied hand,
Intemperance takes his ready stand—
    A bloated mass;
And prompts the feast, and circulates the glass:
    Health flies the revelling board;
Still 'midst fresh fields and dews she loves to stray,
To sip the sweets of young-born day,
    Far from Temptation's scourging rod.

    Then keep thy boasted gifts, O Wealth!
    Be thou my better portion—Health.
    Thee, Goddess, with the rosy crest,
    Florid cheek, and azure vest,
    Sparkling eyes of heavenly blue,
    Shall my eager homage woo!
    With thee from smoky towns I'll fly;
    To scenes of rural peace we'll hie;
    Inhaling Zephyr's balmy breath,
    Sweeten'd o'er the yellow heath;
    Blown from beds of scented broom,
    Open'd now, and all in bloom;
    Climbing up the mountain's side,
    To behold the prospect wide;
    Dells, and woods, and lawns, and streams,
    Gilded with the sun's bright beams;
    Now to view the lessening sail

Sink beneath a cloudy veil;
Now to hear the feather'd throng
Tune their magic-breathing song;
Now to roam thro' grove and dale,
To listen to the shepherd's tale,
Drawn from softly-breathing reed,
And, listening, check our eager speed;
While exercise gives sweetest zest
To each short interval of rest.
Thus would I live, and live content,
To know with thee my days were spent;
Far from the witchery of wealth,
Bless'd with thy better portion—Health!"

When Rosalind laid down her pen, she perceived that Gertrude still slept, and she hoped that it might prove an omen of her returning health. Her wish was accomplished; for on the morrow Gertrude shewed signs of approaching convalescence, and Rosalind once more entertained a hope that her only companion of her own sex would be spared her.

Twelve days the Baron, her father, had been absent, and no tidings of him had reached De Mowbray Castle: every day increased the anxiety of Rosalind for his fate; she knew not whether to believe him the victim of a powerful foe, or delayed from returning by pursuing the freebooters to their holds. She had no beam of comfort to cheer her desponding mind, but that which Heaven had kindly granted her in the life of Gertrude; and situated as she was at the moment of its favour, she felt a more than common gratitude for its indulgence.

On the eighteenth day after the departure of the Baron from his castle, Gertrude's health was so far improved, that Rosalind felt no hesitation in quitting her, for the hours which she had before her illness been accustomed to spend in devotion, by the side of her mother's tomb in the chapel.

Ambrose attended her, and opened for her the gates, which had lately been kept locked, on account of the communication of the vaults with the northern rampart. Rosalind knelt on her accustomed stone, and with her eyes raised to heaven, she mingled her prayers of request and thanksgiving: when her devotions were ended, her eyes fell upon the marble which enclosed the ashes of her loved and lamented parent; and upon a white spot of its surface, where the veins of jet which variegated the stone did not interfere with its purity, she perceived a glittering trinket, which arrested her observation; she looked closer, and discovered it to be the very cross of rubies set in gold, which had been the legacy of her deceased parent to her lost Edward!

The sight startled her, and a thousand distracting ideas rushed into her brain.—"Ambrose!" she exclaimed—"Ambrose, who has been into the chapel? can you explain this mystery?"

Ambrose entered hastily, and inquired the meaning of her question.

A secret instinct, for which she could not account, whispered to her heart to be silent on the occurrence of the foregoing minute, and she replied—"It is so long since I have left my chamber, in attending to your niece, that I tremble at my own shadow; my momentary alarm is past and forgotten."

"No one has been within the chapel, I am certain," replied Ambrose; "the keys have not been from my side."

Rosalind attempted to change the subject, and to chat with Ambrose on other matters, as they together returned towards the castle hall; but she observed that he saw her mind occupied by some recent impression, and she felt that her efforts to conceal the emotions of her heart were very inadequate to her design. She repaired quickly to her chamber, and here her first action was to draw the cross from its hiding-place in her bosom, and to assure herself that it was indeed the same which the Baroness de Mowbray had bequeathed to her beloved Edward. The same it was, beyond all doubt; she recollected a small fracture in a rim of the gold which enclosed one of the stones, and which certified it to be the very cross that she had at first believed it.

She considered that in Gertrude's present weak state, it would be wrong to make her the confidante of this discovery; and that she would be an equally unfit subject for the deriving of an opinion from: accordingly, she was doomed to confine her thoughts to her own breast.—"By what means," she began with asking herself, "could this cross have been conveyed into the chapel? and for what purpose, but to meet my observation?" Then succeeded the question of—"By whom had it been placed there?" At this demand, a sensation approaching to frenzy, seized her brain; she almost dared to hope that Edward might himself be alive!—The chapel gates, Ambrose had said, were constantly kept locked; but Edward was acquainted with the entrance to the vaults from the rampart, and the passage which led from thence into the chapel. Through them had Edward gained admittance on the night which had made her his wife. Could it be possible that Edward was himself alive?

A flood of tears came to the relief of her overburdened heart; and as the first impression of hope wore away, she began to chide herself for the weak latitude which she had allowed to her thoughts and expectations. Edward was a corpse, and had been so for six long months—sad testimony of his death had reached her father, and no doubts could hang on the heart-rending fact.

Thought is ever busy to torment the breast that it inhabits, and thus it whispered in the ear of Rosalind:—"Never would Edward have parted from this bequest of her whom he considered as his mother, but in death. He died far from his native soil, in Flanders. Who then could have been sufficiently acquainted with the history of this trinket, to have returned it to the spot from whence it was brought; or, if any one had gained this knowledge, or, from his intimation, had learnt that it would be regarded as valuable by her, why not bring it to her in person, and place the sacred relic in her hands?—why commit it to the chance of never reaching her, by leaving it on the spot where she had discovered it?"

The finding of this cross, so well known, and highly revered, on account of those to whom it had belonged, in so peculiar a situation, must have some meaning, some reference to herself; and to discover what this might be, she wanted no spur to goad her on; where alone she failed, was in devising the means for discovering what design lay concealed beneath her finding it where she had done.

The day passed in thought and anxiety unequalled by any she had ever before experienced; she knew not what to expect, or what to believe. The gates of the chapel Ambrose had declared to have been kept locked; thus, whoever had placed the cross there, must have gained admittance from the vaults which opened upon the northern rampart. A chaos of ideas filled her brain, and from the mass, she determined (she could scarcely answer to herself why) to ask of Ambrose the keys of the chapel that night, under pretence of going, earlier than usual, to prayer on the following morning; and to visit the chapel at that hour of the night at which she had met Edward there previously to their marriage.

With the dusk of the evening, she accordingly called Ambrose into her presence, and having required of him the keys, she indulged him with half an hour's conversation, spent in surmises on the fate of her father in his present attack upon the forces of the freebooter; and then retired to her chamber, where the hours crept heavily on till the clock of the castle struck twelve.

CHAPTER VII.

> Oh that I were a God, to shoot forth thunder
> On these paltry, servile, abject drudges!
>
> His army is a ragged multitude
> Of hinds and peasants, rude and merciless.
>
> HENRY VI, PART II.

SHE directly took up her lamp, and, with a heart trembling with agitation, she left her chamber: she reached the great hall of the castle, without meeting a single observer; as she was turning into a passage, which led from it to that wing of the castle which she was under the necessity of passing in her way to the chapel, sounds, which startled her, met her ear. She was, at first, at a loss what to conclude them; but as she moved a few steps towards a casement, of which an upper compartment had been left open, she clearly distinguished the approach of martial music.

Before she had time for reflection, an alarm was sounded from the watch-tower of the castle; the sentinel at the drawbridge replied to it with his horn; the trumpet in the watch-tower sounded a second and a third blast—"To arms! to arms!—an enemy!—to arms!" ran from sentinel to sentinel on the ramparts; and in a few seconds, the soldiers of the castle burst from all parts into the great hall, in quest of their arms.

The first who recognised Rosalind was Ambrose: he had no suspicion but that the terror of the moment had drawn her from her chamber, and addressed her with—"Dearest lady, be of good cheer; Heaven still protects the innocent amidst the din of war. We have sturdy fellows in our castle, who will oppose the enemy's force to the last drop of their blood."

"But should their courage be overpowered by numbers?" said Rosalind.

"Even these ravagers must shew mercy to females," answered Ambrose.

Seymour, the leader, on whom the command of the troops belonging to the castle had devolved, during the absence of Lord William and Irwin, now advanced, and requested Rosalind to suffer herself to be conveyed, with the other females, into an interior apartment, where they might in safety await the issue of the attack.

Rosalind accepted his counsel, and retired to the room which he had pointed out.

Already was the combined force of the musketry and the bow levelled from the ranks of the enemy against the defenders of De Mowbray Castle. Rosalind threw herself into a chair, and in that dread of mind which imposed silence on her tongue, she sat awaiting the event, and endeavouring to catch an idea of the fortunes of the hour, from the mingled sounds which assailed her ear. Now a shout beneath the ramparts caused her to believe the invaders victorious; now the voices of her father's soldiery seemed to bespeak them conquerors. Of the women who were, at this trying moment, her companions, some wept from cowardice, some from their apprehension for the safety of individuals amongst the soldiery to whom they had attachments. Gertrude was too weak and ill to express her sensations, and Rosalind was without a consoler.

Ambrose alone visited the chamber; he was the only male whose age exempted him from an active share in the contest: the intelligence of hope which he one moment brought, his entrance on the next crushed; a third visit would again perhaps revive the sensation; and a fourth once more banish it entirely from the heart.

Thus did Rosalind pass three hours, between the extremes of hope and despair. The dawn of day was now beginning to break, and with the first approach of twilight she distinctly heard the cry of—"Quarter," from her father's troops. Dreadful was the sound, and still more terrible was that which succeeded it; for in a few seconds more she heard the castle gates burst open, and the riotous band of conquerors rushing through the building.

Ambrose came again into the apartment.—"Oh, lady!" he exclaimed—"dear lady!—that I should live to bear you these tidings!—we are the prisoners of the freebooter Allanrod. Oh that I had died, ere I had seen this wretched day!"

"We are still the creatures of Providence," cried Rosalind; "in its mercy I trust."

The gleam of torches which now played upon the roof of the vaulted passage leading to the apartment where Rosalind sat awaiting her fate, announced the approach of the freebooters. About thirty were seen advancing: the females in the apartment fled to the remotest extremity it afforded them, and united their shrieks for mercy. By an effort almost superior to her strength, Rosalind rose from her seat, and moving a few steps towards the door, she said—"If you are men, sully not your pretensions to the name by cruelty to the defenceless; stain not your conquest by inhumanity to helpless woman!"

One alone, whose dress bespoke him superior to his fellows, entered the apartment; the rest remained without, closing up the entrance.—"You are, I presume," he said, "the Lady Rosalind?"

"I am that Rosalind," she replied.

"Fear nothing, lady," returned the man; "no injury is intended you: comply willingly with my demands, and you are safe and happy."

"Will you extend the same promise to my poor attendants here?" asked Rosalind.

"At your request, they shall be safe," returned the Moss-trooper. "Come, lady," he added, taking the hand of Rosalind, to lead her forth.

"Whither do you require me to go?" she said.

"To a place better suited for your abode than the despoiled castle of your father," answered he.

"Oh, where is my father? tell me that, I conjure you?" asked Rosalind.

"More of that anon," returned her conductor, still leading her away from the apartment.

"Tell me whither it is that I am required to go; only tell me that," said Rosalind.

"I have already told you, to a place of safety and happiness," he replied.—"Nay, lady," he added, drawing Rosalind's arm through his, "be not reluctant to your own good; no force will be used with you, but in this particular."

It was in vain, she knew, for her to resist the power which had conquered her father's soldiery, thus suffered herself to be led by him through the hall of the castle, where spoil and rapine presented themselves to her sight at every step: they proceeded to the outer court, where the light of the morning rendered the torches no longer necessary; and here she beheld a carriage, which, from the preparations making about it, she doubted not awaited her. Her conjecture, was not ill founded; she was desired to get into it, and the Moss-trooper who had led her to it, having once again requested her to lay aside all apprehensions for her safety, the door was closed, and the carriage put into motion.

Rosalind threw herself back in the carriage, and with her handkerchief held to her eyes, she sat for some time in wretched thought; when she again opened them, and looked around her, no light met them, except a faint gleam which burst through a crevice in one of the shutters that occupied the space of the windows. She attempted to open them, but they were too securely fastened to be moved by her. Patience and resignation she now perceived to be alone left her, and with a mournful silence she endeavoured to retain her composure of mind.

They travelled during the whole of the day, stopping only at intervals for refreshments, which were brought to her by the same Scotchman who had in the morning been her conductor to the carriage: about the dusk of the evening, they arrived at a house of rather mean appearance, where she found they were to repose that night. Her guard led her to an apartment which seemed to have been prepared for her reception; a delicate repast was served up to her by a decent-looking woman and girl, and the Moss-trooper remained standing in a remote part of the room.

Rosalind questioned him upon various subjects, and gained his ready replies to them all, except that of her own destination, from which he still assured her she had nothing to fear: relative to her father's fate, he declared himself ignorant. She wished to have been left alone with her hostess; she believed that she might have it in her power to reveal what her guard withheld from her; but this opportunity was not given to her; for when the hour of rest arrived, her conductor to her chamber was still this man. She found it a comfortable apartment, with a lamp burning ready for her on a table, and both a key in the lock, and a bolt on the door, to secure her from interruption in the night.

Still waiting respectfully at the door, the guard enquired if she would have any objection to pursuing her journey at five on the following morning, or if the hour was too early for her pleasure? She replied, that she could not have any pleasure in an action of force, like the one she was now constrained by, except of accelerating, as much as possible, her journey, that she might the sooner know her fate.

The Moss-trooper bowed, and retired, after telling her that he and his companions were to occupy the adjoining apartment through which she had passed to her's, and that she need entertain no fears for her safety during the night. Of this assurance, the strangeness of her fate would not allow her to feel certain herself; but apathy had for so many years benumbed her feelings, that she was almost indifferent to the event of her captivity. She sat for some time dwelling on her fate; and knowing herself to be the prisoner of the freebooter Allanrod, with whose name she had heard her father threatened on the evening previous to his departure from De Mowbray Castle, she concluded that she was now carrying to his fortress, as an hostage for an immense ransom. Her thoughts dwelt also on the circumstance of the cross which she had found on the tomb of her mother; and what she lamented by no means the least in her present captivity, was that it had prevented her from visiting the chapel at that hour, when a combination of strange circumstances seemed to have promised her some occurrence of surprise or pleasure. She thought of Gertrude, and hoped the Moss-trooper had kept his promise of sparing her, and the other females of the castle: she thought also of her father; cruel as he had been to her, she prayed for him, and then laid herself down, without undressing, upon the bed.

In a short time, her guards entered the adjoining chamber; but none of the riot attendant on conquerors marked their approach;

their footsteps seemed to be lightly set, and every mark of silence and respect observed by them towards her. The fatigue of the day had brought on the attacks of sleep, and re-assured by the conduct of her guards, she presently sunk into repose.

When she awoke in the morning, she heard her guards stirring in the adjoining chamber. She arose, and looked out of the casement; a landscape presented itself to her view; a few scattered cottages appeared amongst the knots of trees that diversified the scene, and she saw that the country she looked upon was a spot perfectly new to her.

When her guide enquired at her chamber door if she was ready to set out, she immediately opened it, and came out to meet him. On entering the carriage, she requested to be allowed to remove the shutters from the windows, which was directly complied with: he who had been her constant attendant rode by the side of the carriage, and she shortly heard him addressed by the name of Sir Maurice.

Their progress was much the same as it had been on the preceding day, and their intervals for refreshment divided in nearly the same manner. The country over which they journied had, during the morning, offered some beautiful diversities of hill and dale, watered by the circling streams that ran amongst them, now glittering under the refulgence of the sun's rays, now hidden by the clustering forest; but they had passed, though not unnoticed, still unenjoyed by Rosalind.

Towards evening those verdant prospects which had hitherto decked the face of nature, began gradually to disappear. The herbage no longer vied in sparkling greenness with the emerald; but brown and withering, it appeared to conceal its meanness beneath the wide-spreading furze and bramble, which overran the earth: the road was now a heavy sand, and a slow walk the only pace at which the horses were able to drag along the carriage. Stony cliffs bounded the road on either side, and the few solitary trees which broke the uniformity of the scene were all bent in one direction, and barely clothed with a few brown and shrivelling leaves.

Rosalind remarked the change to Sir Maurice, and he replied—"We are approaching towards the sea."

The ocean was a sight entirely new to Rosalind, with which she was yet acquainted only by description; and even in her present state of anxiety, she felt something like pleasure at the idea of beholding it.—"Shall we see it?" she asked of her guide.

"It will burst upon us," he answered, "at the next turn of the road."

"Indeed!" said Rosalind—"we are not far from it then?"

"Scarcely three miles," was the reply.

The shades of night were now descending fast, and when the carriage arrived at the anticipated spot, the object from which Rosalind expected gratification was scarcely visible even to one unaccustomed to behold it; for, in the duskiness of the evening, the horizontal line was lost, and the sea appeared but a continuation of the clouds, ultimately losing themselves amongst the cliffs.

But as her eye roved over the scene, it fell suddenly upon an object, on which it rested with a kind of superstitious awe and dread: this was a building whose towers seemed mingling with the skies, and which, in the present twilight, she could only discover to be immense.

"What is that?" she asked Sir Maurice, pointing to it with her finger.

"Rockmount Castle," he replied.

She had heard the name before, but could not immediately recollect where or by whom, and echoed his words.

"Yes, Rockmount Castle," he repeated, "the mansion of Lord Rufus de Madginecourt."

"Oh God!" exclaimed Rosalind—"am I then in the power of Lord Rufus?"

"You are under his protection, lady," returned Sir Maurice.

"Oh! why am I not rather the captive of Allanrod?" continued Rosalind. "I should expect more humanity from that freebooter, than from Lord Rufus."

"It is from his savage ferocity," answered Sir Maurice, "that Lord Rufus has rescued you."

The senses of Rosalind became bewildered, as in a hurried dream. The name of Lord Rufus brought with it the remembrance of never-to-be-forgotten horrors; a thousand ideas crowded on her mind, but she could dwell on none: recollection of the past united with it bitter regret; anticipation of the future the most sickening terrors—she burst into tears, and sunk back in the carriage.

CHAPTER VIII.

> Eye me, bless'd Providence, and square my trial
> To my proportion'd strength.
>
> MILTON.

THE roaring of the waves dashing their milky foam against the foot of the rocks, roused Rosalind from the trance into which she had fallen. Just sufficient of the light of day was remaining to shew her that she was on the point of entering the lofty gateway that led to the castle; the building itself appeared equally gloomy and sublime. The numerous lights which were moving within it, and constantly passing and repassing the high and narrow casements, shewed it to be immense and dreary.

While Rosalind was lost in contemplation, the carriage entered the castle court; the open door of the building presented to her sight a spacious and lofty hall, of grey stone, thickly illumined with lamps, which cast their reflection on various trophies of highly-polished armour, that were hung upon the pillars, and formed a dazzling contrast to the gloomy scene without, where nothing was visible but the dusky rocks on one side, and the agitated bosom of the ocean on the other; each sinking under the veil of night.

A number of richly clad attendants approached to receive her; Sir Maurice handed her from the carriage, and conducted her through the hall: they ascended a flight of steps, leading to an apartment, of which the attendants who preceded them with lights threw open the door; and as Rosalind arrived at it, Sir Maurice let go her hand, and Lord Rufus advanced to receive her.

"Welcome, fairest, dearest Lady Rosalind!" he cried—"the happiest moment of my life is that in which I am enabled to afford protection to such divine excellence and beauty."

He took the hand which Sir Maurice had just quitted, and led her to a seat, placing himself by her side; the attendants retired, and they were left alone.

"My Lord," said Rosalind, addressing him in a trembling voice, as soon as she could command the power of utterance, "all that passes now before my senses appears to them as a dream. Do not, I beseech you—do not trifle with the feelings of a wretched woman; tell me, I conjure you, why I am brought hither?"

"It is my proudest boast," returned Lord Rufus, "to explain to you the cause:—you cannot, lady, require to have it repeated to you that your father's castle is fallen a prey to the Scottish freebooters, commanded by the famed Allanrod—famed for his cruelties, his oppressions, his brutal ferocity! Need I tell you what horrors, females, young, beautiful, and alluring, like yourself, have to expect from such a conquest, and from such a conqueror? Dreadful the bare idea!—too horrible for tongue is the relation! Such a fate awaited you; but Heaven, which ever guards the innocent and deserving, by a strange fate; placed it in my power to rescue you from the brutality that threatened you."

Strange appeared this information to Rosalind, and not less strange the soft accents in which Lord Rufus delivered it: but universally benevolent as were her feelings, she could not still give credit to the vaunted friendship of Lord Rufus; she could not but believe that some fraud was lurking behind in his heart.

"My Lord," she said, "the man whom I have so long considered as the cause of all my misery in life, my avowed and unfeeling persecutor, I cannot thus easily be induced to consider as influenced to serve me by any motive but a selfish one: I cannot therefore feel gratitude for your protection from Allanrod, till I have proof that it is disinterested."

"What proof can I give to convince you that I am your slave?" asked De Madginecourt.

"Convey me instantly," returned Rosalind, "to my sovereign; place me under the willing protection which she will afford me; and receive her thanks for saving one whom I dare believe dear to her."

"Wise is your request," returned Lord Rufus, "and dictated by that sense and modesty which are the ornaments of your mind."

These words he uttered in a slow and hesitating tone, his eyes averted from Rosalind as he spoke, and fixed upon the floor. The expression of his countenance was that of mingled reflection and sorrow.

Without observing him, Rosalind spoke again,—"You applaud my wish then," she said, "and consent to my proceeding immediately to the court of Queen Elizabeth?"

"Would it were in my power to give that consent!" returned Lord Rufus; "but, alas! it is not. There is a tie—a bond, subsisting between myself and Allanrod, which denies me the power of allowing you to pass these walls."

"Am I then your prisoner?" exclaimed Rosalind.

"Oh no, no, no!" replied Lord Rufus; "name not so harsh a word, I entreat you; there is no indulgence which my power does not allow me to shew you within this castle; you are therefore not its prisoner, but its queen."

"The name cannot alter the reality," answered Rosalind; "and whatever you may call me, I shall still feel myself a captive. You are endeavouring to amuse me from my purpose, like a child, with toys and promises:—if you had the power of bringing me hither, why have you not equally the power of conveying me hence?"

"You know not," returned Lord Rufus, "fair Rosalind, the strait in which I am placed—the hazard I have encountered, to save you from brutality, or you would bless the fate that has preserved you, and ask no more than the protection you enjoy. To disobey the commands of Allanrod would, after what he has given up to me, in respect to yourself, endanger my life; nay, it would endanger the life of one most nearly connected with your own—your father, lady."

"Oh! where is my father?" exclaimed Rosalind. "I implore you to tell me what you know of my father!"

"He is, and has been long," returned Lord Rufus, "a prisoner in the fortress of Allanrod: unsuccessful in his sally against the freebooters, with his vanquished men, he was conveyed to their stronghold, where he now enjoys all the comforts which captivity can give him—and those he owes to me: without my interposition, he had been the inhabitant of a dark and loathsome dungeon, where his necessities would have been so scantily supplied, as merely to give a keener edge to famine."

Rosalind shuddered at the idea, and a deep sigh escaped her lips. Lord Rufus was silent, and Rosalind, after a pause, spoke thus:—"It is strange, my Lord, that in some instances you should possess the power of turning this Allanrod from his purposes, and that in others you should appear to dread his resentment! It seems also equally strange by what means you should be thus well acquainted with the proceedings of the enemy of your country, and that you should appear so well content to live in awe of him whom you might raise a force to quell, serving at once your sovereign and yourself!"

"Oh, lady," replied De Madginecourt, "you know not what you urge; for your sake, I have disclosed to you a tie, a union, which no one but yourself knows to exist between Allanrod and me. Do not, I conjure you, by endeavouring to frustrate the counsels I give you, by an attempt to act in opposition to the conduct I mark out to you as necessary, drive to perdition the man who has rescued you from the extremity in which you stood: let it satisfy you to be assured, that your father suffers no ill treatment, though a prisoner; and that you, although restricted for a time to these walls, are still their mistress. In the name of mercy, for your own sake and mine, be guided by my advice!—none but myself can save you from Allanrod; and Allanrod is the director of De Madginecourt's fate."

"Strange, inexplicable declaration!" was on the point of bursting from the lips of Rosalind; but as Lord Rufus ceased speaking, he rose suddenly from his seat, and taking her hand, led her towards a door at the end of the apartment, which he threw open, and discovered to her view an elegant saloon splendidly illuminated; in the centre of which a repast was spread, and at its extremity in a gallery, appeared a number of musicians, who instantly awakened to sound the chords of their instruments. Lord Rufus led her to the table, and placing her at its head, he said—"Does this look like captivity, Lady Rosalind?"

Rosalind knew not whether to believe him friend or foe, and, absorbed in thought, she forbore to reply.

Her entertainer pressed her to taste the numerous delicacies of which the feast was composed; but anxiety deprived Rosalind of all power to eat. The minstrels sang, and their plaintive notes produced an oppression of spirits which drew the tears into her eyes; a sickly faintness at the same time stole over her senses, and she could scarcely support herself upon her seat.

Lord Rufus perceived her emotion, and every restorative was called in by him to animate her drooping strength—but in vain; the roses fled from her cheeks, and she fainted in his arms.

On reviving, Rosalind found herself extended on a bed, and several females surrounding her, one of whom she heard say—"Inform my Lord that the Lady Rosalind recovers."

As she moved her eyes round the chamber, she perceived that it was of the same superb order with the other apartments of the castle that she had already seen; the bed and hangings were of rich velvet, sumptuously embroidered in gold, and loaded with tassels and devices: the females who stood round her were all in a similar dress, which bespoke them attendants, and all of them young, except one, whose appearance particularly struck her from its singularity.

Under the burden of apparently a century of years, she was the very essence of alacrity, and no sense seemed defective in her but her eyes, which were assisted in their function by a pair of spectacles, of which the bows clasped down to her cheeks two locks of perfectly white hair; if she had more, it was concealed by a point-lace cap, of which the lappets hung down upon her shoulders; and this was surmounted by a large hat of black silk, with a conical top, that seemed to emulate the length and erectness of a church spire: her gown was of black silk, drawn up behind through the string of her apron, to prevent its being an impediment to her moving as quickly as the present occasion of Rosalind's illness might require: her petticoat was of rose-coloured satin, over which hung her short apron of lace, and from the string of this depended an immense bunch of keys, and a pincushion: yellow stockings of worsted, with black clocks, and a pair of embroidered shoes, with square toes and high heels, completed her dress.

This good lady had, for three successive generations, been the housekeeper and superintendant-general of the economies of the castle; she had been brought to it when a girl, and had never stirred beyond the limits of Rockmount, since her first becoming an inhabitant of it: her name was Edith, to which the title of Dame had, for the last thirty years, been added.

"See, see! the sweet lady-bird revives!" said Dame Edith, as Rosalind opened her eyes. "Oh, bless her! she is as beautiful as the Lady Helen, that the siege of Troy was fought about—Go, go away, all of you," she added, addressing the other females: "the quieter my Lady is kept, the better, after the fatigue of travelling; so I'll put her to bed myself.—You won't be ashamed of an old nurse to put you to bed, will you, my Lady? I dare say you have read that Penelope had her old nurse Euryclea."

Rosalind did not attend to the old dame's learning, but merely to the voice of tenderness in which she addressed her, and replied thankfully in the affirmative to her question, upon which the other females retired.

"The blessings of Heaven fall upon us!" said Edith—"how weak you are, sweet lady!—but you'll soon get better, now my Lord has rescued you from that brutal robber;—why, he is quite another Nero in his cruelties, I hear!"

Silence prevailed until Rosalind was undressed, and put into bed. Dame Edith then said—"Good night, sweet lady-bird; may Morpheus visit you!—and should you want any thing, only call Dame Edith, and you shall be replied to immediately from the adjoining apartment: you sleep here, lady, quite in security, like Semiramis in her bower, surrounded by your virgins, of which I am one;" and with these words the good dame departed, leaving two wax tapers burning on a table.

Rosalind knew not the hour of the night, but the castle appeared perfectly still, and no sound met her ear but the soft murmuring of the waves. Reflection, for a time, drove off repose from her pillow; but Dame Edith's wish at length prevailed, and she sunk into the arms of the God of Sleep.

CHAPTER IX.

> Smooth runs the waters where the brook is deep;
> And in his simple shew he harbours treason.
>
> SECOND PART OF HENRY VI.

Rosalind awoke early in the morning, and the same stillness prevailing as when she had fallen asleep, she justly concluded that no one was yet stirring in the castle; the tapers burnt no longer, and the light of day peeped through the curtains of her bed; busy reflection haunted her mind, and rendered her suspicious of her security in her present abode, and of the friendship of him who professed himself her deliverer from the cruelties of Allanrod. She judged that it might have been possible, and she had often believed it to have been the case, that her father had been more culpable in regard to urging the addresses of Lord Rufus, than he had himself been; and upon this belief she considered that he might desire, by his present protection, to repair to her the former injuries to which he had exposed her.

But even with this allowance for his present conduct, she felt it impossible to place immediate confidence in a man whose actions she knew to be veiled with that degree of mystery which clouded those of Lord Rufus. What but an evil one could be his tie to Allanrod, that he should fear to bring him to justice, and award to him the punishment due to his unwarranted depredations? Who could Allanrod be, that Lord Rufus should fear him? What motive could induce Allanrod, in any point, to yield to the entreaties of Lord Rufus?

Again she reflected on the strange conduct of Lord Rufus, during the time he had been an inmate of her father's castle; of his returning by moonlight to the castle, from some nightly ramble; of his still more extraordinary conversation with his page, in his bedchamber, in the dead of the night, of which she had overheard a part, and that part of a most dreadful nature, bespeaking unfair death.

Every fresh idea, as it came across her mind, tended only to render her more dissatisfied with her present situation. There was but one point of view in which it appeared tolerable, and that was, that she was delivered by it from the brutality of a ferocious freebooter, and that for the present she was safe. She arose, and went to the window of her apartment; it looked upon a garden, gaily luxuriant in every blooming flower, which was enclosed within a square formed by a part of the castle walls: this alone, and the lofty turrets which bound it on every side, were visible from her apartment.

She wandered across her chamber, and an open door into an adjoining apartment drew her eye; within it, she beheld sitting Dame Edith, with a large folio volume on a table before her, and her hands clasped as in prayer.

"Good morrow," said Rosalind—"but I fear I disturb you."

The dame did not reply, and Rosalind, concluding her at her devotions, walked away from the door, and returned to the window. In a few minutes Dame Edith tripped into the room.—"Many pardons, my sweet lady," she said, "for not answering your kind salutation just now: I hope you'll not take offence at me; but the first I address in the morning is always my Maker; for eighty years past, I have always said my prayers, and read two chapters in the Bible, as regularly as the morning came, and then I am ready to attend to my business for the rest of the day."

The family of the castle, Rosalind learnt, were all risen; but the apartments appropriated to her use were too far removed from those which were occupied by them, for her to be disturbed by their movements.

Rosalind's breakfast was prepared for her in an elegant apartment, to which she passed through two other rooms, which Edith informed her were all set apart for her use, as were an equal number on the other side of her chamber, for the domestics which were appointed to attend upon her.

When her repast was removed, Lord Rufus requested permission to visit her. He entered the apartment in the most respectful manner, and enquired, with the greatest tenderness, after her health; informed her that the garden which she had beheld from the window of her chamber was for her particular use, and that a part of the ramparts which commanded a view of the sea, had been prepared for her to walk upon at her pleasure. He particularly questioned her whether every attention had been shewn to her by Dame Edith and his domestics; urged her to inform him whether there were any means by which he could add to her happiness, or the tranquillity of her mind; and so great was the interest which he appeared to take in bestowing comfort on her, that Rosalind was half won to feel gratitude for his kindness.

In the same respectful manner, he inquired whether it would meet her inclination to join him at dinner, in the castle-hall, or whether she judged it most consonant with the delicacy of her present situation to dine alone in her own apartment? of which latter Rosalind made choice.

During the whole of the day Rosalind had been oppressed by a faintness and head-ache, which the agitation of her mind tended greatly to increase; and in the afternoon she requested Dame Edith to lead her to the garden, hoping to gain a little relief from tasting the air.—The sea-breeze was serene and refreshing, and from it alone she could derive any enjoyment, save what the many-coloured *par-*

terre, studded thickly with flowers, afforded her; for nothing could be seen from it but the sky and the surrounding walls.

As Rosalind was returning from the garden, through a hall in the castle, to her apartments, the sound of boisterous mirth drew her eye, and she beheld a youth, in an extremely rich dress, gamboling on a staircase, near the foot of which she was passing, with some females, who immediately, on seeing her, stifled their laugh, and fixed their eyes upon her.

"Who are those?" asked Rosalind of Dame Edith, when they had passed the group which had attracted her attention.

"Some of the foolish virgins, who do not put oil into their lamps," returned the dame, "wasting their time in folly and idleness, instead of laying up treasure for a rainy day; and that silly boy, Alwin (or man, I suppose he calls himself now), thinks he is a very Apollo amongst them."

"Is that the page Alwin?" said Rosalind.

"Yes, my Lady," returned Edith, "it is Alwin; and a rare job his pageship is to him, for he is as much lord of this castle as my Lord himself is."

"Indeed!" said Rosalind—"is he so great a favourite with Lord Rufus as that?"

"Heaven forbid I should question my Lord's actions!" replied the Dame,—"but I can't think what good qualities he finds in him, to set such store by him as he does; but if he asked for gold to eat, he'd have it of my Lord.—I blush to tell your Ladyship, but those girls you saw on the stairs with him are all kept to be his playfellows."

Rosalind was silent; she recollected the conversation which had passed betweens herself and Gertrude some years before, on the partiality of Lord Rufus to Alwin, and believed, as she had then done, that she was perhaps the only person who could solve the enigma.

"Are you not fond of reading, my Lady?" asked the Dame. "There is a large library in the castle, full of excellent books, which there is not above one person in the house ever enters."

"Lord Rufus, I suppose?" said Rosalind.

"Blessings on the heads of us!—No, my Lady, not he—I don't think he has been into the library these fifty years: the last time I saw him there was when I carried him in my arms into it, to shew him the illuminations in the histories of Colbrand, the Danish champion, and strong Guy, Earl of Warwick. *I am* the only reader."

"And you seem to remember well what you have read," said Rosalind, "for I have remarked your quoting many passages both from true and fabulous history."

"I hope I am not wickedly vain," went on the Dame, "but I do pride myself a little on what I have learnt by book-reading. It is now more than eighty-seven years since I have crossed the castle moat, and yet I know more than any one in it, except his Lordship, saving your Ladyship's presence, now you are here. But it is a hard thing upon me that there is not any one soul in the castle with any learning besides myself: if I mention the name of an old hero amongst them, they all stare, and grin; and if I talk of the Gods and Goddesses, they laugh right out in my face, and call me an old Bedlamite."

Rosalind could not help laughing herself.

"Hours, days, months, and years, as I may say," rejoined Dame Edith, "I have passed in that library; for it suits my taste, my Lady, far batter to read in wise books, than to converse with foolish men and women. Had Socrates been my husband, I had never behaved to him as Xantippe did."

"You shall shew me the library in the morning," said Rosalind.

The remainder of the present evening she spent alone; she felt uneasy at the conviction of such scenes of wantonness as the one she had just broken in upon, where Alwin was the principal actor, being too common in her present abode, to excite a comment, even in the apparently well-disposed Dame Edith: she also reflected, with horror, on the ascendancy which Alwin possessed over the man in whose power she now was, as she accounted for it, in her own mind, by the words which she had overheard him utter in De Mowbray Castle.—She went to bed, and passed a sleepless night.

Towards noon, on the following day, Dame Edith reminded Rosalind of the library, and she directly expressed a wish to visit it. A long vaulted corridor upon one end of which a door in the bedchamber, Rosalind opened, led to the library, which was situated at the other extremity. Dame Edith opened the door, and Rosalind entering beheld a large and lofty apartment; such parts of the wainscot as were not hidden by shelves of books, or almost illegible maps and charts, the hand of Time had turned nearly to a black; the windows were of painted glass, and the dust which had gathered upon them from neglect, lending its assistance to the paint to keep out the rays of the days, increased the gloomy and dismal appearance of the place.

"Your ladyship sees what a state it is in; you can't want to be told it is neglected," said Dame Edith, as she followed Rosalind; "every volume is an inch thick of dust: any that your Ladyship wishes to peruse must be brushed before you can touch them."

Rosalind opened several of the volumes, and found, with satisfaction, that there was here some amusement for her solitary hours. She continued some time in the library, in conversation with Dame Edith, and when she was about to leave it, and was turning towards a door for that purpose, the Dame said—"Not that way, my Lady, you are wrong; that is not the door we came in by—it is on the other side of the room: but you might easily mistake it, for the two doors are exactly alike. That door," continued she, after a short pause, "leads to a set of apartments that I have not been into for some years myself, and I believe I am the only person that has been into them at all, since she who inhabited them died."

"Who was she?" asked Rosalind, with some degree of interest.

"She was, as I may say, a Venus from the ocean," returned Dame Edith, "for she came hither by sea, and landed on the beach below the castle;—she was the wife of my Lord and master."

"The wife of Lord Rufus!" echoed Rosalind.

"Aye, my Lady," returned Edith, "for one short year, and scarcely that: her death was sudden; a malignant fever brought her to the grave, and I doubt not she went to heaven, although she was a Catholic and a Frenchwoman."

Rosalind stood wrapt in thought; words which she wished she had never heard returned to her memory, a chill stole over her blood, and she felt sick at heart.

"Will you like to see her apartments?" continued Dame Edith, opening the door which led to them.

Rosalind followed her, without speaking.

They passed through a suite of apartments, of which the fourth was a bedchamber, and beyond this an oratory, which commanded a view of the sea.

"Nothing has been moved," said Edith, "since the sad event

which so greatly affected my Lord; it is now full twenty-three years since the death of my Lady, and still he can't bear to hear her name mentioned, or to see any thing that ever belonged to her. These apartments have no communication with the rest of the castle, and nobody ever comes near them now."

"Did you attend the Lady de Madginecourt in her last illness?" asked Rosalind.

"No, my Lady," replied the Dame, "I was at that time confined to my bed with a sprain I had received in my back, by a fall I had down stairs. My Lord himself was her principal attendant; he left her neither day nor night."

Having taken a cursory view of the apartments, Rosalind returned to her own, and shortly after dismissed Edith: her thoughts were too busily engaged for her to need a companion, and they rested on the information she had just gained of Lord Rufus being a widower. Strange, that she should never have heard this before! that her father should not have mentioned it to her, when he first introduced to her Lord Rufus!—still more strange, if the circumstance had never been known to him! —Why this concealment? why this mystery with regard to his first marriage? Could it have been of his wife that he had spoken on that dreadful night, when she had overheard him in his chamber in De Mowbray Castle?—"God forbid it!" she cried, as she sunk upon her couch, and gave vent to those tears which she could not repress, although she could not explain why they flowed from her eyes.

CHAPTER X.

I could a tale unfold, whose lightest word
Would harrow up thy soul, freeze thy young blood,
Make thy two eyes, like stars, start from their spheres,
Thy knotted and combined looks to part,
And each particular hair to stand on end,
Like quills upon the fretful porcupine!

HAMLET.

On the following day Lord Rufus de Madginecourt requested to see Rosalind: her dislike to him was now again strengthened by a combination of circumstances, which she could scarcely for a moment drive from her mind; and she felt more averse than ever to beholding him: but she considered that however great her suspicions of his evil conduct, still she had *but* suspicion to rest her opinion upon, and that the certainty of her being in his power taught her, for her own sake, to act towards him with complacency: she recollected also, how often her deceased mother, in those precepts which she had been in the constant habit of giving her for the regulation of her conduct, had enjoined her, as a principal virtue, to act with every lenity of opinion towards those who shewed kindness to her; and to disregard whatever of evil the world might prattle of them.—"Remember, my child" she had frequently repeated to her, "how *many* good actions are required, in the opinion of the world, for a man to be accounted worthy by it; and on the other hand, how decidedly it stamps him a villain for one single crime. The unfair judgment of the world, it becomes the individual, whose opinion is perhaps of more consequence to him, to rectify, and to remember that it is the general tenor of a man's conduct from which his heart should be judged, not from a single action. The most depraved frequently practise a single virtue in its greatest purity; the law of universal imperfectness, which governs this sublunary world, may lead one of the purest of its inhabitants into a single crime. From no *single* action should a man's worth be rated."

She desired that he might come to her apartment, and in a few moments he appeared in it.

After the usual salutations at meeting, Lord Rufus spoke thus:—"Lady Rosalind, I am suddenly obliged to leave my castle; my absence will, I trust, be but for a few days, but I could not quit it without informing you in person of my departure."

He had himself commanded all the attendants to retire on his entering Rosalind's apartment; but once more casting his eyes around it, to be assured they were gone, he added—"I have summoned Allanrod to a meeting; for your sake I have done that, which no extremity of my own should have induced me to: when we are together, it is my intention to urge him for his permission to conduct you to the protection of the Queen: should he comply, may I rely on your not revealing to our sovereign that you are privy to the subsistence of any union between myself and the freebooter? may I rely that you will join me in saying that fate led me to the spot whither you had been dragged by the lawless Scottish freebooter, after the despoiling of your father's castle, and that fortune granted me the triumph of rescuing you from his power?"

"Shall I not, my Lord," asked Rosalind, "by joining in your fabricated tale, perhaps hereafter render myself accountable for actions in which I may be deemed an accomplice, although I have had no share in them?"

"I see your fears," answered Lord Rufus, and cannot but commend them, and the purity of your heart, which recoils, even for its own safety, at the idea of falsehood; but trust me, you have nothing to fear of the nature which you apprehend; and I hope that it will not be necessary for you to become a party in any fallacy. I have every expectation, that at my return I shall be allowed to conduct you to the presence of your sovereign, in a manner that will render any inquiry on her part into my conduct unnecessary. Let this idea cheer your spirits, and keep alive your happiness: my stay will be short—with to-morrow's dawn I shall depart, and the evening of the succeeding day will, I doubt not, mark my return to my castle. Trust me, Lady Rosalind, that I have terms to offer the freebooter in your behalf, which I think he will know his own interest too well to refuse."

Lord Rufus pressed the subject of his request no further, but immediately changed the conversation. After he had passed some time in her apartment, he said—"I must request you, Lady Rosalind, ere my departure, which will be with the dawn of day, to accompany me into the hall of my castle."

"For what purpose, my Lord?" asked Rosalind.

"For a mere matter of form," answered he, smiling, "but one under which I shall depart happier than I else could do; and then you will live here in more security of your own peace than you might do without it."

He took her hand, and she suffered him to lead her into the hall of the castle. Here she found assembled a numerous body of attendants and vassals, who appeared to be awaiting her coming: they received Lord Rufus and herself, on their entrance, with every mark of humility and respect; and Lord Rufus, leading her into the midst of them, said—"My friends and servants, I have convened you here, to request that, in my absence from my castle, ye consider her whose hand mine now clasps as your lady-mistress; that ye obey her as myself, and tend to her every duty, affection, and willing service, which ye could render to me."

The hall rang with united promises of obedience to Rosalind, from the assembled servants and vassals; and Lord Rufus bowing to them his head, in acknowledgment of their compliance with his request, reconducted Rosalind to her apartment.

The present action of Lord Rufus was not more extraordinary to Rosalind than every other part of his conduct had been, and she remarked it in silence.—Having returned with her to her apartment, he again expressed his hope that the issue of his conference with Allanrod, concerning her, might be such as it would be satisfactory to her to hear; and took his leave of her with a wish for her happiness during his absence.

How earnestly did Rosalind desire that the intention which Lord Rufus had expressed, of endeavouring to obtain the grant of Allanrod for placing her under the protection of Elizabeth might be sincere, and that good angels might smile upon its issue! She breathed a prayer to Heaven for its event, and sunk upon her pillow, more composed than she believed she could have done in the castle of Lord Rufus, since her conversation with Dame Edith in the library.

At early morn the sound of wind instruments awakened Rosalind, and Dame Edith, who was also aroused by it, informed her that it was the signal of Lord Rufus de Madginecourt's departure.—The general bustle throughout the castle appeared great, for it was the first time that any of the movements of its inhabitants had reached the ears of Rosalind. In the course of an hour the sounds began to die away, and she beheld the cavalcade which accompanied Lord Rufus descending into a valley on the heath, from one of the windows of an adjoining apartment, which overlooked the country.

It was a morning of peculiar serenity, and Rosalind, for the first time, desired Dame Edith to accompany her to that part of the rampart which Lord Rufus had informed her was prepared for her to walk on.

The glassy bosom of the ocean, reflecting the golden beams of the rising sun, and sprinkled with the white sails of passing vessels, presented to her a scene of novelty which called forth in her mind emotions unknown before, and which had the happy effect of silencing for a while the cares of her aching bosom.

After her morning repast, Rosalind repaired to the library, which Dame Edith informed her she would find in a better state than on her former visit, for she had ordered a couple of female servants to brush the books, and dust the furniture.

Rosalind took a volume, and sat down with it on one of the window-seats; Dame Edith stood at some little distance from her, with one of her favourite authors in her hand.

Rosalind had frequently requested the good Dame, when with her, to sit without restraint, which she had regularly refused to do; once more Rosalind desired her to take a seat, and Dame Edith replied—"Since you are so good as to permit me, my Lady, I will sit down to-day, and not be ashamed of my familiarity either; for to-day I think I have gained something like a right to sit in the presence of any one, saving your Ladyship's presence." She placed herself in a chair, and then continued—"And that right, my Lady, is, that I am this day one hundred years old: till that time I think it a servant's duty to stand in the presence of their superiors; at that age, I think they may have an excuse for wanting a seat, wherever they are."

Rosalind paid the Dame some compliments on her hundredth birthday, which proved gratifying to her feelings; and she told Rosalind that she had a request to make of her, which was, that she would allow her to be absent from her apartment for a few hours in the afternoon, as she had long promised a treat to her fellow-servants on her birthday; and that it would hurt her to break her word to them.

Rosalind desired her to use her time as her own, assuring her that the library was capable of affording her sufficient amusement for that day, and many more, should she so long continue an inmate of Rockmount Castle.

The volume which Rosalind had first taken up was one with the contents of which she was well acquainted, and she shortly replaced it, desiring to exchange it for one which she had not read before. As her eye roved along the shelves, a small volume, which was laid across the tops of the other books, caught her attention: she took it down, and turning to its title-page, found written on it the following sentence, in French:—

"Let those who think their own lot the most unfortunate, their own sufferings the most acute, read the following pages; and learn that a still greater wretch than themselves has existed—even she who wrote these words."

Rosalind turned the leaf, and on the other side she found written—

"The History of Eloise de la Valois, unlawfully made the wife of Lord Rufus de Madginecourt."

The book almost fell from her hands; curiosity and surprise shook her every nerve: she turned towards Dame Edith, to ascertain whether she had noticed her agitation, but her eyes were fixed on her book.

Rosalind instantly replaced the volume on the shelf, resolving to use the time of the Dame's absence in the afternoon for its perusal, and rejoicing that such an opportunity would be given her.

"Has your Ladyship done reading?" asked Edith, as Rosalind walked away from the spot where she had found the manuscript.

"For the present I think I have," replied Rosalind.

"And so have I, Lady," returned the Dame: "when I come to a grand climax, I always close my book; and I am at such a one now; I have just left Juno on her visit to Jupiter, when she was girt with the cestus of Venus; and there I shall leave her, till I have made the cakes for my treat."

"Can you read French?" asked Rosalind.

"Heaven forbid!" replied the Dame; "it might only lead me into evil reading."

Rosalind was satisfied. The manuscript she had just found was then probably a secret to all the world but herself.

CHAPTER XI.

List, list, oh list!

HAMLET.

It appears almost needless to say that Rosalind seized the first moment of Dame Edith's absence in the afternoon for returning to the library, and beginning to peruse those pages which seemed to implicate the real character of Lord Rufus de Madginecourt. Their contents were as follows:—

"Oh, may a heart of feeling peruse the lines which I now write! may it drop a tear of sympathy to my sufferings!—it will be a balm to my sad spirit, if it shall haunt the spot where my miseries were endured.

"I am the only daughter of the Marquis de la Valois; I lost my mother at an early age, and for some years my father was to me the kindest of parents, till love in my heart, and interest in his, disunited from me his affection.

"My father's marquisate was situated in the neighbourhood of La Valence, and on a small adjoining estate lived a youth named D'Altonville; whose slender possessions did not prevent me from desiring that his petition to my father for my hand might be accepted. But, alas! my father sternly repulsed his suit, and bade me think of him no more, on pain of falling under his eternal anger. How common is it for parents to issue a command against the thoughts of their children, without considering how impossible it is for those children to restrict their thoughts according to their bidding!

"After the declaration of his passion for me, D'Altonville was refused admittance to my father's house; and from the terms of intimacy on which we had before lived, as neighbours, we now saw each other no more; we had not even the opportunity of correspondence, and I was ignorant of all that related to my D'Altonville, except that I was certain his sentiments with regard to me were the same as when we had last met; he had breathed the most solemn vows of unceasing love, and judging of his heart by my own, I doubted not their truth, nor was I deceived in him.

"About six months after my father had refused to him my hand, a stranger from England, who brought with him a recommendation from our king to the hospitality of my father, arrived at our castle. This was—oh, bane of my peace! poison of my earthly happiness! the wretch, Lord Rufus de Madginecourt, within whose hated walls it is now my only consolation to commit to paper the events of my wretched life; and as I see the characters flow from my pen, it is something like happiness to me to know that the miseries already endured cannot return, and that I am so much nearer the termination of a wretched existence.

"At my first introduction to Lord Rufus, it was my misfortune to please him: my person was handsome, and this is all he is capable of valuing in woman. My father heard his sentiments of me with unfeigned pleasure: his high rank, and great wealth in England, were well known to him; and he now doubly applauded himself for having broken off my acquaintance with the less wealthy, but more worthy D'Altonville.

"In less than a week after the arrival of Lord Rufus, my father informed me that he had done me the honour of asking my hand in marriage, and that I was destined to become his wife.

"I fell on my knees before him, and besought him not to sacrifice me to a man who, though almost a stranger to me, I was well convinced that no length of time could induce me to love; rather than marry him, I entreated to be immured within a convent's walls, where I declared myself prepared to make a vow of retirement for ever from the world.

"He pretended to smile at what he called the frenzy of a girl's disappointment in her first love, and told me that in a few years' time I should return him thanks for the excellent choice he had made for me, and rejoice that the beggar D'Altonville was not my husband.—'Besides,' added he, 'your D'Altonville is by this time probably no more, for he has joined the naval force which our king has just sent out against Spain, and it is rumoured that a bloody engagement has taken place;' and with this humane information he left me.

"I was still on my knees, and breathing a fervent prayer for the safety of him I loved; I concluded it with a wish that if his soul had fled from earth, mine might be called to follow it.

"Wretched beyond description, I continued for two days alone in my chamber; in the evening of the third, my father came to me, and exerted his parental authority to compel me to dress myself, and join a party which I found he had invited to a dance that night, in honour of Lord Rufus.

"Constrained to obey, I dressed myself and went down; to my astonishment, I found that the festivities of the night were to be held in the air, and that the gardens were illuminated for that purpose. I entered them: various groups of dancers in the dresses of shepherds, shepherdesses, and other fantastic characters, met my eyes; and Lord Rufus, the gayest of the festive crowd, came directly to me to claim my hand as his own. Heart-rending congratulations on my approaching marriage were poured into my ear from every tongue.

"The music, and various sounds of mirth which filled the gardens, almost maddened me; and with the first opportunity I retired into a corner, where I burst into tears. The only individual who observed my retreat was a person in the garb of an old shepherd, whose grey hairs and grizly beard almost concealed his countenance: I saw him pass two or three times before the arbour where I sat; at length he spoke.—'Eloise, do you not know me?' he said. It was the voice of D'Altonville.

'Good Heavens!' I exclaimed,— 'are you here?'

'Yes,' returned he; ' but to-morrow I depart. I am thankful that I have found this opportunity for bidding you farewell. Angels guard you, and make you blest and happy!' he cried, pressing me to his breast—'we may perhaps never meet again!'

'Are you then going to join the fleet?' I asked, in trembling accents.

'My destiny has reached you,' he said. 'Yes, Eloise, I cannot be happy here; and it is immaterial to me whither I fly to seek death, since peace in life is denied me.'

"Again he clasped me to his breast; footsteps approached the spot where we were standing. 'Farewell for ever!' he exclaimed, and darted amongst the trees.

'Stay, stay, I entreat you!' I cried. More I could not utter, ere I sunk fainting to the earth: when I revived, I found myself supported in the hated arms of Lord Rufus; a faint shriek escaped my lips—my father stood by me, and his presence awed me from further expressing my sensations of horror.

"When the festivities of the night were over, and I was permitted to retire to my chamber, I did not attempt to enter my bed, but sat deliberating with my own mind how it would be possible for me to act, in order to prove the 'farewell for ever,' of D'Altonville fallacious.

"On the morrow he had said he was to depart; the midnight hour had sounded, and that morrow was already come—already he might be some leagues proceeded on his journey towards the sea; a few more hours might indeed render his parting address prophetic;

the thought was frenzy—intolerable even in idea, and I resolved immediately to follow his steps.

"The point of greatest difficulty was how to escape unobserved from my father's house; disguise I had none, nor had I any hope of procuring one where I now was: I had no friends in the house who would not be overawed from lending assistance to me, by their dread of my father's resentment, if they were discovered in it. I had, accordingly, nothing to depend upon but the smiles of fortune, in suffering me to depart undetected; and judging that no time could be more favourable to my design than the present, at which all the inhabitants of the castle were wrapt in sleep, after the fatigues of the preceding night, I lost no time in dressing myself as plainly as my wardrobe would permit; and taking with me nothing but a small sum of money, of which I was possessed, I boldly sallied forth into the garden, from which a private door opened upon the high road.

"In reaching this, fate smiled on me, and I left my father's territories without a sigh of regret: I lost not a moment in gaining ground on my journey, while I considered my departure as yet unknown. I passed near the small estate which had been rented by D'Altonville, but for many reasons I judged it most prudent not to stop an instant longer than necessary within view of it, although my heart panted to inquire whether its master was yet set out on his journey.

"I knew that the fleet destined against Spain was to sail from Toulon; from this place my father's residence was deemed only a journey of three days; thus I doubted not but the energy of my mind in the pursuit I was bent on, would support me in strength and spirits for the time I should require them to bear me to the spot of my destination.

"About an hour after sunrise, I arrived at a small town, which I judged to be five leagues from the spot from whence I had begun my walk; I felt myself already extremely weary, and still more subdued with the agitation of my spirits than fatigue of body: I dreaded to enter any house of public refreshment, lest I should be pursued, as such houses would naturally be the first where I should be sought; I therefore stopped at the door of a mean cottage, of whose inhabitants, an old man and his daughter, I requested a basin of milk, promising to reward them for their kindness, if they would comply with my request.

"The daughter readily tendered me every service in her power: the old man I found to be blind, and this was some relief to my mind, as the old are more suspicious, and inspire us with greater dread, when we are acting under any deceit, than those of our own years. In the course of my meal, I informed the girl that I had a brother on board the fleet, whom I had an earnest desire once more to see before he should sail, and that I was for that purpose travelling towards Toulon. I had been travelling some time, I added, and was not only very weary with my journey on foot, but also extremely fearful that he might have sailed before I should reach the place; on both which accounts, I wished to procure some conveyance forwards, if it were but for a part of my journey.

"She informed me, that if I turned aside to the right, about a league and a half from the road I was in, I should come into the high road from Paris to Toulon, and that upon it I should find numerous conveyances proceeding with the seamen to the port of embarkation. 'But surely,' added she, 'though the method is easy, it is both hazardous and disagreeable, as you will be the only woman amongst them, to join so large a company of men as you will meet with.'

'That,' said I, 'alarms me, I confess, and I wish very much I could procure a disguise for my sex: could you contrive to get me one, I would willingly reward you for your trouble, and feel more grateful to you than I can express.'

'There is nothing to be procured in our town,' she replied; 'if you thought you should soon be back this way, I would, with all my heart, lend you my brother's Sunday clothes; he is younger than you, and I think they would fit you.'

"I told her, if she would accommodate me with them, I would leave her the value of them, and my own clothes into the bargain, as a surety of my returning them. She readily and unsuspiciously assisted me to equip myself; and when I was attired, I set forward to cross the forest which she had said would bring me into the high road from Paris to Toulon.

"About noon I reached a small village; at the entrance into it I perceived two vehicles standing before a house, at the door of which sat some sailors; and from this circumstance I directly concluded that it was one of the places of refreshment for the seamen on their journey to the fleet. I accosted them, and found my conjectures to be just. 'Will you,' said I, 'have the charity to admit me into your party? I have run away from a cruel master, and have no resource against famine but entering on board the fleet.'

"They pitied me, and readily agreed to my petition. I thanked them from my heart, and directly begged leave to get into the vehicle, where a seat appeared to me at that moment the most enviable treasure in the world. They brought me refreshments, both of meat and drink; but I durst not offer to pay any part of my own expences, lest I should draw suspicion on myself for being possessed of money, after the story I had told of my unfortunate case.

"I inquired of them whether I should be allowed, on my arrival at the port, to enter on board any ship I pleased; for that a kind lady, who knew my situation, had instructed me to make use of her name as a recommendation to an officer on board the fleet, of the name of D'Altonville, and that I should like to sail in the same ship with him.

"To this they could give me no satisfactory answer, but said that the point would be easily ascertained when we arrived at the post, which would be in little more than two days.

"Towards the evening of the second day, we saw before us a carriage of a superior order to those in which I and my companions were journeying, which had broken down on the road. When we came up to it, our driver stopped to offer assistance to the passengers, and one of the first countenances which I beheld amongst those who had alighted from it in consequence of the fracture was—blessed chance! D'Altonville himself!

"This occurrence took place in the dusk of the evening, and as I had resolved not to let myself be recognized by D'Altonville, if I could possibly prevent it, till the fleet should have sailed, lest he should find means of preventing me from embarking, for my safety's sake, I judged this a favourable opportunity for speaking to him; I accordingly said—'Pray can any of you gentlemen inform me where I may be likely to find an officer of the name of D'Altonville, when I reach the port?'

'That is my name, boy,' he instantly replied.

'Is it, sir?' I said: 'then I hope you will be a friend to me, and get me a situation on board your ship.'

'On what pretensions do you ground this hope?' asked he—'who are you?'

'I am a poor boy, an orphan,' I answered, 'without any other means of gaining my subsistence; and my hope of your kindness is founded on the promise of a good lady, who bade me address you in her name.'

'Indeed!' said he—'who is she?'

'The Lady Eloise de la Valois,' I returned, 'who said she was sure you would be kind to me, if I mentioned it to you as her wish that you should be so.'

"He sighed, and said—'Whatever she desires, it is a happiness to me to perform—depend on my protection.'

"He then directed me on board what ship to find him on my arrival at the port, and gave me a paper signed with his name, which he told me would prove a passport for my admission on board, should he be absent from his ship at the time I went to make my demand.

"My mind was now comparatively at ease, and I dropped a silent tear of gratitude to the kindness of my fate.

"The carriage in which D'Altonville was journeying was in a short time repaired, and then set forward again with much greater speed than that in which I was a passenger was able to travel; I thus quickly again lost sight of the only man whom the earth possessed of value to me.

"On our arrival at Toulon, we learnt that an unexpected order had been received by the fleet to leave the port; and that twelve hours only were allowed them for preparing to sail.

"D'Altonville was himself on board his ship when I went to it; but the hurry of the time so much engrossed his mind, that he paid no further attention to me than to appoint me to my station, which was that of a cabin-boy, to serve him—a task which I, with rapture, heard assigned to me, on account of the frequent opportunities it would give me of seeing him, and being near his person.

"I found that I was one more than the ship had been intended to contain, but admitted to the number of the crew, merely on account of the fabricated message I had delivered to its captain from her he loved; and on this account, as there was no hammock for me, a small cot, made up in one corner of the captain's cabin, was appointed for my sleeping-place.

"It was about nine in the morning when I reached the port, and three of the twelve hours allowed for preparing the fleet to sail were already elapsed: thus about six in the evening, the whole of the French squadron was under weigh. Throughout the day, D'Altonville had been too busily employed in giving instructions to his men, and receiving on board the stores necessary for his voyage, to suffer his attention to rest for above a minute at a time upon me; and when it did so, I always turned aside from him my features, or managed to conceal them beneath the face-piece of my cap; still dreading that a discovery of who I was might frustrate my darling scheme of living or dying with the man of my heart.

"With the object of our sailing I was unacquainted, except that the general voice informed me it was to the annoyance of Spain; but how or in what manner that was intended to be effected, I neither learnt, nor did I feel a wish to know: one idea, and that alone, occupied my whole soul.

"When I was informed that my attendance for the night could be dispensed with, and that I might retire to my cot, how fearful, yet how pleasurable, were the feelings of my heart! Possessed I seemed of every earthly bliss, in being the partner of my D'Altonville's fate—blessed beyond the power of fate to torture me, in the certain knowledge that in one fortune the lives of us both were involved: but then, might not D'Altonville upbraid me for the excess of my love, in having so far forgotten the softness of my sex, the effeminacy of my education, as to have endangered my morals, my peace, in a society so little adapted to the delicate tenderness in which every hour of my past life had been nursed? might he not judge that my presence would lead him into difficulties, involve him in situations of hazard, which had not been known to him had I been absent, and render him perhaps a coward in the hour of battle, when his own natural spirit might, without my presence, stamp him the hero of the fight?

"I shuddered at the idea; the tears forced themselves into my eyes, and lifting my clasped hands to Heaven, I fervently prayed that my presence might not prove a bane to the sight of him, for whom, and whose love, life appeared to me of little value. My fears almost subdued my spirit; a new and inexpressible feeling rendered me alarmed at the thought of beholding him for whom I had sacrificed all again to see and to be near, and I resolved not to let him know me, if it were possible to conceal the secret from him, but to rest satisfied that I was the witness of his fate.

"An hourglass stood upon a table in the cabin, and by its side burnt a lamp. By the darkness of the night, I conjectured it to be about ten o'clock, when I was dismissed from the deck to my cot, and according to this calculation, the running sand pronounced it near two in the morning, ere the fall of footsteps announced the approach of D'Altonville.

"I had only thrown myself upon my bed, without undressing, and upon his coming, I turned my face downwards, to avoid meeting his eyes, and experienced a sensation doubtless new to every bosom but my own.

"D'Altonville entered with a slow step: after a momentary pause, and turning the wasting sand, he threw his hat upon the ground, and let himself fall upon his bed: at first I conjectured him overpowered with the fatigues of the day, and thought that he had sunk hastily to sleep; but a short time convinced me of the contrary. He turned frequently upon the bed, clasped his hands in the wildness of frenzy, struck them frequently upon his forehead, and during all these actions of a disturbed mind, he held converse with himself, and many a long-drawn sigh, laden with my name, escaped his lips.

"My breathings probably informed him that I was no more asleep than himself, for after a short interval, he addressed me with—'What is your name, my lad?'

'Albert, sir,' I replied.

'How long have you been known to the Lady Eloise de la Valois?'

'Ever since I can remember myself,' I returned.

'And you esteem her?' he went on.

'And love her,' I rejoined, 'as tenderly as I do myself.'

"He sighed.—'What drives you from your home and country?' he inquired.

'Love,' I falteringly replied.

'Indeed!' said he; 'you are very young, to feel it thus acutely, and I pity you the more on account of your youth, for it is a passion which but too often holds war with reason, and your youth must therefore render you less able to struggle against its attacks. I well know myself what is the power of love.'

'And is your love, sir,' asked I—'pardon the question—at variance with reason?'

'You cannot ask that question seriously, I am sure,' he replied; 'as you have known Eloise from her infancy, you cannot but know the mutual attachment which long has, and I trust, ever will subsist between us; and you cannot but know also, that it was founded on every pretension that can render love worthy of applause.'

"He turned hastily on his bed, as he pronounced these words, and the emotions of his soul were too audible to admit a doubt of his sufferings. A long silence ensued: I durst not venture to break it. At last he spoke.—'I have,' he said, 'prepared my mind to meet death in the engagement which we have daily to expect; and all the anxiety I now feel proceeds from my fear that the apathy with which disappointment oppresses my soul will make me appear a coward in the fight. Oh that it were possible that the countenance of my Eloise could shine upon me at that moment! her smile would arouse in my mind the sensations of a hero, and I should then die a death of glory and honour, becoming the man who had sought and possessed her love.'

"This was an exclamation not to be passed over.—'Oh, D'Altonville!' I cried, 'be blest in the accomplishment of your wish—the countenance of your Eloise shall shine upon you in the battle's heat; her smile shall be the excitement of your heroism; her form shall be your shield against death, and her prayers preserve you for a life of glory and honour!'

"I had pronounced these words in my own natural voice, without the disguise under which I had concealed its real tones, whilst I had desired to remain unknown to him; and starting wildly up, he exclaimed—'Almighty God! do you mock me, or is it—is it indeed my Eloise who speaks?'

'It is, indeed, she who now addresses you,' I said, in reply. 'what reception will she meet for her temerity in following your fortunes?'

"He sunk on his knees before me, and pressing my hand to his lips—'Exalted paragon of thy sex's constancy and truth,' he exclaimed, 'what reward, what recompence, can one honoured like myself dare to offer in return for such heroism of affection? My hand, my heart are all I *have* to offer: long have those been your own; and witness for me, Heaven, while yet I kneel in adoration of your constancy, that none but yourself, either in your life or death, shall ever possess them.'

"Oh what an hour of bliss was this! too exquisite to be permanent, and so richly laden with happiness as to be the certain forerunner of misery as acute. It was one of the last happy moments I was doomed to enjoy on earth; in heaven it may yet be reserved for me, as my recompense for all the woes that have been heaped upon my unoffending head, again to meet my D'Altonville in scenes of purer bliss—in scenes where the tempestuous passions of the heart have no influence, and the more refined feelings of the mind yield happiness in its state of utmost purity.

"A short interval of silence restored a calm to the feelings of D'Altonville, and he then began to express his dread of the perils to which I had exposed myself, in becoming the partner of his voyage.

"After the confession I had already made of my heart, and the steps I had taken, any concealment would have been folly: I therefore assured him, and I spoke the truth, that in his presence I could brave any danger which I might be fated to encounter; and told him that the only thing which could render me otherwise than satisfied with my present situation, would be to see him unhappy in his fears on my account.

"He received my acknowledgment with the utmost delicacy as well as gratitude; he instantly insisted on giving up to me the cabin appropriated for his own use; assuring me that he could easily procure a bed in another part of the ship; and with this assurance he directly left me, saying that I must greatly require rest, after the fatigue of body and mind I had been undergoing for the last few days; and having directed me how to fasten myself within the cabin, where he told me I might lie down to repose with the utmost security of no interruption being offered me, he retired.

"His conjectures were just, for my strength was greatly exhausted by my journey; and notwithstanding the novelty of my situation, I soon closed my eyes in sleep.

"The two succeeding days I passed entirely in D'Altonville's cabin, in a calmness of mind to which I had long been a stranger:

he visited me at such intervals as his presence on deck could be dispensed with; and the delicate conduct which he observed towards me rendered me more than ever convinced that he merited from me the step I had taken for his happiness and my own.

"On the evening of the third day intelligence was brought by a frigate which had been sailing somewhat in advance of the ship we were on board of, that the enemy's fleet was bearing down upon us.

"D'Altonville brought me information of these tidings; he besought me to keep my spirits as calm as possible during the scene I was constrained to pass through, and conveyed me to a part of the ship beneath the surface of the water, where, almost in total darkness, the sounds of hurried preparations over my head, and on each side of me, distinctly reached me.

"One hasty embrace was all that his call to duty allowed him.—'The God of battles shield thee, my D'Altonville!' I exclaimed, and he disappeared from my sight.

"In less than an hour the cannon began to send forth their dreadful thunder. How terrible were the sounds! Each explosion my hurried imagination fancied might have borne with it the *fiat* of D'Altonville's existence. My fears worked on my senses, till every nerve became fixed in dread, and my brain swam in a chaos of sensations which almost maddened me. My senses were recalled to their functions by the shrieks and groans of the wounded, who were bringing down from the scene of action into a part of the ship which was only divided by a slight partition from the spot where I was placed.

"Unspeakable were the horrors which assailed my ears—dreadful were the groans of the dying! still more piteous were the shrieks of those whose wounds compelled them to seek the preservation of life from the amputating knife of the surgeon.

"The thunder of war still roared with unabated violence, and to complete the sum of my terrors, the flickering lamp which had hitherto afforded me the slender consolation of light, in my awful solitude, now died away in its socket; and by leaving me the exercise of only one sense, rendered me more capable of distinguishing all the wretched sounds that were passing around me.

"About nine in the evening, as nearly as I could guess the hour, the cannons suddenly ceased to roar, and in a few minutes D'Altonville appeared, to conduct me from my confinement.—'Thank God, he lives!' I exclaimed—'I am blessed!' Little did I foresee, at the moment of this exclamation, how short might yet be the life of him I adored!—little did I suspect that the darkness of the evening had put a stop to the engagement, and that it was to be renewed with fresh vigour at the break of the succeeding day!

"I know not whether the moments of suspense which intervened between this hour and the morning were not more dreadful than those of the actual fight.

"D'Altonville was slightly wounded in the arm, but his mental anxiety for the event of the contest rendered him almost insensible to bodily pain; his spirits wanted both refreshment and strength. I pressed him to eat; prepared for him an invigorating beverage; and after I had induced him to swallow it, I urged him to seek the repose of a few hours sleep. Nature was greatly exhausted in him; he sunk at my feet, and let his head fall into my lap: his slumbers never lasted above five minutes together, and then they were broken by starts and involuntary exclamations to his crew.

"At length the twilight began to penetrate through the windows of the cabin, and the dreadful signal gun for all to meet on deck was fired. D'Altonville again led me to my retreat from danger: in our way thither, I ventured to enquire of him whether he believed the French would gain the victory? He did believe it, he answered me. 'The hand of God be stretched out to them!' I cried.

"As he closed the door upon me, I sunk, exhausted by the violent emotions of my mind, upon the ground, and anticipating a repetition of the horrors which had before assailed me on this spot. Had my senses been awake to any idea but the danger of him I loved, I might justly have apostrophized to the all-powerfulness of love, which had driven me to the present crisis of my fate.

"Yet, oh reader of this my fate, whoever thou art, if thy gentle nature already bleeds for my sufferings, already leads thee to exclaim—'Is she thus punished for flying a cruel father and a hated lover, for the arms of whom reason and whom every virtuous principle taught her to adore?'—oh, do thou read no further of my wretched story! What I have yet to relate of my destiny will sink what I have already unfolded to thee, in the scale of comparison, till thou wilt forget that these were sufferings at all. I warn thee, and proceed. Yet grant me one word more of digression; nor, as thou readest it, judge that a wretch like me can advance aught from vanity—oh no! all the unhappy speak is truth: affliction wears out all the subtlety of human nature, and leaves the feelings too much weakened for the practice of hypocrisy. Believe then that amidst the many sufferings of my life, I have never yet doubted the justice of the God who permitted their infliction; that I have never ceased to doubt that some future recompence will await my many trials; that the veil which at present separates me from penetrating the wisdom of their infliction, will, at some future day, be withdrawn from my eyes, and that I shall then bless the cause to which I now bend. True it is, that I have wept over my sorrows; it is allowed a woman's privilege; and it is a relief no sufferer need blush at; it is a balm with which sorrow soothes itself, by Nature's law, by which Providence unburdens the heart of grief, when man would choak it with a load of agony, to swell and break it.

"Again the struggle of the war raged with its bloodiest fury, and the dreadful sounds which pierced my ears exceeded even those of the foregoing evening; every moment I believed too much laden with horror for the next to equal it in the power of communicating terror to the senses; but each outweighed the last in shrieks, confusion, and thunder.

"Thus elapsed three hours, at the expiration of which sounds of a different nature succeeded to those I had before heard; running to and fro upon the deck, and a confusion of French and Spanish voices, were all that I could now distinguish, for the cannon had for some minutes ceased to fill the air with their vibrations.

"The intelligence of our fate soon reached me; the Spaniards were victorious, and we were boarded by the crew of an enemy's ship, who were come to secure us prisoners. With all possible expedition, we were conveyed from our own ship into theirs; our own had been much injured in the action, beyond the power of preventing her from sinking; and the utmost celerity was necessary to save the crew from going down with her.

"The Spanish vessel on board of which we were taken was a first-rate ship of war; but the damage she had received in the engagement was so considerable, as to render her wholly incompetent to sailing at an equal rate with the rest of the victorious fleet, indeed she could scarcely sail at all; only one of her masts was left standing, and the small quantity of canvas this was capable of bearing rendered her progress scarcely perceptible.

"The captain of the Spanish ship we found to be a man of a humane and friendly disposition, who did not wish to make his prisoners feel the rigours of captivity, while he had it in his power to lighten to them the misery of their fate. D'Altonville and myself were kindly invited by him to his cabin and table: he looked upon me with surprise; the unusualness of a female in a situation similar to mine, made him inquisitive on the singularity of the adventure; and D'Altonville, believing him a man of honour, entrusted to him the secret of my case.

"He was the man of honour which my lover believed him, and his kindness to us was redoubled as he became acquainted with the peculiarity of our fortunes.

"The shattered situation of our ship rendered her extremely unruly, and we were tossed about for several days on the ocean, without making any advance of consequence towards the Spanish port. The captain said he conjectured that his admiral must have concluded his ship to have sunk, by the distant situation which her disabled state had obliged her to maintain from the rest of the fleet, or he undoubtedly would have sent a frigate to her assistance.

"We were five days at sea in the situation I have just described, and the captain entertained hopes of making the desired port in two days more, when a vessel was descried bearing down upon us, which proved to be an Algerine corsair: the alarm occasioned by this sight was immediately conveyed to every individual on board, and with one emotion, we all ran upon deck. When the Algerine was arrived within gunshot of our ship, she fired upon us: we directly struck our colours, which was an act of necessity on the part of our captain, as he had not a single charge of powder left; his whole stock having been exhausted in the fatal engagement which had made us his prisoners.

"The Algerines now sailed boldly up, and immediately boarded us. I fancied their appearance more horrid than that of any men I had yet beheld, and my heart sunk within me. If such were my feelings at the bare sight of these new directors of the unhappy fate of D'Altonville and myself, what must they have been when I saw him, in common with all his fellow-captives, French and Spanish (for the conquerors of the last hour were now sunk to an equality with the vanquished), loaded with chains, and secured from rescuing the vessel from the hands of her new possessors. I alone, on account of my sex, was spared the galling chain, and conveyed to a separate cabin, where my savage keepers confined me far away from my D'Altonville, heedless of my tears, my shrieks, my prayers, to breathe my last sigh in the arms of my beloved. My strength was at that moment so dreadfully exhausted, that I believed the last hour of my existence to be fast approaching; but I lived to experience how capable was my nature of sustaining still greater struggles with misfortune.

"The terrific ideas which I had formed of the treatment I should be doomed to undergo from the Algerines was, happily, not verified; they behaved towards me with kindness, placed before me luxuries both of wine and viands, at which my sick heart palled; and what was infinitely more acceptable to me, as I was not permitted to see my D'Altonville, they left me almost continually to solitude.

"After a voyage of nearly a week, during which my imagination had been harrowed up with the miseries which it had pictured to me that both my D'Altonville and myself would be doomed to encounter, we arrived at Algiers.

"On our landing, I saw not my D'Altonville, except that I perceived a vast number of captives leading along the shore, and conjectured him to be one amongst them. Every care and attention was shewn to me on my leaving the vessel; and I was conducted to a magnificent palace, which I understood to be a seraglio belonging to the Dey, and that I was a present to him from the captain of the corsair.

"Wretched, it may easily be conceived, was my fate; I sat, heartbroken, in the midst of splendour, and regarded the costly habiliments which were put upon my person as tacit mockers of the misery I was enduring. The females with whom I had intercourse expressed surprise that I did not rejoice at the honour, as they called it, which had fallen upon me: most of them had, I found, been educated in ideas favourable to the easy mode of providing for their daughters, which their parents had taken advantage of, in placing them under the roof of the Dey; and they could not be brought to comprehend the feelings of one whose affections were placed on an object to whom any sensation but that of grandeur had led her heart, and appeared wholly unacquainted with the criminality which I dreaded every hour to be forced into.

"Earnestly did I wish to see the Dey. I thought it possible that my grief might penetrate his heart, and that he might, at least, for my sake, ameliorate the fate of D'Altonville, if he would not spare me the hated honour of his favour; and I expressed my wish to obtain an interview with him.

"This desire my female associates construed into my eagerness for an opportunity of trying the effect of my charms on him; and, stung by envy and jealousy, the only passions of which their minds appeared to be capable, they told me that I might lay aside my hopes, for that the Dey had for two years been constant to a beautiful slave, whom he yet passionately loved; and that, if he were to forsake her, they believed that many in the seraglio had claims on his heart, that would, for as many years longer at least, keep it from feeling that power of which I seemed to believe my person possessed.

"I heard their reply in silence: it would have been impossible to have convinced them that for myself I considered their information the happiest that ever fell from tongue. For D'Altonville's sake, I still secretly wished that I could have seen the Dey, although I felt, at the same moment, persuaded that any interference of mine would be without avail. Alas! what could my insignificant voice have effected with him? He was, doubtless, too happy himself to have leisure for the cries of grief to enter his soul; perhaps too fearful of the power of his transient joys to continue their charm over his senses, to hazard the listening to any sound that might whisper to his heart—'Canst thou laugh alone, when all who make thee blest are weeping around thee?'

"How many exist, who dare not look into the causes of their pleasure, and who possess the power of swelling their joy into heavenly ecstacy, would they but assume the courage to investigate its source, and to resolve that the rose which perfumes their senses with delight should pierce no other hearts with its cancerous thorn!

"Not the slightest intelligence could I gain of D'Altonville, either from my female companions or the eunuchs who attended on me; and I could not even gather from their replies to my inquiries, whether they were ignorant of him and his fate, or concealed their knowledge from me; it was most probable, I judged, that they were wholly unacquainted with his name.

"I must now pursue the story of D'Altonville, rather than my own, as it more fully explains the progress of our fate during our captivity in Algiers.

"D'Altonville and his fellow-captives, on being taken out of the ship, were led, chained in pairs, to a large square in the city, where a public market for slaves was held; himself, the Spanish captain, and six others, were bought by the superintendant of the Dey's gardens, and appointed to work in those which ran under the northern side of the seraglio. Within these walls, D'Altonville had found means of learning that I was held a captive, though all access to me, even by message or letter, was denied him; and it was some slight alleviation of the hardships of his toil, that he beheld the roof which sheltered me: my apartments were on the opposite side of the building to that which overlooked the gardens he was employed in; but of this he was ignorant; and often did he incur the anger of the taskmaster, for desisting from his labour, to fix his eyes on the lattices of the seraglio, in the vain hope of seeing me appear at one of them.

"One day, nearly three months after the commencement of his captivity, as he was reclined, at noon-tide, by the foot of a tree, beneath the boughs of which he sought shelter from the meridian rays of a powerful sun, his frame being equally exhausted by mental and bodily fatigue, a shrill whistle, which seemed to issue from one of the windows of the seraglio, drew his attention; and as he raised his eyes to the spot from whence he believed it to proceed, a small white parcel, which he perceived flying through the air with great velocity, caught his eyes: it fell near his feet; he picked it up, and found it superscribed—'For the French slave.'

"He opened it: it contained a jewel of value, set in a ring. On the paper were these words:—

'By your voice, which I accidentally overheard, I find you are my countryman. I am grieved to see you in your present humiliating situation, as there is something in your mien which informs me that you were not born to endure hardships: the melancholy air of your countenance has sunk into my heart. If you will be to-night, at eleven, in the arbour between the two date-trees, perhaps you may hear of comfort.

'Farewell! Believe me one sincere in her professions.'

"Having twice perused this extraordinary note, he shewed it to his friend, the Spanish captain (for captivity had firmly bound them in the ties of amity), and asked of him his opinion how he should act under it. His friend recommended him, by all means, to comply with the invitation contained in it: his situation, he remarked, could not be worse than it at present was; and on this consideration, as in the case of a drowning man who seizes at a rush for support, he would be wrong not to place himself in the way of any chance which might ameliorate his condition.

"In opposition to this advice, D'Altonville urged that the invitation wore the appearance of an invitation to love; that his heart, placed irrevocably on me, was callous to the witchery of any sigh which might be breathed to him as a lure to passion; and that, with his heart thus steeled against the practice of that softness which might alone be calculated to gain him favour with her who had just written to him, he judged it better to avoid her presence, lest her coldness at their interview, if her intentions were directed to his heart, should provoke her to seek revenge, for his not throwing himself immediately at her feet.

"To this the Spaniard replied, that if such were the temper of the writer, she might be as likely to revenge the slight shewn her in neglecting to keep her appointment, and that it was undoubtedly better to risk the termination of the adventure, than to incur an equal hazard, without having sought the opportunity of receiving a benefit.

"Over-ruled by the arguments of his friend, D'Altonville resolved to be in the arbour at the appointed time.—The walls of the garden were too high for the idea of effecting an escape over them to be for a moment entertained by any of the slaves; they were therefore left to the liberty of perambulating the gardens at any hour of the day or night. The mean huts where they lodged were situated in a remote corner of these gardens, and sheltered from observation by knots of luxuriant shrubs.

"D'Altonville arrived first at the arbour; the night was one of those in which a refulgent moon shines upon the world, scarcely inferior in brilliancy to the orb from which she receives her splendour; and by the force of contrasted shade, leaves various dark nooks upon the earth, directed, as it were, to the very purpose of concealment. In one of these stood the arbour mentioned in the letter of the unknown; and here, according to the appointment of the writer, he placed himself. The path leading to it lay immediately exposed to the light of the silver planet, and he awaited, with a degree of anxiety, the appearance of an expected, but undefined form, coming to seek him in his retreat.

"The path was strait and long, and at its extremity he presently discerned a moving body, which, on its nearer approach, he discovered to be one of the mutes of the seraglio. He entered the arbour, and signifying to D'Altonville that he was the person he was in quest of, he untied a bundle, containing a suit of apparel similar to that worn by himself, and directed D'Altonville to strip off his own garments, and put on those he had brought him. D'Altonville had proceeded too far in the adventure not to pursue it boldly, thus easily complied with the instructions of the mute, who hid D'Altonville's clothes under a bush on one side of the arbour, and then beckoned to him to follow him.

'Oh that it were to my Eloise,' mentally exclaimed D'Altonville, 'that thou wert about to conduct me! May the God of mercy, who directs the finger of fate, grant that my present compliance may place in my power the means of rescuing her from the oppression she now groans under!' and with this silent prayer he followed the steps of the slave.

"His conductor traversed an angle of the garden, and arriving at a small door in the wall of the seraglio, he entered it, and invited D'Altonville to do the same.

"They passed on through a long passage, which led to the foot of a handsome staircase; this they ascended, and entered a gallery of lofty dimensions and rich workmanship: at a door on one side of this gallery the mute stopped—D'Altonville did the same. The mute motioned to him to make no noise—D'Altonville obeyed. The mute hit the door twice with his knuckles, in a manner that gave his action the appearance of a signal agreed upon between him and some person within the apartment: the lock was immediately heard to move in its wards; the mute pushed open the door, and by his signs directed D'Altonville to enter. He did so, and the mute following him in, closed the door, and pointing to him to pass through an arch to the right, disappeared hastily himself through another which corresponded with it on the left.

D'Altonville proceeded according to his instructions; and penetrating the arch which had been pointed out to him, he perceived a beautiful female reclining on a couch, amidst all the voluptuousness which an eastern monarch's favourite could command, and with a smile of countenance, happy as the most satisfied votary of pleasure could be dressed in.

"The fair form which D'Altonville now, for the first time, beheld, was named Clotilda; she was the natural daughter of a French nobleman; and having been left, by the death of her father, dependant on an uncle of a dissolute and mercenary disposition, had been sold by him to the providers of beauty for the seraglio of the Dey. Born of a woman whose immorality had raised her to the only notice and consequence which she had ever obtained in the world, Clotilda had inherited, both by birth and precept, ideas which had rendered her a fit inmate for the walls she now resided in; and her arts and beauty combined, had gained her so great an ascendency over her master and lover, the Dey, that no woman had ever been known to sway his inclinations in the manner she possessed the power of doing:—Clotilda was, in fact, the female whom my companions had informed me had for the two last years fixed the heart of the Dey solely on herself.

"The pride of Clotilda was indeed gratified by the chains in which she alone held him for whom all hearts panted; but her passions had no share in the gratification; for the Dey was a man whose person she disliked; and to repay herself for this sufferance, the spirit of intrigue with which she was born was continually mounting, in some varied form, to her brain.

"Many plans she had already formed for allying to herself a favourite, but she had not yet ventured to put any one of them into execution; perhaps as much because she dreaded a discovery depriving her of that ascendency she now possessed over the Dey, as that her attachments were of an unstable nature, and that she felt a difficulty in deciding on whom to select.

"Slaves were all the males whom it was possible for her to see; but the condition of those amongst whom her choice must unavoidably fall, did not weaken her inclination to sin. Those who give themselves up to the practice of deliberate criminality, it is remarked, are seldom nice in the objects of their selection—a proof of the unworthiness of that indulgence which sinks the use of every rational sense in its gratification.

"On D'Altonville then fell the destiny of her smiles; her ascendancy over the slaves that attended on her person was too great to cause her long to wish an interview, and wish in vain: she watched the first absence of the Dey from his palace, and having given D'Altonville the intimation of her favourable intentions towards him, in the note which I have already given a copy of, and in which she placed the jewel it contained, more to give it sufficient weight to ensure its reaching the spot where he lay than from any other motive, she instructed the mute who conducted him to her apartment from the appointed arbour in the part he had to perform in the business—a failure in which the poor tacit instrument of her plan well knew would cost him his life.

"The moment Clotilda perceived D'Altonville in her apartment, she ran forward to meet and welcome him; and taking both his hands in her's, she led him to the couch, and placed him upon it.—'Welcome, my countryman!' she said, 'We are both slaves, and must endeavour to soften to each other our lot: the toils you suffer are imposed on your bodily strength—mine on my heart; I am the tool of pleasure to a man I hate.'

'And you wish, doubtless, to fly from your galling captivity,' replied D'Altonville. 'Alas! your wish, I fear, is vain; these walls are impervious.'

'You mistake me,' returned Clotilda; 'I do not wish to fly them, but to ensure myself happiness within them. Every wish of my heart has here been long gratified, except one: I cannot love the Dey; all I desire, in addition to the luxuries he heaps on me, is a heart, not which I can call my own, for such is the Dey's, but a heart to which I can feel satisfied in giving mine;—such a one, countryman, I regard your's to be.'

'You are flattering in your selection,' returned D'Altonville, 'and your frankness demands justice on my part;—I have no heart to receive your's in.'

'Perhaps you are married?' she said.

'No, I am not,' he answered.

'Or intend to be so?' she asked.

'I hope the blissful moment, although protracted, will one day arrive,' exclaimed D'Altonville.

'And is the anticipation of that blissful moment,' returned Clotilda, 'to interdict to you every happiness till it arrives?'

'The anticipation of it,' answered D'Altonville, 'grants me every happiness of which the interval is capable; without that happy period for my thoughts to dwell upon, life would be a blank, captivity and labour insupportable miseries; but that idea cheers the void with many prospects of delight, and wrests from toil and bondage half their power to gall my spirits under them.'

'And is the bliss of idea so great, that you mock all substantial pleasure, when it presents itself to your acceptance?' asked Clotilda.

'That,' returned D'Altonville, 'is alone substantial which will give a second pleasure on reflection; while a retrospect capable of calling a blush, though even a secret one, into the cheek, must curtail the enjoyment of that felicity towards which I hope to be advancing through my present pilgrimage.'

"Clotilda burst into a satirical laugh at the resolute calmness with which my D'Altonville uttered these sentiments; her mind could not comprehend their delicacy, and her heart spurned their tendency.

"D'Altonville remained unmoved by her reproofs.

"It is but too often that a sneer can subdue a virtuous inclination, and that a jest can damp the fervour of a religious intention; but the principles and affection of D'Altonville were both too firmly grounded to be shaken by the breath of fleeting pleasure, and rising from his seat he said—'If the friendship or the advice of D'Altonville can be serviceable to you, you may command them. As one sunk in criminality, I pity you, and feel it my duty to offer you such admonitions as I think may reclaim you from that part of the immorality of your conduct into which you voluntarily plunge yourself: if you will resolve to listen to me, I shall never judge my time ill spent in giving you my society. Suffer me now to depart; reflect on what I have already said; and if you determine to profit by my future visits; send for me again; you will find me ready to comply with your invitation—but on no other terms let me hear of you more.'

"Disappointment was the only passion which at that moment swayed the breast of the lost Clotilda; her breathings were almost choked by the repression of the entreaties which she could scarcely smother, and which wounded pride yet restrained her from uttering. D'Altonville had moved to the door by which he had entered, and now demanded to be reconducted to the garden. Clotilda sprang towards him; she seized his hand, and endeavoured to carry it to her lips. D'Altonville drew it resolutely back, and placed his fingers on the lock of the door.

"Personal danger stared her in the face, when she perceived him attempting to rush out alone into the gallery; as he might mistake his way, and a discovery of her wantonness be immediately conveyed to the Dey. She struck the ground with her foot, and the mute appeared to attend him.

'For the love of Heaven, stay yet one moment!' she exclaimed.

'For the love of honour, no!' replied D'Altonville—and rushed out of the apartment.

"On arriving at the arbour, the mute assisted him in taking off his disguise, and dressing him again in his own clothes; and this done, he left him.

"D'Altonville directly repaired to his hut, where he communicated to his friend, the Spanish captain, the issue of his adventure; they agreed that he had nothing to fear from the revenge of Clotilda, as she had shewn herself a coward of any discovery, by immediately allowing him to depart from her apartment, on his demanding to leave it; and D'Altonville slept peacefully that night in the consciousness of having acted rightly.

"Ten days passed on with D'Altonville unmarked by any occurrence; on the eleventh he was informed by the superintendent of the gardens, that himself, and some others of the slaves, were to be sent, on the following morning, to a spot at the distance of about three hours journey from the grand seraglio, where the Dey had lately erected a light elegant building, to which his favourite mistress was sometimes permitted to retire; and that she who now possessed his favour had obtained leave of him to carry thither a certain number of gardeners, to decorate the ground contained within its walls more fancifully than it now was.

"D'Altonville knew not that Clotilda was the sole regent of the Dey's heart, and little imagined, when he received the superintendant's information, that it was into her service he was going.

"The discovery was very quickly made to him; the day after his arrival at the villa, as he was digging the earth, by the order of the superintendant, in a part of the garden remote from the other slaves, he heard a voice address him in the language of his own country; and, on turning round his head, perceived by his side Clotilda, attended only by two mutes, who stood at some distance from her.

'You perceive,' said she, 'that though I excited only your scorn, at our former interview, I cannot forbear renewing our acquaintance.'

'I hope,' replied D'Altonville, 'that you are convinced of the value of those admonitions which I gave you, and are come prepared to reap a further benefit from my tongue.'

'Foolish man!' she went on, 'to slight my favour, the only alleviation of your captivity which you can expect or hope for.—Ungrateful man! to permit a woman to suffer for your sake, who descends from her own sphere, and humbles herself by entreaties to a slave for his smiles!—You have not even complaisance enough to desist from your labour whilst I am speaking to you.'

'In so doing,' answered D'Altonville, 'I should only incur the displeasure of the superintendant of the gardens, to listen to that which I had rather not hear.'

'Camazin, the superintendant of the gardens,' replied she, 'is my friend; you have nothing to fear from him, although every hour we remain here were passed by you without labour: I have acquainted him with my passion for you, and bribed him to leave you always apart from the other slaves.'

'Then if this Camazin ever receives the wages of the Dey again, he is a villain, and it is fit he should be disgraced,' exclaimed D'Altonville.

'Folly!' cried she. 'He who knows not of his wrongs, does not suffer by them; thus you ought to think of your mistress, and we should then both be blessed.'

'Impossible!' answered D'Altonville; 'he who acts wrongly cannot be happy under the reflection, although he to whom the wrong is done be unconscious of its existence.'

'You are a coward,' she returned, 'who have nothing to lose; I have risked every thing for my love to you: should the Dey discover the motive of my visit to this spot, which was undertaken solely that I might here enjoy your conversation without interruption, I should be undone for ever. The Dey is employed in affairs of state, which I understand must confine him to the city: do not then cast the gloom of disappointment upon the few days of happiness which I have promised myself with you in this seclusion.'

'If for me the journey was undertaken,' replied D'Altonville, 'let me entreat you instantly to return to the city, as your remaining here will but provoke your indignation and my contempt.'

"The same arguments were continued for some time to be repeated on either side, without their making any impression on the object to whom they were directed; and with the evening D'Altonville saw no more of the infatuated Clotilda.

"In the morning he encountered Camazin.—'Having seen me only in the habit of a slave,' said D'Altonville, addressing him, 'you probably conceive my mind as abject as my situation; you know not the heart that animates this breast, or you would not have brought me hither to expose me to the licentious passion of Clotilda: words are the only means which captivity does not deprive me of for asserting that my nature is not of the mean texture you gave it credit for being, in acceding to her infamous plan; or words should not be the means I would employ to tell you so.'

"Instead of the haughty reply which D'Altonville awaited from the powerful Camazin, something like an air of humility overspread his features, and he said—'I have a large family, and Clotilda has been my benefactress.'

'But you owe your first obligations to the Dey,' pronounced D'Altonville, 'from whom you derive your regular employment; believe me that your family will prosper better under the honesty, than the craft of their father.'

"Camazin muttered something like an apology, and slunk off to a different part of the garden.

"For several successive days Clotilda continued to haunt

D'Altonville, and to repeat to him those arguments in favour of her passion by which he had resolved not to be moved: he continued uniform in treating her with indifference and contempt, except at those moments when he endeavoured, by the effect of reasoning, to open her eyes to the atrocity of her conduct; but every method proved inadequate to the subduing of the passions which devoured her soul.

"During this time Camazin was not met by him.

"At length a day arrived on which he saw not the favourite of the Dey, and he began to entertain a hope that her ill-founded passion was beginning to evaporate before the influence of returning reason; but in the evening, about the hour of twilight, a paper was brought to him, which contained these words:—'Clotilda desires to see you in her apartment.'

"He tore the paper into atoms, and scattered them into the air, as a signal to the mute who had brought it, that he did not intend to comply with the request contained in it.

"The mute beckoned to him to come; but with a frown of indignation on his brow, he turned from him, and moved along in an opposite direction. The mute immediately slapped the palms of his hands together, and several of his fellows darted out from behind a bush, who caught hold of D'Altonville, and confining his arms, dragged him forcibly towards the building inhabited by Clotilda.

"They led him into an apartment, which Clotilda was traversing with a hasty step, and the wildest emotion painted on her countenance: she stopped, and faced him as he entered, her full dark eyes resting on his, and describing the war of love and anger which was raging in her soul.

'Why this outrage against my person?' asked D'Altonville, calmly—'why am I brought hither?'

'Because, inhuman man!' returned Clotilda—the lost, the shameless Clotilda, 'I cannot live without you. I cannot exist under your contempt; and, for the last time, I entreat you to become the partner of my joys.'

'For the last time, then,' replied D'Altonville, 'take my answer to your importunities. No earthly power can shake my resolution. I know my duty to an absent being, who merits every consideration I can pay to her; and knowing my duty, I perform it. Once more, be advised by me to perform your's towards the Dey;—and now let us part for ever.'

'No, no,' exclaimed Clotilda, 'you are more a slave here than you imagine. Part! What, suffer you to go, that you may bear to another woman that love which I have humbled myself to be refused! Believe it not; Clotilda has pledged an oath to Heaven, that you either requite her love, or yield your breath upon the spot you stand on.'

"The fury of a disappointed woman raised no fears for his safety in the breast of D'Altonville: he trusted that her threats would never be put into effect; he neither conceived her authorized by the Dey to take away the life of one of his slaves, nor did he fear, that if the naked sword were presented to his throat, she would not herself again recall it, as while he lived her hopes might still be kept alive.

'You do not tremble, I perceive,' she said; 'but your calmness probably arises from your not giving credit to my words. I will convince you what my design is.' She turned to one of the mutes, and commanded him to bring the bowstring.

"The mute complied, and two others advanced with him, to perform the dreadful act; one of whom held in his hand a cloth to shade the features of the sufferer in his last moments.

'Now, then, thy choice—Clotilda, or the bowstring?' she exclaimed.

'When death and sin are placed in opposition,' D'Altonville replied, 'the grim tyrant loses all his terrors; if, by flying to his arms, I avoid the evil that might make me dread to meet his touch hereafter, suffering unwarrantably here, I have nothing to look forward to but recompence—'

'Bind him!' exclaimed the female fury.

"The mutes obeyed, and one of them held the noose ready to slip over his head.

'Whilst thou,' continued D'Altonville, with an unfaltering voice, 'at some unexpected moment, wilt meet thy merited punishment!'

'Truly hast thou spoken!' exclaimed a voice, which proceeded from one of those whom D'Altonville had hitherto believed to be all mutes: 'be that cord her instant fate—obey me!'

"As it were by magic, the noose which had been presented to the neck of D'Altonville encircled that of Clotilda; the cloth was thrown over her face, and a low moan bespoke her in the agonies of death.

"Wonder seized the frame of D'Altonville, and he stood gazing on the scene before him.

"The apparent mute again spoke.—'Thus ever perish licentiousness and ingratitude joined!'—then turning to D'Altonville, he continued—'Frenchman, know in me the Dey of Algiers; that woman possessed my heart—my soul! You perceive how she has trifled with the good she enjoyed, and how deservedly she has suffered.—I confess I loved her; but I had rather mourn a disappointment than know myself a dupe. Camazin, the superintendant of the gardens, discovered to me the injustice that was practising against me, and concerted for me the plan of this disguise, by which I have had personal conviction of her guilt: he informed me also of the nobleness of your mind, which refused to wrong in his affections, even the man who held you in bondage; I have myself also seen the workings of your glorious spirit; I have punished the bad; it now alone remains for me to reward the worthy; ask of me any boon, it is your's, in addition to your freedom, and safe convoy to your own country.'

"Need I tell my reader that the gift which D'Altonville asked was his Eloise?

"The Dey heard his story with interest, and invited him to return with him immediately to Algiers.

"I was that night on the point of retiring to my bed, when a slave came to my apartment, and informed me that the Dey requested to see me directly; alarm seized me; I apprehended consequences of the worst nature from the message, but I had no alternative but to obey it, for if he were determined on seeing me, my simple refusal could be of no avail. I threw my veil over me, and with a slow and trembling step, I followed the messenger, who conducted me to an apartment brilliantly lighted, in the midst of which I saw a repast spread, and cushions of purple and gold surrounding it.

"From behind a curtain of flowing silk, at the upper end of the apartment, a personage richly habited, and whom I could not mistake for the Dey, from the humble obeisances of the slaves, as he passed along through the midst of them, advanced towards me. He took one of my hands in his, without which support I believe I should have sunk at his feet, and thus addressed me—'Fair lady, I invite you here to present you with a lover truly worthy of your highest esteem;—tremble not, it is not myself I am recommending to your heart;—here comes the man!'

"I looked towards the curtain, and beheld my D'Altonville, no longer habited as a slave, but with the naval uniform of his country restored to him.

"We flew into each other's arms, and for some succeeding moments I was wholly insensible.

"The Dey invited us to pass the evening in his apartment, and our gratitude to him was too great not to make us feel a true pleasure in complying with any request which came from his lips. At the present moment, I learnt but slightly the cause which had restored to me my lover, as D'Altonville, from delicacy to the feelings of the Dey, forbore to revert to the conduct of one whom, it was yet evident, the Dey had loved better than she had deserved.

"What bliss! what ecstacy did I enjoy, during the hours we passed in the apartment of the Dey, to feel myself once more in the presence of my D'Altonville!—to know myself secure from danger, in those very walls, and in conversation with that very man from whom I had dreaded the destruction of my peace—the eternal separation of my lover and myself! the joy was super-human, and transient as it was great: the last happy moments of my existence had now been nearly all enjoyed.

"Against the following evening, the Dey had promised to provide us with a vessel, which should convey us to any port of France of which we should make choice, and D'Altonville fixed upon Toulon.

"Encouraged by the suavity of manners of the Dey, and the openness of his heart at the present moment, D'Altonville ventured to request of him the liberty of the Spanish captain, whose conduct towards us I have before remarked as kind in the extreme, during the time of our being prisoners on board his ship, and whose friendship had been the only consolation of D'Altonville's bondage.

"The Dey acceded to his request, and the poor Spaniard was made happy in the morning, by the intelligence of his unexpected reverse of fortune.

"I passed the night in golden dreams of bliss to come—of blessings which never rose to light, fostered alone within my breast, and over-shadowed at their birth by the lowering clouds of affliction.

"At the appointed hour on the following day, after receiving a most friendly farewell from the Dey at parting, we embarked on board the vessel destined to convey us to France; the Spanish captain, as had been already settled, being our fellow-passenger.

"On the third day of our being at sea, a rough gale sprang up, and as the waves washed over the deck, I went down into the cabin. I was assured by the Spanish captain, who was himself, as well as my D'Altonville, an excellent mariner, that there was not the slightest danger to be apprehended; and thus satisfied, I retired to bed.

"The sudden change from grief to joy which I had experienced within the last few days, had entirely exhausted my strength and spirits; and when I sunk to sleep, I slept soundly, and for a length of time.

"Oh God! so great are now my emotions at the recollection of the scenes which followed my waking, that my hand almost refuses to trace them upon the paper before me; but the task shall be fulfilled; the wretch of hereafter shall be shewn that as miserable a being as herself has existed before her.

"On my waking, oh, what strange events had taken place during my sleep!—on my waking, the first object in the cabin, on which my eyes fell was—Lord Rufus de Madginecourt!

"Ere I speak of my alarm, let me relate what had preceded it.

"The violence of the wind had increased with nearly every hour of the night, and towards morning it was almost grown into a storm. A little after the break of day, D'Altonville had espied, through the mists of the morning, a vessel, about the size of the bark we were on board of, as he believed, in distress.

"The Spanish captain and himself directed the mariners to make towards her. In a very short time, they perceived that she was foundering, and in a few minutes more, she entirely disappeared beneath the waves. D'Altonville, who kept his eyes fixed on the spot where she had sunk, declared that he saw some of the crew struggling with the waves. Our vessel soon came up with them, and succeeded in preserving the lives of two men, who were buffetting the foaming billows on a mast, to which they were clinging. These two men were no other than Lord Rufus de Madginecourt and his adherent Ravil. They had been on their passage in an Italian ship from Genoa to Cette, and by bad weather and adverse winds had been blown out of their course; their vessel had sprung a leak, and every one on board but themselves had perished.

"Ravil was the son of a gentleman of small fortune. Chance had introduced him to the acquaintance of Lord Rufus, who finding him to be one of those young men who prefer submitting to the drudgery of making themselves useful to a wealthy patron, rather than undergoing the toil of earning for themselves an honest maintenance, free from such dependance, had made him his companion; and his abilities in the accomplishment of his patron's views, of whatever nature they might be, had raised him extremely high in the good favour of Lord Rufus.

"This young man had accidentally seen D'Altonville, during his residence with Lord Rufus, on the marquisate of my father, and lost not a moment in conveying to his patron information of who the person was to whom he owed his life. Upon receiving this intelligence from Ravil, Lord Rufus directly enquired of the captain of our vessel, if there was any female on board, which he, doubtless, suspected to be the case, as no hesitation was made in France, at saying that I had eloped with D'Altonville. The captain satisfied him in this point, and he directly bought his services with a purse of gold, which he had preserved about him.

"With the most rancorous villany brooding in his heart, he returned to that part of the deck where D'Altonville was standing, and while in the act of acknowledging him as the preserver of his life, he drew from his girdle a pistol, which he aimed at his head: fortunately the murderous weapon missed fire; of this the Spanish captain being unconscious, and only sensible of the danger in which he saw his friend, darted forward to wrest the implement of death from the hand of the wretch who grasped it; in the struggle the pistol discharged itself, and the Spaniard was shot through the heart.

"The consternation of D'Altonville at the scene just past was so great, that both his power of utterance and action failed him. It was by accident that the pistol which Lord Rufus happened to have upon him, had been loaded; a second charge he had not at command, so threw from him the useless tube; but in the moment of the action, whilst he was reflecting on the present inutility of the weapon, his sentiments underwent a change, which he expressed in these words, unintelligible to D'Altonville—'No, thou shalt live to see my triumph over thee!'

"Ravil and Lord Rufus then bound him to the foremast of the vessel. D'Altonville called upon the mariners for assistance, and upbraided them for suffering him to undergo the evil treatment he was enduring from two strangers, whom his humanity had just rescued from death; but the Algerines had been bought to passiveness by gold, and they religiously adhered in faith to the god they worshipped.

"D'Altonville now turned himself to the strangers, and began to remonstrate with them on the ingratitude of their conduct, and to demand the reason of the cruel treatment they were shewing him?

"A thunderbolt bursting upon his head could not have occasioned a greater pang to his senses, than he received in the information that Lord Rufus, the persecutor of his Eloise, stood before him. In the wildness of his agony, he called upon Heaven for assistance; his eyes fell on his bleeding friend; he perceived his bosom still heaving with the gaspings of expiring life; he called upon him by name, in the vain hope that the sound of his voice might reanimate his closing powers. Lord Rufus commanded the mariners to throw the body into the sea, fearful, as it were, of its recovery. The eyes were not closed, and D'Altonville believed that they rested on him, as the body sunk beneath the waves.

"These particulars I learnt at a future period from Ravil.

"Having secured D'Altonville beyond the power of disengaging himself, Lord Rufus ordered Ravil to remain with him upon deck, to ensure his receiving no assistance from the sailors; for vice is always doubtful of those engines which are merely bought to assist in its purposes, without possessing any interest in their being effected; and with this caution he came down into the cabin, where I lay sleeping.

"Whether the sound of his voice, or his more hated touch, awoke me, I know not; I can only now recollect, that on opening my eyes, my sight fell on his detested form. On perceiving it, I uttered a frantic exclamation, which I seconded by calling for assistance on D'Altonville.

'Lay aside your fears, dearest lady, I beseech you,' he pronounced; 'you see before you one too much devoted to your happiness, to render it necessary for you to call on any being for assistance but himself!'

'My Lord,' I replied, 'I acknowledge but one protector; there can be but one man whom a woman's heart tells her she has a right to confide in, and you already know that you are not he.'

'I am, at least, blest in thinking, that since a chance, which I revere, has brought me once more into your presence, I shall soon be the envied man you describe,' answered Lord Rufus.

'You!' I exclaimed—'never! never! Were my D'Altonville at this moment on his bed of death before me, and were his last request to me, to admit you to my affections after his decease, not even in compliance with his dying breath, could I tolerate you—could I feel any sensation but aversion for the man who leagued himself with a cruel father, against an injured daughter's cause. By what authority you are here, I know not; but whatever it be, I trust my request to you immediately to depart, will supersede it.'

'Though an angel utter the command,' returned the artful man, 'we are slow in obedience, where death must follow compliance; I can only live in your presence; from the first moment I saw you, my passion for you was extreme, and I care not what sacrifices I undergo to call you my own; you can make no terms to which I shall not accede, so you do but give me yourself; but urge me not to desperation by your obstinacy, for on whatever terms it be, you must be mine!'

'Never in my life, my Lord,' I replied; 'nor can this declaration, on my part, wound any generous feeling of your heart: after the sentiments you have just avowed, I am sufficiently convinced that a passion far inferior to love, stirs your warmth; the noble sensation of love is unacquainted with the *force* your Lordship talks of, and feels its greatest happiness in that forbearance which blesses the object of its selection.'

"Lord Rufus smiled contemptuously.

'Besides,' I continued, 'you are already well acquainted that I have pledged my faith to one whom empires should not tempt me to renounce; and though the perversity of fate has hitherto prevented our union, the hour is not now, I trust, far distant.'

"Oh, would my tongue had cleaved to my lips, ere I had uttered that sentence! Fierce joy sparkled in the eyes of Lord Rufus, and he exclaimed—'Not yet his! Am I then so blest? Are thy beauties yet untasted, and the first fruit of thy charms reserved for me? Fear no intemperance, on my part now, lady; thou art my *destined wife!*'

'Where is my D'Altonville?' I cried. 'Why is he not here? Why does he not appear to vindicate my fame—to protect me from insult? D'Altonville! D'Altonville! oh, where art thou, my D'Altonville?'

"Of what succeeded these moments, I have no perfect recollection; I alone remember that I felt sick and giddy, and sunk upon the floor, before the monster who was exercising his inhumanity over me.

"When I awoke from my trance, Lord Rufus was still with me. The sounds with which I opened my lips were the same that I had closed them with—'Where, where is my D'Altonville?'

'Acknowledge yourself my destined bride,' returned De Madginecourt, 'and you shall instantly see him.'

"There are emotions of the heart which no tongue can express—there are souls which no arguments can move; of the former were my sensations, of the latter class Lord Rufus. I clasped my hands in agony towards Heaven, and remained silent."

Rosalind, for the first time, turned her thoughts from the eventful page she was reading.—"Oh, Heaven!" she exclaimed, "in the power of this monster am I at the present moment!—Shield me, Omnipotence, with thy protecting arm; encircle me with thy guardian spirit from the machinations of this fiend!" She paused a while, in comparative reflection on the fate of Eloise and herself. Again she spoke. "Am I destined to be the second victim of his licentious desires? or is the friendship which he now professes towards me real, and exercised as an atonement for his past transgressions? God of mercy, do thou, in pity to my friendless state, soften and ameliorate his rugged heart!"

The shades of evening were already descending to the earth, and when Rosalind again turned her eyes to the manuscript, desirous of pursuing the narrative it contained, she found that the retiring of the light of day had rendered the characters no longer discernible; and not choosing to carry it with her to her own apartment, she reluctantly replaced it on the same spot where she had found it, and left the library.

Dame Edith met her in her chamber, with many apologies for her absence during the afternoon.

Rosalind felt disinclined to conversation, and alledging an headache as an excuse for retiring early to rest, dismissed the good old dame for the night, and sunk upon her pillow, where reflection on the past, and anticipation of the future, rendered the visit of sleep broken and unrefreshing.

CHAPTER XII.

Mighty God!
What had I done to merit such affliction?

HOME.

ANXIOUS for the conclusion of Eloise's fate, Rosalind left her bed at an early hour, and repaired to the library, unobserved by Dame Edith, who was either still asleep, or occupied with her morning devotions; she opened at the page where she had left off the evening before, and found the narrative continued thus:—

"For several days I was kept a prisoner in the cabin, and saw only Lord Rufus, and his equally vile adherent, Ravil; not a single reply could I gain to my inquiries relative to D'Altonville; and at times I believed that the wretch who aspired to my hand had freed himself by death from the rival whom he saw me resolute in preferring to himself.

"At length, when Ravil was one day alone with me in the cabin, I thought he appeared more than usually disposed to reply to my questions, and I urged him, in the most imploring terms, to inform me what was the fate of D'Altonville. He told me that he was alive, but not allowed to descend into the cabin to me.

'Whither are we sailing?' I next asked. 'We must have reached France long ere this, had not the destiny of the vessel been changed.'

'We are sailing towards England,' he replied. 'Lord Rufus de Madginecourt has a castle on the margin of the shore, where we are to land.'

'Then that castle is destined to be my grave!' I exclaimed.

"Ravil fixed his eyes on me; I thought they gleamed pity, at least they did not appear to exult in my agonies.

'More likely the grave of D'Altonville,' he replied. 'It is not the nature of Lord Rufus to suffer those to live whom he hates. D'Altonville is a brave fellow,' he added, after a short pause; 'he saved my life, so did he also that of Lord Rufus; but Lord Rufus has a heart unacquainted with gratitude.'

"He then proceeded, unasked, to relate to me the accident which had introduced Lord Rufus and himself on board our vessel; he expatiated on the death of the Spanish captain; dwelt on the villany of Lord Rufus, who had attempted the life of D'Altonville, a moment after he had owed his own to his humanity; and added—'Would it were in my power to save the life of D'Altonville!'

"The iniquity of Ravil's heart was not then so fully known to me as it was soon after; and catching at the expressions which had fallen from his tongue, as if the lips of an angel had breathed a sound of comfort in my ear, I said—'Are you then as fully convinced as myself of Lord Rufus's villany, and will you stretch out your arm in the cause of the innocent?'

'Most willingly,' he returned; 'it would be my pride to rescue you from the power of Lord Rufus.'

'But the means?' I returned. 'Lord Rufus has bought the captain to his side; my D'Altonville is bound: what can your single arm, or mine to back it, avail against numbers?'

'The numbers might soon be our own,' rejoined Ravil: 'I have twice the sum of gold about me with which Lord Rufus bought his services; no fear but a double bribe would as quickly bind him to me.'

'O, for the love of Heaven, make the attempt!' I said.

'It remains with you, lady, to give the signal,' he answered: 'say but that the heart which you cannot give to Lord Rufus shall be mine, and I pledge my soul to you that the life of D'Altonville shall be sacred.'

"To express what were my sensations at that moment is not in the power of language. 'Wretch!' was the only sound that escaped my lips; my eyes spoke volumes of indignation and contempt.

'Be not so hasty in your decision, lady,' he rejoined, with the utmost calmness of tone; 'you have not yet heard all the arguments I can advance in favour of my passion. If Lord Rufus be allowed to maintain his present power over you, little do I believe that his promise of marriage will be attended to, when you are once within the walls of his castle; and certain I am that the life of D'Altonville will be as short as the period of your honour: if, on the contrary, you will accede to my proposal, Lord Rufus, who feels no repugnance at attempting the life of a man to whom he owes his own, shall be cut off, and buried in those waves whose murmurs blab no secrets; you shall become a lawful, honoured wife, and D'Altonville shall live to see you happy.'

"I spoke not; the expression of my countenance was sufficient to convince him of the abhorrence in which my soul held him.

"Requesting me to reflect on what he had said, he shortly after left the cabin.

"The misery of my mind was now, if possible, increased. I dreaded more at the moment from the calm villany of Ravil, than from the haughty brutality of Lord Rufus. I considered that I might free myself from the importunity of the former, by a representation of his conduct to his patron. But would not this very act of self-defence be an inimical step to my own peace? Would not a complaint to Lord Rufus of his creature be allowing Lord Rufus an ascendancy over him in my heart? would it not be saying that Lord Rufus was not the being most hated by me in the creation? and would not this confession lead him into the opinion of his having obtained some influence over my heart?—Horrid idea! Whatever I might suffer from the persecutions of Ravil, I resolved not to owe my release from them to Lord Rufus.

"On the following day, Ravil attempted to win upon me by a display of passion, which he artfully pretended to make a merit of restraining within the bounds of respect: more disgusted by this hypocrisy than by his open fallacy, I commanded him to leave me, on pain of my informing Lord Rufus of his conduct. He laughed contemptuously at my threat, and told me that Lord Rufus entertained too good an opinion of his fidelity to be easily shaken from it. He mentioned a large sum, which he said Lord Rufus had willed to him for his honest services, (on these words he laid an ironical emphasis, as if he gloried in the deceit which he had lived in), and added, that ere long I might probably see him in possession of it.

"His words made no impression on me; I regarded them as the froth of villanous disappointment.

"A few nights after, I had fallen into a slumber, in which horrid dreams haunted my sickening fancy; a loud blow upon the door of the cabin awoke me, and a confusion of tongues at the same time met my ear; a second blow upon the door burst it open, and from the light of the lamp which was suspended from the top of the cabin, I saw Lord Rufus pursuing Ravil with his drawn sword. Ravil was unarmed, and his violent efforts to escape the threatened danger, had forced him a way through the door in the cabin.

"The struggle was as short as any contest must necessarily be, where one man has the superiority of arms over a naked opponent: Ravil fell, the blood gushing from a wound in his breast, and another in his side.

"Although contempt alone had met Ravil's infamous proposals to me, he had vigorously pursued the desperate plan which had entered his diabolical mind, of wresting me from Lord Rufus to himself, and of stepping through blood into that independence which his knowledge of the concerns of Lord Rufus ensured to him on his death. Accordingly he had, during the day, appointed the captain of the vessel to meet him at midnight at the foot of the cabin stairs, the spot which, of all others, he conceived the least liable to interruption, informing him that he had something of consequence to communicate to him.

"At the time fixed on, Ravil was repairing to the place of appointment. The night was very dark, and he could merely distinguish a moving figure which appeared to be on the point of ascending the stairs, as he was going down them. 'Remain there,' he said; and the figure ceased to move. Ravil went down, and taking from his pocket the purse of gold he had mentioned to me that he was possessed of, he put it into the hands of the person before him, and said—'Your services are now given to Lord Rufus; take this purse, and let them henceforth be given to me; your compliance shall be rewarded with treble the sum when we arrive in England.'

"The hand which received the gold was not that of the supposed captain, but of Lord Rufus himself, who was coming upon deck for air.

"Needless must it be to observe that vengeance was the sole passion which animated the heart of Lord Rufus, on this unexpected and unequivocal discovery of the perfidy of a man who owed to him his all; his sword was in an instant drawn from its scabbard, with an exclamation sufficient to convince Ravil whose arm he had to dread; and terror lending him strength, he had burst his way into my cabin, in his vain attempt at flying from the avenging steel.

"The icy hand of death was upon Ravil, but still neither remorse for the past, nor dread of the hereafter, occupied his mind; true to the vicious principles under which he had lived, and which had raised him to the rank of De Madginecourt's favourite, in the last moments of his life, he only thought of revenging the failure of his ungrateful villany. His head had fallen near my feet, and I stood hanging over him, my faculties suspended in horror. He fixed his eyes on me. 'D'Altonville,' he said, 'is bound to the mast—take this dagger, to defend yourself,' (drawing one, as he spoke, from his girdle,) 'and fly to his release.'

'God forgive thee!' I exclaimed, snatching the dagger from his hand, and flying towards the spot he had named. The whole was but the transaction of a moment

"Ardent hope gave wings to my feet, and I reached the deck without scarcely touching the stairs that led to it.—'D'Altonville,' I cried, 'thy Eloise calls upon thee!'

'Eloise!' replied the well-known voice, and in an instant my hands were upon the cords that bound him. He was sitting upon the deck, and his arms were confined to the mast in such a manner as to prevent him from rising. Scarcely was one arm unbound, ere the hand of Lord Rufus, calling vehemently on the mariners for assistance, held mine; my shrieks were mingled with his cries: the night was too dark for me to be able to discover whether I had given D'Altonville the power of wholly unbinding himself; and my dread of Ravil's prophecy concerning his life being at that moment fulfilled, wound me up almost to frenzy, and I raved for mercy for my D'Altonville.

"Lord Rufus snatched me in his arms, and was returning with me into the cabin; at that moment I recollected the dagger; with all the violence of my strength, I darted it at his breast. Forgive me, Heaven, for the deed! At any other time but that of the most wretched desperation, I would not have attempted the life even of so cruel an enemy; notwithstanding the sufferings I have since endured from him, I thank God that the blow was not fatal; I had not died in that peace with my own heart which, I trust, will now attend my last moments.

"But although the blow was not fatal, the point of the dagger had entered his arm just below the shoulder; he contrived to stagger with me into the cabin, and there he let me drop. My garments were covered with the blood which had issued from his wound. The loudness of the noise which I heard upon the deck, filled me with the hope that D'Altonville was at liberty, and triumphing over the attempts of the sailors to rebind him; but alas! the hope was futile. The captain brought information to Lord Rufus, that the villain was safe. Villain! oh, what was Lord Rufus, if my D'Altonville was a villain?

"Ravil had ceased to breathe, and the dead body was removed, at the command of Lord Rufus, whose wound, I perceived, gave him pain; he darted at me a look which was meant to upbraid me, but checked by his consciousness of the provocation I had received; he took a linen girdle from his waist, and bound it round his arm; this done, he called to him one of the mariners; and having seen the door sufficiently repaired for again acting as a prevention to my leaving the cabin, he departed in silence, turning the lock upon me, as he went out.

"I tore off such of my garments as were stained with the blood of my detested enemy, and threw them upon the floor; this done, I sunk upon my bed, my brain and heart endeavouring, as it were, to exceed each other in their throbbings; an immense weight appeared to press down my eyelids; my ideas were bewildered; my heart seemed to require the relief of weeping, but the tears would not flow.

"A deadly coldness stole gradually from my feet towards my heart; I believed the termination of my life to be fast approaching, and I prayed only of Heaven to grant D'Altonville resignation under my loss.

"The pain I endured was great, yet were my sufferings for my D'Altonville still greater; exposed to the inclemency of the night air, confined to the most irksome of positions, perhaps denied those aliments which could alone render his strength capable of bearing up under the affliction he was doomed to undergo.

"A violent shivering fit seized me, and unable to resist the acceptance of present relief for my feelings, though, in reality, heedless of the protraction of my life, I, for the first time, drank a small cup of some wine, which Lord Rufus had a few days before brought me into the cabin. I feared not that it should be drugged with any sleepy potion, as the power of instilling such a drug, had it been his inclination so to do, would have been the same into any drink brought to me; nor did it seem likely that such should be his idea; I could not, in the deepest sleep, be more in his power than I was at every moment of my present existence.

"Towards morning I sunk to sleep; the wine had probably invited its approach; although the quantity I had swallowed was small, still, upon exhausted spirits, it had possessed the power of a larger dose; when I awoke, I found my accustomed morning repast by my side, and I saw that the blood-stained garments which I had taken off the night before, were gone.

"My brain was more capable of thought than it had been before I had slept. 'What,' I inquired of myself, 'is the fate of D'Altonville? to what end does the tyrant spare his wretched life?' I could find no reply to these mental questions, but that the wretch who was usurping an unwarrantable right over my liberty felt averse to the commission of deliberate murder, and therefore suffered him to live till some new fit of passion should drive him on madly to the deed.

"It is not uncommon for villains to juggle thus with their own conscience, and not to appear sensible that the cool determination of an evil action is the same as the performance of it.

"When Lord Rufus entered the cabin, he said—'To-morrow, lady, it is probable that we shall reach England; a very short time will now, therefore, place you in the situation your charms were born to shine in;—two days more will make you my wife.'

"I did not reply; my determination was more fixed than ever, rather to die than to suffer myself to be allied by the tenderest name to the man I hated; but I considered it useless at the present moment again to express it.

"In the night, as I lay upon my restless bed, I imagined that I heard some one over my head, singing; the tones were those of the deepest melancholy, and the songster sighed with the most bitter sobbings. At length I heard my name pronounced. I could no longer be deceived in the voice; it was that of D'Altonville. Again he sang, and at the close of a long and mournful cadence, he exclaimed—'Oh, Eloise, why hast thou fled to Heaven before me?'

'Fled to Heaven!' I voluntarily echoed. 'Does he then believe me dead? Impossible!—it is his sleeping fancy that speaks!'

"I sprang upon the table in the cabin, in order to approach as near to him as possible, and exerting my voice to its fullest extent, I called upon him by name. He either did not hear me, or did not attend to my invocation, for he did not reply to me, but continued sighing.

'Eloise!' he presently exclaimed.

'Here, here,' I replied, for I then doubted not that he heard my voice.

'That blessed star is Eloise,' he added; and I heard him move quickly away from the spot.

"It was now impossible for me to admit any opinion concerning what I had heard, but that D'Altonville believed me dead; the fabrication must have been conveyed to him by Lord Rufus; but could I imagine that D'Altonville would, in this point, give credit to his tongue? Oh no; and yet, might not the weakness of his harrassed brain conspire with his enemy to gain his credit to the last pang he could ever be capable of feeling on earth?

"Again I heard his voice pronouncing my name, and singing a melody which he had in former days often heard me play to him upon my lute. Again I heard his footsteps move on the deck. On what account was he now at liberty, when he had hitherto been so closely bound?

"A tide of agony rushed upon my brain, and each moment appeared to predict that it would burst the next.

"Truly was that night a night of horrors; at every interval of the roaring waves and rustling breeze, I heard his wretched, his frantic voice. About an hour after daybreak the wind rose higher, and excluded every sound but the hoarse roarings occasioned by itself.

Lord Rufus did not, as had been usual with him, visit me in the morning; my breakfast was brought me by one of the mariners. About noon, certain words, which heard upon deck led me to believe that we were within sight of land. I stood by the door of my cabin, anxiously endeavouring to catch the sound of my D'Altonville's voice, whose brain, I now firmly persuaded myself, had been affected by his misfortunes; but I heard him not. I placed my hand by accident on the handle of the lock of the door, and my action having, without design, turned it, it flew open; my surprise at finding that it was not barred was great; but I determined to profit by the happy chance for once more seeing D'Altonville; I rushed out, and turned my steps towards the cabin stairs; but, alas! the door at their top, which opened upon the deck, was closed, and refused me a passage.

'She is not dead—it is a villanous fallacy—she is not dead! Suffer me once more to see her—to die in her arms!' These words, in the voice of D'Altonville, I distinctly heard.

'Frantic at the sound, I flew to another part of the ship, where I had some recollection of having seen an entrance to the deck; I gained it, and once more stood before the only man on earth that I could ever love! but oh, how changed since last I had beheld him! With the characters of death legibly written on his countenance, and clasping my blood-stained garments to his heart, lay D'Altonville extended upon the deck.

'Monsters! I knew she lived!' he exclaimed on seeing me; and at the same instant endeavoured to spring from the ground, but the effort overpowered him, and he sunk down by my side.

'Do not, at the peril of your souls, attempt to tear me from him!' I cried, addressing Lord Rufus and the wretches allied to him by gold. 'Ye have murdered him, and I will receive his last breath.'

"I believe there was something in my manner which struck awe even to the hearts of those around me, for they suffered me to remain on my knees by his side.

'Blessed God! I thank thee that I see her once again!' said D'Altonville, endeavouring to fix on me his eyes. 'They gave me these,' pointing to the garments I have already mentioned, 'and told me thou wert dead! Frenzy seized my brain; I broke my bonds. He came, and found me once more at liberty,' (he pointed to Lord Rufus as he spoke) 'and his sword—' He could no more; his hand explained the rest, by placing itself beneath a wound in his side.

'Oh, save him! save him!' I exclaimed; 'inhuman villains! will ye let him die for want of aid?'

'It would come too late,' said D'Altonville, once more opening his lips; 'the pangs of death recalled my reason—it convinced me thou wert still alive! I prayed only to breathe out my last sigh in thine arms!—Oh Eloise, it is accomplished! Almighty Heaven! shield——' The words died on his tongue—his spirit was fled for ever.

"Without a groan, without a sigh, I saw him expire; for a minute all my senses seemed stiffened into apathy, then burst a maddening tide of grief into my veins; one heart-drawn shriek escaped my lips, and I ran to plunge myself into the deep, and end my woes in death.

"An arm snatched me back, and all sense fled from me.

"Oh, why was not that moment my last? Why did not Heaven kindly close my eyes in death, and spare me the horror of opening them upon the murderer of my D'Altonville?

"I cannot dwell on the remainder of my narrative as I have done on that already written; it is my desire to complete it before my death: It is a singular, an inexplicable consolation to me to commit my fate to paper: perhaps I am animated by the idea that those sorrows which during my lifetime were shut from the knowledge of the world, may excite a tear of compassion after my decease. I must hasten in my self-imposed task, for I feel a presentiment, a foreboding, that my miseries on earth will not endure much longer. Lord Rufus scorns the wretch he has made.

"Upon recovering my senses, I found myself in the apartment where I am now writing, and from which I have never been permitted to stir, except into the library adjoining to it, where I shall deposit my sad recital, when I have concluded it, if that power be ever granted me.

"Lord Rufus and some attendants were in the apartment with me; he dismissed the latter, and a priest, at his call, entered from the library. 'The moment of my happiness is now come!' was the short intimation which he gave me of his intention respecting myself. My tears, my prayers, my remonstrances, were unheeded alike by him and the priest; and a ceremony, which was by them called marriage, having been performed, the priest left the chamber.

"And here I must for awhile lay down my pen. I can dwell with comparative composure on the death of my D'Altonville, to the sensations which my mind at this moment experiences in the recollection of the hour which followed that mockery of religion.

"When a month had expired, Lord Rufus, probably judging of me by the impression which any occurrence of joy or grief made on his own unfeeling mind, and conceiving the time of affliction for the loss of my D'Altonville to be past, was urgent with me in his entreaties for me to quit my chamber, and to shew myself to his household, and to the world, as the wife of his choice. He should experience much pride, he said, in carrying me to the court, and introducing me there, in a stile becoming the rank to which he had raised me.

"I replied, that I should ever consider myself the victim of a tyrant; and feeling that I was so, I would, if possible, shut myself out from my own sight, much more from that of the world.

"The policy of Lord Rufus was too great to force me into society against my inclination, how strongly soever he might desire to see me emerge into the world. The tale of his villany at present lay buried in his own breast and mine; within the walls of his castle, I had no means of making my wrongs known to any human being. The domestics I saw were few, and those as wholly unacquainted with the French language, as I was with that of England. Had I suffered myself to have been led into the world, with the splendour which would have accompanied my introduction into it as the wife of Lord Rufus de Madginecourt, he probably conceived that vanity would have dazzled my thoughts from a recollection of the past, or that if I had ever made the disclosure of my situation to any heart, little credit would have been given to the misery of a woman who was blazing in what the world knew to be grandeur, and therefore would conceive to be happiness.

"My thoughts frequently reverted to the living as well as to the dead. I thought of my father, and I prayed for him; he was, indeed, the author of all my misery, but he was still my father—I still owed to him the duty of a child, though he had omitted to perform towards me the part of an indulgent parent. Sorrow softens the heart into universal benevolence; it is the channel through which Providence pours the greatest balm into the breast of affliction, by rendering it conscious that it suffers undeservedly, when it unexceptionally forgives.

"The conduct of Lord Rufus continued consistent with the crimes he had already committed. Indifference quickly succeeded possession, and he did not hesitate to offer me insults, when he found me about to become the mother of a progeny more wretched than myself, because condemned in the very womb to lie under the hatred of a monster and a father.

"Alas! I shall write little more; I feel the moment of my pains approaching; the only consolatory sensation I have for some time experienced is a whispering at my heart, that my existence will now be short; the belief would be exquisite, were it not that a wretched being may receive life from my death, whose unhappy state might be somewhat ameliorated on earth, even by the little share of comfort it would be in its hapless mother's power to bestow on it.

"My hour of suffering is at hand. May it be no crime to wish that Heaven would hear my prayer, to snatch my babe to the arms of its mercy, rather than consign it to those of its miserable mother!"

A chasm in the manuscript here ensued; and when it was again continued, the characters were hardly recognizable for those of the same writer; they appeared to have been traced by a hand almost too feeble to commit them to paper.

"Once more I resume my pen, but my hand, weak and tremulous with illness and suffering, almost refuses to perform the office I require of it.

"Still, even on the margin of the grave, the desire of leaving a record of my afflictions haunts me, and gives me that strength which I could not exert for any other purpose.

"The hour that was destined to make me a mother gave birth to a female infant, which was followed by one of the other sex. Nature never fails to call forth the affections of the parent for her progeny; and much as I had supposed I should lament the birth of a child, I instantly felt that it would be an increase of my sufferings to be deprived of them, now they were given to me.

"Lord Rufus did not appear to welcome his children into existence.

"On the third day after their birth, the girl closed her eyes to the light. I now almost wept that my prayer to Heaven had been heard. Still my boy was left me, to console my sad and solitary moments. On the following morning, Lord Rufus came into my apartment. Instead of one observation relative to the recently created claim upon his affection—instead of one word, even of pretended tenderness to me, he abruptly informed me, that as the girl had died under my care, he had resolved to remove the boy to the superintendance of a nurse, and required me immediately to take leave of him for that purpose.

"In vain I remonstrated with him—in vain I endeavoured to convince him that the nurse which Nature has appointed to each child, in its mother's breast, must be its ablest rearer. He made no reply to my arguments, but merely repeated his own determination. I pressed my lips upon the cheek of the babe, and held him to my bosom. Lord Rufus put his hand upon the child, to tear him from me—I was not able to speak—I raised my eyes to him in eloquent silence; his heart could not relax to pity, and he bore the child away.

"That moment I learnt that there are still fresh pangs in nature for every sufferer's bosom, although he may believe himself already arrived at the climax of his misery.

"Sometimes I dreaded lest the life of my child should be unsafe in the hands of its unnatural father; at others, I almost wished that, whatever the means, it might be snatched from life while its sufferings could only be short and bodily, rather than that its existence should be spared for the lengthened and more acute pangs of the mind.

"In a few days, the conduct observed towards me served to convince me that my boy had been taken away from me, merely that he might never have a knowledge of his unfortunate mother, who was now reduced to that humiliating situation which should attend the lost to virtue, but which, for some unknown end, in the wisdom of Providence, is too frequently transferred to the innocent sufferer.

"The mere necessaries of life were now alone brought to me; and the apartments, which it had before been a voluntary act in me not to quit, were now, I found, become my prison. Heretofore the domestics, who did not understand my language, had made it their study to comprehend my wants from the signs I had given them; now, only one servant, and that of the opposite sex to my own, appeared in my apartment, once, or at most twice, in each twenty-four hours, and he obeyed no signal, nor observed towards me the slightest respect.

"Even at this time a reflection came across my brain, which administered something like peace to my afflicted mind—What, in a situation similar to mine, I considered, must be the feelings of a wretched object, who has voluntarily bent to infamy, and sacrificed her innocence for gold and splendour? When the clouds of adversity and disdain overwhelm her, where can she fly for consolation? That which the world denies her, she cannot receive from her own heart; her present existence is misery, and she has nothing to look forward to but punishment. Dreadful state of mind! While I have still a friend in my conscience, and can indulge in the delightful view of the mind, which presents to me the sun of eternal reward rising upon me, as my recompence for having leant firmly to the anchor of religious hope, whilst tossed on the sea of worldly calamity.

"Thus passed on two months, during which I saw not Lord Rufus. One day my attendants laid before me, upon my table, a small parcel. I found it to contain a *dagger*, and a paper, on which were written the following words in the hand-writing of Lord Rufus:—

'Perhaps you will not immediately recollect this dagger; it is the one which you once aimed at my life!'

'Where,' I involuntarily exclaimed, 'is the sword with which you drew the life-blood of my D'Altonville? The tears burst from my eyes, and for some moments prevented me from returning them to the paper in my hand; it was continued thus:

'You have long since informed me, that your life was a burden to you. Your existence now stands as much in the way of my projects, as it can do of your own happiness: you are therefore at liberty to part with it as soon as you please. I doubt not but that you will receive my present thankfully, and for once acknowledge a benefit at the hands of

'Rufus de Madginecourt.'

"This note I have transcribed into my narrative, the moment after my receiving it, as I would not that this last act of cool-blooded villany should be unknown to the future peruser of my fate. I consider myself as now writing for the last time. His letter plainly expresses that Eloise *must die*, and *shortly too!* If she will not commit suicide, it but remains to close the scene with her murder.

"So then it shall be. Having endured thus long, worlds should not purchase me to fly even the cruel death he may intend me, by an action that would destroy my hope of meeting D'Altonville in Heaven.

"Prepared myself to die, with every soothing sensation that can attend a sufferer to the margin of the grave, my thoughts still lean towards the less fortunate than myself, in their mental composure at so awful a moment; and I pray to Heaven that I may be the last victim of his villanous heart!

"This is probably the last time I shall ever hold a pen. The night is closing in fast. I shall, as usual, place my narrative in the station I have chosen for it in the library, and retire to rest.

"Reader, whoever thou art, that hast thus far accompanied me through the journey of my sufferings and afflictions, I thank thee for thy patience—I thank thee for the tear which I take to myself a pride and pleasure in believing that thou hast shed over them.—Farewell, should I never return to my task—shouldst thou never know how I died, believe, and remember, that Eloise will never *lift her hand against her own existence!*"

CHAPTER XIII.

Can such things be,
And overcome us like a summer's cloud,
Without our special wonder?

MACBETH.

HERE ended the manuscript.

"Thou didst never return to thy task, then, unfortunate Eloise!" exclaimed Rosalind, "and didst, doubtless, perish by the hand of villany! The tear that thou didst pray for falls upon thy writing, and the sigh that thou didst desire is heaved to thy memory, by one whose fate is equally wretched as thine own."

Rosalind now heard the step of Dame Edith approaching towards the library, and replaced the manuscript on the shelf where she had found it.

"It is strange," said Rosalind, addressing her, "that I should never have known Lord Rufus to have been married, till you mentioned it to me the other day."

"Why," replied the Dame, "your Ladyship can hardly have been born when the Lady de Madginecourt died; it is now full twenty-three years ago: besides, as I have before told you, she was a French lady, whom my Lord fell in love with on his travels, and made his wife. She was wholly unacquainted with the English language, and also of a very melancholy turn of mind; from both which causes, as I guess, she disliked mixing with society; for I can't say that I remember her ever quitting this suite of apartments which she inhabited."

"I think you said she was his wife but a short time," remarked Rosalind.

"Not quite a year," returned Edith: "she bore him twins; they both died on the third day after their birth; the poor lady was desperate at their loss; her fever ran high, in addition to which her milk flew to her brain—and—she died," added the Dame, hesitatingly.

"Poor unfortunate!" sighed out Rosalind, fixing her eyes on the Dame;—they probably bore in them a suspicion that Edith knew more than she had spoken; for the Dame advanced a few steps closer to Rosalind, and in a lower tone of voice added—"Unfortunate indeed, my Lady; for it is asserted that the frenzy of her malady caused her to lay violent hands on herself."

Rosalind shuddered at the account: she recollected the last lines of the narrative, which had declared that whatever her fate, she would never lift her hand against her own existence; and she doubted not but that the wretched Eloise had been the victim of unfair death, and had been falsely stigmatized with the crime under which she had suffered.

"Such accidents are dreadful to reflect upon," the Dame continued; "but we trust they are forgiven, because the sense is defective when they are performed. For the sake of her soul, I hope that Queen Dido was frantic, when she immolated herself upon the funeral pile."

Rosalind herself felt so strongly interested in the subject she was discussing, that she could hardly forbear an exclamation of anger or contempt at the last remark made by the Dame, who had plainly displayed that her feelings were of the languid kind, by the easy transition which she could make from fact to fable, and lay an equal emphasis of feeling on both; and she could not, for some time, have commanded her emotions sufficiently to have addressed the Dame with complacency, had not her ardent desire to learn all she was able of the fate of the unhappy sufferer on whom her thoughts were bent, over-ruled every other propensity.

"Did you see her children during the short period of time they lived?" asked Rosalind.

"No, my Lady," answered the Dame, "I never saw the lady herself above two or three times; I could not speak her language, or she mine; so, as I had not the power of offering her my services, I did not intrude myself into her presence; and at the time her children were born, as I think I have told you before, I had been a couple of months confined to my bed with a sprain in my back; and I had not the use of my limbs again till some time after her death."

"Had she any French servants?" asked Rosalind, conscious that she had not, but still unwilling to drop the subject in which her mind was wrapt, and at a loss how to continue it, without betraying herself acquainted with those particulars of which she did not at present chuse to avow a knowledge.

"No, she had not one French servant," answered the Dame; "and those English domestics who were particularly in her service have all left the castle, or are since dead."

A silence ensued.

"The secret then lies buried in the breast of him who will hereafter have to account for it," thought Rosalind.

"She was a beautiful lady, indeed!" continued Dame Edith; "and I dare say as amiable as she was beautiful, for my Lord cannot forget her to this day;—that is, he never suffers himself to be put in mind of her; for these rooms have been uninhabited, though not locked up, ever since her death. His Lordship does not so much as enter the gallery that leads to them; and I well remember once, about five years ago, when he was giving directions to some workmen on the ramparts, and his eye fell upon these apartments, seeing him turn hastily away, put his hand to his face, and shudder."

"To me at least thou standest convicted of thy guilt," said Rosalind, mentally. "Heaven grant that the secret of which I am possessed, may give me power to shield myself from the villany thy heart may intend against me!"

The remainder of the day passed on to Rosalind in painful reflection; she wished to taste the air, but she forbore to visit the garden, or the rampart, not chusing to witness a repetition of the scene she had once caught a glimpse of, in passing through the castle hall.

That hour of the evening at which Lord Rufus had acquainted her, at his departure, that he expected to return to his castle, and to bring with him the reply of Allanrod to her petition of being placed under the protection of the Queen, at length arrived.

She awaited his approach with a degree of impatience natural to the unpleasant situation in which she was placed, and with an anxiety which could not fail to harass her mind, as she dwelt on the mystery which formed the inexplicable union that subsisted between Lord Rufus and the Scottish freebooter.

The supper hour came, but Lord Rufus did not arrive. The spirits of Rosalind sunk at his absence. If he really intended to act towards her the part of friendship, this delay seemed to bespeak Allanrod unwilling to comply with her request. If he were in heart still her enemy, she wished his conduct rather to be shewn to her at once in its true colours, than thus to endure the pangs of suspense. On either consideration, she prayed that his return might not longer be protracted.

Whilst she sat with painful thought for her only companion, in an apartment which received a faint light from the thin crescent of a growing moon, that was rising slowly above the ramparts of the castle, Dame Edith entered the room, with a much more hasty step than she usually moved with, and throwing herself, without ceremony, into a chair,—"I am terrified out of my senses, my Lady," she cried; "I know not whether I stand on my feet or on my head, with fear! Heaven send my Lord may return to the castle to-night, or I shall never dare to go to my bed!"

The Dame had brought with her a lamp, and Rosalind saw real terror depicted on her countenance.—"What is it that has alarmed you?" she asked.

"A spirit!—a most wicked and abominable spirit, that haunts the castle!—Blessed be the Holy Ghost, and grant that its appearance be not the foretelling of the death of some of us!" replied the Dame.

Rosalind's incredulity, with regard to spirits, has already been shown. Much as she had heard them talked of, no report concerning them had ever yet reached her, which had gained her credit to their existence; and she had as regularly found that no arguments can reason those who are disposed to place belief in them, out of the conceit: accordingly, as she easily discovered old Edith to be one of that class, she remained silent, hoping that she would receive her taciturnity as a proof of her incredulity, and go elsewhere to tell her story, which Rosalind, at the present moment, felt particularly disinclined to be teazed with.

But no; Dame Edith was not to be disappointed of her tale; she was willing to believe that Rosalind maintained silence for the purpose of inviting her to continue her narrative, and she proceeded to recount, that the spirit had appeared to several of the household, in the course of the preceding night, who had some taken to their beds, and some gone half distracted, in consequence of what they had seen; that she knew she should die, if it appeared to her, which she did not seem at all inclined to do just yet, old as she was; and that her anxiety for the return of Lord Rufus proceeded, not from any particular receipt which he possessed for returning such airborn forms to their original vapour, but in order that his permission might be obtained to send for a priest who was competent to perform the task for him.

The Dame would talk, and therefore Rosalind was obliged to hear a long account of the different situations in which the alarming spirit had been seen, and of the different persons who had beheld it, and their degrees of bravery under the sight, which she concluded by saying, that the ghost was dressed, from top to toe, in black armour, and that its face was pale and livid, like that of a corpse, with a streak of blood down the left cheek.

This last sentence arrested the attention of Rosalind: she was struck with the resemblance that Dame Edith's description bore to the ghost which Gertrude had some time before informed her had been seen at De Mowbray Castle, and which had passed the drawbridge, to the great terror of old Ambrose, the porter, and Philip Watkins, the sentinel.

The singularity of the incident made a forcible impression on her mind:—on the evening of her father's departure from his castle, she believed that she had heard herself called upon by name, when wandering for air on the ramparts, and that at the same moment she had seen a dusky figure in the act of rising above the parapet wall, which had immediately disappeared, on the sound of Gertrude's voice. On the same evening of this occurrence, Gertrude had informed her of the appearance which had been witnessed at De Mowbray Castle. No sooner was she arrived at Rockmount, than its inhabitants were terrified by a vision exactly similar to that which had been described to her to have occasioned alarm to her father's household: there was something undefinably strange in this coincidence, which she could not so easily reconcile to her mind as she would have done the appearance of any spirit which had been said to have assumed a different form:—according to the description which Dame Edith had given her, it seemed as if that particular appearance flew in her path, and flitted around the spot which she inhabited.

END OF VOLUME TWO

THE *MYSTERIOUS* FREEBOOTER

CHAPTER I.

Is it come to this?

JULIUS CÆSAR.

For the first time in her life, Rosalind felt a sensation approaching to a belief in the existence of supernatural forms; why she now felt it, it was difficult, nay, indeed impossible, for her to account, even to her own heart. She was, however, too conscious that she did feel it, and almost joined Dame Edith in her apprehensions of some fatal event awaiting on one of the inhabitants of the castle—which one she did not doubt to be herself; and her eyes were turned slowly and fearfully around the apartment, in united expectation and dread of encountering the vision pictured on her fancy.

The shrill blast of a horn caused her to spring from her seat. Dame Edith jumped up hastily from her's, and exclaiming—"Thank Heaven! my Lord is home—now we shall hear what is to be done," rushed out of the room.

The sound indeed, as she imagined, announced the return of De Madginecourt to his castle, and the intelligence of his arrival gave a fresh turn to the thoughts of Rosalind, who momentarily expected to see him enter her apartment, with the reply of Allanrod to her request.

An interval of some length elapsed, and still he came not. Some of the attendants appeared with her evening repast, and, judging that Dame Edith's conjecture, concerning his arrival, might have been a mistaken one, she inquired of them whether it was so or not?

One of the domestics replied, that Lord Rufus was returned to his castle, and had retired to his chamber.

The information appeared strange to her; she knew not whether to believe that it augured good or evil: she feared the latter, and she endeavoured to combat the disquietude of her mind, by traversing, with hasty steps, the floor of her apartment. But, alas! the mind cannot fly from itself, nor are momentary oblivions of care an actual relief to an overburdened soul; memory, chased by art from its seat, resumes its empire with a more powerful and painful claim.

In about half-an-hour, Alwin, the page, entered her apartment, for the first time since she had become an inhabitant of the castle.—"Lord Rufus requests me to inform you, Lady Rosalind," he said, "that he is returned to his castle to-night, much fatigued with the journey of the day; he therefore trusts that you will receive this message as an apology for his not visiting you to-night, and will allow him to see you after the hour of breakfast in the morning."

Rosalind made a slight answer, and Alwin retired.

Every delay towards a knowledge of her fate increased the anxiety of Rosalind; and, desirous of passing the interval between the present hour and the morning, in that state of forgetfulness which she hoped sleep might grant her, she retired to her chamber. Dame Edith followed her to it immediately. The dame was, by no means, in a pleasant humour. Lord Rufus had instantly retired to his chamber on entering his castle, without paying the slightest attention to the tale of terror she had made an attempt of communicating to him; and the old lady seemed in actual fear of a summons to the other world, by the spirit in armour, with the streak of blood down its left cheek, before the morning.

Of the thoughts of Rosalind, when her head rested on her pillow, the spirit in armour had by no means an inconsiderable share. Her mind reverted to occurrences of years gone by; she recollected the voice which had called to her father "to spare her," when, in the chamber where her mother died, she was sinking at his feet, overwhelmed by the cruelty of his commands to give her hand to Lord Rufus, and forget her Edward. What interceding voice that was she had never been able to learn; she now fancied that there had been a resemblance between that voice, and the one which she had heard pronounce her name a few weeks before on the ramparts of her father's castle: still this idea afforded her no assistance in solving the enigma which appeared to encompass her.

One consolatory reflection alone arose out of the mass of ideas which crouded her mind: the voice had been a friendly one, and if the voice and the appearance therefore were one, she could have nothing to dread; if they were not, if any ill were haunting her, she had still this consolation within her own breast—that she had not one evil action to reproach herself with, and that innocence has never any cause to fear!

At that hour in the morning, at which the message Lord Rufus had sent her, by Alwin, on the foregoing evening, had taught her to expect his coming, he entered her apartment.

He moved into it with a slow step and sorrowful countenance, his eyes bent towards the ground.

Rosalind was standing by a window: he approached her, and making an inquiry after her health, in scarcely audible accents, he led her to a chair, and placed himself in one by her side.

Rosalind shuddered at his touch: never had she regarded him in any point of view but that of dislike. The narrative of the unfortunate Eloise had now heightened her aversion, almost to an insupportable pitch.

Lord Rufus spoke thus—"The most unpleasant moment of my life, Lady Rosalind, is now arrived. It is impossible for me to express to you how ardent has, for a long time past, been my desire to convince you, that when I first rendered myself hateful in your eyes, by the profession of that love which swelled my heart—when I first ventured to ask, as mine, the only hand which could have blessed my life, I was urged into the declaration of my feelings by your father—who, instead of informing me that there were prior claims on your affection, induced me to believe your sentiments congenial with my own. This encouragement, given to the fondest wish of my heart, made love the tyrant of my soul; and when I found my hopes deceived in you, that master-passion of the human mind poured an inflaming madness through my veins, that led me blindly into a conduct, of which the cause alone can be the apology."

He hesitated, as if expecting that Rosalind should acknowledge, for truth, the avowal he had just made.

"Proceed, my Lord," said Rosalind; "the past has lost its power to wound; it is the present that I wish you to speak of—Proceed."

"Briefly then," continued Lord Rufus, "believe, that I have, for a length of time, most sincerely repented, that one so excellent, so deserving of happiness as yourself, should, from her first knowledge of me, have dated her acquaintance with sorrow; that every moment of my latter years has been employed in plans for proving to you that repentance, and, as far as lay within the limits of my slender ability, restoring you to comfort. From this avowal your father's changed opinion of me has debarred me; no opportunity was given me for entering your presence, or imploring your forgiveness, and I almost began to despair of ever having it in my power to make confession to you of my penitence. At length—Oh, blessed chance!—the hour arrived at which it was given me to serve you. The lawless ruffian, Allanrod, besieged your father's castle, and Heaven made me the engine of your rescue from brutality."

A pause ensued. Lord Rufus rose from his seat, and moved to the other side of the apartment, apparently overpowered by the emotions of his heart; in a few moments he returned to his seat, and proceeded thus—

"Oh, Lady Rosalind! I once loved, but the esteem, the reverence I now feel, points out to me, that there is a greater joy in giving happiness than in receiving it. Oh! had my feelings then been what they now are! Had my kind genius whispered to my heart—'Receive thy bliss from seeing her thou lovest happy in the arms of him to whom her heart is given; make it thy felicity to know that thou hast constituted theirs!' But that hour is past; that moment cannot be recalled; and all that is now left me, is to repair, what I would give worlds that I had placed beyond the need of reparation."

"Even in your power as I am at this moment, and repentant as you profess yourself," replied Rosalind, "I am too much hardened in the school of suffering, to fear to tell you, that your declaration makes not the impression on my mind which you probably expected it would; but I will also tell you, how you may gain my future credit, if you will say that your interference has procured me the grant of being placed under the immediate protection of my Queen."

"There is the sting!—there is the wound that galls!" exclaimed Lord Rufus. "Oh, that villain Allanrod!—the monster refuses your petition—Ill fortune be his recompence!—Oh, Lady Rosalind, have I not reason to exclaim that this is the most wretched moment of my life, when the perversity of my fate withholds me from the performance of that action which might gain me the only esteem I covet to be blessed with?"

Rosalind fixed her eyes on those of Lord Rufus; she would have darted them, if possible, into his soul, and have read in it whether she was *his* prisoner or *Allanrod's*. His warm declarations of repentance for a moment led her to believe them real; then again, a vivid recollection of the past burst upon her mind, and she saw him all a villain.

On the countenance of Rosalind, Lord Rufus read what was passing in her heart.—"You doubt me still, I perceive," he said; "you are placed, Lady, in a situation that authorizes your suspicions, but you shall have proof that, with regard to myself, they are ill founded—though my own ruin ensue, you shall be preserved spotless—No, though De Madginecourt perish in your defence, your lips shall not be sullied by the kiss of a base robber; your bosom shall not be contaminated by the embraces of a freebooter!"

"Oh, Heavens!" exclaimed Rosalind, "what mean these words?—What new terrors are those you hint at? Explain—explain; do not, in mercy, do not torture me thus with maddening apprehensions!"

"Fear nothing; thou shalt be saved!" cried Lord Rufus.

"From what?—From what?" asked Rosalind.

"From becoming the *wife of Allanrod*," returned De Madginecourt.

"The *wife of Allanrod!*" echoed Rosalind. "Does he seek to make me his *wife*?—The *wife of Allanrod!*"

"This is the secret that my bosom laboured with; this is the secret that has thus long detained me from your presence, since my return to my castle," replied Lord Rufus. "Skilful in plans, the freebooter projects an alliance with you, that, by becoming connected with the family of De Mowbray, its intercession may procure him pardon from the crown, to which he is in momentary dread of his lawless life becoming forfeit."

"And it is really your wish to save me from his wiles?" asked Rosalind.

"So witness for me, Heaven!" replied De Madginecourt.

"Then give up Allanrod to the crown," pronounced Rosalind, with emphasis, "as his lawless existence merits, and I *am* saved."

Lord Rufus clasped his hands with violence together, and let his head fall upon them. After a pause—"That cannot be," he pronounced in a low voice.

"You say you wish to save me," continued Rosalind, "and yet reject the means that would preserve me. I feel myself justified in considering your repentance of the same character with your professions, and, regarding you as I have ever done, a combination of fraud and perfidy."

"You know not," returned Lord Rufus, "in how dreadful a strait I am placed; you despise my actions, because you are ignorant of the motive from which they spring; you doubt my fervour in your cause, because I dare not shew you the secret ties by which I am bound to extend it to you only within certain limits. Is it not enough for me to say, that you *shall* be saved, if my power, my wealth, my arm can effect it?—But it cannot, must not, be done by means of placing you under the protection of the Queen; such a step would be certain perdition to myself. Give a patient moment to consideration, and then tell me whether it can be the principle of your heart to return evil to me for the good I pant to confer on you?—No, no; such, I am certain, are not the sentiments of your breast."

Once more Rosalind inclined towards his arguments, and almost believed him her friend. It was *not* the nature of her heart to wish to return evil for good; her feelings were the immediate reverse. She looked at Lord Rufus, and beheld him pacing the room in a hurried manner, that bespoke his mind ill at ease. Her heart again softened towards him, as she conceived it possible that his desire to make her reparation for his past conduct, might be the principal cause of his present involvements—"If," she said, "you reject the obvious means of ensuring my security, you will not doubtless hesitate to inform me what those are which you intend to adopt in their stead?"

"Allanrod," replied Lord Rufus, "gives us but till to-morrow's eve for our separate decisions—to me, whether I will surrender you at his request, or submit to the besieging of my castle? to you, whether or not you will voluntarily become his victim? I have heard *your* resolution, Lady Rosalind, and my *own* has been long formed. Let him and his myrmidons come; let them direct their unjust force against my castle; let them dash down stone from stone, until the entire fabric become a pile of ruins—they shall not, in their victory, find the spoil they seek. The triumph of Allanrod shall lack the only prize he pants to obtain; Rosalind shall not be found by him in Rockmount Castle, nor upon the spot it stands on."

"You speak in riddles," returned Rosalind.

"I will solve my last declaration to you, if you enrol it amongst the other riddles I have been constrained to put to you," answered De Madginecourt. "You shall, Lady, be removed from hence to a place of security, before the freebooter comes. I have fixed my plans for your disposal; the consideration of a sleepless night has presented me with the means. I fear to send you away from my castle openly, lest there should be spies from Allanrod lurking in the neighbourhood, who might either detain you on your road, or convey to him intelligence of your route; in either of these cases, I should be equally miserable with yourself, in the failure of my earnest desire to save you from his justly hated power."

"Pray proceed, my Lord," said Rosalind, almost breathless with agitation, and impatient for the conclusion of his plan.

"Beneath this castle," he continued, "is a secret passage, which leads nearly half a league into the country westward; at its extremity is a habitation—I know not scarcely what to name it, a cell or grotto—once possessed by a solitary man, my friend; thither will I, during the night which shall succeed this day, myself conduct you; a faithful attendant, who shall be your companion during your stay there, shall alone accompany us, and alone be acquainted with your retiring thither; which precaution must inevitably secure us from treachery. There you shall remain till the issue of the threatened siege be past, and I will then, myself, appear to conduct you to some spot of future safety."

The eyes of Lord Rufus were raised to Rosalind; they bespoke him awaiting her affirmative to his proposition. The lights and shades of his character were alternately passing before her mind, and she leant successively to each. There might be some secret enmity to her peace, her life, depending on her compliance with becoming the inhabitant of the cell he had described, which, once arrived there, it might be too late for her to repent not having guarded against, by refusing to go to it: but then, want of compliance might yield her up to the brutality of Allanrod, when the advice of Lord Rufus promised to preserve her from his power. The moment of indecision was dreadful; it was laden with apprehensions that racked her brain.

At length Lord Rufus urged her reply. With an emphatic tone she spoke thus:—"Lord Rufus, you have already, during our conference this day, yourself allowed that my suspicions of your fair conduct towards me, after what is past, are not without justification. They must sufficiently explain to you the hesitation which you now see me labouring under—my reply is still wanting. I feel myself entirely in your power; I feel that I cannot be more so on any spot of the globe than I am under the roof of your own castle, where every domestic is doubtless the submissive performer of his Lord's actions. Thus, assured that you need not carry me hence to inflict on me any barbarity which you may have doomed me to suffer in revenge for your once-slighted love, I think it probable, from your offer just made to me, that it may indeed be your intention to save me from the misery of becoming the victim of this inhuman Allanrod. Carry me therefore to the spot you have described; my thanks I must reserve till you again call upon me to leave it."

With numberless repetitions of the ecstacy he derived from befriending her, Lord Rufus received her reply to the proposition he had advanced to her consideration, and then left her, to prepare his soldiery for the attack upon his castle by the mysterious freebooter.

The strangeness of her fate overwhelmed Rosalind with terrors inseparable from open danger, and which increase in proportion to the mysterious shade which envelopes it. She knew that Lord Rufus had an invention equal to the conception of any project, and daring talents to carry him through its execution; and she had also learnt enough of his past life, during her residence in his castle, to convince her that he had a heart too void of feeling to forego the perpetration of any act which his interest or his desires might require the performance of. As she dwelt on these considerations, a thousand nameless terrors, which exist in the most enlightened minds, and which set reason and examination equally at defiance, added horror to her thoughts; and her present situation appearing to her more tolerable than the offered change, she now resolved to await the event of the siege where she was.

Towards evening Lord Rufus again entered her apartment. He came, he said, to inquire which of his household she would prefer as her attendant and companion, during the time it would be necessary for her to remain at a distance from the castle?

Almost trembling to speak it, Rosalind informed him that her sentiments were changed, and that whatever danger might await her remaining in the castle, she felt a reluctance to quit it.

"Dearest Rosalind!" exclaimed Lord Rufus, "pardon the familiarity of the expression—I entreat you to be guided by my advice; for your own safety, do not distrust my words. Were my intentions towards you evil, were my aim even at your life, would it not be as easy to me to take it here as on any other spot?"

"Do you mean to avow by that question," asked Rosalind, pointedly, "that you have already found this castle a spot suited to a deed of that horrid nature?"

His countenance fell; the throbbings of his breast could not lie concealed beneath the corslet of mail which he wore, and he said, in a voice of tremor, which he sought to disguise under a forced smile—"What means the Lady Rosalind?"

The reflection of an instant convinced Rosalind that she had hazarded too much by this hint; a confession of the knowledge she was possessed of relative to the fate of his wife, might turn him into her most deadly foe, at the very moment when he was, perhaps, sincere in his friendship. She checked her rising feelings, and, with all the calmness she could command, she replied—"Women's fears often lead them to speak without meaning, as well as to feel sensations they cannot account for. The long and gloomy passages, and vaulted halls, which compose a building of the extent of this castle, when my spirits are depressed, always seem to convey to my senses some tale of horror in the breeze that rustles through them; and my Lord cannot suppose that my fate, at this moment, leaves my mind its wonted strength."

Lord Rufus did not look as if he were perfectly satisfied with her explanation, but he forced a second smile upon his countenance, and began to renew his entreaties to her to leave the castle. Again the mind of Rosalind wavered, and once more she acceded to his plan.

He urged her to name the companion she should prefer. She believed all those who composed his household to be alike indifferent to her, and replied to that purpose. "Then," said De Madginecourt, "your companion shall be Edith, and your attendant my own page, Alwin."

This proposition convinced her that all who composed his

household were *not* equally indifferent to her. To Alwin, a combination of circumstances had given her an insuperable aversion. Policy again withheld her from confessing all she felt, and she merely said—"I shall feel happier with only Edith for my companion."

"So then it shall be," he answered; "and at the hour of your departure, Edith shall select some vassal, whom she approves, that you may not be destitute of the means of sending, upon any emergency, to the castle."

Rosalind continued silent. Lord Rufus promised to come to her apartment when the castle was buried in sleep, and again retired.

Rosalind then threw herself upon a couch, and gave vent to her tears; her overburthened heart required the relief of weeping. "How strange!—how inexplicable is my fate!" she exclaimed. "Could I ever have believed that there could exist a man on earth whom I should dread more than Lord Rufus?—that I should ever have consented to have fled for protection, under his escort, from a being more terrible to my imagination than himself? Almighty Providence! thine omniscience sleeps not to the miseries of an imperfect being like myself. I know thee merciful; I know thee just; I ask of thee only strength to endure the trials thy wisdom has ordained me to pass through; grant me thy support, and I am still blessed."

With her mind thus impressed, Rosalind retired to the solitude of her chamber, and passed some time in addressing herself to Heaven for support and protection; and she rose from her devotions with a composure of feeling which seemed to promise her that her prayers were accepted at the throne of comfort.

CHAPTER II.

> Such are those thick and gloomy shadows damp,
> Oft seen in charnel vaults and sepulchres,
> Lingering and sitting by a new-made grave.
>
> MILTON.

About the hour of twilight, Dame Edith joined Rosalind in her apartment, with all the pride of consequence, at being the only person in the castle considered worthy of being entrusted with Rosalind's temporary departure from it, by her Lord. She informed Rosalind, that the person she had fixed upon, as their attendant, was a grand-nephew of her own, who was almost the only well-behaved male in the castle, for he had profited somewhat by her instructions, and she had at least taught him to hear, see, and say nothing.

The whole evening the old dame was employed in packing up a couple of baskets of provisions, and deciding on what books she should take with her in her pockets. She must have food, she said, for the mind as well as the body; it was not her way to feast on meat, and starve for sense. She did not doubt, she added, but that they should pass the time very pleasantly; the grotto was a charming place, in her opinion, and situated in a beautiful grove.

"I thought it was buried beneath the rocks," said Rosalind, "at the extremity of a subterraneous passage leading from the castle."

"Aye, that's the way you get to it," replied the dame, "and part of it is under ground, sure enough, when you are got there, but the other part is like a neat cottage above ground. I have often seen it formerly; I can't say that I have been there of late at all. No—no, your Ladyship, you are mistaken if you thought it was a dull place, like the cave of Polyphemus; it is, I dare say, almost as pleasant as the grotto of Calypso.

"Now I think of it, my Lady," continued the dame, after a pause, "I'll take that book of the Odyssey in my pocket, and then we can read about Calypso, and compare her grotto with our's."

Fortunately for Rosalind, if the dame did but talk herself, she cared not whether the person whom she addressed replied to her observations or not; thus Rosalind was allowed to indulge herself in silent reflection, whilst Edith continued talking without cessation. "It is a glorious thought of my Lord's, sending you to this grotto," she went on, "to preserve you from the malice of this freebooter; for such love as his I can only call malice, as he has never seen you, and only wants you for the wickedest of purposes. Pray Heaven he may get shot through the head in the siege! But I'll tell you what surprises me, my Lady—don't it you?—that if my Lord knows where to see this Scotch robber, and hold conferences with him, and so forth, he does not contrive at once to make him his prisoner, and deliver him up to justice."

Without a reply to this remark, Dame Edith would not rest satisfied. Whatever Rosalind's own opinion of Lord Rufus was, she scorned to give it to any one but himself, and answered—"There are, doubtless, obstacles in the way of his effecting it, which are not known to us."

"True, my Lady; the men say we are no politicians," returned the dame, "but I am a woman of courage, and if I were a lady of rank—"

At this moment a rap upon the door frightened away both Dame Edith's courage and rank, and she dropped into a chair, exclaiming—"Heaven preserve us! what noise is that?"

The pleader for entrance was no other than her nephew, Zachary, the destined companion of their temporary seclusion, who overheard her exclamation, and removed her alarm by announcing himself to his grand-aunt; she immediately opened the door to him, and apologised for the indifferent specimen she had given of her vaunted courage, by saying, that ever since the ghost in the black armour, with the streak of blood down its left cheek, had haunted the castle, she had not been like the same woman in fortitude that she used to be before—that is, Dame Edith, like many others, both before and since her time, was very courageous when she saw nothing to be afraid of.

The figure in armour had not recurred to the memory of Rosalind till the present moment, since the time of her conversation in the morning with Lord Rufus; and she now enquired, with some degree of eagerness, whether it had again been seen since the dame had given her an account of its appearance?

"No—no, Heaven be praised," returned the dame, "not that I have heard of;" and Zachary confirmed that it had not been seen during the last night.

Rosalind eyed Zachary with an enquiring eye, on account of the part which had been assigned him by his aunt, who, she imagined, might have been actuated in her choice of an attendant by a hint from her Lord; but with his appearance she felt satisfied.

He had a countenance which plainly bespoke its affinity to a heart devoid of the abilities for fraud or stratagem. Zachary was one of those beings who bear a continual smile on their countenance, and seem content to wear out life with eating and sleeping.

Zachary himself had not been one of those who had seen the spirit, and his senses were too dense to have been alarmed by the sight, if ever he had. One of the grooms, he said, who had been one of those to whom it had appeared, believed that it had vanished round a nook which led to the subterraneous passage, along which Rosalind had agreed to pass that night.

Dame Edith's terrors began now to be excited, lest they should meet the spirit in their way to the grotto. Zachary laughed at her apprehensions, and promised if they did, to give the ghost a black eye, or knock out some of its teeth; upon which Dame Edith began a long harangue to him upon his ignorance, which she followed with a learned dissertation upon the ærial nature of spirits.

At the end of her discussion Zachary burst into a loud laugh.—"You may as well leave off talking," he said; "I am sometimes afraid of flesh and blood, but your learning will never persuade me to be afraid of air, I can promise you."

"Oh, what a blessing," pronounced Rosalind, mentally, "is insensibility! Why do philosophers labour to be wiser still, when they can never return to that blissful state of ignorance from which they began their career after knowledge?"

A few minutes after the castle clock had struck eleven, Lord Rufus came to Rosalind's apartment; he had a cloak thrown over his shoulders, which, he said, was to protect him from the damps of the subterraneous passages, and he had brought with him another, of skin, for Rosalind, which he assisted her in putting on. When Dame Edith and Zachary were laden with their respective stores, they all left the apartment; Lord Rufus prevailed on Rosalind to support herself on his arm, and with every encouragement which words could give her to believe him her friend, he led her along.

They passed through various parts of the castle, all alike unknown to Rosalind, who had only once visited the garden, and once the rampart bordering on the sea, since her residence in it. After some time they arrived in a long vaulted passage, which Rosalind would have concluded to have been the aisle of a church, had the corresponding parts of the building confirmed the idea; but she soon found that it was an outlet from the castle to the concealed path through the rocks leading to the grotto.

"The subterraneous passage we are approaching," said Lord Rufus, "was, doubtless, dug out of the rocks at some distant period from the present time, when men sought refuge from their enemies in the bowels of the earth."

"Alas!" said Rosalind, "that the hours of that necessity were passed for ever!"

"May it please Heaven," returned Lord Rufus, "since the necessity still exists, that we may owe them our thanks for having afforded you the protection which you are doomed to seek from them. At the extremity of the subterraneous passage," he continued, "on the spot where the habitation I mentioned to you now stands, was once situated, as I have understood, a tower of great strength, connected with this castle; its vestiges are still to be traced, and it was doubtless for the purpose of escaping thither from the castle in the time of assault, that this passage was constructed."

On arriving at the end of the vaulted passage, which grew narrower towards its extremity, a range of dark wainscoting presented itself to their view. Lord Rufus disengaged his arm from that of Rosalind, and placing his hand upon a particular part of the wall, which concealed a spring, a door flew immediately open. Again he drew the arm of Rosalind through his, and led her on; they entered, what appeared, the ruins of a chapel, and her conductor confirmed her in her opinion, by saying, that it had once been so to Rockmount Castle. Rosalind cast her eyes almost fearfully around on the walls, green with damps, and the high and pointed window frames, which had become the supporters of the creeping ivy, and the luxuriant night-shade, in whose clusters roosted the owl, the bat, and the rook, which, on the interruption given to their midnight meridian by the intrusion of the light emitted from the flambeau carried by Zachary, sent forth those dismal shrieks which communicate superstitious shiverings to the hearts of those whose ears they assail.

They proceeded onwards, and as they passed through a deep vault, which Rosalind conceived to have been the cemetery of the castle, her eye fell on some broken columns, which had once supported the roof, and whose capitals were now hidden by the overshadowing briony; and as they rested on them, she fancied she saw a figure in black dart from behind one of them, and disappear again amidst a cluster of tombs, which were barely discernible through the thick shadow of night.

She started at the sight, and Lord Rufus enquired what affected her? She felt averse to confessing her alarm, as she was resolved not to communicate to him the impression which had been made on her mind by the various rumours which had reached her ear concerning the figure in armour, and pretended that she had only stumbled over a part of the rugged and broken pavement.

Zachary and Dame Edith were silent, of course they had not seen the figure glide from behind the shaft of the pillar; her imagination, she conceived, might have deceived her, and she was inclined to believe it had. Still she proposed to her own mind a question, which proved that she did not believe the appearance to have been solely the offspring of imagination; and this question was, whether, if she had really seen a figure at that moment, it had been the one described to her in black armour?

On leaving the chapel and its precincts, Rosalind and her companions entered the subterraneous passage. The cavity they were to pass through was hewn out of the bosom of the solid rock; dank vapours there assailed their senses, and the damps distilled their aguish drops upon their heads.

They had proceeded only a few steps into it, when Lord Rufus said—"My motive, Lady Rosalind, for conducting you, myself, away from my castle by night, you are already well acquainted with; it is to confute the treachery of such as might not be proof against the bribes or threats of Allanrod, should he be the conqueror of my castle, and hold out to the weak the promise of reward for the discovery of your place of concealment, or the terror of punishment for the withholding of the desired information. The shorter the time therefore that I am absent from my chamber this night, the safer our plan, as any knowledge of my leaving it might lead to a suspicion of the cause, and thus to a discovery of the transaction that has marked the hour. The path hence to the grotto is strait—dangerous it cannot be; I will therefore here bid you farewell. Good angels guard you, Lady; depend on seeing me, the instant I can appear to you without danger to yourself."

As Rosalind had already acquiesced thus far in his plan, she had no reason for dissenting from this immaterial part of it; and accordingly, with an entreaty that he would, as soon as possible, give her information of her doom, she suffered him to depart, and proceeded onwards with Dame Edith and Zachary.

As she moved along, her faithful Gertrude recurred to her imagination, and she lamented more than ever her separation from the affectionate girl. At his departure from Rockmount Castle to his meeting with Allanrod, Lord Rufus had promised to make the restoration of Gertrude a part of his request to the freebooter. Weightier matter to her own happiness had occupied her mind since his return, and she had not made any enquiry of him concerning her attendant; but she doubted not that every other consideration had been sunk in the demand Allanrod had made of her person.

About half an hour brought them to the extremity of the subterraneous passage. A low arch, hewn out of the rock, presented itself to them; they stooped, and passed through it. It was the entrance into what Dame Edith called the grotto; to Rosalind it appeared solely as a small apartment cut out of the earth, which owed its walls merely to the spade. In the middle of it stood a rude table, and seats, of an equally indifferent workmanship, were scattered about; on one of these, Dame Edith, panting and puffing with her long walk, sought immediate rest, and Rosalind instinctively followed her example.

"This is not the apartment we are to inhabit," said the dame, "that is up those stairs," pointing to some steps in one corner of the place; "we will go up them in a minute; but I am so unused to walking, that my bones ache as if I had been beaten."

Rosalind's eye kept roving round the place, although there was no object of sufficient importance for it to fix upon.

In a few minutes the dame was ready to ascend into the upper apartment. She took the light, and Rosalind followed her; the stairs led them to a neat room, furnished in the style of a cottage; a door, opposite to the one they entered by, led them into a second room, similar to the first; and these were all the apartments of which the building consisted. There was in each of them only one long and narrow casement; Rosalind raised her eyes to that in the first room, and, from the blank it presented to her sight, she imagined the night to be dark; but from the second, she caught a view of a resplendent moon, glittering through the foliage of some surrounding trees, which convinced her that some interposing substance threw a shade upon that in the first apartment.

Trivial as these circumstances may appear to a mind at ease, they are such as the heart, suspicious of treachery, investigates with the nicest scrutiny.

A door in the second apartment, which was bolted within, next attracted her observation. "Whither does this lead?" she asked her companions. "Out upon the country," returned the dame; "here are a few knots of trees on this side the cottage, then a field, and next the high road; for every step we have set to-night from the castle, has been a step away from the sea-shore into the land: you can hardly hear the roaring of the sea here."

The possibility of an escape now struck the mind of Rosalind, and darted a flash of joy across her heart; but, upon a moment's reflection, the pleasing impression faded away. Whither should she fly? The roads were utterly unknown to her, and if she were acquainted with them, faintness and fatigue must overwhelm her ere she could reach a place of safety, as she was entirely ignorant where to seek her father, and had no protector but the Queen, towards whom she could bend her steps. If she were even to hazard the event of flying from Lord Rufus, (could she escape the vigilance of her companions, who were doubtless commanded to keep a strict watch over her actions) and trust to the guidance of any friendly stranger to whom chance might lead her, she might, ere such a friend was found by her, be encountered by Allanrod's band, and her flight for safety become her ruin. Restoration to peace, she concluded, might be the issue of her remaining where she was; to wander forth alone upon the world, was to court certain danger.

In one of the apartments stood a couch; this Dame Edith prepared, with some clothes which she had brought with her, in addition to some which she found on the spot, for Rosalind to repose upon. After some time the dame prevailed on her to retire to it, but was resolute in not accepting that share of it which Rosalind would willingly have given up to her comfort; and wrapping herself up in the skin cloak which Rosalind had worn during her walk, she placed herself in a chair, by the side of the couch, saying, that "she could sleep as well sitting as lying, and that if she did not sleep quite so long, or so easily, she should enjoy her bed the more when she returned to it, which she hoped would be the next night, as she had understood from her Lord, that the freebooter threatened to attack Rockmount Castle the next day, and she doubted not, from what she knew of the bravery of its troops, that half an hour's fighting with them would cool his courage, and send him quietly about his business."

"Pray Heaven it may be so!" exclaimed Rosalind, and sunk on her couch, not to sleep, but to waking reflection.

Zachary, according to his own account, could have slept on a cannon; so the dame advised him to take the stairs for his resting-place, and use the threshold of the door, at their top, for a pillow, in order that he might be near enough to hear her call in case she wanted him. He would have preferred going down into the grotto, but the dame would be obeyed; and in a very few minutes his snoring informed her, that he did not sleep the worse for her having selected his resting-place.

Rosalind slept as little as it can be supposed she could do in her present novelty of situation, and with her mind thus ill at ease; as soon as the first streaks of returning day beamed through the casement, she left her couch.

She wandered about her apartment, till the light of day became sufficiently powerful to invite her to the window. The first objects which struck her sight, were the distant battlements of the castle, rising above a cluster of trees that grew at their base, and just tinged with the yellow gleam of the rising sun; beyond them rose majestic hills, cloathed with oak and beech, which retired into a long perspective, and ultimately seemed to mix themselves with the clouds.

Immediately before the window at which she stood, lay a flat country, of which the verdure was scanty, and the vegetation barren; it extended almost as far as her eye could accompany it, and at length seemed to terminate at the foot of some craggy steeps.

Having gazed some time on the scene which this casement afforded her, she went to the other, which, on the foregoing evening, she had imagined to have been obscured by some outward object, and she found that a bush of holly had been courted to twine its spreading branches before it, so as almost to deprive it of the power of giving light to the apartment it was in. The ground immediately before the cottage was marked by no track which bespoke its door to have been lately in use; unchecked weeds were growing thickly around it, and the swallows flew to its roof with a security that seemed to bespeak that they had never met with any interruption from its inhabitants.

Dame Edith, who had slept but indifferently during the night, was endeavouring to make herself amends in the morning, and therefore Rosalind moved about unnoticed by her; as for Zachary, he was already at breakfast in the grotto below.

When Rosalind retired from the window, several papers fastened upon the walls attracted her attention; she went up to them, and found that they contained different pieces of poetry; some of them she perused, they pleased her fancy, and she sought for others. In pursuing her amusement, to her surprise, she encountered some lines which were perfectly familiar to her. They had been given to her by her lost Edward; he had informed her, that they had been written by the old man who had brought him up, and at the supplication of whom, when on his death-bed, Lord William de Mowbray had taken him under his protection. These were not only the same lines, but in the same hand-writing as those which Edward had given to her as the composition of old Matthews. Rosalind eagerly examined, in turn, each separate piece contained on the walls of the cottage, and found the characters of them all to have been evidently traced by the same hand. The lines with which she was already acquainted were the following—

THE SEA SIDE.

When evening's balmy breezes mildly blow,
And the bright orb of day is sinking low,
I wander to the shelvy ocean's side,
Where billows foam, or gently rolls the tide.

Sooth'd by the scene, discordant passions cease,
The soul is lull'd to happiness and peace;
While contemplation takes the guiding rein,
And leads remembrance through a pleasing train.

Who can the starr'd expanse unmov'd behold,
Or see its azure surface ting'd with gold,
But must th' omnipotence of God adore,
And cease to doubt, if doubt he could before?

Of life, an emblem is th' incessant change
From high to low, through which the billows range!
How like to pain, when boisterous, rough, and wild!
How like to pleasure, when serene and mild?

Yon distant sail, an image too appears,
Of present pleasure, damp'd by future fears;
For yonder clouds a threat'ning gloom portend;
The present calm may in a tempest end.

Thus in the noon-tide of our early days,
When joyous hope in expectation plays
About the heart, we feel its transports beat,
In sweet vibrations round its native seat.

Ah! happy moments, sources of delight!
Why thus on hasty pinions wing your flight?
Ah! happy days of innocence and ease!
Why do you fly for those less sure to please?

Less sure to please—because each passion grows
As age increases; thus the riv'let flows,
At first soft murmuring o'er its pebbly bed,
Till swell'd by rains, its roaring torrents spread.

Not a single word through all the stanzas varied from the copy which Rosalind had, years before, received of the same lines from her Edward, at De Mowbray Castle; and the more she examined the writing, the more fully she was convinced that it was the same. The strangeness of the circumstance awakened in her mind an ardent curiosity to learn who had been the former inhabitant of the grotto—she might from such a knowledge unexpectedly learn who were the parents of her never to be forgotten Edward; she might discover the existence of some beings to whom she was at present unknown, and to whom it might require her only to acknowledge herself as his wife, to constitute them her friends, as well as relatives.

The idea cheered her more than any which had for some time received birth in her imagination, and she impatiently awaited the waking of Dame Edith, to whom she panted to propose the questions rising in her mind. The dame listened attentively to her enquiries, without knowing the cause from whence they sprang; the verses, she said, had often charmed her, and she doubtless considered this a sufficient reason for any other person being desirous of knowing by whom they were written; but of the author she could give no farther account, than that he was a man of a solitary disposition, and had resided there some two and twenty years ago; but that she knew not either his name, or whence he had come.

"Did he die here?" asked Rosalind.

"No, my lady," returned the dame; "he grew, I have understood, weary of the solitude he lived in, and left the country."

"It is strange," said Rosalind, "as he has been reported to me, both by Lord Rufus and yourself, as his Lordship's friend, that he was not invited rather to make the castle his abode than this lonely spot, especially as the want of society appears to have been a cause of dissatisfaction to him."

"Why, indeed, so it does seem, true enough," replied the dame, "but I can't tell why it was or was not so."

"Did he live quite alone here?" asked Rosalind.

"Entirely so, I believe," answered the dame.

"He had no companion at all then," said Rosalind—"no son, no child?"

"Not that I ever heard of, my Lady; what makes you ask the question?" returned Edith.

"Only," replied Rosalind, endeavouring to conceal her feelings, "because in that case it must have been lonely indeed."

The subject was dropped; Dame Edith prepared the breakfast, and Rosalind continued silent.

The day passed on heavily and mournfully to the daughter of De Mowbray.

A companion, who knows not sufficient of our secret history, to feel that interest in our fate, which can alone render conversation acceptable to our feelings, is less pleasant than solitude; and in order to avoid the necessity of listening, at least for a while, to the old dame's prattle, Rosalind took a pencil from her pocket, and reflecting on the bliss which might have been her's with her Edward, in a cot like the one she was now an inhabitant of, had she been the child of humble cottagers, rather than the offspring of wealth and splendour, she composed the following lines—

THE PEASANT'S NEST.

Far in the depth of yonder glade,
Where plenty smiles around,
The peasant's nest uprears its head,
With moss and ivy crown'd.

Embower'd within the friendly shade
Of oaks encircling arms,
It asks not art's insidious aid,
To deck its native charms.

A little garden, trimm'd with skill,
Boasts not each flow'r that blows;
But waters with its murmuring rill
The jess'mine and the rose.

Peace smiles beneath its humble roof,
Love dwells in every breast;
Each morn brings joy, for ah! content
Has bless'd the peasant's nest.

"Whoever thou art," exclaimed Rosalind, "by whom the lines I have this day perused were written, whether thou art still on earth, unconscious of my present action, or from the blest abode of saints lookst down upon me—pardon the sympathy by which my mind is drawn to an emulation of thine, and despise not the impulse which leads me to place my unadorned composition amongst thine, which are graced by genius and understanding;" and with these words Rosalind placed them upon the wall, amidst those which she had already found there.

Dame Edith put on her spectacles to peruse them. "Well, they are sweetly pretty," she cried, "and the first that I ever read that were written by a lady. Whatever the men may say to the contrary, we don't know what we can do till we make the attempt; and it is my opinion, that any woman might fix a pair of horns on the head of some man or other, as Diana did on Acteon's, if she had but the courage to try."

CHAPTER III.

What are these,
So wither'd, and so wild in their attire,
That look not like the inhabitants o' the earth,
And yet are on't?

MACBETH.

THE evening approached without any intelligence arriving to Rosalind from Lord Rufus, or any sounds meeting her ear which she could construe into a supposition of the attack upon the castle being begun. At times she hoped that Allanrod's threats would end in words; at others, that Lord Rufus might still come to an accommodation with him, and induce him to relinquish the demand of her hand.

The twilight had scarcely begun to expand its raven wings, ere Dame Edith obliged her nephew to have recourse to the flint and steel, to produce a substitute for the waning light of the sky, which appeared absolutely necessary to the keeping up of her spirits in her present solitary abode.

The lamp was accordingly placed upon the table, and Rosalind and the dame drew round it. "It appears strange to me," said Rosalind, "that, if it is now two-and-twenty years since the former inhabitant of this place left it, it should still remain in the good order in which we found it, and the furniture appear so little injured by the hand of time."

"Oh, my Lady," returned Edith, "it has had another inhabitant since then."

"Indeed!" rejoined Rosalind, "who might that be?"

"A person my Lord was good to," answered the dame, casting a significant glance upon her nephew, who was at that time performing some office in the apartment; "only a pensioner of my Lord's."

Rosalind perceived her disinclination to speak before Zachary, and therefore said no more. In a few minutes he went down into the lower apartment. "I did not like to answer your question before him, my Lady," went on the dame, "because it is not fit that such as he should know secrets with which there can be no harm in your Ladyship's being acquainted. The last person who lived here was——" Zachary's foot was heard upon the stairs, and again his grand-aunt became silent. "When you have got what you want," she continued, after a pause, addressing him, "I desire you will keep below; my Lady and I are busy."

"So am I going to be," replied Zachary, "for I am going to get my supper;" and he was on the point of again descending the stairs when the sound of a horse's feet caught the attention of Rosalind and her attendants. It appeared to be moving at full speed, and as they continued to listen, it seemed to approach towards their habitation. The eyes of Rosalind and Dame Edith rested in silent enquiry on each other. Rosalind could not suppose that Lord Rufus would send her information, except by the subterraneous passage. Dame Edith actually believed that Allanrod had discovered Rosalind's retreat, and was coming in person to demand her; but she forebore to express her thoughts. "What can it be?" broke, at the interval of some moments, from the lips of each; and the insensible Zachary mechanically replied to their question—"Only a horse."

The clattering of the hoofs drew nearer and nearer, and at length stopped immediately opposite to the cottage; a rap with a stick upon the door followed, and, almost at the same instant, the voice of a person, who had discovered through the casement that there were inhabitants within, called out—"For the love of mercy, if ye are not callous to every impulse of feeling, give us shelter beneath your roof."

"Oh, Heavens, what a demand!" exclaimed Dame Edith. "What is to be done?"

"Whatever our own situation," replied Rosalind, "we should still have a hand of succour ready for the children of distress. Let us enquire who makes the demand."

"Surely you would not let any body in here!" cried Dame Edith.

"I know not that it is in my power to do so," returned Rosalind; "but we may be otherwise able to afford them assistance on a knowledge of their wants."

Again the same petition was advanced by the pleader without, and Rosalind could discern that the voice which uttered it was that of a female.

Rosalind mounted upon the step at the foot of the casement, and opening a small portion of it, which just admitted her face through the aperture, she perceived a woman, whose countenance bore marks of the deepest affliction, sitting nearest to the head of the horse; in one hand she held the bridle, and with her other arm she supported a man, who was placed behind her upon the saddle, and whose countenance bespoke him suffering under the severest pressure of illness.

"Oh, for the love of Heaven!" the woman again began, "admit us into your dwelling; my wretched, my unfortunate husband, must else die where you now behold him, when a little succour from you may protract, perhaps recover him his existence."

"Oh, indeed, we can't let in any body to die here," cried Dame Edith; "we are very sorry you are going to lose your husband, but we can't do that."

Rosalind was in this instance the mistress of her own actions, and attended not to the exclamation of the dame. She looked stedfastly upon the countenance of the woman, and believed it to be one of those which bespoke a heart incapable of ingratitude—one which would sooner have suffered wrong than inflicted it. The duty of charity had, from her earliest youth, been impressed upon the heart of Rosalind, as that of which the performance raised her the nearest to him, who, though clothed in every virtue, did not escape earthly suffering. The afflictions she had herself endured, had rendered her heart every day more susceptible of the calamities of her fellow creatures, and she would rather have suffered from the perfidy of an object who had proved undeserving of her commiseration, than to have lived under the self-reproach of having refused to stretch out her hand to a being who might have perished from her neglect. "If it is in my power to assist you," she said, "I will." She called to Zachary, and, in a decisive tone of voice, bid him make the attempt of opening the door, which silenced Dame Edith, and left her only her grimaces to shew her discontent of Rosalind's proceedings by.

The bolts were rusted in their sockets, and the door itself had sunk upon its hinges, and settled itself an inch or more into the ground; but these obstacles the strength of Zachary soon overcame, and an entrance to the dwelling was opened to the unfortunate strangers. The female requested assistance to take her husband from the horse; Zachary went out to her aid, and in a few minutes the sick man was brought in, and laid, at Rosalind's command, upon the couch where she had slept the night before.

The woman, whose accent Rosalind perceived to be Scotch, was unceasing in her thanks for the kindness she was experiencing, and pronounced a blessing on Rosalind, with every effort which she made, but made in vain, to induce her husband to taste the wine which she had received at the hand of her benefactress.

The dress of both struck Rosalind as extremely peculiar, and she knew not whether to conclude it the dress of the Scotch, or a garb which would, in any part of the world, have been considered as uncommon as it appeared to her. The dress of the man was less particular than that of his wife; he wore buskins, and a philibeg of plaid, over which his coat hung down almost to his knees, but was unbuttoned before, and discovered his plaid, mounting in the form of a corslet to his neck. On his head was a skin bonnet, bound down under his chin with a handkerchief, which seemed to be intended to preserve him from the cold, out of consideration to his ill health.

The woman appeared about forty years of age, well made, tall, and stout of limb; her countenance was more interesting than handsome; it owed its fascination principally to a pair of full black eyes, of which the expression was very great, and which gave an animation to the rest of her features. Her dress was not confined by stays, but formed of stuff, and bound round her waist with a strip of the same material which composed her outer garment, and which ligature gave it the only distinction it had between waist and petticoat; from under this peeped out a pair of russet boots: upon her shoulders hung a cloak, and the hood of this was thrown over a plaid bonnet on her head.

Still, extraordinary as were their dresses, they did not bespeak poverty; nor did the manners of the female represent her as a woman of a mean rank in life.

"It avails not," she said, after a time, "he must die—I see he must. If thou hearest me," she continued, addressing her husband, whose head was rested on her arm, "grieve not to leave me behind thee; I rejoice that thou art going so soon to join our sainted mistress."

"You see they are only servants, my Lady," whispered Dame Edith to Rosalind.

In a few moments the man opened his eyes. "Margaret," he said, "this hour is my last. I have not been insensible, although unable to speak to thee; I shall never, never be able to execute my vow."

"Have not I told you already not to let that thought vex you?" returned the woman. "Have not I promised to execute it for you?"

"Will you—will you *indeed*, Margaret?" replied the man; "will you assume the courage to revenge the murder of that blessed——?" The word which should have followed died away on his tongue.

"Yes, *by Heaven!*" answered the woman; "may I never enter those blessed regions of eternity, where she now receives her recompence for all her wrongs on earth, if I do not, with mine own hand, justify her on her murderer."

"I shall die happy, Margaret—I shall die happy!" faintly pronounced the man, pressing her hand to his lips.

A silence ensued.

"Ye have been sufferers, it should seem," said Rosalind, "from the unfair death of some lamented friend?"

"The death of an angel," replied the woman, emphatically. "It is true that she was too good for earth—too pure to live in this wicked world; but still the crime of her murderer deserves equal punishment, and it shall meet its merited recompence."

The time passed melancholily on. Rosalind could not induce the woman to be more explicit as to herself than she had already been; and the mystery observed by her, added to the evidently approaching termination of the man's existence, made her almost repent her charity, although she carefully concealed her thoughts from Dame Edith, who would only have triumphed in her feelings, without comprehending the sentiment that occasioned them.

"Wherever I go," said the woman, the tears streaming down her cheeks as she spoke, "your angelic benevolence will never be effaced from my heart. There was a time when I knew only prosperity, but it is now long since my husband or myself have experienced such kindness as we have this night received at your hands; we had once a friend, a saint, an angel, like yourself."—Her tears now entirely choaked her utterance.

"May I not know who that friend was?" asked Rosalind, again self-satisfied that she had admitted the strangers to her hospitality.

"No, no," she replied, "that is the only request which, in the gratitude of my heart towards you, I could withhold from you; but that must not be *now*. You will shortly know who was my friend, and who I am too; but that must not be till that friend is *revenged*."

The hour-glass on the table had just told the second hour of the morning, when the dying man made an effort to raise himself upon the couch. "Margaret," he whispered forth. "I am here," she replied—"I am here."

"Margaret," he repeated, *"remember thy promise!"*

"So bless me, Heaven, with life," she returned, *"it shall be done."*

A faint smile stole over his countenance, which was followed by a convulsive sigh, and in a few moments after he ceased to breathe.

The woman clasped her hands, and stood bending over the corpse. "I lament thee not," she said; "all thy comforts on earth were fled, and thou art now with the blessed in Heaven—Soon, soon shall I join thee there—Prepare, my sainted mistress, to give me welcome!" She continued for some time hanging over the body, and Rosalind, by the motion of her lips, believed that she was in silent prayer; one word only she heard of her oraisons, and that was the word "mistress," of which, at her first use of it, Dame Edith had so readily explained the meaning, but which Rosalind could not induce herself to regard by any means in the same light.

Her prayer ended, she kissed the inanimate lips of her husband, and then turning away from the couch, wiped the tears from her face. This done, she approached Rosalind, and falling upon her knees before her, she caught her hand in her's—"Whoever thou art," she said, "it is needless for me to implore on thee the blessing of Heaven; thou hast a heart that must ensure it to thee. In words adequate to my feelings, it is impossible for me to express my thanks, that your pity has saved him, who now lies cold in death, from breathing out his last sigh unsheltered from the biting air; give his remains a little earth, and if thy inheritance in Heaven be not already secured to thee, accept for it the prayer of a *dying* woman."

Having uttered these words, she rose from her knees, and ran hastily out of the cottage; Rosalind followed her with her eyes, and saw her spring upon her horse, on which she instantly set off at full speed.

CHAPTER IV.

Thou seest we are not all alone unhappy—
This wide and universal theatre
Presents more woeful pageants, than the scene
Wherein we play in.

AS YOU LIKE IT.

THE countenance, bleached by the hand of Death, had no terrors for the mind of Rosalind, and drawing towards the couch, she examined the features of him who lay extended upon it; they were calm and serene—a satisfying assurance that he had died at peace with Heaven.

"Well," cried Dame Edith, "of all the histories I ever read, I never met with any thing equal to what I have seen this night!—To bring an utter stranger to die under one's roof, and to leave him there too!—but some people have no consideration at all."

This last sentence was probably intended as a reproof to Rosalind, if she chose to take it, for having admitted the dead man under her roof; for Dame Edith, with a courage very natural to piqued inferiors, ventured to express her dislike of what had taken place when it was past, though she had not dared to utter a syllable on the subject whilst the action was yet undone, and her interference likely to meet with a reprimand.

But Rosalind was too well satisfied with having acted rightly, to be moved by the displeasure of the old dame. On the morrow she had every reason to expect a recall from her present abode, and she felt no inconvenience in giving up her couch for that night to an unfortunate man, whose lifeless body must else have been exposed to the rude attacks of animals of prey upon the open road.

"And what are we to do with the body?" enquired Edith.

"Nothing," replied Rosalind; "we will return into the other apartment, and leave it; when we are recalled to the castle, it shall be buried."

"My Lord will think it finely odd to find a dead man here when he comes back," exclaimed the dame.

"If the sentiments which your Lord professes towards me are unfeigned," replied Rosalind, "he will not see any thing reprehensible in my having performed a charitable action."

"I hope you will tell him I had nothing to do with it," the dame went on.

"He will perfectly understand that without explanation," answered Rosalind, "as he made me the mistress of this abode."

This was a hint to Dame Edith to put a stop to her observations, which if she did not much relish, at least produced the effect Rosalind desired to obtain from it.

Rosalind and the dame wrapped themselves up in cloaks, and placed themselves in chairs in the first apartment. "I durst not sleep, on any account," said the latter, "in a room next a dead man, especially a Scotchman."

Rosalind could not forbear an inward smile at the idea of the dead being feared in proportion as they were natives of one or another country.

The dame went on—"I am a true English subject, my Lady; I revere our Queen with all my soul, and hate the Scotch from my heart."

The period at which Dame Edith was talking, was a few weeks after the unfortunate Mary Queen of Scots had bowed her neck beneath the axe; and the people of England having been influenced into a belief, that, by her death, their Queen had been freed from a most iniquitous foe, who had endeavoured to hurl her from her throne, and usurp her seat on it, condemned promiscuously all her countrymen with herself.

Although Elizabeth was the godmother of Rosalind, and she had heard only one side of the question during the trial of the Scotch Queen, still, from circumstances which she had singly gathered, but which had rested on her mind, she had been led, privately, to pity Mary's unfortunate lot, and to believe her, if not innocent, at least less guilty than she had been represented, and most rigorously punished by the privation of life.

The dame, although shut for nearly a century within the walls of Rockmount Castle, considered herself by no means a less able politician than those who visited the court; and she now began to descant, with all the fury of bigotry, on the heinousness of Scotch principles, and the universal wickedness which must of necessity be inherent in the Scotch nation, when they had the example of most atrocious crimes set them in the person of their monarch: but that she trusted and hoped that the punishment which had overtaken her, would lead them all to repentance, and that before they died, they would bless the Queen of England, as the instrument of their reformation.

The narrow-minded principles of the dame were as much beneath the attention of Rosalind, as she considered her arguments too contemptible for reply. Rosalind was a firm adherent of Elizabeth's, and bore her that love and respect which the honour she had conferred on her at her birth demanded from her; but still she was not so blind in her affection, as not to be able to distinguish that the most perfect may be liable to single actions, but for the performance of which the fame of their even rectitude would raise them above the level of mortality; and she could not forbear considering the death of Mary, as the single shade which dimmed the otherwise unsullied lights of Elizabeth's character.

The dame passed the night in intervals of sleep and conversation. Rosalind was content to wear away the hours in passive expectation of the ensuing morn, which at length arose with peculiar serenity and brightness. Rosalind rejoiced at the approach of day, because it enabled her again to look towards the castle, and form some idea whether the threatened attack upon it had yet been made. The dame rejoiced, because the light of day dispelled from her mind her superstitious fears.

Rosalind stood at the casement some time, before the increasing light enabled her to discern the battlements of the castle, and when she could see them, she discovered no cause to believe that the forces of the freebooter had yet been planted before them; indeed she believed it hardly possible that the attack should be made without various sounds reaching her. The dame endeavoured to persuade her to suffer Zachary to go back to the castle, and make enquiry; but this appeared, in every respect, so openly to be frustrating De Madginecourt's plan for her security, that she would not for an instant admit the idea.

"We have no provisions to last us longer than till night," said the dame.

"When that hour arrives," said Rosalind, "it will be time enough to think of procuring more; besides, Lord Rufus is acquainted with what stock we brought with us, and will doubtless not allow us to remain here in want: much may occur in the course of the next twelve hours."

The dame went to breakfast, with an appetite that seemed to bespeak her determined not to suffer their stores to last beyond the time she had named, probably from her dread of remaining another night under the same roof with an unburied Scotchman.

Rosalind continued standing before the window, her mind occupied alternately by the mysterious occurrence of the preceding night, and the strange uncertainty of her own fate. Her eyes rested on the grandeur of the scene before her, closed in on every side by distant rocks, whose spiral tops were illuminated by the rays of the rising sun, which was creeping slowly above them into an azure firmament, unspotted by a single cloud. At the foot of the mountains, beyond the castle, she descried a broad stream, which wound amongst the trees that cloathed their sloping sides, and was then seen falling over the crags of a more perpendicular steep; now it appeared flickering beneath the golden sun-beams; now gliding in a silver current under the shadowing foliage of the woods.

The solid mass which composed the castle, gave a feature of the sublimest kind to the landscape; and the extent of the fortifications, which spread along the plain, appeared the work of centuries, and seemed to frown defiance on the attempts of an enemy to invade them. As her eye drew nearer home, the ground sparkled beneath the dew-drops gemmed by the sun; and the song of the sky-lark, flying in circles round the spot where its nest lay concealed, gave a momentary glow to her spirits.

About two hours after sun-rise, as her eyes were stretched out towards the mountains, she perceived a moving body descending from the summit of one of them, on which the light of the sun rested with peculiar brightness, and she concluded that it must be a body of troops, whose arms glittered beneath the reflection of its beams. She called upon Zachary to assist her conjecture, and he confirmed the one she had already drawn.

These then, Rosalind concluded, were the troops of Allanrod, advancing to their attack upon Rockmount Castle. She enquired of Zachary, at the distance of how many hours march they were from it? and he replied, "that they were a good way off, although they seemed so near; for at the foot of the mountain they were now crossing, there ran a river, over which there was no bridge, and which was not fordable in that part: thus, on reaching the foot of the mountain, they must turn to the left, away from the castle as it were, in order to reach a shallow elbow of the stream which they could pass."

His account appeared to be a just one; for, in the course of some time, Rosalind saw the moving body, on which her eyes had been fixed, wind round a knot of trees at the base of the mountain, and disappear from her view.

Several hours elapsed, during which no object met the aching sight of Rosalind; at length the faint sound of a trumpet broke the silence of expectation. "That is our trumpet upon the battlements of the castle," said Zachary; "I wonder whether it will sound again."

"What if it does?" asked Rosalind, "what will that imply?"

"A second blast, like the one we have just heard, Lady," he answered, "will announce the approach of an enemy."

A few minutes passed, and, at their expiration, a second sound, similar to the first, was heard.

"Was not that somewhat louder?" asked Rosalind.

"You only heard it plainer," he returned, "because the wind happened to catch it, and send it this way."

"The attack will soon begin now, I warrant me," added Zachary, after a pause.

"Thank Heaven, we are not there!" exclaimed his aunt. "Should those ruffians conquer, which the saints forbid, we might have shared the fate of the Sabine virgins."

Ever anxious to fathom the mystery which subsisted between the freebooter Allanrod and Lord Rufus, Rosalind began to inquire into the history of the former, hoping that Zachary might, in his intercourse with the soldiery of the castle, have learnt some particulars relating to him, of which the present moment might make him communicative; but he appeared to know only the common story—that he was a Scotchman, and headed a band of freebooters.

"If the siege is going to begin," said Dame Edith, "do, my Lady, take my advice, and let us go down into the cave below for safety; only think of the consequence, if any of the wretches should come this way, and discover our retreat."

"We have nothing to apprehend from that," replied Rosalind. "On the level between us and the ramparts of the castle, we could discover any one who was approaching hither, long before they could discern us, and it would be then time enough to fly from them to the protection the cavern would afford us. It is also very unlikely that any individual of a troop like Allanrod's, bent on plunder, should turn aside from the siege, to wander to a mean cot like this. Lord Rufus, doubtless, knew us secure in this situation, or he would not have placed us in it," she added; for every apprehension of De Madginecourt's infidelity to her cause had vanished, since the ocular demonstration which she had received of the freebooter's troops advancing to the attack of his castle; and she now only wondered what concealed motive could have withheld Lord Rufus from delivering so determined an enemy into the hands of justice.

"Yes, yes, we are safe here," said Zachary; "if any of them were within arm's length of the cottage, we could escape them. This trap," kicking his foot against the door at the head of the steps, leading into the cave below, "has a spring that they could never find out, and strength can't master it; for it is so made, that the harder it is pressed upon, the faster it is—so let them come if they will, say I."

The sun was already past the meridian, and the day, which had risen in cloudless splendour, was now become overcast, and seemed to threaten a storm; the wind had rapidly risen to a considerable height; and the swallow, skimming in uneven mazes, scarcely above the level of the earth, mixed its screams with the whistling gust.

The clouds moved heavily, and almost imperceptibly, along the sky, their weight upborne by the strength of the breeze, and prepared to fall in torrents upon the earth, as soon as they should lose its sustaining aid.

"Hark!" cried Zachary, suddenly, "there they go!"

"What?—What?" asked Rosalind.

"A fire from the castle, Lady," he replied; "the work's begun."

Rosalind listened, but heard nothing; and she was inclined to believe, from the appearance of the clouds, that if Zachary had heard any sound, it had been that of distant thunder.

How awful is suspense!—How much more tolerable is the hour of actual suffering, than the period of doubt!—Apprehension swells the worst of evils beyond the magnitude of which we find them in endurance. Rosalind had reasoned with her mind, till her arguments, by repetition, had lost all their weight; and she now beheld futurity, robed in the most gigantic horrors.

"Was it not distant thunder you heard?" asked Rosalind.

Zachary's countenance indicated that he thought it was not, and also bespoke him in the act of endeavouring to catch a repetition of the sound.

In a few moments it was repeated, with sufficient strength to leave the less acute senses of Dame Edith no reason to doubt that it proceeded from musketry either on the ramparts of the castle, or of the enemy before its walls.

At intervals the volleys of firing were continued with great rapidity, then again they ceased for several minutes together; at each of these intervals Rosalind believed that some decisive blow had been struck; but Zachary told her, that it required a longer time to decide the event of an attack of this nature, and that the cessation of the musketry was occasioned by the occasional resources which each party had to the bow and the sling.

The smoke rose in columns above the battlements of Rockmount Castle, and spreading itself along the plain, appeared like a snowy vapour, floating between the eyes of Rosalind and the sable terrors of the gloomy atmosphere.

Dame Edith sighed and groaned at every fresh sound; and by the closing of her eyes, and the motion of her lips, Rosalind believed her to be in prayer. Zachary did not speak when he was not spoken to; and Rosalind experienced that dreadful sensation of seeing human beings around her, and yet being conscious of their inability to pronounce a sentence which could convey to her heart a single particle of the consolation it so much stood in need of.

Her head had fallen upon her hand, which was rested on the frame of the casement, and she perceived not how quickly the shades of darkness were descending to the earth, till a vivid flash of lightning, which passed immediately before her sight, drew her eyes again to the window.

The castle was now barely discernible; indeed she believed that her imagining she saw its towers at all proceeded merely from her knowing where to direct her eye in search of them, and the strength with which their situation was impressed on her mind. A loud clap of thunder followed the flash just past, and the rain and hail began to burst, in mingled torrents, from the skies.

With every moment the darkness continued to increase, and the tempest to grow more violent. Rosalind begged that a lamp might be lighted, and Dame Edith warmly seconded the proposition. Zachary accordingly proceeded to strike a light. "Now, for Heaven's sake, my Lady," said the dame, "do be persuaded, and let us go down into the grotto; should our lamp be seen by any of the assailants, it may betray us to them, and we cannot now, as we could in the day-time, be apprized of their approach by our eyesight."

Rosalind concurred in the dame's opinion, and declared herself willing to comply with her request, Zachary having promised to take his station at the head of the steps, that he might catch the passing sounds, which was an indescribable consolation that Rosalind could not be induced to give up; as she drew conjectures from each that was heard respecting the progress of Allanrod's attack, although she could not at the same time forbear confessing to herself, how inaccurate, in all probability, were her ideas, founded on so deceitful a basis.

The lamp being lighted, they rose to quit the apartment for the grotto below; as they were moving towards it, the dame, in passing the door of the room in which lay the inanimate object of Rosalind's charity, and which Zachary had opened, to fetch from thence the steel and flint, uttered a loud scream, and would have precipitated herself down the steps before her, but for the interposition of her nephew, who caught her in his arms.

For some moments the dame's eye-balls appeared fixed with terror, and all her efforts to speak proved fruitless; at length—"Oh, Heaven, save us!" she cried; "some judgment awaits us. Heaven save us!" she repeated, "I saw him wave his dead hand at me."

For the first time in her life, Rosalind was moved by the superstitious fears of another person; she shuddered at the fact the dame had advanced, and, instead of smiling at her idea, as she would at any other time have done, she moved hastily up to Zachary, upon whom she looked, not less as a comforter, at that moment, than she regarded the lamp which he held in his hand.

The dame persisted in what she had advanced; the dead man, she resolutely declared, had waved to her his hand, as she had passed the door of the room where he lay, and she hurried down the steps, entreating Rosalind to follow her. Rosalind complied, but no sooner had she gained the bottom, than the folly of listening to the terrors of her companion struck her, and she felt half inclined to go up again, and resolve herself whether there were indeed any remaining life in him whom she had believed dead.

"He is not alive," cried the dame, "I am certain; his corpse is bewitched—in the name of the blessed Jesus, go not near him. Oh that you had not let him into the cottage!—Some punishment awaits us, for the kindness you have shewn to the enemies of our good Queen." A clap of thunder rolled with tremendous loudness at that instant over the grotto, and Dame Edith declared that she heard a groan from the chamber above, notwithstanding the violence of the crash.

Rosalind was now strongly led to believe, that life might not have been entirely flown from the unhappy man above, when they had thought it so, and that timely assistance might still recover him; and she declared, that she would take Zachary with her, and go and examine into the truth of the dame's fears.

The dame wept, shrieked, and implored her not to commit this rashness; but Rosalind could not be withheld, by any personal apprehension, from an act of duty, and was resolute in ascending the steps. Dame Edith saw her determination, and, fearing not less for her safety above, than she did for her own, in being left alone below, after her recent alarm, she shrieked her commands, in so forcible a tone, to Zachary to shut the door at the top of the steps, for the sake of the soul and body of the Lady Rosalind, entrusted to their care, that he complied rather from surprise than actual intention of obedience to his aunt, and fastened the spring beyond his power to unfix it again.

CHAPTER V.

I will advise you where to plant yourselves,
Acquaint you with the perfect spy o' the time,
The moment on't—for't must be done to-night.

MACBETH.

ROSALIND was not satisfied that the spring was immovable, till she had ascertained, with her own hand, that it was so; and she then descended again into the grotto.

Neither the sounds of the thunder, nor of the musketry at the castle, lost any part of their strength by being heard in the grotto, and both continued to rage with unabating ferocity.

With every moment the unpleasantness of Rosalind's situation continued to increase. The dame persisted in the cause of her alarm not having been ideal. The insensible Zachary, unmoved by surrounding circumstances, was sinking to sleep; and the oil, which fed the solitary flame that cheered their dismal abode, was almost wasted.

The dame's fears were wound to a pitch of uncontroulable terror at the idea of the darkness in which they must soon be inevitably involved, and wept aloud. Rosalind stood too much in need of comfort herself, to be able to bestow any on her companion, thus continued to sit in painful silence.

Presently the thunder began to die away in scarcely audible murmurs, and the sounds of the musketry were no longer heard in lengthened echoes through the cavern, as they had a few minutes before been. "Now then," thought Rosalind, "the die is cast!" Anxiously did she pant for information of the event of the siege from Lord Rufus, and as the hour crept on, and no footstep was heard approaching towards the grotto, she began to dread that the ruthless Allanrod was the conqueror.

The lamp gave a dying flash, and expired.

A general silence prevailed. The dame, who had been afraid of stirring from her seat, even while the lamp was still burning, appeared to be now fearful even of hearing the sound of her own voice; her stifled sobs were alone audible, and the unfortunate daughter of De Mowbray sat, worn by expectation, till she almost lost the faculty of thought.

At length the sound of distant voices played upon the air, but whether they proceeded from the plain without the cottage, or from the subterraneous passage, Rosalind could not for some time distinguish. In a short time footsteps were mingled with the voices, and the rays of approaching torches already gleamed on the vaulted roof of the grotto.

Scarcely were these discernible, ere the page, Alwin, was seen running towards the grotto.—"Fly, Lady Rosalind; fly to the fields for succour!" he exclaimed, as he entered it. "Allanrod is the conqueror—Lord Rufus himself in chains—Your retreat, by some villainous treachery, is discovered to the freebooters, and his ruffian band already presses on my heels in search of you."

"Then save me, Heaven!" exclaimed Rosalind, her hands clasped, and extended towards the power in whom her only hope was placed.

"Fly, fly, I entreat you," continued Alwin, running up the steps towards the door into the cottage. "The spring is fastened!" he exclaimed, on reaching it—"then submission is alone left you."

These words were scarcely uttered, ere a number of the freebooters, some bearing arms, others carrying torches, burst into the grotto. The sight struck horror to the heart of Rosalind; and, falling upon her knees before them, she exclaimed—"Oh, save me!—save me!"—from Allanrod, she would have added, but the words died on her lips.

"Fear nothing, fair Lady," said one of the foremost, raising her as he spoke from the ground; "the powerful Allanrod sends you joy by us. The conqueror commands us to lead you to him in the chapel of Rockmount Castle, where he awaits to make you the wedded partner of his victory and wealth."

"Tell your conqueror," replied Rosalind, "that I would sooner he awaited me there to entomb me, living, in the dust beneath his feet, than for the hated act you set a praise upon—tell him, that Rosalind de Mowbray dares him to violate the rights of *her* existence, who is under the immediate protection of her sovereign Queen."

The exertion of uttering these words, which she had spoken with a pretended courage, overpowered her, and as she ceased to speak, the tears burst from her eyes.

"You find, by the present instance," returned one of the men, who had something in his appearance superior to the rest, "that the protection of your Queen is not so powerful or extensive as that which Allanrod is able to afford you; it were therefore wisdom in you, Lady, to let this proof of his superiority open your eyes to the honour he intends you."

"You know me little," replied Rosalind, "if you suppose that it is in the power of any sophistry to win my heart into becoming the willing partner of one, of whose criminality I have every conviction, as I have of Allanrod's; if, therefore, your leader believes to meet in me a woman who will bend in humility before him, because the adventitious fortune of a moment makes him a lawless conqueror, forbear, for his sake, as it is evident you value not mine, to lead me into his presence—be he ever so great, I carry with me a mortification for his pride."

"We must obey," returned the freebooter; and he and one of his companions then began to force her along the cavern.

"You are not the first of your sex, Lady, he has had to deal with," observed one of the men.

"Perhaps you mean to imply," said Rosalind, calmly, "that he owes his name for prowess to the unfeeling conduct which he exercises towards our sex."

"How, Lady!" returned the man.

"It is a natural conclusion," answered Rosalind, "that the wicked man should be unfeeling."

"He is not cruel, unless opposition to his wishes drives him to hasty actions," returned the soldier.

"A glorious character you give him," replied Rosalind; "he is just so little of a tyrant, as to be able to act with lenity towards those who do not thwart his wishes."

"For your own sake," rejoined the man, "moderate your expressions; remember that you are in his power."

"That I do not allow," returned Rosalind; "my soul and my opinions he can never bend to his detested purposes. Let his brutality extend to what lengths it may, he can never enjoy the triumph of having subdued my heart. When he has bent me to his villainous ends, whatever they may be, or taken from me a life, which is already a burden to me, what can he boast of having done?—tortured with his brutality, a form of mouldering clay, cast in the weak impression of a woman, whose mind could not be conquered even by the savageness of his cruelties, and whose resolution baffled the triumph of his enormities."

Her conductors continued to lead her on towards the extremity of the subterraneous passage, and thence she was made to retrace the steps which had led her to the grotto, through the mouldering cemetery, and ruinous chapel. The shadow, which had flitted before her eyes the last time she had passed through the vaults, returned to her imagination, but nothing now met her sight, except various individuals of the freebooter's band.

Having passed through the secret door in the wainscot paneling, which opened into the long and vaulted aisle that connected the ruinous chapel with the castle, they continued to move on through various turnings and windings, which were terminated by a flight of stone steps. On reaching these, all the freebooters, but the two who led Rosalind, remained below; by the two who held her, she was constrained to ascend the steps, and, arrived at the top, one of her conductors pushed back on its hinges a heavy door, which they entered.

Numerous torches had hitherto accompanied their progress from the grotto, and, for a moment, utter darkness appeared to Rosalind to have usurped the place of the streaming lights which had so lately been shedding their vivid influence around her; but in a very short time a couple of lamps, suspended from the roof of the building she was now in, just served to point out to her, that it was a place appointed for religious uses. She distinguished a lofty marble tomb, on which, as she passed, the partial light from one of the lamps fell, and she discerned the name of *Eloise*; she doubted not but that *de la Valois* had followed; but neither the light, nor the hasty pace she was moving at, were favourable for observation.

The lamps were hung at some distance from each other, and as she was now moving in the intermediate space between them, a confused medley of pillars and monuments, shaded by the pervading gloom, were alone discernible. As she continued to proceed, by the influence of the second lamp, which fell on the objects she was approaching, she saw a semicircle of railing in brass, in the centre of which a part of the workmanship swung back on hinges to form a passage towards an altar, which was raised a few feet beyond it in the depth of a stone recess.

By the side of this altar she perceived standing a priest, before whom lay an open volume.

"Here," said one of the borderers, "our Lord, Allanrod, will shortly appear, to claim the hand which ensures the felicity of his future life."

The horror which assailed Rosalind's mind—the peculiarity as well as the cruelty of her situation, choked her utterance. For some time she endeavoured, in vain, to speak; at length, with difficulty, she faintly breathed out—"Priest, I charge thee, by thy hopes of Heaven, be not an accomplice in this act of infamy!"

No sooner had she spoken, than distant footsteps, the echoes of which played through the chapel, drew her eyes to the spot from whence they proceeded, and she perceived, approaching towards her, a man of tall stature, and of a robust frame; he was clad in the Highland habit, and every part of his dress bespoke him a Scottish freebooter, except that on his head he wore an English helmet, of which the visor was down.

"This, Lady," said the freebooter, who had before spoken, "is the great Allanrod."

Rosalind felt her strength gradually dying away; she gazed, but could not speak. Allanrod approached towards her, and, in silence, placed himself by her side. Every object danced before the eyes of Rosalind, and she felt as in a lethargic trance, from which she had not the power to awake herself.

Allanrod waved his hand to the priest, who instantly began to read the ceremony that was to unite her to the wretch into whose power she had fallen.

Again she endeavoured to speak, but her efforts were more ineffectual than before; a faint exclamation of horror alone was she able to articulate.

The priest proceeded, and Allanrod took the hand of Rosalind in his; at the moment he touched it, an unknown voice proclaimed—"Hold! Monster, hold!" and at the next instant a figure, in black armour, whose countenance was pale and emaciated, save where a streak of blood ran down its left cheek, stood between them.

"Oh, God!" exclaimed Allanrod, and sunk into the arms of his attendants who had followed him to the altar.

Rosalind turned her eyes upon the figure; a shriek burst from her lips, and all sense fled from her.

CHAPTER VI.

I know a discontented gentleman,
Whose humble means match not his haughty mind;
Gold were as good as twenty orators,
And will, no doubt, tempt him to any thing.

KING RICHARD III.

We have hitherto scarcely spoken of Edward since the hour of his departure from England, except to mention the intelligence which Lord William de Mowbray professed himself, about a year from the present time, to have received of his death. It now becomes us to recur to the period of his setting out for Flanders, and to enquire into the correctness of this information, and the events which had marked his life since his leaving Cumberland.

It will doubtless be remembered, that Rosalind saw her Edward no more after the night which made her his wife; that on the day subsequent to this event, Lord William brought her intelligence of his departure with a levy of troops for Flanders, and alledged, as the reason of his not having visited her previously to his leaving the country, the apology which she had on the prior evening urged as an excuse for refusing to see Lord Rufus de Madginecourt—"that she was not well enough to receive visitors;" and which sentence the Baron de Mowbray pretended that he had supposed must extend equally to every individual.

On the morning subsequent to that night which had made Edward the husband of his beloved Rosalind, Irwin arrived at early morn at the tower in the village, and informed him, that Lord William had just received a command from the court, to dispatch a levy of his own private troops to join the army which was on the point of embarking for Flanders; and that he had resolved on sending one hundred of his stoutest men, of which he gave the command to Edward, who was ordered to be ready to depart within three hours.

Mingled were the sensations with which Edward received this mandate from Lord William. To leave his Rosalind at that moment, although he had placed it beyond the power of fate to give her lawfully to the arms of Lord Rufus, occasioned him a regret, which the honour conferred on him, in the command of the company over which he was placed, could not balance; still his eternal honour, his only chance of promotion in arms, and progress towards glory—the only attainments by which he could ever hope to advance sufficiently into the favour of the Baron de Mowbray, to be acknowledged by him as his son-in-law, were at stake. At the present moment, any hesitation on his part would for ever condemn him; accordingly nothing remained for him but to accept the command with apparent cheerfulness.

Thus convinced, his good sense overcame every latent, lingering wish of remaining on the spot he now stood on, and he directly proceeded to the castle, to return his thanks to its Lord, for the honour conferred on him, in his promotion to the command of the body of men devoted to foreign service, and to bid him farewell previously to his departure.

Lord William received him with that complacency which was necessary to gloss over his self interested views in sending him out of the kingdom; and when Edward made a request to kneel at the feet of the Lady Rosalind, and receive her good wishes for the success of his arms, De Mowbray artfully replied, that it was with regret he was compelled to refuse his petition, but that Rosalind was much indisposed, and had particularly desired that no one should, on any cause whatever, be admitted to her apartment.

Edward durst not advance the only plea on which he might have enforced his petition, and with a heavy heart, pronouncing a silent blessing on her name, he was constrained to place himself at the head of his men, and begin his melancholy march.

The heart of Lord William de Mowbray bounded with triumphant joy, when the refulgent blades of the soldiery, headed by the devoted Edward, no longer cast their reflection on the plains of Cumberland. A sigh of ecstacy escaped from his bosom, and he mentally exclaimed—"Farewell, bane to the pride of my house!—Farewell, thou minion of a fond, foolish daughter!" The Baron had yet to learn that the indissoluble knot of love was tied between those bosoms, which had only virtue and affection for their guide; and the unfortunate pair, thus united in love, were still ignorant, that the machinations of a pride-devoted father had driven Edward, as he hoped, for ever, from the presence of her in whose sight alone he lived.

Little imagining that his daughter had possessed the firmness of soul to repair to herself his neglect of her dying mother's petition to him, "to give her Rosalind to the man of her heart," he had vainly judged, that Edward, once removed from her sight, time and his arguments would be efficacious in removing him equally from her thoughts; and that when he was once rooted out from them, it would be by no means a difficult matter to place Lord Rufus in his vacated seat: for this reason, therefore, had Lord William given to Edward the command of the hundred men chosen for foreign service, as the most ready and least suspicious method of sending him out of the kingdom—an honour which belonged by right to his elder chieftains, and which, but for this secret cause, had doubtless been theirs.

And here Lord William intended to have stopped, trusting either to the continuation of the war for detaining Edward abroad till Rosalind should have been prevailed on to receive Lord Rufus as her husband, or to the accidents of the field, for precluding the possibility of his ever returning at all. But when the suffering Rosalind disclosed to him that she was already a wife—the wife of an unknown—the wife of the foundling, Edward! Lord William, for the first time, experienced a proof of that power which the insignificant sometimes possess of overthrowing the greatest plans of those who conceive themselves the most mighty; and in the first heat of his rage, he determined on the immediate death of him, whom he wanted strength of invocation to curse with the emphasis he desired to condemn him.

But his idea of depriving Edward of his life, was soon overruled by various considerations which crowded on his mind; principally he reflected on the expression of "*noble*," which old Matthews had used on his death-bed, in reference to his young charge, and which the Baron had always felt a doubt in determining whether it had been applied to his mind or his birth. If it had referred to the latter, the time might come when the youth might be reclaimed by his family, from the bosom of which, perhaps, some mysterious circumstances had hitherto shut him out; and should the progress of his life, in such case, be traced by those anxious for his welfare and existence, and its thread be discovered to have been cut by him, (for the grave itself is not always silent, and foul deeds will sometimes speak, though there be no tongues to tell of them) what would not be his disgrace, his punishment, for the act into which his hasty intemperance had driven him! These thoughts sunk deeply into his mind—and terrified out of his plan by the chimeras of his brain for the most determined villains have their moments of fear, he resolved, by some other means than death, to prevent Edward from ever returning back to England.

Edward meanwhile pursued his journey, unsuspicious of any fraud practising against him, but that which had ostensibly torn him from the arms of his beloved Rosalind. The company which he headed embarked from England, and landed, after a prosperous voyage, at Ostend; in the neighbourhood of which place they were encamped, amidst various other troops, just landed from England.

When the tower of strength was first begun to be erected in the village, of which the scattered roofs reared their humble heads in the valley which ran at the foot of an amphitheatre of hills, on the summit of the highest of which stood the proud castle of De Mowbray, engineers were sent by the Queen from London, for the purpose of constructing its foundation. When the building was completed, and the task, for which the workmen had been hired, concluded, two of the number enlisted themselves into the service of Lord William, as pioneers.

Of these two men, neither was English; the one was a rude and ignorant Cambrian—the origin of the other it was not so easy to define. His father had been a Spaniard, his mother a French woman; they had been stragglers for the greater part of their lives over the face of the globe, and had ultimately settled in the Netherlands, as the keepers of a prison. The name by which he called himself was Sanchez Xavia; at the age of manhood, he had been cast upon the world by his parents, to fight his way through life, according to his own confession, not as a reward for his good conduct previously to that time. He had entered into the service of an Irish gentleman of fortune in France, and returned with him to his own country; no very honourable occurrence, it appeared, had driven him from that situation. To England he had wandered during the preceding reign, and here there existed a stronger proof than suspicion, of his having assisted in the barbarous executions of murdered martyrs, which will for ever stain the memory of Elizabeth's predecessor, and render her claim undoubted, to the bloody fame under which her memory lives.

How he had lived, without punishment, till nearly his sixtieth year, as he had done, is one of those enigmas which puzzle the good, while the evil are insensible that their preservation is not their just and merited due. Too often is it the case in life, that those who deserve to be reprobated by their fellows, gain their esteem; while such as truly merit approbation from the world, are obliged to rest contented with the single applause of their own heart. This instance is peculiarly exemplified in the cases of Hubert and Sanchez Xavia. The rough, but honest, Hubert, was constantly saluted with the epithet of "*Surly*," and found but few who sought his companionship; while the smooth tongue, and smiling countenance, of the rascally Sanchez, gained him a nod of welcome, and a friendly shake by the hand, wherever he went. So true is it that the majority cast their eyes no farther than the surface, and that the skilled in art are well acquainted that *appearance* is accepted by the multitude for *reality*.

Sanchez Xavia had particularly requested of the Baron de Mowbray, that he might be one of the pioneers included in the number of men under the command of Edward. "His father and mother were both dead, but he had," he said, "a brother, on whom the government of the prison which had lately been held by his father, had devolved, and he wished to see him, now an opportunity offered of so doing, without expence to himself." That he was going to fight against the country of which his father and mother had, by residence, become subjects, he cared not; war was his trade, and therefore it was indifferent to him where and against whom he exercised it. He was not cruel from disposition, but from interest—he would not have dealt a painful blow to any one which he had not been paid to do; but he would hire himself to the performance of any action whatsoever, and having once let himself to perform it, most religiously did he act up to the interest of his employer.

Although we have seen, in the instance of Hubert, that Lord William de Mowbray could be mistaken in his opinion of character, still the fawning villainy of Sanchez was of too common a cast for a man, of even a less acute perception than Lord William, to be deceived in; rumour had also whispered in his ear, that gold was the deity of Sanchez, and that he religiously observed his tenets of faith towards those who showered it on him.

His recollection of Sanchez, at the present moment, was a most assuasive balm to the feelings of the pride-wounded Lord; he united with the apt character of Sanchez to stratagem, the convenient stronghold of the prison of which his brother was keeper; and doubted not that an annuity, equivalent to the charge imposed on them, would render both the brothers willing to find the means of decoying Edward into its recesses, and retaining him their captive for the term of his existence.

His heart leapt with exultation at the idea; he doubted not a ready affirmative to his plan from Sanchez. What alone distressed him, was the means of making known his scheme, and the price he was willing to pay for its performance, to him whom he desired to appoint the instrument of it, without the hazard of a discovery of his intentions, or without leaving on record a paper of his own hand-writing, containing his black purposes; which, by some gust of chance or fortune, might damn him as the actor of so nefarious a proceeding.

After much deliberation with his own mind, he decided on leaving his castle for a short time, under pretence of his presence being required by the Queen, to cross the sea unattended, and to see Sanchez Xavia himself. His absence he commanded to be kept a profound secret from his daughter; and her mind, occupied with matter of nearer import to her own happiness, made not that enquiry relative to a father, from whose hand she had received the mortal stab to her felicity, to subject her to the fallacy which had been prepared, as a reply to such question, had she advanced it.

The Baron accordingly left his castle, and having disguised himself as a man of mean rank, he proceeded without delay to the coast, and securing himself a passage on board a ship bound to the continent, was soon landed there.

On reaching Ostend, the Baron took up his abode at a little inn on the side of the town nearest to the camp, and here concealing himself till the shades of evening began to fall, he dispatched a messenger to the English camp, to summon Sanchez to his presence. No sooner did Sanchez perceive who was the stranger that had sent to seek him, than his artful brain prophecied, that there must be some secret cause for the Baron's having undertaken the voyage; and a mutual explanation quickly took place between them, on which they parted, fully satisfied with the promises of each other.

CHAPTER VII.

Could great men thunder
As Jove himself does, Jove would ne'er be quiet;
For every pelting, petty officer,
Would use his Heaven for thunder!
Nothing but thunder! Merciful Heaven!
Thou rather with thy sharp and sulphurous bolt
Split'st the unwedgeable and gnarled oak,
Than the soft myrtle. But man!—proud man!
Drest in a little brief authority,
Most ignorant of what he's most assur'd,
His glassy essence—like an angry ape,
Plays such fantastic tricks before high Heaven,
As make the angels weep.

MEASURE FOR MEASURE.

On the following day, when the exercises of the morning were concluded, Sanchez, approaching his captain, said—"Sir, I have a boon to request of you."—"Name it," Edward replied.—"Do you not, Sir," said Sanchez, "behold that building on yon distant hill?"—"Yes," answered Edward; "what is it? it appears both strong and large."—"And so it is," rejoined Xavia; "it is a prison where captives of a superior order are kept—my brother is the governor of it. To-morrow is his wedding-day; he is about to marry a rich widow of Ostend, and if you would condescend to grace his nuptials with your presence, he would deem it a high honour conferred on him. Your brother officers will also be invited, as he wishes to be in amity with all the British troops. I have besides to request leave of absence for myself from my regiment, for the day, that I may be present at the ceremony."

Edward smiled inwardly at this invitation from the keeper of a prison; but, aware how essential are friends of any description, in a country which we enter as enemies, he agreed on the following day to partake of the wedding-dinner of Garcias Xavia.

"My brother, Gentlemen," said Sanchez, addressing his officers, "is in a very different situation in life to myself; his place, as governor of the prison, is worth several hundred pounds a-year to him; and the lady, whom he is going to marry, is worth an annuity equal to his own—every child of the same mother has not the same good fortune."

At the hour of invitation, Edward and his brother officers, conducted by Sanchez, repaired to the governor's, for by that appellation only was he known in the country. As they approached nearer to the prison, every feature bespoke strength, and every part of its construction seemed to bid defiance to the captive to escape from its holds. The building itself stood on the summit of a rocky hill, whose sloping sides fell into a deep moat, from the centre of which arose a flinty wall, of at least fifteen feet in height; thus, while the prison appeared utterly unprotected, its situation, on the crown of a summit, rendered escape impossible, as every step which was set from the building only sunk the passenger still lower beneath the outer wall, which it had been rendered by art an impracticable labour to climb.

Having passed the outer gate, the governor met them as they ascended the hill; he was a man of a handsome person, and appeared to be at least ten years younger than his brother. His address was polite and easy; and, in the words of a gentleman, he thanked them for the honour they conferred on him by their presence.

He ushered them into a handsome apartment, where he introduced them to his newly-married bride, a middle-aged woman, whose appearance had in it nothing remarkable, and a number of guests of both sexes, who all bore the marks of being persons of some condition in life: but the most interesting personage of the party, was the daughter of her who had that day become Madame Xavia, by her first husband. Belise, for such was her name, had just completed her nineteenth year; her figure, although not tall, was beautiful in the extreme—her countenance was handsome, and full of expression—her dark brown eyes conveyed in them sensibility, soul, and good humour—and her hazel tresses flowed in the most luxuriant ringlets on her delicate bosom.

The repast was handsome and profuse: of the many apartments which were in use, not one bore the slightest mark of its affinity to a prison; and Sanchez himself, although admitted to the feast as the brother of the donor, retired with humility to the bottom of the table, and forbore to intrude his conversation upon the guests of the governor. Sanchez was indifferent about the dissimilitude of situation between himself and Garcias: the villainy which he was hatching against the unsuspicious Edward, produced him inward gratification, equal to what his brother derived from the acquisition of property which had attended his marriage, and the guests of distinction which he saw placed round his table. Nor was Garcias himself, although thus wealthy, much less delighted than his brother, at the idea of some increase to the income which he already possessed being about to flow to him from the intended captivity of Edward; for rare is the instance when the rich do not delight in the idea of becoming richer still, whatever the means which are to make them so.

It appears unnecessary to say, that the brothers had already held a private conference upon the agreement, which had been made between the Lord Baron de Mowbray and Sanchez Xavia, relative to the imprisonment of Edward, and that their plan had already been laid for preventing him from leaving the walls of the prison, where he was now entertained as a wedding guest; to which feast he and his brother officers had been invited, solely to colour over the treachery which was to be executed upon him before the arrival of midnight.

When the repast was ended, and the cheerful glass went round the table, the smiling Belise was requested to produce her lute, and indulge the party, by accompanying its tones with her voice. With that readiness which bespoke a willingness to oblige, rather than a consciousness of excellence, she immediately took up her instrument, and sang the following words—

As Learning o'er his fountain hung,
Two infants wander'd by;
The eldest boy, was Genius nam'd,
The other, Industry:
Beneath the stream, they had been told,
A treasure lay conceal'd;
So both plung'd in to gain the prize,
The waters were to yield.
Firm Industry kept diving on,
Nor turn'd aside his eye;
While Genius swam across the tide,

To catch a golden fly:
With joy the insect he ensnares,
But ah! his pleasure flies!
When mounting from the deep, he sees
Industry with the prize.

Every one present complimented Belise, not less on the sweetness of her voice, than the subject of her song; and when it was understood that the music and words were both her own composition, their encomiums were greatly increased.

Belise happened to be placed at table next to Edward, and his commendations were amongst the warmest bestowed on the fair songstress; for there was something in her voice and expression, which so strongly reminded him of his absent Rosalind, that every pulse in his composition glowed under the words which flowed from her tongue.

In return to his compliments, she said—"My song contains a simple truth; I have ever remarked through life, at least as far as I have had experience for my years, that perseverance always gains us the accomplishment of such desired ends as the too ardent and impetuous mind fails to obtain for itself."

"May thy words be prophetic, fair maiden," thought Edward; "may the lingering hand of destiny still reward my perseverance with the happiness of being acknowledged the lawful protector of my beloved Rosalind!" At this idea a sigh escaped him.

"Let me fill your glass, Sir," said Belise; "you are melancholy. Have you the head-ache, or the heart-ache?"

Edward made some common-place apology for his absence, and emptied his glass to the health of his lively companion.

"It is not the head-ache," went on Belise, "or you would not take your wine thus freely; therefore it must be the heart-ache, and what can cause that in so young a man as yourself? It must surely be love—am I right?"

"If it be so, I must not be a tell-tale of my love," replied Edward, endeavouring to force a smile, "or I should be undeserving a return of my passion."

"That is very well said," answered Belise, significantly; "but you should put the same restraint upon your eyes that you do upon your tongue—they are tell-tales in spite of your precaution."

"And suppose I were to assure you I was not in love at all?" replied Edward.

"Then I should say," returned Belise, "that the air of this prison has infected you with melancholy; it has me already, I freely confess. I love my mother, and have no great dislike to the man whom she has taken for her second husband; but I feel extremely averse to the necessity I am under, from my dependence upon my mother, of being the inhabitant of this gloomy building. I have visited every part of it, *once only*, and I hope I shall never do so again, for it is piteous indeed to see the unhappy persons who are immured within its walls; they have certainly every comfort which captivity can bestow, but what are all the luxuries it can give, compared with the privation of liberty, and absence from those connexions which form the charms of life, and without which existence is a blank, nay a misery?"

"Your feelings," said Edward, "are such as do infinite credit to your heart."

"I would I had the free exercise of them," replied Belise, "and there should not be a prisoner within these walls. Oh! it is dreadful to see those in affliction, to whom the power is denied us of alleviating their sufferings."

"This building is however of such extent," returned Edward, "that you will not be constrained to see those whom you pity."

"I shall equally think of them," answered she; "and I am sure no threats of my father-in-law will ever deter me from rendering them every assistance in my power. When I see men in misfortune, I cannot help forgetting the cause from which they are doomed to suffer, and remembering only that they are in a situation which deserves the commiseration of the benevolent, and the succouring hand of such as are able to extend it towards their misfortunes."

The sentiments of Belise opened a way for her into the noble heart of Edward, and he listened to her conversation with the utmost pleasure and interest. "I have myself," he said, "in many instances, been the child of misfortune from my cradle; and having known how acceptable to a heart of grief is the sympathy of those on whom we have no other claim than the common tie of humanity, I have learnt the respect due to feelings which are so highly honourable to the breast that cherishes them."

"This," said Belise, "is not the exact moment for a conversation of this nature; we must defer its conclusion to some other opportunity, or our gravity will seem to cast a reflection upon the wedding we are celebrating. The dance is going to begin—let us enjoy the pleasure which the hour presents us with."

The party was now rising from table, and in the course of half an hour, the dancing began in an adjoining apartment.

Edward regarded it as a necessary compliment to his entertainers, to take a share in the dance, and accordingly selected Belise for his partner. The amusement they were joining in did not admit of their conversing much together while thus employed; and when the dances, for which Edward had engaged her hand, were concluded, another partner directly claimed her attention.

Edward was far from being in spirits to enjoy an evening of this festive nature; he felt it a painful exertion to go through the ceremony of a single dance, even with the engaging Belise for his partner—thus he had resolved to dance no more, and moved towards the door of the apartment for air. Here stood in conversation the two brothers, Sanchez and Garcias; Edward joined them. Sanchez directly began to speak of the immensity of the building they were in, and to direct Edward's attention to various architectural points about it; one remark naturally produced another, and Edward expressing his surprise at the elegant apartments which he had that day seen connected with a prison, the governor began to explain to him that it was a prison of a superior order, merely used for criminals of rank, and upon a widely different construction to such buildings as were usually distinguished by that name. Sanchez seconded what his brother had said, and added, "If you please, Sir, to walk with me a few minutes, I am sure my brother will give you his permission to take a view of its different parts; and it is well worth your while so to do—I will answer that you have never before seen a building at all resembling this. I have visited the principal prisons in England myself, and the difference is great indeed."

Edward's curiosity was raised by these remarks, and he accepted the offer made him of gratifying it.

The season of the year was the latter end of May, and the hour about six in the evening; thus, notwithstanding the gloominess of the building, of which the narrow casements admitted but partially and sparingly the rays of day, it was still sufficiently light to allow of the investigation which Edward had been allowed to make, without the assistance of a lamp. Edward, following his conductor Sanchez, stole, unobserved, from the company in the dancing-room, and passing through a stone corridor, they arrived at a few steps which led to an iron-grated door, that, Sanchez said, divided that part of the edifice which was set apart for the governor, from that which was allotted to the purposes of imprisonment.

They passed on through various passages and apartments, some of stone, others of wainscot, differently furnished, and containing, in different proportions, accommodations and comforts for such as were destined to be their inhabitants. One apartment, or rather cell, particularly arrested the attention of Edward; it was evidently a place where the torture was accustomed to be exercised on the unhappy victims of bigotry or criminality. At one end was an immense fire-place, which was scattered over with cinders, the remnants of the torturing fire which had scorched the supposed truth from the lips of some unhappy sufferer. In the centre of the apartment stood an iron chair, in which the wretched being had, doubtless, been seated at the hour of punishment; and on the floor were fastened iron rings, which had been constructed for the purpose of confining his feet.

"For Heaven's sake, let us pass on," said Edward; "this scene brings to the mind images too terrific for the heart which is not entirely devoid of feeling, to dwell upon with any degree of composure."

"Yes," replied Sanchez, "the torture by fire is bad enough for those who feel it; it is worse than being burnt to death—in that case the smoke soon does the business, and takes away all feeling."

"You have then, it should seem, been a witness of both instances," rejoined Edward.

"Oh, aye," replied Sanchez, "I had my hands charmingly full of business, when Queen Mary indulged her spleen against the Protestant church, by roasting bishops."

Edward fixed his eyes for a moment in silent surprise on Sanchez. It had so happened that those unfavourable rumours of his character, which were whispered in the world, had never met the ear of Edward, and this unexpected avowal of his having been an actor in scenes of such violent atrocity, both astonished and vexed him; nor did the confession lose any of the horror which attended it to the mind of Edward, by being made on the spot where they now stood, and with which Sanchez seemed to possess all the familiarity of old acquaintance.

Sanchez smiled at the concern with which Edward regarded even the tacit instruments of punishment, and said, "I see, Sir, your's is a tender heart; pardon me, but such strong feelings, as you express, are dangerous sentiments to gain ground in any community. What would become of the good, if the evil were allowed to exercise their villainy unpunished? Your heart recoils at these instruments of punishment, and probably feels a deadly hatred against the common executioner, whose office it is to rid the world of those whose crimes make them unfit members for existence; and still it is to them, and to him, that you owe the security and happiness of your own life."

There was undoubtedly truth in this remark, but it was that kind of truth which proceeds from an unfeeling mind. Edward's was indeed, as Sanchez had remarked, a tender heart; and he heard, with displeasure, that philosophy which appears an apology for a mind incapable of sensibility.

Although these remarks, on the part of Sanchez, had opened to Edward the nature of his heart, still he was entirely unsuspicious of any treachery being intended towards himself; conscious that he merited no evil from any existing hand, he feared none, and continued to proceed in his investigation of the prison. Ascending another short flight of steps, they arrived in a stone gallery of about twenty feet in breadth, which they crossed, and entered an apartment handsomely furnished, in which was a bed and every appertenance of a bed-chamber; beyond this was another room of equal dimensions, and through the latter a closet, where on a table lay scattered some books, and implements for writing.

"It is not long since these rooms were inhabited by a man of rank," said Sanchez; "he has, I understand, been dead only about two months."

"What was the crime for which he was confined here?" asked Edward.

"I believe only that of being one more than his family wished to have belonging to it," answered Xavia, with a significant smile.

This assertion increased the dislike which the last half-hour had given Edward to Sanchez Xavia; and he was also surprised that he should so suddenly have become careless of developing the evil sentiments of his heart.

"I will entreat you to stay here a few minutes," said Sanchez, "till I get a lamp from an adjoining apartment; it is growing so dusk, that we shall not be able to retrace our way to the governor's apartments without a light, much less to pursue our circuit of the building."

Edward answered, that he would await his return, and Sanchez, saying that he would be back in a minute, departed.

Edward was surprised to see him shut the door after him, and still more was he astonished when he heard him double-lock it, and slip a heavy bolt into its socket; he called aloud to him, enquiring the reason of his so doing, but received no answer; he heard his footsteps dying away as he proceeded along the stone gallery; and an universal silence then prevailed, broken only by his own quick breathings, caused by the agitation of his mind, at the strangeness of the circumstance just past.

CHAPTER VIII.

I will despair, and be at enmity
With cozening hope: he is a flatterer,
A parasite—

RICHARD II.

ILL-STARRED Edward! thy doom is then sealed; the tyrant of thy fate holds thee the captive of his triumphant bonds, and exults in the drops of agony which chase each other down thy fevered cheek—which spring from thy racked heart, as it dwells on the painful idea that thy Rosalind may never again meet thy embrace. But despair not, thou suffering youth: however delayed the hour of retribution, its arrival still is certain; the hand of Cruelty shall wither, when it stretches itself out to execute the master-stroke of its unfeeling purpose; and the victim of its machinations, although every ray of cheering hope be fled from its heart, shall meet that reward which is indivisible from the firm exercise of virtuous principles.

For several hours no step approached the apartments in which the anxious and astonished Edward was confined. At length, the fall of feet was audible, they stopped near the door, and he called aloud to have it opened; no answer was returned, but he heard a creaking noise, and suddenly a lighted lamp appeared in the apartment: he went up to it, and found that it had been introduced into the room by means of a shelf, which turned upon a pivot in the wall; on the same shelf was also some fruit and bread in a basket, a flask of wine, and a pitcher of water.

Again Edward called aloud, demanding enlargement; but the steps of the person who had brought him this supply of necessaries, hastily receded from the spot, and all was again solemnly silent.

The mind of Edward was on the rack: he had no hesitation in determining why he was made a captive; not a doubt remained to him of his marriage with his adored Rosalind having been discovered by her father, and of his having taken this method of preventing him from ever returning to claim her as his wife. To what torments might not she be doomed by a father, whose ruling passion of pride had met with so unexpected, so severe a disappointment in the resolution of his daughter! he shuddered at the sufferings to which the intemperate rage of the Baron might have condemned her, and sinking on his knees, he breathed forth a prayer to Heaven for her preservation and protection.

The night was passed by Edward in waking thought; he augured it the forerunner of a train of others similar to it, and despair almost benumbed his faculties.

On the following morning, the shelf introduced into his apartment a change of linen, and various other articles requisite to the comfort of life; and a paper lying on the top of them, directed him to write for whatever he wanted, and to place his demands upon the shelf, by which means they would be received on the other side, and attended to with the greatest punctuality; as there was only one thing which was desired to be interdicted to him, and that one thing was his liberty.

Well assured that the governor, Garcias, was better paid for his detention than he was able to reward him for his enlargement, he forbore to offer him terms, which he was convinced he should only receive the additional mortification of having refused. From endeavouring to make any impression on the hearts of his keepers, the sentiments expressed by Sanchez on the preceding evening deterred him. The man who had lately died in those very apartments which he was now doomed to inhabit, Sanchez had said, "was detained a prisoner in them, only because he was one more than his family wished for." In a place where atrocities of this nature were spoken of with such cool indifference, the voice of the sufferer could not expect to be attended to, nor the cries of the innocent victim to reach the heart.

When the dancing at the governor's broke up, and the brother officers of Edward were about to return to the camp, they inquired for him, and not being able to discover him in any of the apartments, they concluded him gone forward towards his tent; and departed, satisfied that they should find him already in bed.

In passing his tent, they enquired of the sentry, whose patrol was before it, whether his captain was returned? his reply in the negative rather surprised them; but Sanchez, who had followed them from the prison, said, he doubted not but that Edward had been decoyed to the abode of some votary of the Cyprian rites, of which many had their dwellings in the neighbourhood, and that he would arrive at the camp ere long.

Under this idea, the officers returned to their respective tents. The morning came, and still Edward had not been seen: every possible enquiry was set on foot concerning him; and as every effort to discover him had proved ineffectual, his lieutenant dispatched to the Baron de Mowbray intelligence of his disappearance. A speedy answer was returned by Lord William, lamenting the untimely fate which, he pretended to suppose, had attended Edward, from his having ventured into dangerous society; and appointing the lieutenant to the command of the troops, the ensign to his station, and Sanchez Xavia to fill the rank of the lowest officer now promoted; but upon condition of their being reduced to their former situations, should Edward again appear amongst them: convinced of the impossibility of which event, the Lord Baron concluded his epistle with an ardent wish that he might still be safe, and his return to his men speedy.

This intelligence the Baron took especial care to prevent getting abroad in England; and it was probably a secret to every breast but his own.

Days and weeks passed on, and as not the slightest information could be gained of him by any one of his troop on the continent, they concluded him to have been murdered by some robbers, who had despoiled him, as a security against their detection; and as he had never been in the habits of particular intimacy with any one of his company, his fate was, for a short time, talked of and lamented, and in a still shorter, forgotten.

The unhappy Edward, meanwhile, dragged on existence through a round of months, unmarked, except by despair and agony. A solitary pleasure still attended his captivity; the livelong day he would sit with his eyes fixed on vacancy, and believe the shadow of his Rosalind present to his sight—address the imagined vision, till he almost believed it real—and then, waking from his trance, give way to the most violent expressions of grief and frenzy.

To one subject only did the thoughts of Edward wander from his Rosalind, and this was the engaging Belise, the daughter-in-law of the governor. Frequently he reflected on the humane disposition which she had evinced in her conversation with him on the day of her mother's wedding; on the pity which she had expressed herself to feel for the captives of the prison; and more particularly on the avowal she had made, that her fear of the governor's displeasure should never deter her from rendering any service, which might lie in her power, to such unfortunates as were the prisoners of its relentless walls. Did she know his situation, he doubted not but she would use every method in her power to endeavour to procure for him his enlargement: should she not succeed, he felt that it would still be an indescribable pleasure to him, to know that there was a being possessed of a feeling heart, who was acquainted with his captivity, and would lose no opportunity of releasing him from his bonds. But the means of giving her such knowledge, appeared to be entirely removed from his power.

Hourly did he rack his brain for schemes to convey to her the information of his captivity—a thousand various plans presented themselves to his mind, but upon cool examination he found them all to be impracticable. Were he to write to her, his letter would doubtless be examined, and its contents once known, it would never reach her hands. Were he to send her any present, the motive of it would be enquired into, and any secret it might contain would be discovered, and his purpose frustrated.

As nearly as he could calculate, he had now been confined thirteen months, during which time, no individual being had entered his apartment, nor had he even beheld a human countenance; every necessary of life, even his fuel, had been conveyed to him by means of the turning shelf; frequent questions in writing had been given to him, enquiring whether his wants were all supplied; but the sound of no voice had, during that time, met his ear; for if he made any demand of the person who came regularly to the shelf, it was not replied to by speech, but a written answer brought to it shortly after.

The light was admitted into his apartments by windows in the roof; but still he conjectured that the rooms he inhabited were by no means the highest in the building, as he could perceive around his windows high circular walls, whose tops he could not discern; and therefore concluded that his rooms were in the centre of the edifice, purposely surrounded by turrets, to deprive the prisoner of the hope of effecting an escape from the casements.

For the first time, it now occurred to him, that the possibility of an escape might present itself to him, were he to climb up his chimney, and take a survey from its top of the surrounding walls. It was now the month of June, the evenings of course long, and the influence of a full moon rendered the night itself almost a rival of the day. No sooner had this idea entered his mind, than he resolved to make the attempt; he awaited with impatience the hour in the afternoon at which his evening meal was brought to him; and the steps of the attendant being no longer audible along the stone gallery, he stripped himself of his outer garments, and summoning that resolution which is given to us by despair, he succeeded in mounting some feet up the channel, which would at least convey him to the light and air, if not to liberty; for already the beams of day met him as he ascended. But, alas! a few moments cast a damp upon his hopes; an iron grating, fixed across the chimney, baffled equally his attempts to remove it, or to crowd his body through its apertures.

Disappointed expectation is one of the worst feelings to bear with any degree of complacency of mind. Edward threw himself upon his bed, and, for a while, gave way to fruitless lamentations; for the mind of greatest strength may be worn down by calamity, into expressing its sorrows in terms equally devoid of self-controul, as the weakest could use in a similar situation. It is very easy to reason upon the wisdom of resignation, when we do not experience the necessity of exercising it; and equally difficult to call it forth, when we are placed in a situation of trial and affliction.

Edward had not a single implement in his possession, with which he conceived it possible for him to wrench the iron grating from its holds, and force himself a way to the top of the chimney. His fire had been constantly of wood throughout the winter, and a pair of tongs were all the furniture of his hearth; and these had been so long in use, that there could be no hesitation in pronouncing them too weak for the task of dislodging the iron grating from its seat in the stone wall. He had no sword about him, when first trepanned into his present confinement; not a single article was there in his apartments which promised him the slightest assistance; and he felt almost decided that his plan must fall to the ground, till he began to reflect, that what he had not articles of strength to effect, might be produced by perseverance and art. He happened to have about him a large clasp knife of tempered steel; could he devise any method of cutting its edge into teeth in the form of a saw, he believed that, with unremitting labour, the iron bars which composed the grating might be cut through.

He searched his apartments narrowly round, but not even a nail could be found with which to begin his experiment of converting his knife into a saw. With fresh disappointment he desisted from his fruitless search. Every thought was strained to find means of effecting his purpose; and, at length, that invention, which seldom fails to spring from spurring necessity, came to his aid. He observed that a single iron bar, which was raised about half a foot from the hearth of his chimney, in order to confine the wood within the limits of security, had a sharp edge towards the front: and against this he resolved to make the experiment of indenting his knife.

The labour of the whole night produced him one tooth, which though neither so sharp, nor so regularly formed as those of a properly finished saw, still seemed to promise him that his desired end might be accomplished; and he hoped, when all the teeth were formed, to be able to discover some means of sharpening their points, which his mode of forming them naturally rendered blunt and jagged.

Carefully avoiding to work at those hours when he expected a supply of necessaries to be brought to his shelf, lest the noise of the process he was pursuing should be heard, and lead to a discovery which might frustrate all his high-raised hopes, and allowing himself but as few hours as nature could be satisfied with for sleep, his saw was completed in somewhat less than three weeks. As he had proceeded in his task, he had gained skill in its performance, and every tooth had improved in sharpness and formation upon the last; thus he felt less anxious than he had before done, about the discovery of a method for giving keenness to their points, and contented himself with what could be effected by means of a flat stone which composed his hearth, and afterwards whetting them upon the leather of his shoe.

Seven weeks of toil, of a nature infinitely more laborious than what he had experienced while employed in making his saw, were passed by him in dividing the grating on three of its sides from the walls in which it was fixed; the fourth he judged he should be able to bend down flat upon the side of the chimney, by hanging upon it with the whole weight of his body; desiring thus to spare himself the additional trouble of sawing it apart from the wall, as he had been constrained to do the three others.

The grating, as he had expected, bent freely downwards impressed with his weight; but suddenly it started from the wall, and Edward, being unprepared for this accident, fell with his head downwards, upon the hearth; a blow which he received on his temple was his least consideration; what he most dreaded was, lest the noise of his fall should have been heard, and bring some one to his prison to investigate the cause. He rose up with all the precipitancy he could command, and thrusting the iron grating into his bed, he drew on his nightcap, in order, if possible, to conceal his wound, should any one visit his rooms on the business of enquiry, and slipping off his clothes, he jumped into bed himself.

A quarter of an hour passed, and no footsteps were heard; thus reassured, he ventured again to quit his bed, and pay such attention as he had it in his power to do to the wound in his head. Having washed and bound it up, he again retired to bed, as a violent pain began to settle in his temples; and he judged that unless he took the precaution of passing some hours in quiet, if possible in sleep, his bruises might be of a disagreeable consequence. Before he entered his bed, he lifted up the mattress, and having concealed the iron grating between that and the canvas bottom of his bed, he laid his head on his pillow, with something like pleasure, at the reflection that he had obtained for himself free access to the roof of his prison, dancing about his heart; and anticipating the moment when he should begin his investigation of the possibility of effecting his escape.

On the following morning, the violent throbbings he had the night before experienced in his head, were considerably abated; but that part of it on which he had fallen was greatly swelled, and still extremely tender and painful. For two days, accordingly, he delayed his ascent up the passage which he had formed for himself into the air; and on the third, he resolved to hazard the execution of his plan. Fearful of a surprise, he chose the hour of evening for his experiment. The moon was now again at the full, and about nine in the evening, he began to climb his dark and perilous way. He feared lest the parting of the iron grating from the wall might not have loosened some stones, which his touch might draw down upon him in his ascent, or whether the rending of the iron from the stone might not have so much weakened the side wall of the chimney, that it might render his passage to the top unsafe, perhaps impracticable; but, in a very short time, he had to congratulate himself on having passed the spot where the iron grating had been fixed, and as he continued to ascend, the full disk of the moon, shining from a clear sky, studded thickly with refulgent stars, met his sight.

The chimney was at least twenty feet in height, and the labour attendant on mounting it, which he effected by resting his back on one wall, and the soles of his feet upon the opposite side, had fatigued him more than he could have believed it possible, for what his eagerness to breathe the air had led him to consider but a slight exertion, to have done.

Arrived at the top, he anxiously cast his eyes around on every side; parapet walls, circular towers, and the sharp angles of massive battlements, met his sight at every turn; even in what he deemed his own exalted situation, he now found himself many feet below the height of the walls; the light of the sky only met his sight from above, and through the vacant embrasures, which were accidentally seen in the parapet walls.

He looked down, and perceived a flat roof, part of which he knew to be the top of his own apartments, for he recognised the windows of particular shape, from which they received light. Upon this flat roof it was his desire to descend; but the chimney on which he was placed, rose at least twelve feet above its surface: could he contrive to slide down its side, he considered that he might find it impossible again to climb up it; and were he even assured that he could compass this difficulty, if his foot should slip in his descent, his fall might be heard by those in the apartments beneath, perhaps by the governor himself; and thus every hope of future escape might be cut off to him, perhaps even punishment be inflicted on him, for having made the attempt at procuring himself liberty. Of this idea he was, however, more careless than any other; no bodily torture could exceed the mental agony which he endured from his confinement, under the circumstances which attended his banishment from England, and the wife of his affections.

As he hung upon the wall, in consultation with his own mind, he heard a sound, which he, at first, imagined to be a pebble falling upon the window glass below him; but it was almost instantly repeated, and he then discovered that it was the string of a lute vibrating beneath the touch of a finger. No sooner did he ascertain the nature of the sound, than the kind Belise recurred to his thoughts. It was unlikely there should be any other musician than herself within the prison; she might, at that moment, be near enough to hear his words, to reply to them, to promise him her assistance; his heart leapt with ecstacy at the bare idea.

The lute sounded again, but it appeared to be farther removed from him, for its tones were scarcely audible, though it was evident that all the strings were moved in their turn, and that some one was playing an air upon it. His first desire was to ascertain from whence the sounds proceeded. After much hesitation, he was convinced that they arose out of a chimney about seven feet distant from the one on the top of which he was placed, and which did not rise to the height of the latter by about the number of feet at which it stood from it.

In the apartment beneath that chimney was, doubtless, Belise—that Belise, whose benevolent heart required but to be informed of his unjust sufferings, to exert herself with the most praiseworthy humanity to procure his enlargement. He doubted not but she would recognise his voice, should he venture to call to her; but then, should she not be alone, should her dreaded father-in-law be in the same apartment with her, what affliction might he not bring upon her, as well as upon himself.

A bell was regularly tolled at ten every night, from the highest tower of the building; and on this signal, every door was locked for the night, the lamps were extinguished, and all the inhabitants retired to their respective chambers, if not to bed. Edward resolved to descend into his apartments till that hour should be past at which the person who brought him his meals should come to demand his lamp for the night, and when he was retired, again to ascend to the spot which seemed to lead to his only hope of enlargement, and endeavour, if possible, to catch from the sounds which might arise to his hearing, whether or not the room, from which the adjoining chimney issued, was the bedchamber of Belise; if he should receive any reason to believe it so, he judged that he then might venture to pursue some method of conveying through it intelligence of his captivity.

His lamp having, as usual, been demanded, he lost no time in repairing to his situation upon the top of the chimney. Several hours were there passed by him in increasing anxiety; but he heard neither the voice nor the lute of Belise, nor, indeed, any sound whatever, except the growlings of the watch-dog at the outer gate, which appeared to be railing at the shadows of the night, as no attention seemed to be paid to his howlings by any of the inhabitants of the prison.

When the clock struck two, Edward again descended, spiritless and heartbroken with his fresh disappointment; but still resolute to pursue his plan for endeavouring to ascertain whether he might address Belise, through the channel which he believed to communicate with her apartment, without the fear of a discovery.

CHAPTER IX.

I'll read you matter, deep and dangerous:
As full of peril and advent'rous spirit,
As to o'erwalk a current, roaring loud,
On the unsteadfast footing of a spear.

FIRST PART OF HENRY THE FOURTH.

For several successive nights, Edward repaired at the same hour to his accustomed station, but could obtain no satisfactory information relative to Belise's apartment.

At length, one night, a few moments after the midnight hour had sounded, a more than usual stillness appearing to prevail around, he heard a voice, which he could not doubt to be her's, singing a plaintive air, unaccompanied by her lute; he listened, and was decidedly resolved that the voice proceeded from the same chimney from whence had issued the tones of the lute.

This decision carried with it to his mind, a certainty that beneath this chimney must be her bedchamber: the bell for retiring to rest had already been tolled two hours, and it was very unlikely that a young girl like Belise, should be, at that time of the night, in any apartment but her own chamber. He had learnt enough for that night, and descended into his apartment, resolved, by some means or other, to convey to her, on the succeeding one, intelligence of his captivity.

But the method by which this was to be effected, was a consideration full as difficult as any of the labours he had yet gone through. To address her in words, he durst not attempt; although he could not hear any sounds near to him when mounted on his chimney, still there might be persons near enough to hear him, if he ventured to speak sufficiently loud for his words to reach her. Should he write to her, it would be almost an impossibility for him to throw the letter with such exactness, as to ensure its sinking through the aperture down which he wished it to fall; it might be carried away by the air to a different part of the building, picked up, and conveyed to the governor: should his aim be correct, there was still a doubt, whether a piece of paper, from the lightness of its weight, would fall through the aperture or not; whether it would not be equally likely, and perhaps more so, to hang upon some part of the chimney, and never descend at all within the reach or knowledge of Belise.

From the various plans which entered his head, he selected one, which shall be developed in the course of its execution. On the following morning, before his breakfast was brought to him, he placed upon the shelf, against it should be turned round, a paper requesting a lemon to be procured for him. Not one of his demands had hitherto been denied him, and in the space of half an hour, a lemon was brought to him. He had previously written the following letter—

"DEAR LADY BELISE,

"The English officer of the name of Edward, whom you must remember to have seen on the day of your mother's wedding with the governor of this prison—whom you honoured by your particular conversation during the repast, and with your hand in the dance—impressed by the exalted feelings of benevolence which you that day expressed towards the unhappy captives under the power of your father-in-law, hesitates not to inform you that he is unjustly a prisoner within these walls, and ventures to implore your humane assistance in procuring his enlargement. He is so thoroughly convinced of the excellent nature of your heart, that he is assured you will serve him, if the ability so to do be yours; he, therefore, only adds, that for those exertions which he is conscious you will make in his cause, you will be rewarded with prayers and blessings from the hearts of himself and his wretched wife, from whom he is inhumanly separated. He was trepanned into the apartments, in which he is now a prisoner, by the governor's brother, Sanchez, on the day of your mother's wedding; and since that hour, the countenance of no human being has cheered his miserable solitude.

"Pardon him that he inflicts the wounds which sympathy will cause in a heart so exquisite in feeling as your own; but conscious that the heart of humanity conceives the opportunity of doing good a blessing, he, on this plea, grounds his excuse for intruding upon you the sorrows of the prisoner,

"EDWARD."

Having folded his letter, Edward had again recourse to his saw, with which he made a small aperture in one end of the lemon, and having extracted from it all the juice and pulp, he nipped his letter into as small a compass as the paper on which it was written was capable of being pressed into, and thrust it into the skin of the lemon.

About half an hour after his lamp had been fetched away for the night, he ascended that path which use had now rendered him somewhat more of an adept in mounting. When he arrived at the top, the moon had retired behind a cloud, and he resolved to await the moment of its emerging, rather than hazard a failure of his plan, from his impatience to execute it.

On this night, he heard not the voice of Belise proceeding from the spot from whence it had before flowed; universal silence prevailed; not even the howlings of the watch-dog interrupted the stillness of the infant morn.

The hour of one was on the point, as Edward conjectured, of sounding, ere the refulgence of the moon tempted him to make his cast. "God speed thee!" he exclaimed, mentally, and threw from him his lemon; he durst scarcely follow it with his eyes, lest his aim should have been faulty, and the next moment present him with the failure of his plan; but chance smiled on his effort, and he saw the paper which contained his petition, enter the aperture at which he had directed it.

An emotion of pleasure, long foreign to his heart, ran through his veins, and he resolved not immediately to quit his station, but to remain there some minutes longer, and endeavour to learn whether any sounds would arise, to inform him that Belise had gotten his packet safe into her possession.

Full half an hour passed, and the universal silence remained unbroken. Edward was now on the point of descending again to his apartment, when he heard the wards of a lock creak; the sound appeared to be at a short distance from him on his left side, and not far from the chimney down which he had just thrown his letter.

He was, at that moment, in the act of beginning to descend the chimney; his hands were rested on the top of the wall, and half his face only rising above it. Fear and expectation equally prevented him from moving, and he heard a voice say—"When you tap at the door, and I ask, who is there? say, the city of Ostend—be that your watchword—I shall know you by it."—"It is well," replied another voice.—"Think you she will be with you?" asked the first speaker.—"I hope she will, but cannot, to a certainty, determine," replied the other.—"Well, well," answered the first speaker, "that is nothing to me: I will be ready for you."

The man who had spoken last now disappeared again through the door by which they had both entered upon the roof, and closed it after him; the other advanced towards the chimney which Edward had conceived to arise out of the chamber of Belise, and taking from under a horseman's cloak (or, at least, such appeared the garment in which he was wrapped) a ladder of ropes, he slung it, by means of a couple of hooks which were fastened to it, upon the top of the chimney wall, and then threw it into the inside. This done, he took off his cloak, and having laid it down, he climbed upon an iron supporter, which ran from the centre of the chimney to the leaden roof beneath, and from this he mounted on the top of the wall, whence he placed his foot upon the first step of his ladder, and immediately began to disappear down the chimney.

The agitated mind of Edward gave him no power of reflecting on what the conversation he had just overheard might mean; all there was room for in his brain was the possibility of escape, which appeared to present itself to him in his knowledge of the stranger's watchword, and his ability of disguising himself in the cloak, which he had left upon the roof.

It was an opportunity too flattering not to be grasped at by one in the situation of the unhappy Edward. Remounting the top of the chimney, he threw his legs over on the outer side, and clinging with his arms to an angle of the wall, by a sudden effort of resolution he suffered himself to drop down; his arms supported him against the wall for several feet of his descent, but here a prominence in the stonework threw him off his hold, and he fell with his back upon the hard roof of lead beneath. His shoulders were excessively bruised, and his left arm benumbed by the blow it had received; still, regardless of bodily injuries, while the power was left him of rising upon his legs, he listened anxiously, dreading lest the noise of his fall should have called any one to the spot. But all remained silent, and judging that every moment might be of the most material consequence to his safety, as the stranger might return, and thus frustrate his attempt at passing for him to the man, whoever he might be, in the turret, he hastily put on the cloak, and tapped upon the door. "Who's there?" immediately asked a voice.—"The city of Ostend," replied Edward, trembling lest his voice should betray him.

The door was opened, and he stepped in: by the lamp held in the hand of the man who admitted him, and whom he conjectured to be one of the keepers of the prison, he saw that he was standing at the head of a winding staircase. The man began to descend, and he followed him. "So you are come alone?" said the man. Fearful of speaking, lest his answers should betray him for an impostor, and equally dreading to remain silent, Edward replied—"Yes, but I shall come again to-morrow night."—"Ah," returned the man, "it is ten to one if I can admit you again to-morrow night; why did you not bring her away now?—What is the use of delay?—No time like the present."

They were now at the bottom of the stairs, and Edward's guide moved hastily along a stone passage, which brought them into a lofty hall, of which the vaulted roof was supported by pillars, beyond the first range of which nothing was visible by the faint rays of the single lamp carried by the man.

They had nearly gained the extremity of the hall, when the man suddenly exclaimed—"Hark!" They both stopped and listened—Distant footsteps were audible—"Yes," cried the man, "we are discovered; fly to the chapel, and conceal yourself in the confessional." So saying, he blew out the lamp, and Edward heard him rapidly descending some steps at a short distance from the spot where he had left him standing.

This information was doubtless friendly, and might have been of infinite service to the stranger whom Edward was personating, but to him it was entirely useless. He cast his eyes around; darkness met them on every side. The steps of his pursuers, if such they were, increased on his ear, and in a very few moments a light was visible on the opposite side of the hall; a second followed it, and almost instantly after a third appeared in view.

He perceived that they were carried by three different men, and in the midst of them he beheld one with a drawn sword in his hand, whom he believed to be the governor. They did not speak, nor did they appear to see him. He slipped hastily behind a pillar, hoping thus to escape their notice. They separated in the centre of the hall, and taking different directions, each moved slowly along, with his lamp held above his head, to assist his search after those of whom he was in pursuit. After some moments, one of the three passed within a few paces of the pillar behind which Edward had screened himself; the light of the lamp borne by this man, shewed him a couple of steps which led into a chapel. Once more something like hope warmed his heart, and as the man receded from him, he ascended the steps, and proceeded forward. The lamps were now so far removed from him, that he was again left in total darkness, save a faint illumination which entered by a lofty window, and which he conjectured to be the light of the moon.

Eager to find some place of concealment, he still moved on; a single step, of about a foot in depth, which the light was not sufficient for him to discern, threw him forwards, and he fell against a wooden substance, which slid from him as the weight of his body sunk upon it, and he fell with it to the ground. A loud noise accompanied this accident. "Here!—Here!—this way!" was directly echoed from different parts of the hall, and in the space of a minute the lamps advanced sufficiently near to discover to him that he had fallen upon a coffin, which he had knocked from its supporters; and as he rested his hands on it to raise himself again upon his feet, he read upon its lid, in brass letters, "Sanchez Xavia, aged LXIV."

Before he had time for reflection, both his arms were caught hold of by the men who had entered the chapel, and the governor, presenting himself before him, said—"Well, Sir, you see you are caught; however, don't be alarmed; those never need be afraid of me who can pay their way into my good graces; so come, deliver up to me the two purses of gold which you have in your pockets; I'll turn them to quite as good a use as you would have made of them."

"You know," replied Edward, surprised out of the reply, and forgetting at the moment that he was mistaken for another man, "you know that I have no gold about me."

"I know you have," replied the governor; "I overheard you tell my daughter-in-law that you had sold your commission for four hundred and fifty pieces, and that they were in two purses, one in each pocket of your horseman's cloak; so give me leave to save you the trouble of delivering them up to me yourself—I'll make you ample recompence for the gift, though you give it me unwillingly—I'll maintain you for it for life—Don't think that I am weak enough to let you go, and inform against me for easing a young fool of his money."

These words he followed by putting his hands into the pockets of the cloak now worn by Edward, from which he pulled two purses, which, by the chinking sound they sent forth, as Garcias shaked them between his fingers, seemed to contain what he had asserted they did: not satisfied with these, but thinking that there might be still more behind, the governor thrust his hands again into each pocket of the cloak, and, in withdrawing them from the examination, he pulled the cloak off one of Edward's shoulders. "What's this I see?" exclaimed he. "Have you got on an English uniform since you sold your French commission? What does all this mean?" added he, raising the cap which had fallen partly over Edward's eyes. "Why, zounds, and the devil, can I believe my sight?" he again burst forth—"My English prisoner!—Am I witched, or do my eyes deceive me? By what mystery do I see you here, in the cloak, and possessed of the money of Adolphus Biron?"

Edward was unable to speak, had he been inclined so to have done; a mist danced before his eyes, and he felt ready to sink into the earth.

"So then," continued the governor, "not satisfied with his attempt to steal my daughter, the brave Adolphus has been lending his assistance to my prisoner in effecting his escape."

"Whomsoever you are speaking of," said Edward, roused to a reply by the unjust accusation preferring against an innocent man, "he is entirely faultless with respect to myself, and my attempts to escape your tyranny; whatever I have done, in the hope of procuring my liberty, I have performed unaided. I do not know Adolphus."

"You soon shall then," replied the governor; "you shall enjoy the happiness of being fellow prisoners: for since you have not known how to be grateful for the benefits and indulgences you enjoyed in the apartments you lately inhabited, you shall for the future be taught the reverse, and learn what you have lost by your folly."

"Wretch!—Wretch!" exclaimed Edward, "there will come a day, when you will learn what you have lost by the exercise of your cruelties upon the innocent and unfortunate. How did your brother in blood, your brother in iniquity, who now lies dead at your feet, expire? Were the last moments of his existence calm?—Were they such as gave you encouragement to die under the performance of such acts as you are now living in?"

The governor's countenance underwent two or three changes from pale to red, and then again from red to pale; and he replied, though by no means in so firm a tone as he had before spoken—"What, do you think Sanchez died like a cowardly priest, and that I am to be awed by your pious sermonizing? Spare your breath, you only waste it on me; when Garcias Xavia has once said, 'I'll do it,' nothing can turn me from my purpose. I owe my faith to my employers, and religiously keep it with them."

"And what regard do you pay to the faith you owe to Heaven?" asked Edward, with emphasis.

"Have not I told you already not to waste your breath on me?" he replied, in a tone of displeasure; then turning to his men, he said, "conduct him to the vacant cell in the southern tower—I'll meet you there presently—do not leave him till I come."

The governor and one of his attendants then turned towards the direction by which Edward had wandered thus far from his prison, intending, as Edward could not doubt, to repair to the chamber of his daughter, in search of the stranger whom he had named Adolphus Biron; and the two men, who already held Edward, dragged him out of the chapel to the opposite side of the hall, from which they constrained him to pass through several passages to the cell of which the governor had spoken. It was a lofty space of about eighteen feet square; it was built of a grey stone, of which material four pillars, placed at equal distances from each other, seemed to be the supporters of the roof. On one side was a chimney, vast and dreary, and which appeared, notwithstanding its size, incapable of giving warmth to the prison, of which the air, even at the present clement season of the year, was damp and chilly.

At each end was a rude bedstead, spread with straw, over which was thrown a ragged quilt, which appeared the only covering belonging to it. The men placed their lamps on a bench which stood near one of the pillars, and kept their hands fixed upon Edward's arms, whilst they awaited the coming of the governor.

In the space of about twenty minutes he appeared, followed by the man who had left the hall with him, and another, who also appeared to be a servant of the prison; and these led between them a young man, of about twenty-three years of age, habited in the military uniform of France.

A couple of chains were immediately produced by the order of the governor, and with these the young man and Edward were chained to opposite pillars; padlocks were placed on the chains where they crossed their waists, to deprive them of the possibility of freeing themselves from them; and this done, the governor, without addressing his prisoners, commanded his men to take up their lamps and follow him: they obeyed—the prison was left in total darkness, and its inhabitants heard the door looked and bolted upon them.

"Unfortunate stranger," said Edward, addressing his companion in captivity, "add not to the many other miseries with which I am already burdened, thy resentment against one equally unhappy as thyself—who is indeed the instrument of thy present bondage, but who is entirely free from the intention of inflicting on another those pangs under which he has himself so long mourned."

Adolphus replied—"I cannot blame you for the method by which you attempted to effect your escape from these walls; it was the perversity of our fate which led us both into a situation where the combination of circumstances has conspired to render us more miserable than we were before.—I," continued he, "have more to dread from the resentment of the governor than you are acquainted with; my fears are not confined to myself alone, my every nerve is strung with agony for the fate of my Belise."

"Heaven avert all danger from her benevolent heart!" exclaimed Edward.

"I am well aware," replied Adolphus, "that you know how to estimate her excellence; a few minutes before I reached her apartment this night, she had received a letter from you, mysteriously conveyed to her, which proves that you entertain just sentiments of her sensibility and benevolence: impressed with the liveliest pity for your situation, she shewed me your petition, and obtained my promise to assist her in attempting to procure your enlargement from captivity."

"Generous girl!" exclaimed Edward, "may the reward of her excellent disposition, although protracted, be ultimately adequate to her merits."

"Should I ever obtain my release from my present bonds," said Adolphus; "should my Belise ever be restored to my arms by the kind interposition of Providence in our behalf—how dismal are the prospects in life to which I am doomed to look forward! I am an outcast from those who should be my protectors, and I am left entirely destitute, by the loss of those pieces of gold which the villainous governor has this night stolen from the pockets of my cloak; they were my all, and should I ever again clasp my Belise to my breast, she will hold a beggar to her heart."

"My lot," replied Edward, "is equally destitute as your own; I have myself never known a parent; and the beloved woman whom I have allied to me, by the tender title of wife, is under the controul of an unjust and imperious father, by whose machinations I am now detained a prisoner in this place, and who labours, with too much success, to prevent her from ever again reposing her aching head on the breast of an affectionate husband."

This mutual confession drew from each enquiries that led to the history of their past lives. Edward freely narrated his to his fellow in misfortune, who then recounted the principal events of his own life in nearly the following words—

"My father," said Adolphus, "was a merchant of considerable repute in the city of Dunkirk; my younger brother, Frederick, and myself, were his only children; I was two years older than my brother; and about the time I had attained my fifteenth year, severe and unavoidable misfortunes attended my father in trade, which reduced him to the mortifying necessity of declaring himself insolvent; and, in the course of the following year, he died of a broken heart.

"At this unhappy period my brother and myself must have been cast destitute upon the world, but for a brother of my deceased mother, a rich old bachelor, residing at Ostend, who invited us to make his house our home.

"My uncle was a man of great pride, and austerity of character, and he took care to make us feel that we were in his debt: however, in the course of a couple of years, he became in some measure attached to us, and gave us to understand, that he intended to leave his fortune between us at his death, though he never explained to us in what proportion he meant to distribute it.

"About two years ago, that is, just after I had completed my twenty-first year, I became acquainted with my adored Belise; I saw her but to love her, and to wish her mine. My brother Frederick, who had also gained an introduction to her, saw her with the same eyes as myself; but his attentions were by no means so pleasing to her as mine were, and upon me fell her choice and her heart.

"Her mother, though a woman of considerable property herself, still experienced infinite pride and satisfaction in seeing her daughter likely to become the wife of the co-heir of one of the wealthiest men in the city, and gave me every encouragement in her power to persevere in my suit.

"My uncle was acquainted with my attachment to Belise, but considered it as one of those impressions which assail the heart of youth, afford it pleasure while they last, and are easily effaced by any other which promises a greater degree of gratification; for at the very same time that he rallied me on my love for her, he informed me, with all the seriousness of a man who believes himself to be communicating pleasing intelligence, that he had ascertained that my hand would be accepted, with the greatest readiness, by a lady of the city, who had already been twice married, besides being double my age, and with whose family he said it had always been his ambition to ally his own.

"I heard his proposal with real surprise, and without hesitation expressed to him my astonishment that he should suppose my heart to be of so fickle a nature, as to relinquish the prepossession which he knew it already to entertain for another object, particularly when he was well acquainted with the highly amiable qualities and engaging manners of her to whom it was devoted.

"He at first laughed at my scruples, but when he found me resolute in my adherence to those principles which justice and honour dictated to me to persevere in, he flew into a violent passion, and loading me with opprobrious terms, all of which he qualified with the epithet 'ungrateful,' he burst out of the room, and left me to my reflections. From these I could receive no consolation but the consciousness of having acted rightly, and the assurance that my Belise would not waver from her attachment, whatever might be the future fate of the man on whom her affections were fixed; for I concluded, from what I had already seen of my uncle's character, that the right I had assumed of thinking for myself, and my having been sufficiently hardy to oppose one of his favourite schemes, would lose me his favour for ever: nor was I mistaken in my idea. From this time his coolness towards me increased every day; and I could perceive that my brother Frederick, who had before stood second in his favour, was now raised to the very summit of his esteem.

"Rather more than a week explained to me the cause of my observations; my brother no longer spoke in raptures of Belise, as he had been accustomed to do, and in whose affections, I believe, he had, to that very time, entertained a hope of supplanting me. He even sought opportunities of undervaluing that disposition, and those charms, the praise of which had before been his favourite topic; and when I remarked to him the change that had taken place in his sentiments, he replied—'Well, then congratulate yourself that you have no longer a rival in your adoration of her. My uncle has selected for me an alliance of which *I* see the value, although *your* honourable heart spurned the many advantages that are attached to it; but you will no doubt be much happier with love and slender circumstances.'

"These words, spoken with a contemptuous sneer, left me no doubt that my brother had been swayed by the voice of interest, and had accepted the alliance which I had rejected. My conjecture was a just one, for within a month he became her husband. On the day of his marriage, immediately after the ceremony had taken place, my uncle thus addressed me—'It is but just that the observance of the duty of obedience, and its neglect, should meet with opposite rewards; know therefore, that for his acquiescence in the favourite wish of my heart, your brother is from this hour the declared heir of my property, with the exception of one legacy—that legacy I bestow on you before my death; it consists of a commission, contained in that paper,' extending his hand towards me as he spoke; 'and learn, that it is not from any personal regard I bear you, that I confer on you this gift, but to deprive the world of the opportunity of saying, that I have cast out an orphan of my late sister a beggar. You will therefore immediately join your regiment, as your presence here cannot give pleasure either to myself, or to your brother, whose happiness consists in seeing me pleased.'

"Humiliating as I felt it to be obliged to accept the charity of one who so unjustly despised me, still more dreadful was the idea of appearing before my Belise, an outcast, and a beggar; and, receiving from his hands the offered commission, I said—'From one on whom I have no direct claim, every gift must be acknowledged as a favour; I thank you, Sir, for what you have been pleased to confer on me, and wish my brother and yourself much happiness in your congenial sentiments.' I was greatly gratified to find that the calmness with which I uttered these words had the effect I desired them to produce, of enraging my unnatural relative; when, probably, had I suffered my own real feelings of passion to have appeared, he might only have reaped from them food for his ill-natured gratification: and while he was studying a reply, I left the house.

"In the heart of my Belise this unexpected change in my circumstances had worked no alteration; but her mother, who was now become the wife of Garcias Xavia, and was probably influenced in her opinion by his crafty avarice, immediately forbade me access to the house, and charged her daughter on no account to entertain any idea of my now ever becoming her husband.

"All access to my Belise was thus debarred me, and I found that her mother had the intention of uniting her to an old man, who had no recommendation but his wealth, from which he had made many handsome presents to the governor, to buy his interest in his favour. No means of communicating with her now remained to me, but by writing: she bribed one of the keepers of the prison to bring me a letter, containing a full account of what was passing, which informed me, that she feared her mother intended to marry her to the man of her aversion in the course of a few days. The keeper, who brought me this letter, proved to be a person who had formerly been in the service of my deceased father; thus his knowledge of me rendered him doubly willing to be our friend. By him I returned an answer to her letter, telling her, that if she would agree to fly with me, I would sell my commission, and that we would retire into some distant country, where the money I should thus have realized would purchase us a small farm, sufficient to afford us a comfortable maintenance.

"In the course of a week I received from her another letter, acquainting me, that if I would be at the prison gate, at the unfortunate midnight which is just past, and provide myself with a ladder of ropes against my coming, our mutual friend would instruct me in a mode of gaining access to her chamber, where she would load me with such articles of value as she possessed, and then fly with me from the tyranny of her mother and the governor.

"That I came at the appointed time, it is unnecessary for me to repeat to you; nor need I inform you of the means which I used, according to the instructions of my friend, the keeper, for gaining admittance into the apartment of my Belise; but, arrived there, fate frowned upon our hopes—for the governor, whose profession renders him naturally suspicious and watchful, was, as he has since explained it, lurking about the prison at the time of my descending into her chamber, and catching the sound of a second voice within it, he immediately laid his ear to the door, and having heard me inform her of the four hundred and fifty pieces of gold which were in the pockets of my cloak, he resolved, at one blow, to make himself master of them, and prevent our escape.

"Having accordingly summoned to his aid some of his servants, he proceeded to the hall, through which he knew we must unavoidably pass in our way out of the prison. Here you, by the error into which my cloak led him, became his victim, and having secured you, he returned to the chamber of his daughter-in-law; we had just left it, and gained the roof, where I was expressing my surprise at my cloak being gone, when his voice assailed our ears: in a few seconds more I was his prisoner, and my Belise torn from my sight."

Here Adolphus paused; his heart swelled with agony at the idea of the torments to which Belise might be exposed by her cruel parents; his frenzied mind presented her to him forced into the arms of unfeeling age, and calling upon him for that protection which he was denied the power of rendering her.

Edward and his fellow captive were both too miserable in their own feelings, to afford each other any portion of that consolation which adds strength to the mind, and pours a healing balm upon the wounds inflicted by the hand of sorrow. They both concluded their sufferings to be doomed to end only with their lives, and the ineffectual sigh alone broke the silence of their lips.

On the morrow some of the keepers entered their prison, and lengthened the chains which bound them, to such an extent as enabled them to reach the straw pallets that were placed at either end of their cell: this action afforded some relief to their aching limbs; but still care was taken to keep them at that distance from each other, which should prevent their affording one another any assistance in freeing themselves from their bonds.

Thus passed several months, during which the bare necessaries of life were brought to them for their support, and during which time they had not been able to extort a single word from any of the keepers who had entered their cell, in reply to the enquiries they had advanced to them.

From Adolphus, Edward learnt that an engagement had taken place a few days before they had become fellow prisoners, in which Sanchez Xavia had been so severely wounded in both his legs, that amputation had become necessary, and that he had died very soon after the operation.

"We are still not the most unhappy beings in existence," said Edward; "we are eminently blessed, when our hearts are compared with those of such men as Sanchez Xavia. Neither liberty, wealth, nor the accomplishment of our most extended wishes, if our minds be the slaves of evil passions, can procure us that true felicity which will be the companion even of imprisonment, poverty, and the most cruel of disappointments, if the heart that suffers be free from self-reproach."

CHAPTER X.

He that of greatest works is finisher,
Oft does them by the weakest minister.
....
———Great floods have flown
From simple sources; and great seas have dry'd;
When miracles have by the greatest been deny'd.
Oft expectation fails, and most oft there,
Where most it promises; and oft it hits
Where hope is coldest, and despair most sits.

ALL'S WELL THAT ENDS WELL.

THREE sad and mournful years had now passed over the head of Edward in his captivity, when a circumstance took place, which once more animated the latent sparks of hope within his breast.

The provisions with which himself and Adolphus were supplied, consisted principally of bread and fruit; amongst the latter of which were frequently mixed chesnuts. On a certain day, their supply being brought as usual to their prison, Adolphus, who had been for some time past indisposed, and unable to rise from his straw pallet, having refused all nourishment but the bread and milk allowed him, the basket was set down near Edward; it contained some apples, some bread, and a few chesnuts. On looking into the basket, Edward perceived that one or two of the chesnuts were peculiarly marked with white lines; he took them up, in order to examine what these could be—for where the mind has but little to amuse it, it eagerly catches at any object which turns it for a while from itself—and found that they were made by particles of the rind being cut away, through which the white nut beneath shewed itself; and on the one which he first took into his hand, he imagined he could decypher those letters which compose the word "*have.*" He eagerly cast his eyes upon a second, and on this was engraved the single letter "*A.*"

A confusion of ideas floated in his brain; and hastily picking out all those which bore on them any characters, he arranged them with a trembling hand in different situations, till they at last presented him with this sentence—

"*You have a friend within these walls.*"

A tumult of joy ran through his veins, and falling on his knees, he exclaimed—"O God, accept my thanks! in firm reliance that the eye of Providence never sleeps to the sufferer who places faith in his benevolence, I have never despaired—and thou hast rewarded my dependance on thy mercy. O God! my soul pours forth its gratitude before thee."

This sudden exclamation on the part of Edward, roused the attention of Adolphus, in reply to whose enquiries of the cause which had thus agitated him, he gave a full account of the occurrence of the last minutes: and a thousand conjectures were then formed by them both, of who could be the person from whom this enigmatical assurance of friendship had proceeded. It was also a doubt with Edward, on cooler reflection, whether the information had been intended for him, or his fellow captive. Adolphus believed it either the work of his Belise, or of their mutual friend the keeper, who might have escaped from the detection of the fault he had committed in admitting him on the fatal night, from which he dated the commencement of his captivity, to the apartment of Belise, and might still retain his situation in the prison, but have been hitherto prevented from giving him information that he was not less than ever interested in his fate.

However, as so great a cloud of mystery hung over the intelligence thus artfully conveyed, they mutually vowed that they would not accept any terms of liberation which did not include them both.

The participation of their sorrows and hardships had rendered them sincerer friends than flippant prosperity could have done; and they experienced the most consolatory sensations, from the strictness of that friendship by which they felt themselves allied to each other.

Several weeks passed on, and no fresh intelligence reached the captives; narrowly did they examine every supply of chesnuts which was brought to them, and with equal nicety did they investigate every article which was introduced into their cell, in the hope of meeting with some farther information which might keep alive the embers of hope within their breasts; but disappointment attended all their researches.

The weeks grew into months, and seven of these had moved on with tardy pace, when, one evening, between the hours of eight and nine, the keeper, who had for some time past solely attended upon them, entered their prison: he closed the door after him, and, in a familiar tone, called out—"How are ye, gentlemen? how are ye?" Adolphus and Edward looked at him in silent surprise: his steps were faltering, and they perceived that he was intoxicated; in one hand he held a flask, his pipe was in his mouth, and in his other hand he grasped the large key of their prison door; he staggered towards the fire, and placed himself upon the bench, which he had drawn to the hearth.

Having applied his mouth to the flask, and withdrawn it again from his lips with a smack, which pronounced him to have relished the draught it had afforded him, he said—"Gentlemen, I have come to have a little talk with you: I am an honest man, though you see me one of the keepers of a prison. My master, the governor, makes a great deal of money by keeping you, and others like you, confined in this place; now I don't see the reason why I should not make a little money as well as he—by letting you out of it—now an't I an honest fellow?"

However serviceable this intention might prove to our prisoners, they did not feel it at all consistent with truth to compliment him on the virtue of honesty; thus with a smile they remained silent.

"Well," continued the keeper, "now I have explained to you my intentions, how much are you willing to give me for your liberty?"

Adolphus and Edward, well acquainted that they were equally poor, cast upon each other a look of mingled enquiry, how they should reply to the question, and of agony and despair, at the certain knowledge that they had no bribe whatever to offer him.

"You hesitate, methinks, a long while," cried he, "for two men who have appeared as miserable as you have both done in captivity, about deciding on a reward for him who offers to become your liberator. Mark this, a trifle won't satisfy me, as I can never return hither again to my present station, when I have once conveyed you out of the reach of danger, and shall therefore be thrown out of employment."

"My friend," said Edward, "you must be sensible that we can have nothing valuable about us here to reward you with; nor will we deceive you in promises that we should not be able to perform. We are far from affluent, and were we enlarged from this spot, our means of life would be to be earned by us, as we have unjustly been deprived of all we once possessed, and have no dependance left us but our own endeavours. One thing alone we can assure you of, that while we have the power of living, you shall never be destitute; our gratitude will teach us to exert every nerve in rendering you a reward equal to your desert: more we have it not in our power to promise."

"You have not!" returned the man, "why then I must try somebody else: promises wont do for me; I have a certainty here, and can't give it up for the chance of living upon promises. I am very sorry for you, but I can't afford to do any thing for you, as I am an honest man."

He rose from the bench, and was moving towards the door.

"Stay," said Adolphus; "take this ring of hair: shew it to the governor's daughter, Belise, and entreat her to return what money she can command to him who sent it."

"What should that be for?" asked the keeper; "do you think she'll lend her money, if she has got any, to a stranger, especially to help him out of her father's clutches? she'd sooner send you a handcuff, I warrant me."

"You mistake, you mistake!" cried Adolphus, "I am no stranger to her, nor is she at all of the disposition of her father-in-law. I entreat you to take it, and make the experiment."

"No, no; there is too much danger in it," said the man: "ten to one but she informs against me to her father."

"I will pledge my soul that she will not!" exclaimed Adolphus.

"Aye, but that would be no recompence to me for the loss of my head," rejoined the keeper, "in case the governor was to chop it off, in consequence of her prattling. I don't like trusting women."

He placed the key in the door, in order to let himself out.

"Do you then absolutely refuse to make the experiment?" asked Adolphus.

"Not absolutely," returned the man: "there is one chance for you; if no other prisoner can pay me for his liberty in any thing better than you have offered me, namely, promises, I'll come back, and make trial of the ring; but if I can get any thing better, you must not expect me. I am an honest man, and tell you the truth;" and having said this, he went out, and locked the door after him.

Their present disappointment bore less hardly on the friends than it would have done, had they possessed no other chance of being delivered from their bonds than the one which their poverty had just obliged them to relinquish. They were not at all surprised at the kind of philosophy practised by the keeper, who was in the daily habit of seeing his master heaping together wealth by the most unfair means; and they entertained some faint hope that he would find it difficult to meet a ready reward for his offered services from any unhappy victim to the avarice of the governor, and that he would still return for the ring.

The night passed on, and the keeper did not return; thus they concluded, that he had either found some captive able to pay him for his enlargement, or that he had sunk to sleep under the influence of intoxication, and had entirely forgotten the ring of Adolphus.

About that hour in the morning, at which their breakfast was usually brought to them, the door of the cell was opened, and a keeper, whom they had never seen before, entered; he was followed by another man, in mean and tattered garments, one of whose eyes was concealed under a bandage, and whose left leg was bent up at the knee, and rested on a wooden supporter. The former addressing Adolphus, spoke first—"We are come to fetch you," he said, "by order of the governor, to a better apartment. Here, comrade, unlock his chain," he added, giving a key into the hand of the other man, who having received the key, moved up to Adolphus, saying to his fellow—"Stand you, meanwhile, by the door."

There was something of such infinite familiarity to the senses of Edward in the voice of the last speaker, that it thrilled every chord in his system: he fixed his eyes penetratingly on the features of the man, a variety of circumstances united in his mind, and he recognised, in the poor, tattered, and disabled figure, which stood before him—the well-known HUBERT.

The eye of Hubert met his; its expression enjoined silence, and painful as was the injunction, Edward obeyed it.

A few moments served to unlock the chain of Adolphus. Had his own inclination been consulted, he would have preferred remaining where he was, and sharing the conversation of Edward, which had been a great consolation to the miseries of his imprisonment, to the enjoyment of a better apartment without his society; but knowing remonstrance to be in vain, as the command proceeded from a voice from which there was no appeal, he suffered himself to be led away without resistance; Edward and he exchanging good wishes for the future welfare of each other at parting.

For some minutes, Edward could scarcely believe himself to be awake, so impossible did he feel it to believe that his senses had presented him with any thing more than an illusion, when he had supposed himself to have beheld the person of Hubert; and as he became convinced that it was indeed a reality which he had seen, he burst into a flood of tears, which gave relief to his overburdened feelings.

When his mind became again sufficiently calm for reflection, he no longer doubted by whom had been planned and executed the artifice of the chesnuts; and his heart glowed with a fervency of gratitude towards Hubert, which surpassed in strength any sensation he had yet experienced; so exquisite is the happiness of finding a sincere friend still allied to us, at the moment when we have believed ourselves to be forgotten and forsaken by the whole world.

How Hubert had introduced himself into the prison, in his present disabled state and mean disguise, did not at all excite his surprise; what most raised his astonishment was, by what means Hubert had learnt him not to be dead, when he doubted not but the report of his death had been currently circulated in England, and had discovered the place of his confinement.

A thousand distracting thoughts bewildered his brain, and pain and pleasure met in it with equal strength. Hubert might be detected in his friendship, might suffer death on his account. Hubert might succeed in procuring his enlargement, and once again conduct him to the arms of his wife. "Oh, Rosalind! dearest, most adored of women! dost thou still live?" he exclaimed. "Oh, that one single instant of communication had been permitted me with Hubert, that I might have received from him intelligence of thy welfare!" The contradictory ideas which swelled his imagination, almost brought on a delirium; he endeavoured in vain to compose his mind, and throwing himself upon his pallet, prayed for sleep, lest reason should fade under the torturing influence of combined hope and fear.

CHAPTER XI.

————————I will follow thee
To the last gasp, with truth and loyalty.

AS YOU LIKE IT.

We must now dedicate a few pages to the adventurous Hubert. It will be remembered, that in the conversation which passed between him and the Lord Baron de Mowbray, relative to the disposal of Rosalind's then unborn child, the Baron had said—"*Edward will see England no more; he is by my design detained in Flanders*." And at the same instant that conveyed to him this intelligence, Hubert resolved, that if human means could discover his retreat, and procure his enlargement, to be himself the instrument of restoring him to his lamenting Rosalind.

Hubert was one of those beings who may be termed the universal friends of man; the benefits of education he had not enjoyed, but nature had gifted him with a heart possessed of those rich virtues which instruction may refine, but cannot better. Whence then had one, whose soul was the seat of every good quality, obtained the name of "*Surly?*" It was because the honest Hubert could neither fawn, smile, nor cringe; it was because the honest Hubert could not see the dignity of man insulted, whether it were clad in the laced robe of prosperity, or in the tattered garb of indigence, without expressing the indignant feelings that arose in his mind; it was because Hubert could not commend an action of which he believed the motive to be dishonourable; it was because, desiring the happiness of every human being, the many wretches whom he saw in existence, caused his brow to wear an almost constant frown of grief.

When Edward, whilst a youth, first addressed Hubert on the ramparts of De Mowbray Castle, and offered him the slice of bread and meat which he so haughtily rejected, Hubert, who had been accustomed only to hear of the great, with descriptions of their comforts, their luxuries, and their affluent ease, and who had seen so much of the poverty, the hardships, and the ill-rewarded labours of the poor, whom it had been his constant question, "why the better provided for, by the hand of chance, did not more amply relieve?" conceiving that there could be only the one motive of Edward's being unable to eat himself what he offered to him, and that any animal had been equally welcome to the gift, his very wants gave him pride to refuse the offer, of which he mistook the nature. Still did the next instant explain that his heart was tender, although proud; for he scrupled not to submit to the most humble supplication, to obtain what he had refused for himself, for the relief of a poor animal, whom he saw hungry like himself, and, like himself, the sport of superior strength and well-faring.

But no sooner did Hubert discover his error, than mingled repentance and gratitude swelled his heart. Edward, unlike the sons of fastidious grandeur, who are irreconcileable on a first offence, and ever hate the object from which it sprung, easily perceived that the young Hubert possessed a degree of character superior to the station he had been born in; and justly conceiving him one of those personages for whom it is peculiarly the duty of the more fortunate in life to feel consideration, took frequent opportunities of conferring on him such little services and attentions, as proved to Hubert equal sources of comfort and gratification to his feelings.

Actions of this nature, when they spring from hearts like that of Edward, seldom go unrewarded; the sensation of gratitude is the noblest feeling which the human mind can experience; and the justice of Providence has not deprived the poor of the power of tasting and exercising it, any more than the rich—a knowledge which ought greatly to induce us to the performance of benevolent actions; since, in the eventful scale of life, nothing is more likely, than that those who rise to-day may sink to-morrow, and rejoice to meet him as a friend, whom they have once thought it a condescension to acknowledge as a dependant.

Every day Hubert became more and more attached to Edward, and he thought himself the happiest of human beings when, through the intercession of Edward, he was admitted a member of the new troops, then raising at the castle.

When Edward was sent to take the command of the newly-erected tower in the village, he first acquainted Hubert with his love for Rosalind, and confided in his already tried friendship to visit the castle (a privilege which was not interdicted to him, although Edward enjoyed not the same liberty), and to bring him intelligence of what was passing in it.

At length, when Hubert brought him the dreadful information, that the Baron had destined his daughter to become the wife of the hated Lord Rufus, in the course of four more short days, and Edward could no longer endure absence from her sight, Hubert repaired in the evening to the castle, under pretence of sleeping there; and in the night he admitted Edward, as they had previously agreed that he should do, by an outlet from the ramparts, which led him into the vaults connected with the chapel.

From hence they had planned, that Hubert should proceed to the chamber of Gertrude, and require of her to give Rosalind information of Edward's wish to see her in the chapel; but that plan, our readers will recollect, was anticipated, by Edward finding Rosalind already in the chapel when he entered it, whither she had come to pray by the side of her deceased mother's tomb.

The events which followed this interview, down to the time of

Edward's hasty departure with his company for Flanders, have been already fully detailed.

At this period, the heart of Hubert experienced as great a pang as that of the forlorn Rosalind; not even the opportunity of saying farewell to his benefactor Edward was given him: anxiously, most anxiously did he wish that he had been one of the number under his command; but the chance had not been his, and he lamented if more severely than any misfortune which had yet befallen him in life. Earnestly did he desire that a second body of troops might be sent to reinforce those already gone; were he not of the chosen number, should such an event take place, he resolved to solicit for leave to become one of them; and in this hope he grew tolerably composed.

Thus had passed on seven months, when the Baron de Mowbray addressed Hubert, upon his post, as sentinel at the tower in the village, offering him five hundred pieces of gold for removing the child of Rosalind from Cumberland. Hubert could scarcely forbear falling on his knees before the Baron, and returning thanks to Heaven that he had selected him as the instrument of his villanous intention.

"Edward will see England no more: he is, by my design, detained in Flanders," said the Baron.

"Then," whispered the soul of Hubert, "the five hundred pieces you offer shall be devoted to his release."

As eagerly did Hubert pant for the moment at which he should receive, from the hand of the Baron, the sum which would enable him to set out in quest of the victim of treachery, as the stag, which escapes from the pursuit of the hunters, pants for the cooling stream to allay its thirst. At length the hour came, and the five hundred pieces which Lord William had promised, were made *six* hundred, and safely deposited in the pocket of Hubert.

Cautiously had he avoided asking a single question relative to Edward, lest it should have led the Baron to suspect that he felt interested in his fate; thus the only clue which he possessed for tracing him out, was the common report which had been circulated throughout the country, on the departure of the troops, that they were destined for Ostend. Having disguised himself in the tattered jacket of a sailor, and assumed the unnecessary support of a wooden leg, he tied a bandage over his left eye, and having, in other respects, disfigured his person as much as he was able, he proceeded to a seaport town, where he took his passage on board a ship bound for Ostend.

Rich as he was at the present time, he took especial care to make his expences correspond with his appearance, that he might not, by any ill-judged display of his ability to procure for himself accommodations superior to what his beggarly outside denoted him possessed of, draw down upon himself suspicion: his money he had sewn within the lining of a waistcoat, which he had chosen for its strength, not its appearance or comfort, and which he judged would prove a faithful safeguard to the valuable trust committed to its care.

A few days landed him at Ostend. Having taken up his abode at a mean house in the town, and signified to its landlord that he was a poor distressed man, who had once been a sailor, and had now been shipwrecked upon the coast of Flanders, from a vessel of which all the crew had perished except himself, he expressed a wish of finding some employment; he was indifferent, he said, of what nature, provided he was capable of performing it, and that it would keep him from want; alledging that all his relations in England were dead, and that every country was now alike to him; to which account, he added his inability of paying his passage to the opposite shore.

The landlord of the house was a humane man, and promised him his assistance in procuring him some work, if any could be had; but he remarked, "that few were willing to engage a servant, whose disabled limbs must render him less useful than another man." To which Hubert replied, "that he was well aware of this objection, and must therefore be satisfied with less wages."

Hubert felt fearful of visiting the English camp, lest, even disguised as he was, some individual in it should recognize him. Earnestly he wished for the means of making some enquiry relative to Edward amongst the English soldiery, but his apprehensions of a discovery forbade him to make the attempt.

Walking abroad one day with the landlord of his little inn, the prison, in which he then little suspected the object of his pursuit to be a captive, caught his attention, and he enquired what it was; the landlord explained to him, that it was a prison where offenders of a superior order were kept, and where no comfort but that of liberty was denied to them. As they walked on, they approached nearer to its walls, and the sound of music struck the ears of Hubert.

"They are very merry, methinks," said Hubert, "for the inhabitants of a prison."

"The prisoners have nothing to do with the mirth you hear," replied the landlord; "this is the anniversary of the governor's wedding-day, and it is celebrated with great festivity. But the rejoicings of today are far inferior to those which took place on the day on which the governor was married; they were splendid indeed: but it is no wonder, when we reflect on the great income his place is said to bring him in. No doubt but that there are many deeds transacted within a place like this, that are kept secret at a high price."

"It is a pity," said Hubert, "that any edifice should exist which is capable of concealing the crimes of those who live at large unsuspected, whilst the unhappy victims of their iniquity sigh out their days in solitude, unheeded and unconsoled."

"It is a necessary evil," returned the landlord, "that there should be such places; and as no good institutions exist without improper encroachments being made upon the power annexed to them, we must be content, that if a little evil, by such means, creeps into society, much good is produced to it from the same causes. But," continued he, "what I was going to remark to you, was an extraordinary circumstance which took place at this same governor's wedding—Amongst the guests invited were the officers from the English camp; when the evening's entertainment was concluded, all the company left the house much about the same time, and, strange to relate, one of the English officers has never been heard of since."

"Indeed!" said Hubert; "what was his name?"

"I never heard him called by any name," returned the host.

Hubert stopped, lost in thought.

"Aye, it is a strange story—is it not?" went on his informer, not at all suspicious that Hubert was more moved than any one might have been by the recital he was making to him. "It is supposed that some villains robbed him on his way to the camp, and then murdered him, to prevent his preferring an information against them."

Of a far different tenor was the opinion which Hubert formed of this mysterious occurrence. *"Edward is, by my design, detained in Flanders,"* Lord William de Mowbray had said; and what place could appear more likely to be the scene of this treacherous confession, than a building of the nature of which the host had just described the prison they were looking at to be? But Hubert closely shut up his ideas within his own breast, and endeavoured to continue his conversation with his companion, without discovering to him the emotions which agitated his mind.

As they returned towards the town, Hubert, scarcely conscious of advancing the question, enquired the name of the governor of the prison they had just seen? His host replied, "that it was Garcias Xavia."

"Xavia!" repeated Hubert, "it is a Spanish name, and an unusual one. I think I have heard that there was a pioneer in the English troops that came over here last year of that name; but, although I cannot recollect his Christian name, I am inclined to believe it was not Garcias."

"No, no," answered Hubert's companion, "it was Sanchez."

"You know him then," said Hubert.

"I am not acquainted with him," rejoined the host; "I have only heard of him; he is the governor's brother."

"The retreat of my loved master is then discovered!" exclaimed Hubert, to himself. "If Sanchez Xavia is the governor's brother, and an English officer disappeared on the evening of his visiting there, no longer doubt remains to me of his fate." The warm blood of joy poured into his heart, and he breathed a silent prayer of thanksgiving to Heaven.

"Did you know him?" asked the host, who suspected nothing from Hubert's question.

"I have seen him, as you may have done," rejoined Hubert, "but it is some time since." He then gave a change to the conversation, wishing that the subject should be discussed as little as possible, lest he should let fall any expression which might draw upon him the eye of suspicion.

Hubert's night was sleepless; no sooner had he reclined his head on his humble pillow, than a thousand various plans, for gaining access to the prison, passed through his brain. He reviewed each separately, and some obstacle presented itself to the execution of them all; he, however, felt an indescribable satisfaction in believing himself possessed of the secret of Edward's concealment, and willingly resolved not to let his impatience to inform him that he was acquainted with it, lead him into any rashness which might for ever blast the hopes he now entertained of one day restoring him to liberty, and to his beloved Rosalind.

The age of miracles, even at that distant period, was past; at least of those open interpositions of Providence which were once permitted to the eye of man: but those which are allowed to reach the mind of observation, will never cease, while the justice of Providence continues to exist. Although the finger which disposes the events of life be concealed from our view, many are the instances which feelingly convey to our senses the immediate interposition of a Merciful Power; which, beholding with pity the sufferings of the innocent, accommodates, what appear to the unthinking, the common accidents of life, to their eventual happiness, and triumph over their oppressors.

To such a cause did Hubert attribute the accident which, in a short space of time, made him an inhabitant of the prison, whose walls enclosed Edward.

Compelled to catch at the first employment which offered itself to his acceptance, as one of the most requisite parts which he had to act in sustaining his present character, he hired himself to an old woman who sold wood about the streets. On the third day of his serving in his new capacity, his mistress took her road out of the town, and stopped at the gate of the prison. "The governor," she said, "is my best customer; I come here regularly twice a-week." A man came to the gate, who received the stinted quantity of wood, placed it in the prison-yard, and having done this, again closed the gate.

Having disposed of her wood, the old woman returned home for a fresh load, and Hubert, with a heavy heart, followed her, disappointed that he had not even been admitted within the outer wall of the prison.

Thus passed on a second, a third, and even a fourth week; Hubert still constrained to lead about the blind horse, which dragged the sledge that contained his employer's logs.

One day about this time, when they stopped as usual at the gate of the prison, a fat dame, who was a kind of superintendant of the household œconomies of the place, came out to the dealer in wood, and addressed her, with an enquiry, whether she could inform her of any poor wretch who was willing, and hard-working, and wanted a place; for that the man who had been accustomed to perform all the menial offices in the prison, had died the day before, and they were in want of some one to fill his station?

"I pray you, good mistress, engage me," said Hubert; "I shall be very thankful indeed for the situation."

"I doubt you are not strong enough for it," returned the fat dame, eyeing him as she spoke from top to toe. "You are lame, I see, and can't be very quick in your movements on that account."

"But my willingness to oblige my employers may make amends for that deficiency," replied Hubert; "and I am strong, very strong, I assure you."

"So, you ungrateful fellow," cried Hubert's mistress, "then you would leave me, that took you when you had not a bit of bread to put into your mouth."

"It is not ingratitude that prompts me to make the change," returned Hubert, "but it is because I should prefer the work I should have here, within the house, to being continually obliged to walk about the streets."

As the dealer in wood contended for Hubert's services, the housekeeper of the prison directly thought them worth having, which she, probably, would not have done had his present mistress seemed willing to part from him; and accordingly said—"Well I have a good mind to try you:" and she then offered him a very small sum, as wages, for which she demanded of him the performance of as many different concerns, as would, upon a moderate calculation, have afforded employment for three others besides himself. However, as the terms were indifferent to Hubert upon which he entered the prison, so he did but get within its walls, he accepted the proffered conditions.

His mistress paid him a parting compliment, in which she wished him ill luck for quitting her service; and his new one gave him encouragement, by saying—"that if he was obliging to her, she would be his friend with his master;" and with this promise he was ushered into the kitchen of the prison.

His labour was full as much as he expected it would be; he was the servant of almost every servant in the prison; but still he was content, for he believed himself near his benefactor, Edward.

Hubert had been about four months an inhabitant of the prison, when he was conducted to the vault set apart for the governor's family, and commanded to dig a grave, which he was informed was for the governor's brother, Sanchez. It was with no little pleasure that he heard the account of his death, and he performed his task with great good will. The night had been the season at which he had been set about this employment; and as he returned from the performance of his task, with the keys of the vault hanging upon his arm, his mattock and spade supported on his shoulder with one hand, and his lamp held in the other, he was surprised at hearing the sound of the governor's voice, and seeing the keepers running about in a hasty manner, that denoted some matter of importance to have taken place.

He durst not stop to ask any questions in the presence of the governor, but of the first keeper who followed him into the kitchen, he enquired the cause of the commotion he had just seen and heard. "Oh," replied the man, "there has been the devil to pay; the governor's daughter-in-law has been very near eloping to-night with a lover, whom neither her mother nor the governor approves; and, as misfortunes never come single, our English captive was as near making his escape at the same time."

"Well, they are not like me," cried Hubert; "I don't want to get away; I never was so well off in my life as I am here."

"One of my comrades is turned out," went on the keeper, "who was discovered to have let in the lady Belise's lover, and who meant to have favoured her elopement."

"Is her lover an Englishman?" asked Hubert.

"No, a French officer," answered the keeper: "the Englishman is an officer too."

"What, is he a grandee, a lord, or a duke, or any thing of that kind?" inquired Hubert.

"I don't know what he is," returned the man; "titles are all sunk here; we seldom know our captives by name; I never heard him called any thing but the English officer."

Hubert was now entirely convinced—"Have you had him long?" Hubert was beginning to say, when the keeper was called away, and no farther opportunity given him of adding to the number of his enquiries.

Almost all the keepers of the prison were men who had for a long time been the servants of the governor, and whose fidelity to their master had been tried. He who had just parted from Hubert was the only talkative man with whom he had yet met; he was a young Frenchman, who had but lately become a servant in the prison, and who, with the address to appear discreet before the governor, and the old servants of the place, still loved to hear himself talk, when he was with any one who would listen to him. Hubert found him to be the only one in the family from whom he was likely to gain any intelligence of what was passing within the walls, and therefore did all in his power to attach the young man to him. Pierre, for such was his name, would probably have scorned an intimacy with a man in Hubert's inferior situation, had he been able to have found any other person about the place who would have indulged him in the use of his tongue; but not being able to do that, he preferred society, which he considered beneath him, rather than to desist from his favourite amusement of tattling.

Amidst Hubert's numerous employments, it was a part of his business to go to the outer gate of the prison, and receive from those who brought them, the bread, the fruit, the milk, and, in short, every article consumed within the prison; after bringing them in, he was appointed to carry them into the hall, and here the keepers received from him, in different baskets, the allotted portions for the prisoners under their care.

Hubert remarked that Pierre brought a larger basket than any of the other keepers, and received into it a double share of fruit and bread; Pierre was also the last of the keepers who received from Hubert the portion for his captives; and this gave Hubert an opportunity of enquiring of him, why he had always a double quantity put into one of his baskets?

"Why," replied Pierre, "ever since that night when our young lady had like to have run away, and the English captive to have made his escape, the unfortunate lover and the Englishman have both been confined in one cell, so the double portion is for them."

Having thus gained the knowledge of which was the basket of provisions conveyed to Edward, Hubert began to consider it no difficult matter to give him information that he had a friend at hand. After many debates with his own mind, he resolved on engraving those words of hope, which have been already laid before our readers, on some chesnuts, which he intended to take the first opportunity of putting into the basket that daily received the double portion of provisions. To his great delight he found his plan by no means a difficult one to execute; he artfully contrived to give Pierre a subject to discuss, and, while he was engaged in talking, Hubert put his prepared chesnuts at the bottom of the basket, and covering them over with apples and bread, he gave the basket into the hand of Pierre, without feeling the least alarm that he should examine it—he was at all times too idle to do more than he was ordered.

From this time the days passed on with Hubert, unmarked by any event, till Madame Xavia paid the debt of life, and he was again sent into the burying-ground, to open the family vault, for the reception of her body; his friend, Pierre, assisted him in carrying his tools to the spot, and in the way thither informed him, that the vault was immediately beneath the prison where the lady Belise's lover, and the young Englishman, were confined.

Possessed of this knowledge, Hubert resolved to use every moment of the night, which he could spare from the labour he was employed on, in endeavouring to make himself heard by Edward, in his prison above him; to this purpose he repeatedly called on him by name, but as he received no answer to his calls, he concluded, that the stone which parted them was impenetrable to his voice, and therefore began to seek some other method of making himself heard. The roof of the burying-place was within the reach of his mattock, and he struck various parts with the iron end of it, hoping that some of the knocks would reach the ear of Edward; but his endeavours proved fruitless, and he was compelled to complete his task, and leave the spot, where he felt a pleasure in lingering, on account of its proximity to Edward.

On returning to the kitchen, he was surprised to find Pierre, who had promised to sit up for him till he came back from the vault, was not there.

During the time that Hubert had been employed in opening the vault, the governor and Belise had repaired, at midnight, to the chapel, to say a *requiem* for the rest of Madame Xavia's soul; and on the governor's return to his chamber, he found his money-box broke open and robbed; nor was this all—his master-key to the various locks in the building, which was usually hung at the head of his bed, was also gone. An immediate search was made after the thief—Pierre alone was missing, and, as he did not return in the course of the succeeding day, no doubt was entertained of his being the purloiner of the governor's gold.

A reward was offered by the governor for his apprehension; but it proved ineffectual, as Pierre was never heard of after.

Pierre's flight was at first a circumstance on which Hubert by no means reflected with pleasure; he had been the only one in the prison whom he had found ready in his communications, and he feared that his absence would deprive him of gaining any intelligence relative to Edward. While Hubert was wondering whether the new keeper would prove a man from whom he might reap equal advantage as he had done from the familiar disposition of Pierre, he was surprised with the information that he was himself promoted to the station.

Hubert received the intelligence with warm but concealed joy; he now believed that he should enjoy the privilege of waiting upon Edward, and thus easily gain an opportunity of conversing with him; but in this hope he was disappointed. The keeper who had heretofore watched over the prison of Edward in the evening, was appointed to attend upon it entirely; and Hubert was deputed to serve two solitary captives, whose apartments were at one end of the stone passage, the other extremity of which led to the prison of the two friends.

CHAPTER XII.

Oh! 'tis excellent
To have a giant's strength; but it is tyrannous
To use it like a giant.

MEASURE FOR MEASURE.

On the eleventh day after the interment of the governor's wife, a stranger arrived at the prison about the hour of noon, who was for some time shut up with the governor in his private apartment, and then departed.

In the evening, the governor, which was by no means usual with him, went out himself, saying, that he was going to meet some friends, who he expected would arrive that night at Ostend.

Each keeper had a small apartment, for his own private use, in some part of the gallery which led to the apartments occupied by the prisoners immediately under his care; that which was now become the property of Hubert, was directly opposite to that of one of his comrades, named Gourtray. While Hubert had been only in a menial capacity in the prison, this man had noticed him but very little; now he was raised to an equality with himself, their acquaintance grew fast, and they usually passed their leisure hours in each other's apartment. Hubert found Gourtray to be, what he, perhaps uncharitably, but probably very justly, supposed every one who filled an office like his, a rogue in his heart—who wanted but opportunity, like Pierre, to make himself rich, at whosever expence he might become so.

Upon this opinion of Gourtray's disposition, the watchful Hubert had formed a plan, by which he hoped eventually to procure the enlargement of Edward; and judging the present evening of the governor's absence to be a good opportunity for opening to Gourtray a conversation of the nature he wished to have with him, he invited him into his little apartment, saying—"Walk in, comrade; you and I have not had a glass together since I have held my office, so let it be this evening: I have a flask of choice brandy, which I will uncork for the purpose."

Gourtray readily accepted the invitation, and they seated themselves over Hubert's fire. With his second draught, Hubert said—"Come, let us drink to the health of the governor; not that his health is any more to you or me than that of any other man, except as being our employer, and it is my maxim always to wish best to those I get the most by."

"Thou resemblest me exactly," replied Gourtray; "if any one else would offer me a better livelihood than his wages afford me, I would kick him off in a minute, I promise thee."

This was exactly the sentiment which Hubert wished to hear proceed from the lips of his companion, and he said—"To my thinking now, I should suppose, that you, who are a native of this country, and have not, like myself, the misfortunes of a maimed leg, and useless eye, might easily procure for yourself some more lucrative employment than that of being a keeper in a prison."

"Why as to that," returned Gourtray, "our wages, you must allow, are well enough; they are, no doubt, made better than they would be, in order to ensure our fidelity to our master; and, upon the whole, the place would not be despicable, if our prisoners were not so stripped by the cursed avarice of the governor, that they have nothing left to fee us for little services that we might render them, if they could pay us for them."

"I warrant me though," replied Hubert, "that if you or I durst show any of them the way to liberty, he'd manage to find us a reward worth the trying for."

"I can't think that any one confined here has a reward in his power," answered Gourtray; "the governor pilfers them all as they come in—No, no, they can have nothing left."

"I would not wager my life on that," returned Hubert. "Misfortune makes men crafty, and there are ways and means of cheating the keenest-eyed. I dare be bound to say, that some of the captives here have been thus cunning, and have either money or valuables about them yet; but, perhaps, if you knew they had, you would not like such means of earning an independent sum?"

"By Saint Francis," cried Gourtray, "I'd about it this instant, if I thought there was one who could make it worth my while. What, man!—do'st think I would not? All we keepers of prisons have the repute of being thieves and rascals, and we may as well have it for something as nothing, according to my opinion."

"Aye, it is but true," replied Hubert, with a smile, "too true indeed;" and again he put the flask to his comrade, who took a hearty draught, and then spoke thus—"Now, who, to your thinking, is there amongst all our captives, that is most likely to have a golden lining to his pocket?"

"Why, I have been so little amongst them till within these few days," answered Hubert, "that I can hardly be so good a judge as yourself. Let me see—you have an Englishman under your care, have you not?"

"Aye, here hard by," returned Gourtray; "know you any thing of him?"

"How should I?" replied Hubert; "you know I have not been into his cell."

"Then how came you to mention him?" asked Gourtray.

"Why," replied Hubert, "I have a pretty good knowledge of the English; they are a crafty people, apt at stratagem, and I should not wonder, whoever he is, but he has managed to secrete the price of a rescue somewhere about him."

"Aye!" cried Gourtray, evidently animated by the idea.

"Why, I think it very probable indeed," went on Hubert; "and if you like to agree to give me a small share out of what he might in such case bestow on you, I'll go with you into his cell, and sound him for you. I understand his language better than you do, and I am also somewhat more acquainted with the manners of the English than you are."

Some time previous to the evening on which this conversation took place, Hubert had taken one hundred pieces of gold from his waistcoat, and put them into a purse, which he carried constantly about him; and which it was his intention, if he could prevail on Gourtray to carry him with him into Edward's prison, on the business of which he had just given him the idea, to slip into Edward's hand, judging that he could not fail to understand their being intended for him to bestow on Gourtray, as the price of his liberty.

Gourtray continued silent for some moments after the last proposition on the part of Hubert. He then said—"I approve thy counsel; it is good, and worthy to be tried: if the attempt fails of procuring us any advantage, we can lose nothing by it, which renders it doubly estimable—but this is not the proper hour for the attempt. If the governor does not return home before midnight, I will come and call upon you to go with me to the Englishman's prison; if he does return, we must wait for the arrival of some more favourable season;" and, with these words, he rose from his seat, and staggered out of Hubert's apartment, carrying with him the flask, which contained but a small portion of the brandy that had lately filled it, and of which he had drunk by much the better half.

Hubert continued over his fire, anticipating the joyful moment at which Gourtray would return to conduct him to the cell of his respected master. Meanwhile the Fleming, who actually possessed all that cunning which Hubert, in order to favour his purpose, had attempted to make him believe the innate principle of his English prisoner, judging it entirely unnecessary to make Hubert a sharer of the profit that was to be reaped from the plan which he had just proposed to him, proceeded alone, as our readers have already been informed, to the cell of Edward and his friend, where we need not repeat the ill success that attended his attempt.

Gourtray, we must suppose, had never known that Adolphus was the lover of the Lady Belise, or it appears unlikely that he should have refused to carry her the ring; or we must suppose, that if the circumstance had been known to him, the fumes of intoxication had driven it from his brain. Whether Gourtray, after his ill success in the prison of Edward, made a similar offer to any other of the captives, is a circumstance of no consequence to this narrative; we have, in this instance, only to speak of what refers to Hubert.

Each of the keepers of the prison took his turn, by night, in attending in the hall, and letting in such of the family as had, during the evening, been absent from the building; and when every one had entered, he was allowed to retire to rest.

On the present evening, this office fell upon Gourtray, and what hour he went to his post was not known, as no one was absent from the prison but the governor, and none but such as immediately entered the prison from the court-yard, had occasion to pass near the hall. Hubert did not retire to his bed at the usual hour, but continued sitting in his room, expecting the return of Gourtray. He had heard the clock strike twelve some time, and as Gourtray did not return, he opened the door of his room to listen whether he was in his chamber on the opposite side of the gallery; this he had scarcely done, ere he recollected that it was Gourtray's turn to keep watch in the hall. He found that he was not in his chamber, and therefore concluding the governor not to be returned, he was on the point of shutting his own door again, when he heard the bell from the gate sounding in the hall.

The distance of his room from the hall was considerable, but the bell was powerful, and the echoes natural to the vaulted roofs of the building, carried the sound powerfully through the air. "That bell," conjectured Hubert, "denotes the governor's return: I shall probably then not see Gourtray again to-night."

He entered his chamber, but did not shut his door, as he felt a wish to speak to him when he came to bed, and learn whether his resolution to make an offer of enlargement to the English officer still continued unshaken.

In a few minutes, the bell from the gate sounded louder than before; a short silence again ensued, and again the bell was rung with redoubled violence. Hubert felt at a loss to conclude from what cause Gourtray had not given admittance to the claimant for it; and judging that if it was the governor, it became him, as he had heard it thrice repeated, to attend to the summons, he took up his lamp, and went down into the hall.

He saw not Gourtray in his way to the gate, which as he approached, the bell was rung a fourth time. Hubert unlocked the heavy gate, and on drawing it back upon its hinges, the governor, and three other men with him, entered.

"What is the reason," exclaimed the governor, "that I have been thus long detained at the gate? you shall repent this negligence."

Hubert directly replied—"Sir, the watch of to-night is not mine: I, by accident, heard the bell sounded repeatedly, and on this account I came down from my chamber to learn the cause."

"Oh, I perceive," returned the governor, "you are not Gourtray—it is his watch. Where is he?"

Hubert was obliged to reply that he did not know.

"Go, call up some of the servants," said the governor; "these friends of mine will sleep here to-night, and they have not yet supped. Do your best to assist in spreading the table immediately."

At the command of the governor, Hubert preceded him and his friends to one of the handsomest apartments in the house; at the foot of a flight of steps, which led to it from the hall, lay Gourtray, locked in an insensible sleep. "How now, rascal!" exclaimed the governor; but he did not awake; the weight of the brandy he had drank sat heavy on him, and he was incapable of hearing or understanding.

At this time, some others of the keepers, who had been roused by the repeated ringing of the bell, entered the hall; and to these the governor gave in charge to convey Gourtray to the dungeon, where he commanded that he should remain a prisoner, till he judged proper to hear his defence of his conduct from his own lips; an order which those to whom it was delivered, durst not venture to disobey.

As the governor entered the apartment into which he conducted his guests, the light of Hubert's lamp fell upon his countenance, and Hubert perceived that he appeared much agitated, although evident marks of savage triumph were visible amidst the various passions that seemed to fill his breast. The guests, Hubert had only opportunity to observe, were in the English dress; one of them was the person who had been closeted with the governor in the morning.

According to the directions he had received, Hubert called up some of the servants, whose business it was particularly to attend to the governor's family; and their presence rendered it unnecessary for him to do more towards the preparations for the entertainment of the guests, than to carry in some wood, and to make a fire of it upon the hearth.

At the first sight of the strangers, Hubert concluded that one of them, at least, was a new victim doomed to the solitude of imprisonment within the dreary walls he had just entered. He had observed that one of the three was habited more costly than the other two; and him he considered the unfortunate man, for no other reason, except that persecution usually appears to exert itself with the greatest energy against those who stand in a situation the most attractive to envy.

As he went into the room with the logs of wood on his shoulder, the governor whispered to him, to demand the keys of those cells which Gourtray had been accustomed to attend, and to visit them in the morning, with the first meals of the day, himself. This command was a cordial to the heart of Hubert; and he promised with true fervour to obey it.

As he was again quitting the room, the best dressed of the three strangers crossed upon him by accident, in such a situation that he could not help catching a full view of his countenance. He was young and handsome, and Hubert felt confident that his features were familiar to his sight. Again Hubert turned his eye upon him, as he moved out of the room, and became still more certain that the contour of his face was by no means that of a person whom he had never seen before; and what was still more extraordinary, he connected unpleasant ideas with the recollection, although he could not recollect where he had seen him before. But he had not proceeded many steps away from the apartment, when memory came to his aid, and, beyond all possibility of error, he remembered that the man whom he had just seen a guest of the governor Garcias, was Alwin, the page of Lord Rufus de Madginecourt, grown to the stature of manhood.

This conviction struck agony to the heart of Hubert. Emissaries from the man, who passionately desired to possess the lovely and constant Rosalind, and amongst these emissaries, the youth who in a particular manner enjoyed the smiles of his favour, must portend evil to the unhappy Edward.

At first, his fears half distracted him; he knew not whither to fly, what to do, or how to prepare himself against any attack which might be made upon Edward's life. Some minutes of deliberation, however, seemed to promise him, that if his existence was in danger from their arrival, it was at least safe for that night, as the governor would not else have commanded him to visit the prison where he was confined, in the morning. Still, he considered that this might be only a subterfuge to baffle suspicion, if it were awakened in any mind, and he resolved not to go to bed. He returned to his chamber, from which he frequently wandered out upon the gallery, and endeavoured, by action, to calm his perturbed spirits. In the course of a couple of hours, he heard the servants of the household retiring again to rest; he made an excuse of fetching some water, which he pretended was for one of the prisoners, and used the opportunity to enquire if the governor and his guests were gone to bed?

He was told that they were not; that the governor had said he had some business to transact with the strangers which would not admit of delay, and had directed all the servants to return to their chambers.

"Oh God!" exclaimed Hubert, mentally, "is it then their intent this very night to——"—he durst not conclude his sentence even to himself. Wretched beyond the power of any intelligence to make him more so, or of any circumstance to add to the torture of his mind, he resolved to go down, and, if possible, to overhear some part of their conversation.

Every step of the building he was well acquainted with; thus he was not under the necessity of carrying a light with him, to expose himself to any one whom accident might lead the same way; unlikely as it was, that any person besides himself should, at that hour, be moving about.

His resolution was no sooner fixed than put into execution. As he approached the apartment in which were the governor and his guests, he, at some distance, heard their voices, apparently in strong debate.

On arriving at the foot of the steps which led to the door of the apartment, he had not occasion to ascend them, for the purpose of being an auditor of their discourse; either secure that they were not attended to by any ear, or heated into loudness by the interest of the subject they were discussing, their words were easily distinguishable.

The first sentence which Hubert heard, appeared to be spoken by Alwin. "Your captive," he said, "may die to-morrow, and where would then be the annuity on which you set so high a value? You could not long impose on the Lord Baron de Mowbray by feigning him still alive; it is impossible he should be thus deceived. Edward *may die to-morrow, and*—"

"'Tis true," replied the governor; "but he is just as likely to live for many years to come."

"And where is the difference," rejoined Alwin, "if your reward in either case be made equal?"

Many more arguments, of the same nature, followed, between the governor and Alwin; at length the former said—"Well, let the two thousand pieces of gold be given into my hands, and I will consent."

Hubert heard a box unlocked, and he supposed the gold was contained in it, for the governor then said—"I am satisfied."

"Well then," demanded Alwin, "when will you give us the opportunity we require?"

"To-night I dare not do it," returned the governor: "the morning almost dawns, and some of my people, I doubt not, are already risen—this must be an action of secrecy. To-morrow, at the hour of midnight, I will conduct you to his cell."

"If we must submit to this delay, we must," rejoined Alwin; "but as we are so decidedly determined together, that his death is certain, let me entreat you, to-night, to write the letter I requested of you, to the Baron de Mowbray, that we may to-morrow dispatch a messenger with it to England; as in the speed you use in conveying intelligence of his ceasing to exist to Lord William de Mowbray, you most essentially serve him, who sends you, through me, the sum contained in that casket."

"Since we are agreed," returned the governor, "I feel no hesitation in writing the letter. Fill your goblets, and whilst you are emptying them again, I will pen the epistle you desire."

Some minutes of silence ensued: the governor then said—"Please to read what I have written, and tell me if it meets your approbation."

Alwin read thus:

"Garcias Xavia greets the Lord Baron de Mowbray.—The prisoner named Edward, whom it is now very nearly four years since the Lord Baron entrusted to his protection, through the means of his deceased brother Sanchez, breathed his last on the evening preceding that of which this epistle bears the date—a violent fever carried him hastily to the grave. Garcias Xavia trusts that the noble Lord Baron de Mowbray will acknowledge him to have been faithful to the trust reposed in him, and will deign to accept his thanks for the liberality with which he has rewarded the services he is proud of having had it in his power to render to so illustrious a noble.

"Ostend, 7th March, 1587."

"It corresponds exactly with my wishes," said Alwin, "and to-morrow I will dispatch one of these, my friends, as a messenger with it to England. Another day, then, we must remain your guests, and to-morrow night at twelve—"

"I will myself conduct you to his cell," said the governor.

"And the instant our purpose in coming hither is effected, you must lead us beyond the walls of this edifice," said Alwin.

"It shall be done," replied the governor.

Alwin now requested the governor to conduct them to their respective chambers; and on hearing this, Hubert directly fled from the foot of the steps to the gallery where he had left his lamp.

If the state of mind in which Hubert passed the remainder of the night cannot be conceived by the reader, the author's attempt to describe it must be ineffectual. At length the morning arrived, and the refulgent rays of the sun once more enlightened the earth.

As Hubert was on the point of repairing to the cell of Edward with his breakfast, and that of his fellow prisoner, Adolphus, one of the keepers came to him, and said, he was sent by the governor to go with him into the prison of the English officer, and bring away from it his fellow captive, the young Adolphus. "The governor," he said, "had expressed himself to relent* having so long condemned him to a dungeon, when his crime had been only that of love; and had resolved to give him a better apartment, to which he and Hubert were to conduct him."

Hubert could not doubt that Adolphus was to be removed from the cell of Edward, in order that he might not be a witness of his intended murder. "'Tis well," he said, in reply to the information delivered by the other keeper, and led the way to the cell. Hubert perceived that Edward recognised him; but the present was not a moment to acknowledge that he did so, and he departed with Adolphus in silence.

The brain of Hubert had been racked, during the night, with a thousand plans for the preservation of his benefactor's life; and that which seemed to promise the greatest hope of success, was, if possible, to find the means of persuading the avaricious governor, that if he suffered the life of Edward to be taken away by the emissaries of Lord Rufus de Madginecourt, he would eventually lose a much greater reward than he had received as the price of his death. The lure he conceived to be good, but the difficulty was how to represent it to the governor. Were he himself to speak upon it to him, he must, at the same time, confess himself an impostor, a friend to Edward, and that he had been a listener to the conversation the governor had, on the preceding night, held with the English strangers; and to give him any anonymous information upon the subject he felt averse, as he feared that it would not produce the effect of carrying conviction to his mind. The idea, however, he considered as being too good to be suffered to fall to the ground. He accordingly resolved, that as he

* Perhaps an error in the original text for "repent."

could not hold out the temptation to him personally, he would do it anonymously; to this end, he wrote the following letter:—

"Garcias Xavia, beware what you do! You are, on this paper, addressed by a friend of the Lord Baron de Mowbray, who writes to you in consequence of a knowledge he has obtained, that you are at this moment entertaining in your house emissaries from Lord Rufus de Madginecourt, whose visit to the continent, from the well-known passion of that nobleman for the daughter of De Mowbray, who is the wife of your prisoner Edward, cannot but portend danger to his life. You are, therefore, again told to beware what you do; for although the Baron de Mowbray has not yet pardoned his daughter's marriage, the day is, in all probability, not far distant, when he will recall Edward to England, and acknowledge him his son and heir: thus you will, in such case, not only lose the reward he would bestow on you for the preservation of his life from his enemy De Madginecourt, but have to answer for his death. Therefore, a third time, *beware.* So enjoins you, a member of the English camp."

This letter, Hubert put, early in the morning, into a letter-box on the outside the prison wall, of which the contents were daily carried to the governor at his breakfast-table.

Throughout the day, it was the intention of Hubert to watch the governor, as much as opportunity would permit him to do; and to endeavour to gather, from his words and his features, whether his letter had made any change in his resolution relative to Edward.

Scarcely had Hubert removed Adolphus into his new apartment, ere he was summoned to the governor in his private closet. Hubert judged it impossible that the deception he had practised should have been discovered, or even suspected; still he feared this might be the cause of his present summons into the governor's presence; however, whether it was so or not, he could not do otherwise than obey it.

He found Xavia pacing his closet, and when Hubert entered, he quickly thrust a letter into his pocket, which Hubert could not doubt to be the one he had written to him in the night. The governor turned towards Hubert, and bade him shut the door; his features betrayed a violent agitation of mind. "I have," said he, "a particular service to require at your hands—the reward will be ten pieces of gold. Will you promise me your secrecy?" Had Hubert been less eager than he was to learn the governor's secret, it became him, in support of his present character, to pretend that he regarded the gaining of ten pieces of gold worthy of any hazard; and he accordingly answered to that purpose.

"But swear to me by thy Saviour," returned the governor, "that what I am about to entrust to thee, thou wilt never communicate to any of thy comrades."

If the secret related to Edward, Hubert wished it, whatever it was, to remain one to his comrades, as much as the governor could do; if not, he could have no motive for desiring to circulate it: he therefore took the oath.

"The reward which I now devote to thee," said the governor, "would have become Gourtray's, had he not last night fallen under my displeasure; I now transfer it to thee, as a recompense for thy diligence in supplying his place at my return with my guests."

Hubert made a suitable acknowledgement for this consideration in his favour, on the part of the governor; who then continued speaking thus—"I have, at this moment, those within my mansion who have been sent hither to purchase of me the life of my English prisoner; and I have already received from them a sum of money for my consent to the deed: but reasons have since arisen in my mind, which point out to me that it is my duty to preserve his life; and you must lend your assistance to me, in a plan which I have formed to that end."

Hubert durst not reply, lest the tones of his voice should discover the joy of his heart at the success which had attended his letter to the governor.

Garcias Xavia proceeded, by saying—"I have promised them to administer an opiate to my prisoner, during the course of the day, and to conduct them to his cell at midnight, when he lies buried in the arms of sleep. I have privately resolved, that before that hour arrives, we will remove him from his cell, and place in his bed the corpse of a young Frenchman, who is now stretched in his coffin in the chapel for interment. One hour, therefore, after the bell has tolled for all the inhabitants of this house to retire to rest, be you in waiting for me at the door of our English prisoner's cell. I will leave my guests, under pretence of ascertaining whether every one is gone to rest, that they may with safety proceed to the purpose of their coming hither; and we will then use the moments of my absence from them, to accomplish the plan I have already made you acquainted with."

Hubert waited to say no more than an humble promise of obeying the governor's orders, and retired from his presence.

The ecstacy of Hubert's mind was almost too great to leave him capable of performing the offices of his station; thrice, during the day, he was under the necessity of visiting the cell of Edward; but he constrained himself each time to maintain a strict silence, which he, by signs, enjoined Edward to do also. He dreaded lest an incautious moment should now destroy the hope he had formed of the adventures of the night. The governor had resolved that night to preserve the life of his prisoner. Hubert believed that he should, that night, be enabled to restore his benefactor to liberty.

CHAPTER XIII.

> The awful hour of midnight now comes on.
>
> HERBERT.

WHEN the clock had struck eleven, Hubert left his chamber, and placed himself at the door of Edward's cell. In a few minutes the governor appeared in the gallery. "All are in bed, I believe," he said, as he approached Hubert. "For nearly an hour all has been quiet," Hubert replied. "Open the door," said the governor; "we need not fear being interrupted in our proceedings; no one can overhear us, except it be some of the prisoners, who have not the power of quitting their apartments. As Gourtray is still in confinement for his last night's offence, there is no keeper in this gallery but yourself."

This Hubert already knew, but it was an additional satisfaction to him to hear the governor assert it, and he obeyed his orders for opening the door.

"Awake—awake," said Xavia, approaching the pallet of Edward. Edward started up at this address, and the governor continued, "we come to conduct you to better faring."

"The condition of my life is indifferent to me," replied Edward, "while I am denied the enjoyment of liberty; it is even a cruelty to protract my days, by bettering my condition, while you deny me all for which I wish to live."

The governor did not answer this address on the part of his prisoner, but having liberated him from his chain, commanded Hubert to assist in leading him to another cell. The present moment was the first time of Edward's beholding the governor since the night on which he had been conveyed, with Adolphus Biron, to the cell he was now about to quit. When he had first replied to the governor's exclamation, he had not, in the moment of his hasty waking, perceived who it was that he was addressing; now he discovered it to be Garcias himself who was leading him along, he could not forbear making an invocation to his humanity, fruitless even as he believed the appeal would be.

A few minutes brought them to an apartment which Edward was commanded to enter, and the lock immediately turned upon him. "Leave the key in the door," said the governor to Hubert, "for we shall reconduct him to his former cell as soon as the business of the night is concluded."

This done, the governor and Hubert immediately proceeded to the chapel, where lay the young Frenchman, of whom the governor had spoken in the morning, prepared for interment on the following day: taking him up in their arms, they bore him to Edward's vacated cell, and binding the chain round his waist, they placed him on the pallet, and threw a coverlet over him. The governor then commanded Hubert to retire to his own room, saying, that when the emissaries from England had, as they supposed, performed the deed of death, for which they had been sent into Flanders, and he had conducted them beyond the outer wall of the prison, he would summon Hubert to assist him in replacing the dead body of the young Frenchman in its proper situation in the chapel, and in reconducting Edward to his cell.

Hubert obeyed Xavia's command of retiring to his chamber, while Garcias himself proceeded to the apartment where he had left Alwin and his companion. He who had made the third on the preceding evening, had set out that morning for England, with the letter, written by the governor to the Lord William de Mowbray, to inform him of the death of his hated son-in-law.

"Come forth boldly," said the governor, addressing them; "you will meet with no interruption in your proceedings." They left the apartment, and followed his steps.

Arrived at the cell where Edward had lately been a prisoner, the governor said, "You need not fear his waking; he has swallowed a potion, that will ensure your security." The governor continued to stand at the door of the cell, extending his hand, which bore the lamp, into it, and pointing with the other to the pallet where lay the dead body. Alwin's companion continued also at the door, standing by the side of the governor. Alwin himself moved up to the pallet; having fixed his eyes for an instant upon the body, of which the single lamp carried by the governor was too faint a light for him to discover the features, he drew a dagger from the folds of his mantle, and having run it twice into the body of the supposed Edward, he exclaimed—"Farewell! thou wilt never tell tales of him who sent thee to thy account!" He let the dagger fall from his hand as he spoke these words, and leaving the cell, he addressed Garcias Xavia, desiring that he would immediately conduct him and his companion out of the prison.

The moment their receding steps were no longer audible to Hubert, he darted into the gallery, and entering the apartment where Edward was, he exclaimed—"My master! My benefactor! Your liberty, your life, depend on the present moment! Follow me, follow me!"

The heart of Edward beat a tumult of joy on these welcome sounds from the lips of the honest Hubert, and he was satisfied to act under his direction, without that explanation for which the urgency of the moment afforded no opportunity.

Hubert led the way back to his own chamber, and the instant they were both within it, he said—"In a very short time the governor will come hither alone, to summon me to his aid, in a point which shall hereafter be explained to you; the moment he appears, assist me to secure him, and we triumph over our enemies."

A few minutes of awful and torturing suspense succeeded. The soul of Edward almost sickened, between the extremes of expectation and the dread of disappointment; the feelings of Hubert were wound to a pitch of the most nervous hope and exultation.

The door of Hubert's chamber was at length pushed open by

the hand of the governor, "Now then!" exclaimed Hubert. Edward understood the meaning of his exclamation, and both darting at the same instant upon the astonished Garcias, made him their prisoner. "This way with him!" said Hubert, and they had led him to the door of the cell, where Edward had so lately been a captive, ere he was sufficiently recovered from the surprise in which the unexpected treatment he was receiving had thrown him, to be able to command the power of utterance.

When he did speak, it was only in broken sentences that his astonishment and passion could gain a passage through his lips. "What means this?" he exclaimed. "Am I betrayed? Wretches, ye shall repent—ye shall experience torments—ye shall—Help!—Help!—What, no help!"

Edward started with alarm at the sound of his exclamations.

"Fear nothing from his cries," said Hubert; "he has already informed me, that no one can overhear us here, but prisoners, who cannot quit their apartments."

"Oh, mercy, Jesu!—Jesu!" exclaimed Garcias, "ye will not murder me?—What is it ye will do with me?"

"Let you live to repent the crimes of your life, and prepare yourself to meet a more awful administrator of justice than you behold in either of us;" and having said this, Hubert thrust him into the cell, and closing the door, turned upon him the lock.

"Now then let us be gone," said Hubert; "the key which you saw me snatch out of his hand at the moment we first seized him, is the master-key of every lock which could impede our escape from these accursed walls."

"Yet one instant stay," responded Edward: "I have a friend within this edifice, Adolphus Biron his name, the youth whom you this morning led away from the cell in which I was then a prisoner. During the melancholy period of our captivity, we made a promise to each other, not to accept the blessings of liberty singly—he must be the companion of our flight."

The apartment to which Adolphus had that morning been conducted, was near the spot where they were standing; and, by the assistance of the master-key, Hubert directly admitted Edward into it.

It is needless to describe with what joy Adolphus beheld his friend, and heard the purpose of his midnight visit; and the moment the first burst of ecstacy, which had been poured into his soul by the promise of freedom, had subsided, his thoughts turned to his Belise. "I cannot depart to leave her here," he said.

"If you mean that Lady Belise, who is daughter-in-law to the governor," returned Hubert, "she is not within these walls; she has fled from hence some days."

"Fled!" echoed Adolphus.

"Yes," replied Hubert; "on the death of her mother, which happened about a fortnight ago, the governor's threats of uniting her to an old man, who had for some time past been her suitor, but into whose arms her mother had, during her lifetime, withheld her from being forced, produced such an effect on her mind, as to induce her to fly from the misery she dreaded, and she has not since been heard of."

"Unhappy, beloved Belise!" exclaimed Adolphus. "Come then, let us instantly hence. Adolphus shall know no rest, till he has found the mistress of his soul."

Conducted by Hubert, they quickly found themselves on the outside of the prison wall; in passing through the court which led to it, Hubert disencumbered himself of his wooden leg, and the bandage which he had worn over his left eye, for the sake of disguise.

To avoid the city of Ostend, Hubert said, must be their first care, as there would, undoubtedly, be made the first search after them in the morning, as soon as the governor was released from his present confinement, and should disperse abroad intelligence of the occurrences of the night. Towards the coast he considered it equally dangerous for them to proceed, lest they should encounter Alwin and his companion, who had, doubtless, sought it immediately on quitting the prison, in order to embark without delay for England: he therefore advised that they should entirely avoid the coast, and endeavour to push their way into Germany, from some part of which empire they might stand a chance of procuring a passage to England, without exciting suspicions of any kind concerning themselves. It might, perhaps, he said, delay their arrival in that kingdom a couple of months beyond the time in which they might reach it, were they to sail directly thither from any part of Flanders; but he judged that Edward, having once obtained his freedom, with the difficulty and perils with which it had been gained, no caution could be too great to ensure his not being again deprived of it.

Adolphus, uncertain whither his road lay, felt only convinced that it became him to get away as speedily as possible from the neighbourhood of Ostend; and accordingly agreed to pursue the road of his friend and Hubert, for at least a day or two.

"As we shall undoubtedly be sought near the coast," remarked Hubert, "as soon as our escape is discovered, let us use the night to proceed, with all possible expedition, as far as we are able, in an exactly opposite direction; at the first town where we shall arrive in the morning, we will procure some conveyance, to transport us towards a spot of greater security."

"But how, good Hubert, are our expences to be defrayed?" asked Edward.

Hubert explained to him, that he was in possession of above five hundred pieces of gold, which were all devoted to his service; but he forbore to inform him how that sum had become his.

Edward began to pour forth to him those eulogiums on his generosity which the gratitude of his heart dictated to his tongue, but Hubert interrupted him, by beginning to relate some of the occurrences of his own life since Edward and he had parted.

"And didst thou leave thy native land purposely to seek me out?" exclaimed Edward; "and hast thou past all these months, in the meanest capacity, in order to be near me, and watch a moment for my enlargement from captivity? Oh, generous, worthy man!—what benefit had I ever conferred on thee, to demand a return of the exalted nature thou hast made me?"

"Had you not acknowledged me *a man*," replied Hubert—"a being possessed of the same feelings, and the same wants as yourself, although placed by destiny in an humbler sphere of life?—and did you not, by every means in your power, endeavour to equalize my comforts with your own? Yes, yes, you had done this to me—could I, in return, do too much for you?"

Tears are expressive of the weakest, as well as of the noblest sensations of the human mind; those which burst into the eyes of Edward, at this address from the excellent Hubert, were of that nature which bespoke him possessed of a heart, upon which the eye of Providence might glance in exultation, and declare itself well pleased with its created being.

Hubert had remained in England so short a time after Edward's quitting it, that he had but little to inform him concerning those whom he had left behind, with which he was not himself already acquainted. The only occurrence of importance which had taken place, during the few months that Hubert had continued in Cumberland after the departure of Edward for Flanders, was the birth of Rosalind's child; and Hubert had reasons, which will hereafter be shewn, for confining this event, for the present, within his own breast.

As Hubert proceeded to relate the adventures of the two last days, the arrival of Alwin and his companions at the prison, the false intelligence which had been dispatched of Edward's death to Lord William de Mowbray, and the use he had made of the knowledge which he had acquired of these circumstances, not only for the preservation of Edward's life, but also for gaining him his enlargement from the tyranny of the vile Garcias Xavia—the desponding husband of Rosalind expressed the deepest apprehensions lest, immediately on the fabricated news of his death reaching England, her father should force her into the arms of the hated Lord Rufus.

Hubert replied, that he conceived his master (as he was still resolute in calling Edward) to have nothing to apprehend on this score; for as the letter from the governor could not yet have reached England, and as the Baron de Mowbray, on the receipt of it, would doubtless allow a due portion of time to the claims of decency, before he compelled his daughter to enter into a second marriage, there was little doubt of their reaching Cumberland before any step of the kind had been taken, how resolutely soever it might have been determined upon between Lord William and De Madginecourt.

Edward derived little satisfaction from these arguments; but he was loath to return only murmurs to Hubert for the zeal he had shewn in his cause; and therefore, as he knew all complaints to be useless, he constrained himself to keep his thoughts locked up in his own breast.

A friendly moon, which rose soon after our travellers had quitted the precincts of the prison, guided them on their way, till the light of day eclipsed the silver splendour of the fainter orb: they had continued to move forward without a single moment of delay, and about an hour after the rising of the morning, they found themselves at the mouth of a valley which led to a knot of cottages, in the midst of which, a church spire, raising its head above the thatched roofs, bespoke it a village of inferior note.

At this village they procured some refreshment, and a conveyance to the next stage, upon the road which Hubert had resolved to be the most judicious for them to pursue. They continued to travel on without interruption, and about four in the afternoon of the following day, they reached a town, where they learnt that there was, on that day, a fair: they entered a house of public entertainment, and were vexed to find that the room they were conducted into fronted a square, where the fair was held. As they dreaded a pursuit, they dreaded equally to be seen, and accordingly kept on the side of the apartment farthest removed from the windows, whilst they were constrained to remain in the house, which was during the time that fresh horses were providing, and a hasty meal was preparing for them.

Amidst the other sounds that ascended to their apartment from the fair, in the course of a few minutes, they heard the voice of a female, whom they supposed to be a common ballad-singer, chanting to the sweetest melody, the following song:

What is power, what is wealth?
Can they free the heart from pain;
Or bestow soft blooming health,
Where disease and sickness reign?

See yon mountain's rugged brow,
Frowning o'er the chrystal stream,
While its crumbling honours show,
Life's a gay, fantastic dream.

Mark ambition, ceaseless toil,
Looks with scorn on humble worth;
Humble worth, unhurt the while,
Pity feels for wealth and birth.

In some sweet sequester'd glen,
Deep embower'd from haughty pride,

Far remov'd from envious man,
Let my life but smoothly glide:
There I'll watch the setting sun,
While soft memory brings to mind,
Days when happiness begun;
Days alas! left far behind.

Adolphus displayed violent emotion, whilst the songstress pursued her ballad: in the midst of the fifth stanza he rose from his seat, and approached the window, and whilst her last cadence vibrated on the air, he exclaimed—"It is she—'tis she, by Heaven! my beloved, my adored Belise!" and with these words he darted out of the apartment.

Edward supposed that his friend had been mistaken, in the opinion he had formed of the songstress; but a few moments afforded him another proof of how keen are the senses of a lover; for Adolphus returned to their apartment, bearing in his arms, neatly habited in the dress of a Flemish peasant, his Belise, who had fainted with the joy and surprise she had experienced, at so unexpectedly meeting him.

When Belise was sufficiently recovered to collect her ideas for speech, she corroborated those particulars which Hubert had already given for the cause of her flight from her father-in-law; and added, that having kept herself concealed, after her first departure from the prison, in a wood in the vicinity of Ostend, till she believed the heat of the pursuit, which she doubted not was set on foot after her, to have subsided, she had emerged from her retreat, had put on the disguise in which we saw her, and was pursuing her way to a relation of her deceased father at Maestricht, whom she meant to inform of the Governor Garcias Xavia's cruelty to her, and the imprisonment of Adolphus Biron, and implore his intercession in her behalf; as she despaired, by any other means, of preserving herself from an union with the man whom her father-in-law had selected as her husband, or of procuring the enlargement of him who possessed her affections.

"But this habit," said Adolphus, "is, my dear Belise, only a change of dress, not the least disguise to your person."

"Is it not?" she replied; "I had hoped that it would be; but no matter—its use is now over. But, to tell you the truth, the principal cause of my putting it on, was not with regard to disguise, but to procure myself a maintenance on my journey. I had but one single ducat in the world, at the time of my escaping from the old governor, and as I knew it very inadequate to support me all the way on my journey to Maestricht, I put on this dress, which I happened to have in my possession at my departure, and trusted to my voice and lute to earn me my livelihood, in the towns and villages I had to pass through."

After Adolphus had, in his turn, gratified the curiosity of Belise, respecting the mode of his escape from the prison, she said—"As I know that we are equally poor, I recommend that we pursue my intention of proceeding to my relation at Maestricht, and entreat his interposition in procuring for me, out of the hands of Garcias Xavia, the sum of money which I inherited from my father at his decease, and which, I fear, my mother, before her death, was sufficiently inconsiderate to trust in the hands of the governor: without the intervention of a friend, who is acquainted what measures ought, in this case, to be pursued, I am convinced I shall never be able to call it mine."

Adolphus joined in her opinion; but the difficulty which still presented itself to them was, how even their journey to Maestricht was to be performed, in the pennyless state they were both in.

This difficulty the generous Hubert easily settled for them: taking from his trusty waistcoat one hundred pieces of that gold, of which it had for years past been the guardian, he begged them to accept it as a tribute of friendship, not from him, but from his master Edward.

"No, no," said Adolphus, "it may never be in my power to repay you."

"You wrong the disposition which makes you this offer," returned Edward, "in the cause from which you hesitate to accept it—his is a heart of that nature, which cannot be more highly gratified, than by proving itself useful to his fellow beings."

Adolphus and Belise poured forth their joint thanks to a benefactor, from whom they had so little expected so useful a service. The grateful Belise seized his hand, and imprinting on it a kiss, exclaimed—"Be this the bond, that I owe to you the happiness of possessing my Adolphus, and——" the tears prevented her further utterance.

"Depend upon it," cried Adolphus, concluding the sentence which she had been unable to finish, "that whenever fortune shall smile upon us——"

"I," exclaimed Hubert, interrupting him, "shall experience an additional pleasure to what I now feel, in considering that I have, perhaps, laid the first stone of your future independance."

Their repast was now brought in; and after they had partaken of it, they rose to bid each other farewell. The route of Belise towards her relation, lay in an opposite direction to the one destined to be pursued by Edward and Hubert. A lack of words is sometimes the most expressive sign of true regret at parting; such was the separation of Edward with Adolphus and Belise; and as their full hearts pronounced blessings on each other, not the least fervent were those which Adolphus and Belise coupled with the name of the exalted Hubert.

CHAPTER XIV.

Lo! as the surplic'd train drew near
To this last mansion of mankind,
The slow sad bell, the sable bier,
In holy musings wrap the mind!
And while their beam,
With trembling stream,
Attending tapers faintly dart;
Each mould'ring bone,
Each sculptur'd stone,
Strikes mute instruction to the heart!

MALLET.

It would be uninteresting to the reader to accompany Edward and Hubert in their wearisome journey into the German empire: suffice it to say, that many unpleasant causes conspired to oblige them to pursue the greater part of it on foot; and that, after the expiration of nine long weeks, they found themselves at the port of Hamburg.

Here, in the course of a few days, they procured a passage on board a French ship, which had been sent thither to load with merchandize, which she was destined to carry to Newcastle. The harbour of her destination appeared to Edward as desirable a spot for his landing as he could have fixed upon, had he himself been consulted relative to her course; and with a heart light as air, now borne on the buoyant wings of expectation towards his adored Rosalind, he went on board the vessel.

For the three first days their voyage was prosperous; on the evening of the fourth, the English shore having, for the greatest part of the last day, been in view, the Captain made towards it, with an intention, as he said, of coasting it up to the mouth of the Tyne. About the time of sunset, the weather was remarkably serene for the season of the year; the golden beams of the grand luminary of earth had quivered on the waves, till it had sunk into the obscurity of its watery bed; and the captain, drawing his conclusion from the proverb, had foretold a morning of equal serenity and brilliancy. But proverbs are not always infallible: towards midnight the wind suddenly veered round to the south, it rose in short and angry gusts, and, in the course of a few hours, swelled into a tempestuous hurricane, which drove the vessel off the coast: with the morning a thick rain began to fall, which obstructed all observation at the distance of half a furlong from the ship; the English shore was no longer visible, and the compass their only direction.

The gale continued to blow with equal violence throughout the day; a hope was entertained by the mariners, that about the hour it had arisen on the preceding night, it might abate on this; but their expectations were deceived, and the captain pronounced, that if the wind continued to blow twelve hours longer in the same point of the compass that it then did, they should be driven farther into the North Sea.

The next night came, and brought with it no change but that of the wind having veered in a trifling degree to the westward. Again the morning rose, and ushered in a day equally stormy as the preceding one had been; at every fresh gust the billows ran mountains high, and the vessel truly seemed the sport of the waves, which, at intervals, rolled in curling circles over the deck, breathing, as it were, vollies of smoke in their hasty passage. The wind now flew to the eastward of the south; all power of directing the course of the ship was at an end, and she had nothing to trust to but the chance of escaping rocks and sands. In the afternoon, a leak of considerable size was discovered in the hold; the pumps were immediately set to work, but their efforts were soon found to be very inadequate to discharging the quantity of water which was forcing its way into the ship. To add to the horror of the scene, two men, who were about this time employed in endeavouring to take in some of the canvas, fell from the yard-arm into the sea, and were seen to rise no more. Every individual on board continued to work at the pumps, with a fervor, which nothing but the desire of preserving life could have given them strength or spirits to have done. Night was yet distant, and still the darkness of the atmosphere encreased with every minute; and, as if the terror of the scene was not already enough to gratify the spleen of nature, the thunder began to roll in tremendous cracks over their heads, and the forked lightning to cut the heavy clouds on every side.

In this extremity, not only the mariners (with the exception of only two men), but the captain himself, lost their resolution, and ran for the support of their courage to such strong liquor as the vessel had on board. Every added draught seemed insufficient to steel their minds against their approaching death; and, in a short time, the resources of their cowardice had so far driven out sense, that none were capable of working the pumps but Edward, Hubert, and the two mariners, who possessed a sufficient command over themselves to refuse the invitation of their companions to drown thought in drunkenness.

These, in a short time, found themselves entirely inadequate to the proper exercise of the pumps; and one of the two mariners declaring that he was certain the vessel must, in another quarter of an hour, go down, so rapidly was she filling with water, they agreed to launch out the boat, and, in this perilous situation, to trust themselves to the mercy of the waves.

At the moment they entered the boat, a crack of thunder rent the air; it appeared to be the master-effort of Nature to dispel the horrors which clouded her face; and a short time proved it to have been so, for, from that instant, the gusts of wind became less violent, the awfulness of the thunder seemed to recede in hollow murmurings, and the lightning was but a faint image of its former fierceness.

The ship sunk before half the quarter of an hour, which the sailor had given her to remain above water, was expired.

It was now about eight in the evening, and although the blackness of the clouds was less threatening, the darkness of night was stealing so rapidly upon the day, that the obscurity of the scene was becoming gradually thicker every moment. Could they defend their little bark from being overset by the violent motion of the waves, it was all they hoped or expected, till the day should rise, and furnish them with light to guide their course. They continued to buffet about in all directions, till about two hours more, as nearly as they could conjecture, had passed by; about this time, the sailors said, that they guessed, from the direction in which the boat was driving, that she was running into some creek, which they almost ventured to believe would carry her ashore.

The violence of the wind continued to abate; their boat rode with more safety upon the waves; the blackness of the night began to fade into a paler grey, and even accidental stars to peep from the atmosphere. At length, the mariners, whose sight use had rendered more expert than that of Edward or Hubert, declared that they were within a cable's length of land. On the sound of this intelligence, an exclamation of joy was poured from every mouth, and every eye bent towards the land, which, in a very short time became discernible to all.

The wind lying on their stern, shortly drove the boat upon the coast; and when the water became too shallow for her to be carried farther up the land, they quitted her, and forded their way to the dry ground.

Edward was no sooner landed, than a thanksgiving to that Power, which had so frequently testified its favour towards him in the many acts of preservation he had experienced at its hands, burst from his lips: the soul of Hubert was not less grateful than that of Edward, but his gratitude was confined to the silence of his breast. The two mariners also who had escaped with them from the wreck, sunk upon their knees, and fervently raised their voices to Heaven.

When their devotions were concluded—"Which way shall we proceed," said Edward, "with the hope of reaching any habitation? We are probably at a considerable distance from any town or village."

The mariners replied, that they had never before sailed near that coast on which it had now been their fortune to be wrecked; that they conjectured it to be the coast of Scotland, but could form no idea upon what part of it they were now standing.

While they were deliberating how to proceed—"Hark!" exclaimed Hubert: they immediately became silent, and, in the space of about half a minute more, they heard the toll of a bell. "I was not mistaken," cried Hubert; "there it is again."

"A bell at this hour! a bell at midnight!" exclaimed one of the sailors; "pray the holy Jesus we be not treading on ground that is witched!"

"I have lost both my beads and my missal!" said the other; "mercy, mercy, good Saint James! protect me, holy martyr, for I have no power of defending myself against evil spirits!"

Edward was too well acquainted with the superstitious minds of seamen, to be moved by what they said: he endeavoured to convince them, that unusual as the hour was for the bell of any religious house to be tolling, yet that such certainly was the sound which they had heard, and which still continued to vibrate at intervals upon the air; that some monastery probably was nigh, and that, if they followed the sound, it doubtless would lead them to a spot where they might obtain relief and comfort, after the extremities to which they had been exposed.

Having said this, Edward directly began to proceed in such direction as the sound of the tolling bell invited him to pursue; and the sailors preferring, probably, rather to run into the jaws of danger, agreeably to their own opinion, in good company, than to remain where they were, with no other counsellors than their own coward hearts, followed close behind him, repeating, with most audible voices, prayers to their tutelar saints.

They moved on for nearly half a mile, the strength of the sound increasing at every step upon their ears, till turning out of the path in which they were proceeding, in order to avoid some piles of stones which choaked up the road, they caught a view of lights at a short distance.

The progress of a few minutes more served to shew them that these were torches in the air, the flames of which played above a wall, that intervened between them and our travellers. Advancing towards this wall as rapidly as they were able, they at length reached a spot of sloping ground, which led immediately up to it; as they ascended this, the sound of female voices became audible; they were chanting a hymn, of which Edward distinctly heard the last lines.

Nurs'd on Heaven's ethereal breast,
Our sister tastes celestial rest;
Freed from the pangs she knew on earth,
The child of Innocence by second birth.
Angels hover round her head,
Angels deck her snow-white bed;
Sister, farewell, more blest than we,
For thou hast gain'd eternity!

After these words had been sung, a solemn silence ensued, the bell ceased to toll, and the lights began to move along. Edward and his companions, who were now divested of all supernatural fears, went up to a gate of iron work, which they discovered in the stone wall that divided them from those whose voices they had heard, and on looking through it, perceived a procession of nuns, headed by their priest, and lighted by the torches, of which they had, for a long time past, seen the flames in the air, entering, with slow steps, a vaulted door, which led into the hall of a convent. In the midst of the nuns they beheld a man, who appeared not many years to have exceeded the prime of life, led by the abbess of the convent, and a youth, whose dress bespoke him the sacristan.

The sight of any male attending on the funeral of a nun excited the surprise of Edward, particularly as he appeared too much in years to be a lover, and as, at the same time, his demeanour bespoke him weighed down with grief.

When the procession had entered the convent, Edward looked round to see upon whom he should call, to request admittance into the holy building; because, although he had seen enough to know it to be the dwelling of religious females, he doubted not, that on account of its proximity to the coast, some part of it was dedicated to the services of humanity and charity, out of compassion to shipwrecked mariners, who, like themselves, might be cast upon its shores.

He saw a couple of men busily employed in throwing the earth into a grave, where, from every circumstance he had observed, it was evident one of the sisterhood had that night been returned to her kindred clay. He accordingly hailed them; they immediately advanced to the gate, and demanded the business of those they saw without it. Edward explained their situation, and enquired where they were? To this question, one of the men replied, that they were cast upon the island of Auskerry, one of the most eastern of the Orkneys; and that the building, on the outside of which they stood, was the convent of Saint Agnes. Edward next demanded, if it would be permitted them to receive from it the offices of humanity due to their necessities, of which the most grateful would be, a place of repose for the night?

His demand was replied to, in terms that proved that his conjectures, concerning the provision which had been made by the founder of the edifice in behalf of the unfortunate, were not erroneous. The man said he would instantly acquaint Saint Matilda, the lady abbess, of their arrival, and bring back with him the keys of the gate to admit them within its walls.

In a short time he returned, and with him came the portress, who though a nun and a virgin, no danger could have been apprehended from her being presented to the gaze of a seaman who had performed the voyage round the world, without having encountered a female during the whole of the circuit; for her age was at least seventy, her teeth were gone, one side of her body she was obliged to support on a crutch, and, in short, no part of her composition appeared to retain the vigour of which it is but natural to suppose the whole had once been possessed, except her tongue.

The moment she had unlocked the gate, old sister Judith began to display her best point, by immediately putting into motion her valuable weapon: she enquired whence they came? how long they had reached the shore? whither they had been sailing? what was become of the rest of the crew? and many more questions, between which she made no pause for a reply.

Edward made her merely such answers as he deemed necessary, in order to win her willing services towards himself and his companions. Hubert spoke not; and the sailors, unable to converse in her language, were satisfied to follow the fortunes of him who could make known their wants for them.

"Well," cried sister Judith, as they crossed the burying-ground, "you are come on a memorable night; we have had a heart-rending funeral. There lies," pointing to the grave, which was not yet filled up, "one of the sweetest flowers that ever bloomed in Scotland."

"Who was she? I pray you tell me," said Edward.

"No other," returned sister Judith, "than the bonny Mabel Monteith."

"I do not recollect ever to have heard of her," replied Edward.

"Not heard of her!—why where have you lived?" cried Judith—"not in Scotland, I am sure, nor in England, I should almost think. You must have heard of her, and her cousin, Lady Margaret Murray; the first the niece, and the other the daughter of the powerful Laird of Lednoch, who, in the last pestilence which raged in our country, fled from the world to the mountains of Athol, where they secreted themselves in a mean hut, partly of their own building, and there escaped the plague, while every body thought them dead of it. But you see, you see," continued she, emphatically, "if we contrive to put off the evil day ever so long, it will come at last. Yes, bonny Mabel Monteith was buried in that grave to-night."

Edward had now some faint remembrance of having heard the story when a boy, and mentioned it to sister Judith.

"Man, woman, and child know their story," rejoined she; "it has been told twenty different ways, in verse;" and as she uttered these words they entered the hall of the convent, where Saint Matilda met them. She received them with that kindness and courtesy of expression, which give the highest value to benevolence and hospitality; and perceiving Edward to be of superior rank to his companions, she addressed herself particularly to him, to enquire in what manner she could be serviceable to him in his present unfortunate situation?

Having told her as much of his history as it was necessary that she should be made acquainted with, she replied, that the French sailors had better remain in a cottage which she would dispose to receive them in the village hard by, till some vessel, bound to the continent, should touch upon the island for water or provisions, which, she said, was generally the case every fortnight, or sometimes more. For himself, she said, she would willingly supply him with money, if he wanted it, which she supposed to be the case, and put him into the road for England, instructing him how to travel it, with the least inconvenience to himself. Of money, he informed her, that he did not stand in need, as his companion, pointing to Hubert as he spoke, had some about him at the time they had been obliged to quit the foundering vessel. For her instructions how to pursue his route into Northumberland, he should be very thankful; but added, "that he felt himself so much weakened and fatigued by the perils he had encountered in his voyage, that he should, in all probability, be compelled to intrude for two or three days at least upon her hospitality, before he should be able to pursue his journey into England."

"My son," replied Saint Matilda, "it is not to me, but to the founder of this mansion, that you are indebted for such comforts as it can afford you; if my welcome to it can add to the gratification with which you receive them, you have it from my heart: this is all which you will owe to me, should you reside with us a month."

Edward returned the abbess thanks, suitable to the benevolent temper of her mind; and having partaken with Hubert of some refreshments that were set before them, they requested to be shewn to their respective chambers.

At the hour of breakfast, sister Judith called them to their meal, and while they were seated at it, Saint Matilda, who did not appear entirely to have forgotten the world, or to have lost her relish for society, visited them; she congratulated them on finding them better, she said, than she expected to have done, from their haggard and weary looks on the preceding night; and told Edward, that if he was able to travel in two days time, she could recommend him company as far as Perthshire—for that there were, at the present moment, a gentleman and his servant, in her convent, who were at that time to set out on their journey thither.

Edward replied, that he doubted not being well enough to undertake the journey, and enquired who the gentleman was at whom she had hinted as a travelling companion for him?

"It is," answered Saint Matilda, "the Laird of Glenross, the disconsolate widower of our sister, Bonny Mabel, as we have always called her, immediately after whose funeral you arrived last night."

"A wife, and still a member of your sisterhood!" exclaimed Edward.

"Even so," returned Saint Matilda. "I do not wonder that you express surprise: for seventeen years she had been one of our sisterhood, ere I discovered who she was, or learnt that she had ever been a wife. At the time of her making this discovery to me, she was on her deathbed. Heaven grant that the portion of charity which I felt for her, on learning the imposition she had practised upon me, at the time of her becoming an inhabitant of this convent, be not less of religion than the severity with which most women, who are placed in situations of authority like myself, would have treated her! If I have erred, I am satisfied that my error has been on the side of humanity."

A pause ensued; the abbess broke it—"I doubt not that she would have died, without confessing to me the secret of her having ever been married, had she not been tortured with remorse for her unjust conduct to her husband, and felt it necessary to the peace of her last moments to see him, and obtain his pardon, ere she quitted life."

The abbess was at this moment called away from the apartment, and Edward, moving towards the window, saw the same man whom he had on the preceding evening observed to be led from the funeral of the deceased nun, by Saint Matilda and the sacristan, standing by the side of the grave, with his hands clasped, and his eyes raised to Heaven, as if imploring its charity for her whose earthly part lay concealed beneath the turf at his feet. As Edward continued to observe him, he could not forbear drawing a comparison, which communicated pleasure to his feelings, between himself and the Laird of Glenross. "Thou lamentest an inconstant and departed wife," he said; "I anticipate the bliss of again clasping to my heart one who lives but for me, and whose existence the fates have spared her, again to behold me in her arms. Destiny is still kind, and I will not arraign her dispensations. Sinful are those who murmur, when one gaze around the world will ever present to their view, beings more unfortunate than themselves."

In the evening Saint Matilda again visited Edward; she informed him, that she had mentioned to Laird Archibald the plan which she had proposed to him of their journeying together, and that he had acceded to it with pleasure, and had agreed to breakfast with Edward on the morning of their setting out; but that he had declined an introduction to him till that time, wishing to pass his hours until that period in solitude, dedicated to the memory of his deceased wife.

Edward began to remark, to the lady abbess, on such parts of the Bonny Mabel's story as the prattling old Judith had made him acquainted with on the preceding night; and Saint Matilda replied, "Her life has, in many instances, been a romance. If it will afford you any pleasure to hear such particulars of it as I am acquainted with, you shall sit an hour with me in my own parlour after vespers, and I will relate them to you."

Edward replied, "that, not from idle curiosity to learn the concerns of others, but from the religious content with which it ever inspired his own mind, to hear in what manner the hand of Providence had interfered in regulating the destiny of his fellow beings, her offered recital would give him satisfaction."

"Thou art wise, my son," returned Saint Matilda; "the great book of learning is the human heart—to study its workings, and to observe in what manner the indulgence and restriction of its passions have been instrumental to the honour or disgrace of such members of society as have preceded us upon the stage of life, is an enquiry worthy of the most exalted philosophy, and a curiosity which cannot be deemed a vice. Experience is the mother of true wisdom, and it is only to be acquired by attention to the conduct of others. I am not talking," she added with a smile, "like one immured for life within the walls of a convent; at least you may judge these sentiments not to be applicable within one: but trust me, that even here, in our small community, where you may perhaps imagine that none of the errors which exist in the world at large are to be found, example has too much sway for the happiness of many—because, my son, it is a sorrowful truth, that such is the force of example, that it does not alone find followers when its actions are praise-worthy, but begets imitators equally of its impurities."

The bell now tolling to assemble the nuns to their evening devotions, the abbess went to join them in the chapel; on her return from it, Edward was summoned to her parlour by sister Judith, and Saint Matilda executed her promise of relating to him the history of the Laird of Glenross, and his faithless wife, the bonny Mabel Monteith.

END OF VOLUME THREE.

THE MYSTERIOUS FREEBOOTER

CHAPTER I.

They bigged a bower on yon burn-brae,
And thick'd it o'er with rashes.

ANCIENT BALLAD.

"It was one evening in the early part of spring, that Laird Archibald Glenross, having been separated from his companions in the chace, found himself alone, and at the distance of several miles from his own castle, in the northern and mountainous part of the county of Perthshire. As no trodden path pointed out to him a ready way for gaining the high road, the more he strove to extricate himself from the intricacies of the chain of mountains he was riding amongst, the more entangled he became; and the dusky clouds of departing day beginning to descend to the earth, he despaired of reaching home that night, and thought only of finding some humble cottage to repose at.

"As the evening closed in, a heavy rain began to fall, and Laird Archibald was wet through all his clothes, before a friendly, though distant, light gave him the comfortable assurance of his being within sight of some habitation. With all speed he made up to it, and alighting from his horse, knocked with his fist upon the door, and implored admittance. He could distinguish the whispering of voices within, but still he heard not the fall of steps, nor any promise of his request being complied with.

"Again and again he hit his hand upon the door, and between the intervals of the roaring gust, he explained his hopeless situation, and entreated shelter from the inclement weather, and the biting air.

"The Laird of Glenross had at that time just completed his twenty-fourth year; his person was handsome, his figure good, his manners universally allowed to be of the most generous and persuasive kind; and by the late death of his father, he was just become the representative of his house; and the benevolent actions which had attended his accession to the dignities of his station, he believed to have rendered his name not alone known, but respected, in the neighbourhood where he resided; accordingly, he failed not, in his petition for admission into the cottage, at the door of which he was now standing, to inform its inhabitants who was their petitioner.

"Laird Archibald looked around him, in the hope of espying a second light in some other cottage, whose inhabitants might prove more impressive to the calls of humanity, but he could discover none; indeed, when he turned round his head from the shelter which the little building he was standing under the cover of afforded him, no object was discernible through the thick darkness of night; nor did he find it scarcely possible to open his eyes at all, on account of the driving rain and sleet, which were borne through the air on the wings of a keen northerly wind.

"Laird Archibald did not quit his station, for even the outside of the cottage was a defence to him against the weather, which he knew not where else to seek; and at intervals he continued to repeat his petition for admittance: after he had passed nearly half an hour in this disagreeable situation, a female voice within the house replied—'We come.'

"Of the most delightful nature was the sound; he placed his foot upon the threshold, and the door was opened by a person whose appearance filled him equally with surprise, as did the delay with which the humane action had been performed; it was a lady, habited in the deepest mourning; and behind her stood another female, dressed exactly the same as herself, and whose appearance denoted her to be of equal rank as the first: the latter held in her hand a lamp; the former, the moment she had opened the door, thus addressed Laird Archibald—'Enter, my Laird; as we know you to be a knight of Scotland, we trust that you will not sully the name, by forgetting the respect due to two unprotected females; we therefore admit you beneath our roof.'

'Good heaven!' exclaimed Glenross, fixing his eyes upon them, 'I cannot be mistaken; surely I behold the niece, and daughter, of the Laird of Lednoch?'

'The same, the same!' they both replied: 'Here, in this seclusion, have we lived, while the world has thought us both long dead. We are at present the sole inhabitants of this cottage; when you hear this, you will not be surprised that we were scrupulous about admitting you into it at this hour of the night.'

'And may I lose every claim to the honour of manhood,' ejaculated Laird Archibald, 'if I forget the reverence due to my benevolent entertainers.'

'Enter, enter freely,' said the daughter of Lednoch: 'we have heard much spoken in your praise, and doubt not to find you equal in honour to the report you bear in the world.'

"They immediately placed a chair for their guest opposite to the fire; and as they had no change of garments to offer him, they heaped additional logs upon the hearth, and produced a cup of wine, which he drank at their invitation.

"When some time had been passed in necessary attentions to the comfort of the weather-beaten Laird Archibald, he besought his fair entertainers to inform him by what miracle he saw them alive and in health, when they had for some months past been supposed to have fallen victims to the pestilence which had at that time raged in Scotland.

"He had once visited, with his father, at the Castle of Lednoch, in Aberdeenshire; its Laird was then a widower, with one son, Sir Alexander, a daughter, the Lady Margaret, and an orphan niece of the name of Monteith, whose beauty had acquired her the title of the Bonny Mabel.

"Since that time, the pestilence had carried off the Laird of Lednoch and his son: his daughter and niece had been reported in the world to have fled from Aberdeen, where the disorder had raged with the greatest violence, but, nevertheless, to have sunk under its power: he now rejoiced that common fame had been a false intelligencer in the instance of their fate, and received from their lips an account of their preservation.

"Lady Margaret satisfied his curiosity in these words:—

'A very short time after the breaking out of that pestilence, to which there is scarcely a Scottish family who does not owe the privation of some loved relative, my dear father and brother having both fallen victims to its fury, my cousin Mabel and myself, at their death, having no one left us in the world to whom we were bound by the ties of affinity—no one but each other to look up to for the mutual kind offices of friendship and consanguinity, bethought us alone of what steps we might pursue that seemed to promise us the preservation of both our lives, which we wished to ensure, more, I believe, for the sake of each other's happiness, than our own love of existence.

'We heard of many who fled from the cities towards uninhabited spots, and died in their way to what they had regarded as places of security; but this did not discourage us—we hoped that all might not be alike unfortunate; and esteeming the chance of prolonging our existence to depend alone on our quitting Aberdeenshire, where the plague raged in its hottest fury, we resolved on setting out for the mountains of Athol, where we knew our old nurse, Mause, to reside in a lonely cot, although we were unacquainted with the exact spot on which her dwelling stood.

'After some days of weary travelling, we reached the mountains, and with little difficulty discovered the humble cot of old Mause; with surprise she saw us step upon her threshold, and with humanity and love she received us as her inmates, till the fury of the raging pestilence should be abated.

'Here we have now resided five months, old Mause having occasionally gone to a neighbouring village to procure us provisions, and bring us the report of the times; upon this business she is now absent, and will not return till the morrow: on this account you find us here alone, and unattended.'

"Laird Archibald congratulated his fair entertainers on the object of their seclusion from the world having been granted them, in the health which he saw them enjoying; and assured them that they had now nothing to apprehend from quitting their concealment, as the alarming disorder from which they had fled was entirely subdued.

"When the hour of retiring to rest arrived, the Laird of Glenross insisted that they should occupy their accustomed chamber, declaring that his repose would be equally good in a chair before the fire, as if he were pressing the finest down in the universe; accordingly, having rendered his resting-place below as commodious as it lay in their power to make it, they ascended to their bedchamber, and locked themselves in for the night.

"Glenross, when left to his reflections by the retiring of the fair recluses, felt more inclined to indulge himself in thought than sleep.

At the time of his visit to the Castle of Lednoch with his father, the charms of the Bonny Mabel had inspired him with feelings which nothing could have damped but the report which had so shortly after been circulated in the world of her death; they now blazed forth again with additional warmth; and circumstances had added such strength to his passion, that he almost feared to sleep, lest his dreams should deny him that bliss of beholding the Bonny Mabel through his mind's eye, which his waking reflections accorded him.

"At bidding him good night, the Lady Margaret Murray had placed a few books upon the table by his side.—'Should you not be able to sleep the night through in your chair,' she said, 'you will perhaps find something in these volumes to entertain you.'

"A short time after their departure, Laird Archibald looked into the books, and found them mostly to contain ancient legends in verse; upon one of these, which contained the history of the loves of King Richard Coeur de Lion and his Queen Matilda, he paused; for lovers feel it a devotion to dwell upon the pages that treat of love; and as he turned over the leaves, a paper fell from them, upon which he, at the first glance, discovered the characters of a female pen; he laid down the book, and unfolding the sheet, he perceived that they were lines of poetry which it contained, and which were thus inscribed:—

On seeing the Funeral of a young English Officer, who fell a Victim to the Plague in Scotland, where he was entirely a Stranger.

Behold the thronging crowd in yonder street,
Where expectation strains each eager eye;
Think they the warrior's dauntless brow to meet,
Crown'd with the laurel wreath of victory?

Alas! no shout of triumph bribes the gale,
To boast of conquest with exulting breath;
The solemn dirge explains the mournful tale,
And chants the final victory of Death!

Ah, what remains of that which once had life?
Mute is the voice that wak'd at pleasure's call;
Youth with the tyrant held unequal strife,
To break the wool that wove the fun'ral pall.

The helmet, once that brac'd his youthful brow,
To fancy's eye his well-known face pourtrays;
The harmless sword directs no fatal blow,
The martial belt but mimic show displays.

The warlike horse, with fun'ral trappings proud,
Paws the rude earth, and champs the frothy reins,
Mistakes for joy the tumult of the crowd,
And fancies still his master he sustains.

No ear paternal caught his parting breath,
No friendly hand reviving cordials gave:
No lifted finger hush'd the voice of Death,
When in harsh tones he call'd him to the grave.

The half-form'd wish his trembling lips betray'd,
Unheeded fell upon a stranger's ear;
His sinking frame no kindred eyes survey'd,
To claim the birth-right of the kindred tear.

Perhaps my wand'ring feet his grave may seek,
May find the spot where his cold ashes lie;
Then shall a sigh from mem'ry's impulse speak,
A stranger's pray'r for frail mortality.

"These verses had been written by the Lady Margaret Murray, who was as highly gifted with the qualifications of the mind, as was her cousin Mabel with those of the person.

"The Laird of Glenross had read them with the utmost pleasure; he was himself a man of refined sense, and he hoped to learn that they were the effusions of his beloved Mabel: the morning brought him the conviction of his error from her own lips.—'Oh no,' she replied to his enquiry if the verses were her's, 'I never wrote a line in my life.'

"He felt rather disappointed, but the confession was made by Mabel with a smile which compensated, by excess of beauty, for every deficiency in poetical skill.

"Laird Archibald readily accepted the invitation of his fair entertainers to breakfast at their cottage; and a short time after their repast was ended, old Mause returned home; she confirmed the information which the Laird of Glenross had given them, that all danger from the late pestilence was removed, and that they might with safety again emerge into the world.

"All obstacles to their quitting the seclusion of the mountains being thus obviated, Glenross promised to go himself in person, on the following day, to the castle of Lednoch, and having assembled an escort of their own servants, to return with them as soon as possible to the cottage, and be himself one of their conductors to their parental habitation.

"With many acknowledgments they accepted his courtly offer; and he then departed, leaving the Bonny Mabel suspicious of the sentiments which she had created in his heart, and by no means displeased at the prophecy of her own.

"Early on the fourth morning, the winding of the horn over the mountains of Athol, announced the approach of the Laird of Glenross with his promised escort; and the Ladies Margaret and Mabel were conveyed back to the Castle of Lednoch, with all the state becoming their rank and birth, where they were received with every demonstration of joy by their assembled clans.

"By constant intercourse with the object of his adoration, Laird Archibald's passion became too violent to be confined to his own breast, and he breathed the confession of his love into the ear of the Bonny Mabel, who acknowledged him the lord of her affections, with blushes that heightened the charms which had inspired him with the consuming fire.

"When a due time had been given to the preparations for their nuptials, they were united at the altar of Lednoch Abbey. By their union, the clans of Glenross and Monteith became consolidated into one vassalage, and the Castle of Glenross was fixed upon as their place of residence.

"The lover has no eyes except for the outward perfections of his mistress—the husband searches for those of the mind. When nearly half a year had passed over the heads of the Bonny Mabel and her Laird in their married state, and the affection he bore her began to calm into the sedateness of a friendly esteem, it was not without regret that he discovered her mind to be as unadorned, as her person was richly ornamented; while in the Lady Margaret, whose person was plain, when compared with that of her cousin Mabel, the alluring graces of a highly cultivated understanding shone with extraordinary brilliancy.

"To the Castle of Lednoch, which was her parental inheritance, the Lady Margaret felt averse to retiring as a residence, saying that she should infinitely prefer being allowed to constitute a part of their family, to the solitude which she must experience as the mistress of a castle—a decision which the Laird of Glenross heard her make with pleasure, as it ensured him many hours of satisfaction in the enjoyment of her conversation.

"But let it not be understood that Laird Archibald regarded the Lady Margaret in any other light than as a woman whose universal knowledge it gave him pleasure to possess an opportunity of referring to with the familiarity he had the power of doing to her's. Where the tenderer emotions were concerned, no woman had ever, for one single instant, entered his heart in competition with his Mabel: but love, even with the most heavenly object, will not always satisfy the mind of reason; it must also banquet on that food in which the understanding holds a share; and this repast of reason, none could, in the opinion of Laird Archibald, spread in richer delicacy to the senses, than Lady Margaret Murray.

"She was," remarked Saint Matilda, "a woman possessed of an uncommon understanding for the age in which she was educated; and was, besides, gifted with that strength of mind which it is very unusual to find the inmate of a female breast."

CHAPTER II.

Ah, gentle pair, ye little think how nigh
Your change approaches, when all these delights
Will vanish, and deliver ye to woe;
More woe, the more your taste is now of joy;
Happy, but for so happy, ill secur'd
Long to continue.

MILTON.

"About two years after the Bonny Mabel had become a wife," continued the Lady Abbess, "was the period at which our unfortunate Queen Mary gave her hand to the Earl of Darnley. In compliment to her people, who expected some expenditure from the royal coffers to be made on this occasion, a week was set apart for sports and tournaments, to be held at Kinnavain Castle, in the county of Dumfries, and to which all the nobility and gentry of Scotland were invited; of the number of the guests, were the Laird of Glenross, with his wife and the Lady Margaret.

"What were the diversions of the first day, I know not; that of the second was a tilt, at which twenty pairs of knights were to display their skill in the wielding of the lance. On the morning of this day, the Queen herself put into the hands of such of her female guests as bore the rank of nobility, elegant scarfs and chains, with which to reward the conquerors of the hour; and the manner in which she directed the prizes to be distributed, was not the common method of each lady presenting the emblem of partiality to any victorious knight whom it best pleased her so to honour, but for such knights as conquered their opponents, to kneel for their reward at the feet of whatever lady they deemed it the highest gratification to receive the mark of their conquest from.

"Of the third pair of knights who contended for the prize which conquest gave them the right of claiming from the hand of beauty, the appearance of one was extremely remarkable; he bestrode a charger of the brightest black, with a flowing mane and tail, that greatly increased the beauty of its form; his dress was an entire suit of sable armour; at his back flowed a cloak of lion's skin, which was fastened upon his shoulders with the paws of the animal in sparkling silver; and upon his head he wore the visage of the lion, cast in massive silver, around the brows of which depended the real mane of the beast.

"During the combat, like the rest of the knights, he wore his visor down.

"Three rounds were allowed to each pair of combatants for the trial of their skill; in the two first of which he broke the lance of his opponent, and in the third he unhorsed him. His victory was the most complete of any one gained that day; and when he ceased to wield the lance, he threw himself at the feet of the Lady Glenross, for the reward of his prowess and skill.

"At the evening board which succeeded the pageant of the day, the victorious knights appeared doffed of their armour, and amongst them, he who had worn the suit of sable with the cloak of lion's skin:

he was tall, handsome, well shaped, and insinuating in his manner. The moment his eye fixed upon the Bonny Mabel, he approached her, and entered into a conversation, for which the arrangements of the morning had given no opportunity.

"On the fourth day, the claimant for the honorary scarf and chain in the gift of the Lady Margaret Murray, was a Sir James Lambrun, a youth firmly attached to the family of the Stuarts, and in particular to its present head, the universally beloved Queen Mary.

"The Laird of Glenross observed the marked attention of Sir James to his cousin Margaret, and also of the sable knight to his wife, and they both afforded him pleasure; he judged that Margaret might be beginning an acquaintance which might eventually lead to the happiness of her life; and it flattered his love for his wife, to see her the object of admiration that she was.

"The Bonny Mabel was more charmed with the attentions of the sable knight than her Lord supposed; he judged the indulgence of her vanity to be guarded by the innocence of her heart, and he forbore to remark upon it to her. The sable knight, on the contrary, persuaded her that the silence of her husband proceeded from indifference; and favouring her own inclination, she trusted to the voice of a new acquaintance, without seeking the advice of an old friend. But I must not anticipate her story—Immediately on the first commencement of her acquaintance with the sable knight, she had enquired his name; this the Laird Archibald had also done, the moment he had seen him kneel to his wife for the pledge of her favour; and to the enquiries of both, it had been replied by the chamberlains of the court, that his esquires had announced him as Sir Allanrod.

"The festive week passed on in the utmost joy and hilarity; a splendid ball on the sixth evening concluded the revelry; and after having attended the Queen and her newly-espoused consort to their devotions at the Abbey of Grey Friars at Dumfries, on the Sunday the nobility were expected to leave Kinnavain Castle, and the royal pair to return to Edinburgh.

"When the dance was breaking up, the Laird of Glenross not perceiving his wife in the ranks of the dancers, concluded her fatigued, and gone to her chamber; and, under this idea, he repaired thither himself. She was not there; and supposing that he had overlooked her in the ball-room, he did not choose to return to it, but sat down to await her coming. Nearly an hour passed away; and as she did not appear, he resolved on going down once more himself; taking up his lamp for that purpose, his eye fell on a letter, upon which, as it appeared, he had set down his lamp at first coming into the room; he took it up, and found it directed to himself, in the handwriting of his wife. Hastily he tore it open, and read nearly these words:—

'I have for a long time perceived that you have preferred the conversation of my cousin Margaret to myself; you may now enjoy it without interruption; you will experience no farther restraint in your inclinations from

'MABEL GLENROSS.'

"The emotions of grief, surprise, and vexation, with which Laird Archibald read these lines, you may easily imagine; how did he lament the improper construction which his wife had put upon the pleasure that he had enjoyed in the society of Lady Margaret; how did he execrate the villain who had robbed him of her charms.

"He could not doubt with whom she had fled from him—it could be no other than the sable knight, Sir Allanrod. He hastened to the porters of the castle, and enquired how long they had passed the gates? the confusion of the evening had been such, that no one was able to reply to his enquiries. He returned to the castle hall, and amidst the assembled esquires and chamberlains, he demanded who was Sir Allanrod, and where he dwelt? No one could reply, with any degree of satisfaction, to his questions.

"In the distraction of his doubts he ran to the queen, and of her, and her royal husband, he made the same enquiries; but they could, not give him the information he desired: Sir Allanrod was known to them only as a knight, whom the general invitation they had issued to all the Scottish nobility and gentry to join in the festivities of the week, had brought to Kinnavain Castle.

"The senses of Laird Glenross were so far bewildered by his loss, that but for the unremitting care and attention of the Lady Margaret Murray, some rash act had, in all probability, been the consequence of his grief: on the following morning he returned with her to his castle, hardly conscious of the change of place he was making; and as every enquiry after the Bonny Mabel, and her vile seducer, proved fruitless, he sunk into a melancholy composure, which threatened a more unhappy termination than had the violence of grief which he had displayed on the first discovery of her inconstancy.

"How did he lament that he had ever felt pleasure in the innocent society of Lady Margaret; and at times he was almost repentant of having married with regard only to the perfections of the face; and having trusted his happiness in the power of one who had shewn herself so little capable of estimating the affection of a husband who had most tenderly loved her.

"One year having been completed, without a single breath of intelligence reaching him concerning either his wife or the mysterious Sir Allanrod, with whom she had fled from him, having lost all taste for the world and its inhabitants, he resolved, from that moment, to consider himself as a widower, and to become a member of the monastery of White Penitents at Perth. Accordingly having witnessed the marriage of Lady Margaret Murray with Sir James Lambrun, at which ceremony he performed the part of father to the bride, he retired from the world, as he then believed, never for a day again to emerge into its deceitful scenes.

"I must now," said Saint Matilda, "part for a while from Laird Archibald, and pursue the narrative I am giving you in my own character.—In the retirement in which I live upon this island, and within the walls of this religious building, the events of the busy world, as you may suppose, seldom reach my ear. I had heard of the manner in which the Lady Margaret, and her cousin, the Bonny Mabel Monteith, had preserved themselves from the pestilence, for it had been chanted all over the kingdom in lays and ballads, but farther I had never heard their names mentioned. That such a noble as the Laird Archibald of Glenross existed, I was not even acquainted: thus it was impossible that I could know any thing of her marriage.

"About two years after her elopement from her Laird, that is nearly twenty years from the present time, one beautifully serene evening in the middle of summer, a female pilgrim rang at the gate of the convent; and when sister Judith replied to the summons, she requested to see the lady abbess.

"I accordingly received her in the very apartment where we are now sitting. The moment she entered it, she said—'I come, good mother, to enclose myself for ever, an inhabitant of these sacred walls; I know the sum which it is required of me to offer up to Saint Agnes for the obtaining of my grant, and I have brought it with me, although not in money; these jewels, I trust, will be accepted as a donation of sufficient value to ensure me my petition.'—And with these words she put into my hand a casket, which contained some large and brilliant diamonds, and a variety of other precious stones.

'Who art thou, daughter?' I demanded. 'Whence comest thou, thus unattended, and, at the same time, mistress of these valuable articles?'

'You have heard of me, I doubt not,' she replied, 'although you knew me not till now: I am the daughter of the late Earl of Monteith, whose escape, with that of my cousin Margaret Murray, from the pestilence which raged three summers ago in our kingdom, has been celebrated in many songs and ballads.'

'Indeed!' said I, 'are you that Mabel Monteith? What is your motive for retiring from the world?'

'My cousin Margaret,' she answered, 'is lately married to Sir James Lambrun, a man in great favour with our Sovereign, and constantly about the court; and as she is so entirely devoted to him as never willingly to be deprived for a day of his society, and as my disposition lies far away from the busy scenes of the world, I have judged this habitation to promise me a happy resource against the solitude in which I must else live, now I am separated from her.'

'But why, my daughter,' I asked, 'are you here alone?—where are your attendants?'

'I parted from them all, for ever,' she answered, 'in the vessel which brought me to this island; I forbade them to follow me on shore, well assured of receiving from these holy walls the protection which I ask of them.'

'Why did you seek this convent in preference to any other?' I demanded.

'Because,' she replied, 'there is one sister in it who knows my family well, although we have never seen each other; and standing almost alone as I do in the world, it was an inducement to me hither, to reflect that I should live beneath a roof which sheltered one to whom my parents had been known. She to whom I allude, was the first cousin of my mother, and I remembered to have heard that she had taken the veil, at a very early age, in the convent of Saint Agnes, in the island of Auskerry; her name was Bertha Lennox—is she still living amongst your sisterhood?'

"I replied in the affirmative; she testified great joy at hearing that our sister Bertha was still alive, and requested to see her; I complied with her petition, by introducing them to each other; and the aged nun appeared to derive much satisfaction from embracing the child of the friend of her youth.

"Feeling thus convinced that the Bonny Mabel was no impostor, I accepted the offering which she had dedicated to our tutelar saint; she was immediately admitted to her noviciate, and at the regular period, took the vows of our order.

"The turn of Mabel's disposition appeared to be a settled melancholy; I knew not whether to believe it her real temper, whether to imagine that she had any secret lying at her heart, which gave her pain, or that she was dissatisfied with the religious life upon which she had voluntarily entered. I frequently spoke to her upon the subject, as did our sister Bertha; and her constant reply was—'I am very happy, quite happy, more happy here than I could be any where else;'—which words always left a doubt on my mind, whether she meant to express her heart at ease, or religiously resigned to her fate.

"About ten years after her becoming an inhabitant of this holy mansion, our sister Bertha died; Mabel and myself were by the side of her bed when her spirit fled from the earthly form which it had just before animated.—'Oh, what a happy death!' exclaimed Mabel, as she bent over her lifeless relative; 'thy endurances are all past, and thou hast no sins to account for in the world to come.'

'Nor hast thou, my daughter, I hope and trust,' I said—'Hast thou?' I added, for her words had increased those doubts concerning the tranquility of her mind which I had before entertained.

'I hope my good mother cannot think otherwise of me than as one fully confident in the mercy of heaven,' she answered, with a smile; and I again thought I had wronged her in my former opinion.

"The years passed on, unmarked by any material occurrence, till about two months ago, when the Bonny Mabel was seized with an illness which, from the first moment of her being assailed by it, seemed to threaten the termination of her existence. In a very short time, our good father confessor, who is alike the practiser of physic in our convent, pronounced it as his decided opinion that her malady must prove fatal.

"I have ever judged it a mistaken kindness to withhold from the sufferer on the bed of sickness, the knowledge we may have of his trembling upon the margin of the grave, and I therefore disclosed to her that the period of her days would be short.

'Am I then about to die?' she cried; 'endue me, heaven, with fortitude!—and do thou, my kind mother, summon hither the good father David, and receive, with tenderness and compassion, the confession of my wretched heart.'

"I complied with her request, and sent to call the father David to her chamber. When we were alone with her, she imparted to us the secret of her marriage with the Laird of Glenross, her subsequent infidelity to him with the sable knight, Sir Allanrod, and concluded by informing us, that having repented of the act of shame which she had committed, and not daring to return to her husband, she had found means of flying from her seducer, and getting herself conveyed to our convent; to enter which, under a false relation of her circumstances, she had judged, she said, to be her only means of procuring herself an asylum which could be grateful to her penitent feelings.

"It was too late to chide; all that remained for us to do, was to exhort her to prayer; but she refused to compose her mind for devotion, till I had given her my solemn promise to send a petition to her husband to come and visit her on her death-bed.—'Did she not see him, and receive her pardon from his lips,' she added, 'she should die without hope of forgiveness in the world to come.'

"The moment I had dispatched a messenger to the Laird of Glenross, she applied herself, in the most contrite manner, to acts of devotion. Thus passed on five weeks, nature growing every day weaker within her: at the expiration of that time, arrived Laird Archibald: never did I behold so affecting a countenance as his was at the moment of his first entrance beneath the roof where lay his perjured Mabel, still beloved, although so many years, blackened by infidelity, had passed since he had beheld her.

"I conducted him to the door of her chamber, and there I left him; he requested that their interview should be private.

"Nearly two hours passed before he returned to my apartment; with the placid sadness of one resigned to misfortune, he then informed me of the frailty of his Mabel, told me that she had with frankness confessed to him her crime, and alledged, as the reason for her having voluntarily plunged into sin, the jealousy which his innocent attentions to the Lady Margaret Murray had excited in her breast, and of which she had not, till too late, allowed herself to investigate the cause. The marriage of the Lady Margaret with Sir James Lambrun, and her husband's seclusion from the world, had opened her eyes to the fallacy of her opinion concerning the nature of the esteem they entertained for each other; and no sooner had this conviction reached her mind, than it was followed by a sense of her own guilty conduct, in having yielded to the delusive persuasions of Sir Allanrod; and thus corrected in her vicious course by the redawning of her reason, she had formed and executed a plan of immediately flying from her seducer, to thc retirement of a religious seclusion from the world, devoting the remainder of her days to the attempt of making her peace with heaven. By the most strict observance of every religious duty since her becoming an inhabitant of the convent of Saint Agnes, her mind, she said, had been cheered with a faint hope of forgiveness in a future state; but still she felt her death would be a most wretched one, unless she were permitted to implore, and to obtain the forgiveness of her injured husband, ere her departure from life.

"This forgiveness the excellent Laird Archibald had already granted her, and now added to it, his prayers for her happiness in a future state.

"In a short time I returned with him to the chamber of the expiring Mabel.—'If true repentance,' she said, 'be the washer out of sin, fear not for the happiness of my soul, my friends: heaven is witness how contrite a heart I have, for the last twenty years, borne within this breast. I have repented, from a conviction of my crime, not from the awe of future retribution. Oh, most exalted husband,' she added, 'there is no reward which heaven can bestow, too great for thy excellence!'

"She closed her eyes as she pronounced these words, and we believed her in silent prayer; but a few moments convinced us that her spirit had fled from its earthly habitation.

"The Laird Glenross sunk on his knees by the side of the bed, on which she lay extended in death; his hands were clasped, his eyes closed, and his head bent downwards; the whisperings of a fervent devotion burst from his lips. When he rose from his kneeling position, he fixed his eyes for a few moments upon the corpse in the most expressive silence, then addressing himself to me, he said—'I have hitherto confined the weakness which I feel within my own breast, but it can no longer be restrained.'

"With these words he burst into a violent flood of tears, and suffered me to lead him away from the chamber.

"Here ends the story of this unfortunate pair," said Saint Matilda: "the grief of the unhappy husband, after the interment of his wife, was as great as if she had never broken to him her vow of fidelity, and the prayers which he has poured forth at the altar of her saint, for the happiness of her soul, as fervent as the most spotless virtue could have drawn for its reward from the lips of a lamenting husband."

The midnight hour was on the point of sounding, when the abbess concluded the history of the Bonny Mabel, and Edward thanking her for her relation, retired to his chamber; but it was some time before sleep visited him after he had entered his bed; he lay reflecting on the baseness of Sir Allanrod's character, and considering that an equally vile seducer might be endeavouring to undermine the principles of his beloved Rosalind; so certain was he, however, of her faith, that he had no apprehensions on the score of her constancy, and only lamented the unpleasant trials to which the persecution of Lord Rufus de Madginecourt, or any other rival of his virtuous love, might expose her constancy. And whilst he was pronouncing expressions of wrath and indignation against the unknown Sir Allanrod, merely as being the seducer of that sex of which he had been born to be the protector, rather than the betrayer, he little imagined that, ere he should again clasp his Rosalind to his heart, she would be driven from the castle of her father by the savage attack made upon it by the freebooters of that very Sir Allanrod, whose character and conduct another instance of his vicious nature was leading him to execrate and condemn.

At the hour on the following morning appointed for the Laird of Glenross and Edward to become travelling companions, they met at breakfast in Saint Matilda's apartment; they were introduced as strangers to each other, and conversed as such till they had crossed that arm of the sea which brought them to the main land of the Scottish kingdom. Here Laird Archibald resumed the dress of the order of the White Penitents, of which he was a member; and shortly after, as they pursued their journey, he spoke of his own story, and the death of his Bonny Mabel.

Edward soon found that the abbess of the convent of Saint Agnes had informed the Laird of Glenross of her having communicated to him the principal events of his life; and he found also that he was not displeased at his having acquaintance with them; and as his own words gave Edward encouragement to speak upon the subject, he enquired of him, "if he was acquainted whether the base seducer of his wife were still in existence?"

Laird Archibald replied—"That he believed him to be alive."

"You will, doubtless, seek him out then," returned Edward, "and revenge on him the infidelity of a wife who was lured, by his seductive tongue, from the path of duty."

"Never, never!" answered the Laird of Glenross, "with the assumption of this habit, I made a vow of holding universal peace with man; it becomes my present character, therefore, not to persecute him for the evil he has done me, but to offer up my prayers for his forgiveness."

Edward, in the warmth of youthful feelings, judged this, if not a mistaken piety in the Laird of Glenross, at least a religious forbearance which he should himself have been averse to have exercised in a similar situation—for the ardent glow of his mind, heated by the expectation of again clasping his Rosalind in his arms, rendered him so sensitive to the passion of love, that he trembled with fancied agony, even at the tale of a seducer's triumph.

"Had you known where to have met Sir Allanrod ere you had pronounced the vows of seclusion from the world, you had not spoken thus forbearingly of the injury he has done to you," returned Edward.

"Probably not," rejoined Laird Archibald, "for I should then have acted without that discretion which the intimate acquaintance that I have since that time gained with religion, has taught me to be essential to a life of future happiness; suffice it, that I know him to be a wretch too infamous to engage the regards of the virtuous man, even in his chastisement; for to the villanous name of a seducer, he adds those of a rebel and a robber."

Here Laird Archibald paused; these particulars of Sir Allanrod he had learnt from the death-bed confession of his wife; but he refused to acquaint Edward either of what country he was a native, to what government he was a rebel, or where he held his residence.—"According to the present religious ideas to which his monastic vows compelled him, he did not," he said, "consider himself authorized to expose any human being, however unworthy he might himself know him to be, to the contumely of those he had not wronged."

"Are she who was the Lady Margaret Murray, and her husband, Sir James Lambrun, still alive?" Edward enquired.

"Yes, they are," replied the Laird of Glenross, "but it is some time since I have heard of them, and I know not whether they are at this moment in Scotland or not; their happiness has been materially broken in upon by the misfortunes of our unhappy Queen Mary, to whom their attachment was of the warmest nature. Perhaps, as you say that you are lately from abroad, you may not yet have heard that our injured monarch has fallen a victim to the hatred borne her by the Queen of England. It is now nearly six weeks since she bowed her innocent head beneath the axe, which was raised against it by the cruel commands of Elizabeth. During the whole period of her imprisonment, Sir James and his lady were her constant companions; and the only consolation which she tasted for many years previously to her death, arose from their steady friendship."

The death of Mary had not yet reached Edward, and he feared that, in the tumult of her state affairs, Elizabeth might not have had leisure to attend to the appeal of her god-daughter, Rosalind, upon her for protection; if to such an extremity she had been driven by the cruelty of her father, or the importunities of De Madginecourt; and upon this idea he became still more anxious than ever to reach England, that he might at least be relieved from the torturing apprehensions occasioned to him by his present suspense.

A few days travelling brought them into Perthshire, where they parted, the Laird of Glenross taking his road towards the monastery of the White Penitents, and Edward pursuing his course towards Northumberland.

Laird Archibald had known no more of Edward's history than that he was upon his return to a beloved wife, whom he had not for many years beheld; and when they bade each other farewell, he promised Edward to tell his beads for his prosperous journey, and safe meeting with the lady of his affections.

Edward pursued his way with all the speed he was able to make; and in the course of another week, his faithful companion, Hubert, congratulated him on the happiness of once more treading on English soil.

CHAPTER III.

Fortune is weary of oppressing me:
Thro' my dark cloud of grief, a cheerful ray
Of light breaks forth, and gilds the whole horizon.

FRANKLIN.

On the first night of their arrival in England, when they had retired to a private chamber in the habitation of a peasant by the road side, where they had obtained leave to repose themselves, Hubert thus addressed Edward—"In two days more, my dearest master, we shall reach Cumberland; it is therefore better to form the plan of our proceedings now, than to defer it till that time. You must be well aware that it becomes you to advance, with the utmost caution, towards De Mowbray Castle; you cannot want to be told, that to approach it at all, will be a task of danger, with your Rosalind for your sole friend within its walls; with her, therefore, it must be your first attempt to gain an interview, as the single person on whose services you can rely; and having communicated to her the joyful intelligence of your existence, let her advice regulate your future conduct."

"But," returned Edward, "there are no means of my gaining access to her without my being seen, and probably recognised, by the servants and soldiery of the castle, if I am so fortunate as to escape the observation of the Lord Baron De Mowbray himself."

"Ridicule not the method which I have devised for your safeguard to her presence," answered Hubert, "but consider that the exigency of the case requires desperate means to be opposed to it. As we travel through Northumberland, I will step aside from the road, to a town near which we shall pass, where I will procure you a suit of armour, such as was worn by the English soldiery on their expedition into Flanders, and as similar as possible to the one in which you left Cumberland; habited in this, you shall approach, and enter De Mowbray Castle; but not as the living Edward; you must represent the apparition of the man you are; and by striking fears, of a supernatural nature, into the minds of such as shall behold and recognise your countenance in your disguise, you will be allowed to shape your course to your own wish, uninterrupted by any one, as a religious awe will withhold every hand from stretching itself out to your molestation."

"Surely this invention will not impose upon the senses of all!" replied Edward.

"Can you, my dear master, who are so well acquainted with the timid and superstitious natures of the inhabitants of Cumberland, doubt it?" returned Hubert. "Any supernatural appearance, I am certain, would be more terrible in the eyes of them all, than a legion of Scottish freebooters drawn up against them in battle array: that which assumes the person of one who has been so well known to the greatest part of them, cannot fail to render them sufficiently cowards for the purpose you require; and having once gained admittance within the castle, by means of your disguise, you are too well acquainted with its secret turns and windings, to require from me instruction where to conceal yourself, till a favorable opportunity shall arrive for you to approach your Rosalind."

It required much persuasion on the part of the wary Hubert, to induce Edward to adopt the advice he gave him.—"It was true," Edward considered, "that he had found him, with regard to his own enlargement from the prison in Flanders, apt at stratagem, and cautious in the construction of his plans; but still he could not immediately reconcile himself to the one he had, in the present instance, devised for his approach to his beloved Rosalind."

"Do any other means, which promise you the accomplishment of your desired purpose with greater security and facility to yourself, offer themselves to your imagination?" Hubert enquired of him.

Edward replied reluctantly in the negative.*

* The text of the first edition reads "affirmative," which does not make sense in this context.

"Then be, at least, willing to make experiment of the *best method* which presents itself," rejoined Hubert; "and listen to a second inducement which I shall give you, strong as the first, for its adoption. Should the vile Alwin, who was commissioned by De Madginecourt to be the instrument of your intended death, or the Lord Rufus himself, behold you in your wanderings round the castle walls, while you shall be awaiting an apt moment for entering within them, it is more than probable that your appearance may strike terror to their guilty souls, and draw from their lips a confession of their crime; nay, if it be even heard by them that such a shape has walked by night, their caution may bend to their apprehensions, and the truth burst from their lips."

Edward was, of course, ignorant of the disagreement which had taken place between Lord William and De Madginecourt during his absence from England, and replied—"I cannot admit the slightest doubt of Lord Rufus and his train being at this time inhabitants of De Mowbray Castle: for what purpose could he have sent emissaries into Flanders, to deprive me of life, but the end of becoming himself the husband of my Rosalind, in which desire he knows that he is possessed of her father's favour?"

"And does not this very supposition point out to you," returned Hubert, "that certain danger must await your approach to the castle, in any form but the one I have proposed to you? If De Madginecourt and his attendants are the guests of the castle, will not any rumour which may be conveyed to him of the living Edward having been seen near it, cause him immediately to issue a reward for the certain performance of that act of death, in which he had been once foiled?—and will not Lord William equally, if the intelligence of your return should meet his ear, redoom you to the imprisonment from which you have escaped?—You must, you must pursue the plan I have marked out for you to follow."

"But," enquired Edward, "where will be your station, while I make the attempt of gaining admittance to the presence of my Rosalind?"

"On our arrival in Cumberland, I must immediately quit you," answered Hubert; "question me not, my dear master, upon what business I leave you, or whither my steps will be bent when we part;

but be satisfied that it is for your eventual happiness that I shall for some time be separated from you."

Edward forbore to trespass upon the request of the generous Hubert, and endeavoured to compose himself to sleep.

On the following morning they again pursued their journey, with the same energetic spirit which had marked their steps ever since they had escaped from the prison of Garcias Xavia. At a small town upon the confines of Cumberland, the suit of armour, of which Hubert had spoken, was purchased, and Edward induced to equip himself in it, according to the directions of his faithful companion.

Edward having agreed to assume the appearance of his own spirit, the deception could not be rendered too complete, and accordingly, Hubert prevailed upon him to mark his left cheek with a streak of blood, and for this reason—he had, from the chamber in his prison, heard enough of the conversation which had passed between Alwin and the governor, while in the cell of Edward, to know that the first time Alwin had wounded the corpse of the French captive who had been placed upon Edward's pallet in the prison, his tremulous hand had unintentionally struck the dagger into its cheek; and therefore thought that a representation of this wound upon the cheek of Edward, would be a mark that must at once convey the history of the supposed spirit, and its appearance on earth, to all such as were in the confidence of De Madginecourt and his adherent Alwin.

Edward's equipment took place towards the close of evening, on the skirts of a wood which divided Cumberland from the more northern county. But three hours travelling lay between Edward and De Mowbray Castle, and he resolved to approach it under the cover of the shade of night, a time which Hubert, with a smile, enjoined him always to choose for leaving his spots of concealment, as a necessary observance for sustaining his present character.

"Here then, for a while, we part," said Hubert; and he again repeated—"Question me not on the business that takes me from you, but rely on my being employed for your eventual happiness."

"When and where shall we meet again?" asked Edward.

"When," answered Hubert, "I cannot with exactness determine; the spot will, in all probability, be De Mowbray Castle."

Hubert having then made a transfer of part of the gold which he had still remaining from the safehold of his trusty waistcoat to the pocket of Edward, they bade each other an affectionate farewell, and took separate roads.

The agitated mind with which Edward pursued his way, may be easily imagined. Again he felt dissatisfied with the disguise he had assumed, and anxious to exchange the plan for some other; but he could devise none, nor had he the means of putting any other into execution, if even it had entered his imagination.

Just as the castle clock struck eleven, he reached the moat; his heart beat with rapture at beholding the walls that enclosed his Rosalind; but the possibility of her having been already forced into the arms of another, on the report of his death, suddenly turned his tide of rapture into the most acute pain.

In a short time he saw a man approaching towards the spot where he stood; he moved up to him, in order to try what effect his disguise would produce upon him; an exclamation of terror burst from his lips, and he fled. Edward was thus satisfied that his appearance was answerable to the expectation which Hubert had formed of it; but he was sorry that it had frightened away from him his old friend Ambrose, to whom he should have felt little reluctance in confiding his secret.

The alarm which was occasioned to Ambrose, and to the sentinel, Simon Williams, by their observation of a figure in armour wandering on the outside of the castle walls, has already been mentioned, and its cause explained in what we have just related of Edward. Suffice it to say, that after having undergone the necessity of hiding himself for three successive days, in a cave with which he was acquainted, in the neighbourhood of the castle, on the fourth evening after his separation from his friend Hubert, chance favoured him in his attempt at crossing the drawbridge, after Lord William and his men had passed over it, at the time of their setting out on their march against the advanced body of Allanrod's troops.

The additional effects of terror which were produced on old Ambrose, and Philip Watkins, the sentinel of the hour, at the foot of the bridge, by beholding what they believed an aerial being, bearing a resemblance in its countenance to the lost Edward, and disfigured with a bloody gash down its left cheek, have also been detailed to our readers; we have, therefore, in this place, only to speak of Edward himself.

Not alone from the testimony which Edward had received that the appearance of his person had struck terror into the minds of all who beheld him, but also from the observation he had made from his spot of concealment hard by, that a large number of the Baron's soldiery had quitted the castle that night, from which cause he knew that the ramparts would be less thickly planted with sentinels than they at other times were; he ventured boldly to pursue his way towards a part of the glacis, from whence arose a portion of the rampart wall that encircled the terrace walk, upon which opened a door communicating with the apartment that had at his departure from the castle been occupied by Rosalind.

From the glacis, he immediately began to climb the intervening wall: the moment his head was raised above it, his eyes fell on a female at a short distance from him, which the glow of his heart instantly informed him could be no other than the mistress of his affections. Trembling with the emotion raised in his breast by a variety of contending feelings, he could not, on his first attempt to address her, command his utterance at all; a second attempt enabled him faintly to pronounce her name, and the instant that she turned her head towards the spot where he was stationed, he heard a door open, and a voice, which the apprehension of a discovery from an enemy prevented him from recognizing to be Gertrude's, addressing her. Thus fearful of detection, he immediately disappeared; and when the return of silence encouraged him again to ascend to the top of the wall, Rosalind was not only gone, but the sentry of the night placed before the turret, through which lay the passage from the rampart to her apartments.

Disappointed, but not discouraged, he turned his thoughts to the reflection of where he should conceal himself during the next day; he had now passed the drawbridge, and the cave, which had before been favourable to his retreat from observation during the hours of day, was no longer attainable. He remembered the communication leading from the northern ramparts to the vaults beneath the castle, and thence to the chapel, through which his friend Hubert had conducted him to his concealed interviews with Rosalind, when he had stolen by night away from the tower in the village. To the privacy of these he resolved to commit himself; and having, with the use of the utmost caution and slow proceeding, reached them without attracting the observation of any individual, he believed himself, for a time at least, once more in safety.

The morning was already beginning to break, ere Edward reached the interior of his hiding-place; he therefore resolved not to emerge from it into any of the avenues which led towards the chapel, till the succeeding night should again have spread the veil of darkness over the earth.

When the hollow-toned clock of the castle had once more sounded the hour of midnight, Edward directed his steps towards the chapel; the beams of the moon peeping through various slender chasms in the rocky ceiling of the vaults through which he was moving, and gliding through the frame-work of the decayed cloisters, which ran at intervals along the side of his path, guided him to it. The full disk of a resplendant moon shone through a spiral window at one end of the building, and its refulgent light rested on the altar at the opposite extremity. The eye of Edward fell on it, and he stood for some time resigned to an overpowering sensation which filled his mind, as he gazed upon the shrine at which he had become the husband of Rosalind.

Places where the most interesting events of our lives have taken place, when beheld at any remote period from the time of their happening, excite in us sensations of the most acute nature. Imagination places around them the same personages, causes them to react the same scenes which are impressed upon our memory, and we encourage the delusion with a warmth amounting almost to the real joy or pain which we experienced at the memorable moments that have inscribed them on our recollection.

By Hubert, Edward had been supplied with the implements for striking a light, and by their means he now applied himself to illumine one of the lamps, of which there were always several dispersed about in various niches in the walls, ready for burning on any solemn occasion which required the evening use of the chapel.

From the chapel he had resolved boldly to pursue his way through the castle to the chamber of Gertrude; and having made himself known to her, employ her to announce his existence to his beloved wife; accordingly, the moment his lamp was lighted, he proceeded to the massive door which opened into the passage communicating with the corridor that led into the great hall of the castle.

To his severe disappointment, and contrary to former custom, he found it locked, and impervious to every attempt he made to open it.

We have already said, that as the incursions of the borderers became more determined, it had been deemed dangerous to suffer it to remain unsecured, and that, on this account, its key had been added to the number of those which it was the duty of old Ambrose, as the porter of the castle, to keep in his custody.

In disappointment and reflection, Edward sunk down upon the base of a pillar, which afforded a resting-place for his harassed and enervated frame. After some time passed in thought, he recollected that at the time of his quitting England, Rosalind had been in the constant habit of praying, once in the course of every revolving day, by the side of her deceased mother's tomb: the intimate acquaintance which he had with the virtuous and steady principles of her heart, led him to suppose that the calamities which she had since that period been doomed to experience, would, if possible, have strengthened her constancy and fervour in her former habits of devotion; and thus assured, in his own opinion, that there could not be the slightest doubt of her accustomary visit to the grave of the Lady de Mowbray being performed in the course of the following day, his first resolve was to remain in the chapel till she should appear in it; but a little farther consideration pointing out to him that she might come to it, attended by those over whose conduct she might not have sufficient power to restrain them from bearing intelligence of his existence to his enemies, his final determination was to place, upon the marble tomb which enclosed the ashes of the late Baroness, the cross of rubies which she had bequeathed to him by the name of mother, and which he had vowed to Rosalind never to part from but in death.

This cross he had constantly worn upon his breast, from the first moment of his receiving it at the hand of Lord William, a short time after the death of the Lady de Mowbray; and he concluded it impossible that Rosalind should not behold it, as she knelt in devotion by the side of the tomb; and equally so, that she should not conclude its being placed there a testimony of his existence, and of his not being far distant from the spot where she should find it. The issue of this plan, he doubted not, would be her devising some means of seeing him alone in the chapel, or of conveying to him instruction concerning the conduct which it would be becoming in him to pursue, for their mutual safety and happiness.

Thus resolved, he took the cross from the ribband by which it was suspended round his neck, and having placed it upon a white speck of the marble which composed the tomb, he returned again to his concealment amidst the vaults.

Night after night, with increased anxiety, he visited the chapel; and to his inexpressible astonishment and grief, the cross was still unmoved from the situation in which he had placed it. This repeated disappointment of his highly raised hope of beholding his cross exchanged for some token placed on the spot for him to find by the hand of his Rosalind, rendered him not alone uncertain what to conjecture of her fate, but equally so how it became him to proceed for gaining any information concerning her, or obtaining an interview with her. To this end his soul was day and night upon the rack of thought; but in every point of view in which he could place it, the idea of his emerging from his present concealment, or attempting to enter into conversation with any of the inhabitants of the castle, appeared so replete with danger, both to himself and the wife of his affections, that he was compelled to decide it an insurmountable necessity for him to keep himself a close prisoner in the vaults, till he should either again see Hubert, or receive intelligence from him.

At parting, Hubert had informed him that their next meeting would be at De Mowbray Castle, although he had not fixed any time when that meeting was to be expected: earnestly he prayed that his arrival might not be long protracted; and as he doubted not, let Hubert come to the castle in what character he might, that the story of an alarming spectre having passed the drawbridge would reach his ear, and be to him sufficient information that his master was secreted in some part of the fabric, the hardships of his case were somewhat softened by the assurance that Hubert would lose no time in discovering his retreat, and console him at least with his friendship, if it was not in his power to conduct him to the happiness at which he aspired.

To the wretchedness of his mind were added bodily inconveniences, which heightened the unpleasantness of his situation; his bed was of no softer material than the uneven clods of earth which composed the floor of the vaults, and his provisions such as he contrived by night to steal from a storehouse near the entrance to the vaults from the rampart, where bread of the coarsest kind was piled on the days of its being baked at the castle, against it should be fetched away by a person appointed for that purpose, to the tower of strength in the village, for the use of the soldiery it contained.

It will be remembered that Rosalind visited the chapel on the morning succeeding the departure of her father from De Mowbray Castle; and that morning, it will be perceived, was the one previous to the night in which Edward placed his cross upon the tomb of the deceased Baroness. In the course of this very night occurred the illness of Gertrude, which our readers have already been informed withheld Rosalind for seventeen mornings from paying her accustomed devotions in the chapel: on the eighteenth, the amendment of Gertrude's health was such, that she again repaired to that spot where her devotions were performed with the greatest satisfaction to her own mind. With her finding the cross, and her subsequent resolution of visiting the chapel by night, at the hour she had, previously to her marriage, been accustomed to meet Edward in it, our readers are also acquainted, and with the sudden discovery of the approach of the freebooters to an attack upon the castle, at the moment she had reached the great hall in her way towards it.

At the same moment of time that Rosalind was descending from her chamber, Edward, who did not relax in his nightly visits to the chapel, although increasing disappointment alone marked the periods of his entering it, made the joyful discovery of his cross being removed from the spot where he had placed it; but scarcely had the rapture which had been admitted at his eyes, communicated itself to his heart, ere his ears were assailed by the blast of the trumpets blown from the advanced body of the enemy, and replied to by similar sounds from the heights of the castle.

For a time he supposed that the sounds might predict the return of that body of men whom he had seen march from the castle on the night in which he had gained a passage over the drawbridge; but when the clangour of contending arms ran through the air, with the discovery of his error, he felt himself entirely at a loss to decide what could be the cause of its present hostilities, as he did not suppose that the audacity of the moss-troopers had arisen to a sufficient height to encourage them to hazard a regular attack, such as he could discover that which was now passing to be.

A prey to the most torturing suspense of mind, Edward wandered about the chapel; a thousand different ideas crowding into his brain, a thousand various plans entering his imagination, and undecided which to select, or indeed whether it became him to put any one of them into execution or not: at one moment, trembling for the safety of his Rosalind, he resolved to rush boldly into the castle, to search her out, and present himself as her lawful champion; at another, he determined to issue from the vaults, and ascertain who were the enemies of the castle: cooler reflection then represented to him that he had not the power of entering the castle walls, and that by issuing out from the vaults, he should expose himself, without the possibility of benefit accruing either to himself or his Rosalind from such an exposure, to the fire and arrows of the soldiers upon its walls.

At length he recollected that from a dormitory, now ruinous and in disuse, behind the chancel of the chapel, there had once been a communication with a small bastion, which had been a spot of defence to the building in its monastic state, but which was now entirely neglected, since it had become a regularly fortified castle. To this he resolved, if possible, to trace out his way, in the hope of obtaining from it a view of the contest which was passing without, and which he considered, by his being able to form a judgment of it only from the single sense of hearing, might thus be magnified to his imagination.

With some difficulty he found the steps, the entrance to which he had once before seen, but never yet attempted to ascend; the iron hand of time had so far misshapen and despoiled them of their former properties, that no one, without the spur of feelings like those by which Edward was at the moment actuated, could have made his way up the ascent which they had once afforded; with much time and labour he effected it. On looking out from the ruined bastion, he found the day already to be rising, and the contention of arms to have ceased; his situation was not a favourable one for viewing the ramparts, being too much confined within the walls of the castle;

and as the enemy were not visible without the moat, he concluded them conquerors, and already within the building.—"Almighty God, preserve my Rosalind!" burst in quivering accents from his lips; and scarcely had the exclamation escaped them, ere he perceived a vehicle, which was drawn by four horses, and attended by some men on horseback, passing over the drawbridge. A secret instinct, inexplicable, except it be that every circumstance of which we know not the exact cause, gives us additional anxiety for the safety of those about whose fate we are uncertain, and at the same time most anxious, instantly caused Edward to believe his Rosalind confined in the carriage he had seen; and without any decided plan in view, he made a hasty effort to retrace his way from the bastion to the dormitory below; and incautious with regard to the ruinous path he had to tread, he fell, and his head struck with such violence against the wall of the turret, through which he was descending, that the blow deprived him of all sense.

CHAPTER IV.

Has pitying Heav'n consented to my pray'r?
It has! it has!——————————
But language poorly speaks the joy I feel;
Let passion paint, and looks express my soul.

HENRY JONES.

WHEN Edward recovered the power of recollection, and again raised himself upon his feet, the first sound which he heard was the castle clock striking the ninth hour of the morning; and when its hollow tones had died away upon the air, a solemn silence prevailed. He returned to the chapel, and his eye falling upon the altar, he found it despoiled of the tripod lamps of silver which had before stood on marble pedestals on the sides of the sacramental table; and the golden eagle, upon which the sacred volume had hitherto been supported, was likewise gone: and these observations convinced him that whosoever had been the enemies of De Mowbray Castle, theirs had been the victory.

He moved towards the door of the chapel leading into the body of the castle; he found it burst from the lock, and standing open. He approached it, and as he stood listening with eager desire to catch some sound which might convey to him information, whether or not the enemy had yet quitted the place, he leaned for support upon the open door, for a faint sickness oppressed him; and although he at present felt little anguish from the blow which he had received upon his head, he was sensible of an aching numbness, which seemed to be the forerunner of much acute pain.

For above two hours he continued to wander at the distance of a few feet from the door of the chapel, near the entrance into the vaulted corridor leading into the great hall of the castle; and as no sound, either within the building, or on its exterior, met his ear, save the periodical voice of the clock, he began to imagine the castle deserted; for even in his concealment in the vaults, he had scarcely ever passed five minutes together without some sound reaching him, either from the sentinels on the walls, the closing of doors within the castle, or similar causes of noise.

Another hour, passed in the same uninterrupted stillness, convinced him that the inhabitants were fled, and he began to proceed towards the marble hall; arrived there, the same scene of devastation, which we have already described Lord William to have witnessed on his return to his castle from the strong-hold of the freebooter Allanrod, met the eye of Edward.

With grief and astonishment he contemplated the scene before him; how altered the appearance of all around him, since those happy days when he had lived the friend of Rosalind, and the friend of the Baron! He ascended to her chamber, and it afforded him a slender gratification to behold the various articles of furniture which it contained; with most of which he had, as it were, an intimate acquaintance, and which still remained in their accustomed places, having been considered of too little value by the enemy to be made part of their pillage.

Burning with thirst, for the fever into which the agitation of his mind had thrown his blood, was increased by the pain which was the consequence of his fall, he descended into a lower part of the building, and proceeded towards a marble cistern, at the extremity of one of the corridors branching out from the great hall; the gilt cups which had been wont to be found in the bason, had been rent by the despoilers of the castle, from the light chains by which they had for years past been fastened to it; and Edward, taking off his casque, received into it the grateful stream for which his parched throat panted.

As he raised his eyes from the casque after his draught, they fell upon the figure of a man in an attitude of surprise, at the opposite extremity of the passage, who almost instantly uttered an exclamation of alarm, and fled.

Scarcely had the man disappeared, ere Edward recollected both his countenance and his name; he was the very Philip Watkins who had been the sentinel at the drawbridge on the night that Edward had passed over it in his disguise, and as Edward was still in the same suit of armour, with the same representation of a streak of blood marked upon his left cheek, he was not much surprised to find that Philip fled from him; what most surprised him was, that he alone should be remaining in the castle when every other inhabitant appeared to have fled from it.

It had so chanced, that on the night of the freebooters' attack upon the castle of De Mowbray, Philip Watkins had been the sentinel at the watch-tower; at the approach of the enemy, he had exerted his lungs with due effect, and blown a hearty blast of alarm to the inhabitants of the castle; and whether he conceived that he had performed all his duty in so doing, or whether he had any particular aversion to oppose the enemy with more substantial efforts than the wind which he had sent at them through his trumpet, is not exactly ascertained; all we are informed of the business is, that when the attack was over, and the castle had surrendered to the enemy, Philip was still safe and snug in his watch-tower, from whence he had seen such of his comrades as had fallen in the contest, buried beneath a tumulus cast up for that purpose on the outside of the walls, and those who had survived, led away prisoners by the conquering party.

The same vaulted passage or corridor, at the extremity of which was the cistern, led also to the kitchens of the castle, and towards them Philip was proceeding, in order to examine whether the freebooters had left him a dinner; his first glimpse of Edward filled him with terror, but scarcely had he fled from him, when recollecting that he had always heard it affirmed that spirits never were visible except by night, he assumed courage to take a second look. For this purpose he returned cautiously to the passage, and the moment he again appeared in sight, Edward hailed him.—"You are Edward alive!—Are you not Edward himself alive?" replied Philip to his exclamation.

Edward advanced hastily towards him. "Yes, I am," he said; "keep my secret, and you have nothing to fear from me; but should you disclose it, you may work my ruin, and thus merit my resentment."

"Alas!" replied Philip, "there is no one left within these walls for me to communicate it to; wheresoever you may have been concealed about them, you must have heard the attack that has been made during the night; all the survivors of the siege are the prisoners of the freebooter Allanrod."

"Allanrod!" exclaimed Edward, for the seducer of the Bonny Mabel immediately recurred to his memory, as did the epithet of 'robber,' which Laird Archibald Glenross had given him: "Allanrod!" he repeated.

Philip immediately began to explain the terror which this mysterious freebooter had, for some time past, been to the English borders, and to recount Lord William's marching against him, and the ill success which it was conjectured, from his not having since that time returned to his castle, had attended his expedition; but Edward, scarcely listening to his words, or permitting him to utter them, urged the most impatient enquiries after his Rosalind.

With astonishment he heard from Philip, the enmity which had broken out between Lord William and Lord Rufus de Madginecourt, and with rapture did he learn that no other suitor had been forced upon her by her father: but the tide of joy which filled his heart on gaining this information, was quickly turned into an opposite feeling, upon the recollection that she was now the prisoner of the infamous, the villanous Allanrod—perhaps already the victim of his lust, or loaded with chains within his strong-hold; and with the wildness of delirium he expressed aloud his apprehensions.

Philip Watkins was one of those to whom Edward had in his boyish days been indebted for his first knowledge of military exercises: when the soldiers of the castle had been drawn out on the ramparts for inspection or exercise, Philip had often indulged him, by suffering him to bear his pike for a short time on his shoulder, and sometimes had given him a lesson in the management of the crossbow. These kindnesses had made an impression on the heart of Edward; and when the Baron, some years after, doubled the number of his troops, as the incursions of the moss-troopers became more formidable, Edward procured for Philip an advance in his profession, which Philip had ever felt pleasure in acknowledging that he owed to the indulgence he had shewn Edward when a boy.

So great had been the esteem in which the urbanity of Edward's manners and the benevolence of his heart had caused him to be held at De Mowbray Castle, that at the time of the false intelligence of his death being circulated in it, few of its household did not let fall a tear to his memory; and amongst the most sincere mourners for his fate, next to his afflicted wife, one in particular had been Philip Watkins: his joy, therefore, at seeing him still alive, was at least equal to the sorrow he had felt for his supposed death; and he instantly demanded how he could be of use to him, declaring himself entirely devoted to his service.

Edward remembered, with equal satisfaction as Philip bore it in his memory, the intimacy which had subsisted between them, when he was about half the length of the pike which he had been so emulous of handling; and Philip being, besides, almost the only person whom he had ever heard Hubert speak of as an honest fellow, he felt no repugnance, situated as they both were, at that moment, to give him a short sketch of what had befallen him since his departure from England.

"Now then," said Edward, as he concluded what he deemed a sufficient account of his adventures to interest Philip in his fate, "now, if thou wouldst indeed serve me, devise some means for bringing me into the presence of my Rosalind; give me thy assistance to rescue her from the power of the freebooter Allanrod."

Philip repeated, "that howsoever it was in his power to serve him, he might command him."—He then proceeded to inform Edward, that he did not believe the Lady Rosalind had been conducted to the fortress of the borderers; from his elevated situation in the watch-tower, he had, he said, been able to command an extensive view of the country. She had, as Edward had imagined, been carried away from the castle in the vehicle which he had seen pass over the drawbridge; but it had proceeded towards the south, in an exactly opposite direction to the track followed by the victorious freebooters, when they had borne off, in triumph, their prisoners and spoil; they had moved directly north, and from the north they likewise had marched when he had first beheld them in the night, approaching to their attack upon the castle.—"It therefore appeared to him," he said, "that the Lady Rosalind had, by the order of the chief of the horde, been conveyed to some place less repugnant to the feelings of a delicate female, than the fortress of a banditti must have proved to them, where it was his design to detain her till a ransom was offered for her person."

All the haunts of the moss-troopers were known to be upon the borders of the Scottish kingdom; few had even ventured to settle themselves upon the confines of England: the idea accordingly formed by Philip, of Rosalind's destination, appeared probable to Edward, and he immediately expressed his wish to endeavour to trace out the road by which she had journied, in order that he might learn the spot where she was detained, and, if possible, by his presence, corroborate that idea of his being still in existence, which he doubted not she must have conceived upon finding his cross on the tomb of her mother; and that by her the cross had been removed from the spot where he had placed it, Philip had convinced him, by assuring him that no one but herself ever entered the chapel, except on the Sunday.

All carriages were at that time so rare throughout the kingdom, especially in the more remote northern counties, that Philip did not despair of very easily gaining information where such a one had passed, provided its route had been taken within view of any of the cottages or sheepfolds, which were scattered about the country.

Accordingly, having prevailed on Edward to take some refreshment, (to induce him to allot a portion of his care to the hurt he had received on his head, and which was now so much swelled as to prevent him from wearing his casque, he was unable,) they set out, Edward having thrown a plain surtout over his suit of armour, and put upon his head a soldier's bonnet as a substitute for his casque.

For more than two leagues, they were able to proceed from the observations which Philip had made upon the vehicle in its progress, from his situation in the watch-tower, which were greatly assisted by the track of the wheels, which was discernable on the sandy roads over which it had passed. Early in the evening, Philip prevailed on his companion to stop for the night at an hospitable cottage, which afforded them accommodation as weary travellers, and whose owner, at the entreaty of Philip, called in a neighbour who had some little skill in surgery, and who applied a healing medicine to the bruise on Edward's head, of which he was himself too careless for his own safety; so true is it, that the wounds of the body are not felt, at least not regarded, when he who bears them suffers at the same moment under any mental calamity.

Pursuing their journey on the following day, by the information which they were able to gather from the shepherds, who had seen the vehicle which they described, pass their folds, and, at intervals, assisted by the marks which the wheels had left of their passage, towards evening they came up with a party of pilgrims, who were returning to their homes, from a pilgrimage they had been making to the lady at Walsingham, and whom, with their minstrels and some other travellers who had joined company with them, in order that their number might prove a defence to them against the freebooters, of whom there was a general terror throughout the northern parts of the kingdom, they found seated on the side of a shady hill, regaling themselves on the contents of their wallets.

With the hospitality customary to their profession, the pilgrims invited Edward and his companion to partake of their homely fare: they were faint with travelling, and readily accepted the offered kindness. Whilst they sat amongst them, it entered the imagination of Edward, that any disguise must be preferable for him to attempt gaining an interview with his Rosalind in, to the suit of armour which he now wore, and which might render him, he judged, a suspicious character to her guards; accordingly, producing some of the gold with which Hubert had, at their last parting, furnished him, he privately offered a couple of pieces to one of the pilgrims, who had informed him that he had now but one more day's journey to his house, in exchange for his robe, his staff, and his hat. The pilgrim had no objection to so advantageous a sale of articles, of which he sincerely hoped he should never stand in need again; and the bargain was, without hesitation, struck.

Having equipped himself, Edward endeavoured to make a similar purchase for Philip; but no other of the pilgrims was sufficiently near home, to authorize his quitting the dress of his present profession; and, therefore, he found his desired end of habiting his companion like himself, unattainable; but Philip entering into Edward's idea, meanwhile made so successful a suit, by the powerful argument of gold, to one of the minstrels, who, he found, loved money better than music, even in the holy service of lightening their way to journeying pilgrims, which was his avocation, that he obtained of him the promise of a spare doublet and cloak, with which he was furnished in a knapsack at his back, and likewise a lute, in playing upon which Philip possessed some little skill; and he judged that it might not prove an unacceptable passport for them to the prison of the Lady Rosalind, if she was at the present moment the inhabitant of one. Accordingly, having made his agreement with the young minstrel, he applied to Edward for the purchase-money of his new accoutrements; and Edward having rewarded the minstrel as liberally as he had done the pilgrim, the lad, on seeing the money, said—"Indeed you have the worst of the bargain, for I shall reach my own town to-morrow, where I can buy all the same articles I have sold to you for two-thirds of the price you have paid me for them."

"The better luck for thyself," said Philip, satisfied that Edward's wish had been gratified in the obtaining of their disguises; and they then bade farewell to the party of travellers by whom they had been regaled, and set forward.

About noon, on the fourth day after their quitting De Mowbray Castle, as they ascended an eminence in the road, the sea, at a short distance, burst upon them; and Edward, on perceiving it, began to suppose that they must, after all, have pursued a wrong track. Whilst they were in debate together, some villagers of different sexes approached them, dressed in what appeared their holiday apparel. Philip addressed them, for it had been agreed between him and Edward, that lest Edward should in his speech betray himself to suspicion, he should pass for the dumb brother of his companion.—"What castle is that?" asked Philip.

"Rockmount," they replied, "the castle of Lord Rufus de Madginecourt."

Edward gave an involuntary start at the sound.

"We are all going thither," rejoined one of the females, "to celebrate the birthday of the old housekeeper, Dame Edith, who is today one hundred years old."

"Then, I suppose, my Lord himself is not at the castle?" enquired Philip.

"I don't know," replied the female who had before spoken.

"But I do," cried one of the males: "Lord Rufus left it this day, at early morn, and it is thought that he is gone to London, to ask our queen's advice about a young lady that he has rescued from a band of moss-troopers."

"The queen's advice!" said Philip.

"Aye," returned the man, "the young lady whom he delivered from her enemies, is our gracious queen's own god-daughter: her name is De Mowbray, the daughter of the richest and greatest noble in all Cumberland."

This act of humanity, on the part of the hitherto unfeeling De Madginecourt, to the woman who had slighted his addresses, was surprising information to Edward; it exceeded all the enigmas in which his life had hitherto been involved.

"Perhaps," said Philip, "as there is to be a merry meeting at the castle, a little of my music would prove acceptable; and it would be a great charity done to my poor brother and myself, if they would admit us for a short time within its walls."

"Oh, I doubt not but ye will be welcome," replied the young man; "I have interest with the housekeeper's niece, who is one of the domestics, and you shall have my recommendation."

They trudged on towards the castle; the villagers walked boldly over the drawbridge, telling Edward and Philip to remain at its foot, till they had given intimation of them at the castle, saying that they would shortly return and inform them whether their presence would be agreeable within it.

The few minutes that Edward and his companion were left alone, they passed in imperfect surmises on the unaccountable information they had just received, of Rosalind being under the protection of Lord Rufus de Madginecourt: thankful, however, that he had gained knowledge of the place of her retreat, all Edward at the present moment desired, was permission to enter the walls within which she was enclosed.

In a very short time, the young peasant who had promised to be their advocate with the servants of the castle, returned at the head of about a dozen of them, who gave the supposed minstrel and his brother a most cordial invitation to enter, and conducted them to the great hall, where they were to be regaled with Dame Edith's treat.

Philip Watkins was but an indifferent performer on an instrument, and the voice with which he accompanied it was by no means one of the best; but he was well stored in old ballads and romances, and luckily for him, it appeared that his audience infinitely preferred the matter which was sung to the manner in which it was executed; thus he proved exactly the musician suited to their taste. What most puzzled him, were the questions which they were continually asking of him concerning his brother, as whence arose his dumbness?—whither he was conducting him?—and various other enquiries of the like nature.

When the night began to advance, Philip excused himself from singing any more, saying that he was exhausted with the amusement he had already given them; but that if they would suffer him and his brother to sleep at the castle that night, he would willingly play and sing to them the whole of the next day, if it gave them pleasure. To these terms they agreed with much satisfaction; and Philip and Edward were accordingly served with their supper, and shewn to a chamber.

Concealed under his pilgrim's garb, Edward still wore the suit of armour which had been provided for him by Hubert. Beneath the roof of Lord Rufus de Madginecourt, where it was probable to suppose that the villanous Alwin was existing, he considered that the supernatural appearance which he had assumed on his entrance into De Mowbray Castle, was, of all other places, the one most likely for him to derive the safeguard from it, which he desired it to afford him: the present night, he also reflected, might be the only one which he should have the liberty of passing within the walls of Rockmount. Thus, if he did not use the passing hour for venturing forth into the castle in quest of the apartment of his Rosalind, he might lose the only opportunity that would ever be granted for endeavouring to gain an interview with her.

Acting under this idea, the moment he believed the inhabitants of the castle retired to rest, he issued from his chamber; he had no clue by which to guide his steps, save a single expression which had fallen from the lips of Dame Edith on quitting her guests.—"I must now," she had said, "return to my charge in the western gallery."—This charge he could not doubt to be Rosalind, and, therefore, towards the western gallery he resolved to bend his course.

Contrary to the opinion which Edward had formed, previously to his quitting his chamber, of all the castle being already locked in sleep, he had proceeded but a very little way in his search of the western gallery, before the sound of voices struck his ear, and before he had time to decide from whence they had proceeded, a door opposite to him was opened, and from it issued about half a dozen of the domestics, in the act of leading to bed two of their fellows, for the strength of whose brains, the mead with which Dame Edith had regaled them, had proved of too potent a nature.

Edward was immediately seen by one of the party, who, with a dreadful outcry, proclaimed his cause of terror to the rest: the cries of fear burst from every mouth; those who were able, fled—and those who required support in their movements, fell to the ground.

Not doubting that an alarm would be raised throughout the castle, Edward, with all precipitancy, returned to his chamber, and giving Philip a hasty command to preserve silence, he drew on his pilgrim's habit, blew out his lamp, and threw himself upon his bed.

The stillness of the mansion continued unbroken, no sound reaching the chamber of Edward and his companion but the hoarse voice of the waves, which beat against the rock it stood upon, and Edward began to suppose that the domestics had not aroused any of their fellows, in consequence of the alarm they had experienced from beholding him; but he durst not again venture to quit his chamber that night, upon the same business which had before led him from it; and he lay beseeching Philip to exert himself to the utmost on the following day, to entertain the servants, in order to give them a chance of being invited to pass a second night in the castle.

As soon as they arose in the morning, a relation was given of the horrible apparition which had been seen by a party of the servants in the night, and Edward could scarcely refrain from a smile at the many exaggerations with which the simple fact was now increased into the most terrific of all terrible histories. To Dame Edith the story was also recounted, and by her, it will be remembered that intelligence of what had been seen was conveyed to Rosalind, who experienced some degree of surprise at the similarity of the appearance to that which had a short time before been witnessed at De Mowbray Castle, still little suspecting how nearly the interest of herself and the spectre were connected.

Philip took advantage of the impression which the story of the spectre had made on the minds of the inhabitants of Rockmount Castle, and sung to them many monkish traditions of ghosts and goblins, which, to his desire, brought on evening again, without any hint having been given to him, and his nominal brother, to quit the place; accordingly, he petitioned that they might have leave given them to retire to their resting-place of the former night; for which permission was scarcely granted them, ere a great bustle was occasioned in the castle, by the return of Lord Rufus, and those who had attended him in his expedition.

The pleasure with which Edward had looked forward to the hour of retiring to rest, was entirely overthrown at the arrival of the anticipated period, for he then found that a second bed in the chamber where he and Philip Watkins had reposed on the preceding night, was to be occupied by two of the grooms who had returned to the castle along with Lord Rufus. Thus circumstanced, he perceived that it would be impossible for him to repeat the attempt in which he had, on the foregoing night, failed, with any hope of greater success attending upon it, and he lay stretched on his pallet, a victim to the agonies of despair. He considered that as soon as the morning should arise, and they should again descend into the hall of the castle, they would be told to depart, and thus every chance of his desired end in coming thither cut off. At one moment he resolved boldly to stalk forth in his disguise, and enter the presence of Lord Rufus, and his villanous associate, Alwin; he doubted not but that his appearance would strike terror to their souls, and wring from their lips a confession of the murder which they believed themselves to have committed; but he, at the same time, reflected that the deceit could not long pass upon their senses; and that the spot he was now on, was one which would, of all others, be the most favourable to his enemies for completing the purpose in which they had once been foiled; and this reflection withheld him from venturing into their presence.

When they arose in the morning, and returned to the hall of the kitchen, the first words they heard from the domestics informed them, that an enemy was shortly expected to besiege the castle, and that every preparation was to be made within it, with all speed and industry, for repelling the attack.

Philip enquired who the dreaded enemy was?

"The united bands of the moss-troopers," was the reply, "who had vowed vengeance against Lord Rufus de Madginecourt, for having rescued the Lady Rosalind de Mowbray from Allanrod, who was one of the most esteemed chiefs."

Again Edward was thrown into astonishment, by hearing Lord Rufus named as the protector of his Rosalind.—"Could it be possible," he reflected, "that Rosalind would submit to owe her protection to the man who had been the cause of all her misery in life—now, too, when enmity had broken out between him and her father!"—The mystery which he had before been unable to solve, was now become still more obscure; the only thing of which he was certain was, that if Lord Rufus was indeed the true friend of his Rosalind, there remained no doubt, from the attempt which had been made to take away his life, that he was still his decided enemy; and this conviction made him infinitely more suspicious of the friendship which he was making a display of rendering her.

"If the freebooters are advancing from their strong-holds to an attack upon this castle," rejoined Philip, "I pray you to permit us to remain within its walls till the contest be decided; for our road lies north, and should we encounter them, little as it is that we have to be plundered of, I very much fear that they would not spare us: I beseech you, therefore, kind masters, to let us abide here till we can proceed with more safety."

His petition produced the desired effect; the servants took pity upon him, and his helpless brother, as they considered Edward, and consented to their remaining at the castle till after the siege.

During the course of the two following days, Philip, in his intercourse with the domestics, lost no opportunity of introducing into his conversation, the name of the Lady Rosalind, and endeavouring to gain some tidings concerning her; but all he could gather relative to her, was, that Lord Rufus had declared he would sooner part with his life or his liberty himself, than surrender her into the hands of the freebooter Allanrod; and that the servants had discovered that she no longer inhabited the apartments in the western gallery, which had been set apart for her use on her first arrival at Rockmount; and that, from the little fear which their Lord testified for her personal safety during the threatened siege, and the sudden disappearance of Dame Edith, and her grand-nephew, Zachary, from the inhabited parts of the building, they conjectured her to have retired, at the advice of Lord Rufus, for protection, to some subterraneous vaults on the left of the castle, in which, they said, there were an apartment or two, which had formerly been fitted up as a dwelling.

The moment the arrival of the freebooters on the outside of the castle called its inhabitants from the interior parts of the walls and ramparts, in order to repel the attempts of the besiegers to subdue it, Edward and his companion, left without any observers of their actions, immediately began to search for the entrance into the subterranean vaults, of which the servants had spoken to Philip Watkins.

They proceeded towards the left, in which direction the conversation of the servants had informed them lay the object of their search, and, after some time, they discovered a long and vaulted passage, growing gradually narrower as they drew towards its extremity, and which, from the singularity of its form tallying with the description which their kitchen friends had given of the entrance of the vaults, they could not doubt to be the same of which they had spoken.

But when they had reached the end, although assisted in their search by the light of a lamp borne by Philip, no door was discoverable in the wainscot, although the hollow sound which it returned to a blow struck upon it by the hand of Edward, convinced them that there was an extensive vacancy beyond it.

It has been already said, in a foregoing part of this history, that the door which formed the entrance into the subterraneous vaults leading to the grotto, opened with a spring; with the situation of this spring Edward and his companion were unacquainted, and without possessing this knowledge, it was utterly impossible that they should gain access to them.

Still, although unsuccessful in their attempts, they did not relax in their endeavours to effect a passage into the subterraneous dwelling, nor could Edward endure the idea of quitting the spot over which Hope stretched out her balmy pinions.

At length the tumult of the war ceased, and the riot of conquest was heard pouring through the castle. In a very short time, several members of the freebooters' band appeared in the vaulted passage, bearing flambeaux; they passed by Edward and Philip, with a sneer upon them, as cowards who had skulked into this recess for safety during the siege, and bursting their way, with the butt-ends of their match-locks, through the wainscot panelling, they entered the vaults. The heart of Edward now turned to ice in his breast; the most agonizing of human sensations assailed his brain; the moment was approaching at which his Rosalind might be lost to him for ever; and, still more torturing idea! he might be a witness of her misery, without the power to save her.

These reflections were but the transitions of a moment; he was awakened from them by the voice of one of the freebooters, who appeared to possess some degree of command over his fellows, and who called to them to return quietly to the great hall of the castle, and to remain there till he should announce to them that the Lady Rosalind was become the wife of their chief. To be a witness to the solemnization of which ceremony, he was himself going to proceed to the chapel.

Edward formed the instant determination of following his steps; the darkness of the hour favoured his design, and he moved along securely in the shade, guided by the rays of the lamp carried in the hand of the freebooter, in whose path he trod. Arrived at the chapel, he secreted himself behind a tomb, by raising his head above which, he could command a view of the altar, at which he saw the priest already standing.

Resolved to make an effort for the preservation of his Rosalind, even though his life should be the price at which he made it, he considered that, alone, opposed to a body of savage freebooters, with whom the spilling of his blood would not be a feather's weight in the scale of those enormities which marked their character, the only chance on which he could rely for being able to afford assistance to his Rosalind, or ensure safety to himself, must be the effect of the disguise which was concealed beneath his pilgrim's garb, and which he entertained a slight hope might produce the same terrific effect on the freebooters, which it had done on the servants of the castle. It was, however, a last hope to preserve the honour of a beloved and suffering wife, and he resolved to hazard.

Accordingly he threw off his pilgrim's habit and hat, and replaced on his head the casque corresponding with his suit of armour, which he had worn slung by his side, and concealed beneath the folds of his garment, during his residence in Rockmount Castle. He was still possessed of the crimson dye with which the gash on his left cheek had been represented; and having found that those who had been alarmed by him in his disguise, had been most terrified by the streak of blood down the side of his lace, he again applied the liquid to his countenance in the same situation as before; and this done, he awaited, with the most torturing anxiety, the approach of his Rosalind and the villanous Allanrod.

At length the dreadful moment arrived, at which he beheld his Rosalind—that Rosalind so tenderly beloved, and on whose adored image his desiring eyes had not rested for five long years, led into the chapel by two of the banditti. Scarcely had she reached the altar, ere, from the other extremity of the chapel, advanced a figure of height and strength, whose habit would have bespoke him to be Allanrod, had he not moved to the altar, and taken the hand of Rosalind in his, as the treasure which the voice of the priest was to make his own.

"Second my endeavours, thou protecting God of the innocent and oppressed!" Edward breathed forth in silent prayer; and darting towards the altar, he rushed between the wife of his sacred affections and the villain who was about to rob him of his earthly paradise. The protecting God of the innocent and oppressed did second the endeavours of him who had prayed to him in agony of heart; for even the savage Allanrod and his bloody horde shrunk back, appalled with supernatural dread, as they beheld him; and Edward, snatching to his arms the only blessing of his existence, bore her, with the rapidity of lightning, from the presence of her astonished enemies.

CHAPTER V.

I had a mighty cause
To wish him dead, but thou hadst none to kill him.
....
Hadst thou but shook thy head, or made a pause,
When I spoke darkly what I purposed;
....
Deep shame had struck me dumb, made me break off,
And those thy fears, might have wrought fear in me:
But thou didst understand me by my signs,
And didst in signs again parley with sin;
Yea, without stop, didst let thy heart consent,
And, consequently, thy rude hand to act
The deed, which both our tongues held vile to name.

KING JOHN.

We now return to the Lord Baron de Mowbray, whom we left extended, in the acutest agonies of mind, on a couch, in the sable gloom of the funeral chamber, in his despoiled castle. To those whose hearts are rent with remorse, it is an imaginary relief to pour forth their souls in exclamations bespeaking the wretchedness of their feelings. Thus impressed, or rather almost insensible that sounds proceeded from his lips, Lord William raved forth the racking sensations of his breast. "Oh that the child of my Rosalind had been spared by me!" he exclaimed. "The miseries which have fallen upon me and my house, had not then perhaps overwhelmed me. The stings of conscience which I now feel, had not then pricked my bleeding heart. I might have risen from the calamities brought upon me by an unjust foe, to future peace of mind; but now—O God!—oh merciful Providence! when, when shall the murderer taste peace?"

"When his crime is expiated by death!" exclaimed a voice.

The Baron sprang from his couch, but his lips refused their office, and he sunk down again upon it: he turned his eyes around the apartment, and they fell upon a dusky substance which was approaching slowly towards him, from the dark shades which enveloped the opposite end of the chamber,—"Who art thou?" he fearfully demanded.

"Hubert," returned the voice.

"Hubert!" echoed De Mowbray; "art thou living, or hast thou

forsaken the confines of the grave, to burst upon my miseries with thy fearful sight?"

The figure approached close to the Baron, and the remaining light of day was just sufficient to shew him the features of the living Hubert.

"Alive *I am*," replied Hubert, "but I come to thee resolved on death."

"If it is my life thou seekest,"' returned Lord William, "take it; I am sunk so low into the abyss of misery, that it will not cost me one pang to yield it to thee."

"No, no," rejoined Hubert, "it is no second *murder* that I seek to do; the death which I demand, is a forfeiture of existence due to justice—the only expiation of guilt which this world can grant—the only act which can make me quit it, devoid of the horrors which a murderer's conscience is so justly cursed with. Are you prepared to die?"

"I know not what you mean," replied De Mowbray; "I tell you to take my life freely; you refuse to stain your hands with my blood, and still demand of me if I am prepared for death."

"Death on the scaffold, I mean!" exclaimed Hubert; "am I understood by you now?"

"Not understood, upon my life," returned the Baron, scarcely able to articulate.

"Did you not," asked Hubert, in an impressive and solemn tone, "seduce me into a promise to murder a helpless innocent babe?"

"You accepted six hundred pieces of gold for the deed," answered the Baron.

"Aye, likely I might," cried Hubert, "but they cannot heal the wound which that devil's act has left upon my conscience. You tempted me to evil, when your better state in life should have taught you to instruct me in what was good, and not to have lured me into the path of wickedness. You saw me poor, and bribed my necessity into the performance of guilt, when it became your station and knowledge to have given me the means of avoiding that which might lead to my eternal ruin."

The Baron groaned aloud.

Hubert continued thus—"That sense which was denied to me from education, I have gained from repentance. The comparison of my own iniquitous heart with that of other men, whose lives have been innocent, makes me recoil with horror at myself; I see them happy all the day, the night repairing to them, with an easy slumber, the labours of their waking. With me the days are irksome, full of fear—the nights are passed in waking misery: each man, I think, suspects me for the criminal I am—a murderer!—and of what degree?—the most atrocious in the scale of murderers!—that of an innocent babe, without the means of defending itself from the attacks of villany.—'On him,' methinks men cry, 'rests the stain of vice; his hands are dyed in infant blood: avoid him, shun the contagion of his breath, the horror of his eye; leave him an outcast to the pangs of conscience.'—Thus do I feel, as if these sounds were hourly breathed upon mine ear."

"But they are not, are they, good Hubert?" asked the Baron, doubtfully.

"Only by mine own conscience," he replied; "the deed of horror hitherto lies buried in ignorance on earth, but it cannot be hid from heaven: and if such would be man's horror of the act, what must be the detestation in which angels hold it?—Where must we expect to go?—what recompense to await us, when the screen of earthly existence no longer defends us from retribution?"

"We will repent, we will repent!" exclaimed De Mowbray.

"Aye, and suffer too," replied Hubert, "or our repentance will be an unsatisfactory reparation for the crime it follows. Where is the punishment of the guilty—where the terror of the wicked—if they shall commit a deed of villany, veiled by their machinations from every earthly eye, and silence all their fears of future retribution, by saying to themselves—'I will repent?'—Thus cannot I stifle the goadings of remorse; I feel that an exposure of my guilt, and my abettor in guilt, to the world, is necessary to the happiness of my soul; and thus resolved, I come to seek you out, that we may together expiate our crime by that death which will give a lesson of caution to those we leave behind us."

"Hear me—I conjure you, hear me," exclaimed the Baron; "your terrors hurry you beyond your reason."

"I will hear you," returned Hubert; "but understand that it is my reason which prompts my utterance, and renders me insensible to all terrors but those I experience in the concealment of my guilt."

"Is not God our only judge?" asked the Baron; "are we accountable to men for our actions?"

"A secret villain," replied Hubert, "living amongst men, under the enjoyment of a fair reputation, is a serpent endued with sense, and uniting the worser part of man with the evil qualities of the reptile. The serpent is known to contain venom in its sting, although its silver skin hides its destructive power. Against the secret villain, man has no instinct implanted in his breast to teach him to fly from him; it must, therefore, be equitable, that at his death, his skin should, like the venomous reptile's, be pulled off, and his poison exposed to the sight, before he can be purified for a second state."

"Hubert, oh Hubert," cried the Baron, taking the hand of him he addressed, "in the name of heaven, I conjure you to become calm; I am the Lord Baron de Mowbray—reflect on that—the Lord Baron de Mowbray a criminal on a scaffold!"

"The Lord Baron de Mowbray is a murderer," returned Hubert—"reflect on that."

"Crimes like mine are committed," said the Baron, "when the heart is on the rack of torture."

"The sufferings of those on whom they fall, are not, on that account, the less."

"The aggravations which drive us to such acts, are great."

"So is the crime that follows them."

"You once appeared my friend. Do you not recollect, when by the tower in the village——"

"Name it not—then it was you worked upon the ignorance you should have instructed; we were then *equally fools*, but *you alone the villain*. Fool you were, to think it friendship in any man who promised you assistance in iniquity—villain, to tempt any man to that iniquity. I was a fool to believe that evil could ever bring me good. Friends indeed! If I then thought that we were so, I am now grown wise enough to know that friends in evil are mutual enemies."

"After your promises, your oaths of friendship, you, Hubert, are you my bitterest enemy?" groaned out the Baron.

"Need I again repeat to you," replied Hubert, "that I knew not then what it was to be the victim of a goading conscience?—that my present actions are the result of reason and religion? Enemy I am not—I am now, indeed, your friend; for in delivering your life up to justice, I preserve alive the happiness of your soul."

"Surely I dream," exclaimed the Baron; "visions are floating before my eyes, and imaginary sounds assail my weakened senses. Thou canst not be Hubert; impossible that thou, entrusted with the secret of my soul, shouldst use thy knowledge thus to goad the victim in thy power. Whence dost thou come?—how arrived here at this critical moment of my wayward fate? Speak—explain, I entreat thee—my brain and heart are alike upon the rack."

"Of my history, anon," replied Hubert; "I shall return to you ere long, perhaps pass the night with you. I would prepare you for the fate that awaits you, and shall not consider any portion of time lost which I use in giving instruction to *you*, though you poured a baneful doctrine into *my* deluded senses. I shall be here again presently."

Hubert moved towards the door; it was now become too dark for the Baron to follow him to it with his eyes, and he stood for a few moments entranced; but the shutting of the door on the part of Hubert, and the sound of the key moving in the lock immediately after, startled him, and he sprang towards the door, which he hastily endeavoured to open, but it resisted his efforts: he called aloud upon Hubert, but no answer was returned to his cries; his knees trembled under him, and he fell against the wall, upon which he leant in a state of existence that could hardly be termed life.

CHAPTER VI.

The great king of kings,
Hath in the table of his law commanded,
That thou shalt do no murder; wilt thou then
Spurn at his edict, and fulfil a man's?
Take heed; for he holds vengeance in his hand,
To hurl upon their heads, that break his law.

KING RICHARD III.

THE situation of the Baron de Mowbray was now even more wretched than it had been when a prisoner in the fortress of Allanrod. What was he to expect from the dreadful menaces of Hubert?—the enforcement of his threats, or that argument might still be able to soften his intentions?—Whence could Hubert be come? How was he alone in the castle, at an hour when the fury of the spoiler had driven from its walls every other inhabitant?—whither was he gone?—when would he return, and what was his immediate design with regard to himself?

These points alone occupied the mind of Lord William; and now indeed was his repentance sincere for the death of his grandchild, if that repentance which proceeded from terror, might be allowed the appellation.

Nearly two hours had passed, and still Hubert returned not; the curtain of night was drawn over the earth, and no speck of light cheered the apartment where Lord William was confined: he searched out his way to the door, and endeavoured, by the imposition of his weight upon it, to force it open; but the hard oak resisted his efforts. Pride and anger began now to mingle themselves with the other sensations which preyed upon his mind. For Lord William de Mowbray to be a prisoner in an apartment of his own castle, and made so by one of the meanest of his dependants, was an idea almost as painful as the disgrace and punishment with which that dependant threatened him.

At length a footstep was audible in the gallery, and the Baron, who had strayed to the farther end of the apartment in the wanderings of his hurried brain, saw the door opposite to him open, and a figure, which could only be Hubert, enter with a dim lamp burning in a lanthorn in his hand.

"Hubert!" exclaimed the Baron.

"Hubert hears you," he returned.

"Hubert," repeated the Baron, "hast thou forgotten me for thy Lord?"

"I acknowledge you as the Lord Baron de Mowbray," returned Hubert.

"Well then," rejoined the Baron, "my wealth, my power of giving happiness, cannot be unknown to thee; thou canst not be ignorant that my riches are still great, notwithstanding the spoil which has been drawn from my castle by a savage enemy. If it is thy intention to exact from me a greater reward for the service I have received at thy hands than that I have already conferred on thee, why dost thou not demand it in terms of respect, of friendship?—why threaten thy superior, when thou hast but to ask of him, and to receive?"

"Have I not already explained to you, my Lord," replied Hubert, calmly, "that nothing this world is capable of bestowing can restore me to happiness, or set me at peace with my own mind—that I place my hope of forgiveness, after death, on the expiation which I shall make of my crime by the forfeit of my life—and that worlds should not bribe me to forego the ray of comfort which this idea glances on my desponding heart?"

"If thou art thus madly bent upon thine own ruin and disgrace," exclaimed the Baron, becoming for the first time impassioned, "on what authority dost thou unite me in the rash act thou hast resolved upon?"

"I shall die but half purged of my iniquity," returned Hubert, "if I suffer him to live unsuspected, who instigated me to the crime."

"Hubert," roared out the Baron, "I command enlargement from this apartment."

"It cannot be, my Lord, till we are both fetched hence by the officers of justice," rejoined Hubert.

"The officers of justice summoned hither!" cried Lord William; "thou threatenest me with falsehoods."

"Time will convince you that I am not deceiving you: the officers of justice are summoned hither by me, and apprized that they here will find us both," Hubert replied.

"Villain!" exclaimed De Mowbray, "or thou, or I, shall not live to see that hour—unless——"

The violence of his emotions choaked his utterance.

"Unless what?" asked Hubert.

"Give me the key, thou monster of iniquity!" roared out the Baron, darting towards the door.

"Never," replied Hubert, calmly.

The Baron put his hand to his side—he had forgotten that he was unarmed—no sword met his hand. He muttered an exclamation of mingled curses and regret, and again threw himself with his whole weight upon the door, in the hope of forcing it from the lock.

Hubert continued standing by the side of a couch, upon which one of his hands was rested.

"Give me the key," repeated the Baron, "or by that God whose vengeance thou dost dread, thy life shall answer the refusal!"

Hubert continued unmoved.

"Villain, the key!—I say the key!" a third time shrieked forth the Baron, and sprang with the fury of a tyger upon the neck of him whom he addressed.

"Forbear, my Lord," said Hubert, "or I must defend myself."

The Baron was unmindful of his admonition.

"Lion," said Hubert, and immediately Lord William felt himself pinioned down to the ground by his cloak.

The Baron turned himself round to enquire by what force he had been torn from the neck of Hubert, and perceived the glaring eyes of a dog, Hubert's faithful attendant, which met the light of the lamp that was placed upon the table, and gleamed with terrible ferocity. The Baron shrunk in terror from the sight.

"Fear nothing, my Lord," said Hubert; "he is under my absolute command, and will not harm you without my order, which I trust you will not drive me to the necessity of giving him, since you see I am prepared with a friend against your attacks.—Come off," added Hubert, addressing the dog, which immediately quitted his hold of Lord William's cloak, and returned peaceably to the side of his master.

The Baron lay groaning on the floor; his only chance of escape, which had been in a trial of strength with Hubert, was now taken from him, and promised rewards the only sparks of hope which were left him; and from these he expected but little friendship, in the present determined state of Hubert's mind.

Mingled promises, threats, and arguments, burst from his lips, but Hubert was not to be won to his suit by any of them. The Baron sunk upon his knees before him.—"In this posture of humiliation, canst thou refuse to grant my prayer?" he exclaimed.

"It pains me to see you in it," replied Hubert, "but it pains me more to reflect on the crime which has reduced you to it."

"Thou art the cause of this humiliation," returned the Baron, "and refusest to feel for the wretch thou hast made."

"And what a wretch have you made me?" replied Hubert—"reflect on that, and then ask yourself if you can justify your wish to have me die without an expiation of my crime."

"Heart of stone!" exclaimed the Baron; "may tortures, powerful as its stubbornness, rend its fibres!"

"It merits such punishment indeed," returned Hubert.

"Weak fool!" roared out De Mowbray, "may curses stronger than those tortures follow thee from the verge of death into eternity."

"For your own sake, my Lord," said Hubert, "forbear to curse one whom you have already sufficiently injured. Let me entreat you to give some portion of this night to prayer."

A silence of some minutes ensued. Lord William broke it.—"Tell me," he said—"by thy hopes of Heaven, I adjure thee to tell me, does the hand of justice pursue us?"

"By my hopes of Heaven," answered Hubert, "the hand of justice is stretched out towards us both, according to our merits."

"Then God have mercy!" feebly articulated the Baron, and again sunk upon the floor, burying his face in his cloak.

Hubert took a book from his pocket, and placing himself opposite to the lamp, read.

In a short time the Baron sprang up again, and paced the room with the wild step of a frenzied mind.

"My Lord," said Hubert, "compose your feelings, and read some passages of this book."

Lord William replied to him only with a deep groan, and continued his pace.

Another silence ensued, which De Mowbray broke.—"My thirst is excessive," he said; "am I to be confined here without the necessaries of life?"

Hubert immediately produced a basket of refreshments, and poured out for the Baron a cup of mead. Although he had impatiently demanded it, he scarcely touched it with his lips, and refused all substantial nourishment. After the Baron was served, Hubert himself partook of the contents of the basket.

"How can you be thus calm?" asked the Baron, observing him.

"Because my repentance is sincere," answered Hubert.

"You repent, then, of one crime, to step more boldly into another," said the Baron; "it looks, indeed, much like repentance to be one of Allanrod's banditti."

"My Lord, I do not understand you," returned Hubert.

"Perhaps it does not suit your purpose to own it; but I recognized you, even in the disguise you wore when you entered my prison in his fortress, bearing a lamp and a dagger in your hand. Confess to me by what means I was conveyed into the subterraneous vaults, where I again saw you passing before me, and how you traced me hither? If you are resolved on dying, as you say you are, it cannot avail you to keep these secrets."

"My Lord, you rave," replied Hubert; "I know not what you are speaking of—the name of Allanrod is to me unknown. A robber I have never been, nor can I understand your words but as those of frenzy."

"If you will not speak of yourself, reply but to this one question," rejoined the Baron; "tell me what mysterious connexion it is that subsists between Lord Rufus de Madginecourt and the freebooter Allanrod?"

"My Lord," answered Hubert, "I can only repeat, that I know not the name of Allanrod."

"Liar!" exclaimed the Baron, in half-smothered accents, and continued to wander about the apartment.

The clock of the castle now sounded midnight. A feebleness of body and mind overpowered the Baron, and he once more threw himself upon a couch.

Hubert trimmed his lamp, and resumed his book.

CHAPTER VII.

'Tis only when with inbred horror smote,
At some base act, or done, or to be done,
That the recoiling soul with conscious dread,
Shrinks back into itself.

MASON.

THE light of returning day had for some hours reanimated the face of nature ere the Baron de Mowbray, sinking under bodily and mental fatigue, fell into a restless slumber; from this he was awakened by the noise occasioned by the shutting of the door of the apartment in which he lay extended upon the floor, with his head rested against the foot of a couch; and on casting his eyes around, he found that Hubert had left the chamber.

Again the most impetuous desire of effecting his escape from the captivity to which he dreaded Hubert had condemned him, entered his mind, and again he sought the means of forcing his way out of the apartment.

The upper compartments alone of the windows in this chamber could be opened, and they were moved by a cord fastened to a spring, which acted upon them for that purpose; these upper divisions were much above his reach, even when mounted upon a table which stood beneath them, consequently unfavourable to the hope of escape. Anxious to obtain a view of the inner court of the castle, which the painting upon the window glass prevented him from gaining through it, he dashed out the panes from the lower frames.

The compartments of glass between the stone work which intersected the long and spiral windows, were too narrow to have admitted his body to pass through them, if even their height from the ground had not been so great as to have rendered it impossible for him to have leapt down, without the hazard of fracturing some of his limbs in the fall. Whilst he stood thus a prey to despair, his eye suddenly fell on an armed figure which issued from one of the arched portals leading into the court. The figure he instantly observed to be in the dress of his own soldiery; two others, in the same attire, almost immediately followed; and with these was a man, in the raw and tattered garments which characterized Allanrod's band of freebooters. His heart bounded with joy at the sight, and he was on the point of calling to them, when the one, whom he had first observed, turned his eye upon the casement, at which Lord William was standing, and he recognised in him his chief leader, Irwin, whom he had believed to be still a prisoner in the fortress of Allanrod.

"Do I behold my Lord de Mowbray?" exclaimed Irwin.

"Oh, Irwin!—my friend!—my friend!" returned the Baron; "blessed be Heaven that thou art arrived to my aid!—Hasten hither instantly, I entreat thee."

"We come, my Lord—we come," replied Irwin; and, with his companions, immediately disappeared from the court.

The Baron flew to the door of the chamber, where he stood

trembling under the alarming possibility of Hubert not having left the key on the outside of the door, but taken it with him. In the course of a few minutes he heard the sound of footsteps in the gallery, approaching towards the cedar chamber, and very shortly after he experienced the ecstacy of beholding the door open. On entering, Irwin immediately enquired from what cause he found his Lord a prisoner in that apartment.

The Baron replied to this demand, by explaining, in as few words as possible, that the surly Hubert, whom, he said, Irwin could not but remember to have been formerly one of the soldiery of the castle, had, at a certain period, a few years past, been entrusted by him with the care of an infant, nearly connected with himself, whom he had, for the most urgent reasons, wished to have reared in obscurity, and which office Hubert had taken upon himself, and received a reward from him to perform. "From that time," continued the Baron, "I had not seen him, nor even heard of him, till he appeared to me by night in the fortress of Allanrod, during my confinement in it; and at the moment of his second appearance in it, I was hastily conveyed away from the spot, in a manner which I am not able to explain or account for. Let it at this minute be sufficient for me to inform you, that I effected my escape from the stronghold of my enemy; that on returning to my castle, I found it despoiled, as you now behold it; and that whilst I stood in this chamber, fixed in agony, and lamenting the unhappy fate of my daughter and myself, Hubert again appeared before me."

"Proceed, my Lord," said Irwin, for the Baron paused, and turned aside his countenance.

"It appears from his account of himself," De Mowbray continued, "that the passion of avarice stole into his heart, and tempted him with the desire of possessing the sum with which I had furnished him for the maintenance of the child, and to this end he became its murderer. His conscience now, it seems, reproves him with the deed, and wrings his heart with tortures of such violence, that they have induced upon his mind a state of frenzy, under the influence of which he believes that I commanded the death of the infant, and that he cannot taste salvation in a future life, unless he delivers up himself and me to justice in this. You cannot, from this account which I give you, doubt the derangement of his brain; when he returns hither, therefore, which I expect he shortly will do, you must assist me to secure him, and I will then deliberate upon what steps it were most advisable for me to take respecting him."

Irwin heard these words, on the part of the Baron, with a degree of astonishment which he could not repress. The Baron's faltering accents gave him a suspicion that his heart was ill at ease within his breast; and the recollection of Edward's hasty departure from Cumberland, and Rosalind's imprisonment from the world, subsequent to that period, connected with the Baron's avowal that there had been a child born, which he had wished to conceal from the public eye, carried with it a train of strange ideas to the mind of Irwin, although he forbore to give them utterance. "Did you suppose, my Lord," he said, "that it was Hubert who twice appeared to you by night in the fortress of Allanrod, within the chest in your prison?"

"I cannot doubt it," returned the Baron.

"You are deceived, my Lord," replied Irwin; "it was myself whom you there beheld."

"You, Irwin!—You!" exclaimed Lord William, in a tone of voice which bespoke him unable to give credit to the words which fell from the tongue of his leader.

"I will immediately explain to you," returned Irwin, "what now appears to you a matter of doubt. Did not you, my Lord, whilst confined in the fortress of Allanrod, throw from the window of your prison, a paper, containing a promise of a thousand pieces of gold to whomsoever should convey intelligence of the place of your confinement to De Mowbray Castle?"

"Yes, yes, I did," answered Lord William; "this was an experiment for regaining my liberty, which I several times repeated."

"One of these papers," said Irwin, "was found by the member of Allanrod's band, whom you now behold—my companion: and he, as chance willed it, was the very person destined to attend upon me in my imprisonment."

The Baron stepped forward to behold the man to whom Irwin alluded, and saw him standing without the door of the chamber, with those two of his own soldiery whom he had before observed in the court below. "Was it he who found that paper?" said Lord William, returning towards Irwin.

"The same, my Lord," replied the leader; "he is a man whom

poverty had urged, in opposition to his natural inclination, to enter into the company of the freebooters, and, burning with the desire of obtaining a reward, which promised him the means of quitting their band, without exposing himself to the miseries of famine; and still fearful of the tortures to which Allanrod might condemn him, if he were either detected in flying as a messenger to De Mowbray Castle, or enlarging you from your prison in the fortress of the freebooter, he resolved to inform me what was passing in his mind; and having done so, he questioned me, whether I would equally ensure to him the thousand pieces of gold, if he gave me instruction for effecting your escape? Your Lordship cannot doubt that I instantly gave the promise which he demanded. Our agreement being made, he informed me, that the point wherein the greatest danger lay to whomsoever should attempt your release, was the act of reaching the turret where you were confined; but, that if I were inclined to hazard the undertaking, he would direct me in the only way by which it could be done. I declared myself ready to make the attempt, and at the dead hour of midnight, putting a lamp into my hand, and presenting me with a dagger for my defence, he led me through the sepulchral vaults of the ancient monastery, and bringing me to the foot of a narrow and spiral staircase, he directed me to ascend it, acquainting me that when I had reached the top I should find bolts, which I must undraw, and then raise up a certain portion of the wainscot, which, he told me, formed the lid of an apparent chest in your prison; and which private connexion with the burying ground below, he supposed to have been constructed in former times, for the purpose of conveying with the greater secrecy and ease into the vaults beneath, such persons as had been deprived of life in the prisons above them—and of crimes of this nature, he said, the place had been a frequent witness, in the days of religious persecution.

"I ascended the stairs, and he remained below, hid in a dark corner of the vaults, which he had chosen for the purpose of concealing himself from view, should any one chance to pass that way. Scarcely had I raised the lid of the supposed chest, ere my companion, seeing a distant light approaching towards the spot, and being fearful of a surprise, which might defeat our intention with regard to you, gave me a signal, which had been agreed upon between us, to return to him; I instantly let fall the wainscot partition, and ran down the stairs. He hid my lamp in a lanthorn, which he had brought with him for that purpose, and we knelt down behind a mouldering tomb, where we screened ourselves from the observation of a freebooter, whom my companion judged to be on his way to steal liquor from the cellars of Allanrod. The moment he had passed us, I returned to my prison, and he to his accustomed sleeping place, as we judged it unsafe to renew our attempt that night."

"But on the following one you repeated it," said the Baron, "did you not?—for the armed figure, which you now explain to me to have been yourself, again appeared to me beneath the lid of the chest."

Irwin replied, that on the subsequent night, the freebooters having nearly all left the fortress, upon an expedition of plunder, which he had now found to have been directed against De Mowbray Castle, the friendly borderer and himself proceeded, with less fear, towards the Baron's prison, in the turret. Having ascended the stairs, he raised the lid of the chest as before, and that he had scarcely done so, ere he perceived the Baron suddenly to vanish from his sight on the opposite side of the apartment. "In the greatest surprise," continued Irwin, "I immediately returned to my companion, and communicated to him what I had seen; equally astonished at the intelligence I brought, as I myself had been at what I had witnessed, he resolved to ascend with me into the turret, and investigate the cause. We directly entered the apartment which had been your prison, and discovered a trap-door in the floor, which had yielded to the imposition of your weight upon it, and through which it was evident that you had fallen.

"Upon perceiving this, I concluded that you had been precipitated into the vaults which we had just left, but my companion informed me, that the ancient burying-ground was intersected by a wall, which ran immediately across the turret in which you had been a captive, and that you had fallen on that side of it, to which we had not the power of gaining access. Dreading that you might there perish, in consequence of the bruises you might have received in your fall, I besought him to make the experiment of conducting me to you. He declared that it was impossible for him to serve you in your present misfortune, for that the ancient tombs, in the opposite division, were used as the receptacles of such articles of value as were brought to the fortress by the banditti; and that, on this account, the entrance to it was guarded by a man named Frasier, and two others, whose fidelity to Allanrod had been tried, and through whose sleeping apartment lay the only passage which led to the spot.

"In this dilemma, we considered that the single chance by which we could be able to afford you assistance, must be that of effecting our escape from the stronghold of the freebooters, and proceeding, with all the speed we were able, to De Mowbray Castle, where it must be my business instantly to collect all your vassals capable of bearing arms, and to lead them to an attack upon your prison. Thus resolved, we stole out from the ruinous building, with all the caution of men who dread that every succeeding moment may be the termination of their existence, and having gained a dell at a short distance, we determined to hide ourselves in one of the rocky cavities, of which it had many, till the approach of night should favour our proceeding on our destined journey, for already was the sun beginning to break from the clouds, and every moment bringing with it the fear of a discovery. We had entered but a few paces into the cave, which we had chosen for our concealment, ere we were alarmed by the sound of voices and footsteps within it; in a very short time, however, our fears were removed, by discovering that its inhabitants were the two of your Lordship's soldiers, whom you now behold before you, and who, like us, had effected their escape from the fortress in the night, and were seeking shelter from the light of day. They had been more provident than ourselves, in bringing with them provisions for their journey; and by sharing with them the contents of their wallet, our strength and spirits were preserved for the undertaking of the ensuing night.

"At the hour of noon we heard sounds indicative of the return of the victorious freebooters from their expedition, and as soon as the shades of night were spread, we set forward on our way, resolving to repose no more till we should have gained the spot of our destination. On our arrival here, you may easily imagine the consternation with which we beheld the castle despoiled, and deserted; but our astonishment and joy were still greater, when our eyes fell upon the countenance of its Lord, for whose safety our fears had been so strongly excited."

In as brief a manner as possible, the Baron then recounted to

Irwin, and his companions, all that had befallen to him, subsequent to his descent into the vaults, and the providential means by which he had effected his escape from them; "but what," he asked, "could be the light which I so long pursued?"

The freebooter answered—"That he doubted not it had been a lamp, borne either by Frasier, or one of his fellow-guards, who were suspected of paying nightly visits, of not a very honest nature, to the treasures which they were deputed to protect."

These explanations having been made on both sides, the recollection of the past was quickly driven from the mind of the Baron, by the anxiety with which he anticipated the future, and his doubts how to act under the trying and perplexing scene with which he was threatened. The only method by which he could shield himself from the dreaded accusation of his enemy, appeared to be that of becoming himself the accuser of Hubert; and to pursue this plan, therefore, he fixed his determination.

The entreaties of Irwin could not prevail upon Lord William to quit the cedar chamber; he persisted in remaining there till the return of Hubert, having commanded the two soldiers, who had arrived with Irwin, to secure him their prisoner, as soon as he appeared in it.

At the expiration of about two hours after the arrival of Irwin and his companions at the castle, a footstep was heard in the gallery, and in a few moments Hubert entered the cedar-chamber bearing in his hand some refreshments, which he had brought with him, for the breakfast of Lord William. Immediately on his coming into the chamber, the command which the Baron had given was obeyed, and he was seized by two soldiers; the action, as well as the presence of Irwin, and the soldiers, appeared to surprise him; but he still retained his composure of countenance, and ere he had time to enquire why he was thus assailed, the Baron explained the cause by saying—"You are now my prisoner, nor shall you again taste liberty, till you have given such an account of the death of the infant, whom I entrusted to your care, as a court of justice shall deem sufficiently satisfactory to acquit you upon."

"I have already, my Lord," replied Hubert, "expressed my desire to meet you in a court of justice; I am therefore rejoiced that you have resolved to accede to my wish."

"Does not my firmness shake thee from thy mad purpose?" enquired the Baron, after a pause.

"No, my Lord, it does not in the least cause me to waver from my determination," returned Hubert.

"Thy confidence is not less strange than thy frantic intention," replied the Baron.

"It is placed in the justice of Heaven," answered Hubert.

CHAPTER VIII.

Oh, sweet my mother, cast me not away!
————I beseech you on my knees;
Hear me with patience but to speak a word.
ROMEO AND JULIET.

We now again turn the page to Edward and his Rosalind. With the rapidity of the lightning's flash, shot from the resistless bolt of Jove, Edward sped his way from the chapel, bearing the treasure of his soul senseless in his arms. Entirely unacquainted with the intricacies of the building, he thought only of removing her from the presence and power of Allanrod, and his vile adherents; and for this purpose he retraced the only path of which he had any knowledge, and which was the one that had led him into the chapel, from the entrance into the subterraneous vaults. Here he paused an instant in reflection how to proceed. In that instant the wonted powers of her mind returned to Rosalind; with an exclamation, long and piercing, she shrieked forth his name. "Edward!" she cried, "my husband lives!—'tis not the pallid spectre of the man I once was blessed in loving!—'tis he!—it is himself that I am again permitted to throw my trembling arms around, and hang upon for succour. Oh, God!—omnipotent and merciful God!—accept my gratitude for the excess of bliss that fills my heart!"

With a fervour not less animated and devout, than the dying zealot holds to his breast the emblem of his Saviour's suffering, and his own forgiveness, and presses upon it, with religious ecstacy, his fevered lips, did Edward clasp to his breast the long-lost wife of his affections; and as he held her in his arms—"Rosalind!—dearest, persecuted, suffering Rosalind!" he exclaimed, "welcome, welcome, to the heart that lives for thee, and thee alone!"

But the instinctive voice of danger quickly whispered an admonition to the heart of Edward, not to lose an instant in flying from the spot where he stood. Various sounds were assailing his ears from every side; at one moment they appeared to be approaching towards him, at the next to be again receding from him. The darkness of the night was relieved only by solitary lamps, which cast a pale reflection on the lofty walls. After some hesitation which way they should bend their steps, he perceived a glimmering of light, which appeared of a different nature to that emitted by the lamps, and, in the hope of its proving an outlet from the castle, they flew towards it; as they approached it, they discovered it to be a window at the end of a vaulted corridor, through which the beams of the moon obliquely shot a sickly light upon the white marble floor beneath it.

At the moment Edward was contemplating, with a full heart, the disappointment of his hopes, the eye of Rosalind discovered a second luminous space, through which appeared the full face of the planet, whose beams had attracted them towards the window; and as they moved a few paces nearer to the inviting scene, the breeze by which they were met, convinced them that no object here intervened between them and the air. In this conviction they endeavoured to increase upon the speed with which they were already moving, and in a few minutes they found themselves arrived at a postern-gate, leading out upon the ramparts, fronting the sea.

That their course had hitherto been uninterrupted, Edward was not surprised; those whom he had left in the chapel he supposed to be withheld from pursuing them, equally by superstitious fears, and the attention which their Lord, Allanrod, was requiring at their hands, in consequence of the alarm he had received. All the adherents of De Madginecourt he concluded to be prisoners; and he had himself heard a command issued for all the freebooters to assemble in the hall of the castle, and there to await the tidings being brought to them of their Lord's marriage with Rosalind being solemnized. He wished that his friend Philip were still by his side, but the wish was a vain one.

Having issued out upon the ramparts, they discovered that they were on the opposite side of the castle to that on which the drawbridge was situated; nothing was discernible from this spot but the buoyant waves rising above each other in silver swells upon the murmuring bosom of the deep. "Let us fly to the beach, and secrete ourselves in some friendly cavity, which one of the cliffs upon the verge of the sea will not fail to afford us!" exclaimed the anxious Rosalind.

"But how will it be possible for you to descend the steep and rugged declivity which leads to the margin of the ocean?" enquired Edward.

"I once wandered by day on this very rampart," replied Rosalind, "and I then discovered a footway down the cliffs, but a few paces to the left of our present situation."

"But the moat—the moat!" ejaculated Edward; "how shall we pass the moat? There can be no doubt of the drawbridge being securely guarded, although the ramparts on this side of the castle are left naked and deserted."

Scarcely had Edward spoken these words ere the sound of voices arrested his attention, and, on turning round his head in the direction from whence they proceeded, he perceived two men moving slowly along, upon what he, at the first glance, supposed to be a part of the rampart wall; but he almost immediately discovered that he was deceived in his idea, and this discovery rendered him wholly at a loss where to suppose them walking, as they appeared to be crossing the moat on a level with the parapet wall. Rosalind confirmed him in his belief that there was no second drawbridge communicating with that part of the castle, and he almost began to think that they moved on air.

Rosalind and himself were at this time concealed by the shade of a high bastion, while on the two men, the objects of their fear, their curiosity, and surprise, the moon cast a vivid light. When they had gained the ramparts, Edward could distinguish from their dress that they were moss-troopers; and from their conversation, as they passed before the spot where Rosalind and he were standing, he found that one of them had been wounded by a sling from the castle, and that his companion had returned to seek him after the victory, and to lend him his assistance in reaching the walls of which they had made a conquest.

Instantly convinced from what he had overheard, that there must be some passage by which these men had crossed the moat, and which might prove instrumental to the flight of Rosalind and himself, no sooner had the two moss-troopers turned an angle of the walls, than, with the trembling partner of his anxieties, he flew to investigate the spot.

The moment they arrived at it, a surprise of the most joyful nature presented itself to their sight; they found that a temporary bridge had been thrown across the moat, in order, as it appeared, to favour the rushing of the enemy upon the castle, at the period of its defenders growing languid in their exertions. Thankful for the beneficial aid it afforded them, they gave but little consideration to the cause of its existence, and having traversed it with winged steps, they flew towards the beach, which they gained in safety, and with overflowing ecstacy of soul.

They moved hastily on, in search of some nook where they might shelter themselves from the pursuit, which they doubted not would shortly be set on foot after Rosalind; and as they proceeded along, they poured forth upon the delighted senses of each other, those sentiments of joy, of thankfulness, and of astonishment, with which their hearts were filled at the restoration to each other, with which they were at that moment blessed.

"To be torn asunder now," exclaimed Edward, "would be a pang exceeding all the miseries that I have hitherto endured."

"Forbid it, pitying Heaven!" ejaculated the tender Rosalind. "Oh, that we could at this instant be wafted to the foot of our sovereign's throne; that it were permitted us to kneel before my royal godmother, and implore her protection for two unfortunate beings, whose natural protectors have cast them off, and who have alone her clemency and justice to repose on for their future peace!"

"Be of comfort, dearest Rosalind," returned Edward; "the hand of Providence appears to be stretched out in our cause, and it will protect us on our journey towards Elizabeth."

"Alas!" replied Rosalind, "you speak of the journey as if it were possible for us to accomplish it ere the morning; consider the distance from hence to the abode of our royal mistress—the dangers, the perils that await unprotected travellers, like ourselves. Oh, pardon me, my beloved husband, that at the moment thou art restored to me, my heart should sink thus fainting in my breast."

The voice of Rosalind faltered as she pronounced these words;

the tears burst from her eyes, and she sunk, fainting, into the arms of Edward.

Words were all the comfort which he had it in his power to bestow on her; and as he called upon her in accents of the tenderest nature to revive, and place confidence in the will of Heaven to preserve them from their enemies, his attention was, for an instant, called from the object of his anxiety, by a rapid cutting of the waves behind him, and on moving round his head, he perceived that the noise proceeded from the motion of the oars with which a man, whom he discovered in a small boat, was rowing his little bark towards the shore.

On perceiving this man, a sudden thought, which communicated both hope and rapture to his heart, darted into his imagination. He had already wiped the crimson stain from his cheek; and the instant animation returned to the frame of Rosalind, leading her towards the man who had just sprung from his boat upon the shore, he addressed him, by saying—"Fear me not—I am a man like yourself; you have nothing to dread at my hands; benefit it is at your option to receive from them, if you have a heart capable of feeling for the miseries of your fellow beings, and are oppressed with wants which the recompence due to a benevolent action would provide you with the means of supplying. Carry us southward from this spot, to any port or harbour, where it is probable that we may obtain a vessel to transport us farther down the coast, and ten pieces of gold shall be the compensation I will bestow on you for your compliance; five of which I will now give you, as an earnest of my promise being made, by one who will not break his word to you."

The fisherman, for such was the man he addressed, appeared not less surprised by the proposition made to him, than by the sudden appearance, as it seemed to him, of two beings, of the superior cast, of which their garb bespoke them, by the side of his boat.

He stared alternately upon each, without replying to Edward's appeal; but when Edward enforced his petition, by producing five of the pieces of gold with which the faithful Hubert had furnished him at their late separation, his tongue immediately became untied; and having received them into his own possession, and reminded Edward of the other five which were to follow, he agreed to row them down to a creek, at the distance of about a league and a half, where, he said, small vessels, sailing southward, were not unfrequently to be found.

The greatest inconvenience which they experienced whilst in the fisherman's boat, was its owner's curiosity to learn the cause from which they had taken refuge in it; and as Edward judged it most safe not to give him their true history, he was not a little puzzled to find evasive replies to his questions, which were very numerous—otherwise the man proved both civil and kind. He threw a wrapping cloak, which had been intended to defend himself from the coldness of the night, over the shoulders of Rosalind, and pressed both her and Edward to partake of such food and liquor as he happened to have on board.

The tide being unfavourable to their progress, day was beginning to dawn when they reached the creek to which the fisherman had promised to transport them. As they arrived near it, they discovered some low cottages planted at the distance of a few yards from the margin of the sea, but no vessel of any description appeared in sight.

Having landed them, the fisherman recommended to them to knock at a door, which he pointed out, and which, he informed them, was the habitation of a man who was in the habit of supplying such ships as touched upon that part of the coast with fresh water and provisions, and who was the most likely person to inform them whether any vessel was shortly expected to pass that way.

They followed his directions, and scarcely had Edward struck his hand against the door, ere the pilot, of whom the fisherman had spoken, followed by a lad who was his son, came out, ready equipped, as it appeared, for the water. They stepped back a pace or two in surprise, at the appearance of Edward and his fair companion; and before they had time to enquire their business, Edward signified what it was.

The pilot replied, that if it was their wish to get themselves transported to London, his son and himself were then going to carry a sheep on board a ship in the service of government, which was lying off at sea, about half a league from the shore, and which was now on her way to the Tower of London; "and this vessel" he added, "he doubted not, would readily receive them on board as passengers."

The desire which Rosalind had expressed to her husband, at the moment of their reaching the beach on the foregoing night, of being able to throw herself at the feet of her sovereign, and interest her in their cause, had governed him in his actions since that time; and hence arose the decision with which, in his flight from Rockmount Castle, he had still taken the precaution of making progress towards the metropolis.

The light of day was not yet sufficient for them to distinguish the ship of which the pilot had spoken; they, however, trusted to his report of her, and entered the boat in which his son and himself were going to row up to her.

As they advanced out to sea, the vessel gradually became visible; and when they had reached her side, at the request of Edward, the captain appeared upon deck; and a very few words ratified an agreement for the passage of Edward and Rosalind to London.

Towards the captain, Edward maintained the same silence and secrecy, with regard to their names and history, which he had done to the inquisitive fisherman. His time was principally passed in the cabin which was allotted to their use, with his Rosalind; and their hours were spent in a relation of the adventures which had befallen them since their separation from each other, intermingled with their doubts, their wishes, and their apprehensions, for the event of the future.

The ship had got under way almost immediately upon their coming on board; and on the evening of the third day they arrived at the mouth of the Thames, where she anchored for that night.

As Edward and Rosalind had dwelt on past occurrences, one circumstance had particularly excited their surprise, and that was, the effect which the sudden appearance of Edward, in his disguise, in the chapel of Rockmount Castle, had produced on Allanrod. It had by no means astonished them, that the lower orders of society, both at De Mowbray Castle, and afterwards at that of Rockmount, should have been alarmed by the appearance which had been purposely planned to inspire with terror the minds of superstitious and ignorant beholders; but that Allanrod, a chief, even though of a banditti, a situation which alone would have bespoken him of no mean origin, even if the account of his courtesy and accomplishments, which Edward had learnt from the history of the Bonny Mabel Monteith, related to him by the abbess in the island of Auskerry, had not met his ears, should have experienced so great an alarm from the sight, as to have sunk senseless, at beholding it, into the arms of his attendants, was a fact for which he could not in any way account, but that the consciousness of the train of evils which had marked his iniquitous life had rendered him more susceptible of fearful impressions than a man whose days have been more innocently passed.

About five in the afternoon of the fourth day after their escape from Rockmount Castle, they were landed in the metropolis of the kingdom; and Edward having satisfied the captain of the vessel for the service they had received at his hands, they proceeded towards that quarter of the city in which stood the royal palace, and where they procured for themselves the use of an apartment in the vicinity, on taking possession of which they tasted the first moment of security with which they had been blessed since their reunion with each other.

A night of undisturbed rest was a refreshment of which the strength and spirits of Rosalind stood peculiarly in need, ere she could be adequate to the undertaking of entering the presence of her sovereign, upon the painful, the difficult business, for which she was to appear before her; and her ideas relative to the reception she should meet with from Elizabeth almost deprived her of the sleep necessary to enable her to go through the arduous task of the succeeding day.

Kindly as she believed the Queen would treat her, and mindful, as she did not doubt to find her, of those promises of love and protection which she had made to her at the moment of her becoming her sponsor at the holy font of Christianity, still the unprecedented peculiarity of her situation, the detail of extraordinary events for which she had to implore her hearing, filled her with apprehension at the idea of approaching her throne; and not least painful to her imagination was the probability of the queen considering the honour which she had conferred on her, in becoming her godmother, sullied by the union which she had contracted with her beloved Edward; she dreaded that Elizabeth might merely dwell on the circumstance of her being become the wife of an unknown, and be unwilling to make any allowance of pity or indulgence for the cruel extremities by which she had been driven to that act.

When they arose in the morning, having, with the assistance

of their hostess, procured a change of habiliments for themselves, of which some pieces that still remained of Hubert's gold enabled them to make the purchase, and Rosalind having been careful to attire herself with the utmost simplicity, they repaired to the royal mansion of Elizabeth; a chamberlain of the household appeared to receive them, and, in faint accents, Rosalind requested to be admitted to an audience of the queen.

The chamberlain replied, "that her majesty was in ill health, and unable to receive any visitors but such as were honoured by her most intimate acquaintance."

"I am one," rejoined Rosalind, "on whom her smiles have hitherto fallen with the most condescending benignity. I entreat you to bear her information, that her god-daughter, Rosalind de Mowbray, implores permission to kneel before her."

"The name of De Mowbray," answered the chamberlain, "is indeed one that is most likely to gain its suit. Your petition, Lady, shall instantly be conveyed to the ear of our royal mistress;" and having said this, he commanded some of the attendants who were in waiting in the hall of the palace, to conduct Rosalind and her husband to an apartment, whilst he proceeded to execute the commission with which she had charged him.

During the time that they remained in this apartment, awaiting the return of the chamberlain, some domestics attended to place them chairs, and throw additional logs of wood upon a fire which was burning upon the hearth; and of one of these, who appeared of a superior order to the rest, Rosalind ventured to enquire, "whether the Queen had been long indisposed?"

He replied, "that her Majesty was not yet recovered from the grief into which the death of her lamented cousin, the Queen of Scots, had thrown her."

Rosalind could with difficulty confine to her own breast the surprise with which this account filled her mind: Queen Elizabeth had been the instrument of the fallen monarch's death; and therefore it appeared to her indefinably strange, that she should now be represented as mourning her loss.

The chamberlain presently returned, followed by a venerable female, in whose person Rosalind recollected the Dowager Lady Butler: she was a woman of the strictest religious principles, and in her conversation the queen at this time found particular delight. From the moment the fatal blow had been struck, which had put a period to the existence of the Scottish Queen, Elizabeth had repented of the step which she had taken to free herself from an innocent rival; and thus impressed, she scorned the consolation and the lessons of those priests, who had a few weeks before urged her to the act of which she now lamented that she had not withheld the performance; and to the pure doctrines of the Lady Butler she now alone listened.

By her Rosalind was conducted to the presence of her sovereign; as she quitted the apartment where she left Edward, he bade her farewell, with a look in which was conveyed the earnest desire of his soul for her appeal to the feelings of the Queen meeting such a reception as might prove a balm to the suppliant's breast.—Rosalind breathed a sigh of hope, and followed her conductress.

Passing through an antichamber into a retired apartment, Rosalind here beheld the Queen reclining on a couch, pale, and apparently as ill in health as the Lady Butler had described her to be in mind. She was unattended, except by two young females, who were embroidering in a distant part of the chamber, beneath a spiral window of painted glass, through which the rays of day were admitted, dyed with yellow tints, that gave a jaundiced hue to the scene, and increased the pallidness of Elizabeth's countenance.

With tottering steps Rosalind approached towards the couch, and unable to give utterance to the words in which she wished to address the queen, she bent her knee, and prepared herself to fall at her feet; but Elizabeth, who had raised herself upon her seat as Rosalind had advanced into the apartment, extending towards her one of her hands, caught in it that of the trembling daughter of De Mowbray, and withheld her by it from prostrating herself before her.

"Rosalind de Mowbray!" the queen exclaimed, "whence arises it that I thus unexpectedly behold you in my presence? Where is the Baron, your father?—Can it be a truth that was reported to me, that you are here wholly unattended?"

"Oh, my beloved, my gracious sovereign!" faintly breathed forth Rosalind, "I am come hither to implore your motherly protection; I am overwhelmed with wretchedness and sorrow, and I fly to you for advice and succour."

"Can it be possible that Rosalind de Mowbray stands in need of either?" returned the Queen: "if it be, she has done wisely to recollect the friendship which Elizabeth pledged to her infant state, and to fly to her for relief, and retribution."

Cheered by these consolatory words, the tide of joy ran through the veins of Rosalind, and again she would have sunk at the feet of her sovereign; but Elizabeth, in the most affectionate and engaging manner, placed her on the couch by her side.

"You behold in me," said the queen, "a mourner for the death of my lost cousin, Mary of Scotland. The law of my country has exacted from me the termination of a life which, as an individual, it would have been my joy to have preserved. In seclusion I have passed my days, since the unhappy hour which gave her to eternity; and nought could have aroused me from the stupor of grief and melancholy, in which your petition to be admitted into my presence found me, but the name of her to whom I have pledged my faith to be a parent; and by breaking a letter of my promise to whom, I will not give myself a second cause for remorse of mind."

"Heaven will return to you, in additional blessings, the interest which you graciously express yourself to take in the fate of one so little worthy as myself, of exciting it within your breast," replied Rosalind.

"Life is a scene of woe," rejoined the queen, "and happiest they who can alleviate those pangs of anguish which gnaw upon the hearts of others. With all, it is a duty to perform this charitable part; but in a sovereign like myself, it were a blasphemy against the Deity, whose image and whose delegate I live on earth, were I to neglect to act upon this principle of benevolence. Yet I fear me, that in one single instance of my life, I have transgressed."

She paused, and contending feelings appeared to agitate her bosom. When she spoke again, she reverted to the death of Mary, and even a tear fell from her eye, as she recounted the godlike resignation with which she died. But still Rosalind, although she endeavoured to check the idea, and desired to believe the penitence of Elizabeth of the most perfect and religious nature, could not forbear imagining that she discovered her to be more repentant of the stain which she dreaded that this action had cast upon her fame, than of the privation of life which the Queen of Scots had suffered from it.

"I forget myself," said Elizabeth, after another pause—"commence the appeal which you are about to make to my heart; and in contemplating how I can serve you, I will endeavour to chase from my remembrance, the scene of affliction which is ever present to my senses."

"I much fear," replied Rosalind, "that however you may pity me for the wrongs I have endured, I shall still, in certain instances, appear to my sovereign to have acted with rashness and with weakness."

"Let those condemn the weakness of their fellow-beings," answered the queen, "whose lives have been a current of undeviating purity; but such there are not, although a blindness to their own errors often leads the vain and conceited to think thus of themselves. Man is, by his nature, prone to error; were he perfect, he were no longer of this earth. You will be judged by a mortal, Rosalind de Mowbray, when you open your heart to me; and although a queen, I have the feelings of a woman."

As Elizabeth ceased speaking, she waved her hand to the young women at the farther end of the apartment; which signal they understood, and immediately obeyed by quitting her presence; the Lady Butler too, without receiving the same hint for retiring, withdrew into the antichamber. By their absence Rosalind felt emboldened, and as soon as they were alone, the queen again urged her to begin her story.

Without farther hesitation, Rosalind entered upon the recital of such events as had marked her sorrowful life since the period of her former visit to the court. She recounted the death of her mother, and the impressive appeal which in her dying moments she had made to the feelings of Lord William, relative to the union of their daughter: she proceeded to the arrival of Lord Rufus de Madginecourt at De Mowbray Castle—to the offer which he had made to her of his hand—to the cruel severity with which her father had commanded her to receive him as her husband—to the month of grace which he had allowed her for preparing herself for becoming his wife; and thence to her solemn interview with him in the cedar chamber.

Here the queen interrupted her.—"Is it possible," she exclaimed, "that De Madginecourt possessed the hardiness to make you an offer of his hand, and at the period too you mention?—at that very period my frowns had driven him from my court—vain, pitiable fool!—for know, Rosalind, that De Madginecourt was once sufficiently presumptuous to believe that England's queen would share her throne with him. It was an error in which a sovereign could not permit a subject to exist, and I quickly opened his eyes to the delusion with which his hopes were feeding him. Stung to the soul by the mortification to which his own weakness and folly had reduced him, he instantly retired from London, conscious of taking with him my displeasure; and I believed him lamenting the presumption which had cast him from my good opinion, in the privacy of his own domains. It is now explained to me that he was otherwise employed; and I am grieved to find that a noble, in whom I had placed the faith which I have till this moment ever done in Lord William de Mowbray, should have fallen into the weakness of becoming the dupe of so designing and crafty a heart as that which animates Lord Rufus. Not less surprised am I that the Baron, your father, should not, in whatever union presented itself to the acceptance of Rosalind de Mowbray, have deemed it a matter of necessary compliment, if not of compunction, to have entreated her royal godmother to grace it with her sanction, ere the alliance were attempted to be formed."

To the queen it appeared incontestibly evident, that in seeking the hand of Rosalind, Lord Rufus de Madginecourt had only been planning the means of ascending to a secondary step in the path towards royal favour, when foiled in his attempt at mounting the most exalted station of honour and of power; and it increased the contempt with which she already regarded him. For the conduct of the Lord Baron de Mowbray, in having omitted to request of her to honour with her countenance the alliance which he had prepared for his daughter, she could devise no cause, but that he dreaded lest she should have been won to sympathize in the feelings of Rosalind, and out of respect to her happiness have withheld her consent to the marriage; and regarding this procedure as a proof that he preferred being himself the agent of the plans for the future life of his daughter, instead of submitting her to the acceptance of such provision as the queen had it, unlimitedly, both in her power and her intention to make for her, she became equally incensed against the blind wilfulness of his conduct, as she was against the united meanness and arrogance which had marked that of De Madginecourt.

Hitherto every observation made by the queen upon the fate of Rosalind, and the authors of the miseries to which she had been condemned, had tended to assure her of the interest which Elizabeth took in her happiness; but when called upon to pursue her narrative, her heart still sunk within her, for the moment was now come at which it was necessary for her to confess to her sovereign, her private marriage with Edward. In accents almost choked by contending feelings the declaration was made.

Till the moment of her acknowledging herself a wife, the queen had listened to her tale of woe with the most compassionate and indulgent attention; when these words fell from her lips, she impatiently enquired, "on whom she had bestowed her hand?"

Trembling, Rosalind replied—"On Edward."

To this reply naturally followed, on the part of the queen, the enquiries of—"Who was Edward?—of what lineage?—of what rank?"

With increased agitation Rosalind recounted the simple history of Edward, previously to his becoming an inhabitant of De Mowbray Castle, expatiated on the brotherly affection which she had experienced from him, and dwelt on the name of *son*, by which her deceased mother had bequeathed to him the legacy of the cross.

After Rosalind had ceased to speak, the queen maintained a silence of some minutes; during which the anxious pleader for her indulgence and pity fixed her eyes upon her countenance, and beheld in it marks of her being deeply engaged in thought. At length, Elizabeth raising herself upon her couch, spoke thus—"That the goddaughter of England's Queen has both erred and degraded herself, in contracting an union with one who, if he be not unknown, is, at best, but the offspring of an inferior subject of the realm, is a point which admits of no controversy. But the pangs which have rent her motherless breast, the painful extremities which have driven her to the action, shall not be increased by a want of feeling towards her on the part of her sovereign. Elizabeth holds the conduct of which Lord Rufus de Madginecourt and the Baron de Mowbray have been guilty in too despicable a point of view, to become in her own person an imitator of their insensibility. Rosalind de Mowbray shall not be excluded from a parental interest in the heart of her queen, because she was withheld from seeking her advice and friendship at the moment of her affliction and necessity."

At the sound of these words, the tears burst into the eyes of Rosalind, and throwing herself at the feet of her who had uttered them, she imprinted on her extended hand a kiss of gratitude, which she accompanied with an exclamation of rapturous thankfulness, rendered nearly inarticulate by the sobs through which it was uttered.

"Calm, calm your transports," said the queen, again raising her god-daughter from her humble position; "while you merit my favour you shall share it; I will never consider as a transgression of your own, an error into which the crimes of others have driven you. But although I am thus resolved in your cause, there are still worldly customs, of which the universal benefit is too certain and too great to be broken through incautiously by a sovereign like myself, whose example should be the excitement of my people's just and honourable conduct; exceptions to beneficial ordinances in society, come with the worst grace from those the highest in authority. But I will explain myself more fully to you when you have unfolded to me the remainder of your narrative; I must know all that relates to you, ere my judgment can be formed with perfect correctness. Suspend, if possible, your emotions, till you have related to me where you have passed your days, in what retirement, in what asylum found refuge, since your ill-judged union: why have you thus long delayed to present yourself before me?"

Again Rosalind resumed the thread of her calamitous history: she spoke of the imprisonment in her own apartment to which her father had condemned her, after the departure of Edward from England, and of the sufferings which Edward had endured in Flanders; she related the attack threatened to be made upon De Mowbray Castle by the freebooter Allanrod, the marching out of her father with his chosen men to meet the divided forces of the enemy, at the instigation of the deserter, Donald, and his subsequent defeat and captivity. Thence she proceeded to describe the despoiling of Lord William's castle by the moss-troopers; the almost incredible circumstance of her having been rescued from them by the interference of Lord Rufus de Madginecourt; the demand which Allanrod had made of her hand, and the determination of Lord Rufus rather to submit to the sacking of his castle, than to deliver her into the power of the freebooter; lastly, she recounted her seclusion in the grotto; the triumph of Allanrod in his attack upon Rockmount Castle; her being dragged to the altar, and placed there by the side of the dreaded chief, in order to be united to him by the bond of marriage; the sudden appearance of her Edward in the chapel, and the rescue of her person from her enemies, which his disguise had enabled him to accomplish.

The queen heard Rosalind's account of such occurrences as had marked the latter years of her own and her Edward's existence, with an interest which their extraordinary nature excited for them in her breast; but the fact which most astonished her was, the change which appeared to have taken place in the sentiments of Lord Rufus with regard to Rosalind; upon this circumstance, Elizabeth dwelt with many an unsatisfactory surmise: like Rosalind, she could not induce herself to believe that he actually repented of his former conduct towards her, and that this repentance had been the cause of the complacency with which he had lately treated her; she did not doubt that some refined motive of a self-interested nature lay concealed beneath his shew of service, although she could not immediately conceive what that motive was.

Although the dislike which the Queen professed herself to bear Lord Rufus, might have been supposed to have prompted and encouraged Rosalind to the disclosure of *all* she knew concerning him, it will still be observed that the pure and virtuous sufferer, incapable of falsehood, sacredly maintained the promise which he had exacted from her at the time she was immediately in his power, within the walls of his own castle, of not disclosing to Elizabeth that any secret bond existed between himself and the freebooter Allanrod; he had informed her that the disclosure of such a tie must inevitably cost him his life, and her gentle soul recoiled from being the instrument of depriving even an enemy and a monster, like De Madginecourt, of his existence.

CHAPTER IX.

To die—to sleep—
No more;—and by a sleep, to say we end
The heart-ache, and the thousand nat'ral shocks
That flesh is heir to;—'tis a consummation
Devoutly to be wish'd.

HAMLET.

I am settled, and bend up
Each corporal agent to this terrible feat.

MACBETH.

After several farther remarks upon the events which the unfortunate Rosalind had recounted to her, the queen recurred to those words which she had before let fall—"of there being certain beneficial ordinances in society, which a sovereign ought to be the last to break through;"—and she explained them by saying—"that although she bore no animosity, no anger to Edward, as an individual, still, it was impossible for her to admit him to her court, as the husband of the daughter of one of her barons—that by such an admission, she should be countenancing the daughters of other nobles in forming alliances derogatory to their rank in life; encouraging them to contract unions with men of inferior circumstances, who might become the poison of the families into which they were admitted; and that she should, likewise, by such a step, be emboldening men of dangerous and designing minds, to insinuate themselves into the hearts of unsuspicious females, for the very purpose of rising, through their means, to situations, from which they ought most carefully to be withheld."

Rosalind's heart acknowledged the justice of the queen's observations; although she could not restrain the tear from starting into her eye, whilst she considered them as embracing the fate of one so tenderly beloved, and whom it had been the most anxious wish of her soul to behold bending his knee at the feet of her royal godmother.

Upon the countenance of Rosalind the queen read what was passing in her mind, and thus addressed her—"Do not suffer yourself to be cast down; I have already pledged myself a friend to you; and I now make the same promise towards him, in whom you are most interested. But for the reasons I have already given you, my favour cannot shine openly upon him, at least for the present. I will make it my study to investigate his character—to discern whether he is worthy of the hand with which he is blessed; and if I find him thus deserving, circumstances may arise to work a change in his favour, which, if too suddenly brought about, could not add to the eventual happiness of himself or you. In cases of this doubtful nature, slow proceedings are the surest; hasty acts lead the multitude to suspect them the veils of improprieties."

Having said this, the queen requested Rosalind to call to her the Lady Butler. When she entered, Elizabeth took a key from her pocket, and directed her to fetch her a purse of gold, which she informed her she would find in a drawer of her escritoir.

Whilst the Lady Butler was absent, executing the queen's commission, Elizabeth, calling Rosalind to her side, said—"The gold which will be brought me hither, is for the use of your husband. You must, for a time, Rosalind, consent to be parted from him; it is necessary for the accomplishment of the plan, which I have formed for your future felicity, and which I will presently explain to you, that as you have now providentially escaped the toils of your enemies, you should no more quit my palace, till I have brought them to account before me, for their conduct towards you."

The Lady Butler entered with the purse, which the queen receiving at her hand, put into that of Rosalind, accompanying her action by saying—"Here are fifty pieces; retire into the antichamber, where you will find the implements for writing; explain to your husband at large all that has passed between us; give him those reasons which withhold me from admitting him an inhabitant of this mansion, as likewise those by which I am actuated in retaining you near my person; and having done this, direct him to procure for himself an abode in the vicinity of my palace; tell him that any communication, which he may desire to convey to you, by letter, I will issue my commands for having safely delivered into your hands, as likewise into his, such as you may wish to send him. Acquaint him, moreover, that Elizabeth professes herself the mother of Rosalind, and will not consequently be the enemy of him in whom her daughter lives."

Infinitely would Rosalind have preferred to have communicated with her own lips to Edward, such matter as the queen had commanded her to write to him; but averse to advancing any request, where so great indulgences were voluntarily granted, she retired to the antichamber, and having committed a full account of her interview with the queen to paper, she concluded, by entreating him to write to her, at least once every day, which rule she promised to observe towards him, during the period which it should be deemed necessary, by the queen, for their separation to continue.

Having folded her epistle, the confidential Lady Butler was charged by Elizabeth with its delivery.

Edward having read the information which it conveyed to him, had no alternative to quitting the palace. With lingering steps, and a heavy heart, he returned to his solitary abode, where his reflections were his only companions, and his sole employment that of placing them on paper, for the perusal of his Rosalind, who was meanwhile continuing to experience, with every hour, additional kindness from the Queen.

In the afternoon Elizabeth summoned into her presence some of the members of her privy council, with whom she had not conversed since the death of Mary of Scotland; and having passed nearly three hours with them in her closet, she returned to the apartment where she had left Rosalind; she entered it leaning on one of her maids of honour for support, and with the burning glow of fatigue painting her cheeks.

Rosalind advanced to meet her, and said—"Alas! my gracious sovereign, it afflicts me much, that I should be the cause of your suffering anxiety, to which your health and strength are so ill adapted."

"Oh no, no, you are mistaken," replied the queen, with a benignant smile; "I trust that both will be amended, by the powers of my mind being called into action."

After she had some moments reposed herself on her couch, she said—"I have resolved, Rosalind, that in the present crisis of affairs, now under my consideration, it is requisite that my first step should be the release of the Baron de Mowbray from his present captivity; and my next, the utter subversion of the daring freebooter Allanrod, and his lawless band. In your father's attempt at uniting you to Lord Rufus de Madginecourt, without any reference being made to me in the business, he has shewn himself so far indifferent about any consideration which it is in my power to evince for his welfare, and that of his family, that it is not from any regard to him that I shall send a force to procure his enlargement; but in order to afford to the other, and worthier nobles of my kingdom, placed in a similar situation to what his has been, a proof that the arm of Elizabeth shall ever be stretched out to redress the wrongs they may suffer, in their attempts to protect her kingdom from the ravaging banditti with which it is at this instant infested. I have therefore commanded, that with the rising of to-morrow's sun, a proclamation be issued throughout the city, announcing to my knights and captains round my throne, that I shall hold, upon the following day, a public court, at which I shall select the leaders of an expedition, which it is my purpose, without delay, to send forth against the borderers."

"Heaven grant that your royal aid come not too late—that they find not my father deprived of life!" exclaimed Rosalind; for it will be remembered that she was utterly ignorant of his escape from the stronghold of Allanrod.

"Such is my prayer also," returned the Queen. "I wish to see him, and receive from himself the motives which induced him to adopt so harsh, and unnatural a conduct, as he has been guilty of towards a child, so particularly favoured in the pledge of protection which it received at its admission amidst the members of christianity; for it is but equitable that both sides of any question be heard, ere a decisive judgment is formed upon it," she added, with an expression, that assured Rosalind that they were only words of favour, and, in her own mind, not the slightest doubt hung upon the truth of the narration she had received from her lips.

"As soon as my deputed forces shall have marched against the freebooters," resumed Elizabeth, "my next concern shall be to dispatch a summons to the Lord de Madginecourt to appear before me. In the recital which you have given me of the calamities experienced by your husband in Flanders, I have seen him guilty of an attempt to deprive an English subject of his life; and although the crime is not amenable with his death, since it was committed beyond the boundaries of my island, it is, nevertheless, my duty not to suffer such a transgression of the virtue of an English noble to pass unreproved and unstigmatized with the censure it merits. Where," after a pause, asked the Queen, "is that Hubert, of whom you speak, as having been witness of the atrocious villainy?"

Rosalind informed the queen where Edward and he had parted, and that Hubert had assured him that they should meet again.

"As he is in the kingdom," replied Elizabeth, "he will no doubt easily be found, when he learns that those to whom his cares are directed, are under the immediate protection of Elizabeth." And to these words the Queen added an encomium upon the nobleness of Hubert's heart, and the gratitude he had evinced towards the benefactor of his youth.—"He is one of those rare and brilliant examples of true merit," she said, "on which it reflects the highest praise upon majesty to confer a reward; and he shall not be forgotten by me."

As the Queen continued to dwell on the circumstances which immediately occupied her mind, she told Rosalind that she conceived the strongest proof of De Madginecourt's sentiments, with regard to herself, during her stay at Rockmount Castle, not to have been of the innocent and friendly nature which he had endeavoured to induce her to believe them, was the attempt which he had made of depriving Edward of his life, during his imprisonment in Flanders, and his having again proposed himself, immediately after his supposed death, to Lord William, as the suitor of her hand. Rosalind coincided in the opinion of the queen, and said, that such had ever been her own idea; and they both agreed that Rosalind could not be sufficiently thankful for having escaped with unsullied honour, from his power, although they were entirely at a loss to conceive on what account he had spared her, in her defenceless state.

After a night, during which the balm of sleep had been almost a stranger to her pillow, Rosalind arose at early morn, and wrote to her Edward a full detail of the resolutions which the queen had formed on the preceding evening. When Edward read the account of the forces which it was the intention of the queen to send against the detested Allanrod, and of the public court, which she had appointed to hold, for the purpose of selecting the leaders of the expedition, his heart beat a tumult of desire within his breast, to be named one of the envied number.

The anxiety which he felt to obtain a post amidst the chosen, was unconquerable; and he determined to present himself before the queen, at her public court, amongst the other captains who should appear there, as an officer that had borne her majesty's arms in Flanders, and to urge his petition to be enrolled in the present expedition.

After some debates with his own mind, he judged it most adviseable not to acquaint his Rosalind with his intention. He considered, that, apprehensive of his safety, she might endeavour to alter his determination; or that, if such was not the case, she might impart to the queen his wish, and that Elizabeth might raise obstacles to the accomplishment of it, of the same nature as those which she had advanced as reasons for not yet admitting him to her presence.

He had both seen and heard so much of the villanies of Allanrod, that he absolutely felt as if the chastisement of the freebooter would be incomplete, unless his arm were one of those stretched out to vanquish and to crush him.

The whole of the present day he spent in preparations for his appearance on the following one. He procured an armourer to polish the suit of mail, which had been his constant habiliment since his arrival in England, till the hour of his reaching London. The purse which the queen had sent to him, supplied him with the means of procuring whatever he deemed appropriate and necessary to his equipment; accordingly he provided himself with a surcoat of scarlet cloth, on which was embroidered an emblem of valour and hope; and in the front of his helmet was placed a knot of waving plumes.

Thus clad, when the hour of repairing to the appointed assembly arrived, he found no obstruction offered to his entering the palace, and the way to the presence-chamber was pointed out to him, in like manner as to the other suppliants for admission to the presence of the queen, by the chamberlains of the court, who were attending in the hall of the royal mansion for that express purpose.

On entering the antiroom to the chamber of audience, he found the croud of those who were pressing to throw themselves at the feet of their sovereign so great, as almost to impede his progress; but in a short time his attempts to approach the door of the presence-chamber were rendered successful, by placing himself in the train of a body of knights, who were advancing towards it, and for whom a passage was cleared.

Arrived within a few paces of the spacious door, which was thrown back upon its hinges, Edward cast his eyes through the aperture, and, for the first time, beheld the Queen of England, the godmother of his Rosalind! At the extremity of a magnificent saloon, Elizabeth appeared, seated on her throne, beneath a superb canopy of crimson velvet, richly embroidered, and fringed with gold; she was surrounded by a vast body of nobles, who were, with herself, divided from the pressing throng, by a semicircle of gilt wire, which was extended round them, at the distance of about ten feet from the base of the throne.

Whilst he stood wrapt in admiration of the majesty and grace which shone conspicuous upon the countenance of the queen, a figure, habited in the marine dress of the times, pressed before him.— The eagerness which the person thus clad testified to place himself immediately in the door-way of the presence-chamber, attracted the observation of Edward, and as he fixed his eyes upon the stranger, he saw him draw from the folds of his dress, a pistol, which, with the utmost dexterity, he levelled at the person of the Queen.

With the quickness of lightning, Edward darted upon him, and dashed from his hand the weapon of destruction. In the momentary struggle, it discharged itself, and the ball, with which it had been loaded, entered the ceiling of the saloon.

The report of the pistol caused a general consternation and alarm throughout the court; every one flocked to the spot from whence it had proceeded, and those who were able to arrive within sight of it, observed Edward wresting a second pistol from the offender, with which he had attempted to put a period to his own existence, after having been foiled in his attempt upon the life of the queen.

Elizabeth herself had been hurried by her nobles into another apartment; but the natural firmness of her mind had not been at all shaken by the danger from which she had just been rescued, and learning that the offender was secured, contrary to the advice of such members of her council as were present, she commanded him to be brought before her, in order that she might herself examine him.

The report of the occurrence had, in the course of a few minutes, been conveyed to every part of the palace, and no sooner did it reach the ear of Rosalind, than she flew to convince herself that her royal protectress was indeed in safety. Scarcely had she reached the apartment to which the queen had retired from the audience-chamber, ere, at an opposite door to that by which she had entered, the offender was led into it, in compliance with the command which the Queen had issued to that effect.

No sooner did the eye of Rosalind fall upon the countenance of the young man, for such he appeared, than she discovered it to be one with which her memory had acquaintance, and in a very few moments, she recollected that the resemblance of his person was extremely great to that of the female whom, with her husband, she had received into the grotto in the vicinity of Rockmount, and the latter of whom had breathed his last sigh there, whilst receiving acts of kindness at her hands. At the same instant, she also recollected the vow of which her husband had spoken to her, the promise which she had made to him of revenging the death of their sainted mistress, and the mysterious declaration which she had made to her at her departure—"that she was a dying woman."

The offender being placed opposite to the queen, at a short distance from her person, Elizabeth said—"Who are you? and upon what provocation have you attempted to take away my life?"

The person thus addressed replied—"Although you behold me in this habit, I am, like yourself, a woman—my name, Margaret Lambrun."

A sudden emotion overspread the countenance of the queen at the sound of these words, and she cast a look of surprise upon those who were standing near her—"Are you the Lady Margaret Lambrun?" she exclaimed.

"I could not doubt that you would recollect me," returned Margaret: "till your inhumanity drove every friend that loved her from sharing her prison with the injured Queen of Scots, you have often seen my husband and myself hovering round her person, with the hope of communicating a single ray of comfort to her afflicted heart. When your hatred towards her became more inflamed to cruelty, by the godlike resignation with which she bore your injustice, and you deprived her even of this slender consolation, we returned to Scotland, to lament the fate which we could not amend, and endeavour to serve her by our prayers, since we were denied the gratification of dedicating to her our personal services. But when we learnt that you had raised your hand against her life, our anguish rose to frenzy—

our entire possessions we distributed amongst the various Catholic churches in Scotland, to buy masses for the repose of her soul: this done, my husband pledged a vow to Heaven to revenge her death, by the extermination of your life, and I resolved to profess myself an accomplice in the act, that I might not survive him; but that my soul might wing its way with his, to a reunion with our mistress in Heaven!—Heartbroken with affliction, he, on our journey hither, sunk into the sleep of death, but not till he had received a promise from my lips to fulfil the oath of retribution, which he had sworn. Arrived in London, I awaited with the greatest impatience an hour, when I should learn that you were about to appear in some public situation, where I might gain access to your presence. This day presented me with the chance I desired—this habit gained me the passport, that I believed it would, into your palace; and had I, with the weapon which I aimed at your heart, effected my purpose, I was provided with a second, to free myself from the punishment of your avengers."

Although the queen heard this hardy declaration with astonishment, still her fortitude and wonted presence of mind did not forsake her, and she replied—"Is it really possible that you could conceive the deed of which you have attempted the perpetration, a duty?"

"Yes, a double duty," returned Margaret: "You have deprived me of a sovereign, dearer to me than existence; and by her death, you have also caused that of my husband: thus, in striking at the root of your life, I endeavoured to revenge both theirs at a blow."

"And what, upon your own grounds of argument," asked Elizabeth, "must you consider *my* duty to be towards my people, whom you have attempted to deprive of *their* sovereign?"

"Do you ask this question of me in the character of a queen, or a judge?" answered Margaret.

After a moment's hesitation, Elizabeth said—"I now address you as a queen."

"Then," returned the offender, with the intrepidity with which she had before spoken, "if I were the Queen of England, I would pardon Margaret Lambrun, that, by the performance of a merciful action, I might endeavour to re-establish my fame, ere it be committed to the annals of history."

The queen, turning to some of her council, expressed her surprise at the singularity and hardiness of the character before her; and then commanded her to be carried to the Tower, for farther examination, at a future period.

The moment Margaret was withdrawn from her sight, the queen exclaimed—"I have been an abuser of time—I have trifled away those moments with the criminal object, which ought to have been employed in gratitude to my preserver.—Where is he who disarmed the hand of my assassin?"

One of the lords in waiting by her side, replied—"that he was attending in the audience-chamber."

"Who is he, and what is his name?" asked Elizabeth.

Upon these points no one present could give her information. They said that he was a young man in the garb of a soldier, but that his person was not known to them.

The queen commanded him to be instantly conducted into her presence.

Every eye was turned eagerly towards the door at which he was expected to enter; and when that of Rosalind beheld, in the preserver of her godmother, her queen, and her protectress, the husband of her tenderest affections, a flood of joy poured into her heart, which overwhelmed all sense in ecstacy, and with a faint sigh she sunk into the arms of the Lady Butler, who was standing by her side.

By those who observed her emotion, it was supposed to be occasioned by the agitation of mind into which the danger of the queen had thrown her, added to the oppression of the heat caused by the crowd of persons which filled the apartment, and she was directly removed from it into purer air.

Edward saw, at his entrance, but one object, and that was the queen. With a modest expression of the satisfaction which glowed in his heart, beaming from his eyes, he advanced towards the spot where she was awaiting his approach, and sunk upon his right knee before her.

Elizabeth raised him, with her own hand, from his posture of humiliation, and, accompanying her words with a smile of the most affable benignity, she said—"Words were a weak expression of the gratitude with which my heart beats for your loyalty; ask of me any boon, as the recompense of your fervour in my cause, and conceive it already granted."

"The gracious recollection which your majesty bears of the service that I have been so fortunate as to render you, would for me be recompense enough," replied Edward, "did I not believe, that by accepting the promise which your generosity has condescended to make me, I may be enabled to render myself a second time useful in your cause."

"Explain yourself," returned the queen.

"I have, for several years past," rejoined Edward, "been honoured by bearing your majesty's arms; permit me now to march under your standard, against the freebooter, Allanrod, and my proudest wishes will be accomplished."

"And is that the only recompense which thou desirest, for having preserved a sovereign's life?" exclaimed Elizabeth: "Whosoever thou art, thy soul is noble, whether thy blood be so or not. Lords of my council and armies," added the queen, bending her looks alternately to the nobles on either side, "I trust there is no Englishman, who does not rejoice in the preservation of Elizabeth: I trust therefore that no Englishman can envy the honour awarded, as the recompense of England's joy.—Elizabeth bestows on her preserver, *the command* of the expedition against Allanrod."

Again Edward fell prostrate at her feet, and kissed the hand which she extended to him.

"Hast thou rank, young man?" asked Elizabeth.

"Neither rank nor fortune, but my sword and honour, Madam," returned Edward.

The queen took a sword from the hand of one of her attendant lords, and having raised it over the head of Edward, she said—"From this hour thou art possessed of both—rise a Knight of England; and for the support of thy title, Elizabeth bestows on thee ten thousand marks of gold."

The keenest feelings are the most difficult to be expressed; such was the case with Edward; joy, confusion, astonishment, and gratitude, met so forcibly in his heart, as to deny him the power of utterance.

"By what name shall I enquire for you when I wish to take my leave of you, previously to your setting out, and give you my wishes for success in your expedition?" asked Elizabeth.

"Edward is my name, so please your majesty," he replied.

"Sir Edward," repeated the queen, with emphasis; "and so farewell, my noble knight!"

Elizabeth now quitted the apartment, and Sir Edward was directed to attend the queen's secretary at war on the following morning, at the hour of eight, to receive the documents of his march.

CHAPTER X.

Oh, happy hour! If I not set thee down,
The whitest that the eye of time e'er saw,
Let me ne'er smile, when I remember thee.

N. LEE.

It must be unnecessary to expatiate on the rapture experienced by Sir Edward, on having risen to the favour of the queen, by means so honourable and gratifying to his feelings. With a heart light as gossamer he returned home, to impart, by letter, to Rosalind the overflowing joy of his soul. Scarcely had he composed himself for writing, ere one of the chamberlains of the court entered his apartment, and presented him with a note, which contained the following words—

"Oh, my husband, our excellent queen has learnt, that it is *my* Edward who is the preserver of her life; this knowledge has removed every obstacle to your being admitted into her presence: hasten then to obey the summons of your gracious sovereign, and your affectionate Rosalind."

When Sir Edward raised his eyes from the paper, the chamberlain, who had brought it to him, said—"We wait, Sir, to conduct you to our royal mistress." Sir Edward obeyed his signal for descending into the street; where he found prepared for him to mount, a horse, richly caparisoned; and a royal guard to march on either side of him, which the love and loyalty of the people rendered a most useful precaution, as the ardour with which all ranks pressed to behold him, would, but for the resolution of the guard, have entirely obstructed his progress to the palace.

On arriving there, every idea which he had ever before been able to form of happiness, was exceeded by the gracious reception which he received from Elizabeth; by the shouts of joy which issued from the lips of the grateful multitude; and, most of all, by beholding the reflection of that honest pride with which his own heart was filled in the eyes of his Rosalind. The sensation was such as none could have felt with the strength with which Rosalind and her Edward were impressed by it, but those who had, for an equal period, like themselves, drank of the cup of misery and despair; it was a transportation, as by the power of magic, from the dark gulph of mourning, to the lightly buoyant clouds of fluttering joy— in the imagination, it may be drawn; by the pen, it cannot be executed with its natural lustre.

Sir Edward was now considered an inhabitant of the palace, till he should march on his expedition against Allanrod.

In the evening the queen summoned to her, her privy council, and her secretary at war, and having presented to them the young knight, she entered into consultation with them upon the most adviseable plan of proceeding against the freebooters. The first object, it was decided, must be the restoration of Lord William de Mowbray to liberty; the next, that of making Allanrod a prisoner, as he appeared to be the chief animator of the raging hordes, and these points being concluded upon, it was referred to the opinion of Sir Edward, what force he deemed necessary for the undertaking?

He replied—"That he desired no more than one thousand men, well acquainted with the use of arms; they were," he said, "at least equal to twice their number, of a raw banditti, who were entirely uninformed of the use of tactics."

Elizabeth directed that the number should be fifteen hundred, and then applied to her secretary at war to determine from what quarters the requisite force should be drawn. After some debate upon this point, it was agreed, that three of the fifteen hundred should be immediately drafted from the troops now lying in the vicinity of the metropolis, and be ready to commence their march on the morn of the second day from the present one; and that expresses should be sent forward upon the road along which the expedition was to proceed, towards the north, for the like draughts to be made from other regiments, and added to Sir Edward's force as he passed through the towns in which they were stationed—and the arrangement was so planned, that the number of the troops should be completed at York.

Before the breaking up of the council, it was suggested to the queen by her ministers, that it would be regarded by her people as a necessary proof of her gratitude to Heaven, for the blessing of her continuing her auspicious reign over them, which had been granted to her in the preservation of her existence, that she should appoint a day for returning public thanksgiving to that effect in the cathedral of Saint Paul; and they therefore entreated her to name one for that purpose.

Elizabeth replied—"That she was not deficient to Heaven in gratitude for the singular protection which she had received at its hands, but that she chose to defer her public acknowledgment of it, till the return of Sir Edward to London should enable him to be present with her at the hour of her devotion; that by beholding him, through whom her providential rescue had been effected, her mind might be the more firmly bent towards the cause in which the benefit had originated."

Her ministers in return ventured to submit to her opinion, whether so long a delay of an act of devotion, might not appear the effect of coolness in its performance.

For the possibility of such a supposition, the queen's countenance immediately expressed, that she would on no account give the shadow of a plea. "It shall then," she said, "be the day after tomorrow; Sir Edward shall defer his setting out till the subsequent morning, and attend us to Saint Paul's."

Matters of public importance being thus decided, the queen reconducted Sir Edward to the apartment where they had left Rosalind, to join the members of the privy-council; and here, amidst many particulars of his own history, he imparted to the queen, at her command, the account which had been given him, at the convent of Saint Agnes, of the Lady Margaret Murray, the cousin of the Bonny Mabel, who had afterwards espoused Sir James Lambrun, a man most devotedly attached to the interest of the Queen of Scotland; and there appeared scarcely any reason to doubt that she was the very person now in custody for her attempt upon the life of Elizabeth.

The queen and her guests had so much matter before them for conversation and reflection, that the night was far advanced ere they retired to rest, although the health and spirits of both Elizabeth and her goddaughter were in a state to require the nourishment of repose.

On the following day, Margaret Lambrun was brought before the queen's ministers for her examination. From the investigation which she underwent, it appeared that she was indeed the daughter of the deceased Earl of Lednoch, who had preserved herself from the contagion of the pestilence, by flying to the mountains of Athol; that having espoused a man, who owed his all to the House of Stuart, and on that account had been attached to it with a strength of affection which bordered upon frenzy, she had imbibed from him his principles, and considered it an act of duty to his memory to fulfil the plan for avenging the death of his mistress, to which his mind had been devoted for some weeks previous to his decease.

"She had," she confessed, "suffered many struggles within her own breast, and made every effort she had been capable of, to divert her mind from her design; but that all the arguments she had used to convince herself that it was better to resign her purpose, had only tended to strengthen her in it. I have experienced," she added, "that reason has no power to restrain a woman from vengeance, when she is impelled to it by love."

It had been feared and suspected, that Margaret might have been a member of some dangerous conspiracy, formed perhaps by the Roman Catholics against the government and the queen; but on the present examination of the culprit, it was fully proved that all apprehensions of this nature were without foundation.

One of the nobles present enquired of her—"Since you confess that you experienced many struggles with your own mind upon the propriety of the action which you have committed, and could not subdue your idea of the necessity you were under of attempting it, are you satisfied with having made the attempt, and happy that it has not been productive of a fatal consequence, or the reverse?"

"Why should I reply to your demand," she replied, "since the law considers only the attempt?"

Her answers to various other questions which were put to her, displayed the same collectedness, and strength of mind; but her examiners still believed her repentant of her crime, although too proud of spirit to make confession of it.

The report of Margaret's examination was laid before the queen, and her majesty at the same time informed that the necessary preparations for the trial would be made without delay.

"She must be found guilty, must she not?" enquired Elizabeth of the Earl of Southampton, who had brought her an account of the examination, at which he had been present.

"There can be no doubt of it, Madam," he replied.

"And death must be the punishment, which the law awards to her crime," rejoined the queen.

The earl returned an affirmative answer to her question, and then retired, upon a signal to that effect from her majesty.

The queen passed nearly the whole of the afternoon and evening alone in her private apartment. On the following morning, at an early hour, Sir Edward received a summons to attend her in her closet.

"I have an embassy, which I shall request of you to perform for me, to the prison of Margaret Lambrun," she said. "This is the day appointed for me to visit the cathedral of Saint Paul, and return my thanks to Heaven for the preservation of my life, of which it chose you as the instrument. The intention of inflicting punishment on those who have injured us, bespeaks resentment against them in our breast; how then can I, without wilfully drawing down upon myself the vengeance of Providence, pray, 'that my trespasses may be forgiven to me, in like manner as I forgive them who may have trespassed against me,' whilst I permit a fellow-being, who has been guilty of an offence towards my person, to be detained my prisoner, for public execution?—Convey to Margaret Lambrun that paper; it contains her pardon."

"By this unparalleled benignity of soul, Madam," exclaimed Sir Edward, "you increase the glory I have been blessed by rendering you; since by it you afford one more proof of the many virtues that had died with you, had the assassin's blow been fatal."

"But," added Elizabeth, "inform her, that ere the expiration of a week, it is my condition that she quit my kingdom for ever; I will provide her an escort out of it, and if she be destitute of them, with the means of life."

Sir Edward immediately proceeded to the Tower, and was

conducted to the apartment of the Lady Margaret. She expressed a haughty surprise at his appearance, the motive of which he explained by putting into her hand the pardon, to which the royal signature was affixed, and which he presented to her with an impressive eulogy on the humanity of the queen, and the gratitude with which the conduct of Elizabeth ought to fill her heart.

Having twice or thrice successively perused the contents of this paper, as if doubtful of the evidence of her senses, she raised her eyes to Sir Edward, and said, in her usual tone of firmness—"Since the Queen of England has vouchsafed to grant me her pardon, be pleased, Sir, to acquaint her majesty, that I have but one poor request to make of her, which she shall receive from me in the course of a few hours, in writing."

Sir Edward having executed the commission with which his royal mistress had charged him, returned to inform her of the reception which it had met with from the object of her humanity.

"Whatever that request, it shall be granted," the queen said; and, decked with the smiles of conscious benevolence, she proceeded to her chamber, to attire herself in a manner appropriate to the business of the day.

At the appointed hour the religious procession, in the centre of which moved Elizabeth, passed in solemn order from the palace to the church; it was graced by the presence of every noble who had received intimation of the design in time to become a part of her train; and the blessings of the populace, and their prayers for the future preservation of their queen from the attacks of disloyalty, were poured upon her ear from every quarter.

On her return to her palace, a letter was delivered to her by the lieutenant of the Tower. "He had been commissioned," he said, "by Margaret Lambrun, to put it into her majesty's own hands."

The queen tore it hastily open, and found the contents to be these—

"Madam,

"Ere you have perused these lines, I shall be at peace for ever. Whilst I feared that an act of suicide might be imputed to the dread of those tortures to which the voice of justice might condemn me, I determined to endure life, rather than submit my reputation to the obloquy of such cowardice; now your gracious pardon has removed that apprehension, and no motive can be attributed to my self-destruction, but my desire of uniting my spirit with those of my esteemed friends, who are no longer of this earth, I do not hesitate to swallow the draught of death; and the only petition which I leave behind me, is that of being committed to the earth, with the ceremonies of the Catholic church, of which I have lived a member—such is the prayer of the dying

"MARGARET LAMBRUN."

With a countenance, on which the greatest consternation and surprise were depicted, the queen turned to the lieutenant, and enquired, "whether he had not left Margaret alive?"

His reply was—"that he had received the letter from her own hands."

Elizabeth communicated to him the contents, and directed that he should immediately return to the Tower, and make personal investigation into her safety; and if he found her still living, to withhold her from committing the act of violence, upon which she appeared determined.

Accompanied by the Earl of Suffolk, and two other gentlemen, commissioned by the queen to attend him, the lieutenant sped to the Tower, and directly led the way to the apartments where Margaret was a prisoner: she was not in the first, and they proceeded to the second chamber, in which stood her bed; upon it they found her extended: her frame was torn with convulsions, and her features fixed in the agonies of death. Medical aid was instantly called in to her assistance, but it arrived in vain; the struggle in which they had found her was her last, and, with a deep and lengthened groan, her spirit fled into eternity.

Upon a table, near her bed, stood a drinking cup, at the bottom of which appeared a sediment of a dark nature, with a few drops of water floating above it; this was the remnant of the poison which she had swallowed: by its side lay a small silver box, in which the drug had been contained.

Although the queen had nothing to reproach herself with, on the score of humanity, in the case of the deceased Margaret, still she received the intelligence of her death with many expressions of regret, and some degree of painful reflection. Her untimely end was a link of the chain of miseries which the death of Mary had wound round the hearts of the Scotch; and once more Elizabeth wished in vain that she could recall the first inimical action of which she had been guilty towards the fallen monarch.

CHAPTER XI.

——'Tis one thing to be tempted,
Another thing to fall———
....
No ceremony that to great one's 'longs,
Not the king's crown, nor the deputed sword,
The marshal's truncheon, nor the judge's robe,
Become them with one half so good a grace,
As mercy does.

MEASURE FOR MEASURE.

THE succeeding day was that appointed for the setting out of Sir Edward against the borderers.

With the first of the morning the queen called to one of her ministers; she had pledged her word to grant the last request of Margaret Lambrun, and to him she issued her commands for the observance of her promise, by directing the body to be removed into Scotland for interment, and ordering that enquiry should be made at Rockmount Castle for that of her husband, Sir James, in order that he might be laid by the side of his wife.

This done, she dispatched a courier to Rockmount Castle, upon a business of a different nature; him she charged with a mandate to Lord Rufus himself, commanding him to appear before her, without delay, in London; for although from Rosalind she had learnt him to have been vanquished by the moss-troopers, she doubted not that he had already paid the ransom fixed upon for his liberty, and returned to his despoiled castle.

Having made these arrangements, she entered her breakfast apartment, and sent to invite Rosalind and her husband to join her at her repast, that she might enjoy the society of the latter for a few hours previously to his departure, which was to take place about noon.

The various concerns which had occupied the mind of the queen that morning, had caused her to begin her meal full an hour after her usual time; and herself and her happy guests had not yet risen from table, when one of her attendant gentlemen entered the apartment, and informed her that Lord William de Mowbray was arrived at the palace, and entreated to be admitted to the presence of her majesty.

Upon the receipt of this intelligence, the greatest surprise was depicted on the countenances of the queen and her guests, while the gentle Rosalind could with difficulty prevent herself from falling off her seat.

The queen perceived her emotion, and immediately addressed her in these words—"Rosalind, you forget that you are under the protection of a mother and a queen, united in one person."

Then turning to the gentleman from whom she had received the information of Lord William's arrival, she said—"Is it known to you whether the Baron de Mowbray is acquainted that Sir Edward and his daughter are the inmates of my palace?"

"So please your majesty, I have no reason to believe that he knows it," was the reply.

"Let him then be kept in ignorance of it," rejoined the queen; and to this command, she added her directions for him to be conducted into an apartment, till she was ready to receive him, which, she said, he might be informed she should shortly be.

When the messenger had quitted the room—"Heaven be praised!" exclaimed Rosalind, "that my father is no longer the prisoner of the dreaded Allanrod."

"I commend thy filial affection, my Rosalind," said the queen, "which shines forth with additional lustre in proportion to the acquaintance which those who behold it, have with the very slender claim that your parent's conduct towards you has left him to excite it in your breast."

"He is still the author of my being," replied the trembling Rosalind, "and I feel it the first duty of that existence, to implore my sovereign to temper the resentment against him, which my past sufferings have excited in her heart, with a lenient consideration for the errors to which human nature is prone."

"Exalted, generous woman!" exclaimed the queen, "worthy the

love and admiration of thy sovereign, the dove-like supplications of thy forgiving nature shall not fall unheeded upon the ear of Elizabeth, because Elizabeth will not neglect the performance of any act whereby she may add to the happiness of her meritorious god-daughter."

Rosalind kissed the extended hand of her sovereign, but her heart was now too full for utterance.

In the course of a few minutes the queen arose from her breakfast table, and telling Sir Edward and Rosalind that it would probably not be very long before she would summon them into her presence, she proceeded to another apartment, into which she commanded the Baron de Mowbray to be conducted to her.

On his entrance, the queen, who had seated herself at the upper end of the apartment, gave him a reception which bore neither the marks of pleasure, nor the reverse. With a countenance dressed in smiles and humility, he advanced towards her, and kneeling at her feet, whilst he touched with his lips the glove that covered her hand, he poured forth many adulative expressions upon the joy which he experienced, at once more entering her presence

"It surprises me, I confess, to behold you here," returned Elizabeth; "for I had learnt that you were the prisoner of the freebooters, and had prepared a force to march to your rescue."

Lord William returned the queen his most grateful thanks for her kind intention, and then besought her to suffer the troops which she had selected for the purpose of his rescue, to proceed without delay to that of his daughter Rosalind, who, he said, had been torn from De Mowbray Castle by the freebooters that had despoiled it, and, he doubted not, been conveyed to the same fortress in which he had himself been a prisoner, as he had understood it to be the residence of the chief of the banditti, the dreaded Allanrod—"And what," he said, "increased his apprehensions for her safety, was the demand which had been made of him by Allanrod, to grant his daughter to Lord Rufus de Madginecourt to wife, as the price of his own ransom."

"And does this demand on the part of the freebooter Allanrod, increase your apprehensions for her safety?" asked Elizabeth. "Surely I do not comprehend you aright; for it has been reported to me, that you had used every means in your power to compel your daughter into the arms of Lord Rufus de Madginecourt."

Lord William felt entirely at a loss what to decide the queen's feelings with regard to the union he had once endeavoured to contract for Rosalind with Lord Rufus; and equally fearful of condemning himself, if her sentiments were unfavourable towards it, by maintaining silence, he said—"There was a time, my sovereign, when I should have approved the alliance of De Madginecourt with my daughter, but——" He hesitated.

"I supposed that you had been misrepresented to me," replied the queen, with coolness, but with point, "for I judged that, had an alliance been in agitation, the approbation of her royal godmother would have been asked to grace it."

The Baron felt the reproof, and eager to turn the thoughts of the queen from himself to one more culpable, he replied—"The conduct of Lord Rufus has since that period been of so different a nature to what it then was, that I would sooner have followed my daughter to the grave, than to the altar as his bride. Since I have been the prisoner of the freebooters, I have discovered him to be guilty, in the point of loyalty, as well as friendship; for the demand which Allanrod caused to be made to me, of giving my daughter's hand to his friend, Lord Rufus de Madginecourt, plainly bespeaks some secret connexion to subsist between them. Thus in his union with an enemy of the state, Lord Rufus proves himself a foe to its interests."

Lord William paused.—The queen passed a few minutes in reflection upon the strangeness of the information winch he had conveyed to her, and doubtful whether to believe it the truth or a fallacy. If it were true that Allanrod had demanded the daughter of De Mowbray to wife for Lord Rufus de Madginecourt, some tie, some friendly union must subsist between them, to have caused this demand on the part of the freebooter; and if Allanrod had been authorized by Lord Rufus to make this demand for him, why had not Lord Rufus profited by the time during which Rosalind had been the inmate of his castle, for forcing her into compliance with his will? From Rosalind she had learnt that, during this period, Lord Rufus had informed her, that Allanrod had demanded her to wife for himself, and Lord Rufus had suffered his castle to stand the attack of a siege, rather than deliver her into his power. These were contradictory circumstances, points from which the queen knew not what conclusion to draw; and if the assertion which Lord William had made to her, of Allanrod having required the hand of Rosalind to be given to De Madginecourt as the price of his liberty, were a fallacy, she could not imagine to what end he had devised and propagated it.

The Baron de Mowbray we have, throughout the series of adventures in which we have witnessed him, perceived to be a man inoffensive towards those who placed no obstacles in the way of his favourite passion of aggrandizement of power and wealth, and heedless what unjust action he committed, where self-interest was concerned; it was therefore, in the present instance, natural to such a character as his was, however he might feel interested in the fate of his daughter, exposed as he believed her to the power of a band of freebooters, to feel still more for his own safety, which was trembling under the threatened accusation of the resolute Hubert.

Accordingly, finding it difficult any longer to restrain that subject which was uppermost in his heart, from mounting to his lips, he broke the silence which had for some minutes prevailed, by saying—"Upon the house of De Mowbray the countenance of my gracious sovereign has ever shone with the most conspicuous and benign partiality; it is, therefore, not only with satisfaction, but with pride, that I inform her, that there is at this moment existing, an attack, a base calumny, levelled against the honour of that house, in which her interference is most materially requisite for the preservation of its fame in the eye of society."

To what he was now referring, the queen was entirely ignorant, and therefore directed him to explain.

With many pauses and hesitations he gave the demanded explanation; but he said nothing of Hubert's having threatened to accuse him of having commanded the murder of the child; he merely acquainted the queen that, having entrusted the care of an infant, whom he wished to have brought up in obscurity, to one of his vassals for that purpose, that vassal had murdered it, for the sake of possessing undivided, the means with which he had furnished him for its maintenance and his own; and that judging some severe punishment due to him for the crime, yet undetermined in what way to proceed against him, he had brought him in chains to London, in order to act under the advice of the queen.

The Baron's story carried with it evidences of its own imperfectness, which could not pass upon the acute senses of Elizabeth, and she said—"But, my Lord, I do not perceive in what manner a crime committed by a vassal, is to reflect that violent disgrace of which you speak, upon the house of De Mowbray. Let me clearly understand upon what grounds your apprehensions of this nature are founded."

With still more hesitation, the Baron was obliged to confess, that the criminal, frenzied by the torture of his own mind, had declared an intention of accusing him of having commanded the death of the child.

"If it be proved," replied the queen, "that the senses of the accuser are really deranged, by the corroding reflections of his mind, his accusation will be of no avail. If this is not the case, the credit given to his accusation will materially depend on the degree of interest which you will be found to have in the death or existence of the child.—Who was the infant whom you desired to have reared in seclusion from the world?" she added.

"One nearly connected with myself," returned Lord William, forcing a smile, and desiring to convey to the queen that it had been an illegitimate child of his own.

Elizabeth probably comprehended him thus, for she answered—"It had been a safer case for you, my Lord, if the infant had not been at all connected with yourself; those are the worst of crimes which are engendered in folly, and matured in vice."

These words she spoke with asperity, and added, after a moment's pause—"and who, my Lord, is this accuser whom you dread?"

"He was once a soldier in my ranks, so please your gracious majesty," returned De Mowbray: "His name is Hubert."

"Hubert!" echoed the queen, and sunk into thought; for the idea of that Hubert, who had been the faithful follower of Sir Edward, immediately entered her mind; and although she could not for an instant admit the probability of a soul noble and disinterested, as his had been described to her, being the agent of a crime of the horrid nature of an infant's murder; still as she dwelt on the gold of which

Sir Edward had found him possessed when enlarged by him from the prison in Flanders, and on the mysterious manner in which he had parted from him soon after their arrival in England, declaring that the business he was going upon, was for the eventual happiness of his master, she believed that his wealth might have been acquired, by his having been made the guardian of this child of which De Mowbray had spoken, and that his strength of attachment, to his master might have led him into the false opinion of conceiving that the accusation he had resolved upon preferring against Lord William, relative to that child, might, by working the fall of the Baron, cause the restoration of Rosalind and her husband to happiness.

This idea once admitted, the queen could not divest her mind of it, and she enquired of Lord William, "how long it was since he had entrusted the child of which he had spoken, to the care of this Hubert?"

He replied, "that it was now full four years, he believed nearly five, since the event had taken place."

This Elizabeth recollected was about the period at which Hubert had been represented to her to have left England, in quest of his captive benefactor Edward. This recollection strengthened the suspicion which she had before entertained; should the time of his return to England tally with that of Edward's follower, she considered that she should be confirmed in it. To this end, she enquired of the Baron, "when he had first seen Hubert after the time of his committing the child to his care?"

In reply to this question, the Baron stated the unexpected appearance of Hubert before him in the cedar chamber of his own castle, when he was lamenting the devastation made in it by the freebooters.

The queen was now fully confirmed in her suspicion of its being the same Hubert to whom the preserver of her life owed his escape from his captivity in Flanders; and unable to reconcile these apparent contradictions, she desired to hear the account which Hubert should himself give of the transaction, and its consequences, as the various occurrences of which she had lately gained acquaintance from the lips of her god-daughter, had given her some insight into the crafty disposition of De Mowbray, and she therefore doubted the correctness of the information he had just laid before her.

"Where is this Hubert to be found?" asked Elizabeth.

The Baron described a particular spot in the vicinity of the Tower, where he had left him in the custody of Irwin, and those two of his soldiers who had escaped from the stronghold of Allanrod.

The queen rose from her seat, and informing Lord William that she would see him again presently, quitted the apartment; and having commanded Hubert to be brought to the palace, she sent to summon Sir Edward to meet her in another apartment. She judged that the nature of the conference which she wished to hold with him, relative to the strange situation in which the Baron De Mowbray had expressed himself to be placed, might be too overpowering to the feelings of a daughter, who had not forgotten the parent the injuries which she had received at the hands of the father, and therefore she forebore to extend her invitation to Rosalind.

Sir Edward heard her account of what had passed between herself and the Baron de Mowbray with the greatest astonishment, and declared that the case was of so extraordinary a kind, that he could not venture a surmise upon its real state, till he had likewise heard the account which Hubert should himself give of it; of the strict honour of whose heart and principles he made an asseveration of that strength which was to be expected from the tongue of a man who stood indebted to him for the blessings of which he was now in possession.

To Sir Edward, the point was one of the most delicate nature; it appeared that either the saviour of his peace and existence, or the father of his beloved wife, must be proved a criminal of the blackest dye; and with the most painful agitation painted on his countenance, he continued to traverse the apartment in silence, whilst the queen sat lost in reflections equally perplexing and distressing.

At length Hubert was announced. In his way to the palace, he had gained intelligence of those facts of which the Baron de Mowbray was still ignorant; and the instant he was conducted into the apartment, rushing towards Sir Edward, he fell at his feet, and clasping his knees, he exclaimed—"Joy, joy to my beloved master! amidst the blessings called down upon thine head by a grateful nation, although the last to greet thy excellence, not the least fervent is the voice of thy faithful Hubert."

Even the presence of the queen, and the awful crisis of the moment, did not prevent Sir Edward from acknowledging the gratitude with which he received these testimonies of joy and fidelity from his tried friend; but, having in few, although expressive words, declared to him the sentiments of his heart, he admonished him of the presence they were in.

Turning his eyes with the utmost humility and reverence towards the queen—"Although my speech," he said, "be not sufficiently refined for the address of majesty, the gracious sovereign in whose presence I now kneel, has, in the instance of my loved master, displayed too forcibly her regard for the heart of worth and honesty, to make me fear that her displeasure should fall on one who has only the sincerity of his loyalty to recommend him to her hearing. May heaven lay up in store for thee to future ages, gracious queen, an hundred fold of that bliss with which my own feelings acquaint me that your benignity has filled his heart!"

The honest fervour of Hubert in the cause of his master, drew a tear into the eye of Elizabeth; and as she wiped it from her cheek, she rejoined—"Were all my subjects like thee, I were a happy queen indeed!"

Then suddenly recollecting the accusation preferred against him by the Baron de Mowbray, which the interesting scene of his meeting with his revered master had for the moment driven from her remembrance, she added, in an impressive tone—"Heaven grant that thou prove as worthy, upon the investigation of thy inmost soul, as it is my desire to find thee!"

"Oh Hubert!—oh my friend!—whose services have entwined thee round my heart," exclaimed Sir Edward, "should it be possible that thou hast committed any action which casts a spot upon thy fame, which must render thee less perfect, less exalted in mine eyes than thou now appearest in them, that heart would, upon such a conviction, feel a pang far, far beyond the bliss of which thy means have made it the possessor."

Whilst Sir Edward was speaking, a smile of the utmost serenity and inward satisfaction of mind, stole over the countenance of Hubert; and in a tone of voice correspondent with it in composure, he replied—"Has then the Lord de Mowbray been preferring an accusation against me here? It is but as I expected, and as I hoped."

"Hoped! say you hoped?" demanded Elizabeth.

Hubert repeated his declaration.

Still more surprised than ever, the queen commanded him to explain his meaning.

Falling again upon his knees, from which he had just before been permitted to rise, Hubert said—"Most gracious sovereign, if the services which I have rendered to my beloved master have any weight in the scale of your good opinion, as having been the mean instruments of enabling him to perform the blessed, the meritorious act which has drawn upon him your royal favour, by the remembrance of those services I implore your majesty, that, in the presence of your gracious self, I may be permitted to hear Lord William state his accusation."

This request appeared to Elizabeth one of an uncommon nature; but the expressive eye of Sir Edward ranked so forcibly on the side of the pleader, that Elizabeth commanded the Baron to be conducted into the apartment.

Hubert's arms were bound together at the wrists, with chains which had been put upon them by the command of the Baron, immediately on their quitting De Mowbray Castle: this circumstance assured the queen that he could intend no treachery against the life of his accuser, as he had not the power of performing it; and thus convinced, she began to fear the discovery of some great evil on the part of Lord William.

Hubert again addressed the queen.—"I beseech your majesty," he said, "that having granted thus much concerning myself to my petition, you will grant still a little more for the sake of my accuser; permit not any of your attendants, so please your gracious majesty, to be present at the discussion which is about to take place between the Baron de Mowbray and myself. I repeat, that I make this entreaty for the sake of my accuser."

From her irresolution how to reply to this demand, the queen was relieved by the entrance of De Mowbray, whose eyes instantly fell upon Sir Edward.

Had a damning fiend, charged with the mandate of futurity to hurl him to the nether world, encountered the sight of the Baron, the life-blood could not have turned colder at his heart, nor the strength of manhood have fled more rapidly from his trembling knees: thrice his bleached lips moved without utterance; he staggered towards a chair, and leant upon it for support.

"Art thou astonished," demanded Elizabeth, "to behold one doomed by thee to languish out a life of misery within a captive's cell, transplanted to a soil where the rays of my favour shall warm him into bliss? Thy senses do not deceive thee; it is the same Edward who, in return for the little bounty which he for a while received at thy hands, has groaned beneath thy tyrannous persecution—an injustice to which I should call upon thee to explain thy cause of provocation, and to make remuneration to the sufferer, were not thy offence, in this particular, lost in the greater guilt of that crime with which thine own lips have informed me that thou art accused by this man."

The Queen paused.

The Baron appeared several different times to be on the point of speaking, but as often closed his lips again with marks of the greatest agitation of mind depicted on his countenance, ere a sound had escaped them.

"Prove thyself innocent of the accusation which thine own tongue hast taught me to know that this Hubert had against thee, and I shall suppose thee likewise falsified in other accusations," said Elizabeth:—and having said this, she waved her hand to her lords in waiting, and they all left the apartment.

The eye of Hubert sparkled with pleasure at this command on the part of the queen; and as soon as they were departed, the Baron De Mowbray appeared more at ease, in consequence of their absence, and addressed Hubert in these words—"Where, vile miscreant, is that child which I entrusted to thy guardianship?"

"Do you, my Lord, speak of that babe," replied Hubert, calmly, "concerning which you said to me, that no art in the hiding up of those that live, can equal the security of the grave?"

"Sovereign of my hopes!" exclaimed De Mowbray, addressing the queen, "canst thou credit that I would speak thus of a babe, which I *have* already declared to have been nearly connected with myself?—because I conceived it conducive to the honour of my house to have it reared in obscurity, am I, therefore, to be judged guilty of having willed its unfair death?"

"Prove to me that you were interested in its existence," answered the queen, "and you will remove my suspicions."

"Is not every one," cried the Baron, with encreasing agitation, "interested in the fate of those whose blood flows from their own?"

"But that interest is sometimes of a nature to bear the most cruel consequences to the hearts of those descendants," returned Elizabeth; "witness the union into which you would have forced your daughter with the Lord de Madginecourt: you were doubtless urged by interest to inflict on her the cruelties which she then experienced at your hands."

"But, Madam," exclaimed De Mowbray, stung to the soul by this evidence of the queen's acquaintance with his former proceedings, "if I exerted my authority over a daughter possessed of reason, to point out to her the utility of my plans, but wilfully blind to her own happiness and mine, is it thence to be inferred that I should become the monster to command the death of her innocent babe?"

"*Her* babe!" exclaimed the queen, "the babe *of Rosalind!* was it then *her* babe which you entrusted to the care of this man?—and was it not born without life, as its unhappy mother was taught to believe it?"

The confession had escaped the lips of the Baron, and every turn of his agonized countenance was a confirmation of its truth.

Hubert again sunk upon his knees—"Blessed Heaven!" he cried, "do thou give ear to this avowal! And thou, O gracious queen! Heaven's choicest delegate on earth, do thou inscribe upon the tablets of thine heart, this joyful confession. Yes, my beloved master, thou art the father of a babe, lovely as blooming parents like yourselves could wish the offspring of your loves! Fearful, if I adopted any other method than the one I have pursued, in the cause of this deserted helpless infant, that the grandsire who had endeavoured to nip the blossom in its bud, might deny it ever to have possessed being—my invention has been turned to the means of obtaining from his own lips a confession of its existence at its birth: that confession is obtained, and the happiness of my life is complete!" With her hands clasped towards Heaven, the queen stood with her eyes half fixed upon De Mowbray, half averted from him in horror: with him, all sense seemed lost in shame, in disappointment, and in the tortures of conscience.

Sir Edward had fallen upon the neck of Hubert, and had the mingled emotions of joy, surprise, and gratitude, left him the power of rendering his words articulate, he would have been heard to pour forth blessings on the man, who, to the salvation of the father, had added that of his helpless and oppressed infant.

"I told you, my loved master, when we parted in Northumberland," said Hubert, "that it was for your eventual happiness that we were about to separate:—the cause is now explained to you—as is, likewise, the declaration that I made to our gracious sovereign, that, in requesting this interview might be without witnesses, I made that demand for the sake of my accuser."

"Monster of criminality!" exclaimed the queen, addressing De Mowbray, "does not thy soul sink within thee, at beholding the virtuous integrity which thy temptations have not been able to shake? Does not thy heart sicken at the lesson of humanity afforded thee by a vassal? I have pledged my promise to thy godlike daughter, who is now, where she ought long since to have been, under my protection, to treat thee with mercy: to her, therefore, and not to Elizabeth, thou owest the lenity that will be extended towards thy crime; but although I do not follow thee with the rigour of the law, mine eyes must never fall on thee again—quit for ever the presence of Elizabeth."

The Baron endeavoured to move towards the door of the apartment, but his tottering limbs refused to bear him to it, and he sank upon a couch near which he was standing. "Shield me! shield me from the sight of my wronged child!" he groaned forth in accents scarcely audible; "bury me within some cloister's walls, where solitude and repentance may be my only companions to the grave."

The queen advanced towards Hubert, and taking with her own hands the chains from his wrists, she said—"Ere this last action of thy excellent heart was known to me, I had decreed thee a reward for thy services to the preserver of my life: what reward that shall be, we will hereafter determine; become, meanwhile, the esquire of that valorous knight, whom it has hitherto been thy pride to follow in a meaner capacity."

Having said this, the queen summoned her attendants, and commanding them not to quit the apartment, but to watch over the

Baron de Mowbray, whom she expressed as ill at ease in his mind, she directed Sir Edward and Hubert to follow her.

She led the way to her closet, and when they had entered it, she said—"You must perceive, Sir Edward, that it is most essential to the happiness of your Rosalind, that she should never again behold her father, or be made acquainted with the crime which he once intended to her innocent child. He has himself spoken of a monastery as a fit retreat for his future life: I will, therefore, furnish him with a letter to the Abbot of the Holy Ghost in Wiltshire, whose members are never permitted again to return into the world, from the moment of their first entering its walls, commanding that he be instantly received as a brother of the order."

The heart of Sir Edward, like that of his Rosalind, ever leant towards the side of mercy; but he foresaw too much danger to the happiness of himself, and those who formed that happiness, in the restoration of a man like the Baron De Mowbray, whose passions were under the controul of neither reason nor religion, to his former rank in life, to consider that it became him to urge any petition to the queen for the permission of his continuance amidst society; accordingly, the moment the queen had composed her epistle, some gentlemen, in whom she placed confidence, were called to her, and the contents having been entrusted to them, they were directed to remove him from the palace, and to lose no time in beginning their journey with him into Wiltshire.

Sir Edward considered, that as the husband of the Baron's daughter, it was a becoming condescension in him to be himself the messenger of the queen's proceedings in his favour to Lord William; accordingly, having obtained the permission of Elizabeth to this end, he returned to the apartment where he had left the Baron; and scarcely had he reached the door, ere a scene of the most affecting nature met his sight.

Rosalind, the tender Rosalind, racked with the tortures of suspense and apprehension, and no longer able to endure absence from the apartment in which she supposed the queen to be closeted with Lord William and her husband, had just entered it with trembling steps, and was flying to the embrace of her father, who, with his face buried in his hands, turned from her imploring arms, and, in a voice of agony, shrieked forth the crime which rendered him unworthy to be clasped in them.

The mother's heart is never dead to the memory of that offspring for which she has borne the pangs of birth; and at the sound of its name, a thousand perplexing ideas of hope and affection burst upon her brain.

"What, what of my child? tell me, I implore you, tell me if my infant lives?" she exclaimed, in a tone of voice almost as frenzied as that in which her father had addressed his frantic exclamations to her.

"Yes, yes, it lives," replied De Mowbray; "but thy father would have snapped its tender stem of life, and hurled his soul to——"

Rosalind heard no more—with a faint shriek she sunk into the arms of her husband, who bore her instantly from the apartment.

In his way with her to a chamber, he was met by the queen, who comprehending, from the few words which Sir Edward let fall, what was the cause of Rosalind's senseless state, conceived nothing so essential to her future peace as to prevent a second meeting between her and her father, which she dreaded that the dutiful and forgiving temper of her god-daughter might induce her to seek; she therefore accelerated the departure of the fallen Baron, who, if he had a wish remaining in life, it was the wish of hiding himself from the scrutiny of every eye.

Till the necessary preparations could be made for his setting out, he was taken to the house of Lord Burleigh, who, as the uncle of his late wife, could not refuse him a temporary shelter beneath his roof; and where the fever of disappointment and remorse rose in his brain to a height that seemed to threaten to strike at the root of his life.

The queen herself watched the return of sense to the overpowered frame of the unfortunate Rosalind; when that period arrived, sad and desponding were the feelings of her mind; but the gentle reasonings of the queen, aided by the persuasions of her beloved Edward, instilled some degree of calmness into her soul, and, after a time, won her into confessing the necessity of her being withheld from farther communication with her parent; and no pains were omitted to convince her, that his own wish had been gratified in his seclusion from the world.

From the gloomy contemplation of her father, she turned to the blissful expectation of clasping in her arms a pledge of her love for her revered Edward. Impatiently she requested to behold the saviour of her child's existence; and Hubert entered the apartment, and knelt by the side of the couch upon which she lay extended.

Tears alone fell from her eyes, and she was unable to advance the enquiries which she had in her own mind prepared to make of him. The soul of Hubert melted in sympathy with the feelings of the mother, and an interval of the most affecting silence ensued.

At length, the desired explanation flowed from his lips; he said—"That having resolved to use the money which the Baron had given him, as the price of his removing the child from Cumberland, for the enlargement of his loved master from captivity, he had immediately, upon receiving the infant at the hands of Lord William, conveyed it to the cottage of a sister of his own, married to one of the shepherds on the mountains, and in whose kindness and motherly attentions to it he knew that he could confide.

"This done," continued Hubert, "I proceeded into Flanders: with all that befell me in that country, you are already acquainted. I have only to explain the reason of my not having informed Sir Edward that he was a father, and that I had been so fortunate as to have had it in my power to preserve the life of his babe. It had then struck me that my single voice would be insufficient to prove its birth—that nothing could effectually substantiate its ever having lived, but the confession of Lord William himself; accordingly, I resolved to tell my loved master nothing of his child, till I could present it to him as the acknowledged grandson of the Baron de Mowbray.

"When we parted in Northumberland, and Sir Edward proceeded in his disguise to De Mowbray Castle, I went in quest of his child. My sister had removed her abode, and several days elapsed before I was able to discover her new dwelling. I found her situated not a day's journey from De Mowbray Castle, and the treasure which I had entrusted to her keeping, well and happy. It had so chanced, that scarcely an hour before the time of my reaching the cottage of my sister, Lord William had left it; he had called at it for refreshment, on his way to his own castle from the stronghold of the freebooters, after having escaped from the captivity in which he had been held by them. I resolved without delay to follow him to his castle, and obtain the interview with him which had been long planned in my mind. On reaching the castle, I found it despoiled by the freebooters, and the Baron its only inhabitant: this appeared a most favourable opportunity for working upon his mind in the manner I had resolved to do, and I entered his presence. It must be needless to describe the surprise with which he beheld me—the fury with which he heard me declare my intention of delivering him into the hands of justice, that he might expiate, in a manner agreeable to the mandates of the law, the crime which he had induced me to commit. I doubted not that this threat, on my part, would provoke him to throw the supposed murder solely upon me; and that, in order to procure the infliction of public punishment upon me for the death of the child, he must first prove it to have had existence: thus, with the greatest satisfaction, I beheld the effect which my declaration had produced on his mind. His passion drove him to such extremes, that, I believe, had I been unattended, and he armed, I had not left his presence alive; but his arms had been taken from him by the freebooters, and I found a most serviceable companion in that dog, my compassion for whose hungry state first drew upon me the good opinion of my revered master, and which I had left with my sister during my absence from England, as one of the guardians of the child which I had entrusted to her care.

"It was my intention," continued Hubert, "to have detained Lord William a prisoner for some days in his despoiled castle, and to have endeavoured to work his mind to repentance; but the arrival of Irwin and his companions defeated that plan, and I was obliged to return to my original device, of drawing him on to confess that the child had been born alive. Those powers which never sleep to the wrongs of the oppressed innocent, stretched out their arms in my cause, and the proudest wish of my soul is accomplished."

It will doubtless be perceived that the beautiful boy on which the eyes of the Baron fell when he awoke from his repose in the cot of the hospitable shepherd, was his own grandchild; with this particular Hubert was acquainted, and made it known to the parents of the babe.

The queen expressed not less impatience than Rosalind and her husband to behold the child, whose interests were so nearly allied with their own, and which had thus long been the sport of fortune;

and Hubert was requested to set out without delay, and conduct him to the arms of his anxious father and mother.

No commission could have been of a more pleasing nature to Hubert, and he insisted on beginning his journey towards Cumberland that very afternoon. Elizabeth observed the impatient fondness of a mother's heart beaming in the eyes of Rosalind, and immediately promised to provide him with horses and attendants for his journey.

Till the hour of his departure, Hubert was not permitted to quit the apartment which contained his master and Rosalind; and as they dwelt on the strange occurrences which had marked their lives, Hubert addressing the Lady Rosalind, said—"There is one circumstance which I doubt not still appears a mystery to you, and which I have often wished to have it in my power to explain to you—I mean the voice which, on the evening of your interview with the Baron in the cedar chamber, called to him 'to spare you;' it was mine, lady; I had discovered a private and disused passage at the back of this chamber, which led towards that of Gertrude; and towards her apartment I was proceeding, in order to deliver to her a request from my master, that you would meet him at the chapel, when overhearing what was passing between you and Lord William, I could not forbear endeavouring to serve your cause, by calling out in the manner I did."

"And were you the form which I beheld on the day subsequent to my marriage, enter my chamber, and afterwards appear in the door-way of the cedar chamber?" asked Rosalind.

This supposition Hubert also confirmed, by saying, "that he had at that time been seeking an opportunity of informing her of the sudden departure of Sir Edward for Flanders, but had been frustrated in his attempt at gaining access to her."

The moment the horses and attendants which the queen had commanded for the use of Hubert were ready to depart, he set out on his journey, carrying with him the blessings of the happy parents whom he left behind, and receiving the farewell of Rosalind in an embrace of affectionate gratitude.

Hubert had not long quitted the palace ere Lord Burleigh arrived at it, and brought with him information that the first violent transports of Lord William's emotions having subsided, he had himself demanded his journey to be accelerated by every possible means, towards the monastery in which the future period of his life was to be passed—"It is now," added Lord Burleigh, "nearly an hour since he quitted London, rejoicing in nothing so much as that a second interview with his daughter had been spared him."

"May this slender proof of his consciousness of that evil repute in which all characters of worth must hold him," said Elizabeth, "lead him to devote the future hours of his existence to such sincere repentance as may purify his soul, and render him worthy to unite, in another state, with those of whose society he is undeserving in this."

The tears stole down the cheeks of the amiable Rosalind; with her hands clasped to heaven, she seconded the wish of the queen; and retiring shortly after to her chamber, spent the evening in prayer for the restoration of peace to the mind of her father, and forgiveness to his crime.

CHAPTER XII.

Like a caught lion, raging in the snare,
He plunges in his passion, spends his force,
And struggles with the toil that holds him faster.

N. LEE.

THE unexpected arrival of the Lord Baron de Mowbray at the palace of Queen Elizabeth, and its consequences, had delayed the setting out of Sir Edward, on his hostile expedition into the North, to so late an hour, that it was judged expedient for him to postpone the commencement of his journey till the succeeding morning.

It may be imagined that, as Lord William was no longer the prisoner of the freebooters, the queen might have become less anxious for the marching of the troops, than she had been whilst she considered herself called upon, as a sovereign, to effect the rescue of one of the barons of her realm, who had lost his liberty in defending the rights of his country; but it must, at the same time, be recollected, that, although his enlargement had been the ostensible business of this expedition, it had, in the private feelings of the queen, been the secondary one, and her chief object that of subduing the daring freebooter, who appeared to mock her power, and who had possessed sufficient audacity to demand her god-daughter to wife. Accordingly, although the setting out of the troops had, from causes of necessity, been postponed, still the ardour of the queen for their marching had not experienced the slightest abatement.

Not less impatient than his royal mistress was Sir Edward, to chastise the notorious Allanrod, who appeared to stand forth, distinguished by crime, from the common race of man—that Allanrod who, to the iniquity of heading a lawless community of robbers, added the atrocious vice of having been the adulterous disuniter of wedded and happy hearts, in the persons of the Laird of Glenross, and his wife, the Bonny Mabel—that Allanrod who, although the open foe of England, had dared to lift his thoughts to an union with Rosalind de Mowbray, the daughter of one of its barons.

Nor was a justifiable enmity to the foes of their country the only passion winch animated the hearts of the Queen and Sir Edward, in the conquest over Allanrod, which they were mutually anticipating: a great degree of curiosity, which they were impatient to have satisfied, had been excited in their breasts, by the unaccountable and contradictory circumstances of the freebooter having demanded the hand of Rosalind for his friend Lord Rufus de Madginecourt, as the price of her father's enlargement from imprisonment in his fortress; and Lord Rufus having been unable, a few weeks after that period, to prevent Allanrod from leading her to the altar as his own destined bride. It was evident that some secret tie subsisted between them, and what that tie was, it appeared probable that nothing but the overthrow of Allanrod and his band of robbers would ever develope.

Irwin, the leader of the fallen Baron de Mowbray, was a man well acquainted with the duties of a soldier, a quality for which Sir Edward had ever prized him; and no sooner did he learn that he was in London, than he sent to request to see him, and at the interview which this message produced, he proposed to Irwin to join him on his expedition into the North. As he had been a captive in the stronghold of the freebooters, Sir Edward judged that his presence might be of infinite use to him in his undertaking, and Irwin readily agreed to march with him.

Amidst other matter, Irwin informed Sir Edward of the freebooter by whose means he had procured his own release from captivity, and who, he said, was now in London, where Lord William had promised to pay him the stipulated reward of his services.

"The poor fellow," replied Sir Edward, "shall not lose the recompence for which he hazarded his life. Let him be brought before me; I will make him this assurance in person, and take the same opportunity for proposing to him some questions relative to his late captain."

The freebooter was accordingly conducted into the presence of Sir Edward, and the generous promise with which our young knight addressed him, stating, "that, as the husband of the daughter of the Baron de Mowbray, he considered himself called upon by the voice of honour to execute his obligations," so far won him the heart of the grateful deserter, that whatever particulars he was acquainted with concerning Allanrod, it instantly became as great a gratification to himself to disclose, as it could be to Sir Edward to hear them.

But it appeared that the knowledge which he had of the chief of the freebooters was very limited. He described him to be a man of an athletic and commanding form, clad in the Highland fashion of dress, and his face constantly hidden beneath the visor of his helmet. Resembling, in every respect, to this account, had he appeared to Irwin, when he had beheld him on the brow of a distant hill, after the combat which had a few weeks before taken place between the freebooters and the soldiery of the Baron de Mowbray; and corresponding with this description had Sir Edward seen him, when advancing towards the altar in the chapel of Rockmount Castle.

The moss-trooper could give no further account of him, except that it was very rarely that he ever headed any expedition of plunder, but that he generally deputed the command to one of his leaders; that he seldom visited the fortress, and then never remained at it above a day or two at a time, during which period he kept himself retired in a couple of apartments adjoining to each other, in a tower at the southern extremity of the building, which was in better repair than any other part of it; that his attendants were a man named Frasier, and two or three others, who enjoyed his favour, and exercised authority, in his name, throughout the fortress.

Of this vague kind was all the information he was able to give. To the name of Lord Rufus de Madginecourt, he was an utter stranger; he knew not that there was such a noble in existence.

About the hour of noon, on the day succeeding that upon which the disconsolate Baron de Mowbray had set out for one of those mansions of seclusion from the active duties of life, of which a few were still existing, which owed their being to the pretended blindness, and not to the open tolerance of the queen, Sir Edward, animated by the good wishes and affectionate farewells bestowed on him by his beloved wife and revered sovereign, marched with the first division of his troops for Northumberland.

As he proceeded onwards, the promised supplies joined themselves to his standard; and, when he quitted York, he found himself at the head of fifteen hundred men.

During his march, his thoughts rested solely on the object for which it had been undertaken: he doubted not obtaining a full victory over the freebooters, and returning to London worthy of the most benignant smiles of the queen. But the information which he had derived from the moss-trooper was, in one point, unfavourable to his desires. He had said, that Allanrod seldom resided at the fortress, and, when he did so, never above a day or two at a time; the chances, therefore, were much against his being an inhabitant of the building, at the moment of his attack upon it—and, without taking Allanrod his prisoner, he considered that his victory would be but half a conquest. To this uncertainty, however, he was compelled to submit, and to trust to the discovery which his vanquished band might be tempted to make of their leader, if he did not fall into his power a captive of war.

Sir Edward was principally guided in his route by the knowledge which Irwin had of the country; and, by his advice, he halted for a day of refreshment to his troops, on a plain about ten miles distant from the haunt of the freebooters, in order that twelve hours, given to repose and ease, might enable his men to exert themselves more effectually in the business of the fight.

During these hours of cessation from the toil of marching, they were allowed every indulgence which could inspire them with vigour and strength, for stretching out their arms with spirit and energy, in the cause of their country and their queen; and, with the first hour of the morning, Sir Edward gave the command for proceeding towards the spot where their services were to be called into action.

The day was just beginning to break, when the advanced guard, at the head of which Irwin was marching, descried the stronghold of the enemy. Irwin accordingly halted, till the main body of the troops had joined him, and then sent forward a herald, as had been agreed upon between Sir Edward and himself, to demand—"Whether the freebooters were willing to surrender themselves to the banner of mercy, which the queen graciously held out to them, or preferred, by opposing their strength to the troops which she had sent against them, to provoke her vengeance?"

On receiving this intelligence from the herald, the freebooters displayed at once their disregard of all military observations, and the undaunted ferocity of their nature, by surrounding him, and dragging him a prisoner into their fortress.

The eminence on which the English troops were halting, was sufficiently near to the fortress, to enable them to distinguish that their herald had been compelled to enter its walls; and, as he remained within them a longer time than could have been necessary to the framing of a reply to the demand with which he had been charged, Sir Edward suspected his mission to have been abused, and gave the word for his troops to march to the attack of the place.

Ere they could reach it, the freebooters were already mounted upon its walls, and discharged at them a treble fire from their matchlocks, which they seconded with a shower of arrows; and, as the troops drew nearer to the building, they hurled down upon them large stones, which they tore, with the fury of savages, from the ruinous towers and parapet walls.

But the vehement exertion with which the freebooters commenced their defence, rendered them unable to prosecute the struggle, with equal spirit, for any length of time; and, as they grew exhausted by the violence of their efforts, the soldiers, under the command of Sir Edward, by a steady and skilful management of their strength, were becoming, with every moment, more able to sustain the conflict.

For about three hours, the contest was carried on, with the most determined spirit, on either side. The numbers which fell, both amongst the freebooters and the assailants, did not appear to slacken a nerve in the cause—nay, the purple tide, which flowed around the combatants, seemed to act as a stimulus to their valour.

At length a projecting turret at one angle of the building, which was supported upon a wall not less mouldering than itself, becoming still more weak by the freebooters having drawn massive lumps of stone from its tottering sides, to cast down upon the enemy, and rocking under the weight of those who were climbing upon it, for the purpose of providing themselves with ammunition for their slings, fell with a crash, which threatened inevitable destruction to those whom it bore with it to the earth, and also to those to whom the rapidity of its fall gave no time to fly from the spot upon which it sank.

This event, which was fatal to no inconsiderable number of the regular soldiery, proved still of worse consequence to the freebooters; they sustained from it a loss of so great importance, as disabled them from carrying on their operations of defence with any farther degree of success; and although their hardy souls scorned to cry for quarter, their arms shortly after fell in despair from their hands, and victory rested upon the crest of Sir Edward's troops.

The tide of fortune being once decidedly turned against the freebooters, a very short time made them the prisoners of the victorious party; and Sir Edward, with Irwin by his side, rushed into the building, making impatient enquiries of all whom they saw, whether Allanrod was himself within the fortress.—But even the threat of instant death could not terrify the required information from the lips of any one of the banditti; and Sir Edward judging that this stern taciturnity carried with it marks of their unwillingness to confess that he was secreted in some part of it, as had he been absent, it appeared unlikely that they should not readily have declared him so, he demanded of Irwin whether he was acquainted with the way to the southern tower, and having learnt that he was, he bade him lead to it, and followed his steps, attended by some of his own soldiers, whom he called upon for that purpose.

Headed by Irwin, they proceeded to the extremity of a long and narrow passage, whence an archway led to a flight of stone steps: these they ascended, and having arrived at their top, Irwin was on the point of entering a door which presented itself to their view, when it was suddenly opened from within, and Frasier, with about a dozen other men, rushed out with their drawn swords, and immediately fell upon Sir Edward and his companions, with the same savage fury that had marked the actions of the other banditti, during the combat. Unprepared for this attack, as they considered the victory already theirs, and therefore the use of arms to have ceased, Sir Edward and Irwin, with their attendants, were for some time in the most imminent danger, owing the preservation of their lives solely to their skill in the exercise of the sword; but the clangor of their arms being heard below, several of their fellow-soldiers hastened to their assistance, and the desperate remnant of the lawless band were secured, in like manner as their brothers in iniquity had just been before them.

Scarcely allowing themselves a moment to breathe, as they judged for whose sake this desperate effort had been made to prevent their entering the apartment, they rushed into it, and perceived a figure, which they both instantly recognized to be Allanrod, in the act of endeavouring to force his way out of a narrow window, through which he had just thrust one leg and arm, and attempting to wrench away an iron bar which prevented the rest of his body from passing through the aperture.

Sir Edward darted upon him, and seizing the arm which was towards him, he dragged him back by it into the apartment, exclaiming—"Thou shalt not escape me, monster! the hour of thy atonement is at length come!"

The position in which Allanrod had been found by Sir Edward, was such as had rendered him unable to resist the force of his arm; and as he fell beneath it, upon the floor of the chamber, turning his countenance, which was, as usual, concealed by the visor of his casque, upon the arbiter of his fate, a convulsive start shook his frame, and bending himself forward, with an effort of the wildest nature, he seized with both his, the hand in which Sir Edward still bore the naked sword, which he had drawn in his own defence against the ruffians whom he had encountered at the door of the apartment, and in tremulous but solemn accents, expressive of mingled agony, horror, and remorse, he shrieked forth—"Hold—hold! point not thy sword against a *father's life!*"

The quivering lips of Sir Edward would have echoed the exclamation, but the shock of astonishment which had communicated itself to his heart, was so excessive as to deny him the power of utterance, or of motion.

"Deceive me not, I charge thee," proceeded Allanrod, in the

same appalling tone of voice in which he had before spoken.—"Art thou not the acknowledged grandson of an aged man, named Matthews, whose residence was on the margin of a small lake, in the vicinity of De Mowbray Castle?"

Still Sir Edward could not unlock the faculty of speech.—To the demand of Allanrod, Irwin replied for him in the affirmative.

"No doubt then hangs upon our affinity," rejoined Allanrod.—"And, oh God, that we should meet *thus*—that I should have been doomed, in ignorance of thy birth, to have been thy persecutor through life! God of justice, what a meeting is this—*between a son and a father!*"

"Art thou indeed my father?" stammered out Sir Edward; and, in a softened tone, he added—"Oh thou distributor of earthly events, *can* THIS be the author of my being?"

"The God who hears thy invocation is the witness!" cried Allanrod. "Scorn me not. Ere this awful moment, I had resolved to make thee retribution for the pangs thou hast experienced at my hands—retribution worthy thy acceptance: thou art the legitimate heir of honours and of rank, and shalt be proved their legal possessor!"

"But who is he that I am called upon to acknowledge as a father?" demanded Sir Edward. "Oh, disclose thyself to me!"

"I will," replied Allanrod; "first my heart, then my countenance; and it is a heart of no common nature: too soaring to have lived trammelled with the galling ties by which common worldlings are bound—too proud to meet death from any hand but this!" and as he spoke, he tore open his corslet, and plunged a dagger into his breast!

The heart of Sir Edward died within him at the sight; every object floated before his eyes: he endeavoured, but in vain, to call in assistance; he sank upon his knees, by the side of the bleeding body, and had not the power to make an effort at staunching the tide of life, which was flowing from the breast of Allanrod.

Irwin snatched the dagger from his hand; but the deed of death was past recall: at his summons, some of the soldiers, who had followed Sir Edward and himself to the door of the chamber, approached, and would have applied bandages to the wound; but the self-destroyer, with the resoluteness of a tyger, maddened by the torture and imprisonment of a toil into which he has fallen, tore away such ligaments as they were endeavouring to wind round him, exclaiming, at the same time—"Protract not my sufferings, for I *will* die!"—Then turning to Sir Edward, he addressed him, by saying—"Having shewn thee my heart, it now alone remains that I suffer thee to behold my countenance. I have sworn an oath that Allanrod should never be seen without this visor whilst alive; I now consider myself in a middle state, between life and death, and my oath thus void. Behold, therefore, thy father; but remember that the period of his having known thee to be his son, is short—remember, and behold me!"—and having spoken these words, he raised his visor, and discovered beneath it the countenance of—LORD RUFUS DE MADGINECOURT!

That excess of surprise which had before filled the mind of Sir Edward, on hearing himself declared the son of the freebooter Allanrod, is a weak expression for the sensations which it now experienced; the mist which had already been floating before his eyes, increased to total darkness; every faculty became lethargized, and, with a groan composed of horror and astonishment, he fell senseless into the arms of Irwin.

Unmoved by feelings like the rest of men, Lord Rufus still retained a resolute composure on the margin of the grave: he called to his son to attend to his dying words; and when the eyes of Sir Edward again opened to the light, De Madginecourt, in accents which the weakness of approaching death rendered scarcely audible, thus addressed him—"Enquire amongst the freebooters for a man, named Frasier; he will furnish you with the key of a cabinet in the chamber adjoining to this, in which you will find an explanation of the circumstances that now move your wonder. It was my wish never to have beheld you again, since the discovery I have made of our affinity; and I wrote the papers which are locked in that cabinet, in order to repair to you the wrongs I had inflicted on you, whilst ignorant that I was the author of your existence. That Frasier, who now possesses the key, I had commanded to seek you out, and place them in your hands, after my death; for I came hither *to die*; my intention has only been hastened by your arrival."—He paused; the powers of nature were almost drawn to their close, and Lord Rufus gasped with a painful and convulsive struggle for breath.

"Speak not of reparation to me," replied Sir Edward, commanding with difficulty the power of utterance.—"Oh, live to make your peace with Heaven!"

The eyes of Lord Rufus appeared starting from their sockets, and the first groan he had breathed passed through his lips: his countenance was writhed with agony, and every feature indicated the near approach of that moment at which soul and body part for ever.

"Or if our efforts cannot save thee," continued Sir Edward, "take with thee to a future state the free forgiveness of thy son: his prayers shall follow thee into eternity."

Again the eyes of Lord Rufus were fixed upon Sir Edward; their expression was of the most pitiable nature; they bespoke the remorse with which he was stung, at the conviction he had just received of the surpassing excellence and nobleness of that heart which he had wronged, when compared with his own, from whence those wrongs had sprung.

"I have but one request to make," said De Madginecourt; "on the nobleness of thy nature, I rely to grant it.— Extend that forgiveness which thou hast, unasked, bestowed on me, to *thy brother*; and when thou hast forgiven, do not desert him."

"Brother!" echoed Sir Edward.—"A brother!"

"Speak quickly, or I die, and hear not thy promise," said Lord Rufus.

"I know him not, but still I promise," replied Sir Edward.

Lord Rufus caught the hand of his son in his, and pressed it with a convulsive grasp of gratitude, for his compliance with his petition; an agonizing pang then rent the last fibre of his life.—"Mercy—mercy, Jesu!" trembled on his lip, and his spirit fled from earth.

CHAPTER XIII.

In nature there's no blemish but the mind:
None can be call'd deform'd, but the unkind:
Virtue is beauty; but the beauteous evil
Are empty trunks, o'er flourished by the devil.

SHAKESPEARE.

It cannot be doubted but that a very short time elapsed after life had fled from the body of Lord Rufus, ere Sir Edward caused Frasier to be brought to him, and having convinced him of his affinity to the man whom he had lately served, received from him the key of the cabinet. On opening it he found a small packet, of which the direction was—"For Edward, the son and heir of Lord Rufus de Madginecourt." With an impatient hand he broke the seal, and applied himself to the perusal of the contents; but, as they contained only partial accounts of occurrences, with which our readers will desire to become more intimately acquainted, for the purpose of developing some mysteries which have been presented to them in the former pages of these volumes, instead of transcribing them, we shall give an unveiled detail of the life of him who has been one of the principal actors upon our stage.

The same year which gave birth to Lord Rufus de Madginecourt, resigned the parent who had borne him to the grave; and scarcely had he completed his sixteenth year, ere, by the death of his father, he became the representative of one of the families of the first distinction in the kingdom of England.

Some years previous to this event, he had been placed under the care of a tutor, introduced into the family for that purpose, who found him by no means secondary in genius and sense, but deficient in application, and infinitely more incorrect in the regulation of his morals than his manners. His father, however, being a man of severe habits, the natural disposition of the son was checked under his observant eye; but no sooner had he paid the debt of nature, than the tempestuous passions of his soul began to break forth.

His tutor, whose name was Ravil, was a clergyman of the episcopal church, who, during the preceding reign of persecution, had been compelled to desist from the exercise of his religious function; and the savings of whose former years of industry had been so nearly exhausted by his having possessed no other source from whence to supply the exigencies of himself and family, as to reduce him to seek the situation in which we have just found him placed.

In the course of the four first years of his residence in the family of De Madginecourt, a fever, which at that time raged in the kingdom, had carried off his wife and two daughters, and he had now remaining to him only one son. This young man, who was about six years older than Lord Rufus, his father had intended to enter into that profession which he had himself followed in his former days of happiness and prosperity; but Lord Rufus happening to gain acquaintance with him, on an occasional visit which he made to his father, at Rockmount Castle, was so much pleased with his society, that he insisted on retaining him as his friend and companion—promising to render the exercise of any profession unnecessary to him through life; and this young Ravil was the very man to whom our readers have already been introduced as the associate of Lord Rufus, in the narrative of the unfortunate Eloise de la Valois.

In the course of that narrative, enough was displayed of his character to shew that he was possessed of a disposition which could not fail to gain him the favour and good opinion of a youth like Lord Rufus, who, in a friend, sought only the bold executor of his vicious plans, the fawning adulator of his actions, and the invariable approver of his sentiments.

No sooner was this tie of mutual corruption of heart, misnamed friendship, formed between the younger Ravil and his patron, than the father and the tutor lost all influence; still that love, which the affinity of blood caused him to feel for the one, and that partiality which, from the habit of constant intercourse, had grown in his mind for the other, rendered him unable to tear himself from them; and he continued an inhabitant of Rockmount Castle, and the kind and the lenient adviser of his son and his pupil, although he sighed to perceive how unprofitably his admonitions were received by them.

The years passed on, unmarked by any occurrence connected with our history, till Lord Rufus, having completed his twenty-first year, visited the court, clad in all the dazzling pomp and splendor, of which he gloried in making a display. Whilst in the metropolis, he conceived a desire to visit France, and having obtained from Elizabeth an introduction to the monarch of the neighbouring kingdom, he departed, taking with him a large and splendid train of attendants, and his friend Ravil as his companion.

On leaving the French court, the mansion of the Marquis de la Valois was one of the first to which the letters, with which he was honoured by the king, gained him admittance; and no sooner had he entered it, than a passion, exceeding in strength any which he had ever before felt, took possession of his beat for the lovely and enchanting Eloise, the daughter of his entertainer.

Utterly unacquainted with the controul of his inclinations, when any end struck him as desireable, he had simply been accustomed to consider by what means it could be made attainable; arguing, therefore, according to his regular system, he found marriage to be the only channel through which the possession of Eloise could be obtained, and therefore resolved instantly to make her an offer of his hand, without a thought given to the repentance into which a tie of this hasty nature might lead him.

When Eloise escaped from the mansion of her father, and it appeared improbable that he should ever behold her again, violent disappointment took possession of his soul; but it was short in proportion to its strength; and after the first week of her flight from the marquisate of La Valois, it was not probable that he would ever have thought of her again, with the affectionate desire that he had as many days before regarded her with, had he not, by the most extraordinary of chances, when shipwrecked on his way from Genoa to Cette, been preserved from perishing, on board the very vessel which was transporting her back to France from her captivity in Algiers.

At this unexpected meeting, the flame of love, which absence had smothered, burst forth again with redoubled heat; but the manuscript of Eloise has already informed us of the dreadful occurrences which took place on board the Algerine vessel, in which were included the death of the villainous Ravil, and the unfortunate D'Altonville; and we may therefore pass on to [De] Madginecourt's arrival in England, with the unhappy victim who had fallen into his toils.

Some time before the departure of Lord Rufus for France, the elder Ravil, whose health and spirits had been materially impaired by various causes of distress, finding himself ill at ease amidst the noisy and dissipated scenes of Rockmount Castle, had requested its Lord, on whom was his sole dependance for the subsistence of his future days, to remove him to some spot of quiet obscurity, where he might pass the evening of his life.

Lord Rufus had in many instances found the counsels of his tutor of service to his interests, and therefore felt averse to removing him far from his presence; accordingly he proposed to build for him, as a retreat, a small dwelling for which he resolved, that the ruins of an antient tower, at the distance of about half a league from the castle, should serve as the foundation. There was still subsisting a subterraneous passage from the castle to this tower, and this he considered would afford an easy communication for supplying him with the necessaries of life; for him therefore was constructed the cottage or grotto, which at a later period formed the retreat of Rosalind—but more of this hereafter.

On landing in England, his heart, burnt up by the fever of desire, was in a most improper state to be addressed with any admonitions contrary to the immediate gratification of his wishes, and therefore he procured a priest to unite his hand with that of Eloise, from whom he had not any of these reasonings to fear, which Ravil might have ventured to breathe in his ear, had he been called upon by him for the performance of the sacred act.

Scarcely had a month been passed in the enjoyment of Eloise's charms, ere the joys of ecstasy began to wane into coolness, and with a second they were succeeded by satiety. He began to consider her as the impediment to his forming a connexion which might increase his wealth, and swell his consequence; and no consideration prevented him from working her immediate destruction, but the knowledge of her being about to become a mother.

At length Eloise gave birth to two infants of opposite sexes. At the time of their entrance into the world, Lord Rufus was absent from his castle; and at the same moment that the intelligence of his being a father was announced to him, he was likewise informed that the girl had ceased to breathe.

Having resolved that no vestiges of his marriage should remain, De Madginecourt seized upon the death of one child as a plea for removing the other from the protection of its mother; and having torn it from her arms, he conveyed it through the subterraneous vaults to the cottage of Ravil. He had already informed the old man of the death of his son, although he had forborne to explain to him by whose hand he had fallen; and his inducement for remaining in the vicinity of Rockmount being thus materially weakened, he prevailed upon him to consent to remove into Cumberland—to change his name to that of Matthews—to take with him the child—and to bring it up there as his own grandson. The old man looked forward with no small degree of satisfaction to the task of rearing an infant, which might grow up to call forth those affectionate principles of his heart which were almost dead within it; and departed into Cumberland with the child, promising to profess himself his grandsire, and never to develop his real origin—Lord Rufus, on his part, returning to him a promise of visiting their abode at least once in every six months.

In this particular Lord Rufus was for some years true to his word, but he always chose the season of the night for his visits, and beheld his son when locked in the arms of sleep—not suffering that son to behold him, lest any difficulty should arise in replying to such questions as he might ask concerning him; and it so chanced, that at the time of Lord William de Mowbray's being thrown from his horse, in the vicinity of Matthews's cottage, Lord Rufus was just arrived at it upon one of his periodical visits: he, therefore, was the second figure whom the Baron beheld in the doorway of the cottage and on his account was Matthews at first reluctant to admit him within his dwelling, and afterwards so particular in exacting from him a promise of secrecy relative to whatever might meet his observation, if received within it.

The child being thus removed from the eye of the world, all the thoughts of De Madginecourt were turned to the disposal of the mother. He had for some time past suffered her to be attended upon by only one confidential servant, and by him he sent to her the dagger and letter, which we have already recorded as having been received by the unhappy Eloise, as predictors of the violence which was intended her.

Lord Rufus hoped that she might become sufficiently weary of a life of pain and misery, to have seized thankfully and greedily upon the means of suicide; but he was deceived in the nature of her heart. Eloise acted rigorously up to the declaration with which she concluded the narrative of her sufferings—"that she would never lift her hand against her own existence;" and Lord Rufus finding her thus resolved, became the monster to strike to her heart the blow of death, which he then accused her of having perpetrated upon her own person.

Thus perished the unhappy mother of Edward, by the hand of that iniquitous being to whom he owed his existence.

Once more a free member of the world, Lord Rufus plunged

wildly into those vices, which, if they do not draw down open punishment upon the exerciser of them in this life, still goad his soul at certain moments with terrors of the future; and, notwithstanding the greatness of his wealth, his extravagance, in the pursuit of pleasure, was so unbounded, as frequently to throw him into the greatest difficulties when called upon for the payment of his debts.

That servant in the confidence of Lord Rufus, whom we have spoken of, as having been the sole attendant of the Lady Eloise for a short period previous to her death, was a Scotchman, named Frasier: he had once been a gentleman; he had broken his fortune by gambling, and since its loss had committed some actions which had driven him from his own country into England: hither he had come, attended by an only sister, whose principles, if not so decidedly corrupt as her brother's, had still been of too relax a kind to cause her to refuse the advances which Lord Rufus had made towards her person. She was now dead, but Frasier had contrived to insinuate himself into the favour of De Madginecourt, so far as to have become a member of his family, and to enjoy almost as much of his confidence as his friend Ravil had done.

Venting one day a paroxysm of rage in the presence of Frasier, which was occasioned by his inability to command a large sum of money, with which he was impatient to purchase some sensual gratification, Frasier said—"Ah, my Lord, Scottish freebooters do not complain thus of the want of money; would that you had a few score under your command, or that I were the captain of as many in your pay." When Frasier first expressed himself in these words, his meaning scarcely extended beyond a joke, and Lord Rufus, hearing them at the time with a smile, dismissed them from his memory; but in the course of a few days they again returned to it in a different shape to that in which they had before met his senses, and he began to reflect whether such a plan, for the increase of his wealth, might not be practicable; and having dwelt on it for some time in the solitude of his own mind, he imparted his ideas to the subtle Frasier, and they employed themselves with seriousness on the formation of a scheme which might render their undigested plan feasible and easy—which affords an additional instance of the slender causes from which the most important undertakings of a man's life almost invariably flow.

Frasier was too well acquainted with the poverty of the lower orders of the Scotch, and their enmity to the English, not to be well assured that a plundering horde might, without any difficulty, be raised from amongst them, who would require to know nothing more of their captain than his name, and his ability to reward them for their services in his cause.

Several bands of this nature, who had obtained the names of borderers and moss-troopers, had already been formed upon the confines of the two kingdoms; they had chiefly been selected from the rude and ill-living Highland peasants, to whom any state of existence was preferable to the miserable one from which they had been taken—and hundreds were, no doubt, still remaining, who would be glad of the same opportunity for changing their condition.

It was accordingly resolved that Frasier should pass into Scotland, and enlist as strong a force as he could find willing to rally round his lawless standard; and that they should know themselves as the freebooters of Sir Allanrod, under which title it was agreed that Lord Rufus should sometimes appear to them, with his countenance concealed beneath the visor of his casque; for there appeared an equal necessity in his case, for not confiding the knowledge of his person to his banditti, as there did for his sometimes shewing himself amongst them.

For a considerable time this ravaging band, headed by the desperate Frasier, had no settled lurking place, but the cavities of rocks, and rude huts and tents, which they built on the mountains; at length, however, they took possession of the ruined monastery upon the borders of Northumberland, of which our readers have already had a full description, and having converted this into a fortress, their depredations became more bold, as they possessed a stronghold to retire to for their personal defence, and the concealment of their booty.

The wealth which they wrested from its lawful possessors was great; it was such as even exceeded the expectations which Lord Rufus had formed of it, even when a private tax had been paid out of it to the joint avarice and knavery of Frasier, who was, upon the whole, perhaps as just an agent as De Madginecourt could have found for his nefarious scheme. To suppose that a man, who served him in the quality of a robber, would be strictly honest to his employer, Lord de Madginecourt knew too much of human nature, and the motives from which all men act, to expect.

In every enjoyment which gold could purchase, Lord Rufus revelled; female beauty was the charm which possessed the greatest power over his heart; and every part of England having supplied luxury to his wishes, the delights of anticipated novelty had for some time rendered him desirous of visiting Scotland; but the differences which subsisted between the two kingdoms, had withheld him from putting his inclinations into effect: at length, auguring that no Englishman would be present at the revelry in which all Scotland was invited to participate, at Kinnavain Castle, upon the marriage of Mary with her cousin, the Earl of Daruley, he resolved to profit equally by that and his assumed title of Sir Allanrod, to visit the Scottish court. He accordingly passed over into Scotland, and causing himself to be announced at the tournament as Sir Allanrod, he perceived that there were none present who were likely to recognize him for the person he really was, and to expose his fictitious character; and being thus assured of security from detection, he resolved to enjoy the week of festivity without restraint.

Here it was his chance to meet the Bonny Mabel Monteith, the wife of the Laird of Glenross; her beauty, so universally acknowledged, was of that enchanting kind which instantly bound his heart a captive in the fetters of adoration, and he resolved to possess her, if earthly means could purchase the ardent desire of his soul.

The Bonny Mabel, of whose heart vanity was the ruling passion, and who had for some time past considered the pleasure which she perceived her husband to take in the society of the enlightened Lady Margaret Murray, as almost a crime committed against herself, listened, with triumph, to the adulating tongue of a man whom she regarded as sensible of the adoration due to her pre-eminent charms; and, from listening, she consented to reward the high opinion which he professed himself to entertain of their perfection.

Accordingly, on the very evening of the ball, which concluded the festivities given by the royal Mary, and her newly married consort, they fled together from Kinnavain Castle, and their flight knew no interruption till they had reached the confines of the English kingdom. Here they paused in their progress, and here the Bonny Mabel, who had not been able to resist the appeal made to her vanity, confessed herself still not entirely lost to shame. She besought Sir Allanrod, as it was impossible that she could ever become his wife, to suffer her to enjoy his affection in obscurity, and to place her in some retired solitude, where none should visit her but himself.

As the Lady Glenross was now entirely in his power, dispossessed, by the rash step she had taken, of any friend to whom she could turn for protection, he, without reluctance, confessed to her his real rank and name; and, at his desire, she consented to become the inhabitant of that cottage which was united to Rockmount Castle by a subterraneous passage, and of which Ravil had lately been the occupier. Here it was agreed that she should live, and be reputed as a peasant girl, who had fallen into the snare of his seduction.

At the expiration of a year, the Bonny Mabel gave birth to a male infant: a mother, like herself, could not be supposed to feel much desire to be the personal inspectress of her child's rearing, and it was therefore, without any opposition on her part, sent into a distant part of the county, under the care of a nurse, who was provided for that purpose.

Before a second year of adultery had flown over the head of the Lady Glenross, the marriage of her cousin, Margaret Murray, with Sir James Lambrun, and the voluntary seclusion from the world, to which her husband had condemned himself, in consequence of her infidelity to his bed, had opened her eyes to the innocence of that friendship which had subsisted between him and the Lady Margaret; and this conviction, added to the coolness with which Lord Rufus now beheld her, when compared to the rapture with which he had, at their first acquaintance, dwelt upon her charms, resolved her, if possible, to execute a plan, which she had formed, for escaping from him into Scotland, and placing herself for life in the convent of Saint Agnes, in the island of Auskerry; for which convent, we have already said, she felt a preference, on account of one of its members being a relation of her deceased mother.

In the habitation where she then dwelt, money had been useless; accordingly she possessed none. All the wealth she had at command was her jewels, in which she had been decked for the queen's ball, on the night of her flight from Kinnavain Castle with Lord Rufus, and which had, ever since that period, been deposited in a chest in the cottage, which contained her clothes.

With a part of these she bribed one of the domestics, who had attended upon her from the time of her arrival in the county of Durham, to become her escort to the island of Auskerry, and to maintain an inviolable secrecy upon her fate.

The man was true to the confidence reposed in him; he found means of procuring her escape, in disguise, from the vicinity of Rockmount Castle, and conducting her to the coast, from whence he provided a vessel, to transport her to Scotland. Of the particulars of her landing on the island of Auskerry, of her reception into the convent of Saint Agnes, and her subsequent death, we are already informed.

The sudden disappearance of the Bonny Mabel was rather a cause of surprise than regret to Lord Rufus de Madginecourt; constancy was not one of the passions of his heart; and she who was now lost to him, had been his a sufficient length of time to have quenched the fire of his passion in possession. She had left for him in the grotto a letter, in which she informed him, that repentance for her past conduct had driven her to fly for ever from his arms; and entreating him, as he had once valued her, to protect the child which she had borne him for her sake. Lord Rufus had loved the Bonny Mabel better than any woman whose affections he had ever shared; he therefore read her letter with a degree of attention, which that of a pleader, who had been less interesting to his feelings, would perhaps not have commanded; and he resolved to fulfil her petition respecting the child.

In compliance with this determination he frequently visited it, in order that he might be certain of its welfaring; and being struck with the resemblance which it bore to its mother, for whom latent sparks of love were still lurking in his breast, he felt a desire to have him more constantly in his sight; to this end he brought him, at the age of six years, to his castle, as the son of a peasant, whom he intended to bring up for a page, to attend upon his person.

The boy's name was Alwin, by which he has already been introduced upon the stage of our history; and it will now be perceived who was the brother, for whom Lord Rufus, in his dying moments, entreated a promise of forgiveness and protection from Sir Edward.

Alwin was a child of sharp and ready talents, and he insinuated himself into the favour of Lord Rufus, unconscious that those arts, which he had at that early age sufficient cunning to perceive calculated to gain him indulgence and praise from his patron, were directed to the author of his existence.

Lord Rufus, on his part, became every day more and more attached to the boy; he appeared to him the only being who had ever been capable of calling forth affections of the nature which he felt for him; and he perhaps loved him the more, for the novel sensation with which he was inspired by him: In short, ere Alwin had attained his eleventh year, De Madginecourt was ever dissatisfied when he was not by his side.

About this time were waged those continental wars, at the commencement of which arose those false hopes and ideas, with which the vain Lord Rufus flattered himself, that the favour extended to him by Elizabeth, in the exalted command which she honoured him, by permitting him to bear in her armies, was of a nature which extended beyond a friendly regard.

At his return from these wars, on the morning of his receiving the thanks of his sovereign, for the judgment and efficacy with which he had executed the trust that had been reposed in him, he first beheld the daughter of his friend, Lord William de Mowbray.

We have already given the history of his views and passions subsequent to that time, down to the period of Rosalind's marriage; we have therefore, in this place, only to revert to certain actions on his part, of which the motives have not been explained.

For the first few years after the birth of that son, which had been borne him by the unfortunate Eloise de la Valois, Lord Rufus performed his promise of visiting the child and his protector, Matthews, once in every six months; but various causes then arose, to make him neglectful in this point of duty; and at the time of his arriving at De Mowbray Castle, in the character of Rosalind's suitor, so long a period had elapsed since he had made any enquiry after Edward, and his nominal grandfather, that he was entirely ignorant of the fate of both: affection he certainly had none for the child, whom he had driven thus unnaturally from his protection; but there was still a certain feeling in his heart, which rendered him desirous of learning whether or not he were in existence. The proximity of De Mowbray Castle to the spot on which stood the cottage of Matthews, urged him to snatch an hour for visiting it; accordingly, dreading that his absence from the castle, by day, might lead to a disclosure of that secret, which he intended never to reveal, he stole, at the dead of night, from his apartments; and having, by means of the sentinel, procured a passage over the drawbridge of De Mowbray Castle, he proceeded to the cottage, by the side of the lake.

He found it deserted; and upon investigation, he discovered that it must have been some time without inhabitants. He wished to know what was become of those who had formerly resided in it; but it was impossible to make an enquiry to that purport, without divulging their fate to be of some importance to him; and therefore he resolved, if not satisfied with ignorance, to endure it, and trust to the hope of their being both removed from earth, by the hand of death; and this was a hope in which he was most ardent; for his affection for Alwin was now become so great, that he had resolved, should his elder son, Edward, never appear, through the advice of Ravil, to claim his birthright, and should Rosalind de Mowbray bring him no male descendants, to declare Alwin the heir to his name and possessions; for which end it was his design to report him the legitimate son, which Edward really was.

Accordingly he, without delay, returned to De Mowbray Castle; and chance had so fated it, that Rosalind, whose slumbers had been disturbed by dreams of an awful nature, and who had left her bed, in her endeavours to compose her agitated mind, was a witness of his entrance within the walls of her father's castle; a circumstance of which it will be remembered, that the mystery heightened that disgust which she already felt for him. This disgust was afterwards swelled into horror, by the words which she heard him pronounce, as she passed the door of his chamber, in her way to the chapel—"Die she must," he had said, "and if she will not kill herself, I must do it for her." And this conviction of his either having been a murderer, or his intention of becoming one, fixed her in the resolution which she had already formed, of never becoming his wife.

There are moments when conscience will goad the hearts of the most hardened in iniquity; and the hours devoted to sleep, were those in which De Madginecourt felt the scourge of a murderer's recollection. At these moments would he, in imagination, react the murder of his sainted wife; and if not awakened from the trance of painful thought, in which sleeping fancy held him, his sufferings were exquisite: as a relief from those attacks of horror, he had for some time past obliged Alwin to sleep in a closet adjoining his bed-chamber, and instructed him to wake him, whenever he should hear him struggling with the fiends of memory. Alwin was faithful to his trust; for the Lord Rufus was liberal to excess, in rewarding him for his services and his secrecy; and Rosalind perhaps the only person, except the page, who had ever been an auditor of his nightly pangs.

Having explained these mysteries, we proceed to that period at which Lord Rufus de Madginecourt, from having first addressed Rosalind, solely on account of the favour in which she stood with the queen, became so strongly enamoured of her person, as to demand an interview with her father; at which he proposed to him to lead her to the altar, and compel her to become a second time a wife, whilst yet the husband of her affections lived.

We have already seen in how contemptuous a manner Lord William received this unnatural proposal, and the enmity by which it was succeeded between him and De Madginecourt. But although the Baron de Mowbray had been sufficiently wary to refuse his adjunction in a step, which, if taken, threatened to unite dishonour with his name, still, either from incaution, or indifference, about concealing the truth in this respect from Lord Rufus, he let fall enough to inform him, that Edward was held in a confinement, to which he had doomed him in Flanders, and from which it was his intention that he should never return to England to claim Rosalind as his wife. No sooner had Lord Rufus obtained this knowledge, than feeling secure in his own imagination, that were Edward once removed from life, the Baron would feel no scruple in compelling his daughter to accept him as her second husband, all his thoughts were bent upon devising the readiest means for depriving him of life.

The Baron had said enough relative to Edward's confinement, to convince Lord Rufus, to whom Flanders was a country well known, which must be the prison, where he had found the means of confining a man who had committed no ostensible crime; accordingly, resolving that the deed of Edward's death should be performed by one, in whose fidelity he could place the most unlimited confidence, he engaged to that end the services of his page, Alwin; promising him, at his departure from England, that, on his return with a confirmation of his rival's death, his reward should be a disclosure to him, on the part of Lord Rufus, which would not only teach him to know himself as the heir of an immense wealth, but empower him to place his inheritance beyond a doubt.

The deluded youth, who had been won alike by precept, example, and indulgence, on the part of his united father and patron, to consider his will as absolute, and all his desires as just, elated by the promise which was to reward his present mission into Flanders, thought lightly, or indeed scarcely at all, of the crime by which it was to be purchased; and, attended by two trusty companions, he set out on his guilty journey.

In the preceding pages we have been informed of such occurrences as took place in the prison of Garcias Xavia, after the arrival of Alwin in Flanders; we have seen that the misguided boy, at the moment of perpetrating his supposed crime, was not master of the same fortitude with which he had undertaken the commission of it. His every sense was unequal to its office; his eyes did not discover the imposition which was practising upon them, in the body of another man having been placed in the situation where he expected to find the rival of Lord Rufus; and his unsteady hand, instead of directing the first blow which it aimed at its victim to his heart, darted the weapon of death into his cheek.

Delighted, however, at the ultimate completion of his task, Alwin returned to England, and delivered to Lord Rufus a particular detail of the transaction; in return for which, the elated De Madginecourt, clasping his son to his breast confessed to him their affinity, and his intention of declaring him his heir at his death. Alwin listened to him with equal ecstacy and surprise; and the knowledge which he had thus gained, whilst it rendered him still more unlimited in those demands which he was constantly making upon the purse of Lord Rufus, for the indulgence of his own inclinations, caused him also to consider himself as more implicitly bound to fulfil the mandates of his nominal patron. Accordingly, when the Lord Baron de Mowbray, contrary to the high-raised expectations of De Madginecourt, refused to give him the widowed hand of his daughter; when the Lord Rufus, struggling between the pangs of indignant pride and disappointed passion, leant alternately to various plans, for obtaining by force the person of her, the willing gift of whose charms was refused to him, and at length resolved to use to that effect, his second character of Allanrod—he confided to Alwin his union with the freebooters, and questioned him whether he would undertake to act the part of a deserter from the band of the dreaded Allanrod's banditti, and proceed as such to De Mowbray Castle, with a tale calculated to draw Lord William into his toils?

Had not the discovery of his affinity to Lord Rufus been already made to him, there is little doubt that Alwin would readily have complied with his demand, so forcibly had the habits in which he had been educated taught him to desire all that Lord Rufus himself wished; but now he had obtained the knowledge, that it was a father to whom his services had, from his infancy, been given, a sense of duty, of which the strength was surprising, in proportion to the deficiency in every other virtue of that heart in which it grew, rendered him enthusiastically warm in the agency of any plan which could add to the happiness of the man in whom all his expectations were centered; and with exultation he assumed the fictitious character which Lord Rufus had proposed to him; and, thus accoutred, he proceeded to De Mowbray Castle, where we have already seen the success that attended his stratagem—for Alwin was the supposed deserter, who, at the opening of our history, introduced himself to the Lord de Mowbray and his leaders, under the feigned name of Donald, as a youth whose family had been the victims of the notorious Allanrod's brutality and lust.

No sooner was the Baron de Mowbray enticed into that encounter with the freebooters, in which his soldiery met with an entire overthrow, than Lord Rufus considered himself as, at length, secure of obtaining the hand of the Lady Rosalind; he believed that every man's love of liberty was too great to suffer him to have any scruples about the terms on which he was to obtain it, so as it were but presented to him as obtainable upon any conditions at all; and, therefore, he doubted not that the demand which he caused to be made to Lord William, from Allanrod, of his promise to bestow his daughter Rosalind in marriage on Lord Rufus de Madginecourt, as the price of his immediate enlargement, would be replied to with a ready affirmative.

But in the firmness of the Baron, in withholding his daughter from the possession of the man whom he now considered as undeserving of her hand, his hopes encountered a fresh disappointment; and his first resolve, upon receiving a negative to his request from the lips of Lord William, was that of assailing De Mowbray Castle, and enjoying her charms by force.

But a little reflection pointed out to him, that the bliss he should thus obtain must be transient, and that its consequences might be fatal to him, while the exercise of some degree of policy might still cause Rosalind to believe that he was deserving of her gratitude, out of which sentiment it was possible that a feeling approaching to love might ultimately spring.

To the accomplishment of this end, therefore, he directed his confidential friend, Frasier, to send a sufficient force against De Mowbray Castle, for its utter subjugation, whilst, to the trusty Alwin, he confided to lead a small detachment of his own soldiery from Rockmount towards it, at the same hour, to whom, at the command of Frasier, the freebooters were to deliver up the Lady Rosalind, who was thence to be conducted under the escort of a faithful English leader of De Madginecourt's, named Sir Maurice, to his castle on the coast of Durham.

Thus far Lord Rufus succeeded in his plan upon the unprotected Rosalind: he imposed himself upon her as her rescuer from the dreaded Allanrod, and his ferocious band of freebooters, and she confessed herself grateful for the deliverance: but a small part only of the plan he had conceived, was accomplished. The next step towards the attainment of his desires was, to teach her to believe that the nefarious Allanrod demanded her as his bride; and having worked upon her mind with this dreadful apprehension, again to sooth her feelings by declaring, that he would submit to the sacking of his own castle by the lawless freebooter, ere the threatened indignity should be offered to her person.

He perceived that this declaration won some degree of faith from Rosalind, to the repentance which he professed himself to feel, for having, at a prior period, been the cause of unhappiness to her, as likewise to his present desire of repairing to her his former conduct; and, glorying in the observation, he desired to make every possible shew of his present merit, and therefore sent a private order to Frasier to inform his horde, that they were commanded by their chief, Allanrod, to march to an attack upon the castle of Lord Rufus de Madginecourt, in the county of Durham, and to lead them on to it without delay, charging him, at the same time, to bring a force capable of subduing his soldiery, as the fruitful issue of his stratagem depended upon the conquest being assigned to Allanrod.

That a man like Lord Rufus made no scruple of sacrificing the number of individuals, whose fall in this siege was unavoidable, is a matter which cannot excite surprise.

Having still farther shewn his zeal for the safety of Rosalind, by conducting her to the grotto, at the end of the subterraneous passage leading from the castle, Lord Rufus passed the interval, till the hour of the expected siege, in contemplating his future prospects of happiness: he had resolved, the moment the freebooters were declared the conquerors of Rockmount Castle, to enter the chapel in his disguise of their chief, to cause Rosalind to be conducted thither to him, and there, in mockery of the rites of religion, to receive her hand from his vile accomplice Frasier, whom he had instructed to appear at the altar, in the habit of a priest, for the purpose of imposing the marriage, as a legal one, upon the senses of Rosalind.

Having drank the nectar of her charms, in his character of Allanrod, it was his design to quit her chamber ere the light of day should enable her to distinguish his countenance, and having then left her, for the space of about a week, to her own reflections, to present himself again before her, as the zealot of her cause, to inform her that, by the acquisition of additional force, he had conquered the freebooters, and that their detested chief had died by his hand.

The greatest joy, he doubted not, would rush into her heart with this intelligence, and, at the moment that it was softened towards him as her deliverer, the master-stroke of his plan was to be effected, by once more throwing himself at her feet, the suppliant of her smiles: he believed that the gratitude with which she would be inspired, for the accumulated services that he had rendered her, would leave her unable to refuse him the boon which he should sue for, as the recompense of his exertions in her cause; but, should it be possible that she should still attempt to withhold from him the possession of her charms, even after she believed them to have been rifled by the chief of a band of robbers, he considered that the indignity with which he should conceive himself to be treated, by a conduct of this nature on the part of Rosalind, would no longer leave him master of his own feelings; that it would prompt him not only to convince her that his deeply planned arts had already obtained for him the blessings of possession, but perhaps spur him on to deprive her, by death, of the power of bestowing on any other object that happiness which she denied to him.

But the hand of Providence stretched itself out towards the too long-afflicted Rosalind, and preserved her from an accumulation of misery, under which the powers of reason must have forsaken her—Edward, the beloved partner of her heart, was sent to preserve her from the pollution of a villain's touch.

And now we are acquainted who Allanrod really was, it will no longer appear strange that his soul sank within him, and his every nerve became palsied with trembling apprehension, when he beheld Rosalind snatched from his arms by the apparent shade of the murdered Edward. But when Lord Rufus had, in some measure, recovered from the excessive terror which had shaken his senses, at beholding what he had, for the time, believed to be the apparition of the man whose death had been perpetrated at his command, he began to suspect that there might be some deception in the appearance which he had seen, and commanded an instant search to be made for Rosalind throughout the castle.

Blessed in the smiles of fate, Rosalind and the beloved partner of her soul had already gained the beach, and her pursuers did not extend their search after her beyond the walls of Rockmount Castle. But whilst the fruitless pursuit was carrying on in every part of the building, Alwin, who, actuated by the zeal which he always felt for the accomplishment of his father's wishes, was the most strenuous in the cause, discovered the pilgrim's robe and hat behind the tomb in the chapel, where Edward had thrown them down. Since the time that Philip Watkins had been admitted as a minstrel into the castle, Alwin had more than once passed through a hall adjoining the kitchen, where he had seen him, and Edward in his disguise, seated amidst the domestics; and recollecting that these were the garments which had been worn by the minstrel's nominal brother, who had been declared to be dumb, a suspicion of some deceit being allied with his character immediately flashed upon his mind, and he commanded the search which was making for Rosalind, to be extended to the minstrel and his brother.

In a very short time, poor Philip was found lurking near the vaults, where Edward had left him when he had followed the steps of one of the freebooters to the chapel. He was instantly dragged before Lord Rufus, who still wore the dress of the freebooters' chief, and to whom Alwin quickly related the cause by which he had been induced to bring him into his presence.

With an air and voice that might have struck terror to a much more courageous soul than that of Philip Watkins, whom we have already perceived not to have been overburthened with valour, Lord Rufus, placing his hand upon the hilt of his sword as he spoke, commanded him to confess the truth, as he hoped to live beyond the present moment.

Philip was an honest and a well-intentioned fellow, although not a brave one, and the threat of death was probably the only one which could have caused him to betray a man to whom he had promised fidelity; but life is a charm from which few are willing to part; and falling upon his knees, with a prayer that his might be preserved to him, he made the required confession.

The astonishment which seized upon the minds of Lord Rufus and Alwin, on the conviction which they received from the lips of Philip, of their having been juggled with in their attempts upon the life of Edward, in the prison of Garcias Xavia, may be easily imagined; and they demanded of Philip, whether he was able to explain how his preservation had been effected.

Apprehensive of the consequences of refusing to reply to any question they advanced, Philip briefly related the services which Hubert had rendered to his benefactor.

The surprise of Lord Rufus increased upon this recital; and he demanded from what extraordinary cause every vassal in De Mowbray Castle appeared to have been thus strongly attached to this Edward? "I perceive two of you," said De Madginecourt, "risking your lives in his service: from what motive arises your partiality to him?"

Philip replied, that the urbanity of his manners and the excellence of his heart, had won him universal esteem in De Mowbray Castle; and added, "that his deserted state had rendered him a peculiar object of regard."

"Deserted!" echoed De Madginecourt. "Did he not enjoy the protection of the Baron de Mowbray?"

Philip replied, that what he referred to was, his not being possessed of any natural protector, upon whom he could call for acts of service or kindness.

"Whence came he then?" asked De Madginecourt, sternly—"who was he when Lord William admitted him into his castle?"

"The grandson," answered Philip, "of an aged man, named Matthews, who resided on the margin of a small lake in the vicinity of De Mowbray Castle; and by whose sudden death he was left dependant on the charity of strangers."

"Matthews!—Edward his grandson!—*he that Edward!* O God of retribution!—mercy, mercy, Heaven!" groaned forth Lord Rufus; and leaning for support on Alwin, he left the chapel, and, with trembling steps, reached his own chamber.

Scarcely had they entered it, ere Lord Rufus spoke, and the tone of his voice was such as, for the first time, awed the senses of him whom he addressed.—"Alwin," he said, "we are accursed of Heaven! I have commanded the murder of a son, and thou hast raised thy hand against the existence of a brother!"

This declaration was an enigma to Alwin: in a brief, but impressive manner, Lord Rufus explained it to him; and if the goaded consciences of the guilty ever were deserving of commiseration, their hearts were rent with pangs most truly pitiable. Oh, how awful is that moment at which the veil of delusion is removed from before the eyes of the sinful wretch, and he at length beholds the heinousness of the course of iniquity through which he has travelled to the summit of his criminality!

In agony of mind, Lord Rufus threw himself upon his bed, and for several days he refused to rise from it: at length he one day called to him Alwin,—"Repent, repent," he said, "and thou shalt yet be happy; the soul of thy brother is of too noble a nature not to forgive the heart that is filled with contrition."—Having spoken these words, he pressed his son to his breast, and then directed him to retire again to the adjoining apartment; which command Alwin obeyed, totally unsuspicious that he had then beheld his father for the last time.

At the dead of night, Lord Rufus, attended by Frasier and a small number of the freebooters, left Rockmount Castle, and proceeded to the fortress on the confines of Northumberland.

Arrived there, he directed Frasier to lead him to the tower in which he supposed the Baron de Mowbray still to be a prisoner;

and on learning that he had effected his escape about the time that his castle had been despoiled, he expressed great regret at being disappointed of the interview which he had anticipated with him. "It was my desire," he said, addressing Frasier, "to have seen him, and informed him of the lineage of his daughter's husband, that he might have accorded to him his pardon, and paternal protection, in addition to the inheritance which I am *shortly* about to bequeath to him."

Frasier remarked on the term shortly, and Lord Rufus replied—"Yes, *very* shortly; I cannot endure life, under the reflections that I am doomed to bear about with it."

He retired to the chambers which were set apart for his private use in the building, and in one of these he applied himself to writing. He first composed an epistle to the Baron de Mowbray, containing such matters as it had been his intention to give him information of, had he obtained a conference with him; this done, he drew out a history of the birth and inheritance of his son Edward, which he addressed to him, and in which he declared to him his ignorance of their affinity at the time that he had been his persecutor; and entreated forgiveness of him for himself and his brother Alwin, whom he, in the strongest terms, recommended to his protection.

The epistle addressed to Lord William, he enclosed in that intended for his son Edward; and he had just summoned Frasier into his apartment, and given him in charge, instantly to search out that injured son, and place the packet safely in his hands, when the herald from the English army, commissioned by the queen, and headed by Sir Edward, reached the fortress.

Although resolved to die, De Madginecourt's apprehensions of death were still so great, that he required some immediate spur to the act of suicide upon which he had determined; and his superior dread of falling a prisoner into the power of the English troops, as a rebel, who had headed a band of robbers, trained to the molestation of his mother country, furnished him with this spur, and he would have fallen upon his sword the instant that information was brought to him of the English forces being in sight, had he not been withheld by Frasier from the deed; but the instant of his resolution being once past, he suffered himself to be entirety guided by Frasier, who represented to him that the defeat of Elizabeth's army was certain; and that if he were resolved on death, it were at least better to die with the satisfactory knowledge of living the chief of a conquering band.

That lingering love of life which exists in every breast, probably prevailed more with Lord Rufus than the arguments of Frasier, who, committing the defence of the fortress to the other leaders, placed himself, with a score of chosen men, within De Madginecourt's apartment, determined, as he declared, to guard his life, or perish with him. To these the defeat of their comrades was not known, at the moment when they opposed the entrance of Sir Edward and Irwin into the chamber where they had stationed themselves, to protect their chief; and the intelligence of the overthrow of the free-booters was so unexpectedly and suddenly conveyed to Lord Rufus, that he was rendered incapable of reflection by the shock; and forgetting, at the instant, that he might rescue himself from captivity, by flying from existence, he attempted to effect his escape from his enemies through the spiral window of his chamber.

Of the awful interview which succeeded this moment, we have already given a description. So powerful was the effect produced upon the senses of Lord Rufus, at beholding, in the person of his injured son, the agent of that royal mistress, to whom his conduct had been equally criminal, as to the child whom he had, without a just cause, discarded from his affections, that it deprived him at once of every desire to live; the grave appeared to him the only veil for his crimes and his shame; and with a degree of triumph at thus escaping from the taunts of men, he plunged the dagger to his heart.

Beyond the tomb we cannot follow him; but impressive are the reflections which arise out of the contemplation of a life like his. Born to the enjoyment of rank and wealth, endued with every quality which can render man a blessing to the society in which he exists, vanity and avarice, the meanest passions which infest the human mind, stole into his heart, and overrunning it like a noxious weed, poisoned in the bud every generous flower which might have sprung up to its ornament. Thus on the soil where virtue might have thriven in its fairest form, the foulness of vice fixed its abhorrent stamp; and every capability which it possessed of scattering comfort on the millions beneath it, was converted into the purchase of enjoyments not less selfish than unsatisfactory to their possessor.

The doctrines of religion instruct us what will be the reward of those who possess the means, and with it the will of distributing happiness to the circle in which they are placed; and awfully do they set before our observation the dreadful reverse to which the amply gifted of Heaven, who have been the bane, and not the comfort of their fellow-beings, will be doomed. May the example of De Madginecourt's death furnish a convincing proof of the incapability of those enjoyments which are purchased by iniquitous means, to confer happiness on the heart which vainly expects to derive it from them!—may it lead to the reflection, that a life of that nature which ensures a calm and peaceful hour of dissolution, is the only life which, in this state of trial, can be deemed a happy one!

CHAPTER XIV.

The gloom that overspread our morn
Is now dispers'd; our late mishaps
Recall'd, shall be th' amusing narrative,
And story of our future evening, oft
Rehears'd.——Our son too—he shall hang upon
The sounds, and lift his little hands in praise
To Heaven: taught by his mother's bright example,
That to be truly good, is to be bless'd.

H. HARTSON.

O HOW delightful is the task which leads us to tell of the happiness which the virtuous enjoy! How exquisite to recount the rewards which attend on the trials endured by superior beings like Sir Edward and his Rosalind!—to behold them removed from the oppression of the vicious, and the tyranny of the unfeeling, to the joy-fraught exercise of that benevolence which is the spontaneous growth of their hearts, and to the enjoyment of that domestic love which is the recompence of every pang undergone to secure its possession!

It must be almost unnecessary, after what we have seen of the exalted sentiments of Sir Edward's heart, to say, that although he discovered the father in the persecutor, he did not, on this discovery, forget the obligations which are due from every created being to the author of his existence.

With affection it was impossible that he should follow a parent like Lord Rufus to the grave, but with that outward show of respect which reflected back upon himself, in its brightest lustre, the sentiment which he bestowed, he attended the earthly remains of his father to their last abode; and, considering that the rights of burial in England could not be permitted to him, as a rebel to the interests of his country, he procured permission for him to be interred in the burying-ground of a monastery upon the confines of the Scottish kingdom.

Alwin was, meanwhile, not forgotten by him; he sent him an assurance, that, although he could not receive him as a brother to his heart, he would not suffer him to feel the loss of his father, in the point of those comforts, which he had been accustomed to enjoy. This message he sent to him by Frasier, who, rejoicing in the opportunity thus afforded him of flying from the punishment which awaited his fellow-freebooters, at the hand of the English government, instead of bearing the commission with which he was charged to Rockwell Castle, fled into Scotland, and secreted himself there, in the assumption of some new character, from the punishment which be feared might overtake him.

From the tongue of common fame, Alwin heard the occurrences which had taken place at the fortress; and, unable to credit that Sir Edward would grant to him that forgiveness which the narrowness and vice of his own heart would probably have withheld him from bestowing on his brother, had he been placed in his fortunate situation, and Sir Edward in that in which he now stood; a victim to apprehensions and regrets, which almost consumed his senses, he precipitated himself into the sea, from one of the towers of the castle, which overhung its bosom; and his corpse was brought to land a few days afterwards, by some fishermen.

At the same time that Sir Edward had dispatched the treacherous Frasier to Rockmount Castle, he had sent forward Irwin to London, charged to deliver an exact account of all that had taken place since his departure from it, to the queen and his Rosalind. Accordingly, the reception which he met with at the palace, on his return, was that of being saluted by a body of nobles, who ushered him into the presence of the queen as Lord Edward de Madginecourt. But if his heart experienced an honest pride at the smiles of pleasure with which he was welcomed by every member of the British court, smiles of which the queen herself set the example—if his heart danced with ecstacy, at the kiss of welcome imprinted on his lips by his beloved Rosalind, what was the exultation with which he received, from the arms of Hubert, the lovely, blooming boy, who was the pledge of her love, for whom all his miseries had been endured, and for the blessing of whose affection he would again have undergone a second pilgrimage of equal hardships!

The tears of overflowing joy started into his eyes; he pressed the babe to his face, and they fell upon his rosy, velvet cheek.—Almost jealous of the delight which her husband was experiencing from his caresses, Rosalind again drew him to her own breast, and kissed off the tears with which his father had bedewed him.—"O bless the child of my beloved Rosalind!" exclaimed Lord Edward—"Angels guard thee, son of my adored Edward!" responded his mother.

"Son of Edward and Rosalind, is thy happiest name," said the queen, hanging over him, as she spoke; "but thou must also be the son of Elizabeth; the godmother of thy parent, I pledge myself in the same degree of responsibility to thee."

In compliance with this promise, the young Edward was, a few days afterwards, christened in the chapel of the palace, with a display of the utmost state and magnificence; and the queen became the sponsor of his faith, in like manner as she had become to his mother.

After a month passed in the royal mansion of Elizabeth, the Lord Edward and his Lady took possession of Rockmount Castle, to which Rosalind obtained her husband's permission to carry with her her faithful Gertrude, and old Ambrose, formerly the porter of De Mowbray Castle, who, with the other vassals of Lord William, had been restored to liberty by the subversion of the freebooters.

To the unequalled Hubert, the queen presented an estate in the vicinity of Rockmount Castle, not sufficiently large to deprive its possessor of comfort, by forcing upon him grandeur, but large enough to give him the wealth of a happy competency;—a situation suited to the just and moderate feelings of him to whom it was assigned; and the greatest happiness of his existence was the contemplation of that felicity of which he had been the glorious author.

Dame Edith was continued by Rosalind in her situation of housekeeper; and dying, at the age of one hundred and sixteen years, her earnest wish was completed, of living a century beneath the roof of Rockmount Castle, of which she had become an inmate when scarcely sixteen years old.

Philip Watkins threw himself at the feet of Lord Edward, and implored forgiveness for the confession which had been forced from his lips, rather by the polished blade of Lord Rufus's sword, than the eloquence of his tongue; and Lord Edward, kindly remembering only the happy consequence which had arisen from his want of fortitude, bestowed on him, with his pardon, the permission, of continuing in his service for life.

The Baron de Mowbray lived only three years in the asylum to which he had flown from the taunts of the world, and sunk into the sleep of death, with a penitent and religious concern for the errors of his life, which afforded a most consolatory balm to the feelings of his daughter, in the expectation which they gave her of his happiness in a future state.

Lord Edward did not, in his prosperity, forget his friend, Adolphus Biron, and the interesting partner of his fate, the lovely Belise; and he had the satisfaction to learn, that, by the interference of her uncle, at Maestricht, the fortune left to her by her father had been recovered from the hands of the Governor Garcias Xavia; and about five years after her union with Adolphus, Garcias, terrified by the approach of death, into a desire of repairing some of the injustice which he had been guilty of in life, bequeathed to her such a portion of his wealth as increased the independence which she and her husband already possessed, into a fund of riches, for the future portions of a numerous offspring.

Not less happy, in repeated pledges of their affection, were the Lord and Lady de Madginecourt; and on their second son, Elizabeth conferred the title of Baron de Mowbray, which had else been extinct at the death of Lord William; and with it she assigned to him that domain which must otherwise, in default of a male heir, have returned into the hands of the crown.

Thus blessed in the favour of a gracious sovereign, and in the conscious rectitude of their own hearts, Lord Edward and his Rosalind lived long, and lived happily. In distributing comfort to the needy, they doubled their own store of happiness—in educating their children to pursue the path of virtue, they felt their own minds ameliorated by the instruction which they conveyed; and the moments which they passed in a return of thanksgiving to that Omnipotent Being, by whom their preservation from a host of foes had been so miraculously wrought, were rewarded with the glorious expectation of joys more exquisite and more exalted still, beyond the grave.

FINIS.

CONTEMPORARY REVIEWS

British Critic 27 (1806), p. 671.

ART. 18. *The Mysterious Freebooter, or the Days of Queen Bess; a Romance, in four Volumes. By Francis Lathom, Author of Men and Manners.* Lane.

Although we have been accustomed to regard the performances of Mr. Lathom in a favourable point of view, we are willing to place the Mysterious Freebooter at the head of his Romantic productions. We certainly think that his talent is most adapted to the composition of humorous works: but, in this instance, curiosity is as much excited, and time as fairly paid, as by almost any of the romances which the terrific genius of modern fable has produced. Perhaps Mr. Lathom might have ranked in the first class of fabulists, had it been his good fortune to write earlier.

This tale has been brought upon the stage at the Circus in the shape of a ballet. Indeed the situations are frequently striking and dramatic, and the work must derive one advantage from appearing in dumb-show, of which we are sorry to perceive that it at present stands in need. We mean that, in a ballet, while our feelings are wrought on by impassioned scenes, our ears cannot be wounded by the numberless inaccuracies of grammar and style which crowd the pages of this amusing story. We remember to have noticed this defect in a former production of our author, and we were in hopes that time, which gives facility, would give also correctness of composition. We have been deceived. The Mysterious Freebooter is really worth the trouble of correction. Even a Scotch pebble is highly improved by the friction of the Lapidary; but he who possesses a diamond, and neglects to polish it, is guilty of a carelessness for which he deserves to suffer.

The characters are some of them forcibly and naturally drawn, particularly those of De Mowbray and Mable Monteith; though the latter is certainly placed in a situation too prominent for her proportionate importance in the work. The general structure of the plot is simple and unembarrassed: it is interspersed with a number of poetical trifles, among the best of which is an *Elegy on the death of a young officer.* The Episode of Eloise de Valois, is interesting, and, which is seldom the case with episodes, pertinent. The moral is in every respect unexceptionable; and the whole is decidedly the production of a man by no means unaccustomed to the labours of the quill.

Critical Review, 3rd ser. 8 (July 1806), p. 327.

Stimulated, we presume, by the applause which he obtained for his 'Impenetrable Secret,' which appeared some months ago, Mr. Lathom has speedily recovered the elasticity of his mind, and returned to the charge in an ancient romance; and a spirited charge it must be confessed to be; for, where he fails to command our approbation, he generally seizes our attention. He has faults which we cannot but loudly condemn, yet he has merits which induce us to read. His plot is various, and not complicated; the incidents that compose it are generally natural and simple. Its principal error, and that is a grievous one, is its prolixity; a most soporific effect being produced by the long reference to preceding events, which occupies almost the whole of the first volume, and by the story of Mabel Monteith, which has little relation to the principal affair. We cannot help observing therefore that this work might have been with great advantage reduced into the compass of two or at most three volumes, for if a great book of any kind be a great evil, how immense a mischief is a great novel! Our author has certainly the principal art of a novel writer, the knack of exciting interest; but scarcely any interest can be strong enough to prop, upon its own single basis, four long volumes. We say on its own single basis, because Mr. Lathom has most disdainfully rejected all assistance from grammar, style, and harmonious construction. And yet, when we had finished the work, we forgot our displeasure at the errors of the composition, in our regret that the story was concluded.

ALSO AVAILABLE FROM VALANCOURT BOOKS

Gothic Classics

THE ANIMATED SKELETON (1798) BY ANONYMOUS
THE CASTLE OF OLLADA (1795) BY FRANCIS LATHOM
THE PHANTOM OF THE CASTLE (1798) BY RICHARD SICKELMORE
THE CAVERN OF DEATH (1794) BY ANONYMOUS
ITALIAN MYSTERIES (1820) BY FRANCIS LATHOM
MYSTERY OF THE BLACK TOWER (1796) BY JOHN PALMER, JUN.
CLERMONT (1798) BY REGINA MARIA ROCHE
BAROZZI; OR, THE VENETIAN SORCERESS (1815) BY CATHERINE SMITH
THE WITCH OF RAVENSWORTH (1808) BY GEORGE BREWER
THE FOREST OF VALANCOURT (1813) BY PETER MIDDLETON DARLING
THE CASTLE OF WOLFENBACH (1793) BY ELIZA PARSONS
THE IMPENETRABLE SECRET, FIND IT OUT! (1805) BY FRANCIS LATHOM
THE VEILED PICTURE (1802) BY ANN RADCLIFFE
TERRIFIC TALES (1804) BY ISABELLA LEWIS
THE MYSTERIOUS FREEBOOTER (1806) BY FRANCIS LATHOM
THE NEW MONK (1798) BY R. S., ESQ. (*forthcoming*)
THE NECROMANCER (1794) BY "PETER TEUTHOLD" (*forthcoming*)
FARMER OF INGLEWOOD FOREST (1798) BY ELIZABETH HELME (*forthcoming*)

VALANCOURT CLASSICS

THE MAGIC RING (1825) BY BARON DE LA MOTTE FOUQUE
GASTON DE BLONDEVILLE (1826) BY ANN RADCLIFFE
THE ITALIAN (1797) BY ANN RADCLIFFE
IN MAREMMA (1882) BY OUIDA
SIX GOTHIC DRAMAS BY JOANNA BAILLIE

www.ingramcontent.com/pod-product-compliance
Lightning Source LLC
Chambersburg PA
CBHW011959050726
47499CB00010BA/3215
9780977784196